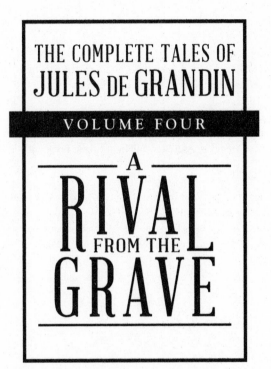

THE COMPLETE TALES OF
JULES DE GRANDIN

VOLUME FOUR

A
RIVAL
FROM THE
GRAVE

SEABURY QUINN

EDITED BY GEORGE A. VANDERBURGH

Night Shade Books
New York

Night Shade books may be purchased in bulk at special discounts for sales promotion, corporate gifts, fund-raising, or educational purposes. Special editions can also be created to specifications. For details, contact the Special Sales Department, Night Shade Books, 307 West 36th Street, 11th Floor, New York, NY 10018 or info@skyhorsepublishing.com.

Night Shade Books® is a registered trademark of Skyhorse Publishing, Inc.®, a Delaware corporation.

Visit our website at www.nightshadebooks.com.

10 9 8 7 6 5 4 3 2 1

Library of Congress Cataloging-in-Publication Data

Names: Quinn, Seabury, 1889-1969, author. | Vanderburgh, George A., editor.
Title: A rival from the grave / Seabury Quinn ; edited by George A. Vanderburgh.
Description: New York: Night Shade Books, [2018] | Series: The complete tales of Jules de Grandin ; Volume four.
Identifiers: LCCN 2018016045 (print) | LCCN 2018018847 (ebook) | ISBN 9781597809696 (Ebook) | ISBN 9781597809689 (hardback: alk. paper)
Subjects: LCSH: Detective and mystery stories, American. | Paranormal fiction, American.
Classification: LCC PS3533.U69 (ebook) | LCC PS3533.U69 A6 2018b (print) | DDC 813/.52—dc23
LC record available at https://lccn.loc.gov/2018016045

Cover illustration by Donato Giancola
Cover design by Claudia Noble

Printed in the United States of America

TABLE OF CONTENTS

*Cover by Margaret Brundage
^Cover by Virgil Finlay

THE COMPLETE TALES OF Jules de Grandin is dedicated to the memory of Robert E. Weinberg, who passed away in fall of 2016. Weinberg, who edited the six-volume paperback series of de Grandin stories in the 1970s, also supplied many original issues of *Weird Tales* magazine from his personal collection so that Seabury Quinn's work could be carefully scanned and transcribed digitally. Without his knowledge of the material and his editorial guidance, as well as his passion for Quinn's work over a long period of time (when admirers of the Jules de Grandin stories were often difficult to come by), this series would not have been possible, and we owe him our deepest gratitude and respect.

Introduction

by George A. Vanderburgh and Robert E. Weinberg

W EIRD TALES, THE SELF-DESCRIBED "Unique Magazine," and one of the most influential Golden Age pulp magazines in the first half of the twentieth century, was home to a number of now-well-recognized names, including Robert Bloch, August Derleth, Robert E. Howard, H. P. Lovecraft, Clark Ashton Smith, and Manly Wade Wellman.

But among such stiff competition was another writer, more popular at the time than all of the aforementioned authors, and paid at a higher rate because of it. Over the course of ninety-two stories and a serialized novel, his most endearing character captivated pulp magazine readers for nearly three decades, during which time he received more front cover illustrations accompanying his stories than any of his fellow contributors.

The writer's name was Seabury Quinn, and his character was the French occult detective Jules de Grandin.

Perhaps you've never heard of de Grandin, his indefatigable assistant Dr. Trowbridge, or the fictional town of Harrisonville, New Jersey. Perhaps you've never even heard of Seabury Quinn (or maybe only in passing, as a historical footnote in one of the many essays and reprinted collections of Quinn's now-more-revered contemporaries). Certainly, de Grandin was not the first occult detective—Algernon Blackwood's John Silence, Hodgson's Thomas Carnacki, and Sax Rohmer's Moris Klaw preceded him—nor was he the last, as Wellman's John Thunstone, Margery Lawrence's Miles Pennoyer, and Joseph Payne Brennan's Lucius Leffing all either overlapped with the end of de Grandin's run or followed him. And without doubt de Grandin shares more than a passing resemblance to both Sir Arthur Conan Doyle's Sherlock Holmes (especially with his Dr. Watson-like sidekick) and Agatha Christie's Hercule Poirot.

Indeed, even if you were to seek out a de Grandin story, your options over the years would have been limited. Unlike Lovecraft, Smith, Wellman, Bloch, and other *Weird Tales* contributors, the publication history of the Jules de Grandin tales is spotty at best. In 1966, Arkham House printed roughly 2,000 copies of *The Phantom-Fighter*, a selection of ten early works. In the late 1970s, Popular Library published six paperback volumes of approximately thirty-five assorted tales, but they are now long out of print. In 2001, the specialty press The Battered Silicon Dispatch Box released an oversized, three-volume hardcover set of every de Grandin story (the first time all the stories had been collected), and, while still in production, the set is unavailable to the general trade.

So, given how obscure Quinn and his character might seem today, it's justifiably hard to understand how popular these stories originally were, or how frequently new ones were written. But let the numbers tell the tale: from October 1925 (when the very first de Grandin story was released) to December 1933, a roughly eight-year span, de Grandin stories appeared in an incredible sixty-two of the ninety-six issues that *Weird Tales* published, totaling well-over three-quarters of a million words. Letter after letter to the magazine's editor demanded further adventures from the supernatural detective.

If Quinn loomed large in the mind of pulp readers during the magazine's hey-day, then why has his name fallen on deaf ears since? Aside from the relative unavailability of his work, the truth is that Quinn has been successfully marginalized over the years by many critics, who have often dismissed him as simply a hack writer. The de Grandin stories are routinely criticized as being of little worth, and dismissed as unimportant to the development of weird fiction. A common argument, propped up by suspiciously circular reasoning, concludes that Quinn was not the most popular writer for *Weird Tales*, just the most prolific.

These critics seem troubled that the same audience who read and appreciated the work of Lovecraft, Smith, and Howard could also enjoy the exploits of the French ghostbuster. And while it would be far from the truth to suggest that the literary merits of the de Grandin stories exceed those of some of his contemporaries' tales, Quinn was a much more skillful writer, and the adventures of his occult detective more enjoyable to read, than most critics are willing to acknowledge. In the second half of the twentieth century, as the literary value of some pulp-fiction writers began to be reconsidered, Quinn proved to be the perfect whipping boy for early advocates attempting to destigmatize weird fiction: He was the hack author who churned out formulaic prose for a quick paycheck. Anticipating charges that a literary reassessment of Lovecraft would require reevaluating the entire genre along with him, an arbitrary line was quickly drawn in the sand, and as the standard-bearer of pulp fiction's popularity, the creator of Jules de Grandin found himself on the wrong side of that line.

First and foremost, it must be understood that Quinn wrote to make money, and he was far from the archetypal "starving artist." At the same time that his Jules de Grandin stories were running in *Weird Tales,* he had a similar series of detective stories publishing in *Real Detective Tales.* Quinn was writing two continuing series at once throughout the 1920s, composing approximately twenty-five thousand words a month on a manual typewriter. Maintaining originality under such a grueling schedule would be difficult for any author, and even though the de Grandin stories follow a recognizable formula, Quinn still managed to produce one striking story after another. It should also be noted that the tendency to recycle plots and ideas for different markets was very similar to the writing practices of *Weird Tales*'s other prolific and popular writer, Robert E. Howard, who is often excused for these habits, rather than criticized for them.

Throughout his many adventures, the distinctive French detective changed little. His penchant for amusingly French exclamations was a constant through all ninety-three works, as was his taste for cigars and brandy after (and sometimes before) a hard day's work, and his crime-solving styles and methods remained remarkably consistent. From time to time, some new skill or bit of knowledge was revealed to the reader, but in most other respects the Jules de Grandin of "The Horror on the Links" was the same as the hero of the last story in the series, published twenty-five years later.

> He was a perfect example of the rare French blond type, rather under medium height, but with a military erectness of carriage that made him look several inches taller than he really was. His light-blue eyes were small and exceedingly deep-set, and would have been humorous had it not been for the curiously cold directness of their gaze. With his wide mouth, light mustache waxed at the ends in two perfectly horizontal points, and those twinkling, stock-taking eyes, he reminded me of an alert tomcat.

Thus is de Grandin described by Dr. Trowbridge in the duo's first meeting in 1925. His personal history is dribbled throughout the stories: de Grandin was born and raised in France, attended medical school, became a prominent surgeon, and in the Great War served first as a medical officer, then as a member of the intelligence service. After the war, he traveled the world in the service of French Intelligence. His age is never given, but it's generally assumed that the occult detective is in his early forties.

Samuel Trowbridge, on the other hand, is a typical conservative small-town doctor of the first half of the twentieth century (as described by Quinn, he is a cross between an honest brother of George Bernard Shaw and former Chief Justice of the United States Charles Evans Hughes). Bald and bewhiskered, most—if not all—of his life was spent in the same town. Trowbridge is old-fashioned and somewhat conservative, a member of the Knights Templar, a vestryman in the Episcopal Church, and a staunch Republican.

While the two men are dissimilar in many ways, they are also very much alike. Both are fine doctors and surgeons. Trowbridge might complain from time to time about de Grandin's wild adventures, but he always goes along with them; there is no thought, ever, of leaving de Grandin to fight his battles alone. More than any other trait, though, they are two men with one mission, and perhaps for that reason they remained friends for all of their ninety-three adventures and countless trials.

The majority of Quinn's de Grandin stories take place in or near Harrisonville, New Jersey, a fictional community that rivals (with its fiends, hauntings, ghouls, werewolves, vampires, voodoo, witchcraft, and zombies) Lovecraft's own Arkham, Massachusetts. For more recent examples of a supernatural-infested community, one need look no further than the modern version of pulp-fiction narratives . . . television. *Buffy the Vampire Slayer*'s Sunnydale, California, and *The Night Strangler*'s Seattle both reflect the structural needs of this type of supernatural narrative.

Early in the series, de Grandin is presented as Trowbridge's temporary house guest, having travelled to the United States to study both medicine and modern police techniques, but Quinn quickly realized that the series was due for a long run and recognized that too much globe-trotting would make the stories unwieldy. A familiar setting would be needed to keep the main focus of each tale on the events themselves. Harrisonville, a medium-sized town outside New York City, was completely imaginary, but served that purpose.

Most of the de Grandin stories feature beautiful girls in peril. Quinn discovered early on that Farnsworth Wright, *Weird Tales*'s editor from 1924 to 1940, believed nude women on the cover sold more copies, so when writing he was careful to always feature a scene that could translate to appropriately salacious artwork. Quinn also realized that his readers wanted adventures with love and romance as central themes, so even his most frightening tales were given happy endings (. . . of a sort).

And yet the de Grandin adventures are set apart from the stories they were published alongside by their often explicit and bloody content. Quinn predated the work of Clive Barker and the splatterpunk writers by approximately fifty years, but, using his medical background, he wrote some truly terrifying horror stories; tales like "The House of Horror" and "The House Where Time Stood Still" feature some of the most hideous descriptions of mutilated humans ever set down on paper. The victims of the mad doctor in "The House of Horror" in particular must rank near the top of the list of medical monstrosities in fiction.

Another element that set Quinn's occult detective apart from others was his pioneering use of modern science in the fight against ancient superstitions.

De Grandin fought vampires, werewolves, and even mummies in his many adventures, but oftentimes relied on the latest technology to save the day. The Frenchman put it best in a conversation with Dr. Trowbridge at the end of "The Blood-Flower":

> "And wasn't there some old legend to the effect that a werewolf could only be killed with a silver bullet?"
>
> "Ah, bah," he replied with a laugh. "What did those old legend-mongers know of the power of modern firearms? . . . When I did shoot that wolfman, my friend, I had something more powerful than superstition in my hand. *Morbleu*, but I did shoot a hole in him large enough for him to have walked through."

Quinn didn't completely abandon the use of holy water, ancient relics, and magical charms to defeat supernatural entities, but he made it clear that de Grandin understood that there was a place for modern technology as well as old folklore when it came to fighting monsters. Nor was de Grandin himself above using violence to fight his enemies. Oftentimes, the French occult investigator served as judge, jury and executioner when dealing with madmen, deranged doctors, and evil masterminds. There was little mercy in his stories for those who used dark forces.

While sex was heavily insinuated but rarely covered explicitly in the pulps, except in the most general of terms, Quinn again was willing to go where few other writers would dare. Sexual slavery, lesbianism, and even incest played roles in his writing over the years, challenging the moral values of the day.

In the end, there's no denying that the de Grandin stories are pulp fiction. Many characters are little more than assorted clichés bundled together. De Grandin is a model hero, a French expert on the occult, and never at a loss when battling the most evil of monsters. Dr. Trowbridge remains the steadfast companion, much in the Dr. Watson tradition, always doubting but inevitably following his friend's advice. Quinn wrote for the masses, and he didn't spend pages describing landscapes when there was always more action unfolding.

The Jules de Grandin stories were written as serial entertainment, with the legitimate expectation that they would not be read back to back. While all of the adventures are good fun, the best way to properly enjoy them is over an extended period of time. Plowing through one story after another will lessen their impact, and greatly cut down on the excitement and fun of reading them. One story a week, which would stretch out this entire five-volume series over two years, might be the perfect amount of time needed to fully enjoy these tales of the occult and the macabre. They might not be great literature, but they don't pretend to be. They're pulp adventures, and even after seventy-five years, the stories read well.

Additionally, though the specific aesthetic values of *Weird Tales* readers were vastly different than those of today's readers, one can see clearly see the continuing allure of these types of supernatural adventures, and the long shadow that they cast over twentieth and early twenty-first century popular culture. Sure, these stories are formulaic, but it is a recipe that continues to be popular to this day. The formula of the occult detective, the protector who stands between us and the monsters of the night, can be seen time and time again in the urban fantasy and paranormal romance categories of commercial fiction, and is prevalent in today's television and movies. Given the ubiquity and contemporary popularity of this type of narrative, it's actually not at all surprising that Seabury Quinn was the most popular contributor to *Weird Tales*.

We are proud to present the first of five volumes reprinting every Jules de Grandin story written by Seabury Quinn. Organized chronologically, as they originally appeared in *Weird Tales* magazine, this is the first time that the collected de Grandin stories have been made available in trade editions.

Each volume has been graced by tremendous artwork from renowned artist Donato Giancola, who has given Quinn's legendary character an irresistible combination of grace, cunning and timelessness. We couldn't have asked for a better way to introduce "the occult Hercule Poirot" to a new generation of readers.

Finally, if Seabury Quinn is watching from above, and closely scrutinizing the shelves of bookstores, he would undoubtedly be pleased as punch, and proud as all get-out, to find his creation, Dr. Jules de Grandin, rising once again in the minds of readers around the world, battling the forces of darkness . . . wherever, whoever, or whatever the nature of their evil might be.

When the Jaws of Darkness Open,
Only Jules de Grandin Stands in Satan's Way!

Robert E. Weinberg
Chicago, Illinois, USA

and

George A. Vanderburgh
Lake Eugenia, Ontario, Canada

23 September 2016

Keeping the Golden Age Alive

by Mike Ashley

EVEN THOUGH THE FINAL Jules de Grandin story appeared over sixty years ago, the series remains the longest running occult detective series—ninety-three stories in total, including one complete novel and several of novella length. Curiously, however, when the subject of occult or psychic detectives arises in discussion, it's unlikely that Seabury Quinn's Jules de Grandin will be the first to be mentioned. He might not even enter the discussion at all, despite the fact that the series remains the longest-running of all occult detective series, with ninety-three stories in total, including one complete novel and several of novella length, all of which appeared over sixty years ago.

Instead, one will think immediately of Algernon Blackwood's John Silence or William Hope Hodgson's Carnacki or Joseph Payne Brennan's Lucius Leffing or, of course, more recent TV examples such as Kolchak in *The Night Stalker* or Mulder and Scully in *The X-Files*. But the occult detective has a long history and a rich tradition, and what is frequently overlooked is the pivotal role that Quinn's de Grandin stories played in developing and even rescuing the character from premature decay—they poured life and vitality into a character role that was becoming dangerously stereotyped and, perhaps more importantly, too closely tied to the British establishment. Indeed, it was Quinn who popularized the psychic sleuth in the United States and gave the archetype a whole new lease on life, as Jules de Grandin's adventures spanned those years between the decline of the traditional British supernatural sleuths at the end of the 1920s and their re-emergence in the 1960s.

The occult detective in Britain has its roots in the medical profession, an approach which has proved ideal for many other detectives—or their companions. Samuel Warren's long-running series, *Passages from the Diary of a Late Physician*, which began in *Blackwood's Magazine* in August 1830, has the nameless first-person narrator investigating all manner of maladies, especially nervous disorders. Many of the stories are macabre, and a few verge on the supernatural, such as "The Spectre-Smitten" (February 1831), in which a patient's madness has arisen out of his apparently seeing the ghost of a recently deceased neighbour. The series proved very popular, not least because Warren's identity was also kept anonymous and many readers believed these were genuine cases.

Even before Warren's series began, the German writer E. T. A. Hoffmann had included an investigative doctor in *"Das öde Haus"* ("The Deserted House") in the second volume of *Nachtstücke* in 1817, but, as this story was not translated into English until 1855, it did not have the impact of Warren's series, which had helped establish the physician as a natural investigator of strange happenings, whether genuine hauntings or delusions. Joseph Sheridan Le Fanu introduced the German physician Dr. Martin Hesselius in "Green Tea," serialized in *All The Year Round* (23 October–13 November 1869), whose investigations were recorded by his anonymous medical secretary. As with Warren's stories, "Green Tea" considers the extent to which hauntings might be psychosomatic. Although Hesselius does not appear in any of Le Fanu's other stories, his casebook was used as a framing device when Le Fanu collected some of his best weird tales as *In a Glass Darkly* (1872).

When Grant Allen started his writing career, masquerading as J. Arbuthnot Wilson, he had two medical students undertake a scientific analysis of a ghost in "Our Scientific Observations on a Ghost" (*Belgravia*, July 1878). Allen was already parodying a genre which had barely got off the ground, but the story highlights the public's growing interest in a thorough investigation of ghosts and the occult. There had been a growth in curiosity about spiritualism and psychic phenomena since the 1850s, notably in the demonstrations given by the Scottish medium Daniel Dunglas Home. This had led to the formation of various spiritualist bodies, such as the British National Association of Spiritualists in 1873, and through these developed the Society for Psychical Research (SPR) in 1881.

The rigorous investigation of psychic phenomena had already been used to great effect by Edward Bulwer-Lytton—who had witnessed some of Home's activities—in one of the best mid-Victorian ghost stories, "The Haunted and the Haunters," also in *Blackwood's Magazine* (August 1859). With the formation of the SPR, though, scientific investigations of hauntings soon featured regularly in fiction. Arthur Conan Doyle, who was cautious early in his career but would later champion the cause of spiritualism, showed how the power of the mind might challenge science in his novella *The Parasite* (1894), wherein the investigator, Professor Gilroy, almost succumbs to the mental strength of a formidable woman.

Although Doyle also wrote other stories of occult investigation, such as "The Brown Hand" (*The Strand*, May 1899), which refers to the SPR, he introduced no recurring investigator, unlike his stories of Holmes and Watson, which had set a new template for detective fiction. One of the pleasures of encountering the occult detective is in pursuing his many and varied explorations and it is the appearance of regular character series that marks the emergence of the field as a distinct sub-genre.

One might point to Arthur Machen's Dyson as the first continuing character, as he appears in four stories, starting with "The Inmost Light" in *The Great God Pan* (1894). But Dyson isn't an investigator by profession; he's a rather dissolute author with a side interest in the scientific understanding of the outré, and he gets dragged into investigations by his colleagues. Much the same applies to Arabella Kenealy's Lord Syfret, who has a sort of sixth sense in detecting the unusual, but whose cases, related in "Some Experiences of Lord Syfret," are only borderline supernatural at best. That series, eleven stories in all, ran in *The Ludgate* from June 1896 to April 1897, but only seven were collected in *Belinda's Beaux* in 1897.

A better example of the first regular-character occult detective is L. T. Meade and Robert Eustace's John Bell, the Ghost Exposer, whose adventures were serialized in *Cassell's Magazine* starting in June 1896 and collected as *A Master of Mysteries* in 1897. A man of private means, Bell has devoted his life to exploring the weird and mysterious and has become an exposer of ghosts. Although these stories are therefore non-supernatural, they are full of atmosphere and challenge the reader to see if they can understand the mundane solution. Bell, then, was an investigator in the true tradition of the SPR.

These precursors lead, at last, to the first true genuine example: the cases of Flaxman Low, a psychologist who, like Bell, has devoted his life to understanding psychic phenomena. When the first set of six stories, written by Hesketh Hesketh-Prichard and his mother Kate O'Brien Ryall Prichard under the pseudonym "E. & H. Heron," were published in *Pearson's Magazine* from January to June 1898, they were presented under the heading "Real Ghost Stories," with each story illustrated by a picture of a haunted house. Low also writes up his investigations for the SPR, giving the stories more than a veneer of verisimilitude. A second series ran in *Pearson's* the following year, and all twelve stories were collected in the landmark, and now quite rare, volume *Ghosts* (1899).

With Flaxman Low, the occult-detective field was ready to blossom. The magazines saw there was a winning formula in feigning veracity, and repeated the guise with Allen Upward's "The Ghost Hunters" in *The Royal Magazine* in 1905 and Jessie Adelaide Middleton's "True Ghost Stories" in *Pearson's* in 1907.

These ushered in a true Golden Age, which really began with *John Silence, Physician Extraordinary* by Algernon Blackwood in 1908. With the Silence stories, the two threads of the occult detective come together; he's both a psychic investigator and a doctor, or "physician extraordinary." Like John Bell and Flaxman Low, Silence has devoted years to studying—or perhaps *experiencing* would be the better word, since he hid himself away from the world for five years—the occult. But, like Samuel Warren's investigator, Silence is also a genuine doctor, interested in psychic afflictions, though he has no consulting rooms!

Blackwood's publisher, Eveleigh Nash, gave *John Silence* huge publicity, which led to not only significant sales and the chance for Blackwood to become a full-time writer, but also sealed the reputation on the occult detective. The floodgates opened and, over the next two decades, almost every popular magazine featured a psychic sleuth.

The Idler ran William Hope Hodgson's Carnacki, the Ghost-Finder in 1910. *The New Magazine* featured Sax Rohmer's Moris Klaw in 1913 (later collected as *The Dream Detective* in 1920). *The Weekly Tale Teller* ran Alice and Claude Askew's Aylmer Vance in 1914. Uel Key's Dr. Arnold Rhymer, the Spook Specialist, appeared in *Pearson's Magazine* in 1917. *The Premier Magazine* featured the first female occult detective, F. Tennyson Jesse's Solange Fontaine, in 1918, followed in 1919 by Mrs. Champion de Crespigny's Norton Vyse. Then, Ella Scrymsour's Sheila Crerar appeared in *The Blue Magazine* in 1920, Elliot O'Donnell's Damon Vane in *The Novel Magazine* in 1922, and Dion Fortune's Dr. Taverner in *The Royal Magazine* in 1926. Even Agatha Christie explored the territory with her character Harley Quin in 1926's *The Story-teller*. The difference here was that Quin was not the investigator, but somehow seemed to influence events off stage.

The link in name between Harley Quin and Seabury Quinn was, of course, entirely coincidental, although it is another interesting coincidence that Seabury Quinn's first appearance in a British publication was just three months before the publication of the first Harley Quin story.[1] The first Jules de Grandin story, "The Horror on the Links," was reprinted from its original October 1925 *Weird Tales* appearance in September 1926's *More Night at Night*, the second volume in what would become the legendary Not at Night series of anthologies edited by the redoubtable Christine Campbell Thomson. Although a hardcover book series, it was treated, contractually, as a British edition of *Weird Tales*, although it also published its own original material and other reprints. Thomson also reprinted two other de Grandin stories, "The House of Horror" and "The Curse

---

1 A further remarkable coincidence was that Sydney Horler had also only just introduced his character Sebastian Quin in "The Clean Wineglass" (*Detective Magazine*, 27 February 1925), and although the story is related as the first of many cases, no further stories appeared until "Black Magic" in 1930, suggesting that Quin had to rest the stories while Christie's Harley Quin had centre stage.

of the House of Phipps," in *You'll Need a Night Light* (1927) and in *At Dead of Night* (1931), respectively, although the Not at Night series ran for a further four volumes until 1936.

It was an indication that the occult detective character had virtually run its course in Britain. A. M. Burrage had contributed his series about Francis Chard to *The Blue Magazine* in 1927 and, rather fittingly, F. Tennyson Jesse brought back Solange Fontaine for a final series in *The London Magazine* in 1929, but the magazines were starting to fold, and the future of the occult detective in Britain, such that it was at the time, was moving to books.

L. Adams Beck, for example, introduced Dr. James Livingstone in *The Openers of the Gate* in 1930. He was a specialist in nervous disorders, just as Samuel Warren's doctor-detective had been a century earlier. Sydney Horler reintroduced Sebastian Quin in two novels, *The Evil Messenger* (1938) and *Fear Walked Behind* (1942). E. Charles Vivian, writing as Jack Mann, switched his detective Gregory George Gordon Green, known as Gees, from investigating mundane cases to supernatural ones with *Grey Shapes* in 1937 and managed to sustain a series of novels over the next few years, but these were exceptions.

The main reason for the gradual disappearance of the occult detective in Britain was because the magazines were themselves fading and there was no suitable market for a continuing short story series. It was not until towards the end of the Second World War that Dennis Wheatley introduced Niels Orsen in four stories in *Gunmen, Gallants and Ghosts* (1943) and Margery Lawrence presented the cases of Dr. Miles Pennoyer in *Number Seven, Queer Street* (1945), though, again, these were exceptions. It would be nearly thirty years before the occult detective truly began to re-emerge in Britain.

But there was also another reason for the loss of interest in psychic sleuths, and that was a lack of originality. Apart from the interesting variations introduced by Agatha Christie and F. Tennyson Jesse—and, to be fair, these were initially only borderline psychic detectives rather than ghost hunters—all of the other series followed a traditional, almost Holmesian, format. Even Carnacki, the most physically active of the ghost finders, still had his consulting room and invited his circle of friends round so he could relate his latest adventure. Some of the detectives had their own special skills: Moris Klaw slept at the scene and dreamed a solution,[2] Norton Vyse had such psychic abilities as psychometry, and Lord Syfret could sense the unusual, rather like Solange Fontaine, who was aware of evil. But despite these skills, the stories still follow a traditional form.

---

2   Even Klaw was not that original, as, in 1904, Harold Begbie had written a series for *The London Magazine* about Andrew Latter, who enters a timeless dreamland where he can witness events leading to crimes.

In the United States, things were very different; until 1912, there had been no true occult investigator series, as in Britain. This all changed with "The Occult Detector," a short serial in *Cavalier* (17 February–2 March 1912) that introduced Prince Abduel Omar, the wealthy son of a Persian nobleman and Russian princess, who lives in a penthouse suite in New York and is known to one and all as Semi-Dual. The odd name comes from the fact that he provides both a natural and a supernatural solution to his investigations, but his entire operation is awesome. Besides being a psychologist—we are back with the medical profession—he is also an astrologer with telepathic abilities. This means he need hardly leave his skyscraper suite, and can instead operate through the team of Bryce & Glace, Private Investigators. Not only can Semi-Dual communicate with them telepathically, but he can divine, via horoscopes, the likely outcome of events. This series, which stretches over twenty-two years through thirty-three stories, many of them short novels, was by the writing team of John U. Giesy, a physician and well-known pulpster, and attorney Junius B. Smith. Despite their length—which almost rivals that of the de Grandin tales—none of the stories was collected in book form until recently, which means they are still relatively unknown except amongst old-time pulpsters. Despite the unusual nature of the plots, or maybe because of them, the series does not fit easily into the occult-detective category. It was much more the progenitor of such hero-pulp adventurers as Doc Savage.

The next occult detective to appear in the United States was equally extraordinary, or even more so, since they were written by an Englishman, but not published in Britain. These were the Simon Iff stories by Aleister Crowley, published under the alias Edward Kelly in the magazine *The International* starting in September 1917. Iff is a Thelemic magician and uses his understanding of the *Book of the Law* (an occult treatise written by Crowley, purportedly under inspiration from an ancient deity) to psychoanalyse his criminals and to help him unravel the inexplicable, though there is no ghost hunting here, the occult element being solely in Iff's abilities. Crowley saw Iff as an extension of himself and thus makes Iff infallible, but the stories are written with a perceptive wit missing from many occult-detective stories. Crowley enjoyed writing them, producing far more stories than were ever published during his lifetime. Iff also appears as a lead character in his novel *Moonchild* (1929), where he leads a group of white magicians in a war with black magicians over the possession of an unborn child. It is not an occult-detective novel.

We can rapidly pass over Herman Landon's Godfrey Usher stories, which ran in *Detective Story Magazine* during 1918. Although they have all the atmosphere of supernatural sleuth stories, there is very little by way of supernatural setting, other than through Usher's preening of his experiences. Crimes are solved far too easily by intuition, and the stories fall flat both as crime fiction and weird fiction.

This background shows that whilst in Britain the psychic sleuth story was getting into a rut, in the United States it hadn't yet grasped its purpose. So, when Seabury Quinn entered the field, courtesy of *Weird Tales*, we could all give a huge sigh of relief.

Quinn was able to blend tradition with exuberance to provide adventures and investigations full of every kind of supernatural and non-supernatural (but crazed) paraphernalia. Jules de Grandin himself seems to bear at least some resemblance to Hercule Poirot, albeit French rather than Belgian, whilst his amanuensis and fellow adventurer Dr. Trowbridge is every inch a John Watson. Both de Grandin and Trowbridge are physicians—in fact, de Grandin's skills are put to the test quite remarkably in this volume in "Malay Horror"—though de Grandin has the additional benefit of having served with the French Sûreté, and has also spent years studying the occult during travels in Asia and Africa. As a result, Quinn's two doctors didn't entirely let go of tradition; there is usually a consulting room scene, tucked away in Trowbridge's house in Harrisonville, New Jersey, even if it never lasts long.

What was exciting about the de Grandin stories is that there were no holds barred. The British breed of occult detectives were usually gentlemanly (or gentlewomanly), followed strict rules (often of their own invention), and dealt with matters that might be psychological or supernatural. The American breed hadn't quite known what they were until Quinn took them by the scruff of the neck and let them fall where they may. There was action a-plenty in the Carnacki stories, for example, but they're all part of his narration, told in the comfort of his home. De Grandin and Trowbridge, on the other hand, don't so much investigate as battle.

They fight against every conceivable type of villain, whether human or bestial, both dead or alive, sometimes all at once, and although Quinn created his own rule book for de Grandin, it was only as extensive as he wished—sharp, pointed knives are a key element in keeping evil at bay. Otherwise, Quinn ignored all the old rules, recognising he was in the twentieth century, not the Middle Ages, and that guns, electricity, and other advances in science were every bit as useful in combatting the horrors de Grandin faced.

Even apart from such usual menaces as werewolves, animated mummies, vampires, and Satanists, Quinn would frequently astonish the reader with his daring. This volume contains some of the most challenging stories, especially considering they were published in the mid-1930s. One of the best, and certainly one guaranteed to raise eyebrows, is "The Jest of Warburg Tantavul," which includes both child abuse and incest, as well as a very original way of disposing of a particularly nasty ghost. That sheer zest and audacity kept readers yearning for more and sustained the character through three decades. And that meant that the occult detective was back with renewed vitality, so that whilst its popularity waned in Britain, it grew rapidly in the States, chiefly in the pulp magazines.

De Grandin soon had his rivals: Pierre d'Artois, a highly Grandinesque character, by E. Hoffmann Price; Dr. Muncing, Exorcist, by Gordon MacCreagh; Cranshawe, "the greatest American authority on poltergeists," by Gordon Malherbe Hillman, Steve Harrison, by Robert E. Howard; Judge Pursuivant and John Thunstone, both by Manly Wade Wellman; Ascot Keane, who fought his deadly nemesis Dr. Satan in a series by Paul Ernst; Hugh Docre Purcell, created by W. Adolphe Roberts; and so many more. And this list doesn't cover the hero pulps, where, leaving aside certain adventures of The Shadow, The Spider, Doc Savage, and The Avenger, there was James Holm, a criminologist who pitted his wits against mad scientist and black magician Dr. Death; Don Diavolo, a stage magician who helped police expose apparent supernatural events; and Val Kildare, who fought the diabolical oriental villain Wu Fang.

The 1920s and 1930s were an exciting time for phantom fighters and psychic sleuths, and, alongside all these characters, Quinn kept de Grandin and Trowbridge alive and kicking—and seemingly ageless—for twenty-six years.

By the time the 1950s and 1960s came around, then, it was not surprising that readers paused for breath and wondered whether all might be calm and collected as, at long last, the traditional occult detective returned with Joseph Payne Brennan's Lucius Leffing.

There is no doubt that during the years between the decline of the traditional British supernatural sleuth at the end of the 1920s and its re-emergence in the 1960s, Jules de Grandin and Seabury Quinn not only helped keep the occult-detective genre alive, but gave it a verve and vitality that revived it for a new generation.

A
RIVAL
FROM THE
GRAVE

The Chosen of Vishnu

"ORDIEU, FRIEND TROWBRIDGE, I am miserable as an eel with the stomach-ache; let us seek the air," pleaded Jules de Grandin. "One little minute more of this and my grandsire's only grandson will perish miserably by asphyxia."

I nodded sympathetically and began shouldering my way toward the conservatory. Once a year all Harrisonville which claimed the faintest right to see itself in the society columns of the local papers attended the junior League's parade at the Bellevue-Standish, and this season's orgy had been even worse than usual. As special added attractions there had been several foreign consuls-general and an Indian princeling, round whom the women fluttered like flies around a freshly spilled sirup-pot, and the scent of flowers, of conglomerate perfumes and faintly perspiring humanity was almost overpowering. I was heartily glad when we finally succeeded in forcing our way to the cool semi-darkness of the deserted conservatory, where we could find sufficient elbow room to light a cigarette, and take a dozen steps without imperiling our feet beneath a wild stampede of high-heeled slippers.

"Eh bien," de Grandin drew a gulp of smoke gratefully into his lungs, "me I think I shall remain here till the ceremonies are concluded; sooner would I spend the night right here than face that crowd to seek my hat and—ah, my friend, is she not the chic, belle créature?" He drove his elbow into my ribs and nodded toward the girlish form emerging from behind the great illuminated fish-bowl at the entrance of the corridor.

He had not over-emphasized the facts. "Belle" she surely was, and "chic" as well. Not very tall, but very slim, her figure was accentuated by a black gown of transparent velvet which reached the floor and swirled about her insteps as she walked. Her eyes were large and wide and far apart, lustrous as purple pansy petals. Her hair, rich blue-black and glistening with brilliantine and careful brushing, was stretched without a ripple to the back of her neck. Her lips were full and darkly made up. Her teeth were very white and very even. Her skin, untouched by color, was faintly tan in shade, and shone as though it were a little moist. As she stepped we saw her heels were extremely high and her stockings sheer and dark. There was something sober, thoughtful, slightly frightened, I thought, in her expression as she faced the flower-and-fern lined corridor and paused a moment beside a lily-studded fountain, then half turned to retrace her steps.

Abruptly she halted, one slender, red-nailed hand half raised to her breast, as though to still the beating of a suddenly tumultuous heart, and stood at gaze, like a living creature frozen into marble at sight of Medusa's head.

Instinctively I followed the direction of her fascinated gaze and wondered at the terror which was limned upon her face. The man who had just stepped into the corridor was not particularly impressive. Undersized, extremely dark, slender, black hair, pomaded till it lay upon his scalp like a skullcap of black satin, he looked as though he would have been much more at home in Harlem than in our fashionable suburban hotel. Shirt studs and waistcoat buttons gleamed with brilliants, and against the lower edge of his evening coat was pinned a gem-encrusted decoration which glittered with a greenish glint in the conservatory's subdued illumination. Rather like a figure from a fancy-dress party I thought him till I saw his eyes. They made a difference; all the difference in the world, for the whole appearance of the man seemed altered instantly when one gazed into them. In odd contrast to his swarthy face, they were light in shade, cold, haughty, ophidian—like frozen agates—and though they were almost expressionless, they seemed to take in everything in the room—to see without beholding, and make a careful note of all they saw.

Apparently oblivious to the half-distracted girl, the man advanced, and, almost abreast of her, turned his freezing, haughty glance in her direction.

The result was devastating. Slowly, like something in a slow-motion picture, the girl bent forward, dropped gently to her knees, raised her arms above her head and bent her wrists till her right palm faced left, and the left palm right, then pressed her hands together and bowed her head demurely.

For a moment she knelt thus; then, still with that slow, deliberate, melting motion, she bent forward to the floor and touched her forehead to the tiles, stretched out her body slowly till she lay in utter prostration, feet straight out, ankles close together, hands extended to fullest reach before her, palms upward, as though inviting him to step upon them.

"Grand Dieu!" I heard de Grandin murmur, and caught my breath with a gasp of utter stupefaction as the dark-skinned man paused a moment in his step, glanced down upon the groveling girl with a look of loathing and disgust and spat upon her.

We saw her slender body quiver, as from a blow, as his spittle struck her on the neck, and:

"*Monsieur*, your face offends me and your manners are deplorable," said Jules de Grandin softly, emerging from behind the stand of potted palms where he had stood and driving a small, hard fist into the other's arrogant face.

The man staggered backward, for he was lightly made, and though de Grandin was of slender stature, his strength was out of all proportion to his size, and when cold fury lay behind his blows they were little less than deadly.

"*Mais oui*," the little Frenchman continued, advancing with a quick light spring, "your features are detestable, *Monsieur*, and spitting serpents are anathema to me. Thus I do to them, and thus—and thus—" With a speed and force and sureness which any bantamweight fighter might well have envied, he drove successive vicious punches to the other's face, striking savagely till blood spurted from the beaten man's cut lips and battered nose, and the cold, insolent eyes grew puffy underneath his stabbing blows. At last:

"A bath may cool your ardor and teach you better manners, one may hope!" the Frenchman finished, driving a final swift uppercut to the other's chin and sending him toppling into the placid waters of the goldfish pool.

"Wha—what's going on here?" a voice demanded and a tall young man rushed into the conservatory. "What—"

"Only a slight lesson in the niceties of etiquette, *Monsieur*," de Grandin answered casually, but stepped quickly back to take advantage of the intervening space if the other should attack him.

"But—" the man began, then ceased abruptly as a sobbing, pleading cry came from the girl upon the floor:

"Edward—Karowli Singh!"

"Karowli Singh? *Here*? Why that's impossible! Where?"

"Here, in this hotel; this room—"

"Yes, by blue, in the fish-pond!" interjected Jules de Grandin, who had been turning his quick, quizzical glance from one of them to the other during their disjointed colloquy. "But do not be disturbed. He will remain in place until I give him leave to move, unless by any chance you would converse with him—"

"Oh, no, no; *no!*" the girl broke in. "Take me away, please."

"Perfectly," the Frenchman agreed with a quick, elfin smile. "Take her away, *Monsieur*. Me, I shall remain behind to see he raises no disturbance."

The man and girl turned to leave, but at the second step she faltered, leaned heavily against her escort, and would have fallen had he not caught her in his arms.

"She's fainted!" cried the young man. "Here, help me get her through the crowd. The house physician—"

"Ah bah!" de Grandin interrupted. "The house physician? *Pouf!* I am Doctor Jules de Grandin and this is my good friend and colleague, Doctor Samuel Trowbridge, both at your instant service. If we can be of help—"

"Can you get us out of here?" the young man asked.

"But naturally, *Monsieur*. We have but to follow our noses. Our coats and hats may stay here for a time. Doctor Trowbridge's car waits without and we can drive all quickly to his office; then, when *Mademoiselle* is restored, I shall return and ransom them from the estimable young female bandit who presides at the check room. *Voilà tout.*"

T̲HE GIRL WAS CONSCIOUS, but strangely passive, lethargic as a fever convalescent, when we readied my house. She walked with trembling, halting steps, supported by her escort's arm, and more than once she stumbled and would have fallen had he not held her up.

"What this one needs is conversation," de Grandin whispered to me as we went down the hill. "Take them into the study, and I shall administer a stimulant, then encourage her to talk. She is beset by fear, and a discussion of her trouble will assist her to regain her mental poise. You agree?"

"I hardly know quite what to say," I returned. "It was the most outlandish thing—"

"Outlandish? You have right, my friend," he agreed with a smile. "It was—how do your so estimably patriotic Congressmen call it?—un-American, that reverence which she made that ape-faced one at the hotel. There is indubitably the funny business here, my old one. Oh, yes."

T̲HE GIRL, THE BOY and I gazed at each other with mutual embarrassment. The incident I had witnessed at the hotel was so utterly bizarre, so degradingly humiliating to the woman, that instinctively I shrank from looking at her, as I might have done had I unwittingly surprised her in the act of bathing. The only one in full possession of his wits seemed Jules de Grandin, who was not only master of himself, but of the situation. Wholly at his ease, he administered a dose of Hoffman's anodyne to the girl, then give her a cigarette, extending his silver pocket lighter to her with the same gay courtesy he would have shown to any usual visitor. At length, when she had set her cigarette alight and her escort's cigar was also properly ignited, he dropped into a chair, crossed his knees, and turned a frank, engaging smile upon the strangers.

"*Mademoiselle, Monsieur*," he began in an easy conversational tone, "as I have told you, I am Doctor Jules de Grandin. But medicine is but an incident with me. In the course of my career it has fallen to my lot to serve my country with sword or wits in every quarter of the globe." He paused a moment, smiling lightly at the visitors, both of whom regarded him with somber, questioning glances. Plainly, they were in no mood for conversation, but more than unresponsiveness was needed to check the loquacious little Frenchman's flow of talk.

"During the great war, of which you have unquestionably heard, though you were only children when it happened, I had occasion to visit India," he pursued, and this time he drew fire, for the girl shuddered, as if with a chill, and the big young man set his lips with sudden grimness, yet neither of them spoke.

"But yes, of course," de Grandin rattled on, gazing with every sign of approval at the polished tip of his patent leather evening pump, "there was a time when our then allies, the British, had good reason to doubt the loyalty of one of their vassal native princes. He was more than half suspected of carrying on an intrigue with the *boches*; certainly he was known to be employing German drillmasters for the tatterdemalion disorganization he liked to call his army, and at any moment he might have loosed his tribesmen on the Indian frontier, causing much annoyance to the British. Oh, yes.

"British spies could not get to him, but his activities must be known, and so, 'Jules de Grandin,' said the French Intelligence, 'you will please dye your hair and mustache and raise a beard, which you will also dye, then you will go to Dhittapur'"—consternation, blank surprise, showed on the faces of his hearers, but de Grandin kept on evenly, still admiring the toe of his pump—"'you will go to Dhittapur, posing as a French renegade, and seek service in the army of his Highness, the Maharajah.'

"*Tiens*, when one is ordered, one obeys, my friends. I went to that benighted country, I served the squint-eyed son of Satan who ruled over it; more, I met and came to know his charming little son and heir—as diabolical a young imp as ever plucked the plumage from a screaming parrot or tortured a caged and helpless leopard with hot irons. His name, unless I am mistaken, was Karowli Singh."

"Karowli Singh!" echoed the girl in a thin, frightened whisper.

"*Précisément, Mademoiselle*, and the opportunity I had tonight to drive my fist into his most unpleasant face was grateful as a drink of water in the desert, I assure you." He paused a moment, then:

"Now that we have established rapport by identifying mutual friendships, perhaps you will be good enough to tell me how and when it was you first became acquainted with the so charming gentleman, *Mademoiselle?*"

There was a long moment's silence; then, in a voice so low that we could barely hear it: "I belonged to him," the girl replied.

"Ah?" de Grandin brushed the trimly waxed ends of his little blond mustache. "You were—"

"I was a *bayadère*, or woman of the inner temple," she broke in. "At the age of five I was affianced to Vishnu, Preserver of the Universe; at seven I was married to him. I was a 'chosen one of the Sacred Bulls of Yama.' I and six other little girls were stripped and tied between the horns of the temple's sacred bulls, and the animals were then goaded into fighting each other. When they drove their heads together, their sharp, brass-tipped horns cut through the bodies of the children tied to them as though they had been bayonets. Of the seven 'choices' I was the only one alive when the cattle had done fighting; so my candidacy for marriage to the god was divinely ordained.

"For another seven years, until I was a full-grown woman according to Hindoo reckoning, I was schooled in the learning of the temple women; for hours each day I practised the devotional dances, working till my muscles ached as though with rheumatism and the skin was braised from my soft, bare feet. Then I learned the gesture dance, which requires years of practise before the performer learns to assume the nine hundred and forty-three symbolic postures and hold them with the rigidity of a statue; last of all I learned the Dance of the Seven Enticements, which is a combination of the Arabian *danse du ventre* and contortionism, the dancer being required not only to swing shoulders, hips, breasts and abdomen in time to the rhythm of the music, but to bend her head backward or forward to the floor without lifting either heels or toes or assisting herself with her hands. I also learned to play upon the *sitar* and tambourine and to sing the adorations, or love songs, which only women of the inner temple are taught, for they are experts in the arts of love and supply the most exclusive clientele in India.

"*Nautchis*—women of the outer temple—are merely *deva-dasis*, or slaves of the gods, and are plentiful in India, every tourist sees them; but *naikin bayadères* are never seen by the public. They keep strict *purdah*, for they are wives of the gods whose shrines they serve, and on the rare occasions when they appear outside the temple are as closely veiled and carefully watched as *ranis* of the mightiest maharajahs. For a low-caste man to touch one of them, or even to look upon her unveiled face, is a capital offense. Not even every Brahmin may approach them; only the higher orders of the priesthood and those of royal blood may speak to them without being first spoken to."

Her full, sad mouth curved in a sarcastic smile as she continued: "But the priests do not spend years in educating these women merely for the glory of the gods—*bayadères* are not like Christian nuns; far from it. When the *naikin* has served her long novitiate and been examined for proficiency in every branch of her learning, she is ready for service. For a stipulated fee she may be hired to dance and sing at the sumptuous entertainments of the rajahs; for a greater sum she may be sent to the zenana of some prince to remain there as long as he pays the yearly rental agreed upon with the priests. But never can she be married, for she is already a wife, wedded to the god whose temple she serves.

"I always hated the temple and the temple life. The priests were foul beasts; lazy, drunken, addicted to drugs and every imaginable form of vice; there was an undercurrent of nastiness running through every word and act and thought inside the temple, and against this I rebelled, but only instinctively, for my background was purely Hindoo, and all my experience since babyhood had been in the poisonous atmosphere of the inner temple.

"Then, one day when I was still a little girl, according to Western ideas, I was taken with some older temple women to assist at a *nautch* given by a great noble, for already my voice had developed and I was clever at playing on the sitar and singing the simpler *ghazals*, or love songs. Traffic was impeded by a herd of sacred cows moving through the street, and our camel-carriage stopped by a corner where a missionary *sahib* was preaching. He talked in the vernacular, and my childish ears drank up his words as sunburned sand absorbs the grateful rain-drops. Never before had I dreamed there could be such a god as that he spoke of. The gods I knew were cruel, lecherous and vengeful; this god the *Englay sahib* told of was gracious, kind and merciful, 'desiring not the death of a sinner, but rather that he should leave his wickedness and lead a new life,' he said—and every god I knew wreaked punishment on his followers through countless incarnations. At last the missionary finished and pronounced his benediction in a foreign tongue. The words were strange to me, but the syllables clung indelibly in my childish memory: '. . . by Thy great mercy defend us from all perils and dangers, through Jesus Christ, our Lord. Amen.'

"Then the traffic was resumed and our cart moved on, but the seed of rebellion had been sown in my heart.

"When I was fourteen it was arranged that I should go to the zenana of Karowli Singh, the new Maharajah of Dhittapur, for he had seen me dancing in the temple and desired me; desired me so much that he paid the priests an annual rental of 30,000 rupees—nearly $10,000—for me in advance.

"The temple slaves dressed me in my finest clothes, put emerald ear-rings in my ears and a golden flower in my nose, loaded my arms and wrists and ankles with bangles and put a ring on every toe and finger. Then I was ready for my royal master—I, a child of fourteen who for seven years had been a wife, yet never felt a man's caress. I was supposed to be elated at my fortune, and they had no thought that I would try to run away. The fact that I was destined for the harem of a rajah was considered sufficient protection; so only one old woman, too old for other service, was sent with me as *ayah*.

"We had almost reached the limits of the city, and my *ayah* had put back the curtains of our bullock cart for air, when I chanced to see a tall, broad-shouldered *sahib* walking by the road. I had not seen many *sahibs* in my life, but this one seemed strangely familiar to me, for while he wore the white-drill clothes and pith sun-helmet common to every *feringhi*, his collar was different, and instead of a cravat he wore a little patch of black cloth on his chest. I recognized him; he was a missionary *sahib* like the one whose sermon had so thrilled me years before.

"Before the old woman or the *gharry-wallah* could restrain me I had leaped from the bullock cart and rushed up to the missionary *sahib*. I knew just what to say, for years I had repeated those unknown but thrilling foreign words in my temple cell. I flung myself down before him, taking the dust from his feet and crying:

"'. . . *defend us from all perils and dangers, through Jesus our Lord. Amen!*'"

"The old *ayah* ran screaming in protest, and the *gharry-wallah* joined her and would have dragged me back, but the *Englay sahib* carried a blackthorn stick and beat them off with it. Even when the *gharry-wallah* drew a knife the *sahib* did not let me go, but struck the knife out of his hand and beat him till he squealed for mercy.

"Then he took me to a mission school and I was baptized as Madeline Kamla, and was no longer Kamla Devi, the temple woman.

"Karowli Singh was furious. He demanded return of the rental he had paid for me, but the priests refused to refund it unless he delivered me to them, and so a feud was started.

"But now I was in double peril, for both the maharajah and the priests desired me. The prince's dignity had been affronted by my flight, and he could not regain the 30,000 rupees rental he had paid till he delivered me at the temple. The priests demanded my return that they might torture me to death as a warning to other *bayadères*, for if other temple women followed my example and escaped, they would lose much money.

"But since I had been married to the great god Vishnu and made a *naikin bayadère* they could not put me to death ceremoniously unless I voluntarily relinquished my rank and titles. They might poison or stab me, or hide a scorpion in my bed, or the maharajah's servants might kidnap or murder me, but only my voluntary relinquishment of my status as a wife of Vishnu could give the priests the right to torture me to death. Still, if they could once get hold of me I knew that some way would be found to make me say the ancient formula of renunciation: 'Do with me as thou wilt.' For a temple woman to forsake her divine husband and her marriage vows and run away, especially to become a Christian, is an unforgivable sin, you know, and merits death by torture here and unending torment throughout the Seven Eternities hereafter.

"They tried to capture me by every means they knew. Twice emissaries from the maharajah attempted to abduct me from the mission, temple girls were sent as pretended converts to the school with poisoned sweetmeats, and even with deadly little kraits, or dust-snakes, concealed in leather bags to be put into my bed; once the mission was set afire. Finally the priests brought pressure on the British *raj*, and threatened an uprising if I were not returned.

"The British did not want to give me up, but it is their policy never to interfere with the religion of the country, and my shelter by the mission was making it very difficult for the government. Finally it was decided that I would be safer in America, where chance of pursuit by the priests or maharajah seemed impossible, so it was decided to send me here; but the question of my entry offered fresh difficulties. Hindoos are not eligible for naturalization, though ethnically we are as much members of the white race as the English and Germans, and the quota barriers prevented my entry otherwise. I could come as a student, but when my studies were completed I should have to return, and that would mean my certain death. Finally"—a flush mantled her olive cheeks—"finally it was decided I might enter as a non-quota immigrant, if I came as—"

She paused, and for the first time her escort spoke:

"If she came in as my wife. It was my father, the Rev. Edward Anspacher, to whom she first appealed, and I met her at the mission three years later when I went out to visit Dad after my graduation from Rutgers. I don't know how it was with Madeline—yes, I do, too, she's told me!—it was love at first sight between us, and I'd have married her and brought her home with me even if that pack of hell-hounds hadn't been yapping at her heels. What I can't understand, though, is whether it's just an evil chance that brings Karowli Singh here, or whether he found out where we lived and came here on purpose to get Madeline. It doesn't matter much now, though; he's seen her."

"But why did you—er—bow to him when you saw him tonight?" I asked the girl. "Surely, you're so changed, with your Western clothes and the passage of time, that you might have ignored his presence, and the chances are he'd never have recognized you."

She gave me a quick, sad smile. "Doctor Trowbridge," she replied, "during the most impressionable period of my life I was under the utter domination of the priests, having no thought or word or act save such as they dictated. I believed implicitly in their power and in the power of the gods of India. Five years among Americans is not enough to overcome the training of a lifetime, and when a person has been reared in the knowledge that a certain class of others hold her life at the dictate of their slightest whim, and when she has been compelled to prostrate herself and kiss the earth before those others— why, when I came suddenly face to face with Karowli Singh tonight, my early training came over me with a sudden rush, and automatically I made him the 'sublime obeisance' with which I had been taught to greet priests and rajahs in my childhood."

It was very quiet in the study as the girl ceased speaking. To me there was something horrible in the matter-of-fact way in which she had related her bizarre story. She was little more than a child, and all the dreadful things of which she told had occurred since the Armistice, yet—

"Eh bien, Monsieur," de Grandin's practical comment broke through my thought, "it seems they have long memories—and arms—these genial gentlemen of Dhittapur. I gave you better advice than I realized when I suggested that you leave your wraps and come with us. If you will excuse me I shall go now and retrieve them. You will await my return?" He rose with a bow, ascended the stairs to his room and employed himself with some mysterious business for a few moments.

"I shall return anon," he announced from the front hall. "Do you entertain *Madame* and *Monsieur*, Friend Trowbridge, and on no account permit yourselves to be enticed from the house till I come back."

"Not much fear of that," I assured the visitors as the door banged to behind my little friend. "It's nearly morning, and my practise is scarcely the kind which brings casual patients to—"

A sudden battering-ram knocking at the front door interrupted, and, though my declaration of intention was still uncompleted, I rose with the medical man's ingrained habit to answer the summons.

"Be careful!" warned the girl as I went down the hall. "Do not open the door, Doctor; look through the window, first, for—"

Some secret warning in my inner consciousness bade me follow her advice and I put back the curtain of the door's sidelight and peered out on the darkened porch.

Tight fingers seemed to close about my throat as I looked, and involuntarily I shook my head to clear my vision. There, crouched upon the door-mat, green eyes shining with malevolent anticipation, was a great, striped tiger, and even as I looked, I saw the beast put forth a pink tongue and lick its chaps. "Good heavens—" I began, but:

"*Kai hai!*" the girl called shrilly as she peered across my shoulder at the crouching beast. Followed a flood of high-pitched, singsong phrases, screamed rather than spoken, and, accompanying them, the girl's slim hands seemed to trace invisible figures in the air.

Amazement gave way to something like superstitious awe in my heart as I saw the gigantic beast slowly become wraith-like, transparent, finally vanish completely, like a slow fade-out in a motion picture.

"Wha—what was it?" I queried. "Was there really something there, or—"

Madeline Anspacher was trembling violently, and her pale-olive face seemed to have gone paler, making her large, purple eyes seem bigger by comparison, but she took control of herself with an effort as she answered: "Yes, it was there, ready to spring on you if you unbarred the door; yet—"

"But I saw it fade away," I cut in. "Was it really a tiger or was it just—"

"I can not explain," she answered quickly. "You have seen yogis do their magic; seen them make a whole tree grow from a planted seed in a minute or so, perhaps? How they do it no one knows, but I have seen it done many times and I have heard some of their charms. The chant I recited was the one they use to make a vision vanish. I do not know the words they use to conjure up a spell, nor do I think that what I said to make it go away would have been effective if the *guru* had been near by; so he must be working his magic from a distance, perhaps as far away as—"

Ron, ron, ron,
Le bleu dragon . . .

Singing blithely, though a trifle bawdily, Jules de Grandin came up the path, his arms laden with our visitors' outdoor wraps.

Sacré de nom,
Ron, ron, ron . . .

"De Grandin!" I cried, caution thrown away as I unlatched the door and leaped out on the porch. "Look out, de Grandin, the tiger's there, and—"

Something tawny-black and horribly agile, a great cat-thing, seemed suddenly to materialize out of the cold morning air and launch itself like a bolt of living fire at my small friend, and my warning changed to a shout of inarticulate terror as I looked.

But, astonishingly, the pouncing beast seemed stopped in mid-spring, as though it came in contact with a barricade of invisible steel bars, and the little Frenchman proceeded on his way as imperturbably as though out for an early-morning stroll. "Do not disturb yourself, *mon vieux*," he bade me almost casually, "it is a harmless pussy-cat they send—harmless as long as I am possessed of this!" he added, unclasping his right hand to display a crumpled marigold blossom in his palm. "For every poison there is an antidote, and this is that which makes them powerless, *n'est-ce-pas, petite?*" he smiled engagingly at Mrs. Anspacher.

The girl nodded. "It is a very holy flower in India," she admitted. "We—the temple women—used to wear wreaths of it on our heads, and garlands of it are draped on Vishnu's idols; but I never understood its real significance or—"

"*Tiens*, how many Christians know the meanings of the prayers they say?" he interrupted with an elfin grin. "It is enough that the flower possesses virtue to protect its bearer against such empty magic as these old ones make. However"—he stepped inside the house, deposited his burden on the hall table and invited our attention to an inch-long tear in his overcoat—"this was no empty gesture, *mes amis*."

"Great Scott!" I exclaimed. "What did it?"

"A knife," he answered easily. "This, to be specific." From his pocket he produced a double-edged dagger, a frightful-looking thing with heavy blade six inches long, wider at tip than base, its shaft set in a hilt of hammered brass.

"A Pathan throwing-knife!" exclaimed the girl.

"Perfectly, *Madame*, a very useful tool for liberating the soul of one whose existence annoys you," he agreed. "I was leaving the hotel, having no more thought of assault than the simple, innocent lamb has of mistreatment from the butcher, when *whish!* I feel the kick of this thing in my back, and the breath is all but knocked from out my lungs. Also, at the same time I hear the beat of running feet. They are not brave, those ones. No, they feared to stand and try conclusions with Jules de Grandin, even though they thought he had been killed to death by their so treacherous knife-in-the-back. Yes."

"But, great heavens, man!" I expostulated. "That hole in your coat is three inches below and three inches to the right of your left scapular. However did it miss your heart?"

"By not reaching it—or my hide, either," he answered with a chuckle. Divesting himself of overcoat and jacket, he displayed a close-fitting, sweater-like garment of finely woven steel chains above his waistcoat. "Jules de Grandin is the simpleton of no one," he informed us gravely. "When I set forth tonight I said to me, 'Jules de Grandin, only an exceedingly brave man or an exceedingly chuckle-headed fool goes into danger unprepared, and the chances of his being a fool are far greater than of his being merely brave. Jules de Grandin, is it that you are an imbecile?'

"'Oh, no; by no means,' I assure me. 'It are far otherwise.'

"'Very well, then, Jules de Grandin,' I inform me, 'you would do well to take precautions.'

"'And by the whiskers of a pink-faced fish, I shall take them, Jules de Grandin,' I replied to me.

"Therefore I went up to my room and took out from my bureau drawer this shirt of chain-mail which I used to wear in Paris when the exigencies of my work took me among the so amiable *apaches*. They are ready workers with their knives, those ones, and more than once I have owed the preservation of my health to this little vest of steel.

"Those ones whom I might meet tonight, I knew, could use a knife for other purposes than to cut their food, and so I did not greatly trust them. Also, lest they add magic to attempted murder, I stopped at the hotel florist's and bought a bunch of marigolds. So I was doubly armed. *Eh bien*, it was as well. Their knife glanced harmlessly away when it should have pierced my gizzard; their magic-summoned tiger was foiled by my flower. It has been a wholly satisfactory night thus far, my friends. Let us take a drink and go to bed while we still have our luck."

How long I had been sleeping I do not know, but it must have been some time, for the rectangle of moonlight from the window had moved perceptibly since I went to bed, and the eastern sky was showing vague streaks of slate-gray when I sat up, stark awake as though some one had slapped me while I slept. "What was it?" I asked myself, looking round the room in which I seemed to sense the presence of something alien, something which had no right to be there. Had I felt something, or dreamed it, or heard—

Instinctively I held my breath, seeking to pierce the smothering half-light with straining ears. I *had* heard something, but what? A cry, a voice, or—

Thin, muffled, like music issuing from a radio when the station is not accurately tuned in, I descried a queer, ululating whine, a rising, a falling, faintly surging and receding monotonous singsong; flat, raucous, metallic, like—what *was* it like, I asked myself, then, for some cause which had nothing to do with conscious reasoning, shuddered as recognition came to me. It was like the dismal, dolorous caterwauling of a juggler's reed pipe when the snake-charmer lifts the basket-lid and the scaly serpents slither out to "dance" upon their tails! "What in heaven's name—" I stammered wonderingly; but:

"Trowbridge, *mon vieux*," de Grandin's soft, insistent whisper sounded from the door, "are you awake?"

"Yes," instinctively I lowered my voice in answer. "What is that—"

"S-s-st," he warned. "No noise, if you please; for the dear God's sake bump into nothing when you rise. Come at once, and walk softly, if you please."

Wondering, I obeyed, and we hastened down the hall to the chamber we had assigned to Mr. and Mrs. Anspacher.

Again I shuddered, for no known reason, as we stopped silently before the door. Unmistakably the whining, droning hum proceeded from the guest room, and the sharp vibrance of it grated on my ears like the cacophony of a buzzing July locust.

De Grandin's lifted finger enjoined silence as he laid one hand on the knob and slowly, deliberately as the minute hand travels round the clock dial, began to twist the handle. The keeper slipped back with the faintest of faint clicks, and with the same slow care he pushed the white door open.

Despite his plea for silence, I could not forbear a gasp of horror and astonishment at the scene revealed. In bed lay Edward and Madeline Anspacher, not sleeping, but very still. Twin bodies in the slumber room of a funeral home could not have lain more quietly upon their biers than these two underneath the silken coverlet; yet their eyes were open wide and both were waking—waking to a horror which was like the insupportable suspense of the poor wretch on the gallows while he waits the springing of the drop. For upon the bed's foot, its dreadful, flattened head backed by a bloated, outspread hood, coiled a great cobra, three feet or so of scale-shod body looped upon the comforter, and three feet more upreared in the air, its forked tongue darting lambently between its thin, cruel lips, its narrow, death-charged head swinging to and fro as it bobbed and swayed and undulated to the measure of the wavering, whining, almost tuneless chant which Madeline Anspacher repeated endlessly, forcing the four quavering notes between stiffened, fear-grayed lips.

Nearly inaudible as our advent was, the sensitive ears of the serpent warned it we had come, and for an instant it turned questioning, threatening eyes in our direction; then, as though it knew that we were there to rob it of its prey, a sort of ripple ran down its body as it flexed itself for a stroke, and we saw the wicked head draw back an inch or so, heard Madeline's despairing scream as her chant broke off, and—

Bang! So swiftly Jules de Grandin fired that though the first shot struck the striking cobra's head even as it darted forward, the second bullet hit the scaly neck less than a half-inch from the wound made by the first; but the taut-drawn body of the reptile did not topple over. Instead it bent deliberately, slowly, toward the far side of the room, as though it had been pushed by an invisible prod, and the Frenchman had time to leap across the floor, draw his heavy hunting-knife and slash the gleaming body clear in two before the supple, coiling thing had fallen to the floor.

"*Parbleu*, I was not sure that I had hit him for a moment," he explained. "These small-bore steel-tipped bullets, they have not the striking power of the leaden ones."

I nodded absently, for my full attention was directed toward the pair upon the bed. Madeline had fainted, and her husband lay half conscious by her side, his lips agape, his tongue against his lower teeth, a smile of semi-idiocy on his face.

"*Mon Dieu*," de Grandin cried, "quick, my friend! Stimulants—ether, brandy, strychnine. They are in a pitiable state!"

They were, indeed. Hot applications and normal stimulants failing, we were forced to resort to intravenous saline infusions before our efforts were successful, and even then our patients' state was not entirely satisfactory.

"Good thing neither of 'em had a weak heart," I muttered grimly as we worked. "We'd surely have had a coroner's case on our hands if they weren't both so young and strong."

"U'm," de Grandin answered as he mixed the saline solution, "there will be a case for the coroner when I lay hands upon the miscreant who inserted that *sacré* snake into this house, you may bet yourself anything you please."

"I DON'T KNOW HOW IT happened," Madeline told us later in the day when, somewhat recovered from their profound shock, she and her husband were able to drink some broth and sit up in bed. "We didn't go to sleep at once, for both of us were badly frightened. Karowli Singh meant mischief, we were sure. We'd seen the tiger phantom which his guru sent against us, and Doctor de Grandin had told us of the attempt on his life. He'd been checked in every move so far, but a man with his capacity for hate and his determination to get revenge wouldn't be stopped so easily, we were certain.

"Finally, we managed to drop off, for it seemed impossible he could harm us so long as we were here; then—" She paused a moment, and de Grandin helped her to a sip of sherry. "I woke up feeling something on my feet. At first I thought it might be the bed clothes tucked in too tightly, and I was about to sit up and loosen them when I felt the weight move. It wasn't quite dawn, but it was light enough for me to make out the shape of the cobra coiling for a stroke.

"For an instant I thought I should die with fright, but one born and reared in India knows snakes, and one reared in a temple as I was knows something of snake-charming, too. I'd seen the fakirs with their dancing snakes a thousand times, and knew the tune they played to lull the venomous things into temporary harmlessness. If I could imitate a fakir's pipe I might be able to keep it from striking long enough for help to come, I thought, and so I began singing. It really wasn't very much of a trick, for I knew the pipe-music as American children know popular jazz songs, and I'd imitated the jugglers' pipes for my own amusement a hundred times.

"I don't know how long I sang. Edward woke at the first note and I was terrified for fear he'd move and break the spell, but fortunately he understood I meant him to lie quiet when I squeezed his hand; so we lay there for what seemed years while I held the snake's attention with my singing. Then when you finally came to help us, the sound of your entrance seemed to break the spell, and the cobra was about to strike when Doctor de Grandin shot it. Oh"—she covered her face with trembling hands—"I can still feel those dreadful coils harden on my feet as it contracted its muscles and braced its tail to strike!"

"Perfectly, *Madame*," de Grandin nodded. "It was a terrible experience you had. One understands."

"WELL, WHATEVER THE TIGER was, that snake was certainly no imaginary thing conjured up by a magician," I remarked as we left the patients and went to seek a bite of luncheon.

"*Tu parles, petit*," he agreed with a grin. "I cremated him in the furnace this morning, and he burned as beautifully as who sent him will eventually roast in hell, I assure you."

"Karowli Singh?" I asked.

"Who else, *pardieu*? Who else would have snakes ready to his hand, and introduce them through your second-story windows, my friend? Me, I think I shall enjoy tweaking that one's nose most heartily. But yes."

A DAY IN BED WORKED wonders for our patients and by evening they were ready to go home, though de Grandin urged them to remain with us a little longer so that he might be prepared to ward off any fresh attempt upon their lives. "He is a clever fellow, that one," he declared, "but Jules de Grandin is cleverer. Consider: I have made a monkey out of him at every turn, and I can continue so to do. Will you not stay with us?"

"Much obliged, sir," young Anspacher answered, "but I think Madeline and I will go home and pack. There's a steamer leaving for Bermuda tomorrow night, and we can make it if we hurry. I'll feel a lot more normal when we've put several thousand miles of ocean between us and Karowli Singh. We may not be as lucky next time as we were last night."

"*Tiens*, if you go away from me you may have no luck at all," the little Frenchman answered with a smile. "You can not have de Grandin at your elbow in Bermuda."

"Guess we'll have to take a chance on that," the young man replied, and so it was arranged.

Shortly after dinner I drove them to their apartment in the Durham Court, and we left them with their doors fast locked and windows tightly bolted. "We shall hope to see you at the ship," de Grandin said at parting. "In any event, call us on the telephone tomorrow morning, and tell us how it is with you."

He was silent through the evening, smoking cigarette after cigarette, staring abstractedly before him into the fire, muttering vague incoherencies to himself from time to time. Once or twice I sought to draw him into conversation, but met with only monosyllabic answers. At ten o'clock I rose and went to bed, for the night before had been a hard one and I felt the need of sleep acutely.

Sometime after midnight the irritable stutter of my bedside 'phone wrenched me from the embrace of a dreamless sleep, and:

"Doctor Trowbridge, can you come right over? This is Mrs. Frierson speaking," an agitated voice announced.

"Mrs. Frierson of the Durham Court Apartments?" I asked, feeling mechanically for the clothes which lay ready folded on the bedside chair.

"Yes—it's Eleanor. Something dreadful's happened."

"Eh? What?" I answered professionally. "Something dreadful," I well knew from past experience with half-hysterical mothers, might mean anything from a wrenched ankle to a case of acute appendicitis, and it was well to have the proper kit assembled ere I set out.

"Yes, yes; she's—they tried to kidnap her, and she's in a dreadful state!"

"All right, keep her in bed with hot water bottles or an electric pad, and give her twenty drops of aromatic ammonia in a wine-glass of chilled water," I prescribed, and I hung up the 'phone and finished dressing.

"Is it Madame Anspacher perhaps?" de Grandin asked, appearing abruptly at the bedroom door. "I heard the night 'phone ringing, and—"

"No, but it's a girl living in the same apartment," I answered wearily. "Somebody tried to kidnap her, and she's in 'a state,' her mother tells me. Want to come along?"

"Assuredly," he agreed. "These midnight calls are often of much greater interest than at first seems likely. Await me downstairs. I shall join you immediately. "

"Queer how cases seem to run in series," I commented as we drove toward Durham Court. "We've just finished treating the Anspachers for shock; now here's another girl, living in the same house with them, needing treatment for the same condition. They usually run in groups of three; wonder who the next one will be?"

"*Parbleu*, if what I damn suspect is true, perhaps it is I who shall need your kindly services," he responded with a smile.

M ISS FRIERSON'S CONDITION WAS not serious, and I found that simple treatment would suffice. Plainly, she had been badly frightened, and just as plainly she desired an appreciative audience to admire her filmy crêpe nightclothes, and listen to her story.

"I went out to Idlewild with Jack Sperry, Mabel Trumbull and Fred Spicer," she told us, "but the place was lousy; nothing doing there and nothing fit to drink, so we decided to cut it and come in town to Joe's place. They always have good liquor there. Know the dump? Hot-cha, it's a regular joint!

"Well, I'd noticed another car trailing us all the way from Idlewild, keeping about the same distance from us whether we went fast or slow, and it got my Billy. Too much of this holdup stuff on the country roads these nights, and though I didn't have anything 'specially valuable in the way of jewelry, I didn't hanker to be mauled around by a gang o' bandits. It's bad enough to have to stand that sort o' thing from your boy friend.

"Everything was jake till we got almost to town; then our left front tire went haywire, and Jack and Fred got out to change it. Mabel and I climbed down to stretch our legs and give the boys moral support, and while we stood there the other car came roaring up like an engine going to a three-alarm fire. They stopped so short the gravel shot in all directions from their wheels, and some of it hit me in the face. Next thing I knew they'd grabbed me and dragged me into their car and were off again, starting in high and running like a streak of greased lightning.

"One of 'em threw a bag or something over my head, so I couldn't see who had me or which way we were going, but I managed to struggle till I could look down under the folds of cloth around my head and catch a glimpse of the hands that held me. It was a colored man."

"*Mordieu*, a colored man, you say, *Mademoiselle?*" de Grandin asked softly.

"Yes," she replied, "and all the rest of 'em were colored, too."

"The rest?"

"Yes. They drove like Lord-knows-what for half an hour or so—we must have covered twenty miles at least—and finally brought up at an old and apparently deserted house. I was peeping between the folds of the cloth over my head as much as I could, and my brain was fairly active, noting all the landmarks, for I was bound I'd make my getaway at the first opportunity, and I wanted to know which way to run.

"They hustled me down a dark hall and flung me into a little room not much bigger than a closet. I felt around the walls and made sure there was no window in the place, then sat down on the floor to think things over. Almost before I realized it they were back—three of 'em—and I saw I'd been mistaken in my first guess. They weren't Negroes, but some sort of dark-skinned foreigners—Turks or something."

"*Eh*, Turks, you say, Mademoiselle?" de Grandin interjected. "How is it that you—"

"Well, maybe they weren't Turks, they might have been Arabs or something like that. All I know is that they were almost as dark as colored men, except that they were more coffee-colored than chocolate-tinted, and they all wore turbans, and when they talked to each other it sounded like smashing china.

"Two of 'em grabbed me and the other one put his nose almost against mine and said something that sounded like 'carbarn,' or—"

"*Dieu de Dieu!*" de Grandin ejaculated. "*Kurban!*"

"Maybe that was it," the girl conceded. "I wasn't paying much attention to exact pronunciation right then; I had other things to think of.

"'Look here, you,' I told the man who spoke to me, 'if you think you can get away with this you're mighty much mistaken. My uncle's an alderman, and you'll have the whole Harrisonville police force on your necks before morning if you don't turn me loose at once!'

"That seemed to sober him, all right, for he looked surprised and said something to the fellows who had hold of me. I guess he was asking 'em if they thought I told the truth, and I guess they said they did, for they weren't so rough with me after that, though they didn't let me go. Instead they took me down the hall to a room where a little, undersized pip squeak was sitting cross-legged on a pile of pillows. He looked as though he'd just come off second best in a bout with a first-class scrapper, too, for his lips were cut and both eyes blackened, and there were two or three bruises on his cheeks.

"Just the same, there was something terrifying about him. I can't remember being really scared of anything since I was a little girl and lay awake in the nursery waiting for the goblins to come and grab me, and—I had just that sort of all-hot-and-weak-inside feeling when I looked into that little dark-skinned fellow's eyes. They were a sort of agate-gray, like the eyes of a bad white man set in an evil mulatto's face, and something seemed to chill me to the bone. It seemed as though his two eyes melted into one, and that one grew and grew till it was as big as the ocean, and the more I tried to look away the more I had to stare at them. All of a sudden I felt myself on my knees—can you imagine? Me on my knees to a little half-portion brown-faced man, sobbing and trembling and so scared I couldn't speak!

"He looked at me for what seemed like a year, got up and came over to me and put my hair back, examining my ears, looking at 'em and feeling 'em—as if I were a horse or something—then he turned and laced it into those three fellows who had brought me. I couldn't understand a word he said, of course, but from his tone I knew he was giving 'em the cussing of their lives, and they crouched there and took it like whipped dogs.

"After that they took me out, put me in the car again and blindfolded me, and the next thing I knew I was out on the sidewalk, right before my own door. Can you imagine?"

"*Eh bien, Mademoiselle*, one can imagine very well indeed; exceedingly, well," de Grandin assured her. "You are a most fortunate young lady."

A S WE DROVE HOME he asked suddenly, apropos of nothing: "Does Mademoiselle Frierson remind you of any one you know, by any chance, my friend?"

"H'm, can't say she—by George, yes!" I answered. "There's a slight resemblance between her and Madeline Anspacher. They're about of a size, and both pronounced brunettes, and—"

"Assuredly," he acquiesced. "One might easily mistake one for the other if one knew neither of them well, especially if the light were indifferent."

"Then you think Karowli Singh's servants abducted Eleanor Frierson by mistake, thinking she was Madeline?"

"Perfectly. One suspects the fox when his poultry disappears, my friend."

"Well, then, why did the rajah, for I suppose it was he to whom she was taken, examine her ears?"

"*Tiens*, to see if they were, or ever had been pierced, of course," he answered in a tone of patient resignation. "Madame Anspacher has lived some time in America; time and different environment and Western clothes might make a big difference in her looks, but the earring holes bored in her lobes, the holes in which great loops of gold hung for nearly all her life, could not be hidden, neither could they have healed. Indeed, she still wears studs in her ears, as I observed last night. Mademoiselle Eleanor's ears have never been pierced for rings. I satisfied myself of that while we interviewed her."

"And that 'car-barn' or whatever it was her captor said to her—what does that mean?" I asked.

"*Kurban* is a Hindoo word denoting human sacrifice," he answered, "a sacrifice at which the victim, in order to attain forgiveness for sins committed in this or a prior incarnation, offers herself voluntarily to death."

"Good heavens, then—" I stopped aghast at the implication his words had raised.

"Precisely, exactly, quite so," he answered in a level, toneless voice. "You apprehend me perfectly, my friend."

N ORA McGINNIS, MY HIGHLY efficient household factotum, has a knack of securing her own way. Devout Catholic that she is, she would as soon think of strangling a sleeping infant in its crib as of eating meat on Friday, or (though I am a vestryman in the Episcopal Church and a past potentate of the Shrine) permitting me to do so. Accordingly, the next morning de Grandin and I found the table set with baked bloaters and waffles when we descended to the breakfast room.

"*Hélas*, I am worried, I am apprehensive and distrait, I can not eat; I have no appetite, me," the little Frenchman told me dolorously as he pushed away his thrice-replenished plate and drained his fourth cup of well-creamed coffee. "Behold, it is already after nine o'clock and Monsieur Édouard has not yet telephoned. I fear for their safety, my friend. That Karowli Singh, he is a rascal of the finest brew. I know him. He is altogether and decidedly no good. While I served as captain in the army of his late and unlamented papa I had abundant opportunity to observe the present maharajah of Dhittapur, then a charming little coffee-colored brat who sadly needed cuffing. I have seen him torture helpless animals for pure love of cruelty; have a peacock plucked alive or a leopard's claws and teeth pulled out before he fought the poor beast with his sword, prodding it repeatedly with his steel until he wearied of the sport and had the maimed and helpless thing thrown to his savage dogs or clubbed to death by his grooms. *Eh bien*, yes; I know him, and I should dearly love to twist his nose."

He lighted a cigarette and blew a twin column of smoke through his nostrils toward the ceiling. "Unless they telephone soon," he began, but the cachinnating summons of the 'phone bell cut him short, and he hastened to the farther room to answer it.

"But certainly," I heard him reply to the caller's query. "And how is Madame— *mon Dieu*, you can not mean it! But certainly, right away, at once; immediately.

"Come, my friend," he bade as he rejoined me in the breakfast room, "let us hasten, let us rush, let us fly with all expedition!"

"Where—"

"To those Durham Courts. She—Madame Anspacher—has gone away, vanished, evaporated completely."

Edward Anspacher met us in the foyer of his apartment, wonder and apprehension struggling for mastery of his features. "We were both pretty well tired with packing and making preparations for our trip," he told us, "and I think Madeline fell asleep at once. I know I did. I was so tired I overslept, for I remember distinctly that the clock was striking nine when I woke up with a raging toothache.

"Madeline was sleeping peacefully as a child and I hated to disturb her; so I got up quietly as possible and went into the bathroom for some aspirin. I couldn't have been five minutes, altogether, but when I came back she was gone, and my toothache had stopped as suddenly as it began."

"U'm?" de Grandin murmured. "You have been suffering with *mal de dents* recently, *Monsieur?*"

"No. My teeth are exceptionally healthy, and I'd finished my semi-yearly visit to the dentist last week. He told me there wasn't a sign of a cavity or diseased root anywhere; in fact, all he did was clean them. Why I should have had that sudden ache is more than I can—"

"But it is no mystery to me, my friend," the Frenchman interrupted. "I damn think it was the same sort of toothache that the tiger which frightened good Friend Trowbridge was a beast—a juggler's trick, by blue!"

The room was in confusion. Two wardrobe trunks, one a man's, one a woman's, stood on end by the door, and beside them rested several kit-bags and suitcases. On the chaise-longue at the bed's foot lay a woman's tan polo coat and a knitted silk-and-wool sports dress neatly folded. A pair of brown suède oxfords stood toe to toe on the floor beneath, dark-brown silk stockings neatly rolled in rings beside them. Beige crêpe step-ins, bandeau and garter belt reposed beside the dress, and a pair of pigskin gloves with purse to match and a hat of brown felt were on the bureau beside a packed, but open, case of toilet accessories.

"Everything else is packed," young Anspacher told us with a nod toward the feminine apparel. "Madeline laid those things out to travel in. She must have gone out in her pajamas, for nothing else is missing—even her mules are here," he indicated a pair of frivolous black-crêpe sandals on the floor beside the bed.

"U'm?" repeated Jules de Grandin musingly, walking toward the bedroom's single window. Parting the pale gold silk-gauze curtains he looked down to the cement-paved areaway beneath. "Ten meters, at the least," he estimated, "and no sign of—ah? A-a-ah? *Que diable?*

"Observe this, if you will be so kind, Friend Trowbridge," he commanded. "What is it, if you please?"

"H'm," I examined the object he had lifted from the sill wonderingly, "I'm hanged if I know. It looks like a strand of hair—human hair, I'd say if it weren't for—" I broke off, regarding his find with bewilderment.

"Yes—yes?" he prompted tartly. "If it were not for what you would classify it as which, my old one?"

"Why, the color," I replied. "It's blue, and—"

"Precisely, it is blue, but if it were brown or black or white, or any color save blue or green or purple, you would say that it is human?" he pressed.

"Yes, I think I should."

"And you should be right. It *is* human hair, my friend."

"Blue human hair?" I replied incredulously.

"Blue hair; blue human hair, no less. Have you ever seen such hair before; do not you know its use?"

"No, I can't say I have—" I began, but Edward Anspacher interrupted:

"*I've* seen blue hair; *I* know its use!" he burst out suddenly. "The fakirs in India when they do their famous rope trick use a strand of human hair dyed blue. I've seen 'em use those ropes in Benares when the pilgrims come to bathe and—"

"*Tu parles, mon vieux,*" de Grandin told him, "and what was it that they did with them?"

"Why, the fakir would uncoil his rope and swish it round his head like a lasso, then toss it up in the air, pronouncing an incantation, and the thing would stand there, straight and rigid as a pole. An assistant would climb up it and disappear, then suddenly reappear and slide down to the ground. Do you"—he broke off as though ashamed to put his guess in words—"do you suppose there's really anything *to* that trick—anything but mere optical illusion, I mean? I've seen it worked dozens of times, but—"

"*Eh bien,* here is one time you did not see it worked, but it was apparently successful," de Grandin interrupted dryly. "Yes, *mon pauvre,* I think that there is decidedly more than mere optical illusion to that trick. How they do it I do not know, any more than they know why a voice comes from the empty air when we dial a radio machine; our science is a tight-shut book to them, theirs is equally inscrutable to us; but I make no doubt that the ache which came into your sound and healthy tooth and roused you from your sleep, driving you from your bed to seek an anodyne, was a fakir's trick, and I also have no doubt that while you ministered to your toothache which was no toothache at all they threw their cursed blue rope up into the air, climbed it and abstracted *Madame* your wife from her bed."

"Good God!" exclaimed young Anspacher.

"Precisely," nodded Jules de Grandin gravely. "Prayers for her are in order, *Monsieur.*" Then:

"And so is action, by damn it! Me, I shall seek the good Costello and enlist his services. We shall turn this city inside out—take it to pieces bit by little bit, but we shall find her, and there shall we find him. Then"—he smiled unpleasantly—"then Jules de Grandin shall deal with the human reptile as he would with one which crawls upon its belly!"

DETECTIVE SERGEANT COSTELLO OF the Harrisonville police force, Captain Chenevert of the State Constabulary and Jules de Grandin bent above the assessor's map in the county building. "Somewhere inside this circle it will be," the Frenchman declared, tapping the chart with his pencil point. "Mademoiselle Frierson declares it was here that she was seized by Karowli Singh's agents, after which, according to her reckoning, she was driven rapidly for some twenty minutes. It is unlikely that they traveled more than sixty miles an hour; accordingly the place where she was taken lies somewhere inside the circle we have traced. Of that much we are fairly certain."

"Sure, an' we may be fairly certain a needle's hidden somewheres in a haystack, but it's a hell of a job sayin' where," Costello answered gloomily. "That circle's twenty miles acrost, Doctor de Grandin, sor, an' that's *some* territory to find one little gur-rl in, 'specially when she's likely to be kilt unless we find her pretty quick."

The Frenchman nodded agreement, but: "That is where you and Captain Chenevert can assist in the process of elimination," he returned. "Here are dwellings indicated. You can identify most of them, and tell something of their tenants. This, for instance"—he indicated the outline of a church and its appurtenant buildings—"is a house of worship. Either you or Captain Chenevert can tell us something of the clergyman in charge. At least you can say definitely that it could not have been here that Karowli Singh was when Mademoiselle Frierson was brought to him by mistake for Madame Anspacher. *N'est-ce-pas?*"

"Sure, I git ye," Costello answered. "I don't know every one whose house is indicated on th' plat, neither does th' Captain, but between us we can git th' necessary information, I from th' city policemen on th' beats, an' he from th' throopers who patrol those parts o' th' country outside th' city limits. How long can ye give us fer to git th' dope, sor?"

De Grandin consulted the watch strapped to his wrist. "It is now half-past two," he answered. "I do not think that they will start their devilment before sundown. Report to me at half-past six at least, and we can then plan our strategy. You agree?"

"Surest thing ye know, sor," the big detective answered; then, to Captain Chenevert:

"Let's git goin', sor; we've a power o'wor-rk to do, an' divilish little time to do it in, I'm thinkin'."

"ARRAH, DOCTOR DE GRANDIN, sor, it's dead I thought ye were entirely when I seen them big, black shiny cars all parked in th' side yard," declared

Costello when he and Captain Chenevert called with their report. "Phwat's th' idea of all th' funeral scenery, if I may ask?"

"I should be desolated if you failed to do so," the Frenchman answered with a grin. "We have a still hunt to make tonight. Somewhere in a quite extensive territory there is secreted a single small woman and we do not know how many miscreants who are spoiling for a slight degree of killing. We must take them by surprise, or all is lost, for they will surely murder her if they realize we are near. Very good. It is, therefore, doubly necessary that we do not advertise our advent. Did we go upon our expedition in police cars and motorcycles we might as well march in battalion formation with field music. Accordingly I have borrowed from Monsieur Martin, the amiable mortician, six limousines, each capable of carrying eight passengers in comfort. These cars will cruise the country over and create no comment. You apprehend my strategy?"

"True fer ye, sor," the sergeant complimented, and Captain Chenevert nodded approbation, "there was one dam' fine policeman lost when ye decided to retire from th' wor-rk."

"*Tiens*, priests, soldiers, doctors and policemen never retire, my friend," de Grandin answered with a smile. "They may enter other lines of work, but always, underneath, they cling all tightly to the instincts of their one-time calling."

So carefully had Costello and Chenevert canvassed their respective divisions of the suspected territory that only ten or a dozen buildings remained on their lists of possibilities. These were mostly vacant residences, deserted factories or houses whose occupants were known or suspected of having traffic with the underworld. It was agreed that a limousine loaded with policemen and state troopers should go immediately to each place, the officer in charge of each detachment being armed with a John Doe search warrant. If no signs of Madeline Anspacher or the retinue of Karowli Singh were found, the cars were to return to their rendezvous at my house, where further strategy would be planned.

An hour, two, passed, and one by one the cars returned, each with reports of failure. Eight strokes were sounding on the Town Hall tower clock when the final car drove up, and de Grandin, the two officers, young Edward Anspacher and I gathered in the study for a council of war.

"Looks like we skipped a bet, afther all," Costello began wearily. "Maybe if ye'd 'a' drawn yer circle wider, sor—"

"*Attendez!*" de Grandin's sharp admonition broke him off. "What place is this, *mes amis?*" he pointed to a sketch upon the map. "Has any one been there?"

"That? Why, it's old St. Malachy's Home," responded Captain Chenevert. "It was used as an orphanage twenty years ago, then turned into some sort of sanitarium for the feeble-minded, taken over as a recuperation home for sick and wounded officers during the war, and finally abandoned when the archdiocese acquired the new home over at Shelbyville. The place is just a ruin and—"

"And we shall go there *tout de suite*, by blue!" de Grandin cut in sharply. "It lies a good five miles outside our circle of suspicion, but Mademoiselle Frierson may easily have been mistaken in her calculations, and we, by damn, we can not afford to reject a single clue. Come, let us be upon our way. *En avant, mes braves.*"

As we drove quietly out the Albemarle Road toward the deserted orphanage, we passed a group of greenhouses, and de Grandin called a halt.

"*Monsieur*, is it that you have the *souci*—how do you call him? the marigold—here?" he asked the florist.

"Plenty," the other answered. "Want a couple o' dozen?"

"A dozen? Two? *Mais non*, I will take your entire stock, and quickly, if you please," replied the Frenchman. "Give them to us right away, immediately, at once, if you will be so kind."

"What the devil—" Captain Chenevert began wonderingly as de Grandin distributed the tawny blooms to each member of the raiding-party with injunctions to wear them fastened to their blouses.

"To circumvent the Evil One and his sworn assistants, my friend," the little Frenchman answered. "Tonight we go out against those who fight with weapons of the flesh and of the spirit also. I would not have it said that we were unprepared."

SILENTLY AS A FLEET of gondolas our motorcade swept out the broad turnpike, circled the rise of ground on which the half-dismantled orphans' home stood, and came to a halt. De Grandin called the officers around him for a final conference before the attack. "You will see strange things, *mes enfants*," he warned, "but do not be dismayed. Press forward steadily, and on no account discharge your weapons until you hear my whistle. You, *mon capitaine*, will take your men, form them in a crescent and proceed up the slope from the south; you, Sergeant, will please deploy your force in another half-moon and advance from the north. Doctor Trowbridge, Monsieur Anspacher and I will take three troopers and two policemen and press forward from this point. Keep in contact with us, if you please, for we shall lead the reconnaissance.

"Should any try to pass you, you will stop them."

"Did you say *stop* 'em, sir?" asked a state trooper, dropping his hand negligently on the butt of his service pistol.

The little Frenchman grinned appreciatively. "Your judgment is unquestionably sound, *mon vieux*," he answered. "Use it.

"When you have drawn your cordon round the house, give a soft owl's hoot," he continued. "You understand? *Bon. Allez-vous-en!*"

CAUTIOUSLY WE TOILED UP the steep slope, taking advantage of such cover as offered, keeping our gaze fixed on the gloomy pile which crowned the hill.

Almost at the crest of the rise we paused a moment, and I thrust my gloved hand into my mouth to stifle the involuntary cry of horror which pressed against my lips. "Look—*look*, de Grandin!" I whispered fearfully. "There—there must be thousands of them!"

Coiling, twisting, hissing, writhing in a horrid living chain about the hill-top was a veritable *chevaux-de-frise* of serpents, their small eyes gleaming balefully in the pale moonlight, peaked heads rearing menacingly, forked tongues darting warning and defiance. Another forward step and we should have walked right into the venomous cordon, and I shuddered as I realized what we had escaped.

"Jeez!" cried the trooper at my right as he snatched his pistol from its holster and leveled it at the seething mass of serpents.

"Fool! Remember my commands; no shooting!" de Grandin hissed, seizing the man's wrist and twisting the muzzle of his pistol toward the ground. "Would you advertise our coming? *Regardez—*"

Plucking a marigold blossom from his lapel he tossed it into the center of the writhing snakes.

Only once before had I seen anything comparable to what resulted. That was when a careless passer-by had dropped a glowing cigarette stump into the curb side exhibit of a peddler of celluloid toys. Now, as the inflammable playthings had caught fire and vanished in a puff of flame, just so did the picket-line of snakes suddenly dissolve before us, vanishing in the twinkling of an eye, and leaving our way clear and unobstructed across the frost-jeweled grass.

"Onward, my friends; quickly, they are at their devil's work already!" the Frenchman ordered in a low, tense voice, and even as he spoke the deep, reverberant tolling of a gong sounded from the darkened house ahead.

Forward we hurried, creeping from tree trunk to tree trunk, crawling on hands and knees from bush to bush, wriggling *ventre à terre* when the cover was too scant to hide us otherwise.

The big old house was dark as Erebus, but as we crouched by the foundation we descried a tiny beam of light leaking from a broken window, and at de Grandin's signal rose and glued our eyes to the cracked and dust-soiled pane.

The room in which we looked had evidently been used as the assembly hall, for it was as large as a small theater, and by the dim light of several oil-lamps swinging from the ceiling we could pick out every detail of the scene. A group of some twenty swart-faced turbaned men squatted tailor-fashion in a circle, while straight ahead, on a sort of dais formed of heaped-up pillows, lolled an olive-skinned young man, handsome in a sinister Oriental way, but with the weak face of a petulant, spoiled child. His head was wrapped in a turban of shimmering silk from the front of which flashed a diamond aigret. Over his shoulders dropped a cloak of leopardskin lined with scarlet, and round his neck and on his breast lay row on row of perfectly matched pearls and emeralds. Three dark-skinned, cameo-featured women, wrapped about head and shoulders with jewel-fringed shawls of red and black, crouched on the cushions at his feet. Naked save for turban and breech-clout, an emaciated old man with the straggling beard and mocking, sardonic eyes of an old and vicious goat squatted cross-legged on a mat before the dais.

A single glance identified the young man lolling on the piled-up cushions; for once seen, that sinister, cruel face could not be forgotten, whatever type of head-gear its owner wore. It was Karowli Singh, Maharajah of Dhittapur, who held his court here—for what purpose we knew all too well.

Once again the deep-toned gong boomed sonorously, and the rajah raised his hand in signal.

The folding doors at the farther end of the room slid back noiselessly, and two black-robed, hooded women entered, leading a third between them. It was Madeline Anspacher, yet it was not Madeline Anspacher, the Christian wife of a Christian American, but Kamla Devi, the Hindoo girl, *naikin bayadère* of the Inner Temple, and wife of Vishnu, the Preserver of the Universe, who stepped with meek, bowed head into this hall of Oriental justice.

Her head was covered with a shawl, or *sari*, of gold and black which fell across her shoulders, crossed at the bosom, then trailed its jewel-adorned fringes at her feet. Between her eyes was set a tiny, fiery-red caste mark, which stood out against the pale flesh like a new wound. Great ear-rings of gold, thick-set with glowing emeralds, caressed her cheeks, a smaller hoop of gold in which a gorgeous emerald solitaire gleamed vividly was in her nose. Her arms were fairly weighted down with bracelets of raw gold close-set with flashing emeralds, and on her rounded bare ankles were broad golden bands adorned with tiny, tinkling bells and fitted with fine golden chains each of which ended in a brilliantly jeweled toe-ring.

And now she stood before the rajah, no longer with bowed head, but proudly, almost arrogantly, like a princess of the blood, straight as a candle-flame in a windless room.

For a moment she stood thus; then, hands palm to palm, fingers pointing down, she bent her head and murmured: "As the gods command I come to thee, my lord, that thou mayest do with me as thou wilt. *Ram, Sita, Ram!*"

The young man on the dais smiled. "Does Kamla Devi come as a *naikin bayadère?*" he demanded.

"Nay, dreadful lord of life and death," she answered, lifting the mantle of black and gold tissue from her head and shoulders and dropping it at her feet, "behold, with unveiled head she stands before thee like a slave. Do with her as thou wilt. *Ram, Sita, Ram!*"

"'Tis not enough," he told her. "Kamla Devi has sinned past hope of pardon. She must taste of utmost degradation."

"Hearing and obeying," she replied, and with a swift brushing motion of her hand effaced the glowing caste mark from her brow, then from round her throat unclasped the triple-stranded necklace of pearls and emeralds and dropped it on the crumpled *sari* at her feet. From her arms she swept the golden bracelets, and slipped the tinkling, bell-hung anklets over her slim feet, laying them beside the other jewels on the discarded mantle; last of all, with a convulsive gesture she ripped the fastenings of her short, gem-embroidered jacket open, and as her breasts were bared, fell forward on her face, elbows to the floor, hands clasped above her bowed neck. As she dropped prostrate in utter self-abasement, I noticed that the palms of her hands and feet and the part in her hair were painted bright vermilion, and with a wondering start recalled hearing that Hindoo women who died before their husbands were thus adorned before the bearers took their bodies to the burning-ghat for incineration.

"As a slave of slaves Kamla Devi lies before thy feet, my lord, divested of her caste and ornaments, her bosoms bared like any casteless woman's, and makes thee offer of her forfeited life. Do with her as thou wilt. *Ram, Sita, Ram!*" she sobbed despairingly.

The aged, goat-faced man turned toward the youth upon the dais. "What shall be the punishment, O Mightiness?" he asked in a high, cracked voice.

The rajah closed his eyes in thought a moment, then answered slowly: "She is too fair to break with stones or burn with fire or smash with flailing clubs, O Holy One. I am much inclined to show her mercy. What is thy thought?"

"*Ahee*," the old man chuckled, "the night is young and death ends everything, my lord; do not drain the cup of vengeance at a single gulp. Let her dance with Nag and Nagaina, and let this be the judgment of her sins."

"*Wah*, thou hast spoken wisely, O brother of the elephant. Let her dance with Nag and with Nagaina," said the rajah.

"Good God!" I heard young Anspacher sob hysterically. "Nag and Nagaina! That means—"

"Be still, you fool!" de Grandin hissed. "We must await the others. Name of a name, why do they not come?"

The bearded, goat-faced man had risen and disappeared into the farther room. In a moment he returned with a pot-shaped basket of woven rushes covered with a scarlet cloth. A silken thong hung round his neck, something gruesomely like a skull dependent from it.

He set the basket down some ten feet from the girl, resumed his squatting posture at the rajah's feet and, unlooping the silk cord from his neck, began swinging the gourd—if it were a gourd—to which it was attached. Backward and forward, right, left; left, right, like a slowly oscillating pendulum he swung the bleached, skull-like sphere. He beat it as it swung, striking short, light taps with finger-tips and palms alternately, and it sounded with a hollow, melancholy murmur, a clucking, syncopated sort of rhythm, every seventh beat accentuated:

Tock, tock-a-tock-a, tock—
Tock, tock-a-tock-a, tock . . .

Monotonously, insistently, endlessly the pounding rhythm sounded:

Tock, tock-a-tock-a, tock—
Tock, tock-a-tock-a, tock . . .

He stared at the rush basket with fixed, hot eyes, and presently the red cloth on its top stirred slightly, as though lifted by a vagrant breath of wind.

Tock, tock-a-tock-a, tock . . .

The red cloth stirred again, slipped back an inch or so, and a flat, wedge-shaped head, set with little, gleaming eyes of green, reared from the opening. Another rose beside it, and now we saw the lamplight glitter evilly on the gray-white scalings of snakes' bellies as two giant cobras, one male, one female, writhed across the basket's lip, dropped thudding to the floor and coiled with upreared heads and outspread hoods, as though seeking to locate the throbbing drum.

"Rise and dance, O Kamla Devi; rise and dance with Nag and Nagaina and sing the snake-song to them as you dance. Sing long, my little nightingale, sing well, little thrush, sing sweetly, little linnet of the slim, white throat, for when you cease to sing you die," laughed Karowli Singh, and as he spoke the drum's soft sobbing ceased, and a silence like the silence of the tomb seemed rushing in to fill the air to overflowing.

"S-s-s-sss!" The great male cobra, Nag, coiled itself, its green eyes flashing evilly, its darting tongue signalling its anger. Then slowly it lowered its head and glided swiftly forward toward the girl's white feet.

"S-S-S-sss!" Nagaina, the female, joined her mate, and twisted her gleaming coils across the floor.

Kamla Devi leaped into the air with the litheness of an acrobat, landing with a little thudding sound some three feet from the snakes, and as she poised on slender, outspread toes, she pirouetted slowly, and from her parted lips there came a chant, a rising, falling, faintly surging and receding monotonous sing-song; raucous, metallic—like the music of a snake-charmer's pipe.

The hooded reptiles paused, reared their heads, and seemed to listen. Suddenly, from right and left, as though by concerted agreement, they raised their heads still higher, opened their jaws till the deadly poison-fangs gleamed whitely in the lamplight, and struck.

The girl rose upward in a soaring leap, and the driving, venom-laden heads passed like twin lightning strokes beneath her, missing her feet by less than three scant inches.

We heard the serpents hiss with fury as they missed their stroke, saw them lengthen out, then coil again, one to the left, the other to the right.

Louder, more insistently rose the chanting, whining wail, and again the snakes poised doubtfully, reddish-black tongues shooting out between blue-black lips, heads swaying as they watched the whirling dancer and listened to her song.

She faltered in the chant. Her throat was getting dry. She stumbled in her step; her feet were growing heavy, and again the serpents hissed their warning signal and struck and hissed again in fury as they missed the twinkling, fear-winged feet.

"Enough of this, *parbleu!*" de Grandin rasped. "If Costello and the captain are not ready we must take our chance against them as we are. We can not linger longer—she is tiring fast, and—"

Quaveringly, lightly through the night came the call of a screech-owl, and as it sounded Jules de Grandin drew his pistol, rested it upon the window-sill for better aim and fired.

He shot with all the daintiness of precision which characterized his every act, whether it were tying his cravat, snipping off a vermiform appendix from a quivering colon or adjusting his silk hat, and as though drawn to their targets by force of magnetism, his bullets struck. Shot followed shot so closely that the second was more like a continuation than an echo of the first. But each one was effective, for ere the startled Hindoos could so much as cry a warning to each other the two cobras lay upon the floor, their gleaming, scale-clad bodies quivering in the agony of sudden death, their poison-freighted heads ripped open by the soft-nosed slugs from his revolver.

"*Wh-e-ep!*" The shrilling of the whistle sounded deafeningly, and as he blew a second blast there came the drumming of heavy feet upon the sagging floors, the hammer of crowbars on the rotting doors, and Captain Chenevert and his men, followed by Costello and his forces, surged into the room. De Grandin mounted to the window-sill and leaped into the house, Anspacher, the officers and I following as best we could.

Cries, shots, the crack of butt-plates on bare skulls, the flash of knives and reek of gunpowder filled the place, mingled with such strange oaths as only soldiers know as the troopers and policemen drove the Hindoos to the wall and held them there.

"Belly th' wall, ye monkey-faced omad-hauns," Costello ordered. "Th' first one as tur-rns round gits a mouthful o' teeth pushed down 'is throat!"

The captives cowered cringingly, all but the maharajah. Scoundrel he was, heartless, unscrupulous, degenerate; but no coward.

"Bhowanee blast thee, Siva smite thee with his wrath!" he screamed at Jules de Grandin, his face gone gray with rage at thwarted vengeance. "Could I but meet thee man to man—"

"*Tiens*, my little vicious one, that can be easily arranged," the Frenchman interrupted. "Though you showed little liking for fair play when you held this poor girl within your power, I will give you one last chance to fight, and—"

"Take them outside," he ordered, motioning to the maharajah's suite. "But leave this one to me. He and I have business to transact."

"Shall we wait? Will ye be comin' soon, sor?" Costello asked.

"But certainly, my friend; either that or—" he raised his shoulders in a shrug as he selected two keen-edged scimitars dropped in the mêlée and thrust them point-downward in the center of the floor. "Friend Trowbridge will remain to see fair play," he added. "Should he come forth accompanied only by this one"—he nodded toward the rajah—"I beseech you to permit him to depart in peace and unmolested. Me, I shall not come out alone, I do assure you. Go out, my friends, for I am anxious to have done."

"Is it to be a dool?" Costello asked.

"More like an execution—but not of the death sentence; that would be too easy," the Frenchman answered. "Now go and leave me to my work.

"*En garde!*" he ordered sharply as the officers went out with their prisoners. "Karowli Singh, thou son and grandson of a stinking camel, if you defeat me you go free; if not I take such vengeance as is just!"

Like savage cats they faced each other, circling slowly round, eyes gleaming with as pitiless a glint as that their weapons caught from the uncertain lamp-light.

Suddenly the rajah charged, scimitar swinging like a whirling windmill—I heard the curved blade whistle through the air. De Grandin gave ground rapidly, skipping lightly back, making no attempt to meet his adversary's steel.

The Hindoo's white teeth flashed in a snarling smile. "Coward, poltroon, craven!" he taunted. "The gods fight with me; I, their chosen one—"

"Will choose no more to torture helpless beasts and women, I damn think!" the Frenchman interrupted. "*Cochon va!*"

The trick was worked so quickly that I could not follow it; but it seemed as if he drove straight forward with his blade, then slacked his thrust in mid-stab and cut a slashing S-shaped gash in the air before the other's face. Whatever the technique, the result was instant, for the rajah's sword seemed to fly from his hand as though he flung it from him, and a second later de Grandin raised his point and dashed his hilt into the other's mouth, sending him sprawling to the floor.

"Thy gods fight with thee, *hein?*" he queried mockingly. "*Pardieu,* I think that you and they alike are helpless when opposed by Jules de Grandin!"

From an inner pocket of his jacket he drew forth a gleaming instrument and leant above his foe. "Look for the last time on the world you know, thou *sacré singe!*" he ordered, and drove the hypodermic needle deep into the other's arm.

"What are you doing?" I demanded. "You promised—"

"I promised freedom if he won; I did not say what I should do if I prevailed," he interrupted coldly, putting the hypo carefully away in its black-leather case.

"What was the injection?"

"A little drug from his own country," he replied. "*Gunga,* it is sometimes called, though it contains other things than hashish. It is the justice of poetry that he should receive it, is it not? Behold how quickly it accomplishes its end."

I looked, and as I looked a chill ran through me. Karowli Singh was sitting on the floor, a silly, vacuous smile upon his face. Saliva dribbled from the corners of his mouth, his tongue hung out flaccidly, pendulously, across his chin, and he kept putting up his hands to stuff it back into his mouth, giggling as he did so. No doctor—no second-year medical student—could misread the signs. Complete, incurable, terminal dementia was stamped upon his features.

"Will—will he recover?" I asked in an awed whisper, knowing all the time what the answer must inevitably be.

"*Eh bien,* in hell perhaps; never in this world," de Grandin replied negligently. "Come, let us send Costello in to him, and—have you any idea how soon we can reach home? Me, I am most vilely thirsty for a drink."

The Malay Horror

T HE STORM WHICH HAD been threatening since noon broke with tropic fury just as darkness dropped upon the northern Jersey hills. Hackensack, where we might have found asylum, was half an hour's steady drive behind us, Harrisonville almost as far ahead, and, as far as I could remember, nothing offering more effective shelter than a road-side tree stood anywhere between, not even a hot-dog stand, a filling-station or a vegetable market.

"Looks as though we're in for it," I muttered grimly, drawing the storm curtains as tightly as I could and setting the automatic windshield-wiper clicking. "If we hadn't stopped for that last drink at the clubhouse—"

"We should have had a ducking, just the same, and should have missed the drink, *parbleu*," Jules de Grandin cut in with a laugh. "A little water is no tragedy, if applied to one's outside, my friend, and—"

The deafening detonation of a clap of thunder and the blinding flash of lightning searing through the dripping heavens interrupted him, and like an echo of the thunderbolt's concussion came the crashing of a tree across the road ahead. Another zigzag of forked lightning ripped the clouds apart and struck its target squarely, hurling a shattered oak athwart the highway just behind us.

Our position was untenable. The thunder had increased to drumfire quickness, and everywhere about us trees were crashing down. Our only safety lay in abandoning the car and taking to the open fields. Turning up our jacket collars, we scrambled from the shelter of the motor-car and dodged among the groaning, storm-racked trees.

The trip through the woods was like running the gauntlet of a barrage, for the lightning was almost incessant and the howling storm-wind bent the tree trunks and ripped off branches, which came hurtling down with smashing impact. More by luck than conscious effort, we struggled through the copse of oak and maple and padded ankle-deep in sodden grass across the open field.

"Yonder—shines—a—light!" de Grandin bellowed in my ear between cupped hands, then pointed to a shifting, fitful gleam which shone through the blinding storm three hundred yards or so away.

I sank my chin a little deeper in the collar of my sopping jacket and, bending my head against the driving storm, began to trot toward the promised shelter.

"Odd," I reflected as we struggled through the drenching rain, "there shouldn't be a light up there, The only house within a mile is the old Haines mansion, and that hasn't been occupied since—"

Shaking the water from my eyes I brought my cogitations to a stop. Only a fool would pause for thoughts like these when shelter from the storm was offered.

"Holà, à la maison!" de Grandin shouted, hammering on the rain-polished panels of the mansion's heavy door. "Make open the door all quickly, pour l'amour de Dieu! We drown, we perish; we are very uncomfortable!"

His hail was twice repeated before we heard a shuffling step and the big door was moved back a scant six inches to permit an old and very wrinkled yellow man to inspect us critically with small, unwinking eyes which somehow reminded me of those of a monkey.

"I am Doctor—" began the Frenchman, and at the title the door swung fully open and the porter motioned us to enter.

"You docta feller?" he asked as we dodged gratefully into the proffered shelter. "You get here pretty quick. Me telefone you ten-twenty minute, you say no can do for long time while God feller make big lain, then you come chop-chop, all same. Me think you dam' good feller for come like that through storm. Missy Lady all same pletty sick. You not chase devil feller out, me think maybe so she die pletty quick, You come now. She wait up stair." Peremptorily he motioned us to follow him.

My surmise had been right. It was the old Haines mansion where we were, though who our strange host and the mysterious "Missy Lady" who waited upstairs for us might be, and what they did in a house of evil memories which had been closed for twenty years, was more than I could guess.

Whoever they were, they had gone far toward making the old ruin habitable. Broken windows had been reglazed, the rosewood wainscoting had been oiled and polished and the oaken floors freshly waxed and strewn with an abundance of warm-colored Indian rugs. Electric light had been in the experimental stage when the foundations of the old house were dug, but some one had evidently rehabilitated the carbide gas plant in the cellar, and flames burned brightly in the ruby-glass globes of the ceiling chandelier with a scarcely audible hiss. Cedar logs blazed comfortably on the newly polished brass fire-dogs beneath the high mantel; curtains of bright silk and lambrequins of split bamboo, such as had been fashionable in the middle eighties, hung at the arched doorways leading from the hall.

We paused a moment by the cheerful fire, but: "You come," our guide admonished in a high, cracked voice, glancing back across his shoulder. "Bime-by dly clothes. Now you come chase devil-devil out Missy Lady's neck. You savvy?" He shuffled almost soundlessly toward the wide stairway above which our unexpected patient waited.

Surprising as the rejuvenated mansion was, our guide was more so. Scarcely five feet tall, he was as thin as almost fleshless bones could make him, and his butter-colored skin was stretched drumtight upon his skeleton everywhere except his face. There it was cut and etched and crisscrossed with innumerable deep-cleft wrinkles till his countenance resembled the rind of a frost-bitten pumpkin. A little green-silk cap was perched rakishly upon his hairless head; a tightly buttoned jacket of freshly washed and starched white drill encased his torso; in lieu of trousers his nether limbs were cased in a length of brightly batiked cotton wound so tightly in a skirt-like drapery that it forced him to proceed with a hobbled, shuffling gait. Heelless shoes of woven straw, like the slippers Chinese laundrymen wear at their work, were on his feet, and their straw soles grated softly with a *whish-whish* at each sliding step he took across the polished floor.

The unmistakably sickly-sweet scent of burning joss-sticks assailed our nostrils as we followed up the stairs and down the upper corridor to a darkened bedroom where our conductor paused and called softly. "Missy Lady, docta fella come all quick for dlive off devil-devil. You see 'um now?"

An odd-sounding, half-articulate gurgle like the cry of some one being slowly strangled, answered him, and he motioned us to enter. No light burned in the room, but here and there the gloom was dotted by the ruddy glow of smoldering punk sticks, and the air reeked with the cloying sweetness of the incense.

"*Morbleu*, it is intolerable!" de Grandin cried. "Lights, my ancient one, and quickly; then fling away these so abominable inventions of the devil. No wonder she is ill! This stink, it is enough to make a camel weep for envy!"

A match scratched, and a moment later a gas flame flared behind the etched glass shade of a wall fixture. By its light we saw a woman lying in a great sleigh bed, pillows heaped behind her till she seemed to sit more than to recline. A silken coverlet was drawn close about her chin. A bunch of bright red flowers, oddly reminiscent of a funeral wreath, lay on the comforter. There was something coppery, almost metallic, about her. Her hair, thick and very glossy, was the color of new-minted copper, and simply parted in the middle, drawn above her ears and knotted low upon her neck. Her eyes were almost bronze in shade, and shone as if with unshed tears. Her features were small and straight and regular, chin pointed, lips rather thin, but exquisitely curved, her skin an even golden tan which told of long exposure to the sun.

"*Eh bien, Mademoiselle*, it seems we are arrived in time to save you from asphyxiation," de Grandin announced. "Your—the excellent old one who admitted us—informed us that you were indisposed. What seems to be—"

He paused beside the bed, and his thin, sensitive mouth drew sharply down at the corners. "*La diphthérie?*" his lips formed the words silently as he looked at me for confirmation of the diagnosis.

I looked sharply at the patient. Her face was slightly cyanotic, her lips were slightly parted and her breathing stertorous. Constantly her throat was working, as though she sought to swallow some obstruction, and, there was no doubt about it, her eyes were definitely protuberant, as from a pressure on the trachea, perhaps a consequence of Graves' disease. No swelling of lymphatics at the angle of the jaw appeared, however, and I withheld my opinion till I had an opportunity of examining the fauces and tonsils.

"Will you open your mouth?" I asked, leaning over her; then:

"I say, de Grandin, look at this!" I cried, incredulity in my voice as I pointed to the patient's throat. Around her neck, midway between the jaw and shoulders, was a plainly marked depression, smooth and circular, as from an invisible ligature which seemed to be drawing steadily tighter with garroting force, for even as we looked we saw the indentation grow white and whiter, saw the shrinking flesh sink further as the unseen tourniquet was tightened.

"*Mon Dieu,*" exclaimed the Frenchman, "she is strangling!" and even as he spoke the girl sat up in bed, clawing at her throat with frenzied hands while he mouth gaped open horribly and her tongue protruded. A choking, gasping sob escaped her tortured lips; then she fell back limply on the pillows, eyes closed, chest heaving, little whimpering noises sounding in her throat.

But the spasm seemed definitely over. Her breath came naturally, though with considerable labor, and the white ring on her throat began to fade.

"*Attendez-vous,*" de Grandin hailed the little yellow man. "Ammonia, aromatic spirits of ammonia—*non*, ten thousand small blue devils, you can not understand!—where in Satan's name is the bathroom?"

"Bathloom?" the other echoed uncomprehendingly.

"*Précisément; la salle de bain*—the place where medicines are kept!"

"Oh, me savvy," said the other in a flat and uninflected voice. "You come; I show you."

They hurried down the hall and presently de Grandin returned with a glass of ammonia and water, which he administered to the patient. "I would we had some belladonna on hand, he murmured as the girl drained the draft and settled back upon her pillows. "It would be of assistance. There is nothing but cosmetics to be had back there, and paint and powder are no use in such a case. If—"

"What do you make of it?" I interrupted, thinking wonderingly of the cincture we had seen form round the girl's slim throat, apparently for no earthly reason.

"*Parbleu,* I do not know," he told me earnestly. "If it were not for certain things I should have said it was the work of—"

A wild, high wail from the little yellow man cut short his words. "*Ahee, ahee—penanggalan, penanggalan!*" he shrieked, falling to his knees and bowing forward like a closed-up jack-knife. "*Ahee, awah!*"

"*Que diable?*" snapped de Grandin; then:

"*Ohé, mon Dieu,* one sees! Behold, my friend, he speaks the truth!" Seizing my shoulder he whirled me round to face the window, and pointed to the rain-glazed pane.

There, limned against the background of the tempest's blackness, hung a face.

I say "hung" advisedly, for it showed against the window in the very center of the pane, and from above and underneath there was nothing to support it. It was a handsome woman's face, beautiful with a sort of eery beauty, but deadly in its look of hatred and malignancy. The skin was an incredibly lovely shade of golden brown, smooth and faintly iridescent, the hair which framed it was a dull cloud of ebon splendor. The features were clear cut, classic, but exotic; high, wide brow, straight, thin nose with faintly flaring nostrils, sharp, pointed chin and thin, black-penciled brows curving like circumflexes above a pair of wide, green eyes with pupils flecked with red, burning like live cinders, unwinking, mesmeric. The mouth was large, with thin, cruel, scarlet lips and white and gleaming teeth which showed their vicious sharpness as the lips curled back in a soundless snarl of leopardine fury.

Beneath the head there was no body, but a length of esophagus hung pendently below the severed neck, and from this in turn hung a stomach sac. It was incredible, impossible, bizarre; but there it was: a living, grimacing face with unsheathed stomach and esophagus was *floating in the air* outside the bedroom window.

"Good heavens," I exclaimed, "what *is* it?"

"The *penanggalan,* did not you hear him say so?" de Grandin answered, and, it seemed to me, he had grown calmer since the dreadful apparition showed outside the window. Whirling toward the bed he snatched up the wreath of scarlet flowers. As he did so I noticed for the first time that their stems were set with long, curved thorns.

"*Allez, Madame,*" he commanded, stepping toward the window. "*Allez-vous-en!* I have here that which will render you decidedly uncomfortable if—" he threw the window open and swept the thorn-set flowers in a wide half-circle. As he did so the half-dissected horror gave ground, hovered menacingly in the swirling rain a moment, then disappeared from view with a shrieking, cachinnating laugh which was half sardonic merriment, half despairing scream.

"So," he murmured as he closed the window and replaced the flowers on the bed. "At last one understands—in part, at least. One might have damn suspected something of the kind, yet it is strange, infernally strange that such a one should be here in New Jersey. If this were Borneo or Flores or the Peninsula, one might look for her, but here? *Non*, we must seek further information."

"Docta *Tuan* blave man!" the little yellow individual complimented with a low, ingratiating bow. "Him not 'flaid Missy Penanggalan; him dlive her off pletty dam' quick!"

De Grandin looked at him with interest. "How long has she been flying round the house, my friend?" he asked.

"Long time, three-four week," the other answered. "Missy Joan bling one piecee coffin here from Manula; bury 'um in glaveyard. Pletty soon Miss Penanggalan come fly all lound house.

"Missy Lady ketchum plenty sickness; get devil-devil in neck. All same maybe turn into *penanggalan* pletty soon if Doctor *Tuan* not come *chop-chop* for dlive devil-devil off.

"Ah Kee ketchum plenty thorn-flower for lay on bed. Maybe Missy Penanggalan not love that thorn-feller velly much. Ah Kee burn joss-stick all lound loom, too. No dam' good. Missy Penanggalan come all time, fly lound house, make bad face outside window. Ah Kee can do no more; he tefelone Docta *Tuan* for come all soon. You dlive devil-devil out Missy Lady's neck, maybe so?"

There was a look of child-like faith and pleading in his wrinkled visage as he spoke. Jules de Grandin beamed on him. "*Pardieu*, that we shall, *mon vieux*, or may I dine upon stewed turnips!" he replied. "And as we speak of dining I remind myself that I have not yet supped. Have you anything to eat about the place? We shall be here all night, it seems, and I would not care to fast till morning."

"All light, me ketchum food," the little man responded. "You stay for look at Missy Lady?"

"We shall most indubitably stay," returned de Grandin. "Bring the food to us when it has been prepared, and do not stint the quantity; this is a very devil of a devil-devil we must fight, and we fight poorly on an empty stomach, my little old one."

As the diminutive yellow man shuffled off, de Grandin turned to me, brows arched, lips pursed quizzically. "This is of interest, my friend," he assured me. "This creature, this *penanggalan* we saw tonight, she is a rare specimen; I have heard of her, but—"

"Ah Kee, Ah Kee, are you there?" a weak voice called. "Did it come again, Ah Kee? I'm afraid; terribly afraid it will come back and—"

"Compose yourself, *Mademoiselle*," de Grandin answered. "Ah Kee is gone but we are here. I am Doctor Jules de Grandin, this is my good friend and colleague, Doctor Samuel Trowbridge. We were driving past your charming house when the storm broke and we knocked upon your door for shelter. It appeared your excellent intendant had summoned medical assistance, but the one he called had been unable to respond. Accordingly he requested that we help you, and we arrived in time to drive away a most unpleasant visitor. Now—"

"It came, then?" the woman interrupted.

"It came, *Mademoiselle*," agreed de Grandin, "but it also went. '*Allez*,' I told it, and *pouf!* like that it went. Me, I am very clever, *Mademoiselle*."

Despite her fear, the girl smiled wanly as he finished speaking. Women, animals and children took instinctively to Jules de Grandin, and our latest patient was no exception to the rule.

"How did you drive it off?" she asked.

"How? By telling it it was not welcome—and by threatening to lacerate its appendages with the thorns of these flowers," he answered with a grin. Then, sobering suddenly:

"*Mademoiselle*, I have said I am a doctor. That is true; I hold degrees from Vienna and the Sorbonne; but I am more than a physician. I am a practised occultist, and have spent as much time grappling with the foes of the spirit as with those of the flesh. Also I have traveled much, and have spent some time in the Malay Archipelago and Peninsula. When we heard your servant cry out in terror that the *penanggalan* was come, I realized the import of his words, and though I have never come to grips with a demon of this order, I welcome the challenge which it brings. Will you permit that I assist you, *Mademoiselle?*"

"Oh, yes!" the girl responded. "I've been so terrified; if you will help me—"

"*Très bon*, it is a bargain, *Mademoiselle*," the Frenchman interrupted, possessing himself of one of the slim hands lying on the counterpane and lifting it to his lips. "Now—as you Americans so drolly say—to business. Begin at the commencement, if you please, and tell us everything leading to the advent of these most unwelcome visits. Your servant told us something of your bringing back a coffin to America and having it interred. How was it that you came to do so?"

"It was the body of my father," the girl replied. "I brought it back from Manura for burial in the family plot in Shadow Lawns, and—"

She paused a moment, and a shudder rippled through her frame; then, taking a firm hold upon her quaking nerves, she began anew:

"My name is Joan Haines. I am twenty years old. I was born in this house, and my mother died when I was born. My father, Henry Haines, had spent several years on the island of Manura, and made a considerable fortune and restored the family home before his marriage. When Mother died he was almost beside himself with grief, declared he never wanted to see this place again, and left almost immediately for the islands. I was taken by my father's cousin, Thomas Haines, who lived in Harrisonville, and reared as a member of his family. I lived with him until a year ago, and his son Philip and I fell desperately in love.

"During all the years when I was growing up my father never wrote me. He sent regular remittances to my uncle—Cousin Tom was so much my senior that

I always called him uncle—for my support and education, but though I wrote him frequent little-girl letters, trying desperately to make him love me, he never answered. Uncle Tom kept in correspondence with him, though, and every time I had a picture taken a print of it was sent my father; so he knew what I looked like, though I had no idea of his appearance.

"My cousin Philip and I had been inseparable as children, went to grammar and high school together, and matriculated at the same college and graduated together. Just after graduation I wrote Father that Phil and I wanted to be married, and then I got the first and only letter which I ever had from him.

"It was stilted and unfriendly, the kind of letter which a stranger might have written, and refused permission for our marriage. He accused Phil and Uncle Tom of wanting my money, and ordered me to come out to Manura at once, as, he said, he had other plans for me.

"I hardly knew which way to turn. Phil and Uncle Tom urged me to ignore Father's orders, but, somehow, I couldn't bring myself to do so. I don't know why it was; perhaps the fact that I'd grown up as a sort of orphan made a difference; possibly the strange, aloof attitude my father had always assumed regarding me piqued my curiosity as much as it excited my vague longings for a real father's affection. At any rate, I decided to go out to him and tell him everything about Phil and me. I was sure that I could win him over. So it was arranged.

"Manura is a little island—just a flyspeck on the map—which lies on the Celebes side of Flores. It took me nearly a month to get out there, and when I finally got there it was too late."

"Too late?" de Grandin echoed.

"Too late, yes," she answered. "My father was dead.

"Manura is nominally under Dutch rule, but it's so unimportant that they haven't a regularly resident administrator there, and the actual government is carried on by the native sultan, Ali Nogoro. When I arrived I discovered that my father had been married for some years to one of the sultan's sisters, a fine-looking native woman named Salanga, who had been given him as wife in return for his promise that he would give *me* to the sultan when I arrived at marriageable age."

"*Mon Dieu!*" exclaimed de Grandin.

"Exactly," she assented with a bitter little smile. "That was the bargain they had made. As Ali Nogoro's brother-in-law, my father had everything his own way in Manura. Other traders were permitted on the island only by his sufferance, and as a consequence of this preferment he had become enormously wealthy. But I was the price he had agreed to pay.

"At the last, though, he must have repented his revolting bargain, for I found a will, duly authenticated by the Dutch district commissioner, which left everything to me, and a note requesting me to bring his body back to Harrisonville for burial beside my mother. 'Go home, child,' the note told me; 'open the old house where I was so happy for a little while, and be happy there with the man you love.'

"Fortunately for me, Father had sent much of his fortune home for deposit in American banks, for when I refused to carry out the bargain and marry Sultan Ali Nogoro, he confiscated everything, and had it not been for Ah Kee, my father's half-caste number one man, I probably shouldn't have been able to escape Nogoro after all. You see, I had practically no money when I landed, and Nogoro absolutely refused to let me take so much as a stick of furniture from my father's house or godown.

"But Ah Kee had some money of his own, and with it he paid the coolies for disinterring my father's coffin, bribed some fishermen to take us to Flores in their boat, then paid our passage to America.

"Bad as Nogoro was to deal with, his sister Salanga, who was, after all, my father's widow, proved far worse. She declared she had 'lost face' by my refusal to carry out the marriage bargain which had been made for me, and the will which virtually disinherited her infuriated her even more. I offered to share everything which Father left with her, half and half, and even had a Dutch notary draw up a quitclaim of half the inheritance, but she tore the paper into shreds, spit at me, and would have done me physical injury if they had not restrained her. The day before I left Manura she committed suicide."

"Suicide?" de Grandin asked. "You mean a sort of vengeance death, like the *hara-kari* of the Japanese?"

"I—I suppose so, sir. Her body was found in the bed she'd occupied in my father's house the day before Ah Kee and I left Manura. But—"

"*Tiens*, now I think that we approach the egg's good meat!" de Grandin cut in softly as she paused in her recital. "Yes, *Mademoiselle?* But—"

"But when the coolies went to the cemetery to disinter my father's coffin they found Salanga's decapitated body sprawled prostrate on the grave. The arms were opened, as though to embrace the mound, and the feet were spread apart, as though to hold down whatever lay beneath. Her neck had been severed close to the shoulders, and the head was nowhere to be found."

De Grandin twisted fiercely at the needle-points of his trimly waxed wheat-blond mustache. "Tell me, *Mademoiselle*," he asked irrelevantly, "who officiated at your father's interment in the grave beside your mother?"

"Why, Doctor Bentley, the rector of St. Chrysostom's; he had been—"

"*Non*, you do misapprehend. I do not mean the clergyman, but the mortician."

"Oh, the undertaker. Why, Mr. Martin, of Harrisonville, who made all the necessary arrangements."

"U'm? Thank you. What then, if you please?"

"Ah Kee and I came out here, and as soon as Mr. Van Riper, our family lawyer, completes the probate of my father's will, I intend having the place completely modernized. My cousin Philip and I are to be married in the fall, if I—"

Once more she paused, and de Grandin leant forward with quick understanding as he patted her hand reassuringly. "Do not be alarmed, *ma chère*; you will assuredly live that long, and much longer, too," he comforted. "I, Jules de Grandin, guarantee it.

"Now," once more his cool, professional manner asserted itself, "when was it that you first observed these untoward occurrences, if you please?"

"I've been home one month tomorrow," she replied. "We'd just come out here, three weeks ago, when one night I wakened from a sound sleep hearing some one laughing at me.

"At first I thought I'd dreamed it, but the laughter persisted, even when I sat up in bed. I looked around; there was no one in the room. Then I rose to light the gas, and as I did so, chanced to look toward the window. *There was Salanga's head.* It hung in midair, with nothing to sustain it, just outside the window, and laughed at me.

"Suddenly I felt a stifling, choking sensation, as though a band were drawn about my throat. I put my hands up to my neck, but there was nothing there. But the throttling feeling grew, and as my fingers touched my throat I could feel the flesh sinking in, as though compressed by an invisible cord. My breath came shorter and shorter, I could hear the heart-beats pounding in my ears, and everything turned black; then bright lights flashed before my eyes. I tried to call Ah Kee, but only a sort of awful gurgle, like water rushing down a drain, sounded when I tried to scream. Somehow I managed to reach the bed and fell there, choking and gasping. Then I lost consciousness.

"When I came to, my throat was sore and bruised, and that awful, bodiless head still hung there just outside the window, mouthing and grimacing at me. Presently it gave a fiendish, screaming laugh and floated away, leaving me half dead with pain and fright.

"As soon as I was strong enough I called Ah Kee, and told him what had happened. He seemed terribly frightened and began mumbling prayers or incantations in Malayan and Chinese. Then he asked me to bolt the door and window, and ran out as though pursued by fiends. In a little while he came back with an armful of Japanese quince, which he twisted into two big wreaths, one of which he insisted on putting on the bed. The other he hung in the window, like a Christmas decoration.

"For the next two nights I rested easily, but the third night I woke up with a feeling of oppression, as though a great weight rested on my chest. I tried to sit up, and instantly the invisible cord tightened round my throat and I began to choke. As I turned my head in agony I saw Salanga's head staring at me through the window.

"Every night it's been like that. I try to stay awake, drinking strong black coffee and tea so strong and bitter that it fairly rasps my throat, but sooner of later I drop off; indeed, it seems as though there is some curse of sleep upon me, for every evening, just at dusk, I find myself so drowsy that no matter how I fight it, I fall asleep, and sleep is the signal for that dreadful head to come again and that awful choking to begin.

"Sometimes I'm tormented by this sensation of strangulation as often as a dozen times a night; other times I suffer only once, then manage to hold myself awake by main strength of determination, but—"

"Can't you sleep in the day?" I interrupted. "The head doesn't appear in daylight, does it?"

"No, it doesn't; but no matter how exhausted I may be, I can't sleep in the light," the girt replied. "I've tried again and again, but just as I can't seem to keep from dozing as soon as it turns dark, I find myself unable to snatch even five minutes' rest by day. It's maddening, and when I say that I'm not speaking figuratively. I really feel that unless I find some way to escape this torment I'll go crazy."

Thoughtfully de Grandin extracted a cigarette from his case of engine-turned silver, set it alight and blew twin columns of gray smoke from his narrow, sensitive nostrils. At length:

"*Mademoiselle*," he announced, "I think I see an avenue of escape. Will you submit to hypnotism?"

"Hypnotism?"

"*Précisément*. Sleep, as you know, can be hypnotically induced; but that is only half the plan. The skilled hypnotist can, by very strength of will, command the blood to flow from the subject's hand or leg, leaving the member totally anemic. It is possible that by exercising a similar command I can induce you to sleep naturally and to ignore the orders of this cursed apparition, thus saving you from torment. Are you willing to experiment?"

"Yes, of course," she answered.

"*Bien*. You will compose yourself, if you please, and gaze fixedly at this—" He drew a silver pencil from his pocket and waved it slowly, like a pendulum, before her eyes. "Sleep, Mademoiselle; sleep, sleep. Sleep soundly and naturally. Obey me only, heed no other's orders; experience no feeling of compression round your neck. Sleep, sleep; sleep—"

A shriek of wild, unearthly laughter sounded from the storm-swept night outside, and to our horror we descried the telltale band of white begin to form about Joan Haines' throat. The indentation deepened, the crimson of her lips took on a violet tinge and between her parted teeth her tongue protruded. Her eyes bulged forward in their sockets and on each cheek appeared small spots of ecchymoses.

With one accord we turned and faced the window. There, like a miniature balloon, hung the severed head of the *penanggalan*, its red lips parted in a mocking smile of hate, green, red-flecked eyes dancing with devilish merriment, sharp, white teeth flashing in the gaslight's rays.

"By damn, I am annoyed, I am angry and enraged!" de Grandin stormed, snatching up the wreath of scarlet flowers from the bed and rushing toward the window. "Be careful how you play your tricks on Jules de Grandin, *Madame*; he is a very dangerous customer!"

Flinging up the sash he lunged out viciously with the thorn-spurred blossoms, and so quick and cat-like was his gesture that the laughing visitant was a thought too slow in darting backward.

A shrill, ear-splitting shriek resounded through the night as a sharp thorn came in contact with the floating horror's stomach sac, and a bloody weal appeared upon the serous coating of the greater curvature. Like a wind-extinguished light the dreadful head was gone, leaving but the echo of its anguished wail to tell us it had been there.

"Ah-ha; ah-ha-ha, I think that she will pause for self-debate before she interrupts our work again," announced de Grandin as he closed the window with a bang. "Now, *Mademoiselle*, if you please. . . ."

Once more he drew the pencil from his waistcoat pocket and began the process of hypnosis. In a few minutes Joan Haines' eyes closed sleepily; then her lips parted as she drew a deep and tranquil breath. Less than five minutes from his opening command she was sleeping naturally, like a tired child, and though we watched beside her till the eastern sky was streaked with gray, there was no sign of strangling marks upon her throat, nor any indication of a further visitation from the dreadful severed head.

THE STORM PASSED WITH the night, and, fortified with several cups of strong coffee brewed by Ah Kee, we left Joan Haines sleeping the sleep of utter exhaustion and set out for town. Highway patrols had cleared away the wreckage from the road, and we made excellent progress through the clear, rain-washed summer morning.

"Tell me," I demanded as we drove along, "what the deuce is a *penanggalan*, de Grandin?"

He twisted thoughtfully at the ends of his mustache a moment; then:

"She is a sort of nocturnal demon closely analogous to the vampire of eastern Europe," he replied, "but she differs from him in a number of respects. First of all, she is, or was, always a woman, whereas the vampire may be either male or female. Again, while the vampire appears with all his members complete, the *penanggalan* possesses only a head, esophagus and stomach sac, either leaving the remainder of her body at her dwelling-place, or—as often happens—permitting it to rot within the grave while only head and stomach retain their evil immortality.

"How one becomes a *penanggalan* is a matter of debate. Some say she was a woman of evil life who uses the magic arts of the devil who is her master to enable her to detach her head and assume volant powers; others declare she is one who died by self-destruction; still others maintain that she is a sorceress who by her magic contrives to remain alive in this fashion after death has overtaken the remainder of her body. However that may be, it is remarkable that the Malay Islands and Peninsula abound with both wizards and witches, and that they are able to perform tricks and work charms which would have turned the witches of Colonial New England and mediæval Europe green with professional envy. Those who have seen the *penanggalan* at her work invariably identify her as some well-known sorceress, either living or dead.

"Her technique differs from the vampire's, too. The vampire, you recall, recruits his grisly ranks by infecting those whose blood he sucks with vampirism, so that they in turn become as he is when he has drained them of their blood and killed them. The *penanggalan*, upon the contrary, can put her seal upon her victim without resorting to physical contact. True, those she drains of blood die, but when they die they die dead. When she desires to make another woman even as she is, it is but necessary for her to infest the house where her victim dwells and gaze upon her prey. By a sort of vile hypnotic spell she works upon her victim, makes her neck to show the signs of thongs upon it; finally she strangles her to death. And when death comes—"

He paused to light a cigarette, and I could have thumped his head in my impatience.

"Yes, and when death comes?" I prompted.

"*Eh bien*, then life—of a kind—begins," he answered. "The strangled victim's head parts company with her body at the point the magic ligature has marked upon her flesh, and, dragging the esophagus and stomach after it, it flies screaming off to join its hideous fellows in the ranks of the *penanggalans*.

"You will recall how certain fathers of the early church enunciated the cheerful doctrine that the only melancholy pleasure which the damned in hell possessed was to rail at the other damned and shrieking with obscene delight when a new soul came to join them in their torment? In some such way the *penanggalan* seems to derive a certain satisfaction from exercising her spells on poor unfortunates, separating their heads from their bodies and making them even as she is.

"Like the true vampire, the *penanggalan* is a blood-sucker, though unlike him, she does not have to have the sanguinary diet to exist. Apparently she drinks warm blood for pleasure, as the drunkard imbibes liquor, not because she must. Also, as garlic, wild rose and wolf's bane are powerful vegetable antidotes to the vampire, so is the jerju thistle, or any bush with strong, sharp thorns, distasteful to the *penanggalan*, though for a different reason. The vampire dare not approach the garlic or wild rose because they exercise a magic influence on him. The *penanggalan* fears a thornbush because its barbs are liable to become entangled in her dangling stomach sac, or even to pierce it. If the first contingency occurs she can not get away, for she is as highly sensitive to pain as any living person; if, by any chance, her stomach sac is perforated, it can not repair itself by healing, and she dies from the wound. It was for that reason that she fled from me when I menaced her with the thorny flowers last night—*ha*, I very nearly had her once, too, you will recall."

"Does she lie dormant by day, as the vampire does?" I asked.

"Yes. And like the vampire, she usually chooses a tomb, a cemetery or an old and long-deserted house as her lair. She need not necessarily do this, but apparently she does it as a matter of choice. Also, she is unable to exercise her powers of flight across bodies of water affected by the tides, as, by example, bays, estuaries and tide-water rivers. Does not the knowledge of that limitation give you an idea? Does not a possible explanation of the mystery of her presence leap to the eye?"

"Not to mine," I answered. "What's your theory?"

"That depends upon the information Monsieur Martin gives us."

"Martin? The funeral director?"

"But certainly. Who else? Will you drive past his place before we go home?"

"Of course," I agreed, wondering what connection any information John Martin might be able to give could possibly have with the presence of an Oriental demon in the quiet Jersey countryside.

J OHN MARTIN, LEADING MORTICIAN of Harrisonville, was seated in his private office when we stopped at his funeral home. "Good morning, gentlemen," he greeted. "What's the bad news today?"

"*Hein?*" replied de Grandin.

The big, gray-haired funeral director laughed. "Some one's always in process of getting in or out of trouble when you're around, Doctor de Grandin," he rejoined. "Can I help 'em out—or in?"

"Perhaps," the little Frenchman answered with a smile. "It is of Monsieur Haines that we inquire. You had charge of his interment, I believe?"

"Yes," replied the other. "I remember the case particularly, because his daughter refused to let me furnish a casket."

De Grandin smiled a thought sarcastically, and Mr. Martin put a quick and accurate interpretation on his grin.

"It isn't the loss of the sale that fixes the case in my mind," he hastened to explain, "but the trouble we had with the Oriental coffin which contained Mr. Haines' body. It was one of those Chinese affairs, heavy as a cast bronze sarcophagus, nearly eight feet long by three feet wide and almost four feet high. Grave space in Shadow Lawns is at a premium, and the Haines family plot is pretty well filled, so burying a coffin of that size was no easy task. We had to get special permission from the cemetery board to have a grave larger than their six foot six maximum dug, and we had to pay seventy per cent above the usual cost of opening a grave for the extra labor. Then, too, our casket coach, which operates with an automatic electric table, wasn't equipped to handle such a large case, and the coffin was too big to fit our lowering-device. I'd almost rather have made the young lady a present of an American casket than go through all the trouble that outlandish foreign coffin caused us."

"U'm? And did you, by any chance, open that outlandish coffin?" de Gran-din asked.

"Lord, no! As I've told you, it was a Chinese coffin, apparently hewn out of a single giant log, heavy as cast iron, and almost as hard, judging by the feel of it. The top was high, like a gabled roof, and fastened to the lower section by invis-ible dowels. I don't know how we'd ever have managed to pry them apart, unless we'd used a buzz-saw, if Miss Haines had decided to let us furnish a new casket."

"And was it airtight and watertight?" de Grandin asked.

"Perfectly. The whole thing had been coated and recoated with red lacquer, smooth and hard as porcelain. Dam' clever people, these Chinese. From the standpoint of utility that coffin was as good as anything our best American factories can turn out."

"Thank you, you have helped us greatly, Monsieur Martin," de Grandin answered. "What you have told is precisely what we wished to know.

"Do you go home and see your silly patients," he directed as we left the Mar-tin mortuary. "Me, I have important duties to perform. I shall return at dinner time or sooner, and I pray that you will be in readiness to accompany me to Mademoiselle Haines' this evening. We must watch with her until we can take steps to obviate the danger which is threatening."

I T WAS NEARLY SIX o'clock when he returned, and his temper was far from amiable. The unmentionable rules of that unnameable cemetery vexed him, he informed me. Because, parbleu! that seven-times-accursed Monsieur Haines had taken it into his never-to-be-sufficiently-anathematized head to die in a miser-able hole of a place like the island of Manura with no physician in attendance, there had been no death certificate, and the cemetery people absolutely forbade disinterment of that Monsieur Haines' eternally accursed body.

"D'ye really think there's any danger of Joan's becoming a penanggalan?" I asked as we drove out the Andover Road toward the old Haines house. "The idea seems so incredibly bizarre that—"

"There is a very real and present danger of her transformation, my friend," he interrupted soberly. "I think the thing which was her stepmother fears me, and will not try to work her spells while I am present, but that makes our need of haste the more imperative. Come, my old one, tread upon the gas; already it grows dark, and darkness is a time of peril for Mademoiselle Jeanne."

Despite our haste, however, darkness had descended before we reached our destination, and the gaslights were flaring brightly in the hall when Ah Kee answered our summons.

"Missy Jo-an all betta," he informed us when we asked him how the patient did. "All day she sleep an' lest. Ah Kee go up to loom one, two, three time for givum bleakfast, tiffin, dinner, she not wake no time. All time she sleep like little baby. Bimeby she call Ah Kee for ketchum food. I takee one piecee day up to loom ten-twenty minute 'fore you come. You like for see her now? Ah Kee think she all finish eat, maybe so."

De Grandin led the way up to the patient's room, talking volubly. "Behold," he boasted, "am I not the clever one? Did not my scheme for hypnotically induced rest work perfectly? But certainly. Shrewd this *sacré* demon from the East may be, but Jules de Grandin is shrewder still. He does not—

"Ah, *mon Dieu!* Too late! Look, my friends, see the desolation she has wrought while we dallied on the road. *Ohé!*"

I looked across his shoulder, saw Joan Haines sprawled face downward on the bed, hands outspread, clutching the mattress with stiffening fingers as if for anchorage; then, as he moved aside, my breath seemed to form a hot and sulfurous bolus in my throat and my heart beat quick with horror. For it was not Joan Haines who lay upon that bed. It was her headless body.

"Missy Lady, Missy Lady; Missy Jo-an!" screamed Ah Kee despairingly, leaping forward to seize one of the stiff, white hands clutching at the bedding; but:

"Back, my little one!" de Grandin ordered sharply. "Touch her not; we must—"

A hideous screaming chorus of discordant laughter drowned his words, and as we turned to face the window we beheld two severed heads staring at us from the darkness.

The Malay woman's gold-bronze face was aflame with evil triumph, and her red lips writhed with devilish merriment as she sent forth peal on ringing peal of mocking cachinnation. Her red-flecked eyes of agate-green glowed brightly in her face, her white teeth flashed, her every feature was instinct with triumphant, hellish jubilation.

Beside the black-tressed head another floated, a little, heart-shaped face with cheeks of golden tan, crowned with long ringlets of copper-colored hair which swirled and floated in the evening breeze like the loosened locks of a drowned woman floating round her still, dead face. And though she joined the other in the duet of derisive laughter, there was no quality of merriment in her tones. Rather, it was the despairing, hysterical shriek of one in whom all hope has died.

And in her eyes there was the helpless, hopeless pleading of an animal in mortal pain, and down her cheeks there coursed. twin trails of shining tear-drops, even as she laughed.

De Grandin suddenly went berserk. "*Dieu de Dieu de Dieu de Dieu!*" he shouted. "Am I to be mocked by this abomination?—made a monkey of by a head without a body?—ten million thousand damn times no!"

Snatching up a heavy vase he struck it on the bedpost, breaking it across the bottom so that it terminated in a jagged, saw-toothed edge, and hurling it with all his frenzied might straight through the window-pane.

The glass crashed outward with a deafening clash and the sharp-toothed missile flew straight to its mark, striking the dangling stomach sac beneath Salanga's head with smashing, devastating impact.

I saw the globular thing sway drunkenly as the broken crockery hit it, heard the anguished scream which cut short the discord of malicious laughter, then shuddered with physical sickness as a spilth of blood-stained liquid spurted from the ruptured sac.

In a second all was quiet—quiet as the tomb. The cord which dangled from the window-blind flapped idly against the sill as a little breath of breeze crept through the broken pane; the gaslight hissed softly in the etched-glass globe; the still, stark body of Joan Haines lay sprawled immovably upon the bed. De Grandin, Ah Kee and I held our breaths in a very œstrum of horror. Suddenly:

"Name of a name, why do we stand here gaping like three *sacré* fools?" the little Frenchman blazed. "Quick, Friend Trowbridge, to your car. Prepare to drive us back to town at once. My little one, I would have your immediate assistance."

He seized Ah Kee by the shoulder and fairly dragged him from the room.

I had hardly had time to seat myself behind the steering-wheel when de Grandin and Ah Kee emerged from the house each bearing a great armful of the red thorn-flowers and a burlap sack.

"Now, Friend Trowbridge, drive; drive like the devil; drive *comme un perdu* to that ninety-times-condemned Shadow Lawns cemetery. We must get there first!" he panted.

"First?" I queried, setting the motor going. "Before whom?"

"Oh, do not stop to talk or argue," he besought. "Go, drive; fly. We must reach that grave before them!"

I PUSHED MY MOTOR TO its utmost. When I bought the car the salesman had assured me that it would be valuable in responding to emergencies, and that night I proved that he had spoken truly. Sixty, sixty-five, seventy miles the speedometer registered. As we came in sight of the long green fence enclosing Shadow Lawns the needle indicated seventy-five, and a little plume of grayish steam was streaming backward from my radiator cap.

"*Très bon*. It is enough," de Grandin tapped me on the shoulder. "Come."

We scaled the cemetery fence and, led by him, hastened on among the quiet graves till we reached a level plot where a tall, imposing granite shaft displayed the one word:

HAINES

"Now quiet, on your lives," de Grandin ordered as we sank to cover in the shadow of the monument and he and Ah Kee fell feverishly to work plaiting long loops of the thorny flower-stalks.

I watched them in bewilderment, but so intent upon their work were they that neither took the slightest notice of my presence. At length:

"Is all prepared?" the Frenchman asked.

"Yup. All flinish; dam' good," Ah Kee returned.

We waited silently for what seemed like an hour, and at last de Grandin seized my shoulder. "Observe, behold; they come!" he told me tensely.

Skimming low above the mounded graves there came what looked like a pair of monstrous birds. They flew heavily, almost blindly, wavering from side to side, swooping near the ground one moment, then suddenly rising to a height of several feet with an awkward, bouncing motion. At last they approached near enough for me to recognize them.

They were two severed human heads, each with a round, balloon-like thing dependent from it. The nearer one flew hesitantly, like a wounded bird, lobbing crazily from side to side, its companion following its flight like a timid, awkward child playing follow-the-leader.

Waveringly they winged their way to a newly mounded grave, hovered in the air a moment, then swooped to earth, wriggling with a terrible, revolting snake-like movement down into the grass.

"*Pardonnez-moi*, I do not think you will go home tonight, *Mesdames*," announced de Grandin, stepping from the shadow of the monument. "I have other plans for you."

Deftly, like a skilled *vaquero* casting his lariat, he threw the loop of plaited thorn-bush over the nearer of the burrowing heads and began drawing in the spike-spurred tether as a fisherman might draw in his line.

Inside the thorny bight the trapped thing bobbed about grotesquely, like a savage, wounded beast, gibbering and shrieking in a high, thin voice horribly reminiscent of the whimperings of a child in pain, and once or twice, when its struggles brought it into contact with the thorny noose, uttering little gasping mewls.

It was pitiful to see the helpless thing's vain struggles, and I felt the same involuntary sympathy which I should have felt at witnessing a beast held fast in the steel jaws of a trap, but pity changed to horror as de Grandin anchored his noose beneath one foot and opened wide his burlap sack, and the captive head sprang at him like a striking serpent. A sharp thorn tore its dangling stomach, widening the rent already made by de Grandin's saw-toothed missile, but rage had made the thing insensible to pain, and, teeth flashing in the pale moonlight, it launched its gaping mouth directly at his throat.

"Ça-ha, diablesse!" de Grandin cried, throwing up his left hand defensively, and the champing teeth fastened in his sleeve, so that the head hung swaying from his cuff, its long hair flowing nearly to the ground, vicious, growling noises issuing from between the tight-clenched teeth.

With a fierce gesture the Frenchman swung his hand away from his face, reached quickly beneath his jacket and snatched out a hunting-knife.

"E-e-e-ur-r-gh!" a kind of screaming grunt issued from the severed head dependent from his sleeve, and the thing fought desperately to free itself, but the saber-sharp white teeth had pierced clear through the cloth and were entangled in the fabric.

De Grandin swung his knife as a woodsman might his ax. The keen blade sheared through the tough muscular tube of the esophagus pendent from the severed neck, and the dangling stomach sac fell to the graveyard grass.

A wild and anguished cry, half screech, half groan, issued from the head, but the little Frenchman's blade was merciless. Flashing in an arc, it swung again, striking heavily, ax-like, upon the vault of the penanggalan's skull, shearing through black, gleaming hair and scalp and bone, burying itself deep in the brain.

The scream of mortal terror died half uttered, like a cry that had been smothered at inception, but the teeth held firmly to his jacket, the jaws fast-locked in cadaveric spasm.

With a wrenching twist he freed his knife-blade from the skull and jammed its gleaming point right in the dead thing's mouth, prying the clenched jaws apart.

Sick at the sight, I turned away.

Ah Kee cast his loop of thorny flowers round the second head, but the savagery which Jules de Grandin had displayed was wholly absent as he gently coaxed the captive toward him. "No be 'flaid, Missy Lady," he crooned softly, twitching delicately at the lasso, lest a sharp thorn wound his catch. "Ah Kee not hurt you; no tly for lun away, you not get hurt!" Slowly, inch by careful inch, he drew the tether in.

"Très bon, good work, my little old one!" de Grandin complimented. "Careful—gently—so!" Leaping forward he drew the opened mouth of his sack over the copper-crowned head as it rose a few inches from the grass in a futile struggle to escape the circling loop of thorns.

Gently, as a lad might soothe a frightened kitten, he stroked the bulge in the big which told where the head lay. "Do not be afraid, *ma pauvre*, we shall not do you injury," he whispered; then leaving the little half-caste to bear the burden, he paused a moment to stuff the knife-slashed remnants of the other head into the other sack.

"Now, my friend, we must make haste," he told me. "Drive first to your house, then to Mademoiselle Jeanne's and do not dally on the road, I beg you; a life—*cordieu*, more than a life!—depends upon our speed this night."

I kept the motor running while he rushed into the house, reappearing in a little while with two emergency kits and a bulging bundle, then, at his whispered order, shoved the throttle forward and forgot there were such things as legal speed limits as we headed for the old Haines mansion.

"There is no time for proper preparation," he told me when we reached our destination; "we must use the things which are at hand."

To Ah Kee he ordered, "Fetch a shutter, quickly, if you please."

The little man departed, returning in a moment staggering under the burden of a tall window-blind, and the Frenchman threw a sheet across it, then seized one end, signing me to take the other. "It is our litter," he explained as we bore the blind upstairs. "Come, make haste, my friend."

We put Joan Haines' stiffened body on the blind and bore it down to the kitchen, where, beneath the glare of unshaded gaslights, we laid it on the sheet-spread table and de Grandin tore open his parcel, drawing forth two surgical robes.

Donning one, he motioned me to put the other on, and unlatched the satchels, laid out a set of knives, artery-clips, thread and needles, last of all a can of ether.

"À *moi*," he told Ah Kee, indicating the sack the other held.

"Do not be fearful, *Mademoiselle*," he soothed as he took the burlap bag between his hands; "this brings forgetfulness and peace—perchance recovery." Gently, caressingly, he stroked the sack, nodding to me to begin dropping ether from the can upon the coarse fabric.

A whimpering cry of fright came from the bag as I dropped the anesthetic on the loosely woven meshes, but as the strong, sweet smell began to penetrate the room, the flutterings and whimpers lessened, finally subsided altogether.

De Grandin drew the bag's closed lips apart, peeked exploringly into the dark depths, then, with a nod of satisfaction, thrust his hand inside, rummaged about a moment, finally drew forth Joan Haines' head.

"We must be swift," he murmured as he laid the pathetic thing on a small table covered with a clean, fresh cloth. "I do not know how long the anesthesia will last. *Parbleu*," he drew on rubber gloves and took a knife up delicately between his thumb and forefinger, "I have operated many times, but never before have I seen ether applied to a patient with no lungs to breathe it!"

"Patient?" I echoed wonderingly. Could he be referring to the dead that way?

I watched him curiously as he set to work with that swiftness and dexterity which always characterized his surgery.

Daintily as a watchmaker working at his delicate mechanism, he commenced the median incision, and I gasped with incredulity as I saw the ruby blood follow the knife in a thin, red ribbon.

There was no time to lose. Snatching sponges and arterial clips, I stationed myself at his elbow. Swabbing, clipping, handing him the instruments, I watched in fascination as he made the Y-shaped transverse cut, laid open the thorax and, as calmly as though he were a toymaker constructing a mechanical doll, proceeded to replace Joan Haines' stomach, connect the duodenum and pylorus, close the throat about the esophagus and matter-of-factly sew the wounds together as though the operation which he had performed were one of everyday occurrence.

"D'ye actually believe she's living?" I asked as he completed his last stitch. "Why, it's preposterous—*rigor mortis*—has set in, and—"

"Did you observe the blood?" he interrupted, busy with his gloves.

"Why, yes, it did seem strangely liquid," I admitted. "You'd have thought coagulation would have started, but—"

"'But' be everlastingly consigned to hell!" he blazed; "see this!"

Leaning forward, he placed his lips against the dead girl's mouth, and, hands beneath her ribs, bore down upon her diaphragm, at the same time forcing a great lungful of breath down her throat.

Once, twice, three times the process was repeated, and as be raised his head to draw a fourth deep breath, I cried out sharply:

"Look; look, de Grandin—*she's alive!*"

She was. There was no doubt of it. Faintly, so faintly that we could hardly see its motion, her chest was fluttering, like the breast of one who breathes his last, but as he leant above her with redoubled efforts, her respiration strengthened visibly. In a moment she was breathing naturally, drinking in the sultry summer air with deep, thirsty gulps, as a desert-famished woman might have drained cool water from a cup.

We wrapped her inert form in blankets, placed it on our improvised stretcher and bore it to the bedroom where Ah Kee waited with a dozen bottles of boiling water which we placed around her in the bed.

"I telephoned Mademoiselle Bradfield before we left the city," de Grandin told me. "She is an excellent *garde-malade* for surgical cases, and *le bon Dieu* knows we shall need such an one for Mademoiselle Jeanne."

He had hardly finished speaking when a taxicab wheeled up to the door and Miss Bradfield, stiff, starched and looking extremely sterile and competent in her hospital whites, alighted.

De Grandin prepared a hypodermic syringe and placed it on the bedside table. "Three-quarters of a grain of morphine in the arm the moment she shows signs of consciousness, if you please, *Mademoiselle*," he told the nurse. "She has been through a serious ordeal, and retching would indubitably prove fatal.

"Now," he signed to me to leave the room, "we have a further duty to perform, my friend; one which shall write *finis* to this chapter of unhappy incidents, I hope."

Downstairs in the cellar Ah Kee had built a roaring fire of oil-soaked wood and shavings in the big, old-fashioned hot-air furnace. Thither de Grandin led me, and paused a moment at the cellar door to take up a blood-soaked burlap sack.

Into the blazing firebox of the furnace he flung the bag, and as the hungry flames enveloped it we saw, for an instant, the beautiful, cruel face of Salanga, the Malay woman, look at us with fixed, staring eyes which, even in the still, set state of death, were freighted with a gaze of deadly hatred.

"*Adieu, Madame Penanggalan; adieu pour l'éternité*," de Grandin raised hand to lips in a sardonic gesture of farewell as the lapping tongue of fire closed above the severed head and blotted it from sight.

"And now, *pardieu*, I think that it is time we left," he told me as he turned upon his heel.

"How was it that you knew we'd find them in the cemetery?" I asked as we drove slowly toward the city.

He chuckled as he lit a cigarette before replying:

"You may recall that I asked Mademoiselle Jeanne who officiated at her father's burial?"

"Yes."

"*Très bien.* And that I told you that my theory of the case depended on the information Monsieur Martin gave us?"

"Of course."

"Very well, then. As I have told you, these *penanggalans* are unable to fly across tide waters; but there is no reason why they can not be carried over. No, certainly.

"*Alors*, I said to me, 'Jules de Grandin, the body of this Malay stepmother of Mademoiselle Jeanne was found breast-down upon the grave of him who was her husband. Is it not so?'

"'It are indubitably so,' I answer me.

"'Very well, then,' I tell me, 'you should know that these Malay demons make their lairs in tombs and graves and old, deserted houses and similar unpleasant places. Are it not possible that she traveled to that grave to shed her head, leaving her body on the earth while the head burrowed downward and found a resting-place inside the coffin with the corpse?'

"'It are entirely feasible, Jules de Grandin,' I agree. 'And if she hid herself in that coffin she would have no inconvenience coming as a passenger across the ocean. No.'

"'Ah, but,' I object, 'that Monsieur Martin, you know him. He is *un homme d'affaires*; surely he would not permit an opportunity for profit to pass by; undoubtlessly he induced Mademoiselle Jeanne to purchase a new casket, and when he transferred Monsieur Haines' body to its new abode he must necessarily have opened that old coffin. Perhaps he saw the *penanggalan?* Perhaps he liberated it from its prison as Pandora let loose the troubles from her box? Who knows?'

"'Perhaps,' I answer, 'but all such speculation is the business of the little fish of April. Why not go see Monsieur Martin? He will tell you truly.'

"And so to Monsieur Martin we did go, and he told us that he had not opened that old coffin. *Par conséquent*, it followed that the *penanggalan* was in there yet, or at least it was highly probable that she still used it for home.

"Accordingly, I decided that I would exhume that coffin my own self and find the cause of all our troubles while she rested there by day and make an end of her. But those *sacré* fools of cemetery people, they would not hear of it. 'It are impossible,' they tell me, and I am balked.

"Then, tonight, when we find we are too late and the wicked *penanggalan* has worked her evil will on poor Mademoiselle Jeanne, I took the chance, played on the hunch, as you Americans say, and hastened to the graveyard to intercept them at Monsieur Haines' tomb. 'For if she really makes that grave her den, then it is probable that she will lead her victim to it, also,' I tell myself. It would be the height of evil vengeance to make the daughter house herself in the coffin with the body of her father. And she is vengeful, that one; oh, but she is vengeful as the devil's self. Yes, of course.

"We were fortunate. The wound which I had given her in my anger made her slow of flight, and so we got there first. We arrived in time to intercept them ere they could burrow out of sight. The rest you know."

"But," I persisted as we turned into my driveway, "how was it possible for the *penanggalan* to force her—its—way down through the earth and into that airtight coffin? The laws of physics—"

"*Ah bah*," he interrupted with a laugh, "I know not whether the laws of physics or of metaphysics govern in such cases; one thing I truly know, however: that is that we saw what we beheld with our own eyes tonight, and no one can say otherwise. And one more thing I know, as well: that is that at present I am greatly conscious of the workings of the law of impenetrability."

"Impenetrability?"

"But certainly, my friend. The proposition is most simple. This monstrous thirst of mine can not continue so to plague my throat when I have poured a pint or so of brandy down it. No, of course not."

The Mansion of Unholy Magic

"**C**AR, SIR? TAKE YOU anywhere you want to go."

It was a quaint-looking figure which stood before us on the railway station platform, a figure difficult to classify as to age, status, or even sex. A man's gray felt hat which had seen better days, though not recently, was perched upon a head of close-cropped, tightly, curling blond hair, surmounting a face liberally strewn with freckles. A pull-over sweater of gray cardigan sheathed boyishly broad shoulders and boyishly narrow hips and waist, while the straight, slim legs were encased in a pair of laundry-faded jodhpurs of cotton corduroy. A pair of bright pink coral ear-drops completed the ensemble.

Jules de Grandin eased the strap by which his triple-barreled Knaak combination gun swung from his left shoulder and favored the solicitor with a look denoting compound interest. "A car?" he echoed. "But no, I do not think we need one. The motor stage—"

"The bus isn't running," the other interrupted. "They had an accident this afternoon and the driver broke his arm; so I ran over to see if I could pick up any passengers. I've got my car here, and I'll be glad to take you where you want to go—if you'll hurry."

"But certainly," the Frenchman agreed with one of his quick smiles. "We go to Monsieur Sutter's hunting-lodge. You know the way?"

A vaguely troubled look clouded the clear gray eyes regarding him as he announced our destination. "Sutter's lodge?" the girl—by now I had determined that it was a girl—repeated as she cast a half-calculating, half-fearful glance at the lengthening lines of red and orange which streaked the western sky. "Oh, all right; I'll take you there, but we'll have to hurry. I don't want to—come on, please."

She led the way to a travel-stained Model T Ford touring-car, swung open the tonneau door and climbed nimbly to the driving-seat.

"All right?" she asked across her shoulder, and ere we had a chance to answer put the ancient vehicle in violent motion, charging down the unkempt country road as though she might be driving for a prize.

"*Eh bien*, my friend, this is a singularly unengaging bit of country," de Grandin commented as our rattling chariot proceeded at breakneck speed along a road which became progressively worse. "At our present pace I estimate that we have come five miles, yet not one single habitation have we passed, not a ray of light or wreath of smoke have we seen, nor—" he broke off, grasping at his cap as the almost springless car catapulted itself across a particularly vicious hummock in the road.

"Desist, *ma belle chauffeuse*," he cried. "We desire to sleep together in one piece tonight; but one more bump like that and—" he clutched at the car-side while the venerable flivver launched itself upon another aerial excursion.

"Mister," our driver turned her serious, uncompromising face upon us while she drove her foot still harder down on the accelerator, "this is no place to take your time. We'll all be lucky to sleep in bed tonight, I'm thinkin', in one piece or several, if I don't—"

"Look out, girl!" I shouted, for the car, released from her guiding hand while she answered de Grandin's complaint, had lurched across the narrow roadway and was headed for a great, black-boled pine which grew beside the trail. With a wrench she brought the vehicle once more to the center of the road, putting on an extra burst of speed as she did so.

"If we ever get out of this," I told de Grandin through chattering teeth, "I'll never trust myself to one of these modern young fools' driving, you may be—"

"If we emerge from this with nothing more than *Mademoiselle's* driving to trouble us, I think we shall be more lucky than I think," he cut in seriously.

"What d'ye mean?" I asked exasperated. "If—"

"If you will look behind us, perhaps you will be good enough to tell me what it is you see," he interrupted, as he began unfastening the buckles of his gun-case.

"Why," I answered as I glanced across the lurching car's rear cushion, "it's a man, de Grandin. A running man."

"Eh, you are sure?" he answered, slipping a heavy cartridge into the rifle barrel of his gun. "A man who runs like that?"

The man was certainly running with remarkable speed. Tall, almost gigantic in height, and dressed in some sort of light-colored stuff which clung to his spare figure like a suit of tights, he covered the ground with long, effortless strides reminiscent of a hound upon the trail. There was something oddly furtive in his manner, too, for he did not keep to the center of the road, but dodged in a sort of zigzag, swerving now right, now left, keeping to the shadows as much as possible and running in such manner that only for the briefest intervals was he in direct line with us without some bush or tree-trunk intervening.

De Grandin nursed the forestock of his gun in the crook of his left elbow, his narrowed eyes intent upon the runner.

"When he comes within fifty yards I shall fire," he told me softly. "Perhaps I should shoot now, but—"

"Good heavens, man; that's murder!" I expostulated. "If—"

"Be still!" he told me in a low, sharp whisper. "I know what I am doing."

The almost nighttime darkness of the dense pine woods through which we drove was thinning rapidly, and as we neared the open land the figure in our wake seemed to redouble its efforts. Now it no longer skulked along the edges of the road, but sprinted boldly down the center of the trail, arms flailing wildly, hands outstretched as though to grasp the rear of our car.

Amazingly the fellow ran. We were going at a pace exceeding forty miles an hour, but this long, thin woodsman seemed to be outdistancing us with ease. As we neared the margin of the wood and came into the dappled lights and shadows of the sunset, he put on a final burst of speed and rushed forward like a whirl-wind, his feet scarce seeming to touch the ground.

Calmly, deliberately, de Grandin raised his gun and sighted down its gleam-ing blue-steel barrels.

"No!" I cried, striking the muzzle upward as he squeezed the trigger. "You can't do that, de Grandin; it's murder!"

My gesture was in time to spoil his aim, but not in time to stop the shot. With a roar the gun went off and I saw a tree-limb crack and hurtle downward as the heavy bullet sheared it off. And, as the shot reverberated through the autumn air, drowning the rattling of our rushing flivver, the figure in our wake dissolved. Astonishingly, inexplicably, but utterly, it vanished in the twinkling of an eye, gone completely—and as instantly—as a soap-bubble punctured with a pin.

The screeching grind of tortured brakes succeeded, and our car bumped to a stop within a dozen feet. "D-did you shoot?" our driver asked tremulously. Her fair and sunburned face had gone absolutely corpse-gray with terror, making the golden freckles stand out with greater prominence, and her lips were blue and cyanotic.

"Yes, *Mademoiselle*, I shot," de Grandin answered in a low and even voice. "I shot, and had it not been for my kind and empty-headed friend, I should have scored a hit." He paused; then, lower still, he added: "And now one understands why you were in a hurry, *Mademoiselle*."

"Th-then, you saw—you saw—" she began through trembling lips, plucked feverishly at the steering-wheel with fear-numbed fingers for a moment, then, with a little, choking, gasping moan, slumped forward in her seat, unconscious.

"*Parbleu*, now one can sympathize with that Monsieur Crusoe," the little Frenchman murmured as he looked upon the fainting girl. "Here we are, a dozen miles from anywhere, with most unpleasant neighbors all about, and none to show us to our destination." Matter-of-factly he fell to chafing the girl's wrists,

slapping her cheeks softly from time to time, massaging her brow with deft, practised fingers.

"Ah, so, you are better now, *n'est-ce-pas?*" he asked as her eyelids fluttered
upward. "You can show us where to go if my friend will drive the car?"

"Oh, I can drive all right, I think," she answered shakily, "but I'd be glad if
you would sit by me."

Less speedily, but still traveling at a rate which seemed to me considerably
in excess of that which our decrepit car could make with safety, we took up our
journey, dipping into desolate, uninhabited valleys, mounting rocky elevations,
finally skirting an extensive growth of evergreens and turning down a narrow,
tree-lined lane until we reached the Sutter lodge, a squat, substantial log house
with puncheon doors and a wide chimney of field stone. The sun had sunk below
the western hills and long, purple-gray shadows were reaching across the little
clearing round the cabin as we came to halt before the door.

"How much?" de Grandin asked as he clambered from the car and began
unloading our gear.

"Oh, two dollars," said the girl as she slid down from the driving-seat and
bent to lift a cowskin bag. "The bus would have brought you over for a dollar, but
they'd have let you down at the foot of the lane, and you'd have had to lug your
duffle up here. Besides—"

"Perfectly, *Mademoiselle*," he interrupted, "we are not disposed to dicker over
price. Here is five dollars, and you need not trouble to make change; neither is
it necessary that you help us with our gear; we are quite content to handle it
ourselves, and—"

"Oh, but I want to help you," she broke in, staggering toward the cabin with
the heavy bag. "Then, if there's anything I can do to make you comfortable—"
She broke off, puffing with exertion, set the bag down on the door-sill and hastened to the car for another burden.

Our traps stored safely in the cabin, we turned once more to bid our guide
adieu, but she shook her head. "It's likely to be cold tonight," she told us. "This
fall weather's right deceptive after dark. Better let me bring some wood in, and
then you'll be needing water for your coffee and washing in the morning. So—"

"No, *Mademoiselle*, you need not do it," Jules de Grandin protested as she
came in with an armful of cut wood. "We are able-bodied men, and if we find
ourselves in need of wood or water we can—*mordieu!*"

Somewhere, faint and far-off seeming, but growing in intensity till it seemed
to make our very eardrums ache, there rose the quavering, mournful howling
of a dog, such a slowly rising and diminishing lament as hounds are wont to
make at night when baying at the moon—or when bemoaning death in the
family of their master. And, like an echo of the canine yowling, almost like an
orchestrated part of some infernal symphony, there came from very near a little

squeaking, skirking noise, like the squealing of a hollow rubber toy or the gibbering of an angry monkey. Not one small voice, but half a dozen, ten, a hundred of the chattering things seemed passing through the woodland at the clearing's edge, marching in a sort of disorderly array, hurrying, tumbling, rushing toward some rendezvous, and gabbling as they went.

The firewood clattered to the cabin door, and once again the girl's tanned face went pasty-gray.

"Mister," she told de Grandin solemnly, "this is no place to leave your house o' nights, for wood or water or anything else."

The little Frenchman tweaked the needle-points of his mustache as he regarded her. Then: "One understands, *Mademoiselle*—in part, at least," he answered. "We thank you for your kindness, but it is growing late; soon it will be dark. I do not think we need detain you longer."

Slowly the girl walked toward the door, swung back the sturdy rough-hewn panels, and gazed into the night. The sun had sunk and deep-blue darkness spread across the hills and woods; here and there an early star winked down, but there was no hint of other light, for the moon was at the dark. A moment she stood thus upon the sill, then, seeming to take sudden resolution, slammed the door and turned to face us, jaw squared, but eyes suffused with hot tears of embarrassment.

"I can't," she announced; then, as de Grandin raised his brows interrogatively: "I'm afraid—scared to go out there. Will—will you let me spend the night here?"

"Here?" the Frenchman echoed.

"Yes, sir; here. I—I *daren't* go out there among those gibbering things. I can't. I can't; *I can't!*"

De Grandin laughed delightedly. "*Morbleu*, but prudery dies hard in you Americans, *Mademoiselle*," he chuckled, "despite your boasted modernism and emancipation. No matter, you have asked our hospitality, and you shall have it. You did not really think that we would let you go among those—those whatever-they-may-bes, I hope? But no. Here you shall stay till daylight makes your going safe, and when you have eaten and rested you shall tell us all you know of this strange business of the monkey. Yes, of course."

As he knelt to light the fire he threw me a delighted wink. "When that so kind Monsieur Sutter invited us to use his lodge for hunting we little suspected what game we were to hunt, *n'est-ce-pas?*" he asked.

COFFEE, FRIED BACON, PANCAKES and a tin of preserved peaches constituted dinner. De Grandin and I ate with the healthy appetite of tired men, but our guest was positively ravenous, passing her plate for replenishment again and again. At last, when we had filled the seemingly bottomless void within her and

I had set my pipe aglow while she and Jules de Grandin lighted cigarettes, the little Frenchman prompted. "And now, *Mademoiselle?*"

"I'm glad you saw something in Putnam's woods and heard those things squeaking in the dark outside tonight," she answered. "It'll make it easier for you to believe me." She paused a moment, then:

"Did you notice the white house in the trees just before we came here?" she demanded.

We shook our heads, and she went on, without pausing for reply:

"That's Colonel Putnam's place, where it all started. My dad is postmaster and general storekeeper at Bartlesville, and Putnam's mail used to be delivered through our office. I was graduated from high school last year, and went to help Dad in the store, sometimes giving him a lift with the letters, too. I remember, it was in the afternoon of the twenty-third of June a special delivery parcel came for Colonel Putnam, and Dad asked me if I'd like to drive him over to deliver it after supper. We could make the trip in an hour, and Dad and Colonel Putnam had been friends since boyhood; so he wanted to do him the favor of getting the package to him as soon as possible.

"Folks had started telling some queer tales about Colonel Putnam, even then, but Dad pooh-poohed 'em all. You see, the colonel was the richest man in the county, and lived pretty much to himself since he came back here from Germany. He'd gone to school in that country as a young man, and went back on trips every year or so until about twenty years ago, when he married a Bavarian lady and settled there. His wife, we heard, died two years after they were married, when their little girl was born; then, just before the War, the daughter was drowned in a boating accident and Colonel Putnam came back to his old ancestral home and shut himself in from everybody, an old, broken and embittered man. I'd never seen him, but Dad had been to call once, and said he seemed a little touched in the head. Anyway, I was glad of the chance to see the old fellow when Dad suggested we drive over with the parcel.

"There was something queer about the Putnam house—something I didn't like, without actually knowing what it was. You know, just as you might be repelled by the odor of tuberoses, even though you didn't realize their connection with funerals and death? The place seemed falling apart; the drive was overgrown with weeds, the lawns all gone to seed, and a general air of desolation everywhere.

"There didn't seem to be any servants, and Colonel Putnam let us in himself. He was tall and spare, almost cadaverous, with white hair and beard, and wore a long, black, double-breasted frock coat and a stiff white-linen collar tied with a black stock. At first he hardly seemed to know Dad, but when he saw the parcel we brought, his eyes lighted up with what seemed to me a kind of fury.

"'Come in, Hawkins,' he invited; 'you and your daughter are just in time to see a thing which no one living ever saw before.'

"He led us down a long and poorly lighted hall, furnished in old-fashioned walnut and haircloth, to a larger apartment overlooking his weed-grown back yard.

"'Hawkins,' he told my father, 'you're in time to witness a demonstration of the uncontrovertible truth of the Pythagorean doctrine—the doctrine of metempsychosis.'

"'Good Lord, Henry, you don't mean to say you believe such non—' Dad began, but Colonel Putnam looked at him so fiercely that I thought he'd spring on him.

"'Silence, impious fool!' he shouted. 'Be silent and witness the exemplification of the Truth!' Then he calmed down a little, though he still continued walking up and down the room twitching his eyebrows, shrugging his shoulders and snapping his fingers every now and then.

"'Just before I came back to this country,' he went on, 'I met a master of the occult, a Herr Doktor von Meyer, who is not only the seventh son of a seventh son, but a member of the forty-ninth generation in direct descent from the Master Magician, Simon of Tyre. He possesses the ability to remember incidents in his former incarnations as you and I recall last night's dreams in the morning, Hawkins. Not only that: he has the power of reading other people's pasts. I sat with him in his *atelier* in Leipzig and saw my whole existence, from the time I was an insensate amoeba crawling in the primordial slime to the minute of my birth in this life, pass before me like the episodes of a motion picture.'

"'Did he tell you anything of this life; relate any incident of your youth known only to yourself, for instance, Henry?' Father asked him.

"'Be careful, scoffer, the Powers know how to deal with unbelievers such as you!' Colonel Putnam answered, flushing with rage, then calmed down again and resumed pacing the floor.

"'Back in the days when civilization was in the first flush of its youth,' he told us, 'I was a priest of Osiris in a temple by the Nile. And she, my darling, my dearest daughter, orphaned then as later, was a priestess in the temple of the Mother Goddess, Isis, across the river from my sanctuary.

"'But even in that elder day the fate which followed us was merciless. Then as later, water was the medium which was to rob me of my darling, for one night when her service to the Divine Mother was ended and temple slaves were rowing her across the river to my house, an accident overturned her boat, and she, the apple of my doting eyes, was thrown from her couch and drowned in the waters of Nilus. Drowned, drowned in the Egyptian river even as her latest earthly body was drowned in the Rhine.'

"Colonel Putnam stopped before my father, and his eyes were fairly blazing as he shook his finger in Dad's face and whispered:

"'But von Meyer told me how to overcome my loss, Hawkins. By his supernatural powers he was able to project his memory backward through the ages to the rock-tomb where they had laid the body of my darling, the very flesh in which she walked the streets of hundred-gated Thebes when the world was young. I sought it out, together with the bodies of those who served her in that elder life, and brought them here to my desolated house. Behold—'

"With a sort of dancing step he crossed the room and swept aside a heavy curtain. There, in the angle of the wall, with vases of fresh-cut flowers before them, stood three Egyptian mummy-cases.

"'It is she!' Colonel Putnam whispered tensely. 'It is she, my own little daughter, in her very flesh, and these'—he pointed to the other two—'were her attendants in that former life.'

"'Look!' He lifted the lid from the center coffin and revealed a slender form closely wrapped in overlying layers of dust-colored linen. 'There she stands, exactly as the priestly craftsmen wrapped her for her long, long rest, three thousand years ago! Now all is prepared for the great work I purpose; only the contents of that parcel you brought were needed to call the spirits of my daughter and her servants back to their earthly tenements, here, tonight, in this very room, Hawkins!'

"'Henry Putnam,' my father cried, 'do you mean to say you intend to play with this Devil's business? You'd really try to call back the spirit of one whose life on earth is done?'

"'I would; by God, I *will!*' Colonel Putnam shouted.

"'You shan't!' Father told him. 'That kind of thing is denounced by the laws of Moses, and mighty good sense he showed when he forbade it, too!'

"'Fool!' Colonel Putnam screamed at him. 'Don't you know Moses stole all his knowledge from the priesthood of Egypt, to which I belonged? Centuries before Moses was, we knew the white arts of life and the black arts of death. Moses! How dare you quote that ignorant charlatan and thief?'

"'Well, I'll have no part in any such Devil's mummery,' Father told him, but Colonel Putnam was like a madman.

"'You shall!' he answered, drawing a revolver from his pocket. 'If either of you tries to leave this room I'll shoot him dead!'"

The girl stopped speaking and covered her face with her hands. "If we'd only let him shoot us!" she said wearily "Maybe we'd have been able to stop it."

De Grandin regarded her compassionately. "Can you continue, *Mademoiselle?*" he asked gently. "Or would you, perhaps, wait till later?"

"No, I might as well get it over with," she answered with a sigh. "Colonel Putnam ripped the cover off the package Father had brought and took out seven little silver vessels, each about as large as a hen's egg, but shaped something like a pineapple—having a pointed top and a flat base. He set them in a semicircle before the three coffins and filled them from an earthenware jug which was fitted with a spout terminating in a knob fashioned like a woman's head crowned with a diadem of hawks' wings. Then he lighted a taper and blew out the oil-lamp which furnished the only illumination for the room.

"It was deathly still in the darkened room; outside we could hear the crickets cheeping, and their shrill little cries seemed to grow louder and louder, to come closer and closer to the window. Colonel Putnam's shadow, cast by the flickering taper's light, lay on the wall like one of those old-time pictures of the Evil One.

"'The hour!' he breathed. 'The hour has come!'

Quickly he leaned forward, touching first one, then another of the little silver jars with the flame of his taper.

"The room's darkness yielded to an eery, bluish glow. Wherever the fire came in contact with a vase a tiny, thin, blue flame sprang up.

"Suddenly the corner of the room where the mummy-cases stood seemed wavering and rocking, like a ship upon a troubled ocean. It was hot and sultry in the house, shut in as it was by the thick pine woods, but from somewhere a current of cold—freezing cold!—air began to blow. I could feel its chill on my ankles, then my knees, finally on my hands as I held them in my lap.

"'Daughter, little daughter—daughter in all the ages past and all the ages yet to be, I call to you. Come, your father calls!' Colonel Putnam intoned in a quavering voice. 'Come. Come, I command it! Out of the illimitable void of eternity, come to me. In the name of Osiris, Dread Lord of the Spirit World, I command it. In the name of Isis, wife and sister of the Mighty One, I command it! In the names of Horus and Anubis, I command it!'

"Something—I don't know what—seemed entering the room. The windows were tight-latched; yet we saw the dusty curtains flutter, as though in a sudden current of air, and a light, fine mist seemed to obscure the bright blue flames burning in the seven silver lamps. There was a creaking sound, as though an old and rusty-hinged door were being slowly opened, and the lids of the two mummy-cases to right and left of the central figure began to swing outward. And as they moved, the linen-bandaged thing in the center coffin seemed to writhe like a hibernating snake recovering life, and stepped out into the room!

"Colonel Putnam forgot Father and me completely. 'Daughter—Gretchen, Isabella, Francesca, Musepa, T'ashamt, by whatever name or names you have been known throughout the ages, I charge you speak!' he cried, sinking on his knees and stretching out his hands toward the moving mummy.

"There came a gentle, sighing noise, then a light, tittering laugh, musical, but hard and metallic, as a thin, high voice replied. 'My father, you who loved and nurtured me in ages gone, I come to you at your command with those who served me in the elder world; but we are weak and worn from our long rest. Give us to eat, my father.'

"'Aye, food shall ye have, and food in plenty,' Colonel Putnam answered. 'Tell me, what is it that ye crave?'

"'Naught but the life-force of those strangers at your back,' the voice replied with another light, squeaking laugh. 'They must die if we would live—' and the sheeted thing moved nearer to us in the silver lamps' blue light.

"Before the Colonel could snatch up the pistol which had fallen from his hand, Father grabbed it, seized me with his free hand and dragged me from the house. Our car was waiting at the door, its engine still going, and we jumped in and started for the highroad at top speed.

"We were nearly out of the woods surrounding Putnam's house—the same woods I drove you through this afternoon—I happened to look back. There, running like a rabbit, coming so fast that it was actually overtaking our speeding car, was a tall, thin man, almost fleshless as a skeleton, and aptly dressed in some dust-colored, close-fitting kind of tights.

"But I recognized it! It was one of those things from the mummy-cases we'd seen in Colonel Putnam's parlor!

"Dad crowded on more speed, but the dreadful running mummy kept gaining on us. It had almost overtaken us when we reached the edge of the woods and I happened to remember Father still had Colonel Putnam's pistol. I snatched the weapon from his pocket and emptied it at the thing that chased us, almost at pointblank range. I know I must have hit it several times, for I'm a pretty good shot and the distance was too short for a miss, even allowing for the way the car was lurching, but it kept right on; then, just as we ran out into the moonlight at the woodland's edge, it stopped in its tracks, waved its arms at us and—vanished."

De Grandin tweaked the sharply waxed ends of his little wheat-blond mustache. "There is more, *Mademoiselle*," he said at length. "I can see it in your eyes. What else?"

Miss Hawkins cast a startled look at him, and it seemed to me she shuddered slightly, despite the warming glow of the fire.

"Yes," she answered slowly, "there's more. Three days after that a party of young folks came up here on a camping-trip from New York. They were at the Ormond cabin down by Pine Lake, six of 'em; a young man and his wife, who acted as chaperons, and two girls and two boys. The second night after they came, one of the girls and her boy friend went canoeing on the lake just at sundown. They paddled over to this side, where the Putnam farm comes down to the water, and came ashore to rest."

There was an air of finality in the way she paused. It was as if she had announced, "Thus the tale endeth," when she told us of the young folks' beaching their canoe, and de Grandin realized it, for, instead of asking what the next occurrence was, he demanded simply:

"And when were they found, *Mademoiselle?*"

"Next day, just before noon. I wasn't with the searching-party, but they told me it was pretty dreadful. The canoe paddles were smashed to splinters, as though they'd used them as clubs to defend themselves and broken them while doing so, and their bodies were literally torn limb from limb. If it hadn't been there was no evidence of any of them being eaten, the searchers would have thought a pair of panthers had pounced on them, for their faces were clawed almost beyond recognition, practically every shred of clothing ripped off them, and their arms and legs and heads completely separated from their bodies."

"U'm? And blood was scattered all around, one imagines?" de Grandin asked.

"No! Not a single drop of blood was anywhere in sight. Job Denham, the undertaker who received the bodies from the coroner, told me their flesh was pale and dry as veal. He said he couldn't understand it, but I—"

She halted in her narrative, glancing apprehensively across her shoulder at the window; then, in a low, almost soundless whisper. "The Bible says the blood's the life, doesn't it?" she asked. "And that voice we heard in Colonel Putnam's house told him those mummies wanted the vital force from Dad and me, didn't it? Well, I think that's the answer. Whatever it was Colonel Putnam brought to life in his house three days before was what set on that boy and girl in Putnam's woods, and it—they—attacked them for their blood."

"Have similar events occurred, *Mademoiselle?*"

"Did you notice the farm land hereabouts as we drove over?" she asked irrelevantly.

"Not particularly."

"Well, it's old land; sterile. You couldn't raise so much as a mortgage on it. No one's tried to farm it since I can remember, and I'll be seventeen next January."

"U'm; and so—"

"So you'd think it kind of funny for Colonel Putnam suddenly to decide to work his land, wouldn't you?"

"Perhaps."

"And with so many men out of work hereabouts, you'd think it queer for him to advertise for farmhands in the Boston papers, wouldn't you?"

"*Précisément, Mademoiselle.*"

"And for him to pay their railway fare up here, and their bus fare over from the station, and then get dissatisfied with 'em all of a sudden, and discharge 'em in a day or two—and for 'em to leave without anybody's knowing when they went, or *where* they went; then for him to hire a brand-new crew in the same way, and discharge them in the same way in a week or less?"

"*Mademoiselle,*" de Grandin answered in a level, almost toneless voice, "we consider these events somewhat more than merely queer. We think they have the smell of fish upon them. Tomorrow we shall call upon this estimable Putnam person, and he would be well advised to have a credible explanation in readiness."

"Call on Colonel Putnam? Not I." the girl rejoined. "I wouldn't go near that house of his, even in daylight, for a million dollars!"

"Then I fear we must forego the pleasure of your charming company," he returned with a smile, "for we shall visit him, most certainly. Yes, of course.

"Meantime," he added, "we have had a trying day; is it agreeable that we retire? Doctor Trowbridge and I shall occupy the bunks in this room; you may have the inner room, *Mademoiselle*."

"Please," she pleaded, and a flush mantled her face to the brows, "please let me sleep out here with you. I'd—well, I'd be scared to death sleeping in there by myself, and I'll be just as quiet—honestly, I won't disturb you."

She was unsupplied with sleeping-wear, of course; so de Grandin, who was about her stature, cheerfully donated a pair of lavender-and-scarlet striped silk pajamas, which she donned in the adjoining room, expending so little time in process that we had scarcely had time to doff our boots, jackets and cravats ere she rejoined us, looking far more like an adolescent lad than a young woman, save for those absurd pink-coral ear-studs.

"I wonder if you'd mind my using the 'phone?" she asked as she pattered across the rough-board floor on small and amazingly white bare feet. "I don't think it's been disconnected, and I'd like to call Dad and tell him I'm all right."

"By all means, do so," bade de Grandin as he hitched the blanket higher on his shoulder. "We can understand his apprehension for your safety in the circumstances."

The girl raised the receiver from the old-fashioned wall fixture, took the magneto crank in her right hand and gave it three vigorous turns, then seven slow ones.

"Hello? Dad?" she called. "This is Audrey; I'm—*oh!*" The color drained from her cheeks as though a coat of liquid white were sprayed across her face. "Dad— Dad—what *is* it?" she cried shrilly; then slowly, like a marionette being lowered by its strings, she wavered totteringly a moment, let fall the telephone receiver and slumped in a pathetic little heap upon the cabin floor.

De Grandin and I were out of bed with a bound, the little Frenchman bending solicitously above the fainting girl, I snatching at the telephone receiver.

"Hullo, hullo?" I called through the transmitter. "Mr. Hawkins?"

"*Huh—hoh—huh-hoh-huh!*" the most fiendish, utterly diabolical chuckle I ever heard came to me across the wire. "*Huh—hoh—huh-hoh-huh!*"

Then click! the telephone connection broke, and though I repeated the three-seven ring I'd heard the girl give several times, I could obtain no answer, not even the faint buzzing which denotes an open wire.

"My father! Something dreadful has happened to him, I know!" moaned the girl as she recovered consciousness. "Did you hear it, too, Doctor Trowbridge?"

"I heard something, certainly; it sounded like a poor connection roaring in the wire," I lied. Then, as hopeful disbelief lightened in her eyes: "Yes, I'm sure that's what it was, for the instrument's quite dead, now."

Reluctantly reassured, Audrey Hawkins clambered into bed, and though she moaned once or twice with a little, whimpering sound, her buoyant youth and healthily tired young muscles stood her in good stead, and she was sleeping peacefully within an hour.

Several times, as de Grandin and I lay in silence, waiting for her to drop off, I fancied I heard the oddly terrifying squeaking sounds we'd noticed earlier in the evening, but I resolutely put all thought of what their probable origin might be from my mind, convinced myself they were the cries of nocturnal insects, and—lay broad awake, listening for their recurrence.

"What was it that you heard in the telephone, Friend Trowbridge?" the little Frenchman asked me in a whisper when her continued steady, even breathing had assured us that our youthful guest was sound asleep.

"A laugh," I answered, "the most hideous, hellish chuckle I've ever listened to. You don't suppose her father could have laughed like that, just to frighten—"

"I do not think Monsieur her father has either cause for laughter or ability to laugh," he interrupted. "What it is that haunts these woods I do not surely know, my friend, though I suspect that the crack-brained Colonel Putnam let loose a horde of evil elementals when he went through that mummery at his house last summer. However that may be, there is no doubt that these things, whatever be their nature, are of a most unpleasant disposition, intent on killing any one they meet, either from pure lust for killing or in order to secure the vital forces of their victims and thus increase their strength in a material form. It is my fear that they may have a special grudge against Monsieur Hawkins and his daughter, for they were the first people whose lives they sought, and they escaped, however narrowly. Therefore, having failed in their second attempt to do the daughter mischief this afternoon, they may have wreaked vengeance on the father. Yes, it is entirely possible."

"But it's unlikely," I protested. "He's over in Bartlesville, ten miles away, while she's right here; yet—"

"Yes, you were saying—" he prompted as a sudden unpleasant thought forced itself into my mind and stopped my speech.

"Why, if they're determined to do mischief to either Hawkins or his daughter, haven't they attempted to enter this house, which is so much nearer than her home?"

"Eh bien, I thought you might be thinking that," he answered dryly. "And are you sure that they have made no attempt to enter here? Look at the door, if you will be so good, and tell me what it is you see."

I glanced across the cabin toward the stout plank door and caught the ruddy reflection of the firelight on a small, bright object lying on the sill. "It looks like your hunting-knife," I told him.

"*Précisément*, you have right; it *is* my hunting-knife," he answered. "My hunting-knife, unsheathed, with its sharp point directed toward the door-sill. Yours is at the other entrance, while I have taken the precaution to place a pair of heavy shears on the window-ledge. I do not think I wasted preparations, either, as you will probably agree if you will cast your eyes toward the window."

Obediently, I glanced at the single window of the room, then stifled an involuntary cry of horror; for there, outlined against the flickering illumination of the dying fire, stood an evil-looking, desiccated thing, skeleton-thin, dark, leather-colored skin stretched tightly as drum parchment on its skull, broken teeth protruding through retracted lips, tiny sparks of greenish light glowing malevolently in its cavernous, hollow eye-sockets. I recognized it at a glance; it was a mummy, an Egyptian mummy, such as I had seen scores of times while walking through the museums. And yet it was no mummy, either, for while it had the look of death and unnaturally delayed decay about it, it was also endued with some kind of dreadful life-in-death; for its little, glittering eyes were plainly capable of seeing, while its withered, leathery lips were drawn back in a grin of snarling fury, and even as I looked, they moved back from the stained and broken teeth in the framing of some phrase of hatred.

"Do not be afraid," de Grandin bade. "He can look and glare and make his monkey-faces all he wishes, but he can not enter here. The shears and knives prevent him."

"Y-you're sure?" I asked, terror gripping at my throat.

"Sure? To be sure I'm sure, He and his unpleasant playfellows would have been inside the cabin, and at our throats, long since, could they have found a way to enter. The sharpened steel, my friend, is very painful to him. Iron and steel are the most earthly of all metals, and exercise a most uncomfortable influence on elementals. They can not handle it, they can not even approach it closely, and when it is sharpened to a point it seems to be still more efficient, for its pointed end appears to focus and concentrate radiations of psychic force from the human body, forces which are highly destructive to them. Knowing this, and suspecting what it is that we have to do with from the story Mademoiselle Hawkins told us, I took precautions to place these discouragers at doors and window before we went to bed. *Tiens*, I have lain here something like an hour, hearing them squeak and gibber as they prowled around the house; only a moment since I noticed that thin gentleman peering in the window, and thought you might he interested."

Rising, he crossed the cabin on tiptoe, so as not to wake the sleeping girl, and drew the burlap curtain across the window. "Look at that until your ugly eyes are tired, *Monsieur le Cadavre*," he bade. "My good Friend Trowbridge does not care to have you watch him while he sleeps."

"Sleep!" I echoed. "D'ye think I could sleep knowing *that's* outside?"

"*Parbleu*, he is much better outside than in, I think," returned the Frenchman with a grin. "However. if you care to lie awake and think of him, I have no objections. But me, I am tired. I shall sleep; nor shall I sleep the worse for knowing that he is securely barred outside the house. No."

R EASSURED, I FINALLY FELL asleep, but my rest was broken by unpleasant dreams. Sometime toward morning I awoke, not from any consciousness of impending trouble nor from any outward stimulus; yet, once my eyes were open, I was as fully master of my faculties as though I had not slept at all. The pre-dawn chill was in the air, almost bitter in its penetrating quality; the fire which had blazed merrily when we said good-night now lay a heap of whitened ashes and feebly smoldering embers. Outside the cabin rose a furious chorus of light, swishing, squeaking noises, as though a number of those whistling rubber toys with which small children are amused were being rapidly squeezed together. At first I thought it was the twittering of birds, then realized that the little feathered friends had long since flown to southern quarters; besides, there was an eery unfamiliarity in this sound, totally unlike anything I had ever heard until the previous evening, and it rose and gathered in shrill tone and volume as I listened. Vaguely, for no conscious reason, I likened it to the clamoring of caged brutes when feeding-time approaches in the zoo.

Then, as I half rose in my bunk, I saw an indistinct form move across the cabin. Slowly, very slowly, and so softly that the rough, uneven floor forbore to creak beneath her lightly pressing feet, Audrey Hawkins tiptoed toward the cabin door, creeping with a kind of feline grace. Half stupefied, I saw her pause before the portal, sink stealthily to one knee, reach out a cautious hand—

"*Non, non; dix mille fois non*—you shall not do it!" de Grandin cried, emerging from his bunk and vaulting across the cabin, seemingly with a single movement, then grasping the girl by the shoulders with such force that he hurled her half across the room. "What business of the fool do you make here, *Mademoiselle?*" he asked her angrily. "Do not you know that once the barriers of steel have been removed we should be—*mon Dieu*, one understands!"

Audrey Hawkins' hands were at her temples as she looked at him with innocent amazement while he raged at her. Clearly, she had wakened from a sound and dreamless sleep when she felt his hands upon her shoulders. Now she gazed at him in wonder mixed with consternation.

"Wh-what is it? What was I doing?" she asked.

"Ah, *parbleu*, you did nothing of your own volition, *Mademoiselle*," he answered, "but those other ones, those very evil ones outside the house, in some way they reached you in your sleep and made you pliable to their desires. *Ha*, but they forgot de Grandin; he sleeps, yes, but he sleeps the sleep of the cat. They do not catch him napping. But no."

We piled fresh wood upon the fire and, wrapped in blankets, sat before the blaze, smoking, drinking strong black coffee, talking with forced cheerfulness till the daylight came again, and when de Grandin put the curtain back and looked out in the clearing round the cabin, there was no sign of any visitants, nor were there any squeaking voices in the woods.

B REAKFAST FINISHED, WE CLIMBED into the ancient Ford and set out for Bartlesville, traveling at a speed I had not thought the ancient vehicle could make.

Hawkins' general store was a facsimile of hundreds of like institutions to be found in typical American villages from Vermont to Vancouver. Square as a box, it faced the village main street. Shop windows, displaying a miscellany of tinned groceries, household appliances and light agricultural equipment, occupied its front elevation. Shuttered windows piercing the second-story walls denoted where the family living-quarters occupied the space above the business premises.

Audrey tried the red-painted door of the shop, found it locked securely, and led the way through a neat yard surrounded by a fence of white pickets, took a key from her trousers pockets and let us through the private family entrance.

Doctors and undertakers have a specialized sixth sense. No sooner had we crossed the threshold than I smelled death inside that house. De Grandin sensed it, too, and I saw his smooth brow pucker in a warning frown as he glanced at me across the girl's shoulder.

"Perhaps it would be better if we went first, *Mademoiselle*," he offered. "*Monsieur* your father may have had an accident, and—"

"Dad—oh, Dad, are you awake?" the girl's call interrupted. "It's I. I was caught in Putnam's woods last evening and spent the night at Sutter's camp, but I'm—*Dad!* Why don't you answer me?"

For a moment she stood silent in an attitude of listening; then like a flash she darted down the little hall and up the winding stairs which led to the apartment overhead.

We followed her as best we could, cannoning into unseen furniture, barking our shins on the narrow stairs, but keeping close behind her as she raced down the upper passageway into the large bedroom which overlooked the village street.

The room was chaos. Chairs were overturned, the clothing had been wrenched from the big, old-fashioned bed and flung in a heap in the center of the floor, and from underneath the jumbled pile of comforter and sheets and blankets a man's bare foot protruded.

I hesitated at the doorway, but the girl rushed forward, dropped to her knees and swept aside the veiling bedclothes. It was a man past early middle life, but looking older, she revealed. Thin, he was, with that starved-turkey kind of lean-ness characteristic of so many native New Englanders. His gray head was thrown back and his lean, hard-shaven chin thrust upward truculently. In pinched nos-tril, sunken eye and gaping open mouth his countenance bore the unmistakable seal of death. He lay on his back with arms and legs sprawled out at grotesque angles from the inadequate folds of his old-fashioned Canton flannel nightshirt, and at first glance I recognized the unnaturalness of his posture, for human anat-omy does not alter much with death, and this man's attitude would have been impossible for any but a practised contortionist.

Even as I bent my brows in wonder, de Grandin knelt beside the body. The cause of death was obvious, for in the throat, extending almost down to the left clavicle, there gaped a jagged wound, not made by any sharp, incising weapon, but rather, apparently, the result of some savage lancination, for the whole integ-ument was ripped away, exposing the trachea to view—yet not a clot of blood lay round the ragged edges of the laceration, nor was there any sign of staining on the nightrobe. Indeed, to the ordinary pallor of the dead there seemed to be a different sort of pallor added, a queer, unnatural pallor which rendered the man's weather-stained countenance not only absolutely colorless, but curiously transparent, as well.

"Good heavens—" I began, but:

"Friend Trowbridge, if you please, observe," de Grandin ordered, lifting one of the dead man's hands and rotating it back and forth. I grasped his meaning instantly. Even allowing for the passage of *rigor mortis* and ensuing *post mortem* flaccidity, it would have been impossible to move that hand in such a manner if the radius and ulna were intact. The man's arm-bones had been fractured, probably in several places, and this, I realized, accounted for the posture of his hands and feet.

"Dad—oh, Daddy, Daddy!" cried the distracted girl as she took the dead man's head in her arms and nursed it on her shoulder. "Oh, Daddy dear, I knew that something terrible had happened when—"

Her outburst ended in a storm of weeping as she rocked her body to and fro, moaning with the helpless, inarticulate piteousness of a dumb thing wounded unto death. Then, abruptly:

"You heard that laugh last night!" she challenged me. "You know you did, Doctor Trowbridge—and there's where we heard it from," she pointed with a shaking finger at the wall-telephone across the room.

As I followed the line of her gesture I saw that the instrument had been ripped clear from its retaining bolts, its wires, its mouthpiece and receiver broken as though by repeated hammer-blows.

"They—those dreadful things that tried to get at us last night came over here when they found they couldn't reach me and murdered my poor father!"

she continued in a low, sob-choked voice. "I know! The night Colonel Putnam raised those awful mummies from the dead the she-thing said they wanted our lives, and one of the others chased us through the woods. They've been hungering for us ever since, and last night they got Daddy. I—"

She paused, her slender bosom heaving, and we could see the tear drops dry away as fiery anger flared up in her eyes.

"Last night I said I wouldn't go near Putnam's house again for a million dollars," she told de Grandin. "Now I say I wouldn't stay away from there for all the money in the world. I'm going over now—this minute—and pay old Putnam off. I'll face that villain with his guilt and make him pay for Daddy's life if it's the last thing I do!"

"It probably would be, *Mademoiselle*," de Grandin answered dryly. "Consider, if you please: This so odious Monsieur Putnam is undoubtlessly responsible for loosing those evil things upon the countryside, but while his life is forfeit for his crimes of necromancy, merely to kill him would profit us—and the community—not at all. These most unpleasant pets of his have gotten out of hand. I make no doubt that he himself is in constant, deadly fear of them, and that they, who came as servants of his will, are now his undisputed masters. Were we to kill him, we should still have those evil ones to reckon with, and till they have been utterly destroyed the country will be haunted by them; and others—countless others, perhaps—will share the fate of your poor father and that unfortunate young man and woman who perished on their boating-trip, not to mention those misguided workingmen who answered Monsieur Putnam's advertisements. You comprehend? This is a war of extermination on which we are embarked; we must destroy or be destroyed. Losing our lives in a gallant gesture would be a worthless undertaking. Victory, not speedy vengeance, must be our first and great consideration."

"Well, then, what are we to do, sit here idly while they range the woods and kill more people?"

"By no means, *Mademoiselle*. First of all, we must see that your father has the proper care; next, we must plan the work which lies before us. That done, it is for us to work the plans which we have made."

"All right, then, let's call the coroner," she agreed. "Judge Lindsay knows me, and he knew Dad all his life. When I tell him how old Putnam raised those mummies from the dead, and—"

"*Mademoiselle!*" the Frenchman expostulated. "You will tell him nothing about anything which Monsieur Putnam has done. It has been two hundred years, unfortunately, since your kin and neighbors ceased paying such creatures as this Putnam for their sins with rope and flame. To tell your truthful story to the coroner would be but signing your commitment to the madhouse. Then, doubly protected by your incarceration and public disbelief in their existence,

Monsieur Putnam's mummy-things could range the countryside at will. Indeed, it is altogether likely that the first place they would visit would be the madhouse where you were confined, and there, defenseless, you would be wholly at their mercy. Your screams for help would be regarded as the ravings of a lunatic, and the work of extirpation of your family which they began last night would be concluded. Your life, which they have sought since first they came, would be snuffed out, and, with none to fight against them, the countryside would fall an easy prey to their vile depredations. *Eh bien*, who can say how far the slaughter would go before the pig-ignorant authorities, at last convinced that you had told the sober truth when they thought you raving, would finally arouse themselves and take befitting action? You see why we must guard our tongues, *Mademoiselle?*"

N EWS OF THE MURDER spread like wildfire through the village. Zebulon Lindsay, justice of the peace, who also acted as coroner, empaneled a jury before noon; by three o'clock the inquisition had been held and a verdict of death by violence at the hands of some person or persons unknown was rendered.

Among the agricultural implements in Hawkins' stock de Grandin noted a number of billhooks, pike-like instruments with long, curved blades resembling those of scythes fixed on the ends of their strong helves.

"These we can use tonight, my friends," he told us as he laid three carefully aside.

"What for?" demanded Audrey.

"For those long, cadaverous things which run through Monsieur Putnam's woods, by blue!" he answered with a rather sour smile. "You will recall that on the first occasion when you saw them you shot one of their number several times?"

"Yes."

"And that notwithstanding you scored several hits, it continued its pursuit?"

"Yes, sir."

"Very well. You know the reason? Your bullets tore clear through its desiccated flesh, but had not force to stop it. *Tiens*, could you have knocked its legs off at the knees, however, do you think that it could still have run?"

"Oh, you mean—"

"Precisely, exactly; quite so, *ma chère*, I purpose dividing them, anatomizing them, striking them limb from limb. What lead and powder would be powerless to do, these instruments of iron will accomplish very nicely. We shall go to their domain at nightfall; that way we shall be sure of meeting them. Were we to go by daylight, it is possible they would be hidden in some secret place, for like all their kind they wait the coming of darkness because their doings are evil.

"Should you see one of them, remember what he did to your poor father, *Mademoiselle*, and strike out with your iron. Strike and do not spare your blows.

It is not as foeman unto foe we go tonight, but as executioners to criminals. You understand?"

W E SET OUT JUST at sundown, Audrey Hawkins driving, de Grandin and I, each armed with a stout billhook, in the rear seat.

"It were better that you stopped here, *Mademoiselle*," de Grandin whispered as the big white pillars of the mansion's antique portico came in view between the trees. "There is no need to advertise our advent; surprise is worth a thousand men in battle."

We dismounted from the creaking vehicle and, our weapons on our shoulders, began a stealthy advance.

"*S-s-st!*" Audrey warned as we paused a moment by a little opening in the trees, our eyes intent upon the house. "Hear it?"

Very softly, like the murmur of a sleepy little bird, there came a subdued squeaking noise from a hemlock thicket twenty feet or so away. I felt the short hair on my neck begin to rise against my collar and a little chill of mingled hate and apprehension run rippling through my scalp and cheeks. It was like the sensation felt when one comes unexpectedly upon a serpent in the path.

"Softly, friends," Jules de Grandin ordered, grasping the handle of his billhook like a quarterstaff and leaning toward the sound; "do you stand by me, good Friend Trowbridge, and have your flashlight ready. Play its beam on him the minute he emerges, and keep him visible for me to work on."

Cautiously, quietly as a cat stalking a mouse, he stepped across the clearing, neared the clump of bushes whence the squeaking came, then leant forward, eyes narrowed, weapon ready.

It burst upon us like a charging beast, one moment hidden from our view by the screening boughs of evergreen, next instant leaping through the air, long arms flailing, skeleton-hands grasping for de Grandin's throat, its withered, leather-like face a mask of hatred and ferocity.

I shot the flashlight's beam full on it, but its terrifying aspect caused my hand to tremble so that I could scarcely hold the shaft of light in line with the leaping horror's movements.

"*Ça-ha, Monsieur le Cadavre*, we meet again, it seems!" de Grandin greeted in a whisper, dodging nimbly to the left as the mummy-monster reached out scrawny hands to grapple with him. He held the billhook handle in the center, left hand upward, right hand down, and as the withered leather talons missed their grasp he whirled the iron-headed instrument overhand from left to right, turning it as he did so, so that the carefully whetted edge of the heavy blade crashed with devastating force upon the mummy's withered biceps. The limb dropped helpless from the desiccated trunk, but, insensible to pain, the creature whirled and grasped out with its right hand.

Once more the billhook circled whistling through the air, this time reversed, striking downward from right to left. The keen-edged blade sheared through the lich's other arm, cleaving it from the body at the shoulder.

And now the withered horror showed a trace of fear. Sustained by supernatural strength and swiftness, apparently devoid of any sense of pain, it had not entered what intelligence the thing possessed that a man could stand against it. Now it paused, irresolutely a moment, teetering on its spindle legs and broad, splay feet, and while it hesitated thus the little Frenchman swung his implement again, this time like an ax, striking through dry, brown flesh and aged, brittle bone, lopping off the mummy's legs an inch or so above the knees.

Had it not been so horrible I could have laughed aloud to see the withered torso hurtle to the ground and lie there, flopping grotesquely on stumps of arms and legs, seeking to regain the shelter of the hemlock copse as it turned its fleshless head and gazed across its bony shoulder at de Grandin.

"Hit it on the head! Crush its skull!" I advised, but:

"*Non*, this is better," he replied as he drew a box of matches from his pocket and lighted one.

Now utter terror seized the limbless lich. With horrid little squeaking cries it redoubled its efforts to escape, but the Frenchman was inexorable. Bending forward, he applied the flaming match to the tinder-dry body, and held it close against the withered skin. The fire caught instantly. As though it were compounded of a mass of oil-soaked rags, the mummy's body sent out little tongues of fire, surmounted by dense clouds of aromatic smoke, and in an instant was a blaze of glowing flame. De Grandin seized the severed arms and legs and piled them on the burning torso so that they, too, blazed and snapped and crackled like dry wood thrown on a roaring fire.

"And that, I damn think, denotes the end of that," he told me as he watched the body sink from flames to embers, then to white and scarcely glowing ashes. "Fire is the universal solvent, the one true cleanser, my friend. It was not for nothing that the olden ones condemned their witches to be burned. This elemental force, this evil personality which inhabited that so unsavory mummy's desiccated flesh, not only can it find no other place to rest now that we have destroyed its tenement, but the good, clean, clarifying flames have dissipated it entirely. Never again can it materialize, never more enter human form through the magic of such necromancers as that *sacré* Putnam person. It is gone, disposed of—*pouf!* it is no longer anything at all.

"What think you of my scheme, *Mademoiselle?*" he asked. "Was I not the clever one to match iron and fire against them? Was it not laughable to see— *grand Dieu*, Friend Trowbridge—*where is she?*"

He leant upon his billhook, looking questingly about the edges of the clearing while I played my searchlight's beam among the trees. At length:

"One sees it perfectly," he told me. "While we battled with that one, another of them set on her and we could not hear her cries because of our engagement. Now—"

"Do—do you suppose it killed her as it did her father?" I asked, sick with apprehension.

"We can not say; we can but look," he answered. "Come."

Together we searched the woodland in an ever-widening circle, but no trace of Audrey Hawkins could we find.

"Here's her billhook," I announced as we neared the house.

Sticking in the hole of a tree, almost buried in the wood, was the head of the girl's weapon, some three inches of broken shaft adhering to it. On the ground twenty feet or more away lay the main portion of the helve, broken across as a match-stem might he broken by a man.

The earth was moist beneath the trees, and at that spot uncovered by fallen leaves or pine needles. As I bent to pick up Audrey's broken billhook, I noticed tracks in the loam—big, barefoot tracks, heavy at the toe, as though their maker strained forward as he walked, and beside them a pair of wavy parallel lines—the toe-prints of Audrey's boots as she was dragged through the woods and toward the Putnam house.

"What now?" I asked. "They've taken her there, dead or alive, and—"

He interrupted savagely: "What can we do but follow? Me, I shall go into that *sacré* house, and take it down, plank by single plank, until I find her; also I shall find those others, and when I do—"

No lights showed in the Putnam mansion as we hurried across the weed-grown, ragged lawn, tiptoed up the veranda steps and softly tried the handle of the big front door. It gave beneath our pressure, and in a moment we were standing in a lightless hall, our weapons held in readiness as we strove to pierce the gloom with straining eyes and held our breaths as we listened for some sound betokening an enemy's approach.

"Can you hear it, Trowbridge, *mon ami?*" he asked me in a whisper. "Is it not their so abominable squealing?"

I listened breathlessly, and from the passageway's farther end it seemed there came a series of shrill skirking squeaks, as though an angry rat were prisoned there.

Treading carefully, we advanced along the corridor, pausing at length as a vague, greenish-blue glow appeared to filter out into the darkness, not exactly lightening into the darkness, making the gloom a little less abysmal.

We gazed incredulously at the scene presented in the room beyond. The windows were all closed and tightly shuttered, and in a semicircle on the floor there burned a set of seven little silver lamps which gave off a blue-green, phosphorescent glow, hardly sufficient to enable us to mark the actions of a group of figures gathered there. One was a man, old and white-haired, disgustingly unkempt, his deep-set dark eyes burning with a fanatical glow of adoration as he kept them fixed upon a figure seated in a high, carved chair which occupied a sort of dais beyond the row of glowing silver lamps. Beside the farther wall there stood a giant form, a great brown skinned man with bulging muscles like a wrestler's and the knotted torso of a gladiator. One of his mighty hands was twined in Audrey Hawkins' short, blond hair; with the other he was stripping off her clothes as a monkey skins a fruit. We heard the cloth rip as it parted underneath his wrenching fingers, saw the girl's slim body show white and lissome as a new-peeled hazel wand, then saw her thrown birth-naked on the floor before the figure seated on the dais.

Bizarre and terrifying as the mummy-creatures we had seen had been, the seated figure was no less remarkable. No mummy, this, but a soft and sweetly rounded woman-shape, almost divine in bearing and adornment. Out of olden Egypt she had come, and with her she had brought the majesty that once had ruled the world. Upon her head the crown of Isis sat, the vulture cap with wings of beaten gold and blue enamel, and the vulture's head with gem-set eyes, above it rearing upright horns of Hathor between which shone the polished-silver disk of the full moon, beneath them the uraeus, emblem of Osiris.

About her neck was hung a collar of beaten gold close-studded with emeralds and blue lapis lazuli, and round her wrists were wide, bright bands of gold which shone with figures worked in red and blue enamel. Her breasts were bare, but high beneath the pointed bosoms was clasped a belt of blue and gold from which there draped a robe of thin, transparent linen gathered in scores of tiny, narrow pleats and fringed about the hem with little balls of gleaming gold which hung an inch or so above the arching insteps of her long and narrow feet, on every toe of which there gleamed a jewel-set ring. In her left hand she held a golden instrument fashioned like a T-cross with a long loop at its top, while in her right she bore a three-lashed golden scourge, the emblem of Egyptian sovereignty.

All this I noted in a sort of wondering daze, but it was her glaring, implacable eyes which held me rooted to the spot. Like the eyes of a tigress or a leopardess they were, and glowing with a horrid, inward light as though illumined from behind by the phosphorescence of an all consuming, heatless flame.

Even as we halted spellbound at the turning of the corridor we saw her raise her golden scourge and point it like an aiming weapon at Audrey Hawkins. The girl lay huddled in a small white heap where the ruthless giant had thrown her, but as the golden scourge was leveled at her she half rose to a crouching posture and crept forward on her knees and elbows, whimpering softly, half in pleading, half in fear, it seemed.

The fixed, set stare of hatred never left the seated woman's eyes as Audrey crawled across the bare plank floor, groveled for an instant at the dais' lowest step, then raised her head and began to lick the other's white, jeweled feet as though she were a beaten dog which sued for pardon from its mistress.

I saw de Grandin's small white teeth flash in the lamps' weird light as he bared them in a quick grimace. "I damn think we have had enough of this, by blue!" he whispered as he stepped out of the shadows.

While I had watched the tableau of Audrey's degradation with a kind of sickened horror, the little Frenchman had been busy. From the pockets of his jacket and his breeches he extracted handkerchiefs and knotted them into a wad, then, drawing out a tin of lighter-fluid, he doused the knotted linen with the liquid. The scent of benzine mixed with ether spread through the quiet air as, his drenched handkerchiefs on his billhook's iron head, he left the shadows, paused an instant on the door-sill, then struck a match and set the cloth ablaze.

"*Messieurs, Madame*, I think this little comedy is ended," he announced as he waved the fire-tipped weapon back and forth, causing the flames to leap and quicken with a ruddy, orange glow.

Mingled terror and surprise showed on the naked giant's face as de Grandin crossed the threshold. He fell away a pace, then, with his back against the wall, crouched for a spring.

"You first, *Monsieur*," the Frenchman told him almost affably, and with an agile leap cleared the few feet separating them and thrust the blazing torch against the other's bare, brown breast.

I gasped with unbelief as I saw the virile, sun-tanned flesh take fire as though it had been tinder, blaze fiercely and crumble into ashes as the flames spread hungrily, eating up his chest and belly, neck and head, finally destroying writhing arms and legs.

The seated figure on the dais was cowering back in fright. Gone was her look of cold, contemptuous hatred; in its place a mask of wild, insensate fear had overspread her clear-cut, haughty features. Her red lips opened, showing needle-sharp white teeth, and I thought she would have screamed aloud in her terror, but all that issued from her gaping mouth was a little, squeaking sound, like the squealing of a mouse caught in a trap.

"And now, *Madame*, permit that I may serve you, also!" De Grandin turned his back upon the blazing man and faced the cringing woman on the throne.

She held up trembling hands to ward him off, and her frightened, squeaking cries redoubled, but inexorably as a mediæval executioner advancing to ignite the faggots round a condemned witch, the little Frenchman crossed the room, held out his blazing torch and forced the fire against her bosom.

The horrifying process of incineration was repeated. From rounded breast to soft, white throat, from omphalos to thighs, from chest to arms and from thighs to feet the all-devouring fire spread quickly, and the woman's white and gleaming flesh blazed fiercely, as if it had been oil-soaked wood. Bones showed a moment as the flesh was burned away, then took the fire, blazed quickly for an instant, glowed to incandescence, and crumbled to white ash before our gaze. Last of all, it seemed, the fixed and staring eyes, still gleaming with a greenish inward light, were taken by the fire, blazed for a second with a mixture of despair and hatred, then dissolved to nothingness.

"*Mademoiselle*," de Grandin laid his hand upon the girl's bare shoulder, "they have gone."

Audrey Hawkins raised her head and gazed at him, the puzzled, non-comprehending look of one who wakens quickly from sound sleep upon her face. There was a question in her eyes, but her lips were mute.

"*Mademoiselle*," he repeated, "they have gone; I drove them out with fire. But *he* remains, my little one." With a quick nod of his head he indicated Colonel Putnam, who crouched in a corner of the room, fluttering fingers at his bearded lips, his wild eyes roving restlessly about, as though he could not understand the quick destruction of the beings he had brought to life.

"He?" the girl responded dully.

"*Précisément, Mademoiselle*—he. The accursed one; the one who raised those mummies from the dead; who made this pleasant countryside a hell of death and horror; who made it possible for them to slay your father while he slept."

One of those unpleasant smiles which seemed to change the entire character of his comely little face spread across his features as he leant above the naked girl and held his billhook toward her.

"The task is yours by right of bereavement, *ma pauvre*," he told her, "but if you would that I do it for you—"

"No—no; let me!" she cried and leapt to her feet, snatching the heavy iron weapon from his hand. Not only was she stripped of clothing; she was stripped of all restraint, as well. Not Audrey Hawkins, civilized descendant of a line of prudishly respectable New England rustics, stood before us in the silver lamps' blue light, but a primordial cave-woman, a creature of the dawn of time, wild with the lust for blood-vengeance; armed, furious, naked and unashamed.

"Come, Friend Trowbridge, we can safely leave the rest to her," de Grandin told me as he took my elbow and forced me from the room.

"But, man, that's murder!" I expostulated as he dragged me down the unlit hall. "That girl's a maniac, and armed, and that poor, crazy old man—"

"Will soon be safe in hell, unless I miss my guess," he broke in with a laugh. "Hark, is it not magnificent, my friend?"

A wild, high scream came to us from the room beyond, then a woman's cachinnating laugh, hysterical, thin-edged, but gloating; and the thudding beat of murderous blows. Then a weak, thin moaning, more blows; finally a little, groaning gasp and the sound of quick breath drawn through fevered lips to laboring lungs.

"And now, my friend, I think we may go back," said Jules de Grandin.

"ONE MOMENT, IF YOU please, I have a task to do," he called as we paused on the portico. "Do you proceed with Mademoiselle Audrey. I shall join you in a minute."

He disappeared inside the old, dark house, and I heard his boot-heels clicking on the bare boards of the hall as he sought the room where all that remained of Henry Putnam and the things he brought back from the dead were lying. The girl leaned weakly against a tall porch pillar, covering her face with trembling hands. She was a grotesque little figure, de Grandin's jacket buttoned round her torso, mine tied kilt-fashion round her waist.

"Oh," she whispered with a conscience-stricken moan, "I'm a murderess. I killed him—beat him to death. I've committed murder!"

I could think of nothing comforting to say, so merely patted her upon the shoulder, but de Grandin, hastening from the house, was just in time to hear her tearful self-arraignment.

"Pardonnez-moi, Mademoiselle," he contradicted, "you are nothing of the kind. Me, once in war I had to head the firing-party which put a criminal to death. Was I then his murderer? But no. My conscience makes no accusation. So it is with you. This Putnam one, this rogue, this miscreant, this so vile necromancer who filled these pleasant woods with squeaking, gibbering horrors, was his life not forfeit? Did not he connive at the death of that poor boy and girl who perished in the midst of their vacation? But yes. Did not he advertise for laborers, that they might furnish sustenance for those evil things he summoned from the tomb? Certainly. Did not he loose his squeaking, laughing thing upon your father, to kill him in his sleep? Of course.

"Yet for these many crimes the law was powerless to punish him. We should have sent ourselves to lifelong confinement in a madhouse had we attempted to invoke the law's processes. Alors, it was for one of us to give him his deserts, and you, my little one, as the one most greatly wronged, took precedence.

"Eh bien," he added with a tug at his small, tightly waxed mustache, "you did make extremely satisfactory work of it."

Since Audrey was in no condition to drive, I took the ancient flivver's steering-wheel.

"Look well upon that bad old house, my friends," de Grandin bade as we started on our homeward road. "Its time is done."

"What d'ye mean?" I asked.

"Precisely what I say. When I went back I made a dozen little fires in different places. They should be spreading nicely by this time."

"I CAN UNDERSTAND WHY THAT mummy we met in the woods caught fire so readily," I told him as we drove through the woods, "but how was it that the man and woman in the house were so inflammable?"

"They, too, were mummies," he replied.

"Mummies? Nonsense! The man was a magnificent physical specimen, and the woman—well, I'll admit she was evil-looking, but she had one of the most beautiful bodies I've ever seen. If she were a mummy, I—"

"Do not say it, my friend," he broke in with a laugh; "eaten words are bitter on the tongue. They were mummies—I say so. In the woods, in Monsieur Hawkins' home, when they made unpleasant faces at us through the window of our cabin, they were mummies, you agree? *Ha*, but when they stood in the blue light of those seven silver lamps, the lights which first shone on them when they came to plague the world, they were to outward seeming the same as when they lived and moved beneath the sun of olden Egypt. I have heard such things.

"That necromancer, von Meyer, of whom Monsieur Putnam spoke, I know of him by reputation. I have been told by fellow occultists whose word I can not doubt that he has perfected a light which when shone on a corpse will give it every look of life, roll back the ravages of years and make it seem in youth and health once more. A very brilliant man is that von Meyer, but a very wicked one, as well. Some day when I have nothing else to do I shall seek him out and kill him to death for the safety of society.

"Can you drive a little faster?" he inquired as we left the woods behind.

"Cold without your jacket?" I asked.

"Cold? *Mais non.* But I would reach the village soon, my friend. *Monsieur le juge* who also acts as coroner has a keg of most delicious cider in his cellar, and this afternoon he bade me call on him whenever I felt thirsty. *Morbleu*, I feel most vilely thirsty now!

"Hurry, if you please, my friend."

Red Gauntlets of Czerni

1. Revenant

OUR VISITOR LEANT FORWARD in his chair and fixed his oddly light colored eyes on Jules de Grandin with an almost pleading expression. "It is about my daughter that I come," he said in a flat, accentless voice, only his sharp-cut, perfect enunciation disclosing that English had not been his mother tongue. "She is gravely ill, *Monsieur*."

"But I do not practise medicine," the little Frenchman answered. "There are thousands of good American practitioners to whom you could apply, Monsieur—"

"Szekler," supplied the other with an inclination of his head. "Andor Szekler, sir."

"Very well, Monsieur Szekler; as I say, I am not a practitioner of medicine, and—"

"But no, it is not a medical practitioner whom I seek," the other interrupted eagerly. "My daughter, her illness is more of the spirit than the body, and I have heard of your abilities to fight back those who dwell upon the threshold of the door between our world and theirs, to conquer such ills as now afflict my child. Say that you will take the case, I beg, *Monsieur*."

"*Eh bien*, you put a different aspect upon things," de Grandin answered. "What are the symptoms of *Mademoiselle* your daughter, it you please?"

Our visitor sucked the breath between his large and firm white teeth with a sort of hissing sigh, and a look of relief, something almost like a gleam of secret triumph, flashed in his narrow eyes. He was a man in late middle life, not fat, but heavily built, blond, regular of features save that his cheek-bones were set so high that they seemed to crowd his light, indefinitely colored eyes, making them seem narrow, and pushing them into a slight slant. Dry-skinned, clean-shaven save for a heavy cavalry mustache waxed into twin uprearing horns, he had that peculiarly well-groomed aspect that denotes the professional soldier, even out of uniform, and though his forehead was broad and benevolent, his queerly narrowed slanting eyes modified its kindliness, and the large, firm mouth, with its almost wolfishly white teeth, lent his face a slightly sinister expression. Now, however, it was the father, not the soldier trained in Old World traditions of blood and iron, who spoke.

"We are Hungarian," he began, then paused a moment, as though at a loss how to proceed.

"One surmised as much," de Grandin murmured politely. "One also assumed you are a soldier, *Monsieur*. Now, as to *Mademoiselle* your daughter, you were about to say—?" He raised his brows and bent a questioning look upon the visitor.

"You are correct, *Monsieur*," responded Szekler. "I am—I was—a soldier; a colonel of hussars in the army of the old monarchy. You know what happened when the war was done, how Margyarország and Austria separated when the poltroon Charles gave up his birthright, and how our poor land, bereft of Transylvania, Croatia and Slavonia was racked by civil war and revolution. Things went badly for our caste. Reduced to virtual beggary, we were harried through the streets like beasts, for to have worn the Emperor's uniform was sufficient cause to send a man before the execution squad. With what little of our fortune that remained I took my wife and little daughter and fled for sanctuary to America.

"The new land has been good to us; in the years which I have spent here I have recouped the fortune which I lost, and added to it. We were very happy here until—"

He paused and once more drew in his breath with that peculiar, eager sound, then passed his tongue-tip across his lower lip. The sight affected me unpleasantly. His tongue was red and pointed like an animal's, and in his oddly oblique eyes there shone a look of scarcely veiled desire.

De Grandin watched him narrowly, his little, round blue eyes intent upon the stranger's face, recording every movement, every feature with photographic fidelity. His air of unsuspecting innocence, it seemed to me, was a piece of superb acting as he prompted gently: "Yes, *Monsieur*, and what occurred to spoil the happiness you found here?"

"Zita, my daughter, was always delicate," Colonel Szekler answered. "For a long time we feared she might be marked by that disease the Turks call *gusel vereni*, which is akin to the consumption of the Western world, except that the patient loses nothing of her looks and often seems to grow more beautiful as the end approaches. It is painless, progressive and incurable, so—"

"One understands, *Monsieur*," de Grandin nodded; "I have seen it in the Turkish hospitals. *Et puis?*"

"Our Magyar girls attain the bloom of womanhood early," answered Colonel Szekler. "When Zita was fourteen she was mature as any American girl four years her senior, and for a time her delicacy seemed to pass away. We sent her off to school, and each season she came home more strengthened, more robust, more like the Zita we would have her be. A month ago, however, her old malady returned. She shows profound lassitude, often complaining of being too tired to rise. Doctors we have had, five, eight of them; all said there is no trace of physical illness, yet there she is, growing weaker day by day. Two days ago I think I found the cause!"

Again that whistling, eager sigh as he drew in his breath before proceeding: "Zita was lying on the chaise-longue in her room, and I went upstairs to ask if she felt well enough to come to luncheon. She was asleep. She was wearing purple-silk pajamas, and a shawl of purple silk was draped across her knees, which enabled me to see it more distinctly.

"As I opened the door to her chamber I saw a patch of white, cloud-like substance, becoming denser and bigger as I watched, issuing from her left side just below the breast. I say it was like cloud, but that is not quite accurate; it had more substance than a cloud, it was more like some ponderable gas, or a great bubble of some gelatinous substance being gradually inflated, and as it grew, it seemed to thicken and become more opaque, or opalescent. Then, taking form as though modeled out of wax by the clever hands of an unseen sculptor, a face took shape and looked at me out of the bubble. It was a living face, Monsieur de Grandin, normal in size, with skin as white as the scraped bone of a fleshless skull, and thick, red lips and rolling, glaring eyes that made my blood run cold.

"I stood there horror-frozen for a moment, repeating to myself: 'Jesus, Mary and Joseph have pity on us!' and then, just as it had come, that cursed, milky cloud began to disappear. Slowly at first, but with ever-increasing speed, as though it were being sucked back into Zita's body, the great, cloudy bubble shrank, the dreadful, leering face flattened out and elongated, melting imperceptibly into its frame of hazy, gleaming cloudiness; finally the whole mass vanished through the fabric of the purple garment which my daughter wore.

"She still continued sleeping peacefully, apparently, and I shook her gently by the shoulder. She wakened and smiled at me and told me she had had a lovely dream. She—"

"Tell me, *Monsieur*," de Grandin interrupted, "you say you saw a face inside this so strange bubble emanating from Mademoiselle Zita's side. Did you by any chance recognize it? Was it just a face, or was it, possibly, the countenance of someone whom you know?"

Colonel Szekler started violently, and a look of frightened surprise swept across his face. "Why should I have recognized it?" he demanded in a dry, harsh voice.

"*Tiens*, why should crockery show cracks, or knives dismember chickens, or table legs be built without knees?" de Grandin countered irritably. "I asked you if you recognized the face, not why."

Szekler seemed to age visibly, to put on ten more years, as he bent his head as though in tortured thought. "Yes, I recognized him," he answered slowly. "It was the face of Red-gauntlet Czerni."

"Ah, and one infers that your relations with this Monsieur Czerni were not always of the pleasantest?"

"I killed him."

De Grandin pursed his lips and raised inquiring brows. "Doubtless he was immeasurably improved by killing," he returned, "but why, specifically, did you bestow the happy dispatch on him, *Monsieur?*"

Colonel Szekler flicked his tongue across his nether lip again, and again I caught myself comparing him to something lupine.

"The vermin!" he gritted. "While I and my son—eternal rest grant him, O Lord!—were fighting at the front for Emperor and country, that toad-creature was skulking in the backwaters of Pest, evading military service. At last they caught him; shipped him off with other conscripts to the Eastern front. Two days later he deserted and went over to the Russians. An avowed Communist, he and Bela Kun and other traitors were hired by the Russians to foment Bolshevist cells among Hungarian prisoners of war.

The colonel's breath was coming fast, and his odd, light eyes were glazed as though a film had dropped over them, as he fairly hurled a question at us:

"Do you know—have you heard how two hundred loyal Hungarian officer-prisoners—prisoners of war, mind you, entitled to protection and respect by the law of nations—were butchered by the Russians and their traitorous Hungarian accomplices, because they could not be corrupted?"

De Grandin nodded shortly. "I was with the French Intelligence, *Monsieur*," he answered.

"My son Stephan was one of those whom Tibor Czerni helped to massacre—the swine boasted of it later!

"Back he came when war was done, led home to Hungary by the instinct that leads the vulture to the helpless, dying beast; and when the puppet-republic fell and bolshevism rose up in its place this vermin, this slacker and deserter, this traitor and murderer, was given the post of Commissar of the Tribunal of Summary Jurisdiction in Buda-Pest. You know what that meant, *hein*? That anyone whom he accused was doomed, that he was lord of life and death, a court from whose decisions there was no appeal throughout the city.

"You heard me call him 'Red-gauntlet'. You know why? Because, when it did not suit his whim to order unfortunate members of the bourgeoisie or gentry to be shot or hanged, he 'put the red gauntlets on them'—had his company of butchers take them out and beat their hands to bloody pulp with mauls upon a chopping-block. Then, crippled hopelessly, suffering torment almost unendurable, they were given liberty to serve as warning to others of their kind whose only crime was that they loved their country and were loyal to their king.

"One day the wretch conceived another scheme. He had been pampered, fawned upon and flattered since his rise to power till he thought himself omnipotent. Even women of our class—more shame to them!—had not withheld their favors to purchase safety for their men or the right to retain what little property they had. My wife—the Countess Szekler she was then—was noted for her beauty, and this slug, this toad, this monstrous parody of humankind determined to have *her*. This Galician cur presumed to raise his eyes to Irina Szekler—*kreuzsakrament*, he who was not fit to lap the water which had laved her feet!

"Out to our villa in the hills beyond Buda he went, forced himself into our house and made his vile proposals, telling my wife that he had captured me and only her complaisance could buy me immunity from the Red Gauntlets. But Szeklers do not buy immunity at such a price, and well she knew it. She ordered the vile creature from her presence as though she still were Countess Szekler and he but Tibor Czerni, son of a Galician money-lender and police court journalist of Pest.

"He left her, vowing dreadful vengeance. Only the fact that he had not brought his bullies with him saved her from immediate arrest, for an hour later a squadron of 'Lenin Boys' drove up to the house, looted it of everything which they could carry, then burned it to the ground.

"But we escaped. I came home almost as the scoundrel left, and we fled to friends in Buda who concealed us till I had time to grow a beard and so alter my appearance that I dared to venture on the street without certainty of summary arrest.

"Then I began my hunt. Systematically, day by day, I dogged the villain's steps, seeking for the chance to wash away the insult he had offered in his blood. Finally we met face to face in a side street just off Franz Joseph Square. He was armed, as always, but without his bodyguard of cutthroats. Despite my beard and shabby clothes he recognized me instantly and bawled out frantically for help, dragging at his pistol as he did so.

"But to draw the rapier from my sword-stick and run him through the throat was but an instant's work. He strangled in his blood before he could repeat his hail for help; so I dispatched the monster and escaped, for no one witnessed our encounter. Next day I fled with my wife and little daughter, and through a miracle we were able to cross the border to freedom."

"And had you ever seen this revenant—this materialization—before the painful incident in *Mademoiselle's* boudoir?" de Grandin asked.

Colonel Szekler flushed. "Yes," he answered. "Once. Though Stephan died a hero, and our loss was years ago, the wound has never healed in his mother's heart. Indeed, her sorrow seems increasing as the years go by. She has been leaning more and more toward spiritism of late years, and though we knew the Church forbids such things, my daughter and I could not bring ourselves to dissuade her, since she seemed to get some solace from the mediums' mummery. A month ago, when the first symptoms of Zita's returning illness were beginning to make their appearance, she prevailed on us to attend a séance with her.

"The sitting was held at the house of a medium who calls herself Madame Claire. The psychic sat at the end of a long table on which a gramophone's tin trumpet had been placed, and her wrists were fastened to the back of her chair with tape which was sewed, not tied. Her ankles were similarly secured to the front legs of the chair, and a blindfold was tied about her eyes. Then the lights were turned off and we sat with our hands upon the table, staring out into the darkness.

"We had waited some time without any manifestation, and I felt myself growing sleepy with the monotony of it, when a sharp rap sounded suddenly from the tin cone lying on the table. *Rat-tat-tat*, it came with a quick, clicking beat, then ended with a heavier blow, which caused a distinct metallic clang. No sooner had this ceased than the table began to move, as though pushed by the medium's feet; yet we had seen her ankles lashed securely to her chair and the knots sewed with thick linen thread.

"Next instant we heard the tin horn scraping slowly across the table-top, as though being lifted with an effort, only to fall back again. This kept up several minutes; then a voice came to us, rather weakly, but still strong enough to be understood:

A, B, C, D, E, F, G,
All good people hark to me,
Where you sit there, one two, three—

"The senseless doggerel was spouted at us through the trumpet which had risen and floated through the air to the far corner of the room. I was about to rise in anger at the childishness of it all when something happened which arrested my attention. The room in which we sat was closed up tightly. We had seen the medium shut and lock the door, and all the windows were latched and heavy curtains hung before them. The place was intolerably hot, and the air had begun to grow stale and flat; but as I made a move to rise, there was a sudden chilling of the atmosphere, as though a draft of winter wind had blown into the room. No, that is not quite accurate. There was no wind nor any stirring of the air; rather, it was as though we had all been put into some vast refrigerator where the temperature was absolute zero. What gave me the impression of an air-current was an odd, whistling sound which accompanied the sudden change of temperature—something like the whirring which one hears when wind blows through telegraph wires in wintertime.

"And as the chilling cold replaced the sultry heat, the piping, mincing voice reciting its inane drivel through the trumpet was replaced by another, a stronger voice, which laughed a cackling, spiteful laugh, then choked and retched and strangled, as though the throat from which it came were suddenly filled up with blood. The words it spoke were almost unintelligible, but not quite. I'd heard them fifteen years before, but they came back to me clearly, as though it had been yesterday:

"'Pig-dog, I'll have her yet. Next time, I'll come in such a way that you can not prevail against me!'

"They broke off with in awful, gurgling rattle, and I recognized them. It was the threat that Tibor Czerni spewed at me that day in Buda-Pest when I ran my rapier through his throat and he lay choking in his blood upon the sidewalk of Maria Valeria Street!

"Just then the trumpet fell crashing to the floor, and where it had been floating in the air there showed a spot of something luminous, like a monster bubble rising from some foul, miasmic swamp, and inside it, outlined by a sort of phosphorescence, showed the grinning, malignant face of Tibor Czerni.

"The medium woke up shrieking from her trance. 'Lights! For God's sake, turn on the lights!' she screamed. Then, as the lamps were lighted: 'I'm a trumpet psychic; my controls never materialize, yet—' she struggled with the bonds that held her to the chair in a perfect ecstasy of terror, crying, groaning, begging to be released, and it was not till we had cut the tapes that she could talk coherently. Then she ordered: 'Get out; get out, all of you—someone here is followed by an evil spirit; one of you must have done it a great wrong when it was in the flesh—*one of you is a murderer!* Out of my house, the lot of you, and take your Nemesis with you!'"

De Grandin tweaked the needle-points of his tightly waxed, diminutive mustache. "And the luminous globe, the one with Monsieur the Dead Man's face in it, did it disappear when the lights went up?" he asked.

"Yes," responded Colonel Szekler, "but—"

"But what, if you please, Monsieur?"

"There was a distinct odor in the room, an odor which had not been present before Czerni's cursed face appeared—it was the faint but unmistakable odor of decomposing flesh. Trust a soldier who has seen a hundred battlefield cemeteries plowed up by shell-fire weeks after the dead have been buried to recognize that smell!"

For a long moment there was silence. Colonel Szekler looked at Jules de Grandin expectantly. Jules de Grandin turned a speculative eye on Colonel Szekler. At length: "Very well, *Monsieur*," he agreed with a nod. "The case intrigues me. Let us go and see *Mademoiselle* your daughter."

2. Zita

COLONEL SZEKLER'S HOUSE FACED the Albemarle Road, a mile or so outside of town. It was a big house, bowered in Norway spruce and English holly and flowering rhododendron, well back from the highway, with a stretch of smoothly mown lawn before and a well-tended rose garden on each side. There was no hallway, and we stepped directly into a big room which seemed to combine the functions of library, music room and living-room. And as a mirror gives back the image of the face which looks in it, so this single room reflected the character of the family we had come to serve. Books, piano, easy-chairs and sofas loomed in the dim light filtering through the close-drawn silken curtains. An easel with a partly finished water color on it stood by a north window; beside it was a table of age-mellowed cherry laden with porcelain dishes, tubes of color and scattered badger-hair brushes.

Beside the concert-grand piano was a music-stand on which a violin rested, and the polished barrel of a cello showed beyond the music-bench. A bunch of snowballs nodded from a crystal vase upon a table, a spray of mimosa let its saffron grains fall in a graceful shower across a violet lampshade. Satsuma ash-trays stood on little tables beside long cigarette boxes of cedar cased in silver. Everywhere were books; books in French, German, Italian and English, some few in Danish, Swedish and Norwegian.

De Grandin took the room in with a quick, appraising glance. "*Pardieu*, they live with happy richness, these ones," he advised me in a whisper. "If *Mademoiselle* makes good one-tenth the promise of this room, *cordieu*, it will have been a privilege to have served her!"

"*Mademoiselle*" did. When she came in answer to her father's call she proved to be a slender, straight young thing of middle height, blond like her sire, betraying her Tartar ancestry, as he did, in her high cheek-bones and slightly slanting eyes. Her face, despite the hallmark of non-Aryan stock, was sweet and delicate as the blossom of an almond tree— "but a wilting blossom," I told myself as I noted white, transparent skin through which showed veins in fine blue lines. There was no flush upon her cheek, no light of fever in her eyes, but had she been my patient I should have ordered her to bed at once, and then to Saranac or Colorado.

"Mother's gone downtown," she told her father in a soft and gentle voice. "I know that she'll be sorry when she hears these gentlemen have called while she was out."

"Perhaps it's just as well she's out," the colonel answered. "Doctor de Grandin is a very famous occultist, as well as a physician, and I've called him into consultation because I am convinced that something more than bodily fatigue is responsible for your condition, dear. Will you be kind enough to tell him everything he wants to know?"

"Of course," she answered with a faint and rather wistful smile. "What is it that you'd like to hear about, Doctor? My illness? I'm not really ill, you know, just terribly, terribly tired. Rest and sleep don't seem to do me any good, for I rise as exhausted as when I go to bed, and the tonics they have given me"—she pulled a little face, half comic, half pathetic—"all they do is make my stomach ache."

"*Ah bah*, those tonics, those noisome medicines!" the little Frenchman nodded in agreement. "I know them. They pucker up the mouth, they make the tongue feel rough and sore—*mon Dieu*, what must they do to the poor stomach!"

Abruptly he sobered, and: "Let us have the physical examination first," he ordered.

At the end of half an hour I was more than puzzled, I was utterly bewildered. Her temperature and pulse were normal, her skin was neither dry nor moist, but exactly as a healthy person's skin should be; fremitus was in nowise more than usual; upon percussion there was no indication of impaired resonance, and the stethoscope could find no trace of mucous rales. Whatever else the young girl suffered from, I was prepared to stake my reputation it was not tuberculosis.

"Now, *Mademoiselle*," de Grandin asked as he completed jotting down our findings in his notebook, "do you recall the night that you and your parents attended Madame Claire's séance?"

"Of course; perfectly."

"Tell us, if you please, when first you saw the face within the globe of light. How did it look to you? Describe it, if you will."

"I didn't see it, sir."

"*Morbleu*, you did not see it? How was that?"

A faint flush crept across the girl's pale cheeks, then she laughed a soft, low, gurgling laugh, half embarrassment, half amusement. "I was asleep," she confessed. "Somehow, I'd been very tired that day—not as tired as I am now, but far more tired than my usual wont, and the air in Madame Claire's drawing-room seemed close and stuffy. Almost as soon as the lights were shut off I began to feel drowsy, and I closed my eyes—just for a minute, as I thought. The next thing I knew the lights were up and Madame Claire was trying to shriek and talk and cry, all at the same time. I couldn't make out what it was about, and it was several days before I heard about the face; the only way I know about it now is from piecing scraps of conversation together, for I didn't like to ask. It would have hurt poor Mother dreadfully if she knew I'd gone to sleep at one of her precious sittings with the spirits."

"Ah? So she has attended these séances often?"

"Gracious, yes! She pretended to Father that the one we went to was her first, but she'd been going to Madame Claire for over a year before she plucked up courage to ask Dad to go with her."

"And had you ever gone with her before?"

"No, sir."

"U'm. Now tell me: have you been subject to unusual dreams since that night at Madame Claire's?"

The blush which mantled her pale face and throat and mounted to her brow was startling in its vividness. Her long, pansy-blue eyes were suddenly suffused with tears, and she cast her glance demurely down until it rested on the silver cross-straps of her boudoir sandals. "Y-yes," she answered hesitantly. "I—I've had dreams."

"And they are—?" he paused with lifted brows, and I could see the sudden flicker in his little, round blue eyes which presaged keen excitement or sudden, murderous rage.

"I'd rather not describe them, sir," her answer was a muted whisper, but the deep flush stained her face and throat and brow again.

"No matter, *Mademoiselle*, you need not do so," he told her with a quick and reassuring smile. "Some things are better left unsaid, even in the medical consulting-room or the confessional."

"INVITE US OUT TO dinner, if you please," he told the colonel as we parted on the porch. "Already I have formed a theory of the case, and if I am not right, *parbleu*, I am much more mistaken than I think."

"DON'T YOU THINK YOU should have pushed the examination further?" I demanded as we drove back to town. "If Zita Szekler's trouble is psychic, or spiritual, if you prefer, an analysis of her dreams should prove helpful. You know Freud says—"

"*Ah bah*," he interrupted with a laugh, "who in Satan's naughty name cares what that old one says? Was it necessary that she should tell her secret dreams to me? *Cordieu*, I should say otherwise! That melting eye, that lowered glance, that quick, face-burning blush, do they mean nothing in your life, my friend, or is it that you grow so old and chilly-blooded that the sweet and subtle memories—"

"Confound you, be quiet!" I cut in. "If externals are any indication, I'd say the girl's in love; madly, infatuatedly in love, and—by George"—I broke off with a sudden inspiration—"that may be it! 'Love sickness' isn't just a jesting term; I've seen adolescents actually made ill by the thwarting of suppressed desire, and Zita Szekler's an Hungarian. They're different from the colder-blooded Nordics; like the Turks and Greeks and even the Italians and Spaniards, they actually suffer from an excess of pent-up emotion and—"

"*Oh là, là*—hear him spout!" the little Frenchman cut in with a chuckle. "You are positively droll, my olden one. And yet," he sobered suddenly, "you have arrived at half—no, a quarter—of the truth in your so awkward, blundering fashion. She *is* in love; sick—drunk—exhausted with it, *mon ami*; but not the kind of love you think of.

"Consider all the facts, if you will be so kind: What do we discover? This very devil of a fellow, Tibor Czerni, has made overtures to Madame Szekler while her husband is away. For that the colonel kills him, very properly. But what does Czerni say while he is dying on the sidewalk? He promises to come back, to have the object of his black and evil heart's desire, and to come in such a way that all resistance to his coming shall be unavailing. *N'est-ce-pas?*

"Very well, then. What next? The years have come and gone. Madame Szekler has grown older. Doubtless she is charming still, but Time has little pity on a woman. She has grown older. Ah, but her little, infant daughter, *she* has ripened with the passing of the seasons. She has grown to sweet and blooming womanhood. Have we not seen her? But certainly. And"—he put his gathered fingers to his lips and wafted an ecstatic kiss up toward the evening sky—"she is the very blossom of the peach, the flower of the jasmine; she is the morning dew upon the rose—*mordieu*, she is not trying on the eyes!

"Now, what turned Madame Szekler's thoughts to spiritism? One does not surely know, but one may guess. Was it only the preying thought of her loneliness at the loss of her first child, or was it not, perhaps, the evil influence of that wicked one who was constantly hovering over the house of Szekler like the shadow of a pestilence; ever dwelling on the threshold of their lives with intent to do them evil?"

"You mean to intimate—" I started, but:

"Be quiet," he commanded sharply. "I am thinking.

"At any rate his opportunity arrived at last. Poor Madame Szekler sought out the medium and let her guard be lowered. There was the opening through which this evil, discarnate entity could inject himself, the doorway, all unguarded, through which he might proceed to spoil the very treasure-house of Szekler. Yes.

"You realize, my friend, that a spiritualistic séance is as unsafe to the spirit as a smallpox case is to the body?"

"How's that?"

"Because there are low-grade discarnate entities, just as there are low-grade mortals, spirits which have never inhabited human form—but which would like to—and the lowest and most vicious spirits whose human lives have been but cycles of wickedness and debauchery. These invariably infest the sittings of the spiritists, ever seeking for an opening through which they may once more regain the world and work their wicked wills. You know the mediums work through 'controls'? Ha, I tell you the line of demarcation between innocent 'control' by some benevolently-minded spirit and possession by an evil entity is a very, very narrow one. Sometimes there is no line at all.

"Now, how can an evil spirit enter in a human body—gain possession of it? Chiefly by dominating that body's human will. It is this will-dominance, which is akin to hypnotism, that is the starting, the danger-point from which all evil things work forward. You have been to séances; you know their technique. The dual state of mental concentration and muscular relaxation which is necessary on the part of everyone for the evocation of the medium's control is closely analogous to that state of passive consent which the hypnotist demands of his subject. If a person attending a séance chances to be in delicate health, so much the worse for him—or her. The evil spirit, striving for control of mortal flesh, can force his way into that body more easily than if it were a vigorous one, precisely as the germ of a physical disease can find a favorable place to incubate where the phagocytic army of defense is weak.

"Now, consider Mademoiselle Zita's condition on the evening of that so abominable séance. She was 'tired', she said, so tired that when she 'closed her eyes just for a moment' she fell into instant slumber. Was her sleep a natural one, or was it but a state of trance induced by the wicked spirit of the wicked Czerni? Who can say?

"At any rate, we know that Czerni's spirit materialized, though Madame Claire declared no spirits ever did so in her séances before. Moreover, while the innocuous control of Madame Claire was making a fool of itself by reciting that so silly verse, it was roughly shouldered from the way, and Czerni's dying threat was bellowed through the trumpet, after which the trumpet tumbled to the floor and Czerni showed his wicked face.

"He has come back, even as he promised, my friend. The materialization which the colonel witnessed in his home the other day establishes the fact. And he has come back to fulfill his threat; only, instead of possessing the mother, as he swore to do when he was dying, he has transferred his vile attentions to the young and lovely daughter. Yes, of course.

"Oh, you're fantastic!" I derided.

"Possibly," he nodded gloomily. "But I am also right, my friend. I would that I were not."

3. The Phantom Lover

MADAME SZEKLER, WHO PRESIDED at dinner, proved as representative of the old, vanished order of Hungarian society as her husband. Well beyond the borderline of middle age, she still retained appealing charm and beauty, with a slender, exquisitely formed figure which lent distinction to her Viennese dinner gown, a face devoid of lines or wrinkles as a girl's, high-browed but heavy-lidded eyes of pansy blue and a pale but flawless skin. Her hair, close-cropped as a man's and brushed straight back with a flat marcelle, was gleaming-white as a cloud adrift upon a summer sky, and gave added charm, rather than any impression of age, to her cameo-clear features.

"Zita was too tired to come to dinner; I left her sleeping soundly shortly after you had gone," Colonel Szekler apologized, and de Grandin bowed assent.

"It is well for her to get as much rest as she can," he answered; then, in an aside to me:

"It is better so, Friend Trowbridge; I would observe *Madame* at dinner, and I can do so better in her daughter's absence. Do you regard her, too, if you will be so kind. Ladies of her age are apt to become neurotic. I should value your opinion."

Dinner was quite gay, for de Grandin's spirits rose perceptibly when the main course proved to be boned squab, basted in wine, stuffed with Carolina wild rice and served with orange ice. When the glasses were filled with vintage Tokay he seemed to have forgotten the existence of such a thing as trouble, and his witty sallies brought repeated chuckles from the colonel and even coaxed a smile to Madame Szekler's sad, aristocratic lips.

The meal concluded, we adjourned to the big living-room, where coffee and liqueurs were served while de Grandin and I smoked cigars and our host and hostess puffed at long, slim cigarettes which were one-third paper mouthpiece.

"But it grows late," the little Frenchman told us as he concluded one of his inimitable anecdotes; "let us go upstairs and see how Mademoiselle Zita does."

The girl was sleeping peacefully when we looked into her room, and I was about to go downstairs again when de Grandin plucked me by the sleeve.

"Wait here, my friend," he bade. "It yet wants a half-hour until midnight, and it is then that he is most likely to appear."

'You think she's apt to have another—visitation?" Madame Szekler asked. "Oh, if I thought that wretched séance were the cause of this, I'd kill myself. I only wanted to be near my boy, but—"

"Do not distress yourself, *Madame*," de Grandin interrupted. "He was bound to find a way to enter in, that one. The séance did at most but hasten his advent—and that of Jules de Grandin. Leave us with her, if you please. If nothing happens, all is well; if she is visited, we shall be here to take such steps as may be necessary."

F OR HOURS OUR VIGIL by the sleeping girl was uneventful. Her breath came soft and regular: she did not even change position as she slept; and I stood by the window, smothering back a yawn and wishing that I had not drunk so much Tokay at dinner. Abruptly:

"Trowbridge, my friend, observe!" de Grandin's low, sharp whisper summoned my attention.

Turning, I saw that the girl had cast aside the covers and lay upon her bed, her slender, supple body showing pale as carven alabaster through the meshes of her black-lace sleeping-suit. As I looked I saw her head move restlessly from side to side, and heard a little moan escape her. I was reminded of a sleepy, ailing child registering protest at being waked to take unpleasant-tasting medicine.

But not for long was this reluctance shown. Slowly, almost tentatively, like one who feels her cautious way through darkness, she put forth one exquisitely small foot and then the other, hesitated for a breath, then rose up from her couch, a smile of blissful joy upon her face. And though her eyes were closed, she seemed to see her path as she walked half-way across the room, then halted suddenly, stretched out her arms, then clasped them tightly, as though she never would let go of what she held. Head back, lips parted, she raised herself and stood on tiptoe, scarcely seeming to touch the floor. It was as if, by some sort of levitation, she were lifted up and really floated in the air, anchored to earth only by the pink-tipped toes of her small feet. Or was it not—my heart stood still as the thought crashed through my mind—was it not as though she yielded herself to the embrace of someone taller than herself, someone who clasped her in his arms, all but lifting her from her feet while he rained kisses on her yearning mouth?

A little, moaning gasp escaped her, and she staggered backward dizzily, still hugging something which we could not see against her breast, her every movement more like that of one who leaned upon another for support than one who walked unaided. She fell across the bed. Her eyes were still fast-shut, but she thrust her head a little forward, as though she seemed to see ecstatic visions through the lowered lids. Her pale cheeks flushed, her lips fell back in the sweet curve of an eager, avid smile. She raised her hands, making little downward passes before her face, as though she stroked the cheeks of one who leant above her, and a gentle tremor shook her slender form as her slim bosom seemed to swell and her lips opened and closed slowly, blissfully, in a pantomime of kissing. A deep sigh issued from between her milk-white teeth; then her breath came short and jerkily in quick exhausted gasps.

"*Grand Dieu—l'incube!*" de Grandin whispered. "See, my friend?"

"*L'incube*—incubus—nightmare? I should say so!" I exclaimed. "Quick, waken her, de Grandin; this sort of thing may lead to erotomania!"

"Be still!" he whispered sharply. "I did not say *an* incubus, but *the* incubus. This is no nightmare, my friend, it is a foul being from the world beyond who woos a mortal woman—observe, behold, *regardez-vous!*"

From Zita's side, three inches or so below the gentle prominence of her left breast, there came a tiny puff of smoke, as from a cigarette. But it was renewed, sustained, growing from a puff to a stream, from a stream to a column, finally mushrooming at the top to form a nebulous, white pompon which whirled and gyrated and seemed to spin upon its axis, growing larger and more solid-seeming with each revolution. Then the grayish-whiteness of the vapor faded, took on translucence, gradually became transparent, and like a soap-bubble of gigantic size floated upward till it rested in the air a foot or so above the girl's ecstatic countenance.

And from the bubble looked a face—a man's face, evil as Mefisto's own, instinct with cruelty and lechery and wild, vindictive triumph. The features were coarse, gross, heavy; bulbous lips, not red, but rather purple as though gorged with blood; a great hooked nose, not aquiline, but rather reminiscent of a vulture; dank, matted hair which clung in greasy strands to a low forehead; deepset, lack-luster eyes which burned like corpse-lights showing through the hollow sockets of a skull.

I started back involuntarily, but de Grandin thrust his hand into the pocket of his dinner coat and advanced upon the vision. "Gutter-spawn of hell," he warned, "be off. *Conjuro te; abire ad locum tuum!*" With a wrenching motion he drew forth a *flaçon*, undid its stopper and hurled its contents straight against the gleaming bubble which encased the leering face.

The pearly drops of water struck the opalescent sphere as though it had been glass, some of them splashing on the sleeping, girl, some adhering to the globe's smooth sides, but for all the effect they produced they might as well not have been thrown.

"Now, by the horns on Satan's head—" the Frenchman began furiously, but stopped abruptly as the globe began to whirl again. As though it had derived its roundness from winding up the end of the smoke-column issuing from Zita's side, so now it seemed that it reversed itself, becoming first oval as it turned, then elliptical, then long and sausage-shaped, finally merging with the trailing wisp of vapor which floated from the girl's slim trunk, and which, even as we watched, was steadily withdrawn until it lost itself in her white flesh.

Zita was lying on her back, her arms stretched out as though she had been crucified, her breath coming in hot, fevered gasps, tears welling from beneath the lashes of her lowered lids.

"Now, look at this, my friend," de Grandin ordered. "It was from here the vapor issued, was it not?"

He placed a finger over the girl's side, and as I nodded he drew a needle from his lapel and thrust it to the eye in her soft flesh. I cried aloud at his barbarity, but he silenced me with a quick gesture, parted the wide meshes of her lace pajamas and held the bedside lamp above the acupuncture. The steel was almost wholly fleshed in her side; yet not only did she not cry out, but there was no sign of blood about the point of incision. It might as well have been dead tissue into which he thrust the needle.

"Whatever are you doing?" I demanded furiously.

"Merely testing," he replied; then, contritely: "*Non,* I would not play with you, my friend. I did desire to assure myself of a local anesthesia at the point from which the ectoplasm issued. You know the olden story that witches and all those who sold themselves to Satan bore somewhere on their bodies an area insensible to pain. This was said to be because the Devil had possessed them. I shall not say it was not so; but what if the possession be involuntary, if the evil spirit of possession comes against the will of the possessed? Will there still be such local insensitive areas? I thought there would be. *Pardieu*, now I know. I have proved it!

"Now the task remains to us to devise some method of attack against this so vile miscreant. He has become as much physical as spiritual; consequently spiritual weapons are of little avail against him. Will the purely physical prevail, one wonders?"

"How d'ye mean?"

"Why, you saw what happened when I dashed the holy water on him—it did not seem to inconvenience him at all."

"But, good heavens, man," I argued, "how can that—whatever it was we saw—be both spiritual and physical? Doesn't it have to be one or the other?"

"Not necessarily," he answered. "You and I and all the rest of us are dually constructed: part physical body, part animating spirit. This unpleasant Czerni person was once the same, till Colonel Szekler killed him. Then he became wholly spirit, but evil spirit. And because he was a spirit he was powerless to work overt harm. He lacked a body for his evil work. Then finally came opportunity. At that cursed séance of Madame Claire's, Mademoiselle Zita was an ideal tool to work his wickedness. It is a well-recognized fact among Spiritualists that the adolescent girl is regarded as the ideal medium, where it is desired that the spirits materialize. For why? Because such girls' nerves are highly strung and their physical resistance weak. It is from such as these that imponderable, but nevertheless physical substance called ectoplasm is most easily ravished by the spirit desiring to materialize, to build himself a semi-solid body. Accordingly, Mademoiselle Zita was ideal for the vile Czerni's purpose. From her he drew the ectoplasm to materialize at Madame Claire's. When the ectoplasm flowed back to her, *he went with it*. This moment, Friend Trowbridge, he dwells within her, dominating her completely while she is asleep and the conscious mind is off its guard, drawing ectoplasm from her when he would make himself apparent. He can not do so often, she is not strong enough to furnish him the power for frequent materializations; but there he is, ever present, always seeking opportunity to injure her. We must cast him out, my friend, before he takes complete possession of her, and she becomes what the ancients called 'possessed of a devil'; what we call insane.

"Come, let us go. I do not think that he will trouble her again tonight, and I have much studying to do before we come to final grips, I and this so vile revenant of the Red Gauntlets."

4. Red Gauntlets of Czerni

"TROWBRIDGE, MY FRIEND, AWAKE, arouse yourself; get up!" de Grandin's hail broke through my early-morning sleep. "Rise, dress, make haste, friend; we are greatly needed!"

"Eh?" I sat up drowsily and shook the sleep from my eyes. "What's wrong?"

"Everything, by blue!" he answered. "It is Mademoiselle Zita. She is hurt, maimed, injured. They have taken her to Mercy Hospital. We must hurry.

"No, I can not tell you the nature of her injuries," he answered as we drove through the gray light of early dawn toward the hospital. "I only know that she is badly hurt. Colonel Szekler telephoned a few minutes ago and seemed in great distress. He said it was her hands—"

"Her hands?" I echoed. "How—"

"*Cordieu*, I said I do not know," he flashed back. "But I damn suspect, and if my suspicions are well founded we must hasten and arrive before it is too late."

"Too late for what?"

"Oh, *pour l'amour des porcs*, talk less, drive faster, if you please, great stupid one!" he shouted.

COLONEL SZEKLER, GRAY-FACED AS a corpse, awaited us in the hospital's reception room. "*Himmelkreuzsakrament*," he swore through chattering teeth, "this is dreadful, unthinkable! My girl, my little Zita—" a storm of retching sobs choked further utterance, and he bowed his forehead on his arms and wept as though his heart were bursting.

"Courage, *Monsieur*," de Grandin soothed. "All is not lost; tell us how it happened; what is it that befell *Mademoiselle*—"

"All isn't lost, you say?" Colonel Szekler raised his tear-scarred face, and the wolfish gleam in his eyes was so dreadful that involuntarily I raised my arm protectively. "All isn't lost, when my little girl is hopelessly deformed?—when *she wears the red gauntlets of Czerni?*"

"*Dieu de Dieu de Dieu de Dieu*, do you say it?" the Frenchman cried. "Attention, *Monsieur*; lay by your grief and tell me all—everything—immediately. There is not a moment to be wasted. I had the presentiment that this might be what happened, and I have made plans, but first I must know all. Speak, *Monsieur*! There will be time enough to grieve if our efforts prove futile. Now is the time for action."

Laying small, white hands upon the colonel's shoulders, he shook him almost as a dog might shake a rat, and the show of unexpected strength in one so small, no less than the physical violence, brought the colonel from his maze of grief.

"It was about three-quarters of an hour ago," he began. "I'd gone to Zita's room and found her resting peacefully; so, reassured, I lay down and fell asleep.

Immediately, I began to dream. I was back in Buda-Pest again during the terror. Czerni was sitting in judgment on helpless victims of the Bolsheviki's vengeance. One after another they were brought before him, soldiers of the king, nobles, members of the *bourgeoisie*—children, old men, women, anyone and everyone who had fallen into the clutches of his rowdies of the Red Guard. Always the judgment was the same—death. As well might a lamb have looked for mercy from the wolf-pack as a member of our class seek clemency from that mockery of a court where Tibor Czerni sat in judgment.

"Then they brought Zita in. She stood before him, proud and silent, as became her ancient blood, not deigning to offer any defense to the accusation of counter-revolutionary activities which they brought against her. I saw Czerni's eyes light with lust as he looked at her, taking her in from head to foot with a lecherous glance that seemed to strip the garments from her body as he puckered up his gross, thick lips and smiled.

"'The charges are not proved to my satisfaction,' he declared when all the accusations had been made. 'At least they are not sufficiently substantiated to merit the death sentence on this young lady. It would be a pity, too, to mar that pretty body with bullets or stretch that lovely throat out of proportion with the hangman's rope. Besides, I know her parents, her charming mother and her proud, distinguished father. I owe them something, and I must pay my debt. Therefore, for their sakes, if not for her own charming self, I order this young lady to be set at liberty.'

"I saw a look of incredulous relief sweep over Zita's face as he gave the order, but it was replaced by one of horror as he finished:

"'Yes, comrades, set her free—but not until you've put red gauntlets on her!'

"And as I lay there gasping at the horror of my dream, I heard a laugh, high, cachinnating, triumphant, and awoke with the echo of it in my ears. Then, as I was about to fall asleep again, thanking heaven that I only dreamt, I heard Zita's scream. Peal after peal of frenzied shrieks came from her room as she cried for mercy, called to me and her mother for help, then, becoming inarticulate, merely wailed in agony. As I ran headlong down the hall her screaming died away, and she was only moaning weakly when I reached her room.

"She lay across her bed, groaning in exhausted agony, like a helpless beast caught in the hunter's trap, and her hands were stretched straight out before her.

"Her hands—*Gott in Himmel*, no! Her stumps! Her hands were crushed to bloody pulp and hung upon her wrists like mops of shredded cloth, sopping with red stickiness. Blood was over everything, the bed, the rug, the pillows and her sleeping-suit, and as I looked at her I could see it spurting from the mangled flesh of her poor, battered hands with every palpitation of her pounding heart.

"'This, too, is a dream,' I told myself, but when I crossed the room and touched her, I knew it was no dream. How it happened I don't know, but somehow, through some damned black magic, Tibor Czerni has been able to come back from that hell where his monstrous spirit waits throughout eternity and work this mischief to my child; to disfigure her beyond redemption and make a helpless cripple of her.

"There was little I could do. I got some dressings from the bathroom and bound her hands, trying my best to staunch the flow of blood, 'phoned to Mercy Hospital for an ambulance; finally called you. We are lost. Czerni has triumphed."

"WILL YOU SIGN THIS, sir?" the young intern, sick with revulsion at the ghastly phases of his trade, stepped almost diffidently into the reception room and presented a filled-in form to Colonel Szekler. "It's your authority as next of kin for the operation."

"Is it absolutely necessary—must they operate?" Colonel Szekler asked with a sharp intake of his breath.

"Good Lord, yes!" the young man answered. "It's dreadful, sir; I never saw anything like it. Doctor Teach will have to take both hands off above the carpus, he says—"

"*Pardonnez-moi, Monsieur*, but who will take what off above the which?" de Grandin interrupted. His voice was soft but there was murderous fury flashing in his small blue eyes.

"Doctor Teach, sir; the chief surgeon. He's in the operating-room now, and as soon as Colonel Szekler signs this authorization—"

"*Par la barbe d'un poisson*, your youngest grandchild will have grown a long white beard before that happens!" the Frenchman cried. "Give me that cursed damned, abominable, execrable paper, if you please!" He snatched the form from the young doctor's hand and tore it into shreds. "Go tell Doctor Teach that I shall do likewise to him if he so much as lays a finger on her," he added.

"But you don't understand, this is an emergency case," the intern swallowed his anger, for Jules de Grandin's reputation as a surgeon, had become a byword in the city's clinics, and my thirty years and more of practise had lent respectability, if nothing more, to my professional standing. "Just look at her card!"

From his pocket he produced a duplicate of the reception record, and I read across de Grandin's shoulder:

Right hand—Multiple fractures of carpus and metacarpus; compound comminutive fractures of first, second and third phalanges; rupture of flexor and reflexor muscles; short abductor muscle severed; multiple contusions of thenar eminence; multiple ecchymoses . . .

"Good heavens!" I exclaimed as the detailed catalogue of injuries burned itself into my brain; "he's right, de Grandin: her hands are practically destroyed."

"*Parbleu*, so will that *sacré* Doctor Teach be if he presumes to lay a hand on her!" he shot back fiercely; then, to Colonel Szekler:

"Retract your order of employment, *Monsieur*, I implore you. Tell them that they may not operate, at least until Doctor Trowbridge and I have had an opportunity to treat her. Do you realize what it means if that *sale* butcher is allowed to take her hands away?"

Colonel Szekler eyed him coldly. "I came to you in the hope of freeing her from the incubus that rested on her," he replied. "They told me you were skilled in such things, and had helped others. You failed me. Czerni's ghost took no more notice of your boasted powers than he did of the efforts of those medical fakers I'd called in. Now she is deformed, crippled past all hope of healing, and you ask another chance. You'd cure her? You haven't even seen her poor, crushed hands. What assurance have I that—"

"*Monsieur*," the little Frenchman broke in challengingly, "you are a soldier, are you not?"

"Eh? Yes, of course, but—"

"And you put the miscreant Czerni to death, *n'est-ce-pas?*"

"I did, but—"

"And you would not shrink from taking life again?"

"What—"

"Very good. I put my life in pawn for my success, *Monsieur!*" Reaching underneath his jacket he drew out the vicious little Ortgies automatic pistol cradled in its holster below his armpit and handed it to Colonel Szekler. "There are nine shots in it, Monsieur," he said. "One will be enough to finish Jules de Grandin if he fails."

"BUT THERE ISN'T A chance; not a ghost of a chance, Trowbridge!" stormed Doctor Teach when we told him that the colonel had withheld permission for the operation. "I've seen de Grandin do some clever tricks in surgery—he's a good workman, I'll give him that—but anyone who holds out hope of saving that girl's hands is a liar or a fool or both. I tell you, it's hopeless; utterly hopeless."

"Do you drink, *Monsieur?*" de Grandin interjected mildly, apropos of nothing.

Doctor Teach favored him with a stare beside which that bestowed by Cotton Mather on a Salem witch would have been a lover's ardent glance. "I don't quite see it's any of your business," he answered coldly, "but as a matter of fact I do sometimes indulge."

"Ah, *bon, meilleur; mieux*. Let us wager. When all is done, let us drink glass for glass till one of us can drink no more, and if I save her hands you pay the score; if not, I shall. You agree?"

"You've an odd sense of humor, sir, jesting at a time like this."

"Ah, *mon Dieu*, hear him!" de Grandin cried as he rolled his eyes toward heaven. "As if good brandy could ever be a cause for jest!"

"WELL, YOU'VE GOT YOURSELF into a nice fix, I must say!" I chided as we sat beside the cot where Zita Szekler lay, still drugged with morphine. "You've no more chance of saving this poor child's hands than I have of flying to the moon, and if I know anything of human nature, Colonel Szekler will take you at your word when he finds you can't make good your promise, and shoot you like a dog. Besides, you've made me look ridiculous by seeming to back you in your insane—"

"S-s-st!" his sharp hiss shut me off. "Be quiet, if you please. I would think, and can not do so for your ceaseless jabbering."

He rose, went to the wall telephone and called the office. "Is all in readiness, exactly as I ordered?" he demanded. A pause; then: "*Bon, très bon, Mademoiselle*; have them bring the sweeper to this floor immediately, and have the saline solution all in readiness in the operating-room."

"What the deuce—" I began, but he waved me silent.

"I arranged for my *matériel de siège* while they were transporting her," he answered with a smile. "Now, if *Monsieur le Revenant* will only put in his appearance—ah, *parbleu*, what have we here? By damn, I think he does!"

The drugged girl on the bed began to stir and moan as though she suffered an unpleasant dream, and I became aware of a faint, unpleasant smell which cut through the mingled aroma of disinfectant and anesthetic permeating the hospital atmosphere. For a moment I was at a loss to place it; then, suddenly, I knew. Across the span of years my memory flew to the days of my internship, when I had to make my periodic visits to the city mortuary. That odor of decaying human flesh once smelled can never be forgotten, nor can all the deodorants under heaven quite drive it from the air.

And now the girl's soft breast was heaving tremulously, and her features were distorted by a faint grimace of suffering. Her brows drew downward, and along her cheeks deep lines were cut, as though she were about to weep.

"She's coming out of anesthesia," I warned; "shall I ring for a—"

"S-s-sst! Be quiet!" de Grandin commanded, leaning toward the writhing girl, his little eyes agleam, lips drawn back from his small, white teeth in a smile which was more than half a snarl.

Slowly, almost tentatively, a little puff of gray-white, smoke-like substance issued from the moaning girl's left side, grew larger and denser, whirled spirally above her, seemed to blossom into something globular—a big and iridescent bubble-thing in which the pale malignant features of the incubus took form.

"Now for the test, by blue!" de Grandin murmured fiercely.

With a leap he crossed the room, swung back the door and jumped across the threshold to the corridor, reappearing in the twinkling of an eye with—of all things!—*a vacuum sweeper* in his hand. He set the mechanism going with a quick flick of the trigger, and as the sharp, irritable whine of the motor sounded, sprang across the room, paused a moment by the bed and thrusting his hand beneath his jacket drew forth his heavy Kukri knife and passed it with a slash-ing motion above the girl's stiff, quivering form. The steel sheared through the ligament of tenuous, smoke-like matter connecting the gleaming bubble-globe to Zita's side, and as the sphere raised itself, like a toy balloon released from its tether, he brought the nozzle of the vacuum cleaner up, caught the trailing, gray-white wisp of gelatinous substance which swung pendent in the air and—sucked it in.

The droning motor halted in its vicious hornet-whine, as though the burden he had placed on it were more than it could cope with; then, sharply, spitefully, began to whir again, and, bit by struggling bit, the trail of pale, pellucid stuff was sucked into the bellows of the vacuum pump.

A look of ghastly fright and horror shone upon the face within the bubble. The wide mouth opened gaspingly, the heavy-lidded eyes popped staringly, as though a throttling hand had been laid on the creature's unseen throat, and we heard a little whimpering sound, so faint that it was scarcely audible, but loud enough to be identified. It was like the shrieking of someone in mortal torment heard across a stretch of miles.

"Ha—so? And you would laugh at Jules de Grandin's face, *Monsieur?*" the little Frenchman cried exultantly. "You would make of him one louse-infested monkey? Yes? *Parbleu*, I damn think we shall see who makes a monkey out of whom before our little game is played out to a finish. But certainly!

"Ring the bell, Friend Trowbridge," he commanded me. "Bid them take her to the operating room and infuse a quart of artificial serum by hypodermoclysis. Doctor Brundage is in readiness; he knows what to do.

"Now, come with me, if you would see what you shall see," he ordered as I made the call. "Leave *Mademoiselle* with them; they have their orders."

Twisting the connecting hose of the vacuum cleaner into a sharp V, he shut the current off; then, always the urbane Parisian, he motioned me to precede him through the door.

Down to the basement we hastened, and paused by the great furnace which kept the building well supplied with boiling water. He thrust the cleaner's plug into an electric wall fixture and: "Will you be kind enough to open up that door?" he asked, nodding toward the furnace and switching on the power in his motor.

As the machine once more began to hum he pressed the trigger sharply downward, reversing the motor and forcing air from the cleaner's bellows. There was a short, sharp, sputtering cough, as though the mechanism halted in its task, then a labored, angry groaning of the motor as it pumped and pumped against some stubborn obstacle. Abruptly, the motor started racing, and like a puff of smoke discharging from a gun, a great gray ring shot from the cleaner's nozzle into the superheated air of the furnace firebox. For an instant it hovered just above the gleaming, incandescent coals; then with an oddly splashing sound it dropped upon the fire-bed, and a sharp hissing followed while a cloud of heavy steam arose and spiraled toward the flue. I sickened as I smelled the acrid odor of incinerating flesh.

"*Très bien*. That, it appears, is that," announced de Grandin as he shut the motor off and closed the furnace door with a well-directed kick. "Come, let us go and see how Mademoiselle Zita does. They should be through with the infusion by this time."

5. Release

ZITA SZEKLER LAY UPON her bed, her bandaged hands upon her bosom. Whether she was still under anesthesia or not I could not tell, but she seemed to be resting easily. Also, strangely, there was not the dreadful pallor that had marked her when we left; instead, her cheeks were faintly, though by no means feverishly, flushed and her lips were healthy pink.

"Why, this is incredible," I told him. "She's been through an experience fit to make a nervous wreck of her, the pain she suffered must have been exquisite, she's had extensive hemorrhages; yet—"

"Yet you forget that Doctor Brundage pumped a thousand cubic centimeters of synthetic serum into her, and that such heroic measures are almost sovereign in case of shock, collapse, hemorrhage or coma. No, my friend, she lost but little blood, and what she lost was more than compensated by the saline infusion. It was against the loss of life-force I desired to insure her, and it seems the treatment was effective."

"Life-force? How do you mean?"

He grinned his quick, infectious elfin grin and, regardless of institutional prohibitions, produced a rank-smelling Maryland and set it glowing. "Ectoplasm," he replied laconically.

"Ec—what in the world—"

"*Précisément, exactement*, quite so," he answered with another grin. "Regard me, if you please: This Czerni person's soul was earthbound, as we know. It hung about the Szekler house, ever seeking opportunity for mischief, but it could accomplish little; for immaterial spirits, lacking physical co-operation of some sort, can not accomplish physical results. At last there came the chance when Madame Szekler induced her husband and child to attend that séance. Mademoiselle Zita was ill, nervous, run down, not able to withstand her assaults. Not only was he able to force himself into her mind to make her do his bidding, but he was able to withdraw from her the ectoplasmic force which supplied him with a body of a kind.

"This ectoplasm, what is it? We do not surely know, any more than we know what electricity is. But in a vague way we know that it is a solidification of the body's emanations. How? Puff out your breath. You can not see it, but you know that something vital has gone out of you. Ah, but if the temperature were low enough, you could not only feel your breath, you could see it, as well. So, when conditions are favorable, the ectoplasm, at other times unseen, becomes visible. Not only that, by a blending of the spiritual entity with its physical properties, it can become an almost-physical body. A materialization, we should call it, a 'manifestation' the Spiritists denominate it.

"Why did he do this? For two reasons. First, he craved a body of some sort again; by materializing, he could make himself seen by Colonel Szekler, whom he desired to plague. He had become a sort of semi-human once again, so far physical that physical means had to be taken to combat him.

"Last night, when I flung the holy water on him, and nothing happened, I said, '*Mon Dieu*, I am lost!' Then I counseled me, 'Jules de Grandin, do not be dismayed. If holy things are unavailing, it is because he has become physical, though not corporeal, and you must use physical weapons to combat him.'

"'Very good, Jules de Grandin, it shall be that way,' I say to me.

"Thereupon I planned my scheme of warfare. He was too vague, too subtle, too incorporeal to be killed to death with a sword or pistol. The weapons would cut through him but do him little harm. 'Ah, but there is always one thing that will deal with such as he,' I remind me. 'Fire, the cleansing fire, regarded by the ancients as an element, known by the moderns as the universal solvent.'

"But how to get him to the fire? I could not bring the fire to him, for fear of hurting Mademoiselle Zita. I could not take him to the fire, for he would take refuge in her body if I attempted to seize him. Then I remembered: When he materialized in her room the bubble which enclosed his evil face wavered in the air.

"'Ah-ha, my evil one,' I say, 'I have you at the disadvantage. If you can be blown by the wind you can be sucked by in air-current. It is the vacuum sweeper which shall be your hearse to take you to the crematory. Oh, yes.'

"So then I know that we must lie in wait for him with our vacuum sweeper all in readiness. It may take months to catch him, but catch him we shall, eventually. But there is another risk. We must sever his materialized form from Mademoiselle Zita's body, and we can not put the ectoplasm back. And so I decide that we must have some saline solution ready to revive her from the shock of losing all that life-force. This seemed a condition which could not be overcome, but this wicked Czerni, by his very wickedness, provided us with the solution of our problem. By injuring Mademoiselle Zita, he made them bring her to this hospital, the one place where we should have everything ready to our hand—the sweeper, the fire which should consume him utterly, the saline solution and facilities for its quick administration. *Eh bien*, my friend, but he did us the favor, that one.

"But her hands, man, her hands," I broke in. "How—"

"It is a stigma," he replied.

"A stigma—how—what—"

"Perfectly. You understand the phenomenon of stigmata? It is akin to hypnotism. In the psychological laboratory you have seen it, but by a different name. The hypnotist can bid his subject's blood run from his hand, and the hand becomes pale and anemic; you have seen the blood transferred from one arm to another; you have seen what appears to be a wound take form upon the skin without external violence, merely the command of the hypnotist.

"Now, this Czerni had complete possession of Mademoiselle Zita's mind while she slept. He could make her do all manner of things, think of all manner of things, feel all manner of things. He had only to give her the command: 'Your hands have been beaten to a pulp, smashed by merciless mauls upon a chopping-block—you are wearing the red gauntlets!' and, to all intents, what he said became a fact. Just as the scientific hypnotist makes his subject's blood reverse itself against the course of nature, just as he makes what appears to be a bleeding cut appear upon uninjured skin—then heals it with a word—so could Czerni make Mademoiselle Zita's hands take on the appearance of wearing the red gauntlets without the use of outside force. Only a strong will, animated by a frightful hate, and operating on another will whose resistance had completely broken down could do these things; but do them he did. Yes.

"When Colonel Szekler told me how his daughter became red-gauntleted while lying in her bed, where she could not possibly have been injured by external force, I knew that this was what had happened, and so sure was I of my diagnosis that I staked my life upon it. Now—"

"You're crazy!" I broke in.

"We shall see," he answered with a smile, crossed to the bed and placed a second pillow under Zita's head, so that she was almost in a sitting posture.

"*Mademoiselle*," he called softly while he stroked her forehead gently, "Mademoiselle Zita, can you hear me?" He pressed his thumbs transversely on her brow, drawing them slowly outward with a stroking motion, then, with fingers on her temples, bore his thumbs against her throat below the ears. "*Mademoiselle*," he ordered in a low, insistent voice, "it is I, Jules de Grandin. I am the master of your thought, you can not think or act or move without my permission. Do you hear?"

"I hear," she answered in a sleepy voice.

"And you obey?"

"And I obey."

"*Très bon*. I bid you to forget all which the evil Czerni told you; to unlock your mind from the prison of his dominance—to restore your hands to their accustomed shape. Your hands are normal, unharmed in any way; they have never been scarred or hurt, not even scratched.

"*Mademoiselle, in what condition are your hands?*"

"They are normal and uninjured," she replied.

"*Bien! Triomphe!* Now, let us see."

With a pair of surgical shears he cut away the bandages. I held my breath as he drew away the gauze, but I wondered as the lower layers were drawn apart and showed no stain of blood.

The final layer was off. Zita Szekler's hands lay on the counterpane, smooth, white, pink-tipped, without a mark, or scar, or blemish.

"Merciful heavens!" I exclaimed. "This is a miracle, no less.

"Here, I say, de Grandin, where are you going, to call Colonel Szekler?"

"Not I," he answered with a chuckle. "Do you call him, good Friend Trowbridge. Me, I go to find that cocksure-of-his-diagnosis Doctor Teach and make him pay his wager.

"*Morbleu*, how I shall enjoy drinking him beneath the table!"

The Red Knife of Hassan

"**M**ON DIEU, IS IT the—what do you call him?—pinch?" asked Jules de Grandin as the traffic policeman's white-rubber mitten rose before us through the driving rain.

"Askin' your pardon. Sir, you're a doctor, ain't you?" The officer pointed to the green cross and caduceus of the medical association attached to my radiator.

"Yes I'm Doctor Trowbridge—"

"Well can you spare a moment to go out to th' dredge?" the other interrupted. "One o' th' crew's hurt bad, an' while they're waitin' for th' amblance it might help if—"

"But certainly, assuredly; of course," de Grandin answered for me. "Lead the way, *mon brave*, we follow."

The grimy, oil-soaked launch which acted as the harbor dredge's tender was waiting at the pier, and within five minutes we were on the squat, ungainly craft which gnawed unsurfeited at the ever-shifting bottom of the bay. The injured man, an assistant in the fire room, was suffering intensely, for an unattached steel cable had swung against him as he crossed the deck, smashing the tibia and fibula of his left leg in a comminuted fracture.

"*Non*, there is little we can do here," said the Frenchman as we finished our examination. "We have no proper fracture box, nor any instruments for cutting through the skin in order to secure the splintered bone, but we can ease his pain. Will you prepare the hypo, good Friend Trowbridge? I would suggest two grains of morphine; he suffers most intensely, and a smaller dose would scarcely help him."

Buttoned to the chin in oilskins and swearing like a pirate, the ambulance surgeon came out in the launch as we completed our administration of the anodyne, and rough but willing hands placed the injured man in the boat which bumped its prow against the dredge's side. Sheltered in the doorway of the engine room, we watched the great dredge at its work while we awaited the return trip of the launch. Like some voracious monster diving for its prey the great clamshell scoop plunged from the tip of the forty-foot boom into the rain-beaten waters of the bay, disappeared amid a ring of oily bubbles, then emerged with water streaming from between its iron teeth, gaped like a yawning hippopotamus, and dropped a ton or more of sand and silt and sediment into the waiting barge.

"Yes, sir, four times a minute, regular as clockwork, she fishes up a mouthful for us," the engineer informed us proudly. "At this rate we'll have this stretch o' channel all cleared out by—God a'mighty, what's that?"

Horribly reminiscent of an oyster impaled upon a fork it hung, feet gripped between the dredge's iron fangs, flaccid arms dangling pendulously, the nude and decomposing body of a woman.

"Easy, Jake, let her down easy!" cried the engineer to the man at the cable-drum. "Don't spring the scoop—we don't want 'er buried in that muck."

"Coming, Doctor?" he cast the question at us impersonally as he jerked the collar of his slicker up about his throat and dashed across the deck through the slanting sheets of winter rain.

"But certainly, of course we come," de Grandin answered as he followed close upon the other's heels, clambered across the rail and let himself almost waist-deep into the ooze which filled the mud-scow's hold. More cautiously, I followed; and as the cable man, with an art which was surprising, lowered the great iron shell, released the gripping metal teeth and let the body slide down gently in the mire, I bent beside the little Frenchman to examine the weird salvage.

"*Non*, we can not see her here," complained de Grandin irritably. "Lift her up, my friends, gently, carefully—so. Now, then, over to the deck, beneath the shelter of the engine-house. Lights, *pour l'amour de Dieu*, shine the light upon us, if you please!"

A big reflector-lamp was quickly plugged into a light-terminal, and in its sun-bright glare we bent to our examination. There was an area of greenish-gray about the face and throat, extending through the pectoral region and especially marked at the axillæ, but very little swelling of either abdomen or mammæ. As I lifted one of the dead hands I saw the palmar skin was deeply etched with wrinkles and slightly sodden in appearance. When de Grandin turned the body over we saw an area of purplish stain upon the dorsal section, but the shoulder blades, the buttocks, backs of the thigh, calves and heels were anemic-white in startling contrast.

"Drowned, of course?" the engineer asked jerkily with the layman's weak attempt at nonchalance before the unmasked face of death.

"No, *non*; by no means," returned the Frenchman shortly. "Observe him, if you please, *le fil de fer*, the—how do you say him?—wire." A slender, well mani-cured forefinger pointed to the slightly bloated throat just above the level of the larynx. I had to look a second time before I saw it, for the softened, sodden flesh had swollen up around it, but as his finger pointed steadily I saw, and as I realized the implication of the thing, went sick with shock. About the throat a length of picture-wire had been wound and rewound, its ends at last spliced tightly in a knot; so there could have been no slipping of the ligature.

"Strangulation!" I exclaimed in horror.

"*Précisément; la garrotte*, the work of the *apaches*, my friends, and very well and thoroughly they did it, too. Had it not been for the dredge she might have lain upon the bottom of the bay for months and no one been the wiser. Observe the coldness of the water has retarded putrefaction, and undoubtlessly she was weighed down, but the iron teeth broke off the weights. One might suppose that—"

"What's that on the left cheek?" I interrupted. "Would you say it was a birth-mark, or—"

The Frenchman drew a pocket lens from his waistcoat held it at varying distances from the dead girl's face, and squinted through it critically. "*Grand Dieu*, a birthmark, a putrefactive stain? *Non!*" he cried excitedly. "Look, Friend Trowbridge, look and see for yourself. What is your opinion?"

I took the magnifying-glass and focused it till the blister-marked and scuff-ing skin enlarged in texture underneath my gaze, and then I saw, rising up from the discolored epidermis like a coat-of-arms emblazoned on a banner, the outline of a scar shaped something like a crescent standing on end, not marked upon, but deeply pressed into the flesh of the left cheek.

"U'm, no, if s not a natural mark," I commented. "Looks almost like a second degree burn or—"

"It *is* a second degree burn, by blue—a brand!" the little Frenchman broke in sharply. "And there is a line of blister round it, showing that it was made on living skin. *Parbleu*, I damn think we have work to do, Friend Trowbridge!"

"Call the tender, if you will, *Monsieur*," he turned to the chief engineer. "We must notify the coroner, then see that an autopsy is made. This is a very evil business, *mes amis*, for that poor one was branded, strangled, stripped and thrown into the bay."

As we stepped into the launch which plied between the dredge and piers he added grimly: "Someone sits in the electric chair for this night's business, my friend."

CORONER MARTIN, DETECTIVE SERGEANT Jeremiah Costello, Jules de Gran-din and I faced each other in the coroner's private office. "The necropsy bears out my diagnosis perfectly, *Messieurs*," the little Frenchman told us as he helped himself to another glass of brandy from Mr. Martin's desk-cellarette. "There was no trace of water in the lungs, showing that death could not have come from drowning, and even though dissolution had advanced, fractures of the larynx and the rings of the trachea were obvious, showing that death had come from strangulation. Taking the temperature of the water into consideration, we may say with fair assurance that the state of putrefaction places her murder at about two weeks ago. Unfortunately the face is too much disfigured to help us with identification, but—"

"How about that scar?" I interjected.

"*Précisément*, how of it?" he rejoined. "Observe it if you will." Unfastening a paper parcel he held out a little square of parchment-like substance stretched tightly on a wire hoop. "I took the liberty of clipping away the scarified skin and impregnating it with formaldehyde," he explained. "The scar which was so indistinct when viewed upon her face may easily be studied now. What do you make of it, Friend Trowbridge?"

I took the little drumhead of skin and held it underneath the light. The mark was not a crescent, as I had at first supposed, but rather a silhouette of a hiltless dagger with an exaggeratedly curved blade. "A knife?" I hazarded.

"*Précisément*, and that suggests—"

"You mean it might have been a sort of ritual murder?"

"It looks that way, my friend—"

"Sure," Costello broke in, "I've heard about them things—ran into one of 'em, once, meself. A dago case. This here now felly'd belonged to one o' them secret societies, an' tried to take a powder on 'em, or sumpin, an' they give 'im th' *sforza*, I think they called it; th' death o' th' seventy cuts. Doctor de Grandin, sor, he were more like a piece o' hamburger steak than anything human when they'd finished wid 'im. Are ye afther thinkin' this pore dame wuz mixed up in sumpin like that?"

"Something like that," the Frenchman echoed; then:

"Will you consult the files of the Missing Persons Bureau, Sergeant, and ascertain if any young woman approximately the size of this one was reported missing in the last month? That may help us to identify her."

But the check-up proved useless. No record of a girl of five feet three, weighing a hundred and ten pounds, was in the missing persons file at headquarters, nor did communication with New York, Newark and Jersey City help us. Mr. Martin, as the keeper of the city mortuary, took charge of the body and buried it in an unmarked grave in the public plot of Rosevale Cemetery, the only record of its disposition being: "Mary Doe, Plot D, Sec. 54, West Range 1458."

Costello went about his duties of pursuing evil-doers with his customary Celtic efficiency, and dismissed the incident from his mind. I reverted to my practise, and thought but seldom of the poor maimed body; but Jules de Grandin did not forget. Several times at dinner I caught him staring sightlessly before him, neglecting the rare tidbits which Nora McGinnis, my highly gifted cook, prepared especially for him. "What's the matter, old chap?" I asked him one night when he seemed especially distrait.

He shook his head as though to clear his thoughts, and: "*Ah bah*," he answered in annoyance, "there is a black dog running through my brain. That *Mademoiselle l'Inconnue*, the poor nameless one whom we saw fished up from the bay, her blood calls out to me for vengeance."

I T WAS A MERRY, though decidedly exclusive party Colonel Hilliston entertained at his big house down by Raritan. Why de Grandin had been so set on coming I had no idea, but from the moment he learned that Arbuthnot Hilliston, world traveler, lecturer and explorer, had returned from the Near East he had given me no peace until I renewed old acquaintance with the colonel, and obtained our invitation as a consequence. A hundred years and more ago some ambitious shipmaster had built this house, and built it solidly as the ships he sailed. Generations had gone by, the old blood thinned and finally trickled out; then Hilliston, weary of globe-trotting, had purchased the old place, rebuilt and modernized it, then with the restlessness of the born traveler had used it more as *pied-à-terre* than home, coming back to it only in the intervals between five-thousand-mile-long jaunts to write his books, prepare his lectures and foregather with his friends a little while.

"You've known Colonel Hilliston long, Doctor Trowbridge?" asked my dinner partner, a tall and more than ordinarily interesting brunette whose name, as I had caught it in the rite of presentation, was Margaret Ditmas.

"Not very, I'm afraid," I answered. "I knew his parents better. They were patients of mine when they lived in Harrisonville, and I attended Arbuthnot for the customary children's ailments, mumps and measles, chickenpox and whooping-cough, you know, but since he's been grown up and famous—"

"Did he ever strike you as a nervous child, or one likely to develop nerves?" she interrupted, and her large and rather expressionless eyes were unveiled suddenly by an odd raising of their upper lids.

"No-o, I can't say he did," I told her. "Just a normal boy, I'd say, rather fond of finding out the reason why for everything he saw, but scarcely nervous. Why do you ask?"

"Colonel Hilliston's afraid of something—terrified."

I glanced along the table with its priceless banquet cloth of Philippine embroidery, its gleaming silver and big, flat bouquets of winter roses, till I saw our host's face in the zone of light which streamed from two tall candelabra. Plentiful dark hair, brushed sleekly back and growing low about the ears, framed a rather lean and handsome face, bronzed as a sailor's and with fine sun-lines about the eyes, a narrow, black mustache and strong, white teeth. A forceful, energetic face, this long-chinned countenance, hardly the face of a man who could be frightened, much less terrified. "What makes you think that Arbuthnot's developed nerves?" I asked.

"You see those doors?" she queried, nodding toward the triple French windows leading to the brick-paved terrace which skirted the seaward side of the house.

"Well?" I nodded, smiling.

"Their panes are set in wood, aren't they?"

"Apparently; but why—"

"They are, but every wooden setting has a steel bar reinforcing it, and the glass is 'burglar glass'—reinforced with wire, you know. So is every window in the house, and the doors and windows are all secured with combination locks and chains while the outside doors are sheathed in steel. Besides, there's something in his manner; he's jumpy, seems almost listening for something, and acts as though he were about to turn round and look behind him every moment or so."

She was so serious and secretive about it all that I smiled despite myself. "And does he turn round?" I asked.

"No. I think he's like that man in *The Rime of the Ancient Mariner*:

Like one that on a lonesome road
Doth walk in fear and dread,
And having once turned round, walks on,
And turns no more his head,
Because he knows a frightful fiend
Doth close behind him tread.

"My dear young lady!" I protested, but Jules de Grandin's voice cut through my words as he spoke jocularly to our host:

"And did you scale the Mount of Evil in Syria, *Monsieur le Colonel?*" he inquired. "The mountain where the ancient bad one dwelt, and sent his minions out to harry those who would not pay him tribute? You know, the Sheik Al-je-bal they called him in the ancient days, and he was head of the *haschisch*-eaters who for two long centuries terrified the world—"

Something flickered momentarily in our host's deep-set eyes, something which if it were not fear seemed very like it to me as I watched. "Nonsense!" he broke in almost roughly. "That's all damned poppycock, de Grandin. Those Assassins were just a lot of ordinary mountain bandits, such as Europe and the Near East swarmed with in those days. All this talk of their mysterious power is legendary, just as half the stories of Robin Hood—or Al Capone, for that matter—are the purest fiction." He gazed around the table for a moment, then nodded to the butler, a small, dark man with olive skin and big, Semitic features.

"Coffee is served in the drawing-room, please," announced this functionary, deftly bringing the meal to a close.

We trooped into the big parlor, and I caught my breath in admiration of the place. The beauty of that room was a sort of mad, irrational loveliness, a kind of orderly arrangement of discordant elements which resulted in perfected harmony. A buhl table out of India, Fifteenth Century Italian chairs, Flemish oak, ponderous as forged iron and beautiful as carven marble, a Chinese cabinet which must have been worth its weight in solid gold, pottery, shawls and hangings from the near and farther East, carved jade, rugs so thick and soft it seemed as though the floor were strewn with desert sand—a very art-museum of a place it was. Thick Turkish coffee and great squares of halwa were handed round by the stoop-shouldered butler, and presently long cigarettes, almost the size of a cigar, were lighted, and I caught the faint, elusive perfume of ambergris as the smoke-wreaths spiraled upward in the dim light sifting through the perforated bronze shades of the lamps.

"Ambergris—for passion," quoted Margaret Ditmas as she lolled beside me on the divan with a cat-like grace of utter relaxation. "You've heard the Easterners believe that, Doctor Trowbridge?"

I turned and studied her. Her hair was very black and glossy, and she wore it smoothly parted and drawn low above her ears. Her eyes were large, dark, queerly unmoving under thin-arched brows. Her mouth was wide, thin-lipped, very red, and her teeth were small and white. Beneath the hem of her black-satin gown there showed an inch or so of gray-silk stocking, and underneath the meshes of the silk there shone a gleam of platinum where a thread-thin anklet encircled her slim leg. I sensed a hard shell over her almost feline suppleness, as though she wore defensive armor against the world. "Where does she fit in?" I asked myself. "And why should she be so attentive to a bald, bewhiskered medical practitioner when there are young and handsome men around? Our host, for instance—"

Colonel Hilliston's voice broke through my ruminations. "Anybody like to play roulette?" he asked. "I've got a set-up here, so if you wish—"

A chorus of enthusiastic assent drowned out his invitation, and in a minute a roulette wheel and cloth were spread across the beautiful buhl table, and Hilliston took his place as croupier. Plaques were placed upon the numbered squares, and: "*Le jeu est fait, messieurs et dames, rien ne va plus,*" he sang out nasally.

The little ball clicked round the spinning wheel, and: "*Vingt-deux, noir, messieurs et dames—*" he chanted.

The play was rather high. My American conscience and Scottish ancestry revolted at the sums I lost, but my losses were as nothing beside those of Miss Ditmas. She hung in breathless interest above the table, her dark eyes dilated, her small, white teeth clamped sharply on her carmine lower lip.

"*Le jeu est fait, messieurs et dames*—what the devil?" Colonel Hilliston broke off his nasal chant as the lights winked out and the room was drenched in sudden, utter, blinding darkness.

"Nejib, Nejib—lights!" It seemed to me there was a thin, hysterical quality in Hilliston's voice as he called the butler.

A soft hand clasped on mine with a grip so strong it startled me, and Miss Ditmas' low-breathed whisper fluttered in my ear. "Doctor Trowbridge, I—I'm afraid *it got in!*"

There was a gentle whistling sound and a gentle draft of air swept on my face, as though an open hand had fanned swiftly past my features, and I thought I heard someone move past me in the dark and stumble clumsily against the roulette table.

"Lights, 'illiston *effendi?*" murmured the butler, appearing at the doorway with a silver candelabrum in each hand.

No answer came from Colonel Hilliston, and the fellow moved silently across the room, the aura of luminance from his burning tapers preceding and surrounding him.

"Look, look—oh, dear God, *look!*" rasped Margaret Ditmas in a choking whisper, then broke off in a wail of mortal terror. It was a terrifying sound, a little, breathless squeak of mortal fear that thinned into a sick, shrill wail of horror. It seemed to hang and linger in the air like the tintinnabulation of a softly beaten gong, until at last I did not know if I still heard it or only thought I did—and would go on thinking that I heard that dreadful, shrilling cry of agonizing panic ever after.

And well she might cry out, for in the center of the roulette table stood the head of Colonel Hilliston. It stood there upright on its severed neck, white eyeballs glaring at us in the flickering candlelight, mouth gaping open as though to frame a cry.

Beneath the table lay the headless trunk, half sprawled, half crouched, one hand extended on the Turkey carpet, the other clasped about the table-leg, as though it sought to drag the body upward to the missing head. Blood was gushing from the severed jugulars and carotids, blood stained and soaked the carpet at our feet and splashed the tip of Jules de Grandin's patent-leather evening pump, and, amazingly, a tiny drop of blood hung like a jewel from the crystal prisms of the ceiling chandelier which swung above the table whence the head stared at us with a sort of silent accusation.

"**B**UT, MY DEAR MAN!" Captain Chenevert of the state constabulary, who had come dashing from the Keyport barracks with two troopers in answer to de Grandin's call, hooked his thumb beneath his Sam Browne belt and gazed at us in turn with something like the look he might have given to a romancing child.

"You tell me you were all assembled in the drawing-room when suddenly the lights went out and when that heathen butler—what's his dam' name? Nejib?—came in with candles, there was Hilliston without his head? Absurd! Preposterous!"

"*Parbleu,* you are informing us?" de Grandin answered with elaborate sarcasm. "Nothing more utterly bizarre was ever fished up from the vapors of an opium-smoker's dream—but there it is. Including Doctor Trowbridge and myself and the late Colonel Hilliston, there were eight persons in that room. You have heard the evidence of seven, while the eighth bears mute but eloquent testimony of the murder. We are all agreed upon what happened: There is light, there is sudden darkness, then there is light again—and there is Colonel Hilliston without his head. Name of a devil, it is crazy; it is impossible; it does not make sense, but there it is. *Voilà tout!*"

"See here, you fellows," I put in; "Maybe this may have some bearing on the case, though I don't see how." Then, briefly, I told them of my conversation with Miss Ditmas at the table, her hand-clasp in the dark and her terrified declaration: "I'm afraid *it got in!*"

"By George, that is interesting; we'll have her in again," said Captain Chenevert; but:

"*Non,* not yet; one little moment, if you please," objected Jules de Grandin. "Me, I have what you call the hunch."

Crossing to the secrétaire, he tore a sheet of note-paper across, then with a match sopped up a little drying blood from the sodden carpet and traced the silhouette of a curved, sharp-pointed dagger on the paper. "Delay your summons for a little while, if you will be so kind," he urged, waving the paper back and forth to hasten drying. "Now, call her in, if you will."

He laid the gruesome picture face-downward on the table beside the objects taken from the dead man's pockets, and lit a cigarette as a trooper ushered Margaret Ditmas in.

"Mademoiselle," he began as she looked at us inquiringly, "we have made an inventory of *Monsieur le Colonel's* effects, the little things he carried in his pockets. Perhaps you can identify them. Here are his keys: you recognize them? No?"

"No," she replied, scarcely glancing at the thin gold chain with its appended key-ring.

A little wad of crumpled banknotes followed, a cigarette lighter, knife, card case, cigarette case, and always, "No, I do not recognize it," she returned as each was shown to her.

Then: "Last of all, we came on this," de Grandin told her. "A strange thing, surely, for a gentleman to have," he turned the sheet of writing-paper with its scarlet dagger up, and held it toward her.

Her face went ghastly at the sight. "You—you found *that* on him?" she exclaimed. "The Red Knife of Has—"

Like a football player tackling an opponent, de Grandin launched himself upon her, grasping her about the knees and hurling her backward several feet before they fell together in a heap upon the floor. And not a fraction of a second had he been too soon, for even as he threw her back, the ceiling chandelier dropped downward like a striking snake, there was a gleam of steel and the *click* of closing metal jaws; then up the fixture leapt again and was once more the harmless glass-hung thing which it had been before.

"*Pardonnez-moi, Mademoiselle*, I did forget that you were standing where the colonel stood, de Grandin told Miss Ditmas as he helped her to her feet. "I hope you are not hurt—but if you are, your injury is slighter than it would have been had I not acted roughly."

"Shaunnessy, Milton!" shouted Chenevert. "Did anybody move?"

"Sir?" asked Trooper Shaunn. "Did the captain call?"

"I'll tell the cock-eyed world he did," the captain answered angrily. "You were on guard in the library, weren't you?"

"Yes, sir."

"Did anybody leave the room?"

"No, sir."

"Anybody get up, press a button or lean against the wall, or anything like that?"

"No, sir. Everyone was seated. No one moved until you called."

"All right. How about you, Milton?"

"Sir?"

"You were in the hall outside this room. See anybody?"

"No, sir; not a soul."

"Bring that butler to me, and bring him *pronto*."

A moment later Trooper Milton came back with the butler, who, arrayed in rubber apron, his sleeves rolled to the elbows had obviously been engaged in the matter-of-fact occupation of washing the silver when summoned.

"Where were you just now?" the captain asked.

"In the pantry, please," the other answered. "Me, I always wash the silver after dinner. The kitchen maids the dishes wash when they come in the morning."

"Humph; you were the only one of the help here tonight?"

"Tonight and every night, please. The cook, the chamber maids, the kitchen girls, they all go home at sundown. Only I remain to serve the dinner and to close the house at night. Me, I sleep here."

"Know the combinations of those door- and window-locks?"

"No, please. 'lliston *effendi*, he knows them only. You shut them so—they lock. But only he can open them."

"U'm; how long have these locks been here?"

"I not knowing, Captain *effendi*. I come here from Damascus with Colonel 'lliston when he come here. He engage to hire me there. I veree good butler and valet, me; serve in the finest English families, and—"

"All right; we'll look into your references later. What are you, an Arab or a Turk or—"

"Captain, *effendi!*" the butler's protest was instinct with injured pride. "Me, I am Armenian. I very good Christian, me, I go to Christian school at—"

"All right, go back to the pantry now, and see you don't leave it unless you have permission."

"Hearing and obeying," replied the other, and turned with a deep bow.

"Well, I'll be a monkey's uncle," Captain Chenevert declared. "I sure will. This dam' case gets tougher by the minute. Now we know how Hilliston was killed, but who the devil worked that guillotine, and who installed it, and—say, Doctor de Grandin, d'ye suppose—"

A crash of breaking crockery, a wild, despairing scream and the noise of heavy objects crashing into one another drowned his question out.

"It's in th' pantry!" Trooper Milton shouted and raced down the long hall with the captain, de Grandin and me at his heels.

"Can't budge th' door!" he grunted as we stopped before the pantry entrance. "Seems like something's wedged against it—"

"Here, let me help," Chenevert cut in, and together they threw their shoulders against the white-enameled door.

It gave slowly, inch by stubborn inch, but at last they forced it back enough to let them in.

The pantry was a ruin. Across the door a heavy table had been pushed, the china closet had been overturned, and scattered on the white-tiled floor were bits of Colonel Hilliston's choice silverware. Also upon the tiles there spread a great red stain, growing fainter and more faint as it approached the window, which, to our surprise, was open.

"Good Lord," the captain muttered, "they—whoever it was got Hilliston with that infernal beheading-machine—got that poor Armenian, too! Run outside, Milton; see if you can find any trace of the body."

De Grandin stooped and scooped a little of the blood from the floor into a bit of envelope he drew from his pocket; then, surprisingly, he fell to examining the pantry walls, completely ignoring the blood train leading to the window.

"Not a chanst o' findin' anything out there, sir," Trooper Milton reported. "It's rainin' cats an' dogs, and any trail they mighta left when they drug 'im away's been washed completely out."

"I was afraid of that," Chenevert responded with a nod. "What's next, Doctor de Grandin?"

"Why, I think we might as well go home," the little Frenchman answered. "You have the name and address of every person present; besides, I am quite sure the murderer has gone. I have made memoranda of some things you might investigate tomorrow, and if you'll kindly give them your attention we shall see each other here tomorrow afternoon. Possibly we shall know more by then."

"O.K., sir. How about that Ditmas dame? Think we'd better give her another going over? She's hiding something, and unless I miss my guess, she knows plenty."

The Frenchman pursed his lips and raised his shoulders in the faint suspicion of a shrug. "I do not think that I would question her tonight," he answered. "Her nerves are badly out of tune, and she might easily become hysterical. To-morrow evening, I think we may learn something of real value from her."

"O.K.," the other repeated. "We'll do whatever you say, but I'd put her on the griddle *now* if it were left to me. See you about three o'clock tomorrow? Right-o."

"WELL, I CHECKED UP on those matters, sir," the captain told de Grandin when we met in the Hilliston drawing-room next afternoon. "It seems the work was done by a Greek or Armenian, or some kind of Syrian named Bogos; he installed the electrical fixtures, and, of course, this chandelier, along with all the other paraphernalia—"

"And how much more? one wonders," de Grandin interjected in a whisper.

"What's that?"

"Nothing of importance. You were saying—"

"This Bogos chap put in all the fixtures on Colonel Hilliston's orders, written from abroad, but when we went to Harrisonville to interview him, he'd skipped."

"Decamped?"

"Evaporated. Left with no forwarding address, you might say. Indeed, when we got to running over his activities, it appears that Hilliston's was the only job he ever did. And he left as soon as it was finished."

"U'm? This is of interest."

"You bet your neck it is. Looks as though this Bogos guy—his name shoulda been spelled 'bogus'—installed a lot of stuff not in Hilliston's specifications. What d'ye think?"

"I think it very likely," returned the Frenchman. "Now, if your men are ready, let us inspect Exhibit A of the machinery of murder."

With hammer and cold chisel two mechanics attacked the frescoed ceiling of the drawing-room, twenty minutes work bringing the diabolical device to light. Concealed behind the innocent-looking mask of a prism-hung chandelier was a pair of strong steel jaws, razor-sharp, and working on oil-bathed bearings. How it was actuated there was no means of telling without tearing down the entire wall and ceiling of the room, but a single glance was sufficient to tell us that when the thing was dropped and the jaws sprung, it was powerful enough to bite through anything less resistant than a bar of iron. Measuring the cable on which it operated, we determined that it was designed to fall and gnash its metal jaws at a height of five feet from the floor.

"Colonel Hilliston was six feet one," Chenevert commented. "Allowing for an inch or so of neck, it was just made to slice his head off right below the chin. And say, wasn't that Ditmas girl lucky when you barged into her? The thing woulda bitten the top right off her head."

He took a turn across the room; then: "She was about to spill something when it started to drop on her, too," he added. "Something about some sort o' knife when you showed her that picture you'd made. Now, how the devil was it timed so nicely, and who worked it?"

"Let us inspect the butler's pantry," answered Jules de Grandin irrelevantly.

"Last night," he told us as we halted in the room from which the butler had been taken, "I made an examination of these walls while you were looking at the blood stains on the floor. Do you observe that clock?" He pointed to a small electrical chronometer set in the wall.

"Yeah, I see it. What about it?"

"Look closely at it, *Monsieur le Capitaine.* Does not it seem unusual?"

Chenevert examined the timepiece from several angles, tapped it tentatively with his forefinger, finally compared it with his watch. "It's half a minute fast, that's all I see," he answered.

"*Ah bah,* you are like the idols of the heathen who having eyes see not!" de Grandin told him irritably. "See how it has been fastened to the wall? Screwed? *Non.* Cemented? Again *non.* Riveted? *Mais non*—it hangs on hinges. Now see." With a quick jerk he drew the timepiece forward like a door, disclosing a small cavity beneath it. In this there hung a little disk of hard black rubber, like a telephone lineman's ear-piece, and in the very center of the hole there was a circular lens shaded by an apron of black metal.

"Look into it," he ordered, "and hold the 'phone against your ear."

I gazed across the captain's shoulder as de Grandin left the pantry. In a moment I beheld him, as though seen through the large end of a pair of opera glasses, standing by the table where Hilliston had met his death.

"It is a kind of periscope," he told us as he re-entered the pantry. "Could you hear me when I spoke to you?"

"Yes, distinctly," answered Chenevert. "You said, 'Do not press the button at the bottom, if you please.'"

"*Exactement.* Now do you and good Friend Trowbridge go into the drawing-room and see what happens."

Obediently we walked to the parlor, and as Chenevert hailed, "All right, Doctor," we heard a sharp and wasp-like buzzing in the ceiling whence the men had moved the hidden guillotine.

"It is as simple as the alphabet when once one masters it," the Frenchman told us. "One in this ninety-times-accursed pantry sees what happens in the drawing-room. Also, he hears the conversation there. Now, if you look there by that china closet, you will see a little metal door. What does it hide?"

"I'll bite," said Chenevert.

"A fuse-box, by blue! You see? Standing here, before this spy-hole, one can reach out and disconnect the lighting-wires from the drawing-room, from that whole section of the house, indeed, at a single motion. Then, when darkness falls upon the parlor, one does but press this button, and *pouf!* someone has his head decapitated with neatness and dispatch. Not only that, by the motion of the guillotine, the head is placed upon the table for all to look at when the lights go on again. Ingenious; ingenious as the schemes of Satan, *n'est-ce-pas?*"

"Why, then, that's what caused the little breath of air I felt against my face," I told him. "It was the guillotine dropping within an inch or so of me. Great heavens—"

"*Ah bah*, an inch was quite enough to spell the difference between life and death for you, my friend," he told me with a grin.

"But who the devil operated it?" Chenevert demanded. "Of course, the butler might have been back here when Hilliston was killed, but they bumped him off, too; so—"

"You are positively sure of that?" de Grandin interrupted.

"Well, nothing's sure but death and taxes, but when we heard him yell, then found this place all smeared with blood—"

"The liquid which you found upon the floor, by example?"

"Yeah, sure; what else?"

"Oh, I thought perhaps you might have found some blood," the little Frenchman answered with an elfin grin. "Last night I took precaution to soak some of that liquid into a piece of paper. Today I analyzed him. He is an exceptionally fine specimen of—red ink, *mon Capitaine*."

"Well, I'll be damned!"

"One hopes sincerely otherwise, though undoubtlessly you would lend a touch of *savoir faire* to hell, my friend."

"So that butler guy did it, after all! H'm. Now, how're we going to put the finger on him? That Ditmas girl—"

"*Précisément, mon Capitaine.* You have said it."

"Eh? Said what?"

"The pretty Mademoiselle Ditmas, she shall be our stalking-horse."

"T IENS, THE THREADS BEGIN to join together in a single cord," he told us as we drove toward Harrisonville.

"I can't see it," I responded. "It seems the most mixed-up hodgepodge I ever heard of. Nothing seems related to anything else, and—"

"You have wrong, my friend," he contradicted. "The relationship is clear, and growing clearer every minute. "Consider—" he checked the items off upon his fanned-out fingers: "Last month we saw a poor dead girl fished up from the bay. Upon her cheek was burned the picture of a knife. Me, I do not know why this should be, but that picture is not merely the representation of a dagger, it is a dagger of one specific kind. The simplest form of dagger-picture is a cross, two straight lines crossing at right angles. Not this one, though. But no, certainly not. It is the carefully prepared picture of a Tripolitan throwing-knife—which may also be conveniently used as a hand-weapon.

"'What should such a picture be doing burned on an American young lady's cheek?' I want to know. This business smells strongly of the East, even to the manner of her killing. Then *zut!* through the so thick head of Jules de Grandin comes a thought. I was in the Service of Intelligence in the War, my friends; besides I have done some service for the *Sûreté*, and I have friends around the world. One of them, serving with our forces in Syria, wrote me but recently of a revival of that sect once called *les Assassins*—the almost mythical but very potent followers of Hassan ibn Sabbah, who from their fortress at Aleppo had terrorized two continents for near three hundred years. Not like a plague, but rather like an epidemic sickness the chapters of this most abominable sect were springing up, now here, now there, throughout the country near Damascus, even as far as Jerusalem and Bagdad. The French had met them with repressive measures, and, believe me, Frenchmen entertain no silly sentimental notions of conciliating native prejudice where law and order are involved. However, we digress.

"The blood-red dagger, exactly like the one burned on that poor girl's face, was the official badge of Hassan's minions in the days of old. 'Now, can it be—' I ask me, and even as I ask, along comes Colonel Hilliston; the soldier and explorer, the *beau sabreur* among the travelers, and providentially, he is back from the Near East. 'This one, will surely know of what is which,' I tell me confidently. 'He will have surely poked beneath the rubbish-heaps of gossip and found the truth. He is a learned man, a fearless man; best of all, he is a curious and most inquisitive man.'

"And so I plague my good Friend Trowbridge till he secures an invitation for us to the colonel's house, and while we all make merry at a most exquisite meal I bring the subject of the Haunted Mountain of the hashish-eaters up; I ask our host if he, by any happy chance, has scaled it for a look around. And does he tell me that he has? Damn no. He shies away from such talk as a nervous horse goes dancing when a piece of paper blows across the road. Ah, but Jules de Grandin is no simpleton. Not he! He can read the signs in people's faces as he reads the print upon the page. And what does he see in the face of Colonel Hilliston? What does he see, I ask it?" He paused dramatically; then:

"Fear!" he said.

"Yes, *mes amis*, most certainly, it was fear I saw shine in his eyes, a fear that might be classified as terror; the terror of the hunted deer when, thinking herself safely hid, she hears the baying of the hounds upon her trail. Yes, certainly.

"*Et puis*—and then? Meantime my good Friend Trowbridge, with a manner highly unbecoming to his eminent respectability, has become most friendly with a pretty little lady who, if ever woman had it, contains a large-sized portion of the devil in her make-up. But do they talk of moonlight kisses and the scent of twice-crushed rose leaves in a lady's flowing hair, or tender nothings spoken underneath the twinkling stars? Damn no, they do entirely otherwise. They talk of Colonel Hilliston and of something which he fears, of the iron reinforcements of his doors and windows, of the locks and bars and bolts which make his house secure. Secure against whom—or what? What is the terror which pursues him night and day?

"And then, when all the lights go out, and we are plunged in darkness deeper than the blackness of the devil's lowest cellar, what does this pretty lady say to Doctor Trowbridge? 'I'm afraid *it got in!*'

"And next we see *Monsieur le Colonel*: wholly headless, lying on the floor of his own house; yet no one knows who struck him down, or how, or why.

"'Oh, do they not, indeed? We shall inquire as to that,' I tell me when I am informed of Miss Ditmas' conversation, and so I make a picture of a dagger. Not *any* dagger, but the kind of dagger which was burned upon the dead girl's face. And when I show it to Miss Ditmas and tell her we have found it on the colonel's body, what does she say? *Cordieu*, she starts to say it is the Red Knife of Hassan, but she does not finish saying it, for from the ceiling falls the guillotine which almost shears her head away, and thereafter she is speechless as an oyster.

"*Tiens*, we are gathering up the threads, my friends. This Mademoiselle Ditmas, Colonel Hilliston and the dead girl in the bay, they are three corners of a square."

"And the fourth?" I asked.

"Is Nejib, Colonel Hilliston's ex-butler."

"But he's an Armenian, a Christian," Captain Chenevert objected. "Those Assassins you're telling of are Turks or Arabs, or something like that, aren't they?"

"Can you distinguish between a Japanese and Filipino?" de Grandin countered.

"Eh?"

"*Précisément.* They look alike; it would be easy to mistake one for the other. So with the peoples of the nearer East—Turks, Armenians, many of the Arabs, they are so much alike to outward seeming that one might easily pass muster for the other. No, this Nejib-butler, he is no Armenian; neither was the Bogos person who did the colonel's electrical work; they may not be Turks, I strongly doubt they are, but certainly beyond a doubt they are Assassins. Yes, of course."

"And you think Miss Ditmas can enlighten us?" I asked.

He raised shoulders, hands and eyebrows in a shrug. "Undoubtlessly she can, but will she?" he replied.

T HE EARLY WINTER DUSK was falling as we stopped before the house where Margaret Ditmas lived. "I'm not sure Miss Ditmas is in," said the attendant at the switchboard; "I'll ring her apartment—"

"Excuse me, you will do nothing of the kind," de Grandin interrupted. "Ringing telephones and sending in cards are only temptations to weak-souled ones to lie. We shall go ourselves to see if she is in, and—do not ring that telephone."

"You heard him, feller," Captain Chenevert added. "If anybody tips Miss Ditmas off we're on our way to see her, you're going to know what the inside of a nice, home-like jail looks like, and I don't mean maybe. See?"

Apparently the operator saw, for it was with an expression of surprise that the trim colored maid met us at the door of the apartment and ushered us in.

Miss Ditmas leant back in a wing chair, a gown of clinging gray swathing her lissome form from throat to insteps. A string of pearls hung round her neck, pearl studs were in her ears, a great pearl solitaire gleamed on the third finger of her right hand, upon her feet were sandals clasped about her ankles with pearl catches, and the little thread of platinum encircling her left ankle shone glimmeringly in the candlelight against her bare, pale-ivory skin. She lay back in the chair like one who slept, or rested after illness, and from the long, thin cigarette which dropped from her right hand a twisting trail of smoke went up, and as I caught its scent I thought of her quotation of the night before: "Ambergris—for passion."

She turned her head listlessly as we appeared, her clear white profile and night-black hair standing out in charming silhouette against the elfin candlelight, and a faint, wan smile stole across her face like the smile of one who sleeps and dreams a sweetly melancholy dream.

"No, Doctor de Grandin, I haven't the faintest idea what it was that Colonel Hilliston feared," she replied in a low, sleepy voice. "Yes, I'd noticed how he'd reinforced his doors and windows, but the house stands in a lonely location, and he had many beautiful and expensive things in his collection. I suppose he wanted to make sure the place wouldn't be burglarized; don't you?"

Once more she smiled that slow, disinterested smile, and inhaled deeply from her amber-scented cigarette.

"I really don't know what I meant by what I said to Doctor Trowbridge when the lights went out," she answered his next query. "What does anybody mean by such hysterical statements? I was startled, terrified, when we were plunged in sudden darkness, and—do you know, I believe I'd taken too much wine at dinner! How I came to say anything about something getting in is more than I can imagine. Nothing got in really, did it? Unless it were the person who made off with poor Nejib just after my escape from that dreadful thing which dropped out of the ceiling?"

"*Mademoiselle*," de Grandin told her sternly, "this is not a *salle d'armes*."

"Really, Doctor, I don't quite understand."

"Very well, let us be frank as friends are frank. This is no place for fencing. We are come to ask you certain questions, it is true; but we have also come to warn you and protect you."

"Warn? Protect me? Whatever from?"

"From the Brethren of the Knife, *Mademoiselle*; from the wielders of the Scarlet Knife of Hassan!"

Her face went blank, then gray-white as a corpse's countenance, as he shot out the bald statement, but she took a sudden grip upon herself, and:

"I haven't the remotest idea what you're talking about," she told him.

"*Au 'voir, Mademoiselle*, even *le bon Dieu* is powerless to help those who will not help themselves," he answered tonelessly, and made her one of his stiff, Continental bows, that straight-backed bow which always suggested uniform and corset to me.

"Come, my friends, we have important duties to perform," he told Chenevert and me as he led us from the room.

"NOW WHERE?" THE CAPTAIN asked as we waited for the automatic elevator.

"Upstairs," the Frenchman answered. "The flat above is vacant."

"What the devil—"

"*Tiens*, not the devil in his proper person, perhaps, but certainly his myrmidons," replied de Grandin with a grin. "Come hurry; we waste our precious time in argument."

Arrived one story up, he tried the handle of the entrance to the suite directly above Miss Ditmas', found it locked and as matter-of-factly as though setting a broken arm, set to picking the lock with scientific neatness and dispatch.

"Softly, if you please," he cautioned as we entered the vacant rooms; "I would not have our footsteps heard below."

Tiptoeing to the window, he inspected the fire escape which zigzagged down the building's side, nodded with a smile of satisfaction and turned again to us. "In half an hour they should come," he whispered. "Do you compose yourselves to wait, my friends; smoke, if you like, but do not speak above a whisper, and keep back from the window. We do not know where they may lurk or how thoroughly they may be watching."

The minutes dragged away and I was getting stiff from sitting on the floor with my back against the un-upholstered wall when: "*P-s-st!*" de Grandin's sharp, admonitory hiss attracted my attention.

"*La fenêtre*—the window; look!" he ordered softly.

I looked up just in time to see a shadow, but a faint shade darker than the outside gloom, go floating downward past the casement, and half rose with an exclamation when his warning, upraised finger and another hiss arrested me. One, two, three times the window was blocked out by downward-drifting shadows, then de Grandin crept across the room, swung the casement back with slow and wary care, thrust his head forth and glanced quickly up and down, then motioned us to follow him.

"What—" Chenevert began; but:

"*S-s-sh*, great stupid one, be quiet!" the Frenchman warned him sharply. "This is no parade we make; leave the music home."

Step by cautious step we clambered down the fire escape, de Grandin in the lead, Chenevert and I near treading on his heels.

No sound reached our ears as we came opposite Miss Ditmas' open window. The room was dark as Erebus.

"Silence!" warned the Frenchman; then, his hand upon his pistol, "Follow me." He stepped through the open window, sweeping the room with his flashlight.

The place was in disorder, showing signs of recent struggle, but was empty of human life.

"*Nom d'un coq!*" exclaimed de Grandin sharply. "After them! We must find them, right away, at once; immediately! God grant that we come not too late!"

The door communicating with the hall was locked, and: "Burst it open," he exclaimed. "We have no time to pick the lock."

Suiting action to his words, we put our shoulders to the panels. It held us back a moment but at the third rush it gave way, precipitating us into the hall.

"This way!" He hurried down the passage to a glazed door marked "Freight Elevator." He pressed the button savagely, but the automatic lift failed to respond.

"Ha, *par la barbe d'un poisson*, undoubtlessly they took her down that ninety-times-damned lift," he panted as we hastened down the winding stairs. "They have wedged the lower door ajar to shut off our pursuit, for the mechanism will not lift unless all shaft-doors have been closed. But we have nimble legs, *parbleu*, and follow fast upon their heels!

"Outside, quickly!" he commanded as we reached the bottom floor. "They have secreted her within the basement, I damn think, but they are no fools, those ones. They will have locked the door behind them, and they would murder her while we were breaking through. This way!"

We burst into the outer air, and de Grandin ran fleetly out into the alley.

"Ah! God be thanked!" he exclaimed, pointing to a row of narrow windows set flush with the ground. "There *is* an entrance from outside. They are small, these windows, but not too small for Jules de Grandin, I damn think."

Cautiously, treading lightly as a cat, he examined each of the windows in turn. They were grimy, and impossible to see through, clearly, but through the glass of one a light could be dimly seen. Just as he knelt in an attempt to peer through, a voice came thickly from the room inside.

"Oh, God!" a woman moaned despairingly. "Have pity on me, Hassan! I didn't tell them anything, I wouldn't—*oh!*" The exclamation cut her speech in half.

"No, you did not tell them—yet," the butler answered in a low and oddly hissing voice. "Nor will you tell, my pretty. The brand, the bowstring and the bay await you, even as they did that other who—"

"Oh, no—*no!* Not that, for pity's sake!" the tortured girl entreated. "I tell you I had no intention of disclosing anything! The Frenchman and the others came to call this evening, but I told them nothing—nothing! I swear it; I—"

The crashing of glass and tearing of rotten wood cut short her plea as de Grandin kicked in the window-frame and launched himself through the narrow opening.

"*Pardonnez-moi, Mademoiselle,* one dislikes to contradict a lady, but you told us much this afternoon," he interrupted as he landed, cat-like, on his feet.

Chenevert and I were close behind him, and our flashlights, stabbing through the cellar's light, disclosed a startling tableau. Upon the rug, birth-nude, knelt Margaret Ditmas. Her ankles were bound beneath her, her wrists were tightly lashed together; her face was a picture of utter despair. Two men stood near her, one slowly whipping a long, thin cord-picture-wire!—back and forth before him, the other heating something in a little charcoal brazier such as plumbers used to carry before the days of the gas-torch. But it was the one who stood with folded arms before her that drew and held my gaze as a magnet draws a needle.

The figure was clothed in a long white robe, with a curious head-piece that completely veiled the face except for two large, square eye-holes covered with gauze that hid the eyes behind them. On the front of the robe a dagger was embroidered in vivid red thread—the red knife of the Assassins, of whom Miss Ditmas had told us.

For an instant the tableau held. Then:

"*Non,* do not move, *Messieurs,* or—*eh bien,* since you request it!"

Three knives flashed from their hidden sheaths even as he spoke, but quicker than the knives were Jules de Grandin's shots. So fast he fired it seemed as if a single line of flame were flashing from the muzzle of his automatic pistol, and the man above the brazier toppled over with his hands clasped to his stomach, while the fellow with the picture-wire hunched his shoulders forward as though about to sneeze, emitted a soft hiccup and fell face-downward on the rug, a spate of blood spilling from his gaping mouth.

The masked figure in front of Margaret Ditmas stood unmovable, swaying slightly, like a person seized with vertigo; then, like a tree which woodsmen have sawn through, his swaying motion quickened, and he toppled sideways, crashing down upon the floor, his long, curved knife still grasped within his hand. It was not till later that I learned de Grandin had shot the butler through the brain (for Nejib, the "Armenian," it was). He must have died upon his feet a full ten seconds before he fell.

"Eh bien, she has had a shock, that one," de Grandin murmured as he looked in Margaret Ditmas' still, set face. "Cut the cursed cords off her and bear her to her bed, Friend Trowbridge. Me, I shall call police and coroner. Her story can await on our convenience, now."

The girl seemed curiously light in my arms as I carried her into the garish modernistic bedroom with its chromium-plated furniture and laid her on the big, flat bed, drawing a down-stuffed comforter over her. In the black-and-silver bathroom I found smelling-salts and a bottle of aromatic bromides, and I brought her from her faint with wet towels and the salts, then gave her thirty grains of bromide. Presently she slept.

I sat beside her, hours, it seemed, while de Grandin and Chenevert moved round the room beyond, inspecting the three bodies, 'phoning to the coroner, examining the branding-iron, shaped like a hiltless knife with exaggeratedly curved blade, attending to the hundred and one things which policemen have to do in such a case.

Day came without dawn. The somber winter blackness of the night faded imperceptibly to smoky gray, at last to something like full daylight, but there was no sun, and in the sky the snow-clouds hovered threateningly.

"She is better? She has slept?" de Grandin asked as he and Chenevert came in quietly.

"Yes," I answered to both questions. "She should be all right, now, though I think a period of rest would do her good."

"Undoubtlessly," he acquiesced, "but she has all her life to rest if she is so disposed, while we are very busy.

"Mademoiselle—Mademoiselle Margot!" he called softly.

She turned restlessly, muttering inaudible words, then, childishly, reached out and took my hand, cuddling it against her cheek, and smiled. A fierce, protective tenderness surged up in me. "For heaven's sake, de Grandin, let the child rest!" I urged him; but:

"Mademoiselle, it is morning!" he persisted.

A KIMONO DRAPED AROUND HER shoulders, Margaret Ditmas sat in bed sipping at the tea de Grandin had prepared for her. "You're sure they're dead?" she asked him with an apprehensive look.

"As dead as forty herring—dead as mutton," he assured her. "Me, I made them so, and I am most particular about my killings, *Mademoiselle*."

Reassured, she went on with her narrative: "I met Arbuthnot Hilliston in Jerusalem when Helen Cassaway and I were touring through the Orient last year," she told us.

"He was a fascinating man, and our acquaintance quickly became an intimate friendship. He knew a lot of places which no tourist ever sees, and the more we went about with him, the more his fascination seemed to grow on us. One day, as we were riding toward the site of the old Joppa Gate, he asked us how we'd like to witness the secret rites of the Assassins. Neither of us had ever heard of them, but the name sounded thrilling, and, of course, we agreed enthusiastically.

"From what he told us it seemed they were a revival of an ancient secret order founded by some old Persian in the Eleventh Century, and in their heyday they were more powerful even than the orders of military knights of the Crusades. They'd exacted tribute from the mightiest, and when the tribute wasn't paid, they killed. The Sultan Malik-Shah, the Califs Mostarshid and Rashid, fell beneath their daggers, as did Count Raymond, Christian ruler of Tripoli. Would seeing a lodge meeting of such an order, even though it were only a sort of pale modern copy of the flamboyant ancient original, be a thrill to any girls? You know the answer.

"Arbuthnot took us to the place. The night was dark, and we went in closed carriages; so neither of us knew where we were going, but when we got there we had to take our Western clothing off and put on long white gowns of some sort of heavy muslin with a scarlet dagger embroidered on the left breast. Then cap-veils were brought us, and we put them on. Not network veils, such as we have here, but heavy cotton *haiks*, which were fastened over our faces just low enough below the cap-like head-dresses to let our eyes look out. Then we put about a dozen silver bracelets on each arm and two or three heavy silver rings about our ankles so that we clanked like moving hardware stores at every step, and went barefoot into the big, bare hall where a lot of veiled women and masked men sat round the wall and stared at us.

"The head Assassin—I suppose you'd call him the high priest?—met us in the center of the hall and held out his hands to us. We knelt and put our folded hands between his and he repeated some sort of welcome in Arabic, and when the right times came Arbuthnot told us to nod, and we nodded. That was all— we thought.

"A little later though, they brought out cups of sherbet spiced with some strong, bitter drug—I learned later that it was hashish!—and it made us crazy as fishes out of water. I remember swaying back and forth in my seat, and having a queer feeling as though the air about me were dissolving; as though I were in a rarer and clearer atmosphere, something like the feeling when you inhale nitrous oxide in the dentist's chair, you know. When some queer-sounding music started I felt I simply had to dance, and I got up, ripped the smothering veil away from my face and did the best imitation of an Oriental dance I could. Suddenly a masked man leaped up from his seat against the wall, seized me in his arms, and—" She paused, and a dull, red flush came to her face.

"Perfectly, *Mademoiselle*, one understands," de Grandin told her evenly. "And later—"

"Next day we learned that we'd been through the ceremony of initiation and were duly enrolled members of the sect, or order. We'd sworn to do the will of the society without question, and—well, it didn't take us long to get away from there.

"We came home, and here, in peaceful, matter-of-fact America, it seemed as though it were all part of some wild and rather unpleasant dream. Then, one afternoon, Helen called me up from her home in Paterson. 'Daisy,' she said, 'something *terrible* has happened.'

"Helen Cassaway was the kind of person to whom something 'terrible' was always happening; so I wasn't particularly impressed, even though her voice seemed charged with terror.

"'What is it this time?' I asked her. 'Has the boyfriend found another girl?'

"'Daisy!' she replied reproachfully, 'please listen. You remember that dreadful lodge we joined with Arbuthnot Hilliston in Jerusalem?'

"You may be sure I began to pay attention then. 'Well?' I asked.

"'Today an Armenian rug-peddler came to our house, and asked for me. I hadn't the faintest idea how he knew my name, but I was interested; so I saw him. Daisy, he was from the Assassins' lodge! He held out a little card with the picture of a red dagger on it—just like the daggers embroidered on the gowns we wore when we joined the society—and said it was the Knife of Hassan. When I asked him what he meant, he said it was the sign of the Assassins, and he had come to demand my services. He wanted me to go downtown with him tonight and help him in a *badger game*. He's got the man all picked out, and all I have to do is obey his orders.'

"'What in the world's a badger game?' I asked.

"'It's a sort of blackmail scheme. A woman flirts with a man, and then goes somewhere with him, and when they're there alone another man who pretends to be the woman's husband comes rushing in, and threatens to make a scandal unless the poor dupe who's fallen for the woman's charms pays him hush money, and—'

"'Did you send him packing?' I asked.

"'I most certainly did, and he was furious—told me that no one could refuse to serve the Red Knife of Hassan, and that the branding-iron, the bow-string and the bay awaited all who were disobedient.'

"'Well,' I told her, 'you'd better go to the police. It may not be very easy, to confess that you're mixed up with such a gang of scoundrels, but it'll be a lot easier than trying to dodge their persecutions on your own account. Besides, that fellow ought to be locked up. He's a dangerous character.'

"'I'm going right now,' she told me as she hung up, and—"

"Yes, *Mademoiselle* and—"

"She walked out of her house on the way to the police and no one ever saw her again."

"And how long ago did all this happen, if you please?"

"About two months."

"U'm, one understands. And then—"

"Arbuthnot Hilliston came home, and I got in touch with him at once. 'You got me into this,' I told him; 'now you've got to get me out. Helen Cassaway's disappeared as though she'd fallen in the bay, and I don't know what minute they'll be putting the finger on me.'

"'My dear girl,' he answered, 'I'd be pleased to help you, but they're after me, too. I was told to do some spying on the French high command in Syria, but I've no desire to be stood up against a wall at sunrise; so I put for home. They tried to get me twice, and nearly succeeded each time, but I think I'm safe, for a while at least. I've got an Armenian servant—they hate the Moslems like sin, you know—and at his suggestion he got in touch with an Armenian workman here who's made my house over into a veritable fortress. If you're game to defy the conventions, you're welcome to come out and stop with me. Nejib, my servant, will attend to everything for us, and we'll have only some local help come in by the day, so there'll be no suspicious characters entering the house. If we play lost for a while, maybe the whole business will blow over.'

"The very night I went to stay at his house, you and Doctor Trowbridge came to dinner. I'd heard of you, of course, Doctor de Grandin, and thought that you could help us if anybody could. I drew Doctor Trowbridge as my dinner partner, and was beginning to lead up to asking him to ask you to help us when we went into the drawing-room. Then Arbuthnot was killed so terribly, and when you showed me the Red Knife of Hassan you'd found on his body, and they almost got me with their infernal machine, I knew that it was hopeless. If they could get into that steel-barred and double-locked house of Arbuthnot's, there wasn't any safety for me anywhere.

"I thought they'd killed poor Nejib when I heard him scream out in the pantry, but this afternoon he called me on the 'phone and said he had managed to escape, though they were hunting for him. He warned me not to tell you anything if you came to see me, and said he and two Armenian friends would come secretly to take me to a place of safety tonight. I was to let Lily, my maid, go home early, and leave the window by the fire escape unlatched, so they could come in without being seen.

"So I pleaded ignorance when you arrived, and waited in a perfect fever of apprehension till Nejib and the others came—and when they did, I found *they* were Assassins, and Nejib's real name was Hassan. Then—"

"*Précisément, Mademoiselle,* the rest we know," de Grandin interrupted with a smile.

"You have, perhaps, a—how do you call him, little cellar?—cellarette?—around?"

"Why yes, over in that cabinet you'll find some Scotch and rye, and some brandy, too, if you prefer."

"Prefer? *Mon Dieu,*" he looked at her reproachfully, "who would drink whisky when brandy is available, *Mademoiselle?*"

The Jest of Warburg Tantavul

Warburg Tantavul was dying. Little more than skin and bones, he lay propped up with pillows in the big sleigh bed and smiled as though he found the thought of dissolution faintly amusing.

Even in comparatively good health the man was never prepossessing. Now, wasted with disease, that smile of self-sufficient satisfaction on his wrinkled face, he was nothing less than hideous. The eyes, which nature had given him, were small, deep-set and ruthless. The mouth, which his own thoughts had fashioned through the years, was wide and thin-lipped, almost colorless, and even in repose was tightly drawn against his small and curiously perfect teeth. Now, as he smiled, a flickering light, lambent as the quick reflection of an unseen flame, flared in his yellowish eyes, and a hard white line of teeth showed on his lower lip, as if he bit it to hold back a chuckle.

"You're still determined that you'll marry Arabella?" he asked his son, fixing his sardonic, mocking smile on the young man.

"Yes, Father, but—"

"No buts, my boy"—this time the chuckle came, low and muted, but at the same time glassy-hard—"no buts. I've told you I'm against it, and you'll rue it to your dying day if you should marry her; but"—he paused, and breath rasped in his wizened throat—"but go ahead and marry her, if your heart's set on it. I've said my say and warned you—heh, boy, never say your poor old father didn't warn you!"

He lay back on his piled-up pillows for a moment, swallowing convulsively, as if to force the fleeting life-breath back, then, abruptly: "Get out," he ordered. "Get out and stay out, you poor fool; but remember what I've said."

"Father," young Tantavul began, stepping toward the bed, but the look of sudden concentrated fury in the old man's tawny eyes halted him in midstride.

"Get—out—I—said," his father snarled, then, as the door closed softly on his son:

"Nurse—hand—me—that—picture." His breath was coming slowly, now, in shallow labored gasps, but his withered fingers writhed in a gesture of command, pointing to the silver-framed photograph of a woman which stood upon a little table in the bedroom window-bay.

He clutched the portrait as if it were some precious relic, and for a minute let his eyes rove over it. "Lucy," he whispered hoarsely, and now his words were thick and indistinct, "Lucy, they'll be married, spite of all that I have said. They'll be married, Lucy, d'ye hear?" Thin and high-pitched as a child's, his voice rose to a piping treble as he grasped the picture's silver frame and held it level with his face. "They'll be married, Lucy dear, and they'll have—"

Abruptly as a penny whistle's note is stilled when no more air is blown in it, old Tantavul's cry was hushed. The picture, still grasped in his hands, fell to the tufted coverlet, the man's lean jaw relaxed and he slumped back on his pillows with a shadow of the mocking smile still in his glazing eyes.

Etiquette requires that the nurse await the doctor's confirmation at such times, so, obedient to professional dictates, Miss Williamson stood by the bed until I felt the dead man's pulse and nodded; then with the skill of years of practice she began her offices, bandaging the wrists and jaws and ankles that the body might be ready when the representative of Martin's Funeral Home came for it.

M Y FRIEND DE GRANDIN was annoyed. Arms akimbo, knuckles on his hips, his black-silk kimono draped round him like a mourning garment, he voiced his complaint in no uncertain terms. In fifteen little so small minutes he must leave for the theatre, and that son and grandson of a filthy swine who was the florist had not delivered his gardenia. And was it not a fact that he could not go forth without a fresh gardenia for his lapel? But certainly. Why did that *sale chameau* procrastinate? Why did he delay delivering that unmentionable flower till this unspeakable time of night? He was Jules de Grandin, he, and not to be oppressed by any species of a goat who called himself a florist. But no. It must not be. It should not be, by blue! He would—

"Axin' yer pardon, sir," Nora McGinnis broke in from the study door, "there's a Miss an' Mr. Tantavul to see ye, an'—"

"Bid them be gone, *ma charmeuse*. Request that they jump in the bay— *Grand Dieu*"—he cut his oratory short—"*les enfants dans le bois!*"

Truly, there was something reminiscent of the Babes in the Wood in the couple who had followed Nora to the study door. Dennis Tantavul looked even younger and more boyish than I remembered him, and the girl beside him was so childish in appearance that I felt a quick, instinctive pity for her. Plainly they were frightened, too, for they clung hand to hand like frightened children going past a graveyard, and in their eyes was that look of sick terror I had seen so often when the X-ray and blood test confirmed preliminary diagnosis of carcinoma.

"*Monsieur, Mademoiselle!*" The little Frenchman gathered his kimono and his dignity about him in a single sweeping gesture as he struck his heels together and bowed stiffly from the hips. "I apologize for my unseemly words. Were it not that I have been subjected to a terrible, calamitous misfortune, I should not so far have forgotten myself—"

The girl's quick smile cut through his apology. "We understand," she reassured. "We've been through trouble, too, and have come to Dr. Trowbridge—"

"Ah, then I have permission to withdraw?" he bowed again and turned upon his heel, but I called him back.

"Perhaps you can assist us," I remarked as I introduced the callers.

"The honor is entirely mine, *Mademoiselle*," he told her as he raised her fingers to his lips. "You and *Monsieur* your brother—"

"He's not my brother," she corrected. "We're cousins. That's why we've called on Dr. Trowbridge."

De Grandin tweaked the already needle-sharp points of his small blond mustache. "*Pardonnez-moi?*" he begged. "I have resided in your country but a little time; perhaps I do not understand the language fluently. It is because you and *Monsieur* are cousins that you come to see the doctor? Me, I am dull and stupid like a pig; I fear I do not comprehend."

Dennis Tantavul replied: "It's not because of the relationship, Doctor—not entirely, at any rate, but—"

He turned to me: "You were at my father's bedside when he died; you remember what he said about marrying Arabella?"

I nodded.

"There was something—some ghastly, hidden threat concealed in his warning, Doctor. It seemed as if he jeered at me—dared me to marry her, yet—"

"Was there some provision in his will?" I asked.

"Yes, sir," the young man answered. "Here it is." From his pocket he produced a folded parchment, opened it and indicated a paragraph:

To my son Dennis Tantavul I give, devise and bequeath all my property of every kind and sort, real, personal and mixed, of which I may die seized and possessed, or to which I may be entitled, in the event of his marrying Arabella Tantavul, but should he not marry the said Arabella Tantavul, then it is my will that he receive only one half of my estate, and that the residue thereof go to the said Arabella Tantavul, who has made her home with me since childhood and occupied the relationship of daughter to me."

"H'm," I returned the document, "this looks as if he really wanted you to marry your cousin, even though—"

"And see here, sir," Dennis interrupted, "here's an envelope we found in Father's papers."

Sealed with red wax, the packet of heavy, opaque parchment was addressed:

"To my children, Dennis and Arabella Tantavul, to be opened by them upon the occasion of the birth of their first child."

De Grandin's small blue eyes were snapping with the flickering light they showed when he was interested. "Monsieur Dennis," he took the thick envelope from the caller, "Dr. Trowbridge has told me something of your father's death-bed scene. There is a mystery about this business. My suggestion is you read the message now—"

"No, sir. I won't do that. My father didn't love me—sometimes I think he hated me—but I never disobeyed a wish that he expressed, and I don't feel at liberty to do so now. It would be like breaking faith with the dead. But"—he smiled a trifle shame-facedly—"Father's lawyer Mr. Bainbridge is out of town on business, and it will be his duty to probate the will. In the meantime I'd feel better if the will and this envelope were in other hands than mine. So we came to Dr. Trowbridge to ask him to take charge of them till Mr. Bainbridge gets back, meanwhile—"

"Yes, Monsieur, meanwhile?" de Grandin prompted as the young man paused.

"You know human nature, Doctor," Dennis turned to me; "no one can see farther into hidden meanings than the man who sees humanity with its mask off, the way a doctor does. D'ye think Father might have been delirious when he warned me not to marry Arabella, or—" His voice trailed off, but his troubled eyes were eloquent.

"H'm," I shifted uncomfortably in my chair, "I can't see any reason for hesitating, Dennis. That bequest of all your father's property in the event you marry Arabella seems to indicate his true feelings." I tried to make my words convincing, but the memory of old Tantavul's dying words dinned in my ears. There had been something gloating in his voice as he told the picture that his son and niece would marry.

De Grandin caught the hint of hesitation in my tone. "Monsieur," he asked Dennis, "will not you tell us of the antecedents of your father's warning? Dr. Trowbridge is perhaps too near to see the situation clearly. Me, I have no knowledge of your father or your family. You and Mademoiselle are strangely like. The will describes her as having lived with you since childhood. Will you kindly tell us how it came about?"

The Tantavuls were, as he said, strangely similar. Anyone might easily have taken them for twins. Like as two plaster portraits from the same mold were their small straight noses, sensitive mouths, curling pale-gold hair.

Now, once more hand in hand, they sat before us on the sofa, and as Dennis spoke I saw the frightened, haunted look creep back into their eyes.

"Do you remember us as children, Doctor?" he asked me.

"Yes, it must have been some twenty years ago they called me out to see you youngsters. You'd just moved into the old Stephens house, and there was a deal of gossip about the strange gentleman from the West with his two small children and Chinese cook, who greeted all the neighbors' overtures with churlish rebuffs and never spoke to anyone."

"What did you think of us, sir?"

"H'm; I thought you and your sister—as I thought her then—had as fine a case of measles as I'd ever seen."

"How old were we then, do you remember?"

"Oh, you were something like three; the little girl was half your age, I'd guess."

"Do you recall the next time you saw us?"

"Yes, you were somewhat older then; eight or ten, I'd say. That time it was the mumps. You were queer, quiet little shavers. I remember asking if you thought you'd like a pickle, and you said, 'No, thank you, sir, it hurts.'"

"It did, too, sir. Every day Father made us eat one; stood over us with a whip till we'd chewed the last morsel."

"What?"

The young folks nodded solemnly as Dennis answered, "Yes, sir; every day. He said he wanted to check up on the progress we were making."

For a moment he was silent, then: "Dr. Trowbridge, if anyone treated you with studied cruelty all your life—if you'd never had a kind word or gracious act from that person in all your memory, then suddenly that person offered you a favour—made it possible for you to gratify your dearest wish, and threatened to penalize you if you failed to do so, wouldn't you be suspicious? Wouldn't you suspect some sort of dreadful practical joke?"

"I don't think I quite understand."

"Then listen: In all my life I can't remember ever having seen my father smile, not really smile with friendliness, humour or affection, I mean. My life—and Arabella's, too—was one long persecution at his hands. I was two years or so old when we came to Harrisonville, I believe, but I still have vague recollections of our Western home, of a house set high on a hill overlooking the ocean, and a wall with climbing vines and purple flowers on it, and a pretty lady who would take me in her arms and cuddle me against her breast and feed me ice cream from a spoon, sometimes. I have a sort of recollection of a little baby sister in that house, too, but these things are so far back in babyhood that possibly they were no more than childish fancies which I built up for myself and which I loved so dearly and so secretly they finally came to have a kind of reality for me.

"My real memories, the things I can recall with certainty, begin with a hurried train trip through hot, dry, uncomfortable country with my father and a strangely silent Chinese servant and a little girl they told me was my cousin Arabella.

"Father treated me and Arabella with impartial harshness. We were beaten for the slightest fault, and we had faults a-plenty. If we sat quietly we were accused of sulking and asked why we didn't go and play. If we played and shouted we were whipped for being noisy little brats.

"As we weren't allowed to associate with any of the neighbors' children we made up our own games. I'd be Geraint and Arabella would be Enid of the dove-white feet, or perhaps I'd be King Arthur in the Castle Perilous, and she'd be the kind Lady of the Lake who gave him back his magic sword. And though we never mentioned it, both of us knew that whatever the adventure was, the false knight or giant I contended with was really my father. But when actual trouble came I wasn't an heroic figure.

"I must have been twelve or thirteen when I had my last thrashing. A little brook ran through the lower part of our land, and the former owners had widened it into a lily-pond. The flowers had died out years before, but the outlines of the pool remained, and it was our favourite summer play place. We taught ourselves to swim—not very well, of course, but well enough—and as we had no bathing suits we used to go in in our underwear. When we'd finished swimming we'd lie in the sun until our underthings were dry, then slip into our outer clothing. One afternoon as we were splashing in the water, happy as a pair of baby otters, and nearer to shouting with laughter then we'd ever been before, I think, my father suddenly appeared on the bank.

"'Come out o' there!' he shouted to me, and there was a kind of sharp, dry hardness in his voice I'd never heard before. 'So this is how you spend your time?' he asked as I climbed up the bank. 'In spite of all I've done to keep you decent, you do a thing like this!'

"'Why, Father, we were only swimming—' I began, but he struck me on the mouth.

"'Shut up, you little rake!' he roared. 'I'll teach you!' He cut a willow switch and thrust my head between his knees; then while he held me tight as in a vice he flogged me with the willow till the blood came through my skin and stained my soaking cotton shorts. Then he kicked me back into the pool as a heartless master might a beaten dog.

"As I said, I wasn't an heroic figure. It was Arabella who came to my rescue. She helped me up the slippery bank and took me in her arms. 'Poor Dennie,' she said. 'Poor, poor Dennie. It was my fault, Dennie, dear, for letting you take me into the water!' Then she kissed me—the first time anyone had kissed me since the pretty lady of my half-remembered dreams. 'We'll be married on the very day that Uncle Warburg dies,' she promised, 'and I'll be so sweet and good to you, and you'll love me so dearly that we'll both forget these dreadful days.'

"We thought my father'd gone, but he must have stayed to see what we would say, for as Arabella finished he stepped from behind a rhododendron bush, and for the first time I heard him laugh. 'You'll be married, will you?' he asked. 'That would be a good joke—the best one of all. All right, go ahead—see what it gets you.'

"That was the last time he ever actually struck me, but from that time on he seemed to go out of his way to invent mental tortures for us. We weren't allowed to go to school, but he had a tutor, a little rat-faced man named Ericson, come in to give us lessons, and in the evening he'd take the book and make us stand before him and recite. If either of us failed a problem in arithmetic or couldn't conjugate a French or Latin verb he'd wither us with sarcasm, and always as a finish to his diatribe he'd jeer at us about our wish to be married, and threaten us with something dreadful if we ever did it.

"So, Dr. Trowbridge, you see why I'm suspicious. It seems almost as if this provision in the will is part of some horrible practical joke my father prepared deliberately—as if he's waiting to laugh at us from the grave."

"I can understand your feelings, boy," I answered, "but—"

"'But' be damned and roasted on the hottest griddle in hell's kitchen!" Jules de Grandin interrupted. "The wicked dead one's funeral is at two tomorrow afternoon, n'est-ce-pas?

"Très bien. At eight tomorrow evening—or earlier, if it will be convenient— you shall be married. I shall esteem it a favour if you permit that I be best man; Dr. Trowbridge will give the bride away, and we shall have a merry time, by blue! You shall go upon a gorgeous honeymoon and learn how sweet the joys of love can be—sweeter for having been so long denied! And in the meantime we shall keep the papers safely till your lawyer returns.

"You fear the so unpleasant jest? Mais non, I think the jest is on the other foot, my friends, and the laugh on the other face!"

W ARBURG TANTAVUL WAS NEITHER widely known nor popular, but the solitude in which he had lived had invested him with mystery; now the bars of reticence were down and the walls of isolation broken, upward of a hundred neighbors, mostly women, gathered in the Martin funeral chapel as the services began. The afternoon sun beat softly through the stained-glass windows and glinted on the polished mahogany of the casket. Here and there it touched upon bright spots of color that marked a woman's hat or a man's tie. The solemn hush was broken by occasional whispers: "What'd he die of? Did he leave much? Were the two young folks his only heirs?"

Then the burial office: "Lord, Thou hast been our refuge from one generation to another . . . for a thousand years in Thy sight are but as yesterday . . . Oh teach us to number our days that we may apply our hearts unto wisdom . . ."

As the final Amen sounded one of Mr. Martin's frock-coated young men glided forward, paused beside the casket, and made the stereotyped announcement: "Those who wish to say good-bye to Mr. Tantavul may do so at this time."

The grisly rite of passing by the bier dragged on. I would have left the place; I had no wish to look upon the man's dead face and folded hands; but de Grandin took me firmly by the elbow, held me till the final curiosity-impelled female had filed past the body, then steered me quickly toward the casket.

He paused a moment at the bier, and it seemed to me there was a hint of irony in the smile that touched the corners of his mouth as he leant forward. "Eh bien, my old one; we know a secret, thou and I, n'est-ce-pas?" he asked the silent form before us.

I swallowed back an exclamation of dismay. Perhaps it was a trick of the uncertain light, perhaps one of those ghastly, inexplicable things which every doctor and embalmer meets with sometimes in his practice—the effect of desiccation from formaldehyde, the pressure of some tissue gas within the body, or something of the sort—at any rate, as Jules de Grandin spoke the corpse's upper lids drew back the fraction of an inch, revealing slits of yellow eye which seemed to glare at us with mingled hate and fury.

"Good heavens; come away!" I begged. "It seemed as if he looked at us, de Grandin!"

"Et puis—and if he did? I damn think I can trade him look for look, my friend. He was clever, that one, I admit it; but do not be mistaken, Jules de Grandin is nobody's imbecile."

THE WEDDING TOOK PLACE in the rectory of St. Chrysostom's. Robed in stole and surplice, Dr. Bentley glanced benignly from Dennis to Arabella, then to de Grandin and me as he began: "Dearly beloved, we are gathered together here in the sight of God and in the face of this company to join together this man and this woman in holy matrimony. . . ." His round and ruddy face grew slightly stern as he admonished, "If any man can show just cause why they should not lawfully be joined together, let him now speak or else hereafter for ever hold his peace."

He paused the customary short, dramatic moment, and I thought I saw a hard, grim look spread on de Grandin's face. Very faint and far off seeming, so faint that we could scarcely hear it, but gaining steadily in strength, there came a high, thin, screaming sound. Curiously, it seemed to me to resemble the long-drawn, wailing shriek of a freight train's whistle heard miles away upon a still and sultry summer night, weird, wavering and ghastly. Now it seemed to grow in shrillness, though its volume was no greater.

I saw a look of haunted fright leap into Arabella's eyes, saw Dennis' pale face go paler as the strident whistle sounded shriller and more shrill; then, as it seemed I could endure the stabbing of that needle-sound no longer, it ceased abruptly, giving way to blessed, comforting silence. But through the silence came a burst of chuckling laughter, half breathless, half hysterical, wholly devilish: *Huh—hu-u-uh—hu-u-u-uh!* the final syllable drawn out until it seemed almost a groan.

"The wind, *Monsieur le Curé*; it was nothing but the wind," de Grandin told the clergyman sharply. "Proceed to marry them, if you will be so kind."

"Wind?" Dr. Bentley echoed. "I could have sworn I heard somebody laugh, but—"

"It is the wind, *Monsieur*; it plays strange tricks at times," the little Frenchman insisted, his small blue eyes as hard as frozen iron. "Proceed, if you will be so kind. We wait on you."

"Forasmuch as Dennis and Arabella have consented to be joined together in holy wedlock . . . I pronounce them man and wife," concluded Dr. Bentley, and de Grandin, ever gallant, kissed the bride upon the lips, and before we could restrain him, planted kisses on both Dennis' cheeks.

"*Cordieu*, I thought that we might have the trouble, for a time," he told me as we left the rectory.

"What *was* that awful shrieking noise we heard?" I asked.

"It was the wind, my friend," he answered in a hard, flat, toneless voice. "The ten times damned, but wholly ineffectual wind."

"SO, THEN, LITTLE SINNER, weep and wail for the burden of mortality you have assumed. Weep, wail, cry and breathe, my small and wrinkled one! Ha, you will not? *Pardieu*, I say you shall!"

Gently, but smartly, he spanked the small red infant's small red posterior with the end of a towel wrung out in hot water, and as the smacking impact sounded the tiny toothless mouth opened and a thin, high, piping squall of protest sounded. "Ah, that is better, *mon petit ami*," he chuckled. "One cannot learn too soon that one must do as one is told, not as one wishes, in this world which you have just entered. Look to him, *Mademoiselle*," he passed the wriggling, bawling morsel of humanity to the nurse and turned to me as I bent over the table where Arabella lay. "How does the little mother, Friend Trowbridge?" he asked.

"U'm'mp," I answered noncommittally. "Bear a hand, here, will you? The perineum's pretty badly torn—have to do a quick repair job . . ."

"But in the morning she will have forgotten all the pain," laughed de Grandin as Arabella, swathed in blankets, was trundled from the delivery room. "She will gaze upon the little monkey-thing which I just caused to breathe the breath of life and vow it is the loveliest of all God's lovely creatures. She will hold it at her tender breast and smile on it, she will—*Sacré nom d'un rat vert*, what is that?"

From the nursery where, ensconced in wire trays, a score of newborn fragments of humanity slept or squalled, there came a sudden frightened scream—a woman's cry of terror.

We raced along the corridor, reached the glass-walled room and thrust the door back, taking care to open it no wider than was necessary, lest a draft disturb the carefully conditioned air of the place.

Backed against the farther wall, her face gone grey with fright, the nurse in charge was staring at the skylight with terror-widened eyes, and even as we entered she opened her lips to emit another scream.

"Desist, *ma bonne*, you are disturbing your small charges!" de Grandin seized the horrified girl's shoulder and administered a shake. Then: "What is it, *Mademoiselle?*" he whispered. "Do not be afraid to speak; we shall respect your confidence—but speak softly."

"It—it was up there!" she pointed with a shaking finger toward the black square of the skylight. "They'd just brought Baby Tantavul in, and I had laid him in his crib when I thought I heard somebody laughing. Oh"—she shuddered at the recollection—"it was awful! Not really a laugh, but something more like a long-drawn-out hysterical groan. Did you ever hear a child tickled to exhaustion—you know how he moans and gasps for breath, and laughs, all at once? I think the fiends in hell must laugh like that!"

"Yes, yes, we understand," de Grandin nodded, "but tell us what occurred next."

"I looked around the nursery, but I was all alone here with the babies. Then it came again, louder, this time, and seemingly right above me. I looked up at the skylight, and—there it was!

"It was a face, sir—just a face, with no body to it, and it seemed to float above the glass, then dip down to it, like a child's balloon drifting in the wind, and it looked right past me, down at Baby Tantavul, and laughed again."

"A face, you say, *Mademoiselle*—"

"Yes, sir, yes! The most awful face I've ever seen. It was thin and wrinkled—all shrivelled like a monkey—and as it looked at Baby Tantavul its eyes stretched open till their whites glared all around the irises, and the mouth opened, not widely, but as if it were chewing something it relished—and it gave that dreadful, cackling, jubilating laugh again. That's it! I couldn't think before, but it seemed as if that bodiless head were laughing with a sort of evil triumph, Dr. de Grandin!"

"H'm," he tweaked his tightly waxed mustache, "I should not wonder if it did, Mademoiselle," To me he whispered, "Stay with her, if you will, my friend, I'll see the supervisor and have her send another nurse to keep her company. I shall request a special watch for the small Tantavul. At present I do not think the danger is great, but—mice do not play where cats are wakeful."

"**I**SN'T HE JUST LOVELY?" Arabella looked up from the small bald head that rested on her breast, and ecstasy was in her eyes. "I don't believe I ever saw so beautiful a baby!"

"*Tiens*, Madame, his voice is excellent, at any rate," de Grandin answered with a grin, "and from what one may observe his appetite is excellent, at well."

Arabella smiled and patted the small creature's back. "You know, I never had a doll in my life," she confided. "Now I've got this dear little mite, and I'm going to be so happy with him. Oh, I wish Uncle Warburg were alive. I know this darling baby would soften even his hard heart.

"But I mustn't say such things about him, must I? He really wanted me to marry Dennis, didn't he? His will proved that. You think he wanted us to marry, Doctor?"

"I am persuaded that he did, Madame. Your marriage was his dearest wish, his fondest hope," the Frenchman answered solemnly.

"I felt that way, too. He was harsh and cruel to us when we were growing up, and kept his stony-hearted attitude to the end, but underneath it all there must have been some hidden stratum of kindness, some lingering affection for Dennis and me, or he'd never have put that clause in his will—"

"Nor have left this memorandum for you," de Grandin interrupted, drawing from an inner pocket the parchment envelope Dennis had entrusted to him the day before his father's funeral.

She started back as if he menaced her with a live scorpion, and instinctively her arms closed protectively around the baby at her bosom. "The—that—letter?" she faltered, her breath coming in short, smothered gasps. "I'd forgotten all about it. Oh, Dr. de Grandin, burn it. Don't let me see what's in it. I'm afraid!"

It was a bright May morning, without sufficient breeze to stir the leaflets on the maple trees outside the window, but as de Grandin held the letter out I thought I heard a sudden sweep of wind around the angle of the hospital, not loud, but shrewd and keen, like wind among the graveyard evergreens in autumn, and, curiously, there seemed a note of soft malicious laughter mingled with it.

The little Frenchman heard it, too, and for an instant he looked toward the window, and I thought I saw the flicker of an ugly sneer take form beneath the waxed ends of his mustache.

"Open it, *Madame*," he bade. "It is for you and Monsieur Dennis, and the little *Monsieur Bébé* here."

"I—I daren't—"

"*Tenez*, then Jules de Grandin does!" with his penknife he slit the heavy envelope, pressed suddenly against its ends so that its sides bulged, and dumped its contents on the counterpane. Ten fifty-dollar bills dropped on the coverlet. And nothing else.

"Five hundred dollars!" Arabella gasped. "Why—"

"A birthday gift for *petit Monsieur Bébé*, one surmises," laughed de Grandin. "*Eh bien*, the old one had a sense of humour underneath his ugly outward shell, it seems. He kept you on the tenterhooks lest the message in this envelope contained dire things, while all the time it was a present of congratulation."

"But such a gift from Uncle Warburg—I can't understand it!"

"Perhaps that is as well, too, *Madame*. Be happy in the gift and give your ancient uncle credit for at least one act of kindness. *Au 'voir*."

"HANGED IF I CAN understand it, either," I confessed as we left the hospital. "If that old curmudgeon had left a message berating them for fools for having offspring, or even a new will that disinherited them both, it would have been in character, but such a gift—well, I'm surprised."

Amazingly, he halted in midstep and laughed until the tears rolled down his face. "*You* are surprised!" he told me when he managed to regain his breath, "*Cordieu*, my friend, I do not drink that you are half as much surprised as Monsieur Warburg Tantavul!"

DENNIS TANTAVUL REGARDED ME with misery-haunted eyes. "I just can't understand it," he admitted. "It's all so sudden, so utterly—"

"*Pardonnez-moi*," de Grandin interrupted from the door of the consulting room, "I could not help but hear your voice, and if it is not an intrusion—"

"Not at all, sir," the young man answered. "I'd like the benefit of your advice. It's Arabella, and I'm terribly afraid she's—"

"*Non*, do not try it, *mon ami*," de Grandin warned. "Do you give us the symptoms, let us make the diagnosis. He who acts as his own doctor has a fool for a patient, you know."

"Well, then, here are the facts: This morning Arabella woke me up, crying as if her heart would break. I asked her what the trouble was, and she looked at me as if I were a stranger—no, not exactly that, rather as if I were some dreadful thing she'd suddenly found at her side. Her eyes were positively round with horror, and when I tried to take her in my arms to comfort her she shrank away as if I were infected with the plague.

"'Oh, Dennie, don't!' she begged and positively cringed away from me. Then she sprang out of bed and drew her kimono around her as if she were ashamed to have me see her in her pyjamas, and ran out of the room.

"Presently I heard her crying in the nursery, and when I followed her in there—" He paused and tears came to his eyes. "She was standing by the crib where little Dennis lay, and in her hand she held a long sharp steel letter-opener. 'Poor little mite, poor little flower of unpardonable sin,' she said. 'We've got to go, Baby darling; you to limbo, I to hell—oh, God wouldn't, *couldn't* be so cruel as to damn you for our sin!—but we'll all three suffer torment endlessly, because we didn't know!'

"She raised the knife to plunge it in the little fellow's heart, and he stretched out his hands and laughed and cooed as the sunlight shone on the steel. I was on her in an instant, wrenching the knife from her with one hand and holding her against me with the other, but she fought me off.

"'Don't touch me, Dennie, please, *please* don't,' she begged. I know it's mortal sin, but I love you so, my dear, that I just can't resist you if I let you put your arms about me.'

"I tried to kiss her, but she hid her face against my shoulder and moaned as if in pain when she felt my lips against her neck. Then she went limp in my arms, and I carried her, unconscious but still moaning piteously, into her sitting room and laid her on the couch. I left Sarah the nurse-maid with her, with strict orders not to let her leave the room. Can't you come over right away?"

De Grandin's cigarette had burned down till it threatened his mustache, and in his little round blue eyes there was a look of murderous rage. "*Bête!*" he murmured savagely. "*Sale chameau*, species of a stinking goat! This is his doing, undoubtedly. Come, my friends, let us rush, hasten, fly. I would talk with Madame Arabella."

"NAW, SUH, SHE'S DONE gone," the portly colored nursemaid told us when we asked for Arabella. "Th' baby started squealin' sumpin awful right after Mistu Dennis lef', an' Ah knowed it wuz time fo' his breakfas', so Mis' Arabella wuz layin' nice an' still on the' sofa, an' Ah says ter her, Ah says, 'Yuh lay still dere, honey, whilst Ah goes an' sees after yo' baby;' so Ah goes ter th' nursery, an' fixes him all up, an' carries him back ter th' settin'-room where Mis' Arabella wuz, an' she ain't there no more. Naw, suh."

"I thought I told you—" Dennis began furiously, but de Grandin laid a hand upon his arm.

"Do not upbraid her, *mon ami*, she did wisely, though she knew it not; she was with the small one all the while, so no harm came to him. Was it not better so, after what you witnessed in the morning?"

"Ye-es," the other grudgingly admitted, "I suppose so. But Arabella—"

"Let us see if we can find a trace of her," the Frenchman interrupted. "Look carefully, do you miss any of her clothing?"

Dennis looked about the pretty chintz-hung room. "Yes," he decided as he finished his inspection, "her dress was on that lounge and her shoes and stockings on the floor beneath it. They're all gone."

"So," de Grandin nodded. "Distracted as she seemed, it is unlikely she would have stopped to dress had she not planned on going out. Friend Trowbridge, will you kindly call police headquarters and inform them of the situation? Ask to have all exits to the city watched."

As I picked up the telephone he and Dennis started on a room-by-room inspection of the house.

"Find anything?" I asked as I hung up the 'phone after talking with the missing persons bureau.

"*Corbleu*, but I should damn say yes!" de Grandin answered as I joined them in the upstairs living room. "Look yonder, if you please, my friend."

The room was obviously the intimate apartment of the house. Electric lamps under painted shades were placed beside deep leather-covered easy chairs, ivory-enamelled bookshelves lined the walls to a height of four feet or so, upon their tops was a litter of gay, unconsidered trifles—cinnabar cigarette boxes, bits of hammered brass. Old china, blue and red and purple, glowed mellowly from open spaces on the shelves, its colors catching up and accenting the muted blues and reds of antique Hamadan carpet. A Paisley shawl was draped scarfwise across the baby grand piano in one corner.

Directly opposite the door a carven crucifix was standing on the bookcase top. It was an exquisite bit of Italian work, the cross of ebony, the corpus of old ivory, and so perfectly executed that though it was a scant six inches high, one could note the tense, tortured muscles of the pendent body, the straining throat which overfilled with groans of agony, the brow all knotted and bedewed with the cold sweat of torment. Upon the statue's thorn-crowned head, where it made a bright iridescent halo, was a band of gem-encrusted platinum, a woman's diamond-studded wedding ring.

"*Hélas*, it is love's crucifixion!" whispered Jules de Grandin.

THREE MONTHS WENT BY, and though the search kept up unremittingly, no trace of Arabella could be found. Dennis Tantavul installed a fulltime highly trained and recommended nurse in his desolate house, and spent his time haunting police stations and newspaper offices. He aged a decade in the ninety days since Arabella left; his shoulders stooped, his footsteps lagged, and a look of constant misery lay in his eyes. He was a prematurely old and broken man.

"It's the most uncanny thing I ever saw," I told de Grandin as we walked through West Forty-Second Street toward the West Shore Ferry. We had gone over to New York for some surgical supplies, and I do not drive my car in the metropolis. Truck drivers there are far too careless and repair bills for wrecked mudguards far too high. "How a full-grown woman would evaporate this way is something I can't understand. Of course, she may have done away with herself, dropped off a ferry, or—"

"S-s-st," his sibilated admonition cut me short. "That woman there, my friend, observe her, if you please." He nodded toward a female figure twenty feet or so ahead of us.

I looked, and wondered at his sudden interest at the draggled hussy. She was dressed in tawdry finery much the worse for wear. The sleazy silken skirt was much too tight, the cheap fur jaquette far too short and snug, and the high heels of her satin shoes were shockingly run over. Makeup was fairly plastered on her cheeks and lips and eyes, and short black hair bristled untidily beneath the brim of her abbreviated hat. Written unmistakably upon her was the nature of her calling, the oldest and least honorable profession known to womanhood.

"Well," I answered tartly, "what possible interest can you have in a—"

"Do not walk so fast," he whispered as his fingers closed upon my arm, "and do not raise your voice. I would that we should follow her, but I do not wish that she should know."

The neighborhood was far from savory, and I felt uncomfortably conspicuous as we turned from Forty-Second Street into Eleventh Avenue in the wake of the young strumpet, followed her provocatively swaying hips down two malodorous blocks, finally pausing as she slipped furtively into the doorway of a filthy, unkempt "rooming house."

We trailed her through a dimly lighted barren hall and up a flight of shadowy stairs, then up two further flights until we reached a sort of oblong foyer bounded on one end by the stair-well, on the farther extremity by a barred and very dirty window, and on each side by sagging, paint-blistered doors. On each of these was pinned a card, handwritten with the many flourishes dear to the chirography of the professional card-writer who still does business in the poorer quarters of our great cities. The air was heavy with the odor of cheap whisky, bacon rind and fried onions.

We made a hasty circuit of the hill, studying the cardboard labels. On the farthest door the notice read *Miss Sieglinde*.

"*Mon Dieu*," he exclaimed as he read it, "*c'est le mot propre!*"

"Eh?" I returned.

"Sieglinde, do not you recall her?"

"No-o, can't say I do. The only Sieglinde I remember is the character in Wagner's *Die Walkure* who unwittingly became her brother's paramour and bore him a son—"

"*Précisément.* Let us enter, if you please." Without pausing to knock he turned the handle of the door and stepped into the squalid room.

The woman sat upon the unkempt bed, her hat pushed back from her brow. In one hand she held a cracked teacup, with the other she poised a whisky bottle over it. She had kicked her scuffed and broken shoes off; we saw that she was stockingless, and her bare feet were dark with long-accumulated dirt and blacknailed as a miner's hands. "Get out!" she ordered thickly. "Get out o' here, I ain't receivin'—" a gasp broke her utterance, and she turned her head away quickly.

Then: "Get out o' here, you lousy bums!" she screamed. "Who d'ye think you are, breakin' into a lady's room like this? Get out, or—"

De Grandin eyed her steadily, and as her strident command wavered: "Madame Arabella, we have come to take you home," he announced softly.

"Good God, man, you're crazy" I exclaimed. "Arabella? This—"

"Precisely, my old one; this is Madame Arabella Tantavul whom we have sought these many months in vain." Crossing the room in two quick strides he seized the cringing woman by the shoulders and turned her face up to the light. I looked, and felt a sudden swift attack of nausea.

He was right. Thin to emaciation, her face already lined with the deep-bitten scars of evil living, the woman on the bed was Arabella Tantavul, though the shocking change wrought in her features and the black dye in her hair had disguised her so effectively that I should not have known her.

"We have come to take you home, *ma pauvre*," he repeated. "Your husband—"

"My husband!" her reply was half a scream. "Dear God, as if I had a husband—"

"And the little one who needs you," he continued. "You cannot leave them thus, Madame."

"I can't? Ah, that's where you're wrong, Doctor. I can never see my baby again, in this world or the next. Please go away and forget you've see me, or I shall have to drown myself—I've tried it twice already, but the first time I was rescued, and the second time my courage failed. But if you try to take me back, or if you tell Dennis you saw me—"

"Tell me, Madame," he broke in, "was not your flight caused by a visitation from the dead?"

Her faded brown eyes—eyes that had been such a startling contrast to her pale-gold hair—widened. "How did you know?" she whispered.

"*Tiens*, one may make surmises. Will not you tell us just what happened? I think there is a way out of your difficulties."

"No, no, there isn't; there can't be!" Her head drooped listlessly. "He planned his work too well; all that's left for me is death—and damnation afterward."

"But if there were a way—if I could show it to you?"

"Can you repeal the laws of God?"

"I am a very clever person, *Madame*. Perhaps I can accomplish an evasion, if not an absolute repeal. Now tell us, how and when did *Monsieur* your late but not at all lamented uncle come to you?"

"The night before—before I went away. I woke about midnight, thinking I heard a cry from Dennie's nursery. When I reached the room where he was sleeping I saw my uncle's face glaring at me through the window. It seemed to be illuminated by a sort of inward hellish light, for it stood out against the darkness like a jack-o'-lantern, and it smiled an awful smile at me. 'Arabella,' it said, and

I could see its dun dead lips writhe back as if the teeth were burning-hot, 'I've come to tell you that your marriage is a mockery and a lie. The man you married is your brother, and the child you bore is doubly illegitimate. You can't continue living with them, Arabella. That would be an even greater sin. You must leave them right away, or'—Once more his lips crept back until his teeth were bare—'or I shall come to visit you each night, and when the baby has grown old enough to understand I'll tell him who his parents really are. Take your choice, my daughter. Leave them and let me go back to the grave, or stay and see me every night and know that I will tell your son when he is old enough to understand. If I do it he will loathe and hate you; curse the day you bore him.'

"'And you'll promise never to come near Dennis or the baby if I go?' I asked.

"He promised, and I staggered back to bed, where I fell fainting.

"Next morning when I wakened I was sure it had been a bad dream, but when I looked at Dennis and my own reflection in the glass I knew it was no dream, but a dreadful visitation from the dead.

"Then I went mad. I tried to kill my baby, and when Dennis stopped me I watched my chance to run away, came over to New York and took to this." She looked significantly around the miserable room. "I knew they'd never look for Arabella Tantavul among the city's whores; I was safer from pursuit right here than if I'd been in Europe or China."

"But, *Madame*," de Grandin's voice was jubilant with shocked reproof, "that which you saw was nothing but a dream; a most unpleasant dream, I grant, but still a dream. Look in my eyes, if you please!"

She raised her eyes to his, and I saw his pupils widen as a cat's do in the dark, saw a line of white outline the cornea, and, responsive to his piercing gaze, beheld her brown eyes set in a fixed stare, first as if in fright, then with a glaze almost like that of death.

"Attend me, Madame Arabella," he commanded softly. "You are tired—*grand Dieu*, how tired you are! You have suffered greatly, but you are about to rest. Your memory of that night is gone; so is all memory of the things which have transpired since. You will move and eat and sleep as you are bidden, but of what takes place around you till I bid you wake you will retain no recollection. Do you hear me, Madame Arabella?"

"I hear," she answered softly in a small tired voice.

"*Très bon.* Lie down, my little poor one. Lie down to rest and dreams of love. Sleep, rest, dream and forget.

"Will you be good enough to 'phone to Dr. Wyckoff?" he asked me. "We shall place her in his sanitarium, wash this *sacré* dye from her hair and nurse her back to health; then when all is ready we can bear her home and have her take up life and love where she left off. No one shall be the wiser. This chapter of her life is closed and sealed for ever.

"Each day I'll call upon her and renew hypnotic treatments that she may simulate the mild but curable mental case which we shall tell the good Wyckoff she is. When finally I release her from hypnosis her mind will be entirely cleared of that bad dream that nearly wrecked her happiness."

ARABELLA TANTAVUL LAY ON the sofa in her charming boudoir, an orchid negligee about her slender shoulders, an eiderdown rug tucked round her feet and knees. Her wedding ring was once more on her finger. Pale with a pallor not to be disguised by the most skillfully applied cosmetics, and with deep violet crescents underneath her amber eyes, she lay back listlessly, drinking in the cheerful warmth that emanated from the fire of apple-logs that snapped and crackled on the hearth. Two months of rest at Dr. Wyckoff's sanitarium had cleansed the marks of dissipation from her face, and the ministrations of beauticians had restored the pale-gold luster to her hair, but the listlessness that followed her complete breakdown was still upon her like the weakness from a fever.

"I can't remember anything about my illness, Dr. Trowbridge," she told me with a weary little smile, "but vaguely I connect it with some dreadful dream I had. And"—she wrinkled her smooth forehead in an effort at remembering—"I think I had a rather dreadful dream last night, but—"

"Ah-*ha?*" de Grandin leant abruptly forward in his chair. "What was it that you dreamed, Madame?"

"I—don't—know," she answered slowly. "Odd, isn't it, how you can remember that a dream was so unpleasant, yet not recall its details? Somehow, I connect it with Uncle Warburg; but—"

"*Parbleu*, do you say so? Has he returned? *Ah hah*, he makes me to be so mad, that one!"

"IT IS TIME WE went, my friend," de Grandin told me as the tall clock in the hall beat out its tenth deliberate stroke; "we have important duties to perform."

"For goodness' sake," I protested, "at this hour o' night?"

"Precisely. At Monsieur Tantavul's I shall expect a visitor tonight, and—we must be ready for him.

"Is Madame Arabella sleeping?" he asked Dennis as he answered our ring at the door.

"Like a baby," answered the young husband. "I've been sitting by her all evening, and I don't believe she even turned in bed."

"And you did keep the window closed, as I requested?"

"Yes, sir; closed and latched."

"*Bien*. Await us here, *mon brave*; we shall rejoin you presently."

He led the way to Arabella's bedroom, removed the wrappings from a bulky parcel he had lugged from our house, and displayed the object thus disclosed with an air of inordinate pride. "Behold him," he commanded gleefully. "Is he not magnificent?"

"Why—what the devil?—it's nothing but an ordinary window screen," I answered.

"A window screen, I grant, my friend; but not an ordinary one. Can not you see it is of copper?"

"Well—"

"*Parbleu*, but I should say it is well," he grinned. "Observe him, how he works."

From his kit bag he produced a roll of insulated wire, an electrical transformer, and some tools. Working quickly he passe-partouted the screen's wooden frame with electrician's tape, then plugged a wire in a nearby lamp socket, connected it with the transformer, and from the latter led a double strand of cotton-wrapped wire to the screen. This he clipped firmly to the copper meshes and led a third strand to the metal grille of the heat register. Last of all he filled a bulb-syringe with water and sprayed the screen, repeating the performance till it sparkled like a cobweb in the morning sun. "And now, *Monsieur le Revenant*," he chuckled as he finished, "I damn think all is ready for your warm reception!"

For something like an hour we waited, then he tiptoed to the bed and bent above Arabella.

"Madame!"

The girl stirred slightly, murmuring some half-audible response, and:

"In half an hour you will rise," he told her. "You will put your robe on and stand by the window, but on no account will you go near it or lay hands on it. Should anyone address you from outside you will reply, but you will not remember what you say or what is said to you."

He motioned me to follow, and we left the room, taking station in the hallway just outside.

How long we waited I have no accurate idea. Perhaps it was an hour, perhaps less; at any rate the silent vigil seemed unending, and I raised my hand to stifle back a yawn when:

"Yes, Uncle Warburg, I can hear you," we heard Arabella saying softly in the room beyond the door.

We tiptoed to the entry: Arabella stood before the window, and from beyond it glared the face of Warburg Tantavul.

It was dead, there was no doubt about that. In sunken cheek and pinched-in nose and yellowish-grey skin there showed the evidence of death and early putrefaction, but dead through it was, it was also animated with a dreadful sort of life.

The eyes were glaring horribly, the lips were red as though they had been painted with fresh blood.

"You hear me, do you?" it demanded. "Then listen, girl; you broke your bargain with me, now I'm come to keep my threat: every time you kiss your husband"—a shriek of bitter laughter cut his words, and his staring eyes half closed with hellish merriment—"or the child you love so well, my shadow will be on you. You've kept me out thus far, but some night I'll get in, and—"

The lean dead jaw dropped, then snapped up as if lifted by sheer will-power, and the whole expression of the corpse-face changed. Surprise, incredulous delight, anticipation as before a feast were pictured on it. "Why"—its cachinnating laughter sent a chill up my spine—"why your window's open! You've changed the screen and I can enter!"

Slowly, like a child's balloon stirred by a vagrant wind, the awful thing moved closer to the window. Closer to the screen it came, and Arabella gave ground before it and put up her hands to shield her eyes from the sight of its hellish grin of triumph.

"*Sapristi*," swore de Grandin softly. "Come on, my old and evil one, come but a little nearer—"

The dead thing floated nearer. Now its mocking mouth and shriveled, pointed nose were almost pressed against the copper meshes of the screen; now they began to filter through the meshes like a wisp of fog—

There was a blinding flash of blue-white flame, the sputtering gush of fusing metal, a wild, despairing shriek that ended ere it fairly started in a sob of mortal torment, and the sharp and acrid odor of burned flesh!

"Arabella—darling—is she all right?" Dennis Tantavul came charging up the stairs. "I thought I heard a scream—"

"You did, my friend," de Grandin answered, "but I do not think that you will hear its repetition unless you are unfortunate enough to go to hell when you have died."

"What was it?"

"*Eh bien*, one who thought himself a clever jester pressed his jest too far. Meantime, look to *Madame* your wife. See how peacefully she lies upon her bed. Her time for evil dreams is past. Be kind to her, *mon jeune*. Do not forget, a woman loves to have a lover, even though he is her husband." He bent and kissed the sleeping girl upon the brow. "*Au 'voir*, my little lovely one," he murmured. Then, to me:

"Come, Trowbridge, my good friend. Our work is finished here. Let us leave them to their happiness."

A N HOUR LATER IN the study he faced me across the fire. "Perhaps you'll deign to tell me what it's all about now?" I asked sarcastically.

"Perhaps I shall," he answered with a grin. "You will recall that this annoying Monsieur Who Was Dead Yet Not Dead, appeared and grinned most horrifyingly through windows several times? Always from the outside, please remember. At the hospital, where he nearly caused the *garde-malade* to have a fit, he laughed and mouthed at her through the glass skylight. When he first appeared and threatened Madame Arabella he spoke to her through the window—"

"But her window was open," I protested.

"Yes, but screened," he answered with a smile. "Screened with iron wire, if you please."

"What difference did that make? Tonight I saw him almost force his features through—"

"A copper screen," he supplied. "Tonight the screen was copper; me, I saw to that."

Then, seeing my bewilderment: "Iron is the most earthy of all metals," he explained. "It and its derivative, steel, are so instinct with the earth's essence that creatures of the spirit cannot stand its nearness. The legends tell us that when Solomon's Temple was constructed no tool of iron was employed, because even the friendly *jinn* whose help he had enlisted could not perform their tasks in close proximity to iron. The witch can be detected by the pricking of an iron pin—never by a pin of brass.

"Very well. When first I thought about the evil dead one's reappearances I noted that each time he stared outside the window. Glass, apparently, he could not pass—and glass contains a modicum of iron. Iron window-wire stopped him. 'He are not a true ghost, then,' I inform me. 'They are things of spirit only, they are thoughts made manifest. This one is a thing of hate, but also of some physical material as well; he is composed in part of emanations from the body which lies putrefying in the grave. *Voilà*, if he have physical properties he can be destroyed by physical means.'

"And so I set my trap. I procured a screen of copper through which he could effect an entrance, but I charged it with electricity. I increased the potential of the current with a step-up transformer to make assurance doubly sure, and then I waited for him like the spider for the fly, waited for him to come through that charged screen and electrocute himself. Yes, certainly."

"But is he really destroyed?" I asked dubiously.

"As the candle-flame when one has blown it out. He was—how do you say it?—short-circuited. No malefactor in the chair of execution ever died more thoroughly than that one, I assure you."

"It seems queer, though, that he should come back from the grave to haunt those poor kids and break up their marriage when he really wanted it," I murmured wonderingly.

"Wanted it? Yes, as the trapper wants the bird to step within his snare."

"But he gave them such a handsome present when little Dennis was born—"

"*La, la,* my good, kind, trusting friend, you are *naïf.* The money I gave Madame Arabella was my own. I put it in that envelope."

"Then what was the real message?"

"It was a dreadful thing, my friend; a dreadful, wicked thing. The night that Monsieur Dennis left that package with me I determined that the old one meant to do him in, so I steamed the cover open and read what lay within. It made plain the things which Dennis thought that he remembered.

"Long, long ago Monsieur Tantavul lived in San Francisco. His wife was twenty years his junior, and a pretty, joyous thing she was. She bore him two fine children, a boy and girl, and on them she bestowed the love which he could not appreciate. His surliness, his evil temper, his constant fault-finding drove her to distraction, and finally she sued for divorce.

"But he forestalled her. He spirited the children away, then told his wife the plan of his revenge. He would take them to some far off place and bring them up believing they were cousins. Then when they had attained full growth he would induce them to marry and keep the secret of their relationship until they had a child, then break the dreadful truth to them. Thereafter they would live on, bound together by their fear of censure, or perhaps of criminal prosecution, but their consciences would cause them endless torment, and the very love they had for each other would be like fetters forged of white-hot steel, holding them in odious bondage from which there was no escape. The sight of their children would be a reproach to them, the mere thought of love's sweet communion would cause revulsion to the point of nausea.

"When he had told her this his wife went mad. He thrust her into an asylum and left her there to die while he came with his babies to New Jersey, where he reared them together, and by guile and craftiness nurtured their love, knowing that when finally they married he would have his so vile revenge."

"But, great heavens, man, they're brother and sister!" I exclaimed in horror.

"Perfectly," he answered coolly. "They are also man and woman, husband and wife, and father and mother."

"But—but—" I stammered, utterly at loss for words.

"But me no buts, good friend. I know what you would say. Their child? *Ah bah,* did not the kings of ancient times repeatedly take their own sisters to wife, and were not their offspring sound and healthy? But certainly. Did not both Darwin and Wallace fail to find foundation for the doctrine that cross-breeding between healthy people with clean blood is productive of inferior progeny? Look at little Monsieur Dennis. Were you not blinded by your silly, unrealistic training and tradition—did you not know his parents' near relationship—you would not hesitate to pronounce him an unusually fine, healthy child.

"Besides," he added earnestly, "they love each other, not as brother and sister, but as man and woman. He is her happiness, she is his, and little Monsieur Dennis is the happiness of both. Why destroy this joy—*le bon Dieu* knows they earned it by a joyless childhood—when I can preserve it for them by simply keeping silent?"

Hands of the Dead

"IF THERE WERE SUCH a thing as a platinum blond tom-cat, I'm sure it would look like Doctor de Grandin." My dinner partner, a long-eyed, sleek-haired brunette in a black-crêpe gown cut to the base of her throat in front and slashed in a V below the waist behind, gestured with her oddly oblique eyes across the table toward Jules de Grandin. "He's a funny little fellow—rather a darling, though," Miss Travers added. "Just see how he looks at Virginia Bushrod; wouldn't you think she was a particularly luscious specimen of sparrow, and he—"

"Why should he watch Miss Bushrod, particularly?" I countered. "She's very lovely, but—"

"Oh, I don't think he's interested in her face, pretty as it is," Miss Travers laughed. "He's watching her hands. Everybody does."

I looked along the candle-lighted table with its ornate Georgian silver and lace-and-linen cloth until my eye came to rest upon Virginia Bushrod. Latest of the arrivals at the Merridews' house party, she was also probably the most interesting. You could not judge her casually. A pale, white skin, lightly tanned on beach and tennis court, amber eyes, shading to brown, hair waved and parted in dull-gold ringlets, curled closely on the back curve of her small and shapely head. The dead-white gown she wore set off her bright, blond beauty, and a pair of heavy gold bracelets, tight-clasped about her wrists, drew notice to her long and slender hands.

They were extraordinary hands. Not large, not small, their shapeliness was statuesque, their form as perfect as a sculptor's dream, with straight and supple fingers and a marvelous grace of movement expressive as a spoken word. Almost, it seemed to me as she raised the spun-glass Venetian goblet of Madeira, her hands possessed an independent being of their own; a consciousness of volition which made them not a mere part of her body, but something allied with, though not subservient to it.

"Her hands are rarely beautiful," I commented. "What is she, an actress? A dancer, perhaps—"

"No," said Miss Travers, and her voice sank to a confidential whisper, "but a year ago we thought she'd be a hopeless cripple all her life. Both hands were mangled in a motor accident."

"But that's impossible," I scoffed, watching Miss Bushrod's graceful gestures with renewed interest. "I've been in medicine almost forty years; no hands which suffered even minor injuries could be as flexible as hers."

"They did, just the same," Miss Travers answered stubbornly. "The doctors gave up hope, and said they'd have to amputate them at the wrist; her father told me so. Virginia gave Phil Connor back his ring and was ready to resign herself to a life of helplessness when—"

"Yes?" I smiled as she came to a halt. Lay versions of medical miracles are always interesting to the doctor, and I was anxious to learn how the "hopeless cripple" had been restored to perfect manual health.

"Doctor Augensburg came over here, and they went to him as a last resort—"

"I should think they would," I interjected. Augensburg, half charlatan, a quarter quack, perhaps a quarter genius, was a fair example of the army of medical marvels which periodically invades America. He was clever as a workman, we all admitted that, and in some operations of glandular transplanting had achieved remarkable results, but when he came out with the statement that he had discovered how to make synthetic flesh for surgical repair work the medical societies demanded that he prove his claims or stop the grand triumphal tour that he was making of his clinics. He failed to satisfy his critics and returned to Austria several thousand dollars richer, but completely discredited in medical circles.

"Well, they went to him," Miss Travers answered shortly, "and you see what he accomplished. He—"

Her argument was stilled as Jane Merridew, who acted as her brother's hostess, gave the signal for the ladies to retire.

CHINESE LANTERNS, ORANGE, RED, pale jade, blossomed in the darkness of the garden. Farther off the vine-draped wall cast its shadow over close-clipped grass and winding flagstone paths; there were rustic benches underneath the ginkgo trees; a drinking-fountain fashioned like a lion's head with water flushing in an arc between its gaping jaws sent a musically mellow tinkle through the still night air. I sighed regretfully as I followed the men into the billiard room. The mid-Victorian custom of enforced separation of men and women for a period after dinner had always seemed to me a relic of the past we might well stuff and donate to a museum.

"Anybody want to play?" Ralph Chapman took a cue down from the rack and rubbed its felt-tipped end with chalk. "Spot you a dollar a shot, Phil; are you on?"

"Not I," the youth addressed responded with a grin. "You took me into camp last time. Go get another victim."

Young Chapman set the balls out on the table, surveyed them critically a moment, then, taking careful aim, made a three-cushion shot, and followed it with another which bunched the gleaming spheres together in one corner.

De Grandin raised a slender, well-manicured hand and patted back a yawn. "*Mon Dieu*," he moaned to me, "it is sad! Outside there is the beauty of the night and of the ladies, and we, *pardieu*, we sit and swelter here like a pack of *sacré* fools while he knocks about the relics of departed elephants. Me, I have enough. I go to join the ladies, if—"

"May I try, Ralph?" Glowing in defiant gayety, lips wine-moist, eyes bright and wandering, Virginia Bushrod poised upon the threshold of the wide French window which let out on the terrace. "I've never played," she added, "but tonight I feel an urge for billiards; I've got a yen to knock the little balls around, if you know what I mean."

"Never too late to learn," young Chapman grinned at her. "I'm game; I'll pay you five for every kiss you make."

"Kiss?" she echoed, puzzled.

"Kiss is right, infant. A purely technical term. See, here's a kiss." Deftly he brought the balls together in light contact, paused a moment, then with a quick flick of his cue repeated the maneuver twice, thrice, four times.

"O-oh, I see." Her eyes were bright with something more than mere anticipation. It seemed to me they shone like those of a drunkard long deprived of drink when liquor is at last accessible.

"See here, you take the stick like this," began young Chapman, but the girl brushed past him, took a cue down from the rack and deftly rubbed the cube of chalk against its tip.

She leant across the table, her smooth brow furrowed in a frown of concentration, thrust the cue back and forth across her fingers tentatively; then swiftly as a striking snake the smooth wood darted forward. Around the table went the cue ball, taking the cushions at a perfect angle. *Click-click*, the ivory spheres kissed each other softly, then settled down a little way apart, their polished surfaces reflecting the bright lamplight.

"Bravo, Virginia!" cried Ralph Chapman. "I couldn't have made a better shot myself. Talk about beginner's luck!"

The girl, apparently, was deaf. Eyes shining, lips compressed, she leant across the table, darted forth her cue and made an expert draw shot, gathering the balls together as though they had been magnetized. Then followed a quick volley shot, the cue ball circled round the table, spun sharply in reverse English and kissed the other balls with so light an impact that the click was hardly audible.

Again and again she shot, driving her cue ball relentlessly home against the others, never missing, making the most difficult shots with the sure precision betokening long mastery of the game. Fever-eyed, white-faced, oblivious to all about her, she made shot follow shot until a hundred marks had been run off, and it seemed to me that she was sating some fierce craving as she bent above the table, cue in hand.

Phil Connor, her young fiancé, was as puzzled as the rest, watching her inimitable skill first with wonder, then with something like stark fear. At last: "Virginia!" he cried, seizing her by the elbow and fairly dragging her away. "Virginia honey, you've played enough."

"Oh?" An oddly puzzled look gathered between her slim brows, and she shook her head from side to side, like a waking sleeper who would clear his brain of dreams. "Did I do well?"

"Very well. Very well, indeed, for one who never played the game before," Ralph Chapman told her coldly.

"But, Ralph, I never did," she answered. "Honestly, I never had a billiard cue in my hands before tonight!"

"No?" his tone was icy. "If this is your idea of being sporting—"

"See here, Chapman," young Connor's Irish blood was quick to take the implication up. "Ginnie's telling you the truth. There isn't a billiard table in her father's house or mine, there wasn't any in her sorority house; she's never had a chance to play. Don't you think I'd know it if she liked the game? I tell you it was luck; sheer luck—"

"At five dollars per lucky point?"

"Word of honor, Ralph," Miss Bushrod told him, "I—"

"You'll find my honor good as yours," he broke in frigidly. "I'll hand you my check for five hundred dollars in the morning, Miss—"

"Why, you dam' rotten swine, I'll break your neck!" Phil Connor leaped across the room, eyes flashing, face aflame; but:

"Gentlemen, this has gone quite far enough," Colonel Merridew's cold voice cut through the quarrel. "Chapman, apologize to Virginia. Connor, put your hands down!" Then, as the apology was grudgingly given:

"Shall we join the ladies, gentlemen?" asked Colonel Merridew.

"IT WAS A RATHER shoddy trick that Bushrod girl played on young Chapman, wasn't it?" I asked de Grandin as we prepared for bed. "He's a conceited pup, I grant, vain of his skill at billiards, and all that; but for her to play the wide-eyed innocent and let him offer her five dollars a point, when she's really in the championship class—well, it didn't seem quite sporting."

The little Frenchman eyed the glowing tip of his cigar in thoughtful silence for a moment; then: "I am not quite persuaded," he replied. "Mademoiselle Bushrod—*mon Dieu*, what a name!—appeared as much surprised as any—"

"But, man, did you notice her dexterity?" I cut in petulantly. "That manual skill—"

"*Précisément*," he nodded, "that manual skill, my friend. Did it not seem to you her hands betrayed a—how do you say him?—a knowledge which she herself did not possess?"

I shook my head in sheer exasperation. "You're raving," I assured him. "How the deuce—"

"*Tiens*, the devil knows, perhaps, not I," he broke in with a shrug. "Come, let us take a drink and go to bed."

He raised the chromium carafe from the bedside table, and: "Name of a devil!" he exclaimed in disappointment. "The thing holds water!"

"Of course it does, idiot," I assured him with a laugh. "You wanted a drink, didn't you?"

"A drink, but not a bath, *cordieu*. Come, species of an elephant, arise and follow me."

"Where?" I demanded.

"To find a drink; where else?" he answered with a grin. "There is a tray with glasses on the sideboard of the dining-room."

The big old house was silent as a tomb as we crept down the stairs, slipped silently along the central hall and headed for the dining-room. De Grandin paused abruptly, hand upraised, and, obedient to his signal, I, too, halted.

In the music room which opened from the hallway on the right, someone was playing the piano, very softly, with a beautiful harpsichord touch. The lovely, haunting sadness of the *Londonderry Air* came to us as we listened, the gently struck notes falling, one upon another, like water dripping from a lichened rock into a quiet woodland pool.

"Exquisite!" I began, but the Frenchman's hand raised to his lips cut short my commendation as he motioned me to follow.

Virginia Bushrod sat before the instrument, her long, slim fingers flitting fitfully across the ivory keys, the wide gold bracelets on her wrists agleam. Black-lace pajamas, less concealing than a whorl of smoke, revealed the gracious curves of her young body, with a subtle glow, as wisps of banking storm-clouds dim, but do not hide, the moon.

As we paused beside the door the sweet melody she played gave way to something else, a lecherous, macabre theme in C sharp minor, seductive and compelling, but revolting as a painted corpse already touched with putrefaction. Swaying gently to the rhythm of the music, she turned her face toward us, and in the wavering candlelight I saw her eyes were closed, long lashes sweeping against pale-gold cheeks, smooth, fine-veined eyelids gently lowered.

I turned to Jules de Grandin with a soundless question, and he nodded affirmation. "But yes, she sleeps, my friend," he whispered. "Do not waken her."

The music slowly sank to a thin echo, and Miss Bushrod rose with lowered lids and gently parted lips, swayed uncertainly a moment, then passed us with a slow and gliding step, her slim, bare feet soundless as a draft of air upon the rug-strewn door. Slowly she climbed the stairs, one shapely hand upon the carven balustrade, the dim night-light which burned up in the gallery picking little points of brightness from her golden wristlets.

"Probably neurotic," I murmured as I watched her turn left and disappear around the pillar at the stairhead. "They say she underwent an operation on her hands last year, and—"

De Grandin motioned me to silence as he teased the needle-points of his mustache between his thumb and finger. "Quite so," he said at length. "Precisely, exactly. One wonders."

"Wonders what?" I asked.

"How long we have to wait until we get that drink," he answered with a grin. "Come, let us get it quickly, or we need not go to bed at all."

BREAKFAST WAS NO FORMAL rite at Merridews'. A long buffet, ready-set with food and gay with raffia-bound Italian glassware, Mexican pottery and bowls, daisies, chicory and Queen Anne's lace, stood upon the terrace, while little tables, spread with bright-checked peasant linen, dotted the brick paving.

De Grandin piled a platter high with food, poured himself a cup of coffee and set to work upon the viands. "Tell me, good Friend Trowbridge," he commanded as he returned from the sideboard with a second generous helping of steamed sole, "what did you note, if anything, when we caught Mademoiselle Bushrod at her midnight music?"

I eyed him speculatively. When Jules de Grandin asked me questions such as that they were not based on idle curiosity.

"You're on the trail of something?" I evaded.

He spread his hands before him, imitating someone groping in the dark. "I think I am," he answered slowly, "but I can not say of what. Come, tell me what you noticed, if you please."

"Well," I bent my brows in concentration, "first of all, I'd say that she was sleep-walking; that she had no more idea what she was doing than I have what she's doing now."

He nodded acquiescence. "Precisely," he agreed. "And—"

"Then, I was struck by the fact that though she had apparently risen from bed, she had those thick, barbaric bracelets on her wrists."

"Holà, touché," he cried delightedly, "you have put the finger on it. It was unusual, was it not?"

"I'd say so," I agreed. "Then—why, bless my soul!" I paused in something like dismay as sudden recollection came to me.

He watched me narrowly, eyebrows raised.

"She turned the wrong way at the stairhead," I exclaimed. "The women's rooms are to the right of the stairs, the men's to the left. Don't you remember, Colonel Merridew said—"

"I remember perfectly," he cut in. "I also saw her turn that way, but preferred to have corroboration—"

The clatter of hoofs on the driveway cut short his remarks, and a moment later Virginia Bushrod joined us on the terrace. She looked younger and much smaller in her riding-clothes. White breeches, obviously of London cut, were topped by a white-linen peasant blouse, gay with wool embroidery, open at the throat, but with sleeves which came down to the gauntlets of her doeskin gloves. For belt she wore a brilliant knit-silk Roman scarf, and another like it knotted turbanwise around her head, its glowing reds and greens and yellows bringing out the charming colors of her vivid, laughing face. Black boots, reaching to the knee, encased her high-arched, narrow feet and slender legs.

"Hello, sleepy-heads," she greeted as she sat down at our table, "where've you been all morning? Making up for night calls and such things? I've been up for hours—and I'm famished."

"What will it be, *Mademoiselle?*" de Grandin asked as he leaped up nimbly to serve her; "a little toast, perhaps—a bowl of cereal?"

"Not for me," she denied, laughing. "I want a man's-sized breakfast. I've ridden fifteen miles this morning."

As she peeled off her white-chamois gloves I caught the glint of golden bracelets on her wrists.

"We enjoyed your playing, *Mademoiselle*," the little Frenchman told her smilingly as, obedient to her orders, he deposited a "man's-sized" plate of food before her. "The *Londonderry Air* is beautiful, but that other composition which you played with such *verve*, such feeling, it was—"

"Is this a joke?" Miss Bushrod looked at him through narrowed eyes. "If it is, I can't quite see the humor."

"*Mais non*, it is no jest, I do assure you. Music is one of my passions, and although I play but poorly, I enjoy to hear it. Your talent—"

"Then you've mistaken me for someone else," the girl cut in, a quick flush mounting to her face. "I'm one of those unfortunates who's utterly tone-deaf; I—"

"That's right," Christine Travers, virtually naked in a sun-back tennis blouse and shorts, emerged through the French windows and dropped down beside Miss Bushrod. "Ginnie's tone-deaf as an oyster. Couldn't carry a tune in a market basket."

"But, my dear young lady," I began, when a vicious kick upon my shin cut my protest short.

"Yes?" Miss Travers smiled her slow, somewhat malicious smile. "Were you going to tell Ginnie you've a remedy for tone-deafness, Doctor? Something nice and mild, like arsenic, or corrosive sublimate? If you'll just tell her how to take it, I'll see—"

"Doctar Trowbridge, Doctar de Grannun, suh, come quick, fo' de Lawd's sake!" Noah Blackstone, Merridew's stout colored butler, burst upon the terrace, his usual serene aplomb torn to shreds by sudden terror. "Come runnin', gen'lemens, sumpin awful's happened!"

"Eh, what is it you say?" de Grandin asked. "Something awful—"

"Yas, suh; sumpin dreadful. Mistu—Mistu Chapman's done been kilt. Sumbuddy's murdered 'im. He's daid!"

"Dead? Ralph Chapman?" Horror mounted in Virginia Bushrod's amber eyes as she seemed to look past us at some scene of stark tragedy. "Ralph Chapman—dead!" Unthinkingly, mechanically as another woman might have wrung her handkerchief in similar circumstances, she took the heavy silver fork with which she had been eating and bent it in a spiral.

SPRAWLED SUPINELY ACROSS THE bed, protruding eyes staring sightlessly at the ceiling Ralph Chapman lay, mouth slightly agape, tongue thrust forward. It needed no second glance to confirm the butler's diagnosis, and it required only a second glance to confirm his suspicion of murder, for in those bulging eyes and that protruding tongue, no less than in the area of bruise upon the throat, we read the autograph of homicide.

"So!" de Grandin gazed upon the body speculatively, then crossed the room, took the dead boy's face between his hands and raised the head. It was as if the head and body joined by a cord rather than a column of bone and muscle, for there was no resistance to the little Frenchman's slender hands as the young man's chin nodded upward. "Ah—so-o-o!" de Grandin murmured. "He used unnecessary violence, this one; see, my friend"—he turned the body half-way over and pointed to a purpling bruise upon the rear of the neck—"two hands were used. In front we have the murderer's thumb and finger marks; behind is ecchymosis due to counter-pressure. And so great a force was used that not only was this poor one strangled, but his neck was broken, as well."

He passed his fingers tentatively along the outline of young Chapman's jaw; then: "How long has he been dead, my friend?" he asked.

Following his example, I felt the dead boy's jaw, then his chest and lower throat. "H'm," I glanced at my watch, "my guess is six or seven hours. There's still some stiffening of the jaw, but not much in the chest, and the forearms are definitely hard—yes, I'd say six hours at the least, eight at the most, judging by the advance of *rigor mortis*. That would place the time of death—"

"Somewhere near midnight," he supplied. Then, irrelevantly: "They were strong hands that did this thing, my friend; the muscles of our necks are tough, our vertebræ are hard; yet this one's neck is snapped as though it were a reed."

"You—you've a suspicion?" I faltered.

"I think so," he returned, sweeping the room with a quick, stock-taking glance.

"Ah, what is this?" He strode across the rug, coming to pause before the bureau. On the hanging mirror of the cabinet, outlined plainly as an heraldic device blazoned on a coat of arms, was a handprint, long slender fingers, the mounts of the palm and the delicately sweeping curve of the heel etched on the gleaming surface, as though a hand, dank with perspiration, had been pressed upon it.

"Now," his slim black brows rose in saracenic arches as he regarded me quizzically, "for why should a midnight visitant especially if bent on murder, take pains to leave an autograph upon the mirror, good Friend Trowbridge?" he demanded.

"B-but that's a woman's hand," I stammered. "Whoever broke Ralph Chapman's neck was strong as a gorilla, you just said so. A woman—"

"Tell me, my friend," he interrupted, fixing me with that level, disconcerting stare of his, "do you not wish to see that justice triumphs?"

"Why, yes, of course, but—

"And is it your opinion—I ask you as a man of medicine—that a man's neck offers more resistance than, by example, a silver table-fork?"

I stared at him dumfounded. Ralph Chapman had publicly denounced Virginia Bushrod as a cheat; we had seen her going toward his room about the time of the murder; within five minutes we had seen her give a demonstration of manual strength scarcely to be equaled by a professional athlete. The evidence was damning, but—

"You're going to turn her over to the police?" I asked.

For answer he drew the green-silk handkerchief peeping from the pocket of his brown sports coat, wadded it into a mop and erased the handprint from the mirror. "Come, my friend," he ordered, "we must write out our report before the coroner arrives."

T HE MORTICIAN TO WHOM Coroner Lordon had entrusted Chapman's body obligingly lent his funeral chapel for the inquest. The jury, picked at random from the villagers, occupied the space customarily assigned to the remains. The coroner himself sat in the clergyman's enclosure. Witnesses were made comfortable in the family room, being called out one by one to testify. Through the curtained doorway leading to the chapel—ingeniously arranged to permit the mourning family to see and hear the funeral ceremonies without being seen by those assembled in the auditorium—we saw the butler testify to finding the body and heard him say he summoned de Grandin and me immediately.

"You give it as your medical opinion that death had taken place some six or seven hours earlier?" the coroner asked me.

"Yes, sir," I replied.

"And what, in your opinion, was the cause of death?"

"Without the confirmation of an autopsy I can only hazard an opinion," I returned, "but from superficial examination I should say it was due to respiratory failure caused by a dislocation of the spinal column and rupture of the cord. The dislocation, as nearly as I could judge from feeling of the neck, took place between the second and third cervical vertebræ."

"And how was the spinal fracture caused?"

"By manual pressure, sir—pressure with the hands. The bruises on the dead man's neck show the murderer grasped him by the throat at first, probably to stifle any outcry, then placed one hand behind his head and with the other forced the chin violently upward, thereby simulating the quick pressure given the neck in cases of judicial hanging."

"It would have required a man of more than usual strength to commit this murder in the manner you have described it?"

I drew a deep breath of relief. "Yes, sir, it would have had to be such a man," I answered, emphasizing the final word, unconsciously, perhaps.

"Thank you, Doctor," said the coroner, and called de Grandin to corroborate my testimony.

As the inquisition lengthened it became apparent Coroner Lordon had a theory of his own, which he was ingeniously weaving into evidence. Rather subtly he brought out the fact that the household had retired by eleven-thirty, and not till then did he call for testimony of the quarrel which had flared up in the billiard room. The painful scene was reenacted in minute detail; six men were forced to swear they heard young Connor threaten to break Chapman's neck.

"Mr. Connor," asked the coroner, "you rowed stroke oar at Norwood, I believe?"

Phil Connor nodded, and in his eyes was growing terror.

"Day before yesterday you won a twenty-dollar bet with Colonel Merridew by tearing a telephone directory in quarters, did you not?"

A murmur ran along the jury as the question stabbed young Connor like a rapier-thrust.

I saw Virginia Bushrod blanch beneath her tan, saw her long, slim hand go out to clutch her lover's, but my interest in the by-play ceased as the final question hurtled like a crossbow bolt:

"Mr. Connor, where were you between the hours of twelve and two last night?"

The tortured youth's face flushed, then went white as tallow as the frightened blood drained back. The trap had sprung. He rose, grasping at the chair in front of him till lines of white showed on his hands as the flexor muscles stood out pallidly against his sun-tanned skin.

"I—I must refuse to answer—" he began, and I could see his throat working convulsively as he fought for breath. "What I was doing then is no affair—"

"*Pardonnez-moi, Monsieur le Coroner,*" de Grandin rose and bowed respectfully, "I do not wonder that the young man is embarrassed. He was with me, and—believe me, I am grieved to mention it, and would not, if it were not necessary—he was drunk!"

"Drunk?" a slow flush stained the coroner's face as he saw his cherished case evaporating.

"Drunk?" the little Frenchman echoed, casting a grin toward the responsive jury. "But yes, *Monsieur.* Drunk like a pig; so drunk he could not mount the stairs unaided."

Before he could be interrupted he proceeded:

"Me, I am fond of liquor. I like it in the morning, I delight in it at noon; at night I utterly adore it. Last night, when I had gone to bed, I felt the need of stimulant. I rose and went downstairs, and as I reached the bottom flight I turned and saw Messieurs Connor and Chapman on the balcony above. They were in argument, and seemed quite angry. 'Holà, *mes enfants,*' I called to them, 'cease your dispute and join me in a drink. It will dissolve your troubles as a cup of coffee melts a lump of sugar.'

"Monsieur Chapman would have none of it. Perhaps he was one of those unfortunates who have no love for brandy; it might have been he did not choose to drink with Monsieur Connor. At any rate, he went into his room and closed the door, while Monsieur Connor joined me in the dining-room.

"*Messieurs,*" he bent another quick smile at the jurymen, "have you ever seen a man unused to liquor making the attempt to seem to like it? It is laughable is it not? So it was last night. This one"—he laid a patronizing hand upon young Connor's shoulder—"he tipped his glass and poured the brandy down, then made a face as though it had been castor oil. Ah, but he had the gameness, as you say so quaintly over here. When I essayed a second drink he held his glass for more, and when I took a third, he still desired to keep me company; but then he scarce knew what he did. Three glasses of good cognac"—he fairly smacked his lips upon the word—"are not for one who does not give his serious thought to drinking. No, certainly.

"Before you could pronounce the name of that *Monsieur Jacques Robinson* our young friend here was drunk. *Mordieu,* it was superb! Not in more than twenty years have I been able to achieve such drunkenness, *Messieurs.* He staggered, his head hung low between his shoulders, and rolled from side to side; he smiled like a pussy-cat who has lately dined on cream; he toppled from his chair and lay upon the floor!

"I raised him up. 'Come, *Monsieur*,' I told him, 'this is no way to do. You are like a little, naughty boy who creeps into his father's cellar and gets drunk on stolen wine. Be a man, *Monsieur*. Come to bed!'

"Ah, but he could not. He could not walk, he could not talk, except to beg me that I would not tell his fiancée about his indiscretion. And so I dragged him up the stairs. Yes, I, who am not half his size, must carry him upstairs, strip off his clothes, and leave him snoring in a drunken stupor. He—"

"Then you think he couldn't 'a' broke th' other feller's neck?" a juryman demanded with a grin.

De Grandin left his place, walked across the chapel till he faced his questioner and leant above him, speaking in a confidential whisper which he nevertheless managed to make audible throughout the room. "My friend," he answered solemnly, "he could not break the bow of his cravat. I saw him try it several times; at last I had to do it for him."

The verdict of the jury was that Ralph Chapman came to his death at the hands of some person or persons to them unknown.

D E GRANDIN POURED A thimbleful of old Courvoiser into his brandy sniffer, rotated the glass a moment, then held it to his nose, sighing ecstatically. "You know, my friend," he told me as he sipped the cognac slowly, "I often wonder what became of them. It was a case with possibilities, that one. I can not rid my mind of the suspicion—"

"Whatever are you vaporing about?" I cut in testily. "What case, and what suspicion—"

"Why, that of Mademoiselle Bushrod and her fiancé, the young Monsieur Connor. I—"

"You certainly lied Phil Connor out of the electric chair," I told him with a smile. "If ever I saw a death-trap closing in on anyone, it was the snare the coroner had laid for him. Whatever made you do it, man? Didn't *you* want to see justice triumph?"

"I did," he answered calmly, "but justice and law are not always cousins German, my friend. Justly, neither of those young folks was responsible for—"

"Beg pardon, sor, there's a lady an' gentleman askin' fer Doctor de Grandin," interrupted Nora McGinnis from the doorway. "A Misther Connor an' Miss Bushrod. Will I be showin' 'em in, I dunno?"

"By all means!" cried de Grandin, swallowing his brandy at a gulp. "Come, Friend Trowbridge, the angels whom we spoke of have appeared!"

P HIL CONNOR LOOKED EMBARRASSED; a darkling, haunted fear was in Virginia Bushrod's eyes as we joined them in the drawing-room.

The young man drew a deep, long breath, like a swimmer about to dive into icy water, then blurted: "You saved my life, sir, when they had me on the spot last month. Now we've come to you again for help. Something's been troubling us ever since Ralph Chapman died, and we believe that you're the only one to clear it up."

"But I am honored!" said de Grandin with a bow. "What is the nature of your worriment, my friends? Whatever I can do you may be sure I'll do if you will take me in your confidence.

Young Connor rose, a faint flush on his face, and shifted from one foot to the other, like a schoolboy ill at ease before his teacher. "It's more a matter of your taking us into your confidence, sir," he said at length. "What really happened on the night Ralph Chapman's neck was broken? Of course, that story which you told was pure invention—even though it saved me from a trial for murder—but both Virginia and I have been haunted by the fear that something which we do not know about happened, and—"

"How do you say, you fear that something which you do not know about," he began, but Virginia Bushrod cut in with a question:

"Is there anything to the Freudian theory that dreams are really wish-fulfilments, Doctor? I've tried to tell myself there is, for that way lies escape, but—"

"Yes, *Mademoiselle?*" de Grandin prompted as she paused.

"Well, in a misty, hazy sort of way I recollect I dreamt that Ralph was dead that night and that—oh, I might as well tell everything! I dreamt I killed him!

"It seemed to me I got up out of bed and walked a long, long way along a dark and winding road. I came to a high mountain, but oddly, I was on its summit, without having climbed it. I descended to the valley, and everything was dark; then I sat down to rest, and far away I heard a strain of music It was soft, and sweet and restful, and I thought, 'How good it is to be here listening—'

"*Pardon, Mademoiselle,* can you recall the tune you heard?" de Grandin asked, his small mustache aquiver like the whiskers of an alert tom-cat, his little, round blue eyes intent on her in an unwinking stare.

"Why, yes, I think I can. I'm totally tone-deaf, you know, utterly unable to reproduce a single note of music accurately, but there are certain tunes I recognize. This was one of them, the *Londonderry Air.*"

"Ah?" the little Frenchman flashed a warning look at me; then: "And what else did you dream?" he asked.

"The tune I listened to so gladly seemed to change. I couldn't tell you what the new air was, but it was something dreadful—terrible. It was like the shrieking and laughing of a thousand fiends together—and they were laughing at me! They seemed to point derisive fingers at me, making fun of me because I'd been insulted by Ralph Chapman and didn't dare resent it.

"I don't suppose you've ever heard of the Canadian poet Service, Doctor, but somewhere in one of his poems he tells of the effect of music on a crowd of miners gathered in a saloon:

"The thought came back of an ancient wrong,
And it stung like a frozen lash,
And the lust arose to kill—to kill . . .

"That's how that dream-tune seemed to me. The darkness round me seemed to change to dusky red, as though I looked out through a film of blood, and a single thought possessed me: 'Kill Ralph Chapman; kill Ralph Chapman! He called you a low cheat before your friends tonight; kill him for it-wring his neck!'

"Then I was climbing up the mountainside again, clambering over rocks and boulders, and always round me was that angry, bloody glow, like the red reflection of a fire at night against the sky. At last I reached the summit, weak and out of breath, and there before me, sleeping on the rocks, was Ralph Chapman. I looked at him, and as I looked the hot resentment which I felt came flooding up until it nearly strangled me. I bent over him, took his throat between my hands and squeezed, pressed till his face grew bluish-gray and his eyes and tongue were starting forward. Oh, he knew who it was, all right! Before I gave his neck the final vicious twist and felt it break beneath my fingers like a brittle stick that's bent too far, I saw the recognition in his eyes and the deadly fear in them.

"I wasn't sorry for the thing I'd done. I was deliriously happy. I'd killed my enemy, avenged the slight he'd put on me, and was nearly wild with fierce, exultant joy. I wanted to call everybody and show them what I'd done; how those who called Virginia Bushrod thief and cheat were dealt with."

Her breath was coming fast, and in her eyes there shone a bright and gleaming light, as though the mere recital of the dream brought her savage exaltation. "The woman's mad," I told myself, "a homicidal maniac, if ever I saw one."

"And then, *Mademoiselle?*" I heard de Grandin ask soothingly.

"Then I awoke. My hands and brow and cheeks were bathed in perspiration, and I trembled with a sort of chilled revulsion. 'Girl, you've certainly been on a wish-fulfillment spree in Shut-eye Town,' I told myself as I got out of bed.

'It was early, not quite five o'clock, but I knew there was no chance of further sleep, so I took a cold shower, got into my riding-clothes, and went for a long gallop. I argued with myself while riding, and had almost convinced myself that it was all a ghastly dream when I met you and Doctor Trowbridge having breakfast.

"When you mentioned hearing the *Londonderry Air* the night before, I went almost sick. The thought crashed through my brain: 'Music at midnight—music at midnight—music luring me to murder!'

"Then, when the butler ran out on the terrace and told you Ralph was dead—"

"Precisely, *Mademoiselle*, one understands," de Grandin supplied softly.

"I don't believe you do," she contradicted with a wan and rather frightened smile. "For a long time—almost ever since my accident—I've had an odd, oppressive feeling every now and then that I was not myself."

"*Eh*, that you were someone else?" he asked her sharply.

"Yes, that's it, that I was someone different from myself—"

"Who, by example, *Mademoiselle?*"

"Oh, I don't know. Someone low and vile and dreadful, someone with the basest instincts, who—who's *trying to push me out of myself.*"

De Grandin tweaked the needle-points of his mustache, leant forward in his chair and faced her with a level, almost hypnotic stare. "Explain yourself—in the smallest detail—if you will be so good," he ordered.

"I'm afraid I can't explain, sir, it's almost impossible; but—well, take the episode in the billiard room at Colonel Merridew's the night that Ralph was killed. I gave him my word then, and I give you my solemn pledge now that never before in all my life had I held a billiard cue in my hand. I don't know what made me do it, but I happened to be standing on the terrace near the windows of the billiard room, and when I heard the balls click I felt a sudden overmastering urge, like the craving of a drug fiend for his dope, to go inside and play. It was silly, I knew I couldn't even hit a ball, much less make one ball hit another, but something deep inside me seemed to force me on—no, that's not it, it was as though my hands were urging me." She wrinkled her brow in an effort to secure a precisely descriptive phrase; then:

"It seemed as though my hands, entirely independent of me, were leading—no, *pulling* me toward that billiard table. Then, when I had picked up the cue I had a sudden feeling, amounting almost to positive conviction: 'You've done this before; you know this game, no one knows it better.' But I was in a sort of daze as I shot the balls around; I didn't realize how long I'd been playing, or even whether I'd done well or not, till Ralph accused me of pretending ignorance of the game in order to win five hundred dollars from him.

"That isn't all: I'd hardly been out of the hospital a month when one day I found myself in Rodenberg's department store in the act of shoving a piece of Chantilly lace under the jumper of my dress. I can't explain it. I didn't realize I was doing it—truly I didn't—till all of a sudden I seemed to wake up and catch myself in the act of shoplifting. 'Virginia Bushrod, what *are* you doing?' I asked myself, then held the lace out to the sales girl and told her I would take it. I didn't really want it, had no earthly use for it; but I knew instinctively that if I didn't buy it I would steal it."

Abruptly she demanded: "Do you approve of brightly colored nails?"

"*Tenez, Mademoiselle*, that depends upon the time and place and personality of the wearer," he responded with a smile.

"That's it, the personality," she answered. "Bright carmine nails may be all right for some; they're not becoming to my type. Yet I've had an urge, almost in irresistible desire, from time to time to have my nails dyed scarlet. Last week I stopped in Madame Toussaint's for a manicure and pedicure. When I got home

I found the nails of both my hands and feet were varnished brilliant red. I never use a deeper shade than rose, and was horrified to find my nails all daubed that way; yet, somehow, there was a feeling of secret elation, too. I called the salon and asked for Héloise, who'd done my nails, and she said, 'I thought it strange when you insisted on that vivid shade of red, Miss Bushrod. I didn't like to put it on, but you declared you wanted it.'

"Perhaps I did; but I don't remember anything about it."

De Grandin eyed her thoughtfully a moment; then:

"You have spoken of an accident you had, *Mademoiselle*. Tell me of it, if you please."

"It was a little more than a year ago," she answered. "I'd been over to the country club by Morristown, and was hurrying back to keep a date with Phil when my car blew out a tire. At least, I think that's what happened. I remember a sharp, crackling *pop*, like the discharge of a small rifle, and next instant the road-ster fairly somersaulted from the road. I saw the earth rush up at me; then"—she spread her shapely hands in a gesture of finality—"there I was, pinned beneath the wreckage, with both hands crushed to jelly."

"Yet you recovered wholly, thanks to Doctor Augensburg, I understand?"

"Yes, it wasn't till every surgeon we had seen had said he'd have to amputate that Father called in Doctor Augensburg, and he proved they all were wrong. I was in the hospital two months, most of the time completely or partly uncon-scious from drugs, but"—her delicate, long-fingered hands spread once again with graceful eloquence—"here I am, and I'm not the helpless cripple they all said I'd be."

"Not physically, at any rate," de Grandin murmured softly; then, aloud:

"*Mademoiselle*, take off your bracelets!" he commanded sharply.

Had he hurled an insult in her face, the girl could not have looked more shocked. Surprise, anger, sudden fear showed in her countenance as she repeated: "Take—off—"

"*Précisément*," the little Frenchman answered almost harshly. "Take them off, *tout promptement*. I have the intuition; what you call the hunch."

Slowly, reluctantly, as though she were disrobing in the presence of a stranger, Miss Bushrod snapped the clasps of the wide bands of gold which spanned her slender wrists. A line of untanned skin, standing out in contrast to her sun-kissed arms, encircled each slim wrist, testifying that the bracelets had been worn on beach and tennis court, as well as in her leisure moments, but whiter still, livid, eldritch as the mocking grin of broken teeth within the gaping mouth-hole of a skull, there ran around each wrist a ring of cicatrice an inch or so above the styloid process' protuberance. Running up and down a half an inch or so from the encir-cling band of white were vertical scar-lines, interweaving, overlapping, as though the flesh had once been cut apart, then sewn together in a dove-tailed jointure.

Involuntarily I shrank from looking on the girl's deformity, but de Grandin scrutinized it closely. At length:

"*Mademoiselle*, please believe I do not act from idle curiosity," he begged, "but I must use the fluoroscope in my examination. Will you come with me?"

He led her to the surgery, and a moment later we could hear the crackling of the Crookes' tube as he turned the X-ray on.

Miss Bushrod's bracelets were replaced when they returned some fifteen minutes later, and de Grandin wore a strangely puzzled look. His lips were pursed, as though he were about to whistle, and his eyes were blazing with the hard, cold light they showed when he was on a man-hunt.

"Now, my friends," he told the lovers as he glanced at them in turn, "I have seen enough to make me think that what this lady says is no mere idle vagary. These strange influences she feels, these surprising lapses from normal, they do not mean she suffers from a dual personality, at least as the term is generally used. But unless I am more mistaken than I think, we are confronted by a situation so bizarre that just to outline it would cast a doubt upon our sanity. *Alors*, we must build our case up from the ground.

"Tell me," he shot the question at young Connor, "was there anything unusual—anything at all, no matter how trivial, which occurred to Mademoiselle Bushrod a month—two months—before the accident which crushed her hands?"

The young man knit his brow in concentration. "No-o," he replied at length. "I can't remember anything."

"No altercation, no unpleasantness which might have led to vengeful thoughts, perhaps?" the Frenchman prompted.

"Why, now you speak of it," young Connor answered with a grin, "I did have a run-in with a chap at Coney Island."

"*Ah*? Describe it, if you please."

"It really wasn't anything. Ginnie and I had gone down to the Island for a spree. We think the summer's not complete without at least one day at Coney—shooting the chutes, riding the steeplechase and roller coasters, then taking in the side shows. This afternoon we'd just about completed the rounds when we noticed a new side show with a Professor Mysterioso or Mefisto, or something of the sort, listed as the chief attraction. He was a hypnotist."

"*Ah*?" de Grandin murmured softly, "and—"

"The professor was just beginning his act when we went in. He was extraordinarily good, too. Uncannily good, I thought. All dressed in red tights, like Mefistofeles, he was, and his partner—'subject' you call it, don't you?—was a girl dressed in a white gown with a blond wig, simulating Marguerite, you know. He did the darndest things with her—put her in a trance and made her lie stretched between two chairs, with neck on one and heels on the other, no support beneath her body, while men stood on her; told her to rise, rose up three feet in the air, as drawn by invisible wires; finally, he took half a dozen long, sharp knitting-needles and thrust them through her hands, her forearms, even through her cheeks. Then he withdrew them and invited us to search her for signs of scars. It was morbid, I suppose, but we looked, and there wasn't the faintest trace of wounds where he had pierced her with the needles, nor any sign of blood.

"Then he called for volunteers to come up and be hypnotized, and when no one answered, he came down among the audience. 'You, Madame?' he asked Ginnie, stopping in front of her and grinning in her face.

"When she refused he persisted; told her that it wouldn't hurt, and all that sort of thing; finally began glaring into her eyes and making passes before her.

"That was a little bit too much. I let him have it."

"Bravo!" de Grandin murmured softly. "And then?"

"I expected he'd come back at me, for he picked himself up and came across the floor with his shoulders hunched in a sort of boxer's crouch, but when he almost reached me he stopped short, raised his hands above his head and muttered something indistinctly. He wasn't swearing, at least not in English, but I felt that he was calling down a curse on us. I got Virginia out before we had more trouble with him."

"And that was all?" de Grandin asked.

"That was all."

"*Parbleu*, my friend, I think it is enough to be significant." Then, abruptly: "This feminine assistant. Did you notice her?"

"Not particularly. She had a pretty, common sort of face, and long, slim graceful hands with very brightly painted nails."

De Grandin pinched his pointed chin between a thoughtful thumb and finger. "Where did Doctor Augensburg repair your injured hands, *Mademoiselle?*" he asked.

"At the Ellis Sanitarium, out by Hackensack," she answered. "I was in Mercy Hospital at first, but the staff and Doctor Augensburg had some misunderstanding, so he took me out to Ellis Clinic for the operation.

The little Frenchman smiled benignly on the visitors. "I can understand your self-concern, *Mademoiselle*," he told Miss Bushrod. "This feeling of otherhood, this impression that a trespasser-in-possession is inside of you, displacing your personality, making you do things you do not wish to do, is disconcerting, but it is not cause for great alarm. You were greatly hurt, you underwent a trying operation. Those things shock the nervous system. I have seen other instances of it. In the war I saw men make what seemed complete recovery, only to give way to strange irregularities months afterward. Eventually they regained normality;

so should you, within, let us say"—he paused as though to make a mental calculation—"within a month or so."

"You really think so, Doctor?" she asked, pathos looking from her amber eyes.

"But yes, I am all confident of it."

"NAME OF A MOST unpleasant small blue devil!" he swore as our visitors' footsteps faded on the cement walk outside. "I must make good my promise to her, but how—death of a dyspeptic hippopotamus!—how?"

"What?" I demanded.

"You know how dreams reflect the outside world in symbolic images. By example, you have kicked the covers off the bed, you are cold. But you are, still asleep. How does the dream convert the true facts into images? By making you to think that you are in the Arctic and a polar storm is raging, or, perhaps, that you have fallen in the river, and are chilled by the cold water. So it was with Mademoiselle Bushrod. She dreams she stands upon a mountain top, that is when she leaves her chamber. She dreams that she descends the mountain; that is when she walks downstairs. She hears a tune, of course she does, her hands, those hands which can not play a single note when she is waking, produce it. She dreams she re-ascends the mountain—climbs the stairs. *Ha*, then she sees before her traducer, sleeping, helpless. She reaches forth her hands, and—

"What then, my friend? Are we to trust the symbolism of the dream still farther?"

"But," I began, and—

"*But* be damned and stewed in hell eternally!" he cut in. "*Attendez-moi*: Those hands, those lovely, graceful hands of hers, are not her own!"

"Eh?" I shot back. "Not—good Lord, man, you're raving! What d'ye mean?"

"Precisely what I say," he answered in a level, toneless voice. "Those hands were grafted on her wrists, as the rose is grafted on the dogwood tree. Her radii and ulnæ have been sawn across transversely; then other bones, processing with the wrist-joints of a pair of hands, were firmly fastened on by silver plates and rivets, the flexor muscles spliced with silver wire, the arteries and veins and nerves attached with an uncanny skill. It is bizarre, incredible, impossible; but it is so. I saw it with my own two eyes when I examined her beneath the fluoroscope."

HE LEFT THE HOUSE directly after breakfast the next morning, and did not reappear till dinner had been waiting half an hour.

"*Sacré nom*," he greeted me across his cocktail glass, "what a day I had, my friend! I have been busy as a flea upon a dog, but what I have accomplished! *Parbleu*, he is a clever fellow, this de Grandin!

"I took down copious mental notes while Mademoiselle Bushrod talked last night, and so this morning I set out for Coney Island. *Grand Dieu des rats*, what a place!

"From one small show-place to another I progressed, and in between times I engaged in conversation with the hangers-on. At last I found a prize, a jewel, a paragon. He rejoices in the name of Snead—Bill Snead, to give him his full title—and when he is not occupied with drinking he proclaims the virtues of a small display of freaks. *Eh bien*, by the expenditure of a small amount of money for food, and something more for drink, I learned from him enough to put me on the trail I sought.

"Professor Mysterioso de Diablo was a hypnotist of no mean parts, I learned. He had 'played big time' for years, but by a most unfortunate combination of events he was sent to prison in the State of Michigan, The lady's husband secured a divorce, *Monsieur le Professeur* a rigidly enforced vacation from the stage.

"After that his popularity declined until finally he was forced to show his art at Coney Island side shows. He was a most unpleasant person, I was told, principally noted for the way he let his fancies for the fair sex wander. This caused his partner much annoyance, and she often reproached him bitterly and publicly.

"Now, attend me carefully. It is of this partner I would speak particularly. Her name was Agnes Fagan. She was born to the theatrical profession, for her father, Michael Fagan, had been a thrower-out of undesired patrons in a burlesque theater when he was not appearing as a strong man on the stage or lying deplorably drunk in bed. The daughter was 'educated something elegant,' my informant told me. She was especially adept at the piano, and for a time entertained ambitions to perform in concert work. However, she inherited one talent, if no other, from her estimable parent: she was astonishingly strong. Monsieur Snead had often seen her amuse her intimates by bending tableware in knots, to the great annoyance of the restaurant proprietor where she happened to perform. She could, he told me solemnly, take a heavy table fork and twist it in a corkscrew.

"*Eh bien*, the lure of the footlights was stronger than her love of music, it appears, for we next behold her as the strong woman in an acrobatic troupe. Perhaps it was another heritage from her many-sided sire, perhaps it was her own idea; at any rate, one day while playing in the city of Detroit, she appropriated certain merchandise without the formality of paying for it. Two police officers were seriously injured in the subsequent proceedings, but eventually she went to prison, was released at the same time that the professor received liberty, and became his partner, the subject of his hypnotism during his performances, and, according to the evil-minded Monsieur Snead, his mistress, as well.

"She possessed four major vanities: her musical ability, her skill at billiards, her strong, white, even teeth and the really unusual beauty of her hands. She was wont to show her strength on all occasions. Her dental vanity led her to suffer the discomfort of having a sound tooth drilled, gold-filled and set with a small diamond. She spent hours in the care of her extremities, and often bought a manicure when it was a choice of pampering her vanity or going without food.

"Now listen carefully, my friend: About a year ago she had a quarrel with her partner, the professor. I recite the facts as Monsieur Snead related them to me. It seems that the professor let his errant fancies wander, and was wont to invite ladies from the audience to join him in his acts. Usually he succeeded, for he had a way with women, Monsieur Snead assured me. But eventually he met rebuff. He also met the fist of the young lady's escort. He was, to use your quaint American expression, 'knocked for a row of ash-cans' by the gentleman.

"*La Fagan* chided him in no uncertain terms. They had a fearful fight in which she would have been the victor, had he not resorted to hypnotism for defense. 'She wuz about to tear him into little bits, when he put 'is hand up and said, "Rigid",' Monsieur Snead related. 'An' there she was, stiff as a frozen statoo, wid 'er hand up in th' air, an' her fist all doubled up, not able to so much as bat a eye. She stood that way about a hour, I expect; then suddenly she fell down flat, and slept like nobody's business. I reckon th' professor gave her th' sleepin' order from wherever he had beat it to. He had got so used to orderin' her about that he could control her at a distance 'most as well as when he looked into her eyes.'

"Thereafter he was often absent from the show where he performed. Eventually he quit it altogether, and within a month his strong and pretty-handed partner vanished. Like *pouf!* she was suddenly nowhere at all.

"By the time the estimable Monsieur Snead had finished telling me these things he could impart no further information. He was, as I have heard it described, 'stewed like a dish of prunes,' for all the while he talked I kept his tongue well oiled with whisky. Accordingly I bid him farewell and pushed my research elsewhere. I searched the files of the journals diligently, endeavoring to find some clue to the vanishment of Mademoiselle Fagan. *Cordieu*, I think I found it! Read this, if you will be so good."

Adjusting my pince-nez I scanned the clipping which he handed me:

GIRL FALLS UNCONSCIOUS WITH
STRANGE MALADY
Collapses on Roadway Near Hackensack—
Absence of Disease Symptoms
Puzzles Doctors

Hackensack, N.J., Sept. 17—Police and doctors today are endeavoring to solve the mystery of the identity and illness of an attractive young woman who collapsed on the roadway near here shortly after noon today, and has lain unconscious in the Ellis Clinic ever since.

She is described as about 30 years old, five feet two inches tall, and with fair complexion and red hair. Her hands and feet showed evidences of unusual care, and both finger- and toe-nails were dyed a brilliant scarlet. In her upper left eye-tooth was a small diamond set in a gold inlay.

She wore a ring with an oval setting of green stone, gold earrings in her pierced ears, and an imitation pearl necklace. Her costume consisted of a blue and white polka-dot dress, white fabric gloves, a black sailor hat with a small feather, and black patent leather pumps. She wore no stockings.

Alec Carter and James Heilmann, proprietors of an antique shop facing on the road, saw the young woman walking slowly toward Hackensack, staggering slightly from side to side. She fell in the roadway across from their store, and when they reached her she was unconscious. Failing to revive her by ordinary first aid methods, they placed her in an automobile and took her to the Ellis Clinic, which was the nearest point where medical aid could be secured.

Physicians at the clinic declared they could find no cause for her prolonged unconsciousness, as she was evidently neither intoxicated nor under the influence of drugs, and exhibited no symptoms of any known disease.

Nothing found upon her offered any clue to her identity.

"Well?" I demanded as I put the clipping down.

"I do not think it was," he answered. "By no means; not at all. Consider, if you please:

"Mademoiselle Bushrod's accident had occurred two weeks before, she had been given up by local surgeons; Augensburg, who was at the Ellis Clinic at the time, had just accepted her case.

"This strange young woman with the pretty hands drops down upon the roadway almost coincidentally with Mademoiselle Virginia's advent at the clinic. Do you not begin to sniff the odor of the rodent?"

"I don't think so," I replied.

"Very well, then, listen: The mysterious young woman was undoubtlessly the Fagan girl, whose disappearance occurred about this time. What was the so mysterious malady which struck her down, which had no symptoms, other than unconsciousness? It was merely that she had been once again put under the hypnotic influence, my friend. You will recall that the professor could control her almost as well when at a distance as when he stared into her eyes? Certainly. Assuredly. She had become so used to his hypnosis that his slightest word or wish was law to her; she was his slave, his thing, his chattel, to do with as he pleased. Unquestionably he commanded her to walk along that road that day, to fall unconscious near the Ellis Clinic; to lie unconscious afterward, eventually to die. Impossible? *Mais non.* If one can tell the human heart to beat more slowly, and make it do so, under power of hypnosis, why may one not command it to cease beating altogether, still under hypnotic influence? So far as the young Fagan person was concerned, she had no thought, no will, no power, either mentally or physically, which the professor could not take from her by a single word of command. No, certainly.

"We were told Mademoiselle Bushrod's accident came from a tire blow-out, *n'est-ce-pas?* I do not think it did. I inquired—most discreetly, I assure you—at and near the Ellis Clinic, and discovered that *Monsieur* the hypnotist visited that institution the very day that she was hurt, had a long conference with Doctor Augensburg in strictest privacy and—when he came he bore a small, high-powered rifle. He said he had been snake-hunting. Me, I think the serpent which he shot was the tire of Mademoiselle Bushrod's car. That was the blow-out which caused her car to leave the road and crush her hands, my friend!

"Now, again: This Professor of the Devil, as he called himself appropriately, visited Doctor Augensburg at several times. He was in the room where the unknown woman lay on more than one occasion. He was at the clinic on the day when Augensburg operated on Mademoiselle Bushrod's hands—and on that day, not fifteen minutes before the operation was performed, the unknown woman died. She had been sinking slowly for some days; her death occurred while orderlies were wheeling our poor Mademoiselle Virginia to the operating-room.

"You will recall she was unknown; that she was given shelter in an institution which maintains no beds for charity or emergency patients? But did you know that Augensburg paid her bill, and demanded in return that he be given her unclaimed body for anatomical research, that he might seek the cause of her 'strange' death? No, you did not know it, nor did I; but now I do, and I damn think that in that information lies the answer to our puzzle.

"I do not have to tell you that the period between somatic death—the mere ceasing to live—and molecular, or true death, when the tissue-cells begin to die, is often as long as three or four hours. During this period the individual body-cells remain alive, the muscles react to electrical stimuli, even the pupils of the eye can be expanded with atropine. She had suffered no disease-infection, this unknown one, her body was healthy, but run down, like an unwound clock. Moreover, fifteen minutes after her death, her hands were, histologically speaking, still alive. What easier than to make the transplantation of her sound, live hands to Mademoiselle Bushrod's wrists, then chop and maim her body in the autopsy room in such a way that none would be the wiser?

"And what of these transplanted hands? They were part and parcel of a hypnotic subject, were they not, accustomed to obey commands of the hypnotist immediately, even to have steel knitting-needles run through them, yet feel no pain? Yes, certainly.

"Very well. Are it not entirely possible that these hands which the professor have commanded so many times when they were attached to one body, will continue to obey his whim when they are rooted to another? I think so.

"In his fine story, your magnificent Monsieur Poe tells of a man who really died, yet was kept alive through hypnosis. These hands of Mademoiselle Fagan never really died, they were still technically alive when they were taken off—who knows what orders this professor gave his dupe before he ordered her to die? Those hands had been a major vanity of hers, they were skilled hands, strong hands, beautiful hands—*hélas*, dishonest hands, as well—but they formed a large part of their owner's personality. Might he not have ordered that they carry on that personality after transplantation to the end that they might eventually lead the poor Mademoiselle Bushrod to entire ruin? I think so. Yes.

"Consider the evidence: Mademoiselle Bushrod is tone-deaf, yet we heard her play exquisitely. She had no skill and no experience in billiards, yet we saw her shoot a brilliant game. For why should she, whose very nature is so foreign to the act, steal merchandise from a shopkeeper?

"Yet she tells us that she caught herself in such a crime. Whence comes this odd desire on her part to have her nails so brightly painted, a thing which she abhors? Last of all, how comes it that she, who is in nowise noted for her strength, can twist a silver table fork into a corkscrew?

"You see," he finished, "the case is perfect. I know it can not possibly be so; yet so it is. We can not face down facts, my friend."

"It's preposterous," I replied, but my denial lacked conviction.

He read capitulation in my tone, and smiled with satisfaction.

"But can't we break this spell?" I asked. "Surely, we can make this Professor What's-his-Name—"

"Not by any legal process," he cut in. "No court on earth would listen to our story, no jury give it even momentary credence. Yet"—he smiled a trifle grimly—"there is a way, my friend."

"What?" I asked.

"Have you by any chance a trocar in your instruments?" he asked irrelevantly.

"A trocar? You mean one of those long, sharp-pointed hollow needles used in paracentesis operations?"

"*Précisément. Tu parles, mon vieux.*"

"Why, yes, I think there's one somewhere."

"And may one borrow it tonight?"

"Of course, but—where are you going at this hour?"

"To Staten Island," he replied as he placed the long, deadly, stiletto-like needle in his instrument case. "Do not wait up for me, my friend, I may be very late."

HORRIFIED SUSPICION, GROWING RAPIDLY to dreadful certainty, mounted in my mind as I scanned the evening paper while de Grandin and I sipped our coffee and liqueurs in the study three nights later. "Read this," I ordered, pointing to an obscure item on the second page:

St. George, S.I, September 30—The body of George Lothrop, known professionally on the stage as Prof. Mysterioso, hypnotist, missing from his rooming-house at Bull's Head, S.I., since Tuesday night, was found floating in New York bay near the St. George ferry slip by harbor police this afternoon.

Representatives of the Medical Examiners' office said he was not drowned, as a stab wound, probably from a stiletto, had pierced his left breast and reached his heart.

Employees at the side show at Coney Island, where Lothrop formerly gave exhibitions as a hypnotist, said he was of a sullen and quarrelsome disposition and given to annoying women. From the nature of the wound which caused his death police believe the husband or admirer of some woman he accosted resented his attentions and stabbed him, afterward throwing his body into the bay.

De Grandin read the item through with elevated brows. "A fortunate occurrence, is it not?" he asked. "Mademoiselle Bushrod is now freed from any spell he might have cast on her—or on her hands. Hypnotic suggestion can not last, once the hypnotist is dead."

"But—but you—that trocar—" I began.

"I returned it to your instrument case last Tuesday night," he answered. "Will you be good enough to pour me out a little brandy? Ah, thank you, my friend."

The Black Orchid

U NDER THE COMBINED INFLUENCE of an excellent dinner and two ounces
of 1845 cognac our guest became expansive. "D'ye know," he told us as he
passed the brandy snifter beneath his nose; inhaling the fruity fragrance of
the ancient liqueur, "I believe I've run across a new disease."

"Ah?" murmured Jules de Grandin courteously, casting a quick wink in my
direction. "You interest me, *Monsieur*. What are the symptoms of this hitherto
unknown disorder?"

Young Doctor Traherne beamed upon us genially. When one is barely thirty,
fresh from his internship and six months' study in Vienna, there is a spice in
being told that your discoveries interest physicians who were practising when
you were in the cradle. "It's a—a bloodless hemorrhage," he confided.

De Grandin's narrow brows receded nearly half an inch toward the line of
his sleekly brushed blond hair. "*Pardonnez-moi, Monsieur,*" he begged. "I fear I do
not understand the English fluently. You said—perhaps I did not hear it right?—
that you had found a bloodless hemorrhage?"

Traherne applied a match to his cigar and chuckled.

"That's it, sir," he answered. "Six months ago they called me to attend old
Mr. Sorensen. At first I thought he suffered from anemia, but a check-up on his
blood convinced me the trouble was more quantitative than qualitative. The
man showed every evidence of hemorrhage exhaustion, and as there was no sign
of external blood escape, I naturally suspected carcinoma and internal bleeding,
but when I tested him I found there was no trace of it. There he was, with no
wound or lesion—absolutely no way by which he could have lost a teaspoonful
of blood—bleeding to death progressively. I put him on a blood-producing diet,
fed him wine and iron and liver enough to fill a fair-sized warehouse, but every
morning he showed fresh evidences of prostration till I had to fall back on glu-
cose injections, and finally resorted to transfusions."

De Grandin's interest showed more than merely formal courtesy as Traherne finished his description.

"And when did this one die?" he asked, a sudden cutting-edge of sharpness in his voice.

"He didn't," answered Traherne with a grin. "Just by luck I hit upon the idea of a cruise—thought he might as well pass out with a ship's doctor in attendance as to have me sign the death certificate—so I shipped him off on a Caribbean trip. He was back in ninety days, hale and hearty as ever, without a sign of the strange condition which had nearly caused his death."

"*Eh bien*, you are to be congratulated," said the Frenchman with a smile. "Our trade is one part science and the other nine parts luck, *n'est-ce-pas?*"

"But here's the funny part," Traherne replied. "Sorensen's been home just six weeks, and he's got it again. Not only that, his niece, who lives with him, has it too, and her condition's even worse than his. Hanged if I can figure it. Whatever influence has caused this condition has undoubtedly been the same in both cases—the symptoms are so exactly similar, but there's absolutely no normal or apparent explanation for it. Think of it, gentlemen. Here are two people, one a man near eighty, but remarkably vigorous and well preserved, without a single trace of degenerative disease of any sort, the other a young woman in her early twenties, and for no apparent reason they both begin to show positively defined symptoms of extensive hemorrhage without a sign of bleeding. They respond to conventional treatment for loss of blood, but lapse into hemorrhage prostration almost overnight. If I were a Negro or a back-county Pennsylvanian I'd say it was a case of voodoo curse or hexing, but being a physician and a man of science I can only conclude these people are victims of some strange and as yet unclassified disease. Quite probably it's contagious, too, since the niece appears to have contracted it by contact with the uncle."

"H'm," de Grandin murmured thoughtfully. "Has it occurred to you, *mon collègue*, that the evil which attacks these two is really old as Egypt's mighty pyramids or Babylon's tall temples?"

"Oh, you mean some old disease which ravaged ancient peoples and has passed out of medical memory, like the Black Death of medieval Europe?"

"*Précisément*, the blackest of black deaths, my friend."

"You know about it—you've seen such cases?" young Traherne asked, a shade of disappointment in his voice.

"I would not say that," de Grandin answered. "I have observed such symptoms, not once, but many times, but only fools attempt a diagnosis at long distance. I should greatly like to have the chance to see the victims of this so strange illness. Could you arrange an interview?"

"Why, yes," the other smiled. "I'm going to drop by Sorensen's house tonight, just to see that everything is going smoothly. Would you care to come along?"

Oscar Sorensen was one of those unusual characters found in many of the small, sub-metropolitan communities which fringe New York. Almost eighty years of age, he had served a rigorous apprenticeship as soldier of fortune, and, unlike most of that breed, he had succeeded. Late in life he retired from service to a half-score countries with military decorations enough to decorate an army corps and a fortune more than large enough to let him end the quiet close of his eventful life in luxury. He had fought in Egypt, China, the Levant, in India and the troubled Balkans, as well as over every foot of Central America. Serving with the Cubans under Garcia, he left the island as a brigadier general of *insurrectos*, his pockets lined with fat commissions from Americans who had seen the wisdom of buying what they wanted. As a commandant of Boer cavalry he had thriftily secured enough tough diamonds to make the unsuccessful war the Dutchmen waged a most remunerative enterprise for him; the loot of half a dozen Spanish cities near the Caribbean Sea had somehow found its way into his pocket, whether he had served the Government or revolutionary forces.

He looked the part which Fate had cast him for. Over six feet tall and proportionately broad, his prominent cheekbones and narrow face bespoke his Viking ancestry, as did his fair skin and light eyes. His face was tanned to the shade of unstained oak by long exposure to the tropic sun, tiny wrinkles splayed out from the corners of his eyes, and a white crescent of scar-tissue outlined the path of an old knife or spear wound from right eye to temple.

Even without having seen the man before, I realized he was little better than a wraith of his former self. Violet half-moons underneath his eyes, a waxed pallor underlying the sunburn of his face and the pinched look of distress about his nose all testified eloquently to the sudden weakness which had fallen on him.

"I've heard of you, de Grandin," he acknowledged as Doctor Traherne finished introductions, "and I think it's time we had you in for consultation. I've been telling myself that what was wrong with me was nothing but a fresh recurrence of malaria, but all along I knew that it was nothing for a sawbones' treatment. You're a ghost-fighter, aren't you? Good. I've got a ghost for you to fight, and it'll take the best you've got to whip it, too!"

The little Frenchman raised his narrow, high-arched brows a trifle. "A ghost, *Monsieur?*" he countered. "But Doctor Traherne informs us that—"

"Excuse me," cut in Sorensen, "but this is no matter for scientific speculation, I'm afraid. Of course Traherne informs you it's some strange form of anemia we're suffering from. You're a doctor, too; but you've traveled. You've seen things outside the dissecting-rooms and clinics, and laboratories. Listen:

"You've been in savage countries; you know there's something to the power that the native witches claim. Here in civilization, with gas to cook our food and electricity to light us on our way to bed, we've forgotten all the old-time powers of the witch, so we say there never was any such thing, and brand belief in it as superstition. *Valgame Dios*," he swore in Spanish, "those who've traveled the remote spots of the world know what is so and what is superstition. In Polynesia I've seen men—whites as well as natives—shrivel and die by inches just because some native witch-doctor prayed them to death. On the African West Coast I've seen owls, owls large as eagles, perch in trees by villages, and next day some dweller in the settlement would die in frightful pain. I've seen Papuan wizards dance around their night-fires till the spirits of the dead came back—yes, by Heaven, with my own eyes I saw my mother, lying twenty years and more in her grave out there in St. Stephen's churchyard, stand across a Dyak campfire from me while a native sorcerer danced about the flames to the rhythm of a tom-tom!"

"*Parbleu*, but you have right, my friend," de Grandin nodded in agreement. "The dwellers in the silent places, they know these things; they have not forgotten; they remember, and they know. Me—"

"Excuse me," Traherne cut in dryly, "I hate to interrupt these reminiscences, but would you mind telling Doctor de Grandin about the onset of your illness, Mr. Sorensen?"

The old man looked at him much as an annoyed adult might regard the impertinent interruption of a child. "You've been in Madagascar?" he demanded of de Grandin.

"But naturally," the little Frenchman answered. "And you, *Monsieur?*"

"I was there with Gallieni in 1895, serving as *sous-lieutenant* of *chasseurs*, later as commandant of a detail of native guides. It was while serving with my detachment that I met Mamba. She was the daughter of an *Andriana*, or noble, family, distantly related to Ranavalona, the native queen just deposed by the French. Her skin was black as a minorca's wing, with a blue, almost iridescent sheen; her features were small and delicate, her body as beautiful as anything ever chiseled out of marble in the Periclean age. She had tremendous influence not only with the *Hova*, or middle-class natives, but with the *Andriana* as well; for she was reputedly a witch and priestess of 'the Fragrant One', and a word from her would bring any native, noble or commoner, from miles around crawling on his belly to lick her tiny, coal-black feet, or send him charging down upon French infantry, though he knew sure death awaited from our *chassepots* and Gatling guns.

"It was good politics to cultivate her friendship, and not at all unpleasant, I assure you. We were married in due state, and I was formally invested with all the rights and dignities of an *Andriana* noble of the highest caste. Things went smoothly at our outpost after that; till—" he paused, and for a moment closed his eyes as though in weariness.

"Yes, *Monsieur*, and then?" de Grandin prompted as the silence lengthened.

Sorensen seemed to wake up with a start. "Then I heard how things were going over in the Caribbean, and decided to resign my commission with the French and try my luck with *Cuba Libre*," he returned.

"Mamba didn't make a scene. Indeed, she took it more calmly than most civilized women would have done. It had never occurred to her that our little domestic arrangement wasn't permanent; so when I told her I'd been ordered away she merely said that she would govern in my place till my return and take good care 'our people' gave no trouble to the French. Then, like a fool, I told her I was through.

"For a moment she looked as though she hadn't understood me; then, when the meaning of my words sank in, she was awful in her anger. No tears, no wailing, just a long and dreadful stare, a stare that seemed to strike right through me and to shrivel everything it touched. Finally she raised both hands above her head and called down such a curse on me as no man has had heaped upon his head since Medea called the vengeance of the gods on Jason. She finished with the prophecy:

"'At the last you shall feel Mamba's kiss, and your blood shall waste and dry away as the little brooks in summer, yet no man shall see you bleed; your life shall slowly ebb away as the tide ebbs from the shore, and none shall give you help; flowers shall feed upon your body while you are still alive, and the thing you most adore shall waste and wither in your sight, yet you shall have no power to stay the doom which crushes her and which shall crush you, too, when she is gone. I have said.'"

Young Doctor Traherne coughed. His manner was discreet, but none too patient, as he asked, "And you think this black woman's curse responsible for your condition, sir?"

"I don't know," Sorensen answered slowly. "In China they've a saying that the three things which age can't soften are a sword, a stone and the hatred of a love-crossed woman. Mamba—"

"Has probably been dead for twenty years," Traherne supplied. "Besides, there's half the earth between you, and—"

"Listen, son," Sorensen broke in, "I've been deluding myself into thinking it was a nightmare which I suffered from—possibly the prickings of a guilty conscience—and that my subsequent illness was merely a coincidence, but I'm far from certain, now. Here's what happened just before we called you in:

"I'd been trap-shooting over at the Gun and Rod Club, and came home thoroughly tired out. Joyce and I had dinner early and I went off to bed almost as soon as the meal was over, falling asleep immediately. How long I slept I've no idea, but I remember waking with a feeling of suffocation—no pain, but utter weakness and prostration—to see something hovering above my throat and to smell a smell I hadn't smelled in years, the hot, half-spicy, half-charnel odor of the Madagascar jungle. I can't describe the thing that hovered over me, for the darkness of the room and its very nearness obscured my vision, but I had an unaccountable but powerful impression that it was a small, black, naked human figure, the figure of a nude black woman a scant four inches high, which poised in midair over me as a hummingbird poises above the flower from which it drains the nectar. How long I lay there in that helpless sort of lethargy I've no idea; but suddenly I became aware of a feeling like a pulling at my throat and Mamba's prophecy came back to me across the years: 'Your blood shall waste and dry up as the little brooks in summer!'

"Gentlemen, I assure you I was paralyzed. Fear held me more firmly than a chain. Move I could not, nor could I cry for help. Then I think I must have fainted, for the next thing I knew it was morning.

"Weakness almost overpowered me when I tried to rise, but finally I managed to crawl from bed and stagger over to the mirror. There was no blood on my pajamas, nor any on my flesh, but on my throat there was a little wound, no larger than a needle-jab or razor-nick would make, and—"

"Tell me, Monsieur," de Grandin interrupted, "this wound of which you speak, was it singular or plural?"

"Eh? Oh, I see what you mean. It was a single little puncture, so small as to be barely noticeable, and with no area of inflammation or soreness round it. At any other time I should have failed to see it, I believe, but the vividness of my nightmare made me especially careful when I looked."

"But this is most unusual," the little Frenchman murmured. "Those punctures, they should be multiple."

"What's that?"

"Nothing of importance, I assure you. I did but indulge in a foolish habit and think with my lips rather than my brain, Monsieur. Please he so kind as to proceed."

"I don't remember a recurrence of the dream, but every morning for a week I rose from heavy sleep not only not refreshed by rest, but successively and progressively weaker. Finally we called Doctor Traherne. He's probably outlined his treatment to you."

"You agree I took the proper measures?" Traherne asked. "We had this condition entirely arrested; then—"

"Précisément," de Grandin nodded, "that is a most unusual feature of the case, my friend; that and the nature of Monsieur Sorensen's wound."

"Oh, Lord!" young Traherne scoffed. "Are you finding a connection between that accidental scratch and this inexplicable pathological condition? What possible—"

"But the wound is constant, is it not?" de Grandin insisted. "It is still there? Either it or a freshly inflicted one remains, n'est-ce-pas?"

"Ye-es," Traherne admitted grudgingly. "But I've never tried to heal it. Even if it is significant, it's nothing but a symptom, and one doesn't bother to treat symptoms."

De Grandin faced Sorensen. "Your niece, Mademoiselle Joyce, she displays symptoms similar to those you first exhibited?" he asked.

"Yes," the other answered. "I'll send for her, if you wish." He pressed a button, and when a small, exceedingly neat and almost startlingly black servant appeared in answer to the summons, ordered: "Ask Miss Joyce to come to the library, please, Marshall."

"Would you object to showing us your throat while we are waiting for your niece to join us?" asked de Grandin.

"Not at all," the other answered, and undoing the collar of his soft silk shirt laid bare a strongly modeled and well-muscled neck.

The little Frenchman leant forward, scanned the patient's sunburned skin with a keen gaze, then, drawing a small lens from his pocket, held it before his eye as he pursued the examination.

"Here, *Monsieur?*" he asked, laying the tip of a small, well-manicured forefinger on Sorensen's neck a little to the right and above the Adam's apple. "Is this the place you first observed the wound?"

"Yes, and that's the spot where it reappeared when I was taken ill again," Sorensen answered.

"H'm," the Frenchman murmured. "It is, as you have said, a single wound striking directly into the skin, not looping through it. It might he from a razor-cut or from a variety of other reasons—"

"Yes, and it wasn't there before my first illness; it disappeared when I recovered, and it reappeared concurrently with my second attack," Sorensen broke in.

"Precisely, exactly; quite so," de Grandin agreed with a quick nod. "There is some connection between the puncture and your trouble, *Monsieur*, I am convinced of it, but the explanation does not leap to the eye. We shall have to think on this. If—"

A rustle at the doorway cut his conversation short as a young girl entered. She was tall and very slender, exceedingly fair-skinned, with a wealth of yellow hair which she wore coiled simply in a figure 8 at the nape of her neck. Her nose and mouth were small and very finely molded, and her brown eyes seemed out of all proportion to her other features, for they were almost startlingly enlarged by the deep violet semicircles which lay beneath them. She walked slowly, haltingly, as though the effort cost her almost every ounce of hoarded strength, and when she spoke her voice was low, partly from the natural softness of its timbre, but more, it seemed to me, from an extremity of fatigue.

"Will you tell Doctor de Grandin about your illness, dear?" Sorensen asked, his hard blue eyes softening with affection as he looked at her. "Doctor Traherne thinks possibly Doctor de Grandin and Doctor Trowbridge may have come across something like it in their practice."

Joyce Sorensen shuddered as though a chilly wind had suddenly blown across her shoulders, and her thin hands clasped together in her lap in a gesture that seemed to entreat mercy from fate. "Everything, Uncle Oscar?" she asked softly.

"Of course."

"I recall my uncle's first attack perfectly," she began, not looking at us, but fixing a half-vacant, half-pleading gaze upon a miniature of the Madonna which hung upon the farther wall. "He'd been out shooting that afternoon and went to bed almost immediately after dinner. I had a theater engagement, and went to the Pantoufle Dorée to dance afterward. It must have been about one o'clock, when I came home. Marshall, the butler, was in bed, of course, so I let myself in and went up to kiss Uncle Oscar good-night before going to my own room. Just as I reached his door I heard him cry out, not loudly, but terribly. It sounded something like the screaming laughs maniacs give in melodramatic motion pictures—it seemed to spout up like a dreadful geyser of insane fear, then died away to a kind of gurgling, choking murmur, like water running down a drain, or a man fighting desperately for breath.

"I tried his door and it was locked—I'm sure of that. Then in terror I ran up to Marshall's room and beat upon his door, calling out that Uncle Oscar was dying; but he gave no answer, so I ran back to the library and snatched a sword down from the wall." She nodded to a row of brackets where mementoes of Sorensen's grim fighting years were displayed. "I was determined to force the lock with the blade," she went on, "but when I reached my uncle's room again the door was partly open!

"Uncle Oscar lay upon his bed, the covers pushed to the floor, his hands flexed and his fingers digging into the mattress. His pajama jacket was open at the throat, and on the white skin of his neck, just below the line of tan, there was a little spot of blood, no larger than a pin-head.

"I hurried back to Marshall's room, and this time he heard me right away. Together we got my uncle back beneath the covers and made him comfortable. I spoke to him and he answered sleepily, assuring me he was all right; so I assumed he must have had a nightmare and thought no more about it. It wasn't till progressive weakness made it impossible for him to rise that we became worried and called in Doctor Traherne."

As she finished her recital de Grandin rose and leant above her. "*Pardonnez-moi, Mademoiselle*," he begged, "but have you, too, by any chance, a stubborn so small wound which gives no pain, but which will not heal? You have noted something of the kind upon your throat?"

The quick blood dyed her face and forehead faintly as she turned startled eyes upon him. "Not on my throat, sir," she answered softly, "here."

She laid her hand upon her breast above the heart.

"*Eh*, death of the devil, do you say so?" he exclaimed; then, very gently: "And may we see, *Mademoiselle*?"

There was something pleading, frightened, timidly beseeching, in the eyes that never strayed from his as she undid the fastenings of her robe and bared a bosom slim as Shakespeare's Juliet's, pointing out a tiny depression which lay against the milk-white skin an inch or so below the gentle swelling of the small and pointed breast.

"Ah?" de Grandin murmured as he finished his inspection. "Trowbridge, if you please, come here and tell me what it is you see."

He passed his glass to me and, obedient to his pointing finger, I fixed my glance upon the girl's pale skin. Piercing directly downward was a tiny punctured wound, semilunar in shape and less than an eighth of an inch in length. There was no area of inflammation round it; indeed, the lips of the small aperture seemed wholly bloodless, like those of a stab-wound inflicted on a corpse.

"There is soreness?" asked the Frenchman, gently touching the skin above the wound.

"None at all," the girl replied.

"And blood?"

"A little, sometimes. Some mornings I wake feeling really rested from my sleep. On these mornings the wound seems nearly healed. Other times I am so weak I can scarcely leave my bed, and I've noticed that at such times there is a little smear of blood—oh, not more than a single drop, and that a very small one—on my skin."

"Thank you, *Mademoiselle*," de Grandin nodded absently, his lips, beneath his trimly waxed mustache, slightly pursed, as though he were about to whistle. "Tell us, if you please, have you been troubled with unpleasant dreams, like that which plagued *Monsieur* your uncle?"

"Why, no; that is, I can't remember any," she replied. "Indeed, I'm perfectly all right, except for this great weakness. Do you know what the disease is, Doctor? Doctor Traherne thinks it may be caused by some strange germ—"

"I make no doubt that he is right," the little Frenchman answered. "A most strange germ, *Mademoiselle*. A very strange germ, indeed."

"WELL," TRAHERNE ASKED AS we left the house after bidding Sorensen and his niece good-night, "what d'ye make of it, gentlemen? Have either of you ever seen anything resembling that condition, or—"

"I have," de Grandin broke in shortly. "On several occasions I have seen such things, my friend, but never with the same accompanying circumstances. If those wounds were perforated, I should be convinced. As it is, I am in doubt, but—"

"But what?" Traherne demanded as the Frenchman failed to bring his statement to conclusion.

De Grandin's voice was flat and absolutely toneless as he answered: "*Monsieur,* if I should tell you what it is I think that lies behind this so strange business of the monkey, you would scoff. You would not believe me. Your mind, *pardieu*, is far too logical. You would say to you, 'Cordieu, I have never seen nor heard of anything like this, therefore it cannot be.' Nevertheless, I am inclined to think the cause of Monsieur Sorensen's illness, and that of his so charming niece, strikes back directly to that night in Madagascar when he pronounced divorcement on his native wife. It is, in fine, a thing which lies below the realms of logic, therefore something to be combated by perfectly illogical counter-measures."

"Humph," Traherne grunted.

"First I advise that you secure a corps of nurses, nurses you can trust implicitly. Have one in attendance on Monsieur Sorensen and another on his niece at every moment of the day and night."

"O.K," Traherne agreed, "I've been thinking of that. They're both too weak to be about. Bed-rest is bound to help them. What next?"

"I suggest that you secure a generous supply of *ail*—how do you say him? garlic?—*allium sativum* in the pharmacopeia—and have it liberally distributed at all entrances and exits of their rooms. See, too, that their windows are kept entirely closed, and that all animals are rigorously excluded from their presence."

Traherne, I could see, was angry, but he kept his temper in control as he demanded: "Then, I suppose, you'd like to have me burn some incense in their rooms, and maybe bring in an Indian medicine man to sing to them? Really, Doctor, you're amusing."

A smile which had no mirth in it swept across de Grandin's mobile lips. "*Monsieur*," he answered acidly, "I regret my inability to reciprocate the compliment, but I do not find you amusing. No, not at all; by no means. I find you distinctly annoying. Your mind is literal as a problem in addition. You believe in something only if you know the cause of it; you have faith in remedies only if you know their application. Smallpox, diphtheria, scarlet fever? Yes, of course, you know them. Dementia præcox, yes, you know it, too. But subtle problems of the mind—a hate, which is malign thought made crystal—hard by concentration—*morbleu*, you will have none of it! 'I have not seen it, therefore there is no such thing,' you say.

"Attend me, *mon petit bonhomme*: When every button which you wore was but a safety-pin, I was studying the occult. 'Ah,' I hear you say, 'occult—magic—balderdash!' Yes, you think I speak in terms of witches riding broomsticks, but it is not so.

"On more than one occasion I have seen men sicken and die when their symptoms were strangely similar to those of Monsieur Sorensen and Mademoiselle Joyce. Yes, by blue, I have seen them die and be buried, then rise again in dreadful life-in-death. Do not laugh, *Monsieur*; I tell you that which I have seen.

"But regard me carefully: I did not say the symptoms were the same; I said that they were similar. Those little, so small wounds the patients show, those little wounds which you think unimportant, may be the key to this whole mystery. One thing disturbs me when I think of them. They are punctured, not perforated, by which I mean they strike down in the flesh but do not wholly pierce it. They have entrances but no exits. Also their form convinces me that they were made with knives or needles or some small cutting instrument, and not by teeth, as I at first suspected—"

"Teeth!" Traherne exploded in amazement. "D'ye mean to tell me you suspected someone had bitten them?"

"Some one—or some *thing*," the Frenchman answered earnestly. "Now I think the contrary, therefore I am greatly puzzled.

"Come, my friend, when doctors quarrel patients die; let us not be stubborn. I will forego the garlic in the sickroom, for a time, at least; also I shall not insist upon their sleeping with their windows closed. Do you, for your part, seek for trusty nurses who shall watch them day and night, and we shall watch them closely, too. Do you agree?"

They shook hands upon their mutual understanding.

B UT THE PATIENTS FAILED to show improvement. Sorensen seemed to grow no weaker, but his strength did not return, while within a week his niece became so utterly exhausted that the mere performance of the vital functions seemed to put too great a tax upon her waning strength. Saline infusions, finally liberal blood transfusions, were resorted to, and while these gave her temporary help, she soon lapsed back to semi-coma.

De Grandin and Traherne were desperate. "Trowbridge, *mon vieux*," the Frenchman told me, "there is something evil here. We have exhausted every remedy of science. Now I am convinced our treatment must pursue another pattern. Will you watch with us tonight?"

We chose the upstairs sitting-room for our headquarters. Sorensen's room lay a dozen steps beyond it to the right, his niece's was scarcely farther at the left, and we could reach either or both in twenty seconds. We made inspections of the patients every hour, and each succeeding visit heightened our morale, for both seemed resting easily, and each time the nurses reported they had shown no sign of restlessness.

"*Mordieu*, but it would seem whatever lies behind this thing knows we are here, and holds its hand in fear," de Grandin told us as the tall clock in the lower hall struck two. "This is the time when vitality is lowest, and accordingly—"

His words were broken by a strangling, choking cry which echoed through the darkened house. "Monsieur Sorensen!" he exclaimed as, with Traherne and me at his heels, he leaped across the threshold of the sitting-room and raced the little distance to Sorensen's room.

The room, which had been dimly lighted by a night lamp, was dark as Erebus, and when we found the switch and pressed it, a sharp metallic click, but no light, followed.

"*Dieu de Dieu de Dieu de Dieu de Dieu!*" de Grandin swore. "Ten thousand small blue devils! What has happened to the lights in this infernal place?"

A rasping, gurgling sound, as of water gushing down a drain, or a man fighting desperately for breath, came through the darkness from Sorensen's bed, and with a string of curses which would have shamed a stevedore, de Grandin groped his way across the room, snatched a pocket flashlight from his pocket and played its beam upon the sick man.

Sorensen lay upon his bed, his bedclothes kicked to the floor, hands clenched in a rigidity like that of death, fingers digging deep into the mattress. His pajama coat was open at the throat, and on the white skin of his neck, just below the line of tan, was a ruby disk where warm blood welled up from a tiny wound. His eyes were open, staring, wide, and on his sun-burned face was such a look of mortal terror as is seldom seen outside the fantasies of a nightmare.

"*Mademoiselle!*" de Grandin challenged sharply. "Where in blazing hell's accursed name is that *sacré garde-malade?*" His flashlight swung around, picking up successive objects in the sickroom, coming finally to rest upon the rocking-chair where sat Sorensen's night nurse.

A chilling sense of cold, as though a freezing wind had blown upon me, made me catch my breath as the flashlight's gleam illumined her. She did not stir. She sat there rigidly, as though she had been carven out of wood. Her head was held uncomfortably downward, as though she listened to something far away; her neck was fixed and firm as though she had been in a trance. She was, to all intents, turned to stone. There was no special look upon her face, no fear, no terror; nothing that might be expected of a woman. in her plight, but she sat fixed, immovable, utterly unconscious of the world about her.

"*Mademoiselle!*" de Grandin cried again.

His hand upon her shoulder brought her back to instant consciousness, and she rose quickly, winking in the strong light of his pocket torch.

"W-why, what's happened?" she demanded.

"Happened?" Doctor Traherne almost shouted. "What's happened? Nothing, only your patient almost died while you sat dozing in your chair!"

"I haven't been asleep," the girl denied vehemently. "Marshall brought me coffee a few minutes ago, and I drank a little, but just as I put the cup down you came shouting here, and—"

"Softly, *mes amis*," de Grandin bade, holding up his hand for silence. "Do not chide her, Friend Traherne, she is not culpable. And you, *Mademoiselle*, what of the coffee which the little black one brought you? Where is it, if you please?"

"Here," she answered, pointing to a half-filled cup upon the table by her chair.

He picked the little vessel up, smelled it cautiously, then, dipping the tip of his forefinger into the brown liquid, put it to his tongue. "*Mais non*," he shook his head in disappointment; then, to the girl:

"You say the Negro butler brought you this?"

"Yes, sir; he's very thoughtful. He brings me coffee every night about this time."

"U'm, one wonders. Let us have a talk with him."

He strode across the darkened room and gave the call-bell button a sharp push.

While we waited for the servant to arrive we made a quick examination of the lights. All were in working order, but each bulb had been twisted in its socket until it just missed contact with the feed line, making the switch entirely useless. "*Parbleu*, it seems there has been business of the monkey here," de Grandin told us as he screwed the bulbs in place. "Now, if we can but—"

"You rang, sir?" asked the colored butler, appearing at the bedroom door as silently as a disembodied spirit from the mists of limbo.

"Emphatically," the Frenchman said. "You brought coffee to the nurse a little time ago?"

"Yes, sir," the black answered, and I thought I caught the sparkle of sardonic humor in his eye. "I bring coffee to both Miss Tuthill and Miss Angevine about this time each night."

"Eh, and drug it, one surmises?" snapped de Grandin.

The servant turned to the nurse, his manner a curious compound of respect and insolence. "How much coffee did you drink, Miss Tuthill?" he asked.

"Not more than half a cup," she answered.

"And is this the cup?"

"Yes."

"Ah," his impudence was superb as he reached out his hand, took up the half-filled cup and drained it at a gulp.

He looked the little Frenchman in the eye, a smile of half-concealed amusement on his face. "If the coffee is drugged, as you suspect, it surely ought to act on me—sir," he announced, just enough pause between the statement and the title of respect to give his words a tone of insolent bravado.

"Sit down, my little one," de Grandin answered with surprising calmness. "We shall see what we shall see anon." He bent above Sorensen, bandaging his wounded throat. "By the way," he flung across his shoulder casually, "you are not American, are you?"

"No, sir," said the butler.

"No? Where is it you were born, then?"

"Barbados, sir."

"U'm? Very well. I apologize if I have accused you wrongfully. That will be all, at present."

Inspection of Joyce Sorensen's room showed the girl sleeping peacefully and the nurse alertly wakeful. "Have you had your coffee yet, *Mademoiselle?*" de Grandin asked.

"No," Miss Angevine replied. "Marshall hasn't brought it yet. I wish he'd hurry, it helps a lot."

The little Frenchman gazed at her reflectively a moment; then: "*Mademoiselle,*" he ordered, "I desire that you join Miss Tuthill in Monsieur Sorensen's room. He is decidedly unimproved, and it is best that both of you stay with him. I shall undertake to watch your patient."

"What—" I began, but his upraised hand checked my question.

"Quickly, my friend," he bade, "behind the lounge!"

"Eh? Behind—"

"Species of an artichoke, conceal yourself with speed, and if you would not die in great discomfort, be sure you make no sound or move which might betray your presence. Me, I shall be the bait, you the silent spectator." He crossed the room and rang the bell; then, as he resumed his seat beside the sick girl's bed: "Remember," he repeated, "on no account are you to move until I give the signal, no matter how great you deem the provocation."

"You rang, sir?" Marshall asked, appearing in the doorway with his silent, ghost-like tread.

"Yes, I should like a cup of coffee, if you please. The nurse is feeling indisposed, and I have taken her responsibility."

Something like a gleam of triumph flickered in the little black man's eyes, but it died as quickly as it came, and with a murmured, "Very good, sir," he vanished in the darkness of the hall.

Five minutes later he returned with a silver tray containing coffee-pot and cup.

De Grandin rose and strode across the room, pausing beside the bed and gazing thoughtfully at the sleeping girl. His back was toward the servant; the opportunity to drug his coffee was perfect, made to order, it appeared to me.

But nothing untoward happened. The butler placed the tray upon the table, stood demurely waiting further orders, then, as de Grandin failed to turn, withdrew with his usual silent tread.

Ignoring my presence completely, the Frenchman resumed his chair, drank his coffee at a draft, and picked up a magazine.

Eight, ten, a dozen minutes passed. Nothing happened. Then suddenly the tomb-like quiet of the room was broken by a gentle guttural sound. I looked out from my ambuscade in fascinated horror. De Grandin's head had fallen forward, the magazine had slipped down to the floor. He was asleep—and snoring.

About to leave my place and seize him by the shoulder, I felt, rather than heard, the butler's quick approach, and hastily retreated to my hiding-place.

Stepping softly as a cat, the servant came into the room, bearing a tray with pot and cup exactly duplicating those which stood upon the table at de Grandin's side. Quickly he exchanged the new utensils for the old, poured out a half-cup of fresh coffee, and arranged the things so carefully that, had I not observed the substitution, I should have been prepared to swear that the cup upon the table was the one from which de Grandin had refreshed himself.

These preliminaries finished, the fellow bent and looked into de Grandin's face; then, satisfied the Frenchman was asleep, he turned and tiptoed to the bed where Joyce Sorenson lay. For a moment he stood looking at her and a smile of wicked malice flickered on his features.

"Broken heart for broken heart, wasted life for wasted life, tears for tears and blood for blood," he murmured. "Thus shall Mamba be avenged."

Drawing a short, wide-bladed knife from underneath his jacket he ripped the girl's silk sleeping-robe from neck to hem with a single quick slash.

There was something devilish in his deftness. Bending close, he drew apart the lips of the slit robe, and gently blew upon the girl's white body. Locked in the thrall of deep, exhaustive sleep, she flinched from the current of his breath, turning slightly from him, and as she did so he tweaked the silk robe gently, pulling an inch or so of it from underneath her. Again and again he repeated the maneuver, slowly, patiently forcing her across the bed, bit by little bit withdrawing the nightrobe, till at last she had shed the garment utterly and lay there like a lovely statue hewn from ivory.

I saw a spot of bright blood form and grow as he pierced the skin below her left breast with the sharp point of his knife, and had flexed my muscles for a spring when his next move struck me stone-still, with amazement.

From beneath his jacket he drew forth something like a bundle of coarse moss, dangled it before him from a silken cord and began to swing it through the air. Faster and faster, till it whirled round his head like a wheel of light, he swung the odd-appearing thing; then, as he reduced its speed and dangled it above the blood-spot on the girl's bared breast, I saw that closely twisted tendrils had worked open, and assumed the form of two capital Y's joined together at the base. Leaning quickly downward he dropped the object on the red-dyed wound which jeweled the whiteness of the girl's uncovered breast, and my eyes almost started from my head in horror as I saw the tiny thing begin to show a dreadful sort of change.

One of the branches of the lower Y had touched the drop, of ruby blood which welled up from the tiny wound he had inflicted on Joyce Sorensen, and like a blotter—or a leech—it drank the ruddy fluid up, slowly swelling, growing, taking on the form of life. Like a tiny balloon, inflated by a gentle flow of breath, the shriveled Y-bars filled out gradually, took on the form of human arms and legs; a head appeared between the outspread branches of the upper Y, and, balanced like a ballet dancer on one toe, a small, black human form pirouetted over Joyce Sorensen's heart.

Strangely life-like, oddly human in form it was, yet with something of the plant about it, too, so that as I gazed in fascination I could not determine whether it was a minute black dwarf which resembled some obscene variety of flower, or some dreadful flower which presented an indecent parody of humanity.

The sleeping girl stirred distressfully, moaning as if in torment, and her hands twitched spasmodically. It seemed as though the dancing horror balanced over her were forcing realization of its presence down through her unconsciousness.

"Trowbridge, *mon vieux*, take him, seize him, do not let him pass!" With a bound de Grandin was out of his chair, every trace of sleep gone from him. He leaped across the room, hands outstretched to seize the black.

With a snarl of bestial fury the little fellow dodged, hurling himself toward the door. I squirmed from my concealment and put myself in his path. As he ran straight at me I let drive my fist, catching him squarely on the point of the jaw and knocking him backward to de Grandin's waiting arms.

"*Bête, chien, chameau!*" the Frenchman whispered fiercely as he seized the undersized man's elbows in an iron grip and forced them to his sides. He slipped his hands down the butler's forearms, gripped him by the wrists and bent his arms upward in a double hammerlock. "Thou species of a spider, thou ninety-nine-times-damned example of a dead and rotten fish, take that flower of hell from *Mademoiselle*, and see that not a root is left to fester in her wound!" he ordered.

The little black man snarled like a trapped cat. "You think that you can make me?" he demanded. "Kill me, French oppressor, cut me in pieces, break my arms and drag my heart from out my breast, but you cannot save the woman. Tomorrow they will find her as she lies, unclothed for all to look on, bloodless and breathless—"

De Grandin bent the speaker's twisted arms a half-inch nearer to his shoulders. "You think so?" he demanded. "*Par les plumes d'un coq*, we shall see if you are right!"

Tiny gouts of perspiration glistened on the little black man's forehead, his mouth drew taut with agony and his eyes thrust forward in their sockets like a frog's as de Grandin slowly tightened his torturing grip upon his arms. Step by step he forced his prisoner toward the bed, hissing epithets in mingled French and English in his car.

As they reached the couch where Joyce Sorensen lay, the captive dropped upon his knees with a short gasp of anguish.

"Let me go," he begged. "Let me go, you French beast. I'll take the flower off of her."

De Grandin eased his grip upon one arm. "Do it with one hand," he ordered.

"I need both."

The Frenchman twisted the bent arms again and the butler crumpled to the floor unconscious.

"Water, if you please, Friend Trowbridge," he commanded. "I am too fully occupied to get it."

I snatched a carafe from the table and dashed a glassful of chilled water in the prisoner's face.

"And now, my little truant out of hell," de Grandin whispered softly as the captive winced beneath the shock of the cold liquid and his eyelids fluttered upward, "you will please remove that thirty-thousand-times-accursed thing from *Mademoiselle*, or I shall surely twist your arms from off your body and thrust them piecemeal down your throat!" Once again he bent his prisoner's arms until I thought that he would surely crack the bones.

One wrist freed, the black man reached out, seized the gyrating black thing and lifted it carefully from the wound in Joyce Sorensen's breast. Like a blow up bladder punctured with a pin, the infernal thing began to wilt immediately. In thirty seconds it had shrunk to half its former size; before a minute passed it had shriveled in upon itself, and was nothing but a ball of moss-like fiber from the fraying ends of which there dripped small drops of ruddy moisture.

"*Bien*," announced de Grandin as he eased his hold upon his prize. "Trowbridge, my friend, go and bid the nurse return, if you will he so kind. Me, I have a few important questions I would ask of this one—and I think I shall elicit better answers if I ask them in the privacy of the garage. I shall rejoin you soon."

"HOLA, MES ENFANTS!" SMILING in complete self-approval, Jules de Grandin joined us in Sorensen's upstairs sitting-room. "The germ which caused this new disease our colleague Traherne found has been isolated. *Morbleu*, he is completely isolated in the *poste de police*—unless they put him in restraint in the hospital. I fear I was a trifle rough with him before his story was completed."

"Then it was a germ disease—" Traherne began, but de Grandin interrupted with a laugh.

"*Mais oui, mon brave*," he chuckled. "A small and wholly vicious germ which traveled on two legs, and bore with him the strangest orchid any botanist could dream of. Attend me, if you please:

"When Monsieur Sorensen told us of his Madagascar interlude, I thought I smelled the odor of the rat. Madagascar, *mon Dieu*, what a place! A land of mystery more terrible than Africa, more subtle than China, more vengeful than India! When our forces overthrew the native government there in 1896 they incurred the never-dying hatred of the *Andriana*, or Malagasy nobility, and that hatred still crops up in strange and inexplicable murders of the French officials.

"You will recall Monsieur Sorensen referred to his native wife as Mamba, and called her a priestess of 'the Fragrant One'? Very good. Mamba, my friends, is a native term for a terrible, strange black orchid said to infest the jungles of inland Madagascar. It is supposed to be a kind of vampire plant, or vegetable leech, and if it be placed upon an open wound it blossoms in the likeness of a human figure and nourishes itself upon the blood of its unfortunate host till he or she is dead. According to the stories I was told in Madagascar, the habitat of this strange plant is strictly guarded by the priesthood which serves 'the Fragrant One,' which is the native name for the more or less mythical man-eating tree of which such dreadful tales are told.

"Very well. What had we before us? A man who had incurred the hatred of a native noblewoman who was also a priestess of a dark, malevolent religion, a noted sorceress, a woman whose very name was identical with that of a strange and dreadful kind of parasitic plant. This man lived beneath a curse pronounced upon him by this woman, and in the curse she foretold that he should be stricken with a malady which should cause his blood to waste away like little brooks in summer. Also that before he died he should see the one whom he loved most slowly wilt away and die.

"And what else did we see? This man was wasting steadily away; his niece, the apple of his eye, was also sinking rapidly. Was it not apparent that the curse had found him out? It seemed entirely possible.

"But, if it were a curse which worked by magic, why had he grown better when you sent him off upon a cruise? And why did his malady return when he came home? Apparently, there was some connection between his house and his disease. What was this link? Ah, that was for me to find out.

"I have seen men die when stricken by a vampire—do not laugh, Monsieur Traherne, I tell you it is so!—but the vampire bites his victim on the throat; Monsieur Sorensen's wound was from a knife or pin, not from a tooth, and a similar wound was on his niece's breast.

"I looked around, I noticed things; it is a habit which I have.

"I saw this colored butler, Marshall. This Marshall is a black man, but he is not a Negro. Neither are the Malagasy. When they are pure-bloods, unmixed with Malay or Chinese or Hindoo stock, their skin is black, but their features are small and straight and fine-cut, without a negroid trace, their hair straight and uncurled, their bodies firmly made, but small.

"Again, this Marshall, as he called himself, spoke with an English accent. I knew he was not reared in this country, but when he said he was from Barbados

I also knew he lied. Negroes from Jamaica speak like Englishmen; those from Barbados, for some strange reason, speak with a strong Irish brogue. 'There is the smell of fish upon this business, Jules de Grandin,' I inform me.

"Tonight we find Miss Tuthill drugged; it is apparent, yet the butler offers a good alibi. I will test him further,' I decide, and so I send the other nurse away, ask him for coffee and pretend to fall into a drug-caused sleep. He rises to the bait. *Mon Dieu*, he rises nobly! He—"

"How did you manage to shake off the effects of the drug so quickly?" I interposed. "The nurse was absolutely paralyzed, yet you—"

"*Tiens*," he broke in with a laugh, "those who would make the fool of Jules de Grandin need to rise early in the day, my friend. Did you think I drank that coffee? *Quelle naiveté! Pah. Regardez!*"

From his pocket he drew out a handkerchief, soaking with brown stickiness.

"When one knows how, the trick is simple," he assured us. "*Le mouchoir*, I stuff him in my collar underneath my chin while my back is turned to Marshall, then *pouf!* I pour the coffee into him when I pretend to drink. *Ah bah*, it is hot, it is sticky, it is most damnably uncomfortable, but it leaves me in possession of my faculties. Yes, certainly; of course.

"Then, while he thinks I am asleep he does the thing he has done many times before, but tonight would have been the curtain for Mademoiselle Joyce. He was prepared to break Monsieur Sorensen's heart by killing his niece before administering the *coup de grâce* to him.

"*Ha*, but I slept the sleep of the pussy-cat, me! When my small, black mouse was too far from his hole to make retreat I pounced upon him with the help of good friend Trowbridge, and thereafter he had many troubles.

"It took persuasion to make him tell his story, but he finally told it, though he finished with a broken arm. He was a nephew of this Mamba, this sorceress, this priestess of 'the Fragrant One,' this orchid-woman who had put a curse on Monsieur Sorensen. Through the years he watched his opportunity, finally coming to this country, taking service with Sorensen, gaining his full confidence, waiting for his chance to plant the strange, black orchid on his throat.

"'You shall feel the kiss of Mamba,' said the Malagasy woman, and it was in truth the kiss of Mamba—Mamba the black orchid, not Mamba the black woman—which had drained him of his blood and almost caused his death when you called us in the case, Monsieur Traherne."

"Where's that black orchid now?" asked Traherne.

"It was not safe to have around. I threw it in the furnace—*morbleu*, it writhed and twisted like a tortured living thing when the flames devoured it!" answered Jules de Grandin with a grimace. "The memory of it nauseates me. Await me here, my friends, I go for medicine."

"I've some tablets in my bag—" Traherne began, but de Grandin made a gesture of dissent.

"Not that, *mon brave*," he interrupted. "The medicine I seek is in a bottle on the sideboard down below. It bears the name of Messieurs Haig & Haig."

The Dead-Alive Mummy

S HE CAME WALKING SLOWLY toward us past the rows of mummy-cases. Not tall, but very slim she was, sheathed in a low-cut evening gown of midnight velvet which set her creamy shoulders off in sharp relief. Her hair, blue-black and glossy, was stretched without a ripple to a knot behind her neck, and contrasted oddly with her eyes of peacock blue. There was contrast, too, between the small and slightly kestrel nose and the full and sensuous mouth which blossomed moist and brilliant-red against the unrouged pallor of her narrow face. One slender-fingered hand was toying with a rope of pearls, and as she stepped there was a glint of golden links beneath the gossamer silk encasing her left ankle. Clouded, but unconcealed, the jewel-red lacquer on her toenails shone through filmy stocking-tips exposed by toeless satin sandals.

"*Mon Dieu*, but she is vital as a flame!" de Grandin whispered. "Who is she, Friend Trowbridge?"

"Dolores Mendoza," I answered, "the sister of the man who gave this collection of Egyptiana to the Harkness Museum. Old Aaron Mendoza, her father, was fanatical about ancient Egypt, and was said to have the third finest collection in the world, ranking next after the British Museum and the *Musée des Antiques* at Cairo."

The little Frenchman nodded. "So we are here," he murmured.

We were, as he had said, there for that very reason.

Aaron Mendoza, son and grandson of our city's foremost merchants, had retired from commercial life at the relatively early age of sixty, turning active management of the Mendoza Department Store over to his son Carlos and devoting himself to Egyptology with an energy amounting to a passion. Honest in all his mercantile transactions with the rigid honesty of a Portuguese-Jewish family which traced its history unbroken past the days of the Crusades, he had not scrupled to resort to any practice which would further his ambition to acquire the finest private Egyptological collection in the world. Men noted for their learning, daring and "resourcefulness" had named what fees they wanted for their services to him, and one by one they brought to him the spoils of Egypt's sands and pyramids and hidden rock-tombs—bits of art-craft wrought in gold and silver, lapis-lazuli and celadon, things whose valuations sounded like the figures of a nation's load of debt, papyri setting forth in picture-writing secrets never dreamt by modern man, desiccated bodies of kings and priests and priestesses whose intrigues shaped the destiny of nations in the days when history was an infant in its swaddling bands.

One morning they found Aaron sitting on his bed, a vacuous grin disfiguring his handsome face, both feet thrust into one trouser-leg. He babbled like a baby when they spoke to him, and smiled at me with child-like glee when I tried to ask him how he felt. His strong, fine brain had softened to a mass of cheesy waste while he was sleeping, and within a week the helplessness of paresis had settled on him. In six months he was dead.

Scarcely had the period of formal mourning ended when Carlos Mendoza announced the gift of all his father's ancient treasures to the Harkness Museum. With antiques went a sum to build a wing for housing them and a fund for their maintenance. This evening the new wing was opened with due ceremony, and the city's notables were gathered for the rites of dedication. Somehow—possibly because I had brought him and his sister into the world and steered them through the mumps and chicken-pox and other childish ills—Carlos had included me and de Grandin in the list of guests invited, and we had traversed miles of marbled corridors, viewing the exhibits with that awe which modern man displays before the relics of the older days. Tired of the flower-scent and chatter and repeated "ohs" and "ahs" of those assembled in the main hall, we had retired to the Gallery of Mummies for a moment's respite, and stood beside the bronze-barred window at its farther end as Dolores entered.

"Would you like to meet her?" I asked as the Frenchman's interested gaze stayed fixed upon the girl.

"*Corbleu*, does the heliotrope desire to face the sun?" he answered. "Yes, my friend, present me, if you will, and I shall call you blessed.

"*Enchanté, Mademoiselle*," he assured her as he raised her fingers to his lips. "You are like a breath of life among these relics of mortality; a star which is reflected in the black tides of the Styx."

The girl looked round her with a little shudder of repulsion.

"I hate these ancient things," she told us. "Carlos wasn't sure he wanted to part with them after Father spent so many years collecting them, but I urged him to present them to the museum. I hope I never have to look at them again. The jewels are ghastly—cold and dead as the people who once wore them, and the mummies—" She paused and looked distastefully at the upright mummy which faced us through the screen of dust-proof glass.

"*Mummy and Coffin of Sit-ankh-hku, Priestess of Isis, from Hierakonpolis. Period XIXth Dynasty (circa. 1,200 B.C.)*" she read aloud from the neatly lettered card. "Can you fancy living in the house with things like that? She might have been a girl about my age, judging by the portrait on the coffin top. Every time I looked at her it was as though I looked at my own body lying in that coffin."

The mummy and its case were usual types. In the open casket stood the mummy, barely five feet tall, swathed in closely wrapped brown cerecloth, banded latitudinally and diagonally with retaining bandages, the head a mere conical hooded protuberance above the slanting shoulders, no trace of arms apparent, feet shown merely as a horizontal shelf beneath the upright body. On the lid, which stood beside the coffin proper, had been carved a face to represent the dead. The features were small, patrician, delicately hawk-nosed and full-lipped, with narrow brows of vivid black arched over eyes of peacock blue. The ancient artist had worked well. Here was no mere mortuary portrait, typical of race and era, but lacking personality. It was, I felt on looking at it, a faithful likeness of the girl who died three thousand years ago, personalized and individual.

De Grandin studied it a moment, then: "One understands, *Mademoiselle*," he told her. "When one looks at that face it takes small imagination to conceive that it resembles you. She had rare beauty, that old one, just as you—*sapristi*, what is it, *Mademoiselle?*"

Dolores stood before the mummy-case, staring at the painted face with a set, unwinking gaze. Her countenance was mask-like, almost totally expressionless; yet something that was lurking terror lay within her eyes, rendering them glassy, shallow. It was as if a curtain had been drawn across them from within, hiding anything that might be seen by one who looked in them and leaving only a suggestion of sheer fright and horror printed on the retina.

"Mademoiselle Dolores!" he repeated sharply. "What is it?" Then, as she swayed unsteadily, "Catch her, my friend," he ordered. "She swoons!"

Even as he cried his warning the girl oscillated dizzily, with a sort of circular motion, as though her feet were fast-pivoted upon the floor, then pitched forward toward the glass-framed mummy-case, and as she toppled forward her eyes were wide and staring, fixed in fascination on the painted face upon the coffin lid. My arm went round her as she swayed, and a gasp of wonder choked my words of sympathy unuttered. From sandal-sole to head she was rigid as a frozen thing; taut, hard, unyielding as a hypnotist's assistant in a trance.

The rigor that affected her was such that we carried her across the room as though she had lain on a litter.

"What in heaven's name is it?" I demanded as we laid her on a Theban couch of sycamore and ivory. We could not chafe her hands, for they were set so firmly that they might have been carved wood, and when I placed my hand upon her breast to feel her heart, the flesh beneath her velvet corsage met my touch unyieldingly. It might have been a lovely waxen tailor's dummy over which we leant rather than the vibrant girl to whom we talked a moment since.

"Perhaps I'd better get some water," I suggested, but de Grandin stayed me with a gesture.

"*Non*," he advised. "Stay here and watch with me, my friend. This is—*sssh*, she is recovering!"

The set and horrified expression in Dolores' eyes was giving way, and in its stead we saw what seemed to be a look of recognition, like that of one who comes upon an old and long-forgotten scene, and fails at first to place it in his memory. The rigid, hard lines faded from her cheeks and jaw, and her slender bosom fluttered with a gasp of inspiration as her lips fell open and a little sigh escaped them. The words she used I could not understand, for they were spoken in a mumbling undertone, strung together closely, like an invocation hurriedly pronounced, but it seemed to me they had a harsh and guttural sound, as though containing many consonants, unlike any tongue with which I was familiar.

She sang softly, in an eery, rising cadence, with a sharply accented note at the end of every measure, over and over the same meaningless jargon, a weird, uncanny tune, vaguely like a Gregorian chant. One single sound I recognized—or thought I did—though whether it really were a word or whether my mind broke its syllables apart and fitted them to the sound of a more or less familiar name I could not tell; but it seemed to me that constantly recurring through the rapid flow of mumbled invocation was a sibilant disyllable, much like our letter S said twice in quick succession.

"What's she trying to say—'Isis'?" I asked, raising my eyes from her fluttering lips.

De Grandin was watching her intently, with that fixed, unwinking stare which I had seen him hold for minutes at a time when we were in the amphitheater of a hospital and a work of unique surgery was in progress. He waved an irritated hand at me, but neither spoke nor shifted the intentness of his gaze.

The flow of senseless words grew slower, thinner, as though the force of breath behind the red and twitching lips were lessening. "*Ah mon . . . sss-sss . . . se-rhus—*" came the softly whispered slurring syllables; then, as the faint voice ceased entirely, a gleam of consciousness came into Dolores' eyes, and she looked from Jules de Grandin to me with a puzzled frown. "Oh, did I faint?" she asked apologetically. "It was so terribly hot in there"—she gestured toward the crowded auditorium—"I thought it would be better here, but I suppose—" She raised her shoulders in the faint suggestion of a shrug, leaving her explanation uncompleted. Then, composedly, she swung her feet to the floor and placed her hand upon my arm.

"Will you take me to the coat room and call my car, please, Doctor?" she requested. "I think I'm about done in. Better be getting home before I have another fainting-fit."

"T HAT WAS ONE OF the most remarkable exhibitions of autosuggestion I've ever seen," I declared as we drove home.

"U'm?" said Jules de Grandin.

"It was," I answered firmly. "I'll admit it was uncanny as the devil, but the explanation's logical enough. That poor child had developed such a detestation of those mummies that it amounted almost to an obsession. Tonight, while she was staring at the face upon that coffin top—you'll recall she said it looked like her?—she suddenly went rigid as a mummy herself. Hypnosis induced by a carefully self-built-up train of thought identifying herself with the mummy of that priestess, then the fatigue of the reception, finally the ideal combination of the polished glass case reflecting a bright light and the face upon the coffin lid to focus her gaze. And, did you notice, she even mumbled some sort of gibberish while she was unconscious? Absolute identification with the character of the priestess. I don't think Carlos got those mummies out of his house one day too soon for his sister's mental health."

"I agree," de Grandin answered heartily. "Perhaps he did not move as quickly as he should. Her case will bear our observation, I believe."

"Oh, then you don't agree with my theory of autosuggestion and self-hypnosis?"

"Eh bien, they are queer things, these minds of ours," he returned evasively. "Hypnotism, what is it? No one rightly knows. Is it the 'animal magnetism' of Mesmer, or the substitution of the operator's mind for that of his subject, or, as some have hinted, the domination of one soul and spirit by another? Me, I do not know; neither do you. But he who plays with it toys with something perilously akin to magic—not always good magic, by the way, my friend."

He paused a moment, drumming on the silver knob of his ebony opera stick with restless fingers; then, abruptly: "Do me a favor, my friend," he begged. "Arrange that we may continue our acquaintance with Monsieur Mendoza and his so charming sister. I would observe her further, if such a thing is possible. I do not like the prospect of the future for that little lovely one."

M ENDOZA'S DINNER WAS PERFECTION; oysters with champagne brut, dry sherry with the turtle soup, pheasant with ripe Conti, Madeira with dessert and '47 cognac with the coffee. De Grandin had been gay throughout the meal brimming with high spirits, recounting anecdote on anecdote of humorous adventure in the tropics, in the war, of student days in Paris and Vienna. When books were mentioned he was equally at home in French and English literature discussing Villon, Huysmans, Verlaine, Lamartine and Francis Thompson with impartial intimacy.

Another guest was with us, a Doktorprofessor Grafensburg whose huge square head topped with close-cut, bristling hair, square spectacles and sweeping handle-bar mustache, no less than his ponderous manner and poorly fitting dinner clothes, labeled him unmistakably a scientist of the Viennese school. He seemed quite lost among the small talk of the table, and occasionally when de Grandin let fly a particularly witty sally he would look up helplessly, as though he sought to mark the flight of some swift-moving insect through the air. Now, cigar between the pudgy fingers of one hand, liqueur glass grasped firmly in the other, he sat foursquare before the fire of blazing apple logs and looked at Mendoza with something like pathetic appeal in his protuberant blue eyes.

"Doktor Grafensburg has consented to go over some of my—some of the mummies in the Harkness Museum," Carlos volunteered with a smile at the big Austrian. "Many of them have never been properly classified, and there's a mass of data to be translated and catalogued."

"*Ach*, yes," replied the savant, his infantile eyes beaming at this chance to take the center of the stage, "there are some most unusual things which your father's curators had completely overlooked, Herr Carlos. That little, small one, for example, the one they call the Priestess Sit-ankh-hku, she had never even been unwrapped, yet in her bandages I found a something truly startling."

"Ah?" breathed Jules de Grandin softly, as a momentary glitter shone in his small blue eyes. "What, by example, *Herr Doktor?*"

Grafensburg rose ponderously and stood before the Frenchman, legs apart, great head thrust forward between his bulging shoulders. "You are, perhaps, familiar with Egyptian beliefs?" he asked challengingly.

"I would not presume to discuss them with the *Herr Doktorprofessor* Grafensburg," replied the Frenchman diplomatically. "Would you not be kind enough to tell us—"

"*Ja wohl*," the Austrian broke in discourteously. "They had no idea of the things we know today, those ancient ones. They thought the arteries were full of air, the seat of the emotions was the heart, that anger generated in the spleen, *nicht wahr?*"

"So we have been told," de Grandin nodded.

"I tell you the same, also," rumbled Grafensburg. "Also I tell you that they had partly grasped the truth when they said that reason resided in the brain. Now, in the wrappings of this Priestess Sit-ankh-hku, I found the customary mortuary tablet, the golden plate on which her name and titles were engraved, with the usual pious invocation to the gods, and the pious hope of final resurrection in the flesh, only it was different. You know the reason for the mummification of Egyptian dead, yes? They believed that when three thousand years had passed the soul returned to claim its body, and without a habitation of the flesh would have nowhere to go. It would have to wander bodiless and nameless in

Amenti, the realm of the damned. As the little lady lived about the time of the Oppression, she should now be ready for reanimation—"

"Perfectly, *Herr Doktor*," de Grandin nodded, "one understands, but—"

"*Ha*, little man, but you do not understand!" the Austrian thrust his cigar forward as though it had been a weapon. "Usually the tablets prayed the gods to guide the *ka*, or vital principle, back to the waiting body. This one does nothing of the kind. It asserts—asserts, if you please, asserts with positiveness—that Sit-ankh-hku will rise again with the help of one who lives, and by the power of the brain. That is most unusual; it is extraordinary. Never before in the annals of all Egyptology have we found an instance where the deceased will rise otherwise than by the help of the gods. This one will rise by the assistance of a man who lives, or perhaps of a woman, the text is not quite clear. But rise she will, by human assistance and by strength of brain. *Donnerwetter*, it is droll, *nicht wahr*? She will reanimate herself by the power of her brain, and that brain was flung into the Nile three thousand years ago, together with her blood!" he finished with a rumbling laugh.

"I do not think that it is droll, *Herr Doktor*," de Grandin answered in a level voice. "I rather think that it is devilish. That statement which you read may go far to explain what—*grand Dieu*, look to Mademoiselle Dolores, Friend Trowbridge!"

At his shouted warning I wheeled round. Dolores stood beside the grand piano, a straight, slim silhouette in lettuce green, pearl-pale and rigid as an image. Even as I leaped to aid her the thought flashed through my mind that she was like a gallant little tree whose roots were severed by the woodsman's ax. She swayed uncertainly a moment, then leant from the perpendicular like a toppling tower. Had I not seized her in my arms she would have fallen flat upon her face, for every nerve and muscle of her slender body had been petrified in the same awful way as on that night at the museum, and as my hands closed round her I was shaken by a feeling of repulsion at the hardness of her flesh.

"Dolores dear, what is it?" Carlos cried as he placed his sister on a sofa.

"Is—is it epilepsy?" he asked fearfully, as he saw the girl's pale skin and set and staring eyes.

De Grandin's face was almost totally expressionless, but anger-lightning flashed in his small eyes as he responded tonelessly: "Monsieur Mendoza, one cannot be quite sure, but I think she is suffering from an attack of the *Herr Doktor's* cursed *drôlerie*."

Treatment was futile. All night Dolores lay as rigid as if petrified. As though she had been dead, her temperature was exactly that of the surrounding atmosphere, the uncanny hardness of the flesh persisted, and she was unresponsive to all stimuli, save that the pupils of her set and staring eyes showed a slight contraction when we flashed a light in them. There was practically no pulse perceptible, and when we drove a hypodermic needle in her arm to administer a dose of strychnine there was no reflex flinching of the skin, and the impression we had was more like that of thrusting a pin through some tough ceraceous substance than through yielding flesh. As far as we could see, every vital function was suspended. Yet she was not dead. Of that much we were certain.

Toward morning the dreadful stiffness, so like rigor-mortis, passed, and as at the museum, she began to hum a chant, a weird and oddly accented tune composed of four soft minor notes. This time enunciation seemed more perfect, and we could recognize a phrase which constantly recurred throughout the chant like an imperative refrain repeated endlessly: "O *Sit-ankh-hku, nehes—O Sit-ankh-hku, nehes!*"

"*Morbleu!*" exclaimed de Grandin as a light of recognition flashed in his eyes. "*Par la barbe d'un bouc vert*, do you apprehend the burden of her song, Friend Trowbridge?"

"Of course not," I replied. "This gibberish hasn't any meaning, has it?"

"Has it not, *ha?*" he shot back. "Me, I shall say it has. It is the tongue of ancient Egypt that she chants, my friend, and that phrase she constantly repeats means: '*Awake, O Sit-ankh-hku; O Sitankh-hku, awake!*'"

"Good Lord, identification with that devilish mummy again!" I exclaimed. "Confound that Grafensburg and his childish talk about the thing, he—"

"He is a species of a camel," cut in Jules de Grandin. "May the fires of hell consume him living—he called me 'little man'!"

DESPITE OUR EVERY EFFORT, Dolores failed to show improvement. Cold compresses on the head, caustics on brow and neck, and repeated stimulants alike seemed powerless to rouse her from her lethargy. Occasionally the delirium in which she chanted thick-tongued invocations lightened the profound coma of absolute unconsciousness; but these spells came unbidden and unheralded, and we were powerless to lift her into consciousness or strike the slightest note of response from her, however much we tried.

"*Dieu de Dieu!*" de Grandin swore when three days of unavailing work had brought us close to nervous breakdown; "me, I am slowly going crazy. This *sacré* coma which has taken hold on her, I do not like it."

"D'ye think there's any chance of her recovering?" I asked, more for the sake of making conversation than from any hope of favorable response.

"*Tiens*; *le bon Dieu* and the devil know, not I," he answered somberly, his speculative gaze upon the patient. For a space of several minutes he continued his inspection, then plucked me by the sleeve. "Do you observe it, *mon ami?*" he asked.

"Eh?"

"Her face, her hands—the whole of her?"

"I don't think—" I began, but:

"Look at her carefully," he ordered. "We have forced the vital functions artificially. Elimination we have had, and nourishment by forcible feeding; moreover, she has lain this way for a scant three days, but observe her if you will. Is she not more than normally emaciated?"

He was right. While some loss of weight was normally to have been expected, emaciation had progressed far past the normal point. The subcutaneous tissue seemed to have dissolved, leaving little more than unfilled skin upon the staring bones. Paper-thin, her cheeks seemed plastered to the jaw-joints of her skull, lips thin as tight-stretched parchment showed the outlines of her teeth, and her very eyeballs seemed deflated, so that the eyes were merely empty pits in a cadaverous face. Wrist processes and radii showed almost as plainly through the drum-tight skin of forearms as though they had no covering at all.

"Good heavens, yes, you're right," I told de Grandin. "Why, she's desiccated as a mummy!"

"*Tu parles, mon vieux,*" he responded grimly. "Like a mummy—yes, by blue, you have put your finger on the word! Come."

"Come?" I echoed. "What d'ye mean? Surely, you'll not leave her—"

"But yes, of course," he interrupted. "The *garde-malade* can watch by her. She can at least report her death, which is all that we could do if we remained. Meanwhile, there is a chance . . . yes, my friend, I think there is a little so small chance. . . ."

"To the Harkness Museum," he ordered the taxi driver, "and hurry, if you please. There is five dollars extra for you if you get us there within ten minutes."

"I'm afraid Doctor Grafensburg can't see you now, sir," said the attendant when de Grandin panted his demand that we be taken to the Austrian at once. "He's very busy in his office, and left strict orders—"

"Ah bah," the little Frenchman cut in. "You tell me *that* when we are come upon an errand that may mean the saving of a life? Where is this pig-dog's utterly, unmentionable office? Me, I will go to him without announcement. Only show us where he hibernates, my friend, and I shall take the full responsibility for disturbing him. Yes, certainly; of course."

"*Kreuzsakrament!* Did I not strict orders leave that I should not be bothered?" Doktor Grafensburg's big face turned toward us with a snarl of almost bestial fury as we wrenched aside his office door and hastened toward him. He was gowned in linen, as for an autopsy, and glared at us across a porcelain operating-table on which there lay a partly unbandaged mummy. A shiver of repulsion ran through me. With his great head hunched forward, mouth disfigured by the stream of curses which he hurled at us, he reminded me of some foul ghoul disturbed at its repast. The furious scowl lightened somewhat as he recognized us, but his effort at cordiality was plainly forced as he drew a sheet across the mummy on the table and came forward.

"So? Is it you, little man?" he asked with ponderous jocularity. "I had thought that you were busy taking temperatures and mixing pills!"

"*Sale bête!*" de Grandin murmured underneath his breath; then, aloud:

"We have just come from Mademoiselle Mendoza's sickroom," he explained. "Something has happened which has made our presence here imperative. Is it the mummy of the Priestess Sit-ankh-hku. you are working on, *Herr Doktor?*"

Grafensburg glared at him suspiciously. "And if it is?" he countered.

"*Précisément,* if it is, we should greatly like to see what you have found, if anything. Her physical condition, the extent of preservation of her body, is of great importance to us. May we inspect it?"

"*Nein!*" the other spread his arms in a protective gesture, as though de Grandin made a threat against the mummy on the table. "She is mine, and only I may look at her. When I have my investigation made and my notes arranged, you may read what I have found; meantime—"

There was the menace of cold hatred in de Grandin's voice as he cut in—"Meantime, *mon cher collègue,* you will kindly stand aside and let me look at that ten-thousand-times-accursed mummy, or I shall give myself the great felicity of sending your fat soul to hell." From his shoulder holster he snatched out a pistol and aimed it steadily at the Austrian's protruding paunch.

"*Allez—en avant,*" he ordered as the other stared at him with dilated eyes. "I do not feel inclined to argue with you, my pig-ugly one."

Muttering thick-throated curses, Grafensburg gave ground, and de Grandin reached his free hand toward the sheet, twitching it from the half-stripped mummy on the operating-table.

"Ah?" he breathed as the cotton covering came fluttering off. "Ah-ha? Ah-ha-ha?"

I stared in blank amazement.

The form upon the table was no mummy. Denuded of their centuries-old bandages, the head and shoulders were exposed, and from the face Herr Grafensburg had lifted the gold mummy-mask. A pale, exquisite countenance looked up at us, clear-cut as cameo. The brow was low and broad, framed in a mass of fine, dark hair bound round the temples with a diadem of woven silver set with lapis-lazuli. The nose was small and delicately aquiline, the mouth a trifle wide and rather thin-lipped, a willful, proud and somewhat cruel mouth, I thought. Long, curling lashes rested on the youthful, rounded cheeks. Bare, creamy shoulders gleamed beneath the little pointed chin, and from the torn and powdered wrappings, still crossed on the breast, a pair of slender, red-tipped hands peeped out like fragile lilies blooming in corruption. I gazed upon the lovely face in awed amazement, realizing that these silk-fringed eyes had looked upon the world three thousand years ago. How many men had lived and died since those pale lips had drawn the breath of life and those closed eyes had looked upon the sun-gilt, star-jeweled skies of ancient Egypt!

De Grandin drew his breath in with a sort of whistling gasp. "*Mon Dieu*," he whispered softly, "cannot you see it, good Friend Trowbridge? Does not the likeness strike you?"

"Yes—yes!" I breathed. "You're right; she does resemble poor Dolores. One could swear that they are sisters, though they lived three thousand years apart."

"*Himmelskreuzsakrament!*" raged Doktor Grafensburg. "You come in here, you crazy, brainless *schmetterling*, and point pistols at me; you interrupt me at my work, you take from me my beautiful, incomparable one, and—"

"Calm yourself, *mon collègue*," broke in Jules de Grandin with a smile. "We would not for the world disturb you at your work, but we desire certain information which only you can give. This is truly an amazing piece of body preservation. I have seen many mummies in my time, but never one like this. Tell me, if you will; have you some theory of the method they employed to keep her as we see her now?"

The Austrian's pale eyes blazed with enthusiasm.

"*Nein, nein*," he answered huskily. "I was unwrapping her when you came in. I was about to make a set of careful measurements and note them down; then I would make an autopsy to find how they performed the work to her preserve this way. By heaven, it is a marvel! It is something never seen before. *Herr Gott*, it is—"

"One agrees entirely," de Grandin nodded, "but—"

"*Nein, lieber Gott*—you do not understand!" the Austrian cut in. "You have seen mummies, *ja*? You know they are deprived of moisture-content, left with nothing but the husk of bone and tissue, *ja*? But—*Donnerwetter!*—did you ever see a mummy which could take up moisture from the air and resume the look of life it had before the old embalmers pickled it, *hein*?"

The little Frenchman's small blue eyes were dancing with excitement, his tightly waxed wheat-blond mustache seemed fairly quivering as he faced the fleshy Austrian. "*Herr Doktor*," he asked half tremulously, "do you tell me that this mummy-thing has seemed revived—"

"*Sehr wohl*," the Austrian broke in, "have I not told you so? When first I took that mummy from its case it was a mummy, nothing more. All moisture had been from it dried; it weighed not more than thirty pounds. I the outer layer of bindings stripped away, then stopped to read and translate the inscription on the pectoral tablet. Three days it lay here partially unwrapped. Today—*Herr Gott!*—I start to take the other bindings off, and what do I discover? Not the mummy I had left three days before, but the lovely, life-like body of a lovely woman! *Herr Gott*, she has begun to blossom like a flower in the moisture of the air! She enchants me; I love her as I never loved a woman in my life; I can scarcely wait to cut her open!"

De Grandin looked at Grafensburg a moment; then: "*Meinherr*," he asked, "does human life mean anything to you?"

The big man stared at him as though he had been something he had never seen before, then raised his shoulders in a ponderous shrug.

"If it does," resumed the Frenchman, "you have now the chance to aid us. This body, this lovely, evil thing must be destroyed, and quickly. Believe me, life depends on it."

"*Nein!*" cried the other in a voice gone thin with sudden panic. "I cannot have it so. Not for a hundred human lives shall you lay hands upon my *liebes liebchen* till I have the autopsy performed on her. Men have died and worms have eaten them ten thousand thousand times since the embalmers of old Egypt finished with their labors on this body. Men will die until the end of time, but here we have a miracle of science. What is one paltry life compared with the disclosures an autopsy on this body will give us? Bah, you little pill-peddler, you tinkerer of broken bones, you set your stupid trade above the cause of science? You would hold the clock-hands back that you might spare some little, worthless life a few years longer? By heaven! I say you shall not touch this body with your little finger! Out, out of my cabinet, out, before I throw you!" Pop-eyes blazing, heavy lips drawn backward in a snarl, he advanced on Jules de Grandin, heedless of the latter's pistol as though it had been but a pointed finger.

"*Halte la!*" de Grandin cried. "I will make the bargain with you. Bring this body which you so adore to Monsieur Mendoza's house this evening, and promise me you will perform your autopsy upon it before midnight, and I will consent. Refuse, and—it would be some loss to science if I had to shoot you dead, *Herr Doktor*, but if I must I will. Make no mistake about it."

For a moment they glared in each other's eyes; then, with a shrug of resignation, the big Austrian turned back. Half the other's size, dandified, almost effeminate, de Grandin nevertheless bore the stamp of the born killer, and in the steady gaze of his little, round blue eyes the Austrian savant had seen the bare-boned face of death. For all his ponderous size and his bloodless, cold devotion to his science, Herr Doktor Grafensburg was something of a coward, and his blustering bravado melted like a snowpatch in the sun before the Frenchman's cold determination.

"*Ja wohl*," he finally agreed. "Leave me to my work this afternoon. I will the body have at Herr Mendoza's house tonight at eight."

"WHAT THE DICKENS DOES it mean?" I asked as we drove toward Mendoza's. "Have you found some explanation for this chapter of strange incidents—"

"*Non*," he broke in, "I am at sea, my friend. I, the clever one, the shrewd, so wily fox, am faced with a blank wall. This business of the monkey passes my experiences. I am a poor and purblind stupid fool. Let me think!"

"But—"

"Precisely—exactly, 'but',' he agreed, nodding. "Consider, if you please: Mademoiselle Dolores has been ill three days. She is unconscious in a coma, and we cannot waken her. She loses weight so quickly that within the little space of seventy-two hours she has become to all appearances a cadaver—a mummy, by blue! Meantime, what happens at the museum? The swinish Grafensburg partially unwraps the mummy of the Priestess Sit-ankh-hku, then stops to read her pectoral tablet. Three days elapse, and in their course the mummy of the Priestess Sit-ankh-hku puts on the semblance of a new-dead body. What is the next step in this dual transformation, *hein?*"

"But there may be something in the theory Grafensburg advances," I argued. "We've seen dehydrated food—apples, for instance. Though shrunken to a husk, and bearing no more resemblance to their original state than a mummy resembles a fresh body, when they're put in water they fill out and almost simulate fresh fruit. Isn't it possible that the embalmers of old Egypt might have hit upon some process of dehydration whereby the body would take up moisture from the air when it had been unwrapped, and—"

"*Ah bah*," he interrupted in disgust. "Grafensburg can read hieroglyphs, Grafensburg knows Egyptology, but also Grafensburg is a great fool!"

A CASE OF LEUCOCYTOPENIA I had under observation at Mercy Hospital kept me later than I had expected, and preparations were complete when I reached Mendoza's house that night. Thin, frail, emaciated, looking more like a cadaver than a living person, Dolores lay swathed in blankets on a lounge. Beside her, close as though ready for a blood transfusion, lay the blanketed body of the Priestess Sit-ankh-hku, and as I looked upon the two pale faces I was struck anew with the strange resemblance each bore to the other. The only light in the room was that given by a red-bowled vigil lamp which de Grandin placed about two feet from, and midway between, the two dark heads pillowed on their couches, and the flickering, fitful gleam of the little lamp's short wick cast a shifting mottle of shadows on the equally immobile faces of the living and the dead.

Silently de Grandin crossed the room drew back the curtains at the window and looked up at the sky. "The moon is rising," he announced at length. "It will soon be time for our experiment."

For something like five minutes he stood at gaze; then, as a shaft of silver light stole through the window and across the floor, splashing a little pool of luminance upon the two still faces, he stepped quickly to the lamp, blew out its flame, and from beneath his jacket drew a roll of silken gossamer.

"*Lieber Gott!*" cried Grafensburg as de Grandin spread the silver tissue out, laying part of it across the dead girl's face, the other end across Dolores' white, still countenance. "Where—where did you get that? It is a portion of the—"

"Silence, *cochon*," bade the little Frenchman sharply. "It is a fragment of the veil of Isis which hung before her altar-throne that the profane might not see her godhead. It will help us get in contact with the past—one hopes."

Now the moonlight shone full on the girls' veiled faces, touching them with argent gilding. De Grandin laid one hand upon Dolores' brow and touched the forehead of the long-dead priestess with the finger-tips of the other. There was something measured, monotonous as a chant, in his voice as he called out softly: "Mademoiselle Dolores, you can hear me when I speak?"

A moment's silence; then, so softly we could scarcely hear, soft as a breath of wind among the leafless branches of a tree, but still distinct enough to understand, there came the answer: "I can hear you."

"You can hear the chiming of the sistra; you can hear the chanting of the priests?"

"I can hear them!"

"Open the eyes of your memory; look around you—tell us what it is you see. I order, I command it."

As the answer came I started violently. Was it a vagary of overwrought nerves, or did my ears deceive me? I could not surely tell, but it seemed that by some odd trick of ventriloquism the reply came not only from Dolores, but from the dead girl at her side, as well. They seemed speaking in soft chorus!

"I am in a lofty temple," came the faltering, halting answer. "Sistra ring and harps are playing, priestesses are chanting hymns. A man has come into the temple. He is young and very beautiful. He is robed in white. His head is shaven smooth. He has paused before the silver veil that hangs between the temple and the face of Isis. He has put aside the veil and gone through a low door. I can no longer see him."

We could hear the soft rustle of the April wind in the budding trees outside; somewhere in the house a clock ticked steadily, and its ticking sounded like the blows of some great hammer on a giant anvil. The sharp staccato yelp of a taxi's horn out in the street was almost deafening in the silence of that darkened room. Then there came another sound. No, not quite a sound; rather, it was like that subjective sense of ringing in the inner ear we have after taking a heavy dose of quinine, more the *impression* of a sound than any actual vibration. Bell-like it was, almost unbearably shrill, unspeakably sweet; nearly toneless, yet utterly fascinating. I felt a sense of drowsiness come stealing over me, and with it the impression of another presence in the room was borne upon me. There was another—some one—some *thing*—among us, and I shivered as though a chill hand had suddenly been passed across my cheek.

"What is the ceremony you are witnessing?" de Grandin asked, and his voice seemed faint and far away.

"A man is entering the priesthood. He is in the sanctuary of the goddess now. She will come to him and flood him with her spirit. He will be her own for time and for eternity. He will put away the love of woman and the hope of children from his heart, and devote himself for ever to the service of the great All-Mother."

"Who is this man?"

"I do not know his name, but he was born a Hebrew. He has put aside his God to take vows of Isis for love of a priestess of the goddess. She has put a spell on him; he is mad for love of her, but because she is forbid to marry by her vows he has abjured Jehovah and become a heathen priest that he may be near her in common worship of the goddess."

"What else do you see?"

"I see nothing. All is dark."

We waited a tense moment; then: "Is it over—have you finished?" I asked, edging toward the light-switch. Somehow, I felt, with the friendly glow of electricity upon us, that sense of being in the room with something alien would fade away.

The Frenchman hushed my question with an upraised hand. "Tell us what you witness now?" he ordered, leaning forward till his breathing stirred the silver veil which lay upon Dolores' face.

"It is daylight. The sun shines brightly on a temple's painted pylon. The sacred birds are feeding in the courtyard. I see a woman cross the forecourt. It is I. I am robed in a white robe which leaves my bosom and my ankles bare. Sandals of papyrus show my feet. Jewels are on my arms and a band of silver crowns my hair. In one hand I bear a lotus bud, and a water-pot is in the other. I am going to the fountain. An old man accosts me. He is very feeble. His hair and beard are white as snow. He wears a blue robe and red turban. He is a Hebrew. He raises his hands and curses me. He tells me I have charmed his son away from God, and have made a heathen of him. He curses me in life and death. He calls the curse of Yahweh on me. I laugh at him and call him Jewish dog and slave. He curses me again and tells me I shall find no rest until atonement has been made. He swears that I must walk the earth again in penance and humility.

"Now I see the youth who took the vows of Isis. He is dead. A wound gapes like a flower in his throat. His Jewish brethren have set on him and killed him for apostasy. I bend over him and kiss him on the lips, and on the gaping, bloody wound. My tears fall on his face. I tear my hair and throw dust on my head. But he does not answer to my cries. I swear that I will join him.

"I seek out Ana the magician. He is old and wise and very wicked. I promise him what he will if he will make it so that I can join the man who forsook his race and God for me. He tells me I must be a Jewess, but I know this cannot be, for I am Egyptian. He says that when the time for my awakening comes and my *ka* comes back to seek its earthly tenement, he can make me rise a Jewess. I ask him what his fee will be, and he says it is I. So I yield myself to his embrace, and then, because I know the priests will stone me with stones until I die because I broke my vows of chastity, I throw myself into the Nile. Ana the magician takes my body and prepares it for the tomb."

Silence heavy as a cloud of darkness settled on the room as the last faint, halting sentence ended. The shaft of moonlight had vanished from the window, and the still, couched forms were barely visible. There was a queer, sharp freshness to the air, as though it had been ozonated by a thunder-storm. Almost, it seemed to me, there was a quality of intoxication in the atmosphere, and mechanically I put my hand upon my wrist to test my pulsation. My heart was almost racing, and throughout my body there tingled a feeling of physical well-being like that one feels upon a mountain-top in summer.

"Lights!" came Jules de Grandin's hail. "*Grand Dieu*—Trowbridge, Grafensburg, make lights; it is incredible!"

I stumbled through the gloom, found the wall-switch and turned on the electricity. De Grandin stood between the silent bodies, a mute forefinger pointed at each.

"Look, observe; behold!" he ordered.

I blinked my eyes and shook my head. Surely this was some gamin trick of faulty senses. Dolores lay in quiet sleep lips softly parted, limbs relaxed, a faint but unmistakable glow of health upon her cheeks. Beside her lay the body of the priestess, and already it seemed undergoing dissolution. The once firm cheeks were sunken in, the eye-holes so depressed they were no more than hollow pits; the lips were drawn back from the staring teeth, and on the skin there lay that hideous tint of leprous gray which is the harbinger of putrefaction.

"Quickly, Grafensburg," de Grandin bade, "if you would make your precious autopsy you had better be about it while there yet is time. Take her away. We follow you soon."

THE HERR DOKTORPROFESSOR GRAFENSBURG stripped off his rubber gloves and looked from me to Jules de Grandin, then back again in blank bewilderment "By heaven!" he swore, "never have I a thing like this seen before. Never; never! She was a mummy first, *kollegen*, as perfect a specimen of embalming as ever I have seen, and thousands of them have I unwrapped. Then she was a woman, almost living, breathing. Next she becomes a *kadaver*, a long-dead corpse, already almost reeking. *Lieber Gott*, I cannot understand it!"

"Yet the autopsy—" de Grandin murmured, "but—"

"*Ach, ja,*" excitedly broke in the Austrian, "it showed hers was a body like the thousand others I have cut apart. *Donnerwetter*, I might have been in hospital dissecting the dead corpse of one who died in bed a little while before! Brain, heart and lungs, viscera—everything she had in life, were all in place. *Herr Gott*, she had not been embalmed at all according to Egyptian custom; only dried and bandaged! I am in the sea of doubt submerged. I cannot tell my right hand from my left; my experience is of no value here. Have you perhaps a theory?"

De Grandin shed his linen operating-gown and lit a cigarette. "I have an hypothesis," he answered slowly, "but I would not care to dignify it by the name of theory. The other night when Mademoiselle Dolores went insensible before that mummy in the museum, she was like one hypnotized. She made a quick recovery, so we thought, but only to be seized again when you told us of the strange inscription you had found upon the pectoral tablet of the Priestess Sit-ankh-hku. Why was this? one wonders.

"Me, I think I have the answer. Thoughts are things, immortal things. Thought emanations, especially those produced by violent emotions, have a way of permeating physical objects and remaining in them as the odor of the flowers lingers in the vase, or the sweet perfume of sandalwood remains for all to smell long after life departs from out the tree. Very well, consider: Too-late-awakened love, perhaps, shook this ancient priestess' being to its very core; she would make atonement for the sin she had committed against the Jewish youth who loved her more than he adored his God. That was the thought which moved her when she struck her so abominable bargain with the wizard Ana; the thought persisted when she cast herself into the Nile. *And though her body died, the thought lived on.*

"When Ana the magician made her body ready for the tomb he mummified it by some secret process of his own, not by the technique of the *paraschites*. And, further to concentrate the thought which dominated her, he carved upon her pectoral mortuary tablet the prediction that she would arise through the agency of her brain—her thought, if you prefer—rather than by intervention of the gods.

"Mademoiselle Dolores is a psychic. As she paused before the mummy of this so unfortunate young girl the tragic history of her life and pitiable death was borne to her as the scent of mummy spices which have been borne to one less susceptible to psychical suggestion. Unwittingly Friend Trowbridge sensed the truth when he said that she 'identified herself with the mummy.'

"My friends, she was infected with the thought-force emanating from that long-dead mummy, even as she might have taken germ-contagion from it. Sit-ankh-hku would expiate her sin of long ago by resurrection as a Jewess. Mademoiselle Dolores is a Jewess. Strangely, by coincidence, perhaps, the two resembled each other. *Voilà*, the thought-cycle was completed. Dolores Mendoza would become Sit-ankh-hku; Sit-ankh-hku would completely dominate—displace—the personality of Dolores Mendoza. Yes, undoubtlessly it was so.

"These things I surmised without knowing them. It was a process of instinct rather than of reason. *Alors*, I blended the modern with the ancient. There is much to say in favor of the Freudian psychology, even though it has been made the happy hunting-ground of pornography by some who practise it. Mademoiselle Dolores suffered from a 'complex', a series of emotionally accented ideas in a repressed state. A thought-thorn was imbedded in her personality. While it remained there it would fester. Accordingly, we must take it out, as we would take out a physical thorn from her physical body if she were not to suffer an infection.

"I had you bring the body of the olden one and lay it close beside her that she might be *en rapport* with things which happened in the long ago. For the same reason I secured the veil of Isis and laid it on her face. It, too, was pregnant with the thought-forms of an ancient day. Finally, I waited for the moon to shine upon her, for the moon was sacred to the Goddess Isis, and each little thing which brought her nearer to the past brought the past nearer us. I sent her questing spirit backward to the days of old. I bade her tell us what she saw and heard, and through her living lips dead Sit-ankh-hku disclosed the tragedy which came to her three thousand years ago.

"*Enfin*, we took the stopper from the jar of scent, and the perfume, liberated in the air, disseminated. Those old tragic thoughts, so long locked tightly in Sit-ankh-hku's little body, were set at liberty; they thinned and drifted off like vapor in a breeze—*pouf!* they were gone for ever. No longer will they ride Mademoiselle Dolores like an incubus. She is forever freed from them. It is doubtful if she will retain the slightest memory of the sufferings she underwent while they possessed her."

"But how do you account for Dolores almost changing to a mummy, while the mummy almost came to life?" I asked.

"In Mademoiselle Dolores' case it was, as you have aptly phrased it, a case of 'identifying herself with the mummy'. Under self-hypnosis, originally induced by the thought-force she had absorbed as she stood before the mummy of the Priestess Sit-ankh-hku, she forced herself to simulate the mummy's stark rigidity, the very physical appearance of a desiccated lich. In the mummy's case—who knows? Perhaps it was as Doktor Grafensburg suggests, that the body was so treated by the wizard Ana's art that it took up moisture from the air, became rehydrated and put on its original appearance. Me, I think it was a transfer of psychoplasm from Dolores to the mummy which drained the living girl of all life-force and gave her the appearance of a mummy, while the dead form put upon it the appearance of returning life. One cannot surely say, these are but guesses, but my opinion is strengthened by the fact that when Dolores had recounted the tragedy of Sit-ankh-hku she all at once regained her normal look, while dissolution seemed to fall upon the dead girl with the suddenness of striking fate. It was as if a tide of life flowed and ebbed from one to the other. You see? It is most simple."

An expression of bewilderment, mingled with horrified incredulity, spread over Grafensburg's broad face as de Grandin finished speaking. I could scarce refrain from laughing, he looked for all the world like William Jennings Bryan reading Darwin, or a leader of the W.C.T.U. perusing a deluxe edition of the Bartenders' Guide.

"*Lieber Himmel!*" he exclaimed. "You—you tell us this? With seriousness you say it? Yes? *Mein Gott, du bist verrückt!* Stay, stay, little man, and rave your crazy ravings. I am going to get drunk!"

A smile of almost heavenly delight lit up de Grandin's face. "*Mon cher ami, mon brave collègue,*" he exclaimed, "for a week I've known you, yet never till this instant have I heard you speak one word of sense!

"Wait till I find my seven-times-accursed hat, and I will go with you!"

A Rival from the Grave

"HOW MANY LOBSTER SANDWICHES is that?" I demanded.

Jules de Grandin knit his brows in an effort at calculation. "Sixteen, no, eighteen, unless I have lost count," he answered.

"And how many glasses of champagne?"

"Only ten."

"By George, you're hopeless," I reproved. "You're an unconscionable glutton and wine-bibber."

"*Eh bien*, others who considered themselves as righteous as you once said the same of one more eminent than I," he assured with a grin as he stuffed the last remaining *canapé homard* into his mouth and washed it down with a gulp of Roederer. "Come, my friend, forget to take your pleasures sadly for a while. Is it not a wedding feast?"

"It is," I conceded, "but—"

"And am I not on fire with curiosity?" he broke in. "Is it a custom of America to hold the celebration in the bridegroom's home?"

"No, it's decidedly unusual, but in this case the bride had only a tiny apartment and the groom this big house, so—"

"One understands," he nodded, finding resting-space for his sandwich plate and glass, "and a most impressive house it is. Shall we seek a place to smoke?"

We jostled through the throng of merrymakers, passed along the softly carpeted hall and made our way to Frazier Taviton's study. Bookcases lined the walls, a pair of Lawson sofas ranged each side the fireplace invited us to rest, a humidor of Gener cigars, silver caddies of Virginia, Russian and Egyptian cigarettes and an array of cloisonné ash-trays offered us the opportunity to indulge our craving for tobacco.

"*Exquise, superbe, parfait!*" the little Frenchman commented as he ignored our host's expensive cigarettes and selected a vile-smelling Maryland from his case; "this room was made expressly to offer us asylum from those noisy ones out there. I think—*que diable!* Who is that?" He nodded toward the life-size portrait in its golden frame which hung above the mantel-shelf.

"H'm," I commented, glancing up. "Queer Frazier left *that* hanging. I suppose he'll be taking it down, though—"

"Ten thousand pestilential mosquitoes, do not sit there muttering like an elderly spinster with the vapors!" he commanded. "Tell me who she is, my friend."

"It's Elaine. She is—she *was*, rather—the first Mrs. Taviton. Lovely, isn't she?"

"U'm?" he murmured, rising and studying the picture with what I thought unnecessary care. "*Non*, my friend, she is not lovely. Beautiful? But yes, assuredly. Lovely? No, not at all."

The artist had done justice to Elaine Taviton. From the canvas she looked forth exactly as I'd seen her scores of times. Her heavy hair, red as molten copper, with vital, flame-like lights in it, was drawn back from her forehead and parted in the center, and a thick, three-stranded plait was looped across her brow in a kind of Grecian coronal. Her complexion had that strange transparency one sometimes but not often finds in red-haired women. A tremulous green light played in her narrow eyes, and her slim, bright-red lips were slightly parted in a faintly mocking smile to show small, opalescent teeth. It was, as Jules de Grandin had declared, a fascinating face, beautiful but unlovely, for in those small features, cut with lapidarian regularity, there was half concealed, but just as certainly revealed, the frighteningly fierce fire of an almost inhuman sensuality. The sea-green gown she wore was low-cut to the point of daring, and revealed an expanse of lucent shoulders, throat and bosom with the frankness characterizing the portraiture of the Restoration. Scarcely whiter or more gleaming than the skin they graced, a heavy string of perfectly matched pearls lay round her throat, while emerald ear-studs worth at least a grand duke's ransom caught up and accentuated the vivid luster of her jade-toned eyes.

"*Morbleu*, she is Circe, *la Pompadour* and Helen of Tyre, all in one," de Grandin murmured. "Many men, I make no doubt, have told her, 'I worship you,' and many others whispered they adored her, but I do not think that any ever truthfully said, 'I love you.'"

He was silent a moment, then: "They were divorced?"

"No, she died a year or so ago," I answered. "It happened in New York, so I only know the gossip of it, but I understand that she committed suicide—"

"One can well believe it," he responded as I paused, somewhat ashamed of myself for retailing rumor. "She was vivid, that one, cold as ice toward others, hot as flame where her desires were concerned. Self-inflicted death would doubtless have seemed preferable to enduring thwarted longing. Yes."

A chorus of shrill squeals of feminine delight, mingled with the heavier undertone of masculine voices, drew our attention to the hall. As we hurried from the study we saw Agnes Taviton upon the stairs, gray eyes agleam, her lips drawn back in laughter, about to fling her bouquet down. The bridesmaids and the wedding guests were clustered in the hall below, white-gloved arms stretched up to catch the longed-for talisman, anticipation and friendly rivalry engraved upon their smiling faces. Towering above the other girls, nearly six feet tall, but with a delicacy of shape which marked her purely feminine, was Betty Decker, twice winner of the women's singles out at Albemarle and runner-up for swimming honors at the Crescent Pool events. The bride swung out the heavy bunch of lilies-of-the-valley and white violets, poised it for a moment, then dropped it into Betty's waiting hands.

But Betty failed to catch it. A scant four feet the bouquet had to fall to touch her outstretched fingers, but in the tiny interval of time required for the drop Betty seemed to stumble sideways, as though she had been jostled, and missed her catch by inches. The bridal nosegay hurtled past her clutching hands, and seemed to pause a moment in midair, as though another pair of hands had grasped it; then it seemed to flutter, rather than to fall, until it rested on the polished floor at Betty's feet.

"Rotten catch, old gal," commiserated Doris Castleman. "You're off your form; I could 'a' sworn you had it in the bag."

"I didn't muff it," Betty answered hotly. "I was pushed."

"No alibis," the other laughed. "I was right behind you, and I'll take my Bible oath that no one touched you. You were in the clear, old dear; too much champagne, perhaps."

De Grandin's small blue eyes were narrowed thoughtfully as he listened to the girls' quick thrust-and-parry. "The *petite mademoiselle* has right," he told me in a whisper. "No one touched the so unfortunate young lady who let her hope of early matrimony slip."

"But she certainly staggered just before she missed her catch," I countered. "Everybody can't absorb such quantities of champagne as you can stow away and still maintain his equilibrium. It's a case of too much spirits, I'm afraid."

The little Frenchman turned a wide-eyed stare on me, then answered in a level, almost toneless voice: "*Prie Dieu* you speak in jest, my friend, and your fears have no foundation."

"There's a gentleman to see yez, sors," Nora McGinnis announced apologetically. "I tol' 'im it wuz afther office hours, an' that yere mos' partic'lar fer to give yerselves some time to digest yer dinners, but he sez as how it's mos' important, an' wud yez plase be afther seein' 'im, if only fer a minute?"

"*Tiens*, it is the crowning sorrow of a doctor's life that privacy is not included in his dictionary," answered Jules de Grandin with a sigh. "Show him in, *petite*"— Nora, who tipped the scales at something like two hundred pounds, never failed to glow with inward satisfaction when he used that term to her—"show him in all quickly, for the sooner we have talked with him the sooner we shall see his back."

The change which three short months had made in Frazier Taviton was nothing less than shocking. Barely forty years of age, tall, hound-lean, but well set up, his prematurely graying hair and martial carriage had given him distinction in appearance, and with it an appearance of such youth and strength as most men fifteen years his junior lacked. Now he seemed stooped and shrunken, the gray lights in his hair seemed due to age instead of accidental lack of pigment, and in the deep lines of his face and the furtive, frightened glance which looked out from his eyes, we saw the symptoms of a man who has been overtaken by a rapid and progressive malady.

"Step into the consulting-room," I said as we concluded shaking hands; "we can look you over better there," but:

"I'm not in need of going over, Doctor," Frazier answered with a weary smile; "you can leave the stethoscope and sphygmomanometer in place. This consultation's more in Doctor de Grandin's line."

"*Très bien*, I am wholly at your service, *Monsieur*," the Frenchman told him. "Will you smoke or have a drink? It sometimes helps one to unburden himself."

Taviton's hand shook so he could hardly hold the flame to his cigar tip, and when he finally succeeded in setting it alight he paused, looking from one to the other of us as though his tongue could not find words to frame his crowding thoughts. Abruptly:

"You know I've always been in love with Agnes, Doctor?" he asked me almost challengingly.

"Well," I temporized, "I knew your families were close friends, and you were a devoted swain in high school, but—"

"Before that!" he cut in decisively. "Agnes Pemberton and I were sweethearts almost from the cradle!"

Turning to de Grandin he explained: "Our family homes adjoined, and from the time her nursemaid brought her out in her perambulator I used to love to look at Agnes. I was two years her senior, and for that reason always something of a hero to her. When she grew old enough to toddle she'd slip her baby fist in mine, and we'd walk together all around the yard. If her nurse attempted to interfere she'd storm and raise the very devil till they let her walk with me again. And the queer part was I liked it. You don't often find a three-year-old boy who'd rather walk around with a year-old girl than play with his toys, but I would. I'd leave my trains or picture books any time when I heard Agnes call, 'Frazee, Frazee, here's Agnes!' and when we both grew older it was just the same. I remember once I had to fight half a dozen fellows because they called me sissy for preferring to help Agnes stage a party for her dolls to going swimming with them.

"We spent our summers in the Poconos, and were as inseparable there as we were in town. Naturally, I did the heavy work—climbed the trees to shake the apples down and carried home the sack—but Agnes did her share. One summer, when I was twelve and she was ten, we were returning from a fox-grape hunt. Both of us were wearing sandals but no stockings; we couldn't go quite barefoot, for the mountain paths were rocky and a stone-bruised toe was something to avoid. Suddenly Agnes, who was walking close beside me, pushed me off the path into the bushes, and dived forward to snatch up a stick.

"'Look out, Frazy, stay away!' she cried, and next instant I saw the 'stick' she had picked up was a three-foot copperhead. It had been lying stretched across the path, the way they love to, and in another step I'd have put my unprotected foot right on it. Copperheads don't have to coil to strike, either.

"There wasn't time to take a club or rock to it, so she grabbed the thing in her bare hands. It must have been preparing to strike my ankle, or the pressure of her hand against its head worked on its poison-sac; anyway, its venom spilled out on her hand, and I remember thinking how much it looked like mayonnaise as I saw it spurt out on her sun-tanned skin. The snake was strong, but desperation gave her greater strength. Before it could writhe from her grasp or slip its head far enough forward to permit it to strike into her wrist, she'd thrown it twenty feet away into the bushes; then the pair of us ran down the mountainside as if the devil were behind us.

"'Weren't you scared, Aggie?' I remember asking when we paused for breath, three hundred yards or so from where we'd started running.

"'More than I've ever been in my life,' she answered, 'but I was more scared the snake would bite you than I was of what it might do to me, Frazier dear.'

"I think that was the first time in my life that any woman other than my mother called me 'dear', and it gave me a queer and rather puffed-up feeling."

Taviton paused a moment, drawing at his cigar, and a reminiscent smile replaced the look of anguished worry on his face. "We were full of stories of King Arthur and the days of chivalry," he continued, "so you mustn't think what happened next was anywise theatrical. It seemed the most natural thing in the world to us. 'When anybody saves another person's life that life belongs to him,' I told her, and went down upon one knee, took the hem of her gingham dress in my hand and raised it to my lips.

"She laid her hand upon my head, and it was like an accolade. 'I am your liege lady and you're my true sir knight,' she answered, 'and you will bear me faithful service. When we're grown I'll marry you and you must love me always. And I'll scratch your eyes out if you don't!' she added warningly.

"God, I wish she'd done it then!"

"Hein?" demanded Jules de Grandin. "You regret your sight, Monsieur?

"Trowbridge, *mon vieux*, you must examine me anon; my ears become impertinent!"

Taviton was earnest in reply: "You heard me quite correctly, sir. If I'd been blinded then the last thing I'd have seen would have been Agnes' face; I'd have had the memory of it with me always, and—I'd never have seen Elaine!"

"But, my dear boy," I expostulated, "you're married to Agnes; Elaine's dead; there's nothing to prevent the realization of your happiness."

"That's what you think!" he answered bitterly.

"Listen: I believed that bunk they told us back in '17 about it's being a war to end all war and make the world a decent place to live in. I was twenty-three when I joined up. Ever seen war, gentlemen? Ever freeze your feet knee-deep in icy mud, have a million lice camp on you, see the man you'd just been talking to ripped open by a piece of shrapnel so his guts writhed from his belly like angleworms from a tin that's been kicked over? Ever face machine-gun fire or a bayonet charge? I did, within three months after I'd left the campus. Soldiers in the advanced sections go haywire, they can't help it; they've been through hell so long that just a little human kindness seems like paradise when they go back from the front.

"Elaine was kind. And she was beautiful. God, how beautiful she was!

"I'd gotten pretty thoroughly mashed up along the Meuse, and they sent me down to Biarritz to recuperate. It was a British nursing-station, and Elaine, who came from Ireland, was out there helping. She seemed to take to me at once; I've no idea why, for there were scores of better-looking fellows there and many who had lots more money. No matter, for some reason she was pleased with me and gave me every minute she could spare. Strangely, no one seemed to envy me.

"One night there was a dance, and I noticed that not many of the Scots or Irish, who were in the majority, seemed inclined to cut in on me. The English tried it, but the Gallic fellows passed us by as though we'd had the plague. Of course, that pleased me just as well but I was puzzled, too.

"I shared a room with Alec MacMurtrie, a likable young subaltern from Highland outfit who could drink more, smoke more, and talk less than any man I'd ever seen. He was in bed when I reported in that night, but woke up long enough to smoke a cigarette while I undressed. Just before we said good-night he turned to me with an almost pleading look and told me, 'I'd wear a sprig o' hawthorn in my tunic when I went about if I were you, laddie.'

"I couldn't make him amplify his statement; so next day I talked with old MacLeod, a dour, sandy-haired and freckled minister from Aberdeen who'd come out as chaplain to as rank a gang of prayerful Scots as ever sashayed hell-for-leather through a regiment of Boche infantry.

"'Mac, why should anybody wear a sprig of hawthorn in his tunic?' I demanded.

"He looked at me suspiciously, poked his long, thin nose deep in his glass of Scotch and soda, then answered with a steel-trap snap of his hard jaws: 'T' keep th' witches awa', lad. I dinna ken who's gi'en ye th' warnin', but 'tis sober counsel. Think it ower.' That was all that I could get from him.

"I was ready to go back to active duty when the Armistice was signed and everybody who could walk or push a wheel-chair got as drunk as twenty fiddlers' tikes. MacMurtrie was out cold when I staggered to our room, and I was sitting on my bed and working on a stubborn puttee when an orderly came tapping at the door with a chit for me. It was from Elaine and simply said: 'Come to me at once. I need you.'

"I couldn't figure what she wanted, but I was so fascinated by her that if she'd asked me to attempt to swim the Channel without water-wings I'd have undertaken it.

"Her room was in a little tower that stuck up above the roof, removed from every other bedroom in the place, with windows looking out across the sea and gardens. It was so quiet there that we could hear the waves against the beach, and the shouting of the revelers came to us like echoes from a distant mountain-top.

"I knocked, but got no answer; knocked again, then tried the door. It was unfastened, and swung open to my hand. Elaine was lying on a sofa by the window with the light from two tall candelabra shining on her. She was asleep, apparently, and her gorgeous hair lay spread across the jade-green cushion under-neath her head. You recall that hair, Doctor Trowbridge? It was like a molten flame; it glowed with dazzling brilliance, with here and there sharp sudden flashes as of superheated gold.

"She was wearing a green nightrobe of the filmiest silk crêpe, which shaded but hid nothing of her wonderfully made body. Her long green eyes were closed, but the long black lashes curled upon her cheeks with seductive loveliness. Her mouth was slightly parted and I caught a glimpse of small white teeth and the tip of a red tongue between the poinsettia vividness of her lips. The soft silk of her gown clung to the lovely swell of her small, pointed breasts, the tips of which were rouged the same rich red as her lips, her fingertips and toes.

"I felt as if my body had been drained of blood, as if I must drop limply where I stood, for every bit of strength had flowed from me. I stood and gazed upon that miracle of beauty, that green and gold and blood-red woman, absolutely weak and sick with overmastering desire.

"She stirred lazily and flung an arm across her eyes as she moaned gently. I stood above her, still as death.

"For a moment she lay there with the blindfold of her rounded arm across her face, then dropped it languidly and turned her head toward me.

"Her glowing green eyes looked up in my face, and the pupils seemed to widen as she looked. Her breath came faster and her body tensed, as though in sudden pain. Swift, almost, as a snake's, her scarlet tongue flicked over scarlet lips and opal teeth.

"'You love me, Frazier, don't you?' she murmured in a throaty undertone which seemed to lose itself in the shadows where the candlelight had faded. 'You love me as only an American loves, with your heart and soul and spirit, and your chivalry and truth and faith?'

"I couldn't speak. My breath seemed held fast in my throat, and when I tried to form an answer only a hoarse, groaning sound escaped my lips.

"The pupils of her green eyes flared as with a sudden inward light, her lithe, slim body shook as with an ague, and she laughed a softly purring laugh deep in her throat. 'Mine,' she murmured huskily. 'Mine, all mine for ever!'

"She raised her arms and drew me down to her, crushed my lips against her mouth till it seemed she'd suck my soul out with her stifling kiss.

"Half fainting as I was, she pushed me back, rolled up my tunic-cuff and bit me on the wrist. She made a little growling sound, soft and caressing, but, somehow, savage as the snarling of a tigress toying with her prey. Her teeth were sharp as sabers, and the blood welled from the wound like water from a broken conduit. But before I could cry out she pressed her mouth against the lesion and began to drink as though she were a famished traveler in the desert who had stumbled on a spring.

"She looked up from her draft, her red lips redder still with blood, and smiled at me. Before I realized what she did, she raised her hand and bit herself upon the wrist, then held the bleeding white limb up to me. 'Drink, beloved; drink my blood as I drink yours,' she whispered hoarsely. 'It will make us one!'

"Her blood was salty and acerb, but I drank it greedily as I had drunk champagne an hour or two before, sucked it thirstily as she sucked mine, and it seemed to mount up to my brain like some cursèd oriental drug. A chill ran through me, as though a bitter storm-wind swept in from the sea; a red mist swam before my eyes; I felt that I was sinking, sinking in a lake of bitter, scented blood."

THE SPEAKER PAUSED AND passed a hand across his forehead, where small gouts of perspiration gleamed. "Then—" he began, but Jules de Grandin raised his hand.

"You need not tell us more, *Monsieur*," he murmured. "In England and America there is a silly superstition that seduction is exclusively a masculine prerogative. *Eh bien*, you and I know otherwise, *n'est-ce-pas?*"

Taviton looked gratefully at the small Frenchman. "Thanks," he muttered.

"MacLeod refused point-blank to marry us. 'I'd sooner gie ye'r lich t' th' kirk-yard turf than join ye wie yon de'l's bairn,' he told me when I asked him.

"When we asked a priest to marry us we found French law required so much red tape—getting baptismal certificates and all that nonsense—that it was impractical; so I applied for leave to London, and Elaine joined me on the ship. We were married by the master just as soon as we were out of French territorial waters.

"I cabled home for funds and we had a grand time shopping first in London, then at the Galeries LaFayette in Paris when my discharge came through.

"But I wasn't happy. Passion may be part of love, but it's no substitute. Elaine was like a quenchless fire; there was no limit to her appetites nor any satisfying them. She wanted me, and all that I possessed. I never saw her eat much heavy food, but the amount of caviar and oysters and pasties she consumed was almost past belief, and she drank enough champagne and brandy to have put a dipsomaniac to shame; yet I never saw her show the smallest sign of drunkenness. No kind of sport or exercise held any interest for her, but she'd dance all afternoon and until the final tune was played at night, and still be fresh when I was so exhausted that I thought I'd drop. Shopping never seemed to tire her, either. She could make the rounds of twenty stores, looking over practically the entire stock of each, then come home glowing with delight at what she'd purchased and be ready for a matinee or *thé dansant* and an evening's session at the supper clubs.

"When I appraised her thus and realized her shallowness and the selfishness which amounted to egotism, I felt I hated her; but more than that I loathed myself for having let her make a slave of me, and against the memory of her branding kisses and the night when we had drunk each other's blood there rose like a reproachful ghost the recollection of the evening I had said good-bye to Agnes just before I went to Dix to proceed to ship at Hoboken. How sweet and cool and comforting that last kiss seemed; there was something like a benediction in her promise, 'I'll be waiting for you, Frazier, waiting if it means for time and all eternity, and loving you each minute that I wait.'

"But when I lay in Elaine's arms so feverishly clasped it seemed our bodies melted and were fused in one, and felt the sting of her hot kisses on my mouth, or the bitter tang of her blood in my throat, I knew that I was weak as wax in her hot grasp, and that she owned me bodily and spiritually. I was her slave and thing and chattel to do with as she liked, powerless to offer any opposition to her slightest whim.

"Her blood-lust was insatiable. Five, ten, a dozen times a night, she'd wound me with her teeth or nails, and drink my blood as though it had been liquor and she a famished drunkard. The Germans have a word for it: *Blutdurst*—blood-craving, the unappeasable appetite of the *blutsanger*, the vampire, for its bloody sustenance.

"Sometimes she'd make me take her blood, for she seemed to find as keen delight in being passive in a blood-feast as when she drank 'the red milk', as she called it.

"Sometimes she'd mutilate herself upon the hands and feet and under the left breast, then lie with outstretched arms and folded feet while I applied my lips to the five wounds. 'Love's crucifixion', she called it, and when she felt my mouth against the cuts upon her palms and side and insteps she would make small growling noises in her throat, and almost swoon in ecstasy.

"I was weak with loss of blood within three months, but as powerless to refuse my veins to her as I was to tell her that the sums she spent in shopping were driving me to bankruptcy.

"Things were changed when I came home to Harrisonville. My parents had both died with influenza while I was away. Agnes' father had committed suicide. He'd been in business as an importer, dealing exclusively with German houses, and the blockade of the Allies and our later entrance into the war completely ruined him. They told me when his bills were paid there was less than a hundred dollars left for Agnes.

"She made a brave best of it. Nearly everything was gone, but she furnished a small flat with odds and ends that no one bid for at the auction of her father's things, got a place as a librarian and carried on.

"She took my treachery standing, too. Some women would have tried to show their gallantry by being over-friendly, calling on us and asserting their proprietary rights as old friends of the bridegroom. Agnes stayed away with reserve and decency until our house was opened, then came to the reception quite like any other friend. Lord, what grit it must have taken to run the gauntlet of those pitying eyes! I don't believe there was a soul in town who didn't know we'd been engaged and that I'd let her down.

"If there were any bitterness in her she didn't show it. I think that my lips trembled more than hers when she took my hand and whispered, 'I'm praying for your happiness, Frazie.'

"God knows I needed prayers."

TEARS WERE STREAMING FROM de Grandin's eyes. "*La pauvre!*" he muttered thickly. "*La pauvre brave créature! Monsieur*, if you spend all of life remaining to you flat upon your face before *Madame* your wife, you fail completely to abase yourself sufficiently!"

"You're telling me?" the other answered harshly. "It's not for me I've come to you this evening, sir. Whatever I get I have coming to me, but Agnes loves me. God knows why. It's to try and save her happiness I'm here."

"*Tiens*, say on, *Monsieur*," the little Frenchman bade. "Relate this history of perfidy and its result. It may be we can salvage something of the happiness you let slip by. What else is there to tell?"

"Plenty," rejoined Taviton. "Elaine could not abide the thought of Agnes. 'That cold-faced baby; that dough-cheeked fool!' she stormed. 'What does she know of love? What has she to give a man—or what can she take from him? Say she's frigid, cold, unloving as a statue, icy-hearted as a fish!' she ordered. 'Say it, my lover. You won't? I'll kiss the words from you!' And when she held me in her arms again and stifled me with bloody kisses—Heaven help me!—I forswore my love, forgot the debt of life I owed to Agnes, and repeated parrotwise each wretched, lying slander that she bade me speak.

"It was a little thing that freed me from my slavery. We'd given up the house here and taken an apartment in New York. Elaine was in her element in the world of shops and theaters and night clubs; she hardly seemed to take a moment's rest, or to need it, for that matter. My old outfit was going to parade on Decoration Day in honor of the buddies who went west, and she set herself against my coming back to Harrisonville, even to participate in the parade. I don't think she cared a tinker's dam about my going, but she'd grown so used to having me obey her like a docile, well-trained dog it never seemed to occur to her that I might go when she forbade me. Perhaps, if she had pleaded or used her deadly, seductive power, she would have prevailed, but she'd grown so she had no respect for me. Seldom did she say so much as 'please' when ordering me about; I was necessary to her satisfaction—there never was a hint of any other man—but only as any other chattel that she owned. She showed no more affection for me than she might bestow upon her powder puff or lipstick. She loved the things providing creature comforts and sensory satisfaction; I was one. The endearing names she called me while she held me in her arms were purely reflex, a sort of orchestration to a dance of Sapphic passion.

"'If you disobey me you'll be sorry all your life,' she warned as I left the house that morning.

"I went and marched with what remained of the old outfit. The excesses I'd been subject to had weakened me, and when the parade was dismissed I reeled and fell. Coroner Martin's ambulance had been assigned for public service, and they put me in it and took me to his funeral home. I thought he looked more serious than a little fainting-fit would warrant when he helped me to his private office and offered me a glass of brandy.

"'Feeling stronger now, Frazier?' he asked.

"'Yes, sir, thank you,' I replied as I handed back the glass, 'quite fit.'

"'Strong enough to stand bad news?'

"'I suppose so; I've stood it before, you know, sir.'

"He seemed at a loss for what to say, looking at his sets of record cases, at his wall safe and the telephone; anywhere except at me. Finally, 'It's Mrs. Taviton,' he told me. 'There's been an accident; she's been—'

"'Killed?' I asked him as he hesitated.

"I felt like shouting, 'That's not bad news, man; that's tidings of release!'

but I contrived to keep a look of proper apprehension on my face while I waited confirmation of my hope.

"'Yes, son, she's been killed,' he answered kindly. 'They telephoned the police department an hour ago, and as you were marching then the police relayed the message to me. They knew I'd always served your family, and—'

"'Of course,' I interrupted. 'Make all necessary arrangements with New York authorities, please, and send for her as soon as possible.' I had difficulty to keep from adding, 'And be sure you dig her grave so deep that she'll not hear the judgment trumps!'

"Elaine had jumped or fallen from a window, fallen fourteen stories to a concrete pavement; but despite the fact that practically all her bones were broken Mr. Martin told me that her beauty was not marred. Certainly, there was no blemish visible as I sat beside her body on the night before the funeral.

"Mr. Martin was an artist. He had placed her in a casket of pale silver-bronze with écru satin lining and had clothed her in a robe of pale Nile green. Her head was turned a little to one side, facing me, and the soft black lashes swept her flawless cheeks so naturally it seemed that any moment they might rise and show the gleaming emerald of her eyes. One hand lay loosely on her breast, the fingers slightly curled as if in quiet sleep; the other rested at her side, and in the flickering light of the watch-candles I could swear I saw her bosom rise and fall in slumber.

"I could not take my eyes off her face. That countenance of perfect beauty I had looked upon so often, those slim red-fingered hands and little satin-shod feet from which I'd drunk the blood at her command—it seemed impossible that they were now for ever quiet with the quietness of death.

"'But it's release,' I told myself. 'You're free. Your bondage to this beautiful she-devil's done; you can—' the thought seemed profanation, and I thrust it back, but it came again unbidden: 'Now you can marry Agnes!'

"It was a trick of light and shadow, doubtless, but it seemed to me the dead lips in the casket curved in a derisive smile, and through the quiet of the darkened room of death there came, faint as the echo of an echo's echo, that whisper I had heard Armistice Night beside the sea at Biarritz: 'Mine! Mine; *all mine for ever!*'

"We buried her in Shadow Lawn, and Agnes sent me a brief note of sympathy. Within a month we saw each other, in two months we were inseparable as we had been before the war. Last winter she agreed to marry me.

"I think I knew how Kartophilos felt when he was reconciled with Heaven the night that Agnes promised she would be my wife. All that I'd forfeited I was to have. The promises of childhood were to be fulfilled. I put the memory of marriage to Elaine behind me like an ugly dream, and a snatch of an old war song was upon my lips as I let myself into my bedroom:

There's a kiss with a tender meaning.
Other kisses you recall,
But the kisses I get from you, sweetheart,
Are the sweetest kisses of all . . .

"That night I'd had the sweetest kiss I'd known since I went off to war; life was starting afresh for me, I was—

"My train of happy thought broke sharply. My bedroom was instinct with a spicy, heady perfume, cloying-sweet, provocative as an aphrodisiac. I recognized it; it was a scent that cut through all the odors of the antiseptics a moment before I had first seen Elaine in the convalescent section of the nursing-home at Biarritz.

"I looked wildly round the room, but there was no one there. Stamping to the nearest window I sent it sailing up, and though it was a zero night outside I left it fully open till the last faint taint of hellish sweetness had been blown away.

"Shivering—not entirely from cold—I got in bed. As the velvet darkness settled down when I snapped off the light, I felt a soft touch on my cheek, a touch like that of soft, cold little fingers seeking my lips. I brushed my face as though a noisome insect crawled across it, and it seemed I heard a little sob—or perhaps a snatch of mocking laugh—beside me in the darkness.

"I put my hand out wildly. It encountered nothing solid, but in the pillow next my head was a depression, as though another head were resting there, and the bedclothes by my side were slightly raised as if they shrouded slimly rounded limbs and small and pointed breasts.

"I dropped back, weak with panic terror, and against my throat I felt the tiny rasping scrape of little fingernails. How often that same feeling had awakened me from sleep when Elaine's craving for a draft of 'the red milk' was not to be denied! And then I heard—subjectively, as one hears half-forgotten music which he struggles to remember—'Give me your blood, belovèd, it will warm me. I am cold.' Then, sharp and clear as the echo of a sleigh's bells on a frosty night, repeated those six words which had been my bill of sale to slavery: 'Mine! Mine; all mine for ever!'

"I woke next morning with a feeling of malaise. Sure I'd suffered from a nightmare, I was still reluctant to rise and look into the mirror, and reluctance grew to dread when I put my hand up to my throat and felt a little smarting pain beneath my fingers. At last I took my courage in both hands and went into the bathroom. Sheer terror made me sick as I gazed at my reflection in the shaving-glass. A little semilunar scar was fresh upon my throat, the kind of scar a curved and pointed fingernail would make.

"Had Elaine come from the grave to set her seal on me; to mark me as her chattel now and ever?"

Taviton was shaking so he could not relight the cigar which had gone dead during his recital. Once again de Grandin helped him, steadying his hand as he held his briquette out; then: "And did this—shall we say phenomenon?—occur again, *Monsieur?*" he asked as matter-of-factly as he might have asked concerning a dyspepsia patient's diet.

"Yes, several times, but not always the same," the other answered. "I had a period of two weeks' rest, and had begun to think the visitation I had suffered was just a case of nerves when something happened to convince me it was not a case of nightmare or imagination that had plagued me. Agnes and I were going to the first recital of the Philharmonic, and—I was luxuriating in renewing our old courtship days—I'd stopped off at the florist's on my way from the office and bought her a corsage of orchids. Of course, I might have had them sent, but I preferred to take them to her.

"I laid the box upon my bureau while I went in to shave. My bedroom door was closed and the bathroom door was open; no one—nothing animal or human—could have come into my room without my hearing it or seeing it, for my shaving-mirror was so placed that its reflection gave a perfect view of the entrance to the bedroom. Perhaps I was five minutes shaving, certainly not more than ten. The first thing that I noticed when I came back to my room was a heavy, spicy scent upon the air, sweet, penetrating, and a little nauseating, too, as though the very faintest odor of corruption mingled with its fragrance.

"I paused upon the threshold, sniffing, half certain that I smelled it, half sure my nerves were fooling me again. Then I saw. On the rug before the bureau lay the box the flowers came in. It was a heavy carton of green pasteboard, fastened with strong linen cord, enclosing an inner white box tied with ribbon. Both the outer and the inside boxes had been ripped apart as if they had been blotting-paper, and the tissue which had been about the flowers was torn to tatters, so it looked as though a handful of confetti had been spilled upon the floor. The cord and ribbon which had tied the boxes were broken, not cut—you know how twine and ribbon fray out at the ends when pulled apart? The bouquet itself was mashed and torn and battered to a pulp, as though it first were torn to shreds, then stamped and trodden on.

"Again: We were going to the theater and I came home a little early to get into my dinner kit. I dressed with no mishaps and was taking down my overcoat and muffler in the hall when a vase of roses on the mantel toppled over, and absolutely drenched my shirt and collar. There was utterly no reason for that vase to fall. It stood firmly on the mantel-shelf; nothing short of an earthquake could have shaken it over, yet it fell—no, that's not so; it didn't fall! I was six or eight feet from the fireplace, and even admitting some unfelt shock had jarred the rose-vase down, it should have fallen on the hearth. If it reached me at all, it should have rolled across the floor. But it didn't. It left its place, traveled the six or eight intervening feet through the air, and poured its contents over me from a height sufficient to soak my collar and the bosom of my shirt. I'm just telling you what happened, gentlemen, nothing that I guessed or surmised or assumed; so I won't say I heard, but *it seemed to me I heard* a faint, malicious laugh, a hatefully familiar mocking laugh, as the water from that rose-jar soaked and spoiled my linen.

"These things occurred in no set pattern. There was no regularity of interval, but it seemed as if the evil genius which pursued me read my mind. Each time when I'd manage to convince myself that I'd been the subject of delusion, or that the persecution had at last come to an end, there'd be some fresh reminder that my tormentress was playing cat-and-mouse with me.

"You were at my wedding. Did you see what happened when Agnes threw her bouquet down; how Betty Decker almost had it in her hands, and how—"

"*Parbleu*, yes, but you have right, Monsieur!" de Grandin interrupted. "By damn, did I not say as much to good Friend Trowbridge? Did I not tell him that this tall young *Mademoiselle* who all but grasped the flowers which *Madame* your charming wife had thrown did not miss them through a lack of skill? But certainly, of course, indubitably!"

"D'ye know what happened on our wedding night?" our guest demanded harshly.

De Grandin raised his shoulders, hands and eyebrows in a pained, expostulating shrug. "*Monsieur,*" he muttered half reproachfully, like one who would correct a forward child, "one hesitates to—"

"You needn't," cut in Taviton, a note of bitter mockery in his voice. "Whatever it may be you hesitate to guess, you're wrong!

"We went directly to Lenape Lodge up in the Poconos, for it was there twenty-eight years ago we'd plighted our troth the day that Agnes saved me from the snake.

"We had dinner in the little cottage they assigned us, and lingered at the meal. That first breaking of bread together after marriage seemed like something sacramental to us. After coffee we walked in the garden. The moon was full and everything about us was as bright as day. I could see the quick blood mount to Agnes' face as she bent her head and seemed intent on studying her sandal.

"'I feel something like the beggar maid beneath Cophetua's window,' she told me with a little laugh. 'I've nothing but my love to bring you, Frazier.'

"'But all of that?' I asked.

"'All of that,' she echoed in a husky whisper. 'Oh, my dear, please tell me that you love me that way, too; that nothing—*nothing*—can or will ever come between us. We've waited so long for each other, now I—I'm frightened, Frazier.'

"She clung to me with a sort of desperation while I soothed her. Finally she brightened and released herself from me.

"'Five minutes I'll give you for a final cigarette. Don't be longer!' she called gayly as she ran into the cottage.

"That five minutes seemed eternity to me, but at last it was concluded, and I went into the house. The bedroom was in shadow, save where a shaft of moonlight struck across the floor, illuminating the foot of the big old-fashioned bedstead. Under the white counterpane I could see the small twin hillocks which were Agnes' feet; then, as I stood and looked at them, my breath came faster and my pulses raced with quick acceleration. There was the outline of another pair of upturned feet beneath that coverlet. 'Agnes!' I called softly, 'Agnes, dear!' There was no answer.

"Slowly, like a man wading through half-frozen water, I crossed the room, and put my hand upon the bed. The linen sank beneath my touch. There was nothing solid there, but when I took my hand away the bedclothes rose again, showing the contour of a supine body.

"'She—it—can't do this to us!' I told myself in fury, and disrobed as quickly as I could, then got in bed.

"My hand sought Agnes', and I felt a touch upon it, soft as rose leaves, cold as lifeless flesh. Slim fingers closed about my own, fingers which seemed to grasp and cling like the tentacles of a small octopus, and which, like a devil-fish's tentacles, were cold and bloodless.

"I drew back with a start . . . surely this could not be Agnes, Agnes, soft and warm and loving, pulsing with life and tenderness. . . .

"Then I almost shrieked aloud in horror—'almost,' I say, because my mouth was stopped, even as I drew my lips apart to scream. A weight, light, yet almost unsupportable, lay upon my chest, my hips, my thighs. Moist lips were on my lips; small, sharp fingers ran like thin flames across my breast and cheeks; nails, small nails of dainty feet, yet sharp and poignant as the talons of a bird of prey, scratched lightly against the flesh of my legs, and a heavy strand of scented hair fell down each side my face, smothering me in its gossamer cascade. Then the quick, sharp ecstasy I knew so well, the instant pain, which died almost before it started with the anodyne of bliss, as the cut of razor-keen small teeth sank in my lips and the salty, hot blood flowed into my mouth. Slowly I could feel the nerve force draining from me. Wave on wave, a flooding tide of lethargy engulfed me; I was sinking slowly, helplessly into unconsciousness.

"When I awoke the sun was streaming in the bedroom windows. Spots of blood were on my pillow, my lips were sore and smarting with a pain like iodine on a raw wound. Agnes lay beside me, pale and haggard. On her throat were narrow purple bruises, like the lines of bruise that small strong fingers might have left. I roused upon my elbow, looking in her face with growing horror. Was she dead?

"She stirred uneasily and moaned; then her gray eyes opened with a look of haunted terror, and her lips were almost putty-colored as she told me: 'It—she—was here with us last night. Oh, my love, what shall we do? How can we lose this dreadful earthbound spirit which pursues us?'

"We left Lenape Lodge that day. After what had happened we could no more bear to stay there than we could have borne to stay in hell. As quickly as I could I made arrangements for a Caribbean voyage, and for a short time we had peace; then, without the slightest warning, Elaine struck again.

"A ball was being given at Castle Harbor and Agnes was to wear her pearls. They had been my mother's and Elaine had always been most partial to them. When she died I put them in a safe deposit vault, but later had them restrung and fitted with a new clasp for Agnes.

"I was dressed and waiting on the balcony outside our suite. Agnes was putting the finishing touches on her toilet when I heard her scream. I rushed into the bedroom to find her staring white-faced at her own reflection in the mirror, one hand against her throat. 'The pearls!' she gasped. '*She* was here; she took them—snatched them from my neck!'

"It was true. The pearls were gone, and within a little while a bruise appeared on Agnes' throat, showing with what force they had been snatched away. Naturally, as a matter of form, we hunted high and low, but there was no sign of them. We knew better than to notify the police; their best efforts, we knew but too well, would be entirely useless.

"I had a terrible suspicion which plagued me day and night, and though I didn't voice my thought to Agnes, I could hardly wait till we got home to prove the dreadful truth.

"As soon as we were back in Harrisonville I saw the superintendent of the cemetery and arranged a disinterment, telling him I had decided to place Elaine's body in another section of the plot. There were several obstacles to this, but Mr. Martin managed everything, and within a week they notified me that they were ready to proceed. I stood beside the grave while workmen plied their spades, and when the big steel vault was opened and the casket lifted out, Mr. Martin asked if I desired to look at her. As if I had another wish!

"He snapped the catches of the silver-bronze sarcophagus, and gently raised the lid. There lay Elaine, exactly as I'd seen her on the night before the funeral, her face a little on one side, one hand across her breast, the other resting at her side. A little smile, as though she knew a secret which was more than half a jest, was on her lips, and in the hand that rested on her breast, twined round the slender fingers like a rosary, was the string of pearls which had been snatched from Agnes' throat that night at Castle Harbor, a thousand miles and more away!

"I don't expect you to believe my unsupported word, but if you'll trouble to call Mr. Martin, he'll confirm my statement. He saw me take the pearls from her, and remarked how she seemed to cling to them, also that he had no recollection they were buried with her, and would have sworn they were not in the casket when he closed it."

Taviton drew a long, trembling breath, and the look of settled melancholy had deepened on his stern and rather handsome face as he concluded: "And that is why I'm here tonight, Doctor de Grandin. Probably the old axiom that every man must bear the consequences of his own folly applies to me with double force, but there's Agnes to consider. Though I don't deserve it, she's in love with me, and her happiness is bound inextricably with mine. I've heard that you know more about these psychic phenomena than anyone, so I've come to see you as a last resort. Do you think that you can help us?"

De Grandin's small blue eyes were bright with interest as our caller finished his recital. "One can try," he answered, smiling. "You have been explicit in your narrative, my friend, but there are some points which I should like to be enlightened on. By example, you have seen these manifestations in the form of force a number of times, you have smelled the perfume which *Madame* your *ci-devante* wife affected. You have seen her outline under cloth, and you, as well as Madame Taviton, have felt the contact of her ghostly flesh, but have you ever seen her in ocular manifestation?"

"N-o," answered Frazier thoughtfully, "I don't believe we have." Suddenly he brightened. "You think perhaps it's not Elaine at all?" he asked. "Possibly it's one of those strange cases of self-imposed hypnosis, like those they say the Hindoo fakirs stimulate among their audiences to make it seem they do those seemingly impossible—"

"*Pardonnez-moi, Monsieur,* I think nothing at all, as yet," the little Frenchman interrupted. "I am searching, seeking, trying to collect my data, that I may arrange it in an orderly array. Suppose I were a chemist. A patron brings me a white powder for analysis. He cannot tell me much about it, he does not know if it is poisonous or not, only that it is a plain white powder and he wishes to be told its composition. There are a hundred formulae for me to choose from, so the first step is to segregate as many as I can; to find out what our so mysterious powder is definitely not before I can determine what it is. You could appreciate my difficulty in the circumstances? Very well, we are here in much the same predicament. Indeed, we are in worse case, for while chemistry is scientifically exact, occultism is the newest of the sciences. Less than half emerged from silly magic and sillier superstition. It has not even a precise nomenclature by which one occultist can make his observations fully understood by others. The terminology is so vague that it is almost meaningless. What we call 'ghosts' may be a dozen different sorts of things. 'Spirits?' Possibly. But what sort of spirits? Spirits that are earthbound, having shed their fleshly envelopes, yet being unable to proceed to their proper loci? If so, why do they linger here? What can we do to help them on their way? Or are they possibly the spirits of the blessèd, come from

Paradise? If so, what is their helpful mission? How can we assist them? Spirits of the damned, perhaps? What has given them their *passeport jaune* from hell? By blue, *Monsieur*, there are many things we must consider before we can commence to think about your case!"

"I see," the other nodded. "And the first thing to consider is—"

"Mrs. Taviton, sor!" announced Nora McGinnis from the study doorway.

She came walking toward us rapidly, the tips of silver slippers flashing with swift intermittence from beneath the hem of her white-satin dinner frock. Time had dealt leniently with Agnes Taviton. The skin of her clear-cut oval face was fresh and youthful as a girl's, despite her almost forty years; her short, waved hair, brushed straight back from her broad forehead, was bright as mountain honey, and there were no telltale wrinkles at the corners of her frank gray eyes. Yet there was a line of worry in her forehead and a look of fear in her fine eyes as she acknowledged my quick introduction and turned to Frazier.

"Dear," she exclaimed, "the emeralds, they're—she—"

"*Pardonnez-moi, Madame,*" de Grandin interrupted. "*Monsieur* your husband has recounted how your pearls were taken; now, are we to understand that other jewels—"

"Yes," she answered breathlessly, "to-night! My husband gave the emerald earrings to me—they had been his great-great-grandmother's—and as the stones were so extremely valuable I didn't dare have them reset in screws. So I had my ears pierced, and the wounds have been a little slow in healing. Tonight was the first time I felt I dared take out the guard-rings and try the emeralds on. I'd brought them from the safe and put them on my dresser; then as I raised my hands to disengage the guard-ring from my left ear I felt a draft of chilly air upon my shoulders, something seemed to brush past me—it was like the passage of a bird in flight, or perhaps that of an invisible missile—and next instant the velvet case in which the emeralds rested disappeared."

"*Eh*, disappeared, *Madame?*" de Grandin echoed.

"Yes, that's the only way that I can put it; I didn't actually see them go. The chill and movement at my back startled me, and I turned round. There was nothing there, of course, but when I turned back to my bureau they were gone."

"Did you look for them?" I asked with fatuous practicality.

"Of course, everywhere. But I knew it was no use. They went the same way that the pearls did—I recognized that sudden chill, that feeling as if something—*something evil*—hovered at my shoulder, then the rustle and the disappearance. And," she added with a shuddering sigh, "those emeralds went to the same place the pearls went, too!"

"Thank Heaven you'd not put them in your ears!" broke in her husband. "You remember how she bruised your throat that night she snatched the pearls—"

"Oh, let her have them!" Agnes cried. "I don't want the vain things, Frazier.

If hoarding jewelry like a jackdaw gives her restless spirit peace, let her have them. She can have—"

"Excuse me, if you please, *Madame*," de Grandin interrupted in a soft and toneless voice. "Monsieur Taviton has placed your case with me, and I say she shall not have anything. Neither your jewelry, your husband, your peace of mind—*corbleu*, she shall not have so much as one small grave to call her own!"

"But that's inhuman!"

The Frenchman turned a fixed, unwinking stare on her a moment; then, "*Madame*," he answered levelly, "that which pursues you with the threat of ruined happiness also lacks humanity."

"Perhaps you're right," said Agnes. "She stole Frazier from me; now she takes the jewels, not because she has a use for them, but because she seems determined to take everything I have. Please, Doctor de Grandin, please make sure she doesn't take my husband, whatever else she takes."

I had a momentary feeling of uncertainty. Were these three sane and grownup people whom I listened to, these men and woman who talked of a dead woman's stealing jewelry, discussing what she might have and what she might not take, or were they children playing gruesome make-believe or inmates of some psychopathic ward in some mysterious way brought to my study?

"Don't you think we'd better have a glass of sherry and some biscuit?" I suggested, determined to negotiate the conversation back to sanity.

D E GRANDIN SIPPED HIS sherry thoughtfully, taking tiny bites of biscuit in between the drinks, more for the sake of appearance than from any wish for food. At length: "Where are the pearls which were abstracted from *Madame* your wife's throat?" he asked Taviton.

"I put them in the safe deposit vault," the other answered. "They're still there, unless—"

"Quite so, *Monsieur*, one understands. It is highly probable they are still there, for these prankish tricks *Madame la Revenante* is fond of playing seem concerned more with your personal annoyance than your valuables. I would that you have imitations of those pearls made just as quickly as you can. Be sure they are the best of duplicates, and match the gems they copy both in weight and looks. You apprehend?"

"Yes, of course, but why—"

"*Tiens*, the less one says, the less one has cause for regret," the Frenchman answered with a smile.

A LTHOUGH I HAD RETIRED from obstetrics several years before, there were times when long association with a family made me break my resolution. Such a case occurred next evening, and it was not till after midnight that I saw the red and wrinkled voyageur on life's way securely started on his earthly pilgrimage and his mother safely out of danger. The house was dark and quiet as I put my car away, but as I paused in the front hall I saw a stream of light flare from beneath the pantry door.

"Queer," I muttered, walking toward the little spot of luminance; "it's not like Nora to go off to bed with those lights burning."

A blaze of brightness blinded me as I pushed back the door. Seated on the kitchen table, a cut loaf of bread and a partially dismembered cold roast pheasant by his side, was Jules de Grandin, a tremendous sandwich in one hand, a glass of Spanish cider bubbling in the other. Obviously, he was very happy.

"Come in, *mon vieux*," he called as soon as he could clear his mouth of food. "I am assembling my data."

"So I see," I answered. "I've had a trying evening. Think I'll assemble some, too. Move over and make room for me beside that pheasant, and pour me a glass of cider while you're at it."

"*Mon Dieu*," he murmured tragically, "is it not enough that I come home exhausted, but I must wait upon this person like a slave?" Then, sobering, he told me:

"I am wiser than I was this morning, and my added wisdom gives me happiness, my friend. Attend me, if you please. First to Monsieur Martin's I did go all haste, and asked him the condition of the body of that pretty but extremely naughty lady who pursues Monsieur and Madame Taviton. He tells me it showed signs of slight desiccation when they opened up the casket to retrieve the pearls, that it was like any other body which had been embalmed, then sealed hermetically in a metallic case. Is that not encouraging?"

"Encouraging?" I echoed. "I don't see how. If a corpse buried eighteen months doesn't look like a corpse, how would you expect it to look—like a living person?"

His eyes, wide and serious, met mine above the rim of his champagne glass. "But certainly; what else?" he answered, quite as if I'd asked him whether three and two made five.

"You recall how I compared myself to an analyst last night? *Bon*, this is the first step in my analysis. I cannot say with certainty just what we have to fight, but I think that I can say with surety what it is not we find ourselves opposed to. You asked me jestingly if I had thought to find a body seemingly alive and sleeping in that casket. Frankly, I shall say I did. Do you know what that would have portended?"

"That Martin was either drunk, crazy or a monumental liar," I answered without hesitation.

"*Non*, not at all, unfortunately. It would have meant that we were dealing with a vampire, a corpse undead, which keeps itself sustained by sucking live men's blood. There lay a dreadful danger, for as you doubtless know, those whom the vampire battens on soon die, or seem to die, but actually they enter in that half-world of the dead-alive, and are vampires in their turn. From such a fate, at least, Monsieur and Madame Taviton are safe. *Eh bien*, I have but started on my work. It is now incumbent on me to determine what it is we fight. I was considering the evidence when you came in:

"From what we know of Madame Taviton the first, she was a person of strong passions. Indeed, her whole existence centered on her appetites. It was not for nothing that the Fathers of the Church classed lust among the seven deadly sins. And she had so surrendered to her passions that she might be called one single flaming, all-consuming lust wrapped in a little envelope of charming flesh. *Tiens*, the flesh is dead, snuffed out of life in all its charm of evil beauty, but the lust lives on, quenchless as the fires of hell. Also hate survives, and hate is a very real and potent force. As yet this evil thing of lust and hate and vanity has not found strength to take material form, but that will come, and soon, I think, and when it comes I fear she will be bent on working mischief. Hatred is a thing that gains in strength while it feeds upon itself."

"But according to Taviton she came first as a perfume, then made him feel her fierce sadistic kisses," I objected. "That's pretty near materialization, isn't it?"

"Near, but not quite," he answered. "Everything which this one wants she takes. When she came as a perfume she had not strength to make her presence physically felt, but by *willing* him to smell the scent she turned his thoughts on her. Thoughts are things, my friend, make no mistake concerning that. Once Monsieur Taviton was thinking of her, she was able from the psychoplasm he thus generated to construct the invisible but able-to-be-felt body with which she fondled and caressed him, ever concentrating his thoughts more strongly on her memory, thus gaining greater strength."

"I don't follow you," I countered. "You say she made him think of her, and merely from that—"

"Entirely from that, *mon vieux*. This psychoplasm, which we cannot certainly define any better than we can electricity, is something generated by the very act of thinking. It is to the mind what ectoplasm is to the body. Apparently it is more substantial than mere vibrations from the body, and seems, rather, to be an all-penetrating and imponderable emanation which is rapidly dissipated in the atmosphere, but in certain circumstances may be collected, concresced and energized by the will of a skilled spiritualist medium—or an active discarnate intelligence. Generally in such cases it becomes faintly luminous in a dark room; again, when very strongly concentrated, it may be made the vehicle to transmit force—to hurl a jar of roses or snatch a strand of pearls, by example."

"Or to inflict a bite?"

"Most especially to inflict a bite," he nodded. "That adds fuel to the ready-blazing fire, more power to the dynamo which already hums with power-generation. The Scriptures speak more categorically than is generally realized when they affirm the blood is the life. With the imbibition of the emanations of big rich, warm blood she gained the strength to make it possible for her to thrust herself between him and his bride upon their wedding night, to choke poor Madame Agnes senseless, and to play the sadist wanton with him after death as she had done so many times in life. But her very wanton wickedness shall put her in our power, I damn think."

"How's that?"

"She follows such a pattern that her acts can be predicted with a fair degree of certainty. She hates poor Madame Agnes so that she will go to any length to plague her. She stole her pearls, she stole her emeralds. Now the pearls have been recovered. If Madame Agnes were to put them on again, do not you think that she could come and try to repossess them?"

"It's possible."

"Possible, *pardieu?* It is more than possible; it is likely!"

"Well—"

"Yes, my friend, I think that it is well. Ghostly manifestations, materializations of spirit-forms, are peculiarly creatures of the darkness and the twilight. Bright sunlight seems to kill them as it kills spore-bearing germs. So do certain forms of sound-vibration, the sonorous notes of church bells and of certain kinds of gongs, for instance. High-frequency electric currents, the emanations of radium salt or the terrific penetrative force of Roentgen rays should have the same effect, *n'est-ce-pas?*"

"I suppose so, but I can't say that I understand."

"No matter, that is not essential, But if you will wait I'll show you what I mean before you are much older. Meantime, the hour is late, the bottle empty and I have much to do tomorrow. Come let us go to bed."

"ALL IS PREPARED," HE informed me the next night at dinner. "I had some little difficulty in assembling my armament, but at last I have it all complete. We are ready to proceed at your convenience."

"Proceed? Where?"

"To Monsieur Taviton's. He telephoned me that the imitation pearls are ready, and—*corbleu*, I think that we shall see what we shall see tonight!"

The Tavitons were waiting for us in their drawing-room. Always poised and calm, Agnes nevertheless displayed something of that look of mingled hope and apprehension shown by relatives when someone dear to them has undergone a major operation. Looking at her pleading eyes, I almost expected to hear the old familiar "How is he doing, Doctor?" as I took her hand in greeting. Frazier was plainly on the rough edge of collapse, his movements jerky, eyes furtive, voice sharpened to the point of shrillness.

"You're sure that it will work?" he asked de Grandin.

"As sure as one can be of anything—which is, *hélas*, not very sure at all," the Frenchman answered. "However, we can make the effort, eh, my friend?"

"What—" I began, but he motioned me to silence.

"*Madame*," he bowed to Agnes in his courtly foreign fashion, "you are ready?"

"Quite, Doctor," she replied, rising to cross the hall and spin the handles of the wall-safe. The tumblers clicked, the little door fell open, and from the strongbox she removed a long jewel-case of night-black plush. For a moment she regarded it half fearfully, then snapped it open, drew out the strand of gleaming pearls it held and clasped it round her throat.

"Why, those are surely not an imi—" I began when a brutal kick upon my shin warned me de Grandin wished me to keep silent.

Scarcely whiter than their wearer's slender throat, the sea-gems glinted luminously as Agnes joined us in the drawing-room, cast an apprehensive glance around, then sank down in a chair beside the empty fireplace.

"Brandy or cream?" she asked matter-of-factly, busying herself with the coffee service on the table at her knee.

"Brandy, *s'il vous plaît*," de Grandin answered, rising to receive his cup and snapping off the light-switch as he did so.

We were playing at the social amenities, but the very air was pregnant with expectancy. The rumble of a motor truck bound for the Hudson Tunnels seemed louder than an earthquake's roar; the howling of a dog in the next yard was eery as the wailing of a banshee. I could hear the little French-gilt clock upon the mantelpiece beat off the seconds with its sharp, staccato tick, and in the hall beyond the more deliberate rhythm of the floor clock. In my waistcoat pocket I could hear my own watch clicking rapidly, and by concentrating on the varied tempos I could almost make them play a fugue. Autumn was upon us; through the open window came a gust of chilling air, fog-laden, billowing out the silk-net curtains and sending a quick shiver down my neck and spine. De Grandin took a lump of sugar in his spoon, poured brandy over it and set the flame of his briquette against it. It burned with a ghastly, bluish light. The dog in the next yard howled with a quavering of terror, his ululation rising in a long crescendo.

The strain was breaking me. "Confound that brute—" I muttered, rising from my chair, then cut my malediction off half uttered, while a sudden prickling came into my scalp and cheeks, and a lump of superheated sulfur seemed thrust in my throat. At the farther corner of the room, like a pale reflection of the alcoholic flare which burned above de Grandin's coffee cup, another light was taking form. It was like a monster pear, or, more precisely, like a giant waterdrop, and it grew bright and dim with slow and pulsing alternations.

I tried to speak, but found my tongue gone mute; I tried to warn de Grandin with a sign, but could not stir a muscle.

And then, before I had a chance to repossess my faculties, it struck. Like a shot hurled from a catapult something sprang across the room, something vaguely human in its shape, but a dreadful parody on humankind. I heard Frazier give a startled cry of terror and surprise as the charging horror dropped upon his shoulders like a panther on a stag, flinging him against the floor with such force that his breath escaped him in a panting gasp.

Agnes' scream was like an echo of her husband's startled cry, but the spirit of the little girl who dared the snake to save her youthful sweetheart still burned gallantly. In an instant she was over Frazier, arms outstretched protectingly, eyes wide with horror, but steady with determination.

A laugh, light, titillating, musical, but utterly unhuman, sounded in the dark, and the visitant reached out and ripped the pearls from Agnes' throat as easily as if they had been strung on cobweb. Then came the ripping sound of rending silk, the flutter of torn draperies, and Agnes crouched above her man as nude as when the obstetrician first beheld her, every shred of clothes rent off by the avenging fury.

Birth-nude, across the prostrate body of the man they faced each other, one intent on horrid vengeance, one on desperate defense.

Agnes' lissome body was perfection's other self. From slender, high-arched feet to narrow, pointed breasts and swaying golden hair she was without a flaw, as sweetly made and slender as a marble naiad carved by Praxiteles.

Her opponent was incarnate horror. Hideous as a harpy, it still was reminiscent of Elaine as an obscene caricature recalls the memory of a faithful portrait. Where red-gold hair as fine as sericeous web had crowned Elaine's small head, this phantom wore an aureole of flickering tongues of fire—or hair which blew and fluttered round the face it framed in the blast of some infernal superheated breeze. The eyes, which glowed with virid phosphorescence, started forward in their sockets, lids peeled away until it seemed that they had broken with the pressure of the eyeballs. The mouth was squared in a grimace of fury, and the white, curved teeth gleamed pale against the blowzed and staring lips like dead men's bones drowned in a pool of blood. Fingers, strictly speaking, there were none upon the hands, but a thick and jointless thumb and two bifurcations of the flesh made beast-paws at the end of either wrist, curved claws like vultures' talons growing at their tips. Upon each heel there grew a horny, spur-like knob, and the knotty-jointed toes were mailed with claws like digits of some unclean carrion fowl. The body was well formed and comely, but the breasts were long and pendulous, like pyriform excrescences hanging half-deflated from the thorax.

I put my hand across my eyes to shut the horrid vision out, for in an instant I was sure the dreadful, claw-armed thing would tear the quivering flesh from Agnes' bones as it had rent the clothing from her body.

A rumbling, like the moving of a heavy piece of furniture, sounded at my back, and as I turned around I saw de Grandin trundling a dental X-ray stand across the floor. As an artillerist prepares his piece for action, the Frenchman swung the lens of his contrivance into line, and next instant came a snapping crackle as the high potential current set the cathode rays to darting through the Crookes' tube.

"*Ha, Madame la Revenante,* you see that Jules de Grandin is prepared!" he announced, the elation of the killer who takes pleasure in his task shining in his small blue eyes and sounding in his voice.

As the Roentgen ray fell on the clawing horror it let out a shriek that pierced my eardrums like a white-hot wire.

As though the devilish form were painted on the atmosphere and de Grandin held a powerful eraser, it was wiped away—obliterated utterly—while he turned the flanged lens of his apparatus back and forth, up and down, like a gardener directing water from a hose.

The last faint vestige of the dreadful apparition vanished, and he snapped down the trigger which controlled the current.

"Look to Madame Agnes, my friend, *elle est nue comme la main!*" he commanded, rushing from the room to seize the telephone, dial a number in hot haste and call, "*Allo,* is Monsieur Martin there? *Très bien, Monsieur,* proceed at once, we wait on you!"

I advanced a step toward Agnes, mute with sheer embarrassment, but I might have been a chair or sofa, for all the notice she gave me. Unconscious of her nudity as though the very beauty of her body were sufficient raiment, she bent above her husband and clasped his head against her bosom. "My dear," she murmured crooningly, like a mother who would soothe her fretful babe, "my poor, sweet, persecuted dear, it's all right now. She's gone, belovèd, gone for ever; nothing more shall come between us now!"

"Come away, thou species of a cabbage plant!" de Grandin's whisper sounded in my ear. "That conversation, it is sacred. Would you eavesdrop, *cochon?* Have you no delicacy, no decency at all, *cordieu?*"

WITH DUE REVERENCE JULES de Grandin raised the bottle with its green-wax seal flaunting the proud N of the Emperor and poured a scant two ounces of the ancient cognac into the bell-shaped brandy snifters. "But it was simple, once I had the cue," he told me smilingly. "First of all, my problem was to find what sort of thing opposed us. Monsieur Martin's assurance that the body was a naturally dead one greatly simplified my task. Very well, then, I must proceed not against a vampire or a vitalized corpse but against a thing which had a psychoplasmic body. *Ha,* that was not so difficult, for I knew all surely that the powerful vibrations of the Roentgen ray would batter it to nothingness if I could but contrive to lure it within range of my machine.

"Good, then. Madame Elaine is cruel, vicious, lustful. Also she is panting for revenge on Madame Agnes, and perhaps she tires of making savage love to Monsieur Frazier, and will do him violence, too. So I contrive my plan. With an imitation of the pearls we lured her to the house. She comes, all fitted with fury to wreak a horrid vengeance on Monsieur and Madame Taviton. She strikes, *mon Dieu*, how savagely she strikes! But so do I, by blue! I have rented from the dental *dépôt* a small X-ray apparatus, one which can be aimed as though it were a gun. When her fierce specter rises in our midst I meet it with my X-ray fire. I wither her, I break her up, *parbleu*, I utterly destroy her, me!

"Meanwhile, I have arrangements made with Monsieur Martin. He has disinterred her body, has it ready at the crematory, waiting my instructions. The minute I have triumphed with my X-ray gun, I call him on the telephone. Immediately into the retort of the crematory goes all that is mortal of Madame Elaine. Into nothingness goes that spirit-form she has constructed with such labor. Body and spirit, she is through, completed; finished! Yes, it is so."

"But d'ye mean to tell me you can destroy a ghost with Roentgen rays?" I asked incredulously.

"Tell me, my friend," he answered earnestly, "were you in the Taviton drawing-room this evening?"

"Why, of course, but—"

"And did you see what happened when I turned the X-ray on that spectral horror?"

"I did, but—"

"Then why ask foolish questions? Are not your own two eyes sufficient witnesses?"

Silenced, I ruminated for a moment; then: "Elaine was beautiful," I mused aloud, "yet that thing we saw tonight was—"

"The death mask of her soul!" he supplied. "The body she was born into was beautiful, but her soul and mind were hideous. When she was no longer able to dwell in her natural body, she made herself a second body out of psychoplasm. And it matched the mind which fashioned it as a plastic cast will duplicate the model to which it is applied. The creature which the world saw while she was in the flesh was a false-face, the whitewashed outside of the reeking charnel which was she. Tonight we saw her as she truly was. *Tiens*, the sight was not a pretty one, I think."

"But—"

"*Ah bah!*" he interrupted with a yawn. "Why speculate? I have told you all I know, and much that I surmise. Me, I am tired as twenty horses. Let us take a drink and go to sleep my friend. What greater happiness can life give tired men?"

Witch-House

S TREET LIGHTS WERE COMING on and the afterglow was paling in the west beneath the first faint stars as we completed our late dinner and moved to the veranda for coffee and liqueurs. Sinking lazily into a wicker deck chair, Jules de Grandin stretched his womanishly small feet out straight before him and regarded the gleaming tips of his brightly polished calfskin pumps with every evidence of satisfaction.

"*Morbleu*," he murmured dreamily as he drained his demitasse and set his cigar glowing before he raised his tiny glass of *kaiserschmarnn*, "say what you will, Friend Trowbridge, I insist there is no process half so pleasant as the combination of digestion and slow poisoning by nicotine and alcohol. It is well worth going hungry to enjoy—ah, *pour l'amour d'une souris verte*, be quiet, great-mouthed one!" he broke off as the irritable stutter of the 'phone bell cut in on his philoso-phizing. "*Parbleu*, the miscreant who invented you was one of humankind's worst enemies!"

"Hullo, Trowbridge," hailed a voice across the wire, "this is Friebergh. Sorry to trouble you, but Greta's in bad shape. Can you come out right away?"

"Yes, I suppose so," I replied, not especially pleased at having my postprandial breathing-spell impinged on by a country call. "What seems to be the matter?"

"I wish I knew," he answered. "She just came home from Wellesley last week, and the new house seemed to set her nerves on edge. A little while ago her mother thought she heard a noise up in her bedroom, and when she went in, there was Greta lying on the floor in some sort of fainting-fit. We don't seem able to rouse her, and—"

"All right," I interrupted, thinking regretfully of my less than half-smoked cigar, "I'll be right out. Keep her head low and loosen any tight clothing. If you can make her swallow, give her fifteen drops of aromatic ammonia in a wine-glassful of water. Don't attempt to force any liquids down her throat, though; she might strangle."

"And this Monsieur Friebergh was unable to give you any history of the causal condition of his daughter's swoon?" de Grandin asked as we drove along the Albemarle Road toward the Friebergh place at Scandia.

"No," I responded. "He said that she's just home from college and has been nervous ever since her arrival. Splendid case history, isn't it?"

"*Eh bien*, it is far from being an exhaustive one, I grant," he answered, "but if every layman understood the art of diagnosis we doctors might be forced to go to work, *n'est-ce-pas?*"

THOUGH GRETA FRIEBERGH HAD recovered partial consciousness when we arrived, she looked like a patient just emerging from a lingering fever. Attempts to get a statement from her met with small response, for she answered slowly, almost incoherently, and seemed to have no idea concerning the cause of her illness. Once she murmured drowsily, "Did you find the kitten? Is it all right?"

"What?" I demanded. "A kitten—"

"She's delirious, poor child," whispered Mrs. Friebergh. "Ever since I found her she's been talking of a kitten she found in the bathroom.

"I thought I heard Greta cry," she added, "and ran up here to see if she were all right. Her bedroom was deserted, but the bathroom door was open and I could hear the shower running. When I called her and received no answer I went in and found her lying on the floor. She was totally unconscious, and remained so till just a few minutes ago."

"U'm?" murmured Jules de Grandin as he made a quick inspection of the patient, then rose and stalked into the bathroom which adjoined the chamber. "Tell me, Madame," he called across his shoulder, "is it customary that you leave the windows of your bathroom screenless?"

"Why, no, of course not," Mrs. Friebergh answered. "There's an opaque screen in—good gracious, it's fallen out!"

The little Frenchman turned to her with upraised brows. "Fallen, *Madame?* It was not fastened to the window-casing, then?"

"Yes, it was," she answered positively. "I saw to that myself. The carpenters attached it to the casing with two bolts, so that we could take it out and clean it, but so firmly that it could not be blown in. I can't understand—"

"No matter," he broke in. "Forgive my idle curiosity, if you please. I'm sure that Doctor Trowbridge has completed his examination, now, so we can discuss your daughter's ailment with assurance."

To me he whispered quickly as the mother left the room: "What do you make of the objective symptoms, *mon ami?* Her pulse is soft and frequent, she has a fluttering heart, her eyes are all suffused, her skin is hot and dry, her face is flushed and hectic. No ordinary fainting-fit, you'll say? No case of heat-prostration?"

"No-o," I replied as I shook my head in wonder, "there's certainly no evidence of heat-prostration. I'd be inclined to say she'd suffered an arterial hemorrhage, but there's no blood about, so—"

"Let us make a more minute examination," he ordered, and rapidly inspected Greta's face and scalp, throat, wrists and calves, but without finding so much as a pin-prick, much less a wound sufficient to cause syncope.

"*Mon Dieu*, but this is strange!" he muttered. "It has the queerness of the devil, this! Perhaps she bled internally, but—*ah-ha, regardez-vous, mon vieux!*"

Searching further for some sign of wound, he had unfastened her pajama jacket, and the livid spot he pointed to seemed the key which might unlock the mystery that baffled us. Against the smooth white flesh beneath the gentle swell of her left breast there showed a red and angry patch, such as might have shone had a vacuum cup been pressed some time against the skin, and in the center of the ecchymosis were four tiny punctures spaced so evenly apart that they seemed to make an almost perfect square three-quarters of an inch or so in size.

The discolored spot with its core of tiny wounds seemed insignificant to me, but the little Frenchman looked at it as though he had discovered a small, deadly reptile coiled against the girl's pale skin.

"*Dieu de Dieu de Dieu de Dieu!*" he murmured softly to himself. "Can such things be here, in New Jersey, in the twentieth centennial of our time?"

"What are you maundering about?" I asked him irritably, "She couldn't possibly have lost much blood through these. Why, she seems almost drained dry, yet there's not a spot of blood upon those punctures. They look to me like insect bites of some kind; even if they were wide open they're not large enough to leak a cubic centimeter of blood in half an hour."

"Blood is not entirely colloidal," he responded slowly. "It will penetrate the tissues to some slight extent, especially if sufficient suction be employed."

"But it would have required a powerful suction—"

"*Précisément*, and I make no doubt that such was used, my friend. Me, I do not like the look of this at all. No, certainly." Abruptly he raised his shoulders in a shrug. "We are here as physicians," he remarked. "I think a quarter-grain of morphine is indicated. After that, bed-rest and much rich food. Then, one hopes, she will achieve a good recovery."

"How is she, Trowbridge?" Olaf Friebergh asked as we joined him in the pleasant living-room. He was a compact, lean man in his late fifties, but appeared younger, and the illusion of youth was helped by the short mustache, still quite dark, the firm-cheeked, sunburned face and hazel eyes which, under clear-cut brows, had that brightness which betokens both good health and an interest in life.

"Why, there's nothing really serious the matter," I answered. "She seems quite weak, and there's something rather queer—"

"There's something queer about the whole dam' case," he cut in almost bruskly. "Greta's been on edge since the moment that she came here; nervous as a cat and jumpy and irritable as the very devil. D'ye suppose hysteria could have caused this fainting-fit?"

De Grandin eyed him speculatively a moment; then: "In just what way has Mademoiselle Greta's nervousness been noticeable, *Monsieur?*" he asked. "Your theory of hysteria has much to recommend it, but an outline of the case might help us greatly toward a diagnosis.

Friebergh stirred his highball thoughtfully a moment; then, "D'ye know about this house?" he asked irrelevantly.

"But no, *Monsieur*; what has it to do with *Mademoiselle* your daughter?"

"Just what I'm wondering," Friebergh answered. "Women are weird brutes, Doctor, all of 'em. You never know what fool tricks nerves will play on 'em. This place belonged to one of my remotest ancestors. You're probably aware that this section was originally settled by the Swedes under William Usselinx, and though the Dutch captured it in 1655 many of the Swedish settlers stayed on not caring much who governed them as long as they were permitted to pursue their business in peace. Oscar Friebergh my great-great-grandfather's half-brother, built this house and had his piers and warehouses down on Raritan Bay. It was from here he sent his ships to Europe and even to the Orient, and to this house he brought the girl he married late in life.

"Theirs was quite a romance. Loaded with silks and wine, the *Good Intent*, my uncle's fastest ship, put in at Portugal for a final replenishment of victuals and water before setting sail for America on the last Sunday in June, 1672. The townsfolk were making holiday, for a company of witches and wizards, duly convicted by ecclesiastical courts, had been turned over to the secular arm for execution, and a great fire had been kindled on the Monte Sao Jorge. My uncle and the master of the ship, together with several of the seamen, were curious to see what was going on, so they ascended the hill where, surrounded by a cordon of soldiers, a perfect forest of stakes had been set up, and to each of these were tied two or three poor wretches who writhed and shrieked as the faggots round their feet took fire. The tortured outcasts' screams and the stench of burning flesh fairly sickened the Swedish sailors, and they were turning away from the accursed place to seek the clear air of the harbor when my uncle's attention was attracted to a little girl who fought desperately with the soldiers to break through to the flaming stakes. She was the daughter of a witch and a warlock who were even then roasting at the same stake, chained back to back as they were said to dance at meetings of the witches' coven. The soldiers cuffed her back good-naturedly, but a Dominican friar who stood by bade them let her through to burn, since, being of the witch-folk, her body would undoubtedly burn soon or later, just as her soul was doomed to burn eternally. The sailormen protested vigorously at this, and my uncle caught the wild girl by the wrists and drew her back to safety.

"She was a thin little thing, dressed in filthy rags, half starved, and unspeakably dirty. In her arms she clutched a draggled-looking white kitten which arched its back and fluffed its tail and spat venomously at the soldiers and the priest. But when my uncle pulled the girl to him both child and kitten ceased to struggle, as if they realized that they had found a friend. The Spanish priest ordered them away with their pitiful prize, saying she was born of the witchpeople and would surely grow to witchcraft and work harm to all with whom she came in contact, but adding it was better that she work her wicked spells on Englishmen and heretics than on true children of the Church.

"My, uncle lifted the child in his arms and bore her to the *Good Intent*, and the moment that he set her down upon the deck she fell upon her knees and took his hands and kissed them and thanked him for his charity in a flood of mingled Portuguese and English.

"For many days she lay like death, only occasionally jumping from her bunk and screaming, '*Padre, Madre—el fuego! el fuego!*' then falling back, hiding her face in her hands and laughing horribly. My uncle coaxed and comforted her, feeding her with his own hands and waiting on her like a nurse; so by degrees she quieted, and long before they raised the coast of Jersey off their bow she was restored to complete health and, though she still seemed sad and troubled, her temper was so sweet and her desire to please everybody so apparent that every man aboard the ship, from cabin boy to captain, was more than half in love with her.

"No one ever knew her real age. She was very small and so thin from undernourishment that she seemed more like a child than a young woman when they brought her on the *Good Intent*. None of the seamen spoke Portuguese, and her English was so slight that they could not ask her about her parents or her birthplace while she lay ill, and when she had recovered normal health it seemed her memory was gone; for though she took to English with surprising aptitude, she seemed unable to remember anything about her former life, and for kindness' sake none would mention the *auto da fé* in which her parents perished. She didn't even know her name, apparently, so my uncle formally christened her Kristina; using the Lutheran baptismal ceremony, and for surname chose to call her Beacon as a sort of poetical commemoration of the fire from which he saved her when her parents had been burnt, It seems she—"

"My dear chap," I broke in, "this is an interesting story, I'll admit, but what possible connection can it have with—"

"Be silent, if you please, my friend," de Grandin ordered sharply. "The connection which you seek is forming like the image as the sculptor chips away the stone, or I am a far greater fool than I have reason to suspect. Say on, *Monsieur*," he ordered Friebergh, "this story is of greater import than you realize, I think. You were informing us of the strange girl your uncle-several-times-removed had rescued from the Hounds of God in Portugal?"

Friebergh smiled appreciation of the little Frenchman's interest. "The sea air and good food, and the genuine affection with which everyone on ship-board regarded her had made a great change in the half-starved, half-mad little foundling by the time the *Good Intent* came back to Jersey," he replied. "From a scrawny little ragamuffin she had grown into a lovely, blooming girl, and there's not much doubt the townsfolk held a carnival of gossip when the *Good Intent* discharged the beautiful young woman along with her cargo of Spanish wines and French silks at the quay.

"Half the young bloods of the town were out to court her; for in addition to her beauty she was Oscar Friebergh's ward, and Oscar Friebergh was the richest man for miles around, a bachelor and well past fifty. Anyone who got Kristina for his wife would certainly have done himself a handsome favor.

"Apparently the girl had everything to recommend her, too. She was as good and modest as she was lovely, her devoutness at church service was so great it won the minister's unstinted praise, her ability as a housekeeper soon proved itself, and my uncle's house, which had been left to the casual superintendence of a cook and staff of Negro slaves, soon became one of the best kept and most orderly households in New Jersey. No one could get the better of Kristina in bar-gain. When cheating tradesmen sought to take advantage of her obvious youth and probable inexperience, she would fix her great, unfathomable eyes on them, and they would flush and stammer like schoolboys caught in mischief and own their fault at once. Besides her church and household duties she seemed to have no interest but my uncle, and the young men who came wooing met with cool reception. Less than a year from the day she disembarked, the banns for her wed-ding to my uncle were posted on the church door, and before the gossip which her advent caused had time to cool, she was Mistress Friebergh, and assumed a leading place in the community.

"For nineteen years they lived quietly in this house, and while my uncle aged and weakened she grew into charming, mature womanhood, treating the old man with a combination of wifely and daughterly devotion, and taking over active management of his affairs when failing sight and memory rendered him incompetent."

Friebergh paused and drew reflectively at his cigar. "I don't suppose you'd know what happened in New England in 1692?" he asked de Grandin.

The Frenchman answered with a vigorous double nod. "*Parbleu*, I do, indeed, Monsieur. That year, in Salem, Massachusetts, there were many witchcraft trials, and—"

"Quite so," our host broke in. "Parish and the Mathers set the northern colonies afire with their witchcraft persecutions. Fortunately, not much of the contagion spread outside New England, but:

"Old Oscar Friebergh had been failing steadily, and though they cupped and leeched him and fed him mixtures of burnt toads, bezoar stone, cloves, and even moss scraped from the skull of a pirate who had been hanged in chains, he died in a coma following a violent seizure of delirium in which he cursed the day that he had taken the witch's brat to his bosom.

"Oscar had sworn his crew to secrecy concerning Kristina's origin, and it seems that they respected the vow while he lived; but some few of them, grown old and garrulous, found their memories suddenly quickened over their glasses of grog after the sexton had set the sods above old Oscar's grave, and evinced a desire to serve gossip and scandal rather than the memory of a master no longer able to reproach them for oath-breaking. There were those who recollected perfectly how the girl Kristina had passed unharmed through the flames and bid her burning parents fond farewell, then came again straight through the flames to put her hand in Oscar Friebergh's and bid him carry her beyond the seas. Others recalled how she had calmed a storm by standing at the ship's rail and reciting incantations in a language not of human origin, and still others told with bated breath how the water of baptism had scalded her as though it had been boiling when Oscar Friebergh poured it on her brow.

"The whole township knew her singing, too. When she was about her household tasks or sewing by the window, or merely sitting idly, she would sing, not loudly, but in a sort of crooning voice; yet people passing in the road before the house would pause to listen, and even children stopped their noisy play to hear her as she sang those fascinating songs in a strange tongue which the far-voyaged sailor folk had never heard and which were set to tunes the like of which were never played on flute or violin or spinet, yet for all their softness seemed to fill the air with melody as the woods are filled with bird-songs in late April. People shook their heads at recollection of those songs, remembering how witches spoke a jargon of their own, known only to each other and their master, Satan, and recalling further that the music used in praise of God was somber as befitted solemn thoughts of death and judgment and the agonies of hell.

"Her kitten caused much comment, too. The townsfolk recollected how she bore a tiny white cat beneath her arm when first she tripped ashore, and though a score of years had passed, the kitten had not grown into a cat, but still as small as when it first touched land, frisked and frolicked in the Friebergh house, and played and purred and still persisted in perpetual, supernatural youth.

"Among the villagers was a young man named Karl Pettersen, who had wooed Kristina when she first came, and took the disappointment of refusal of his marriage offer bitterly. He had married in the intervening years, but a smallpox epidemic had robbed his wife of such good looks as she originally had, and continued business failures had conspired to rob him of his patrimony and his wife's dowry as well; so when Oscar Friebergh died he held Karl's notes of hand for upward of five hundred pounds, secured by mortgages upon his goods and chattels and some farming-land which had come to him at marriage.

"When the executors of Oscar's will made inventory they found these documents which virtually made the widow mistress of the Pettersen estate, and notified the debtor that he must arrange for payment. Karl went to see Kristina late one evening, and what took place at the interview we do not know, though her servants later testified that he shrieked and shouted and cried out as though in torment, and that she replied by laughing at his agony. However that might be, the records show that he was stricken with a fit as he disrobed for bed that night, that he frothed and foamed at the mouth like a mad dog, and made queer, growling noises in his throat. It is recorded further that he lay in semi-consciousness for several days, recovering only long enough to eat his meals, then lapsing back again into delirium. Finally, weak but fully conscious, he sat up in bed, sent for the sheriff, the minister and the magistrate, and formally denounced Kristina as a witch.

"I've said that we escaped the general horror of witch persecution which visited New England, but if old records are to be believed we made up in ferocity what we lacked in quantity. Kristina's old and influential friends were dead, the Swedish Lutheran church had been taken over by the Episcopacy and the incumbent was an Englishman whose youth had been indelibly impressed by Matthew Hopkins' witch-findings. Practically every important man in the community was a former disappointed suitor, and while they might have forgotten this, their wives did not. Moreover, while care and illness and multiple maternity had left their traces on these women, Kristina was more charmingly seductive in the ripeness of maturity than she had been in youth, What chance had she?

"She met their accusations haughtily, and refused to answer vague and rambling statements made against her. It seemed the case against her would break down for want of evidence until Karl Pettersen's wife remembered her familiar. Uncontradicted testimony showed this same small animal, still a kitten, romped and played about the house, though twenty years had passed since it first came ashore. No natural cat could live so long; nothing but a devil's imp disguised in feline shape could have retained its youth so marvelously. This, the village wise ones held, was proof sufficient that Kristina was a witch and harbored a familiar spirit. The clergyman preached a sermon on the circumstance, taking for his text the twenty-seventh verse of the twentieth chapter of Leviticus: 'A man also or woman that hath a familiar spirit, or that is a wizard, shall surely be put to death.'

"They held her trial on the village green. The records say she wore a shift of scarlet silk, which is all her persecutors would allow her from her wardrobe. Preliminary search had failed to find the devil's mark or witch-teat through which her familiar was supposed to nourish itself by sucking her blood; so at her own request Mistress Pettersen was appointed to the task of hunting for it *coram judice*.

"She had supplied herself with pricking-pins, and at a signal from the magistrate ripped the scarlet mantle from Kristina, leaving her stark naked in the center of a ring of cruel and lustful eyes. A wave of smothering shame swept over her, and she would have raised her hands to shield her bosom from the lecherous stares of loafers congregated on the green, but her wrists were firmly bound behind her. As she bent her head in a paroxysm of mortification, the four-inch bodkin in the Pettersen woman's hand fleshed itself first in her thigh, then her side, her shoulder, her neck and her breast, and she writhed in agonizing postures as her tender flesh was stabbed now here, now there, while the rabble roared and shouted in delight.

"The theory, you know, was that at initiation into witch-hood the devil marked his new disciple with a bite, and from this spot the imp by which the witch worked her black magic drew its sustenance by sucking her blood. This devil's mark, or witch-teat was said to be insensible to pain, but as it often failed to differ in appearance from the rest of the body's surface, it was necessary for the searcher to spear and stab the witch repeatedly until a spot insensible to pain was found. The nervous system can endure a limited amount of shock, after which it takes refuge in defensive anesthesia. This seems to have been the case with poor Kristina; for after several minutes of torment she ceased to writhe and scream, and her torturer announced the mark found. It was a little area of flesh beneath the swell of her left breast, roughly square in shape and marked off by four small scars which looked like needle-wounds set about three-quarters of an inch apart.

"But the finding of the mark was inconclusive. While a witch would surely have it, an innocent person might possess something simulating it; so there remained the test of swimming. Water was supposed to reject a witch's body; so if she were tied and thrown into a pond or stream, proof of guilt was deemed established if she floated.

They cross-tied her, making her sit tailor-fashion and binding the thumb of her right hand so tightly to the great toe of her left foot that the digits soon turned blue for lack of circulation, then doing the same with her left thumb and right great toe, after which she was bundled in a bed-sheet which was tied at the corners above her head, and the parcel was attached to a three-fathom length of rope and towed behind a rowboat for a distance of three-quarters of a mile in Raritan Bay.

"At first the air within the sheet buoyed up the bundle and its contents, and the crowd gave vent to yells of execration. 'She floats, she floats, the water will have none of her; bring the filthy witch ashore and burn her!' they shouted, but in a little while the air escaped from the wet sheet, and though Kristina sank as far down in the water as the length of rope permitted, there was no effort made to draw her up until the boat had beached. She was dead when finally they dragged her out upon the shingle.

"Karl Pettersen confessed his error and declared the devil had misled him into making a false accusation, and, her innocence proved by her drowning, Kristina was accorded Christian burial in consecrated ground, and her husband's property, in which she had a life estate, reverted to my ancestor. One of the first things he did was to sell this house, and it went through a succession of owner-ships till I bought it at auction last autumn and had it reconditioned as a summer home. We found the old barn filled with household goods, and had them recon-ditioned, too. This furniture was once Kristina Friebergh's."

I looked around the big, low-ceilinged room with interest. Old-fashioned chintz, patterned with quaint bouquets of roses, hung at the long windows. Deep chairs and sofas were covered with a warm rose-red that went well with the gray woodwork and pale green walls. A low coffee table of pear wood, waxed to a satin finish, stood before a couch; an ancient mirror framed in gilt hung against one wall, while against another stood a tall buhl cabinet and a chest of drawers of ancient Chinese nanmu wood, brown as withered oak leaves and still exhal-ing a subtly faint perfume. Above the open fireplace hung an ancient painting framed in a narrow strip of gold.

"That's Kristina," volunteered our host as he nodded toward the portrait.

The picture was of a woman not young, not at all old; slender, mysterious, black hair shining smoothly back, deep blue eyes holding a far-off vision, as though they sensed the sufferings of the hidden places of the world and brooded on them; a keen, intelligent face of a clear pallor with small, straight nose, short upper lip and a mouth which would have been quite lovely had it not been so serious. She held a tiny kitten, a mere ball of white fluffiness, at her breast, and the hand supporting the small animal was the hand of one in whom the blood of ancient races ran, with long and slimly pointed fingers tipped with rosy nails. There was something to arrest attention in that face. The woman had the cold knowledge of death, ominous and ever present, on her.

"*La pauvre!*" de Grandin murmured as he gazed with interest at the portrait. "And what became of Monsieur Pettersen and his so highly unattractive wife?"

Friebergh laughed, almost delightedly. "History seems to parallel itself in this case," he answered. "Perhaps you've heard how the feud resulting from the Salem persecutions was resolved when descendants of accusers and accused were married? Well . . . it seems that after Kristina drowned, executors of Oscar

Friebergh's will could not find clue or trace of the notes and mortgages which Pettersen had signed. Everybody had suspicions how they came to disappear, for Mistress Pettersen was among the most earnest searchers of Kristina's private papers when they sought a copy of the compact she had signed with Satan, but—in any event, Karl Pettersen began to prosper from the moment that Kristina died. Every venture which he undertook met with success. His descendants prospered, too. Two years ago the last male member of his line met Greta at a Christmas dance, and"—he broke off with a chuckle—"and they've been that way about each other from the first. I'm thinking they'll be standing side by side beneath a floral bell and saying 'I do' before the ink on their diplomas has had much chance to dry."

"All of which brings us back three centuries, and down to date—and Greta," I responded somewhat sharply. "If I remember, you'd begun to tell us something about her hysterical condition and the effect this house had on her, when you detoured to that ancient family romance."

"*Précisément, Monsieur*, the house," de Grandin prompted. "I think that I anticipate you, but I should like to hear your statement—" He paused with interrogatively raised brows.

"Just so," our host returned. "Greta has never heard the story of Kristina, and Karl Pettersen, I'm sure, for I didn't know it very well myself till I bought this house and started digging up the ancient records. She'd certainly never been in the house, nor even seen the plans, since the work of restoration was done while she was off to school; yet the moment she arrived she went directly to her room, as if she knew the way by heart. Incidentally, her room is the same one—"

"Occupied by Madame Kristina in the olden days!" supplied de Grandin.

"Good Lord! How'd you guess?"

"I did not guess, *Monsieur*," the little Frenchman answered levelly; "I knew."

"Humph. Well, the child has seemed to hate the place from the moment she first entered it. She's been moody and distrait, complaining of a constant feeling of malaise and troubled sleep, and most of the time she's been so irritable that there's scarcely any living with her. D'ye suppose there's something psychic in the place—something that the rest of us don't feel, that's worked upon her nerves until she had this fainting-fit tonight?"

"Not at all," I answered positively. "The child's been working hard at school, and—"

"Very likely," Jules de Grandin interrupted, "Women are more finely attuned to such influences than men, and it is entirely possible that the tragedy these walls have witnessed has been felt subconsciously by your daughter, Monsieur Friebergh."

"DOCTOR TROWBRIDGE, I DON'T like this place," Greta Friebergh told me when we called on her next day. "It—there's something about it that terrifies me; makes me feel as though I were somebody else."

She raised her eyes to mine, half frightened, half wondering, and for a moment I had the eery sensation of being confronted with the suffering ghost of a girl in the flesh.

"Like someone else?" I echoed. "How d'ye mean, my dear?"

"I'm afraid I can't quite say, sir. Something queer, a kind of feeling of vague uneasiness coupled with a sort of 'I've been here before' sensation came to me the moment I stepped across the threshold. Everything, the house, the furniture, the very atmosphere, seemed to combine to oppress me. It was as if something old and infinitely evil—like the wiped-over memory of some terrifying childhood nightmare—were trying to break through to my consciousness. I kept reaching for it mentally, as one reaches for a half-remembered tune or a forgotten name; yet I seemed to realize that if I ever drew aside the veil of memory my sanity would crack. Do you understand me, Doctor?"

"I'm afraid I don't, quite, child," I answered. "You've had a trying time at school, and with your social program speeded up—"

Something like a grimace, the parody of a smile, froze upon de Grandin's face as he leant toward the girl. "Tell us, *Mademoiselle*," he begged, "was there something more, some tangibility, which matched this feeling of malaise?"

"Yes, there was!" responded Greta.

"And that—"

"Last night I came in rather late, all tired and out of sorts. Karl Pettersen and I had been playing tennis in the afternoon, and drove over to Keyport for dinner afterward. Karl's a sweet lad, and the moonlight was simply divine on the homeward drive, but—" The quick blood stained her face and throat as she broke off her narrative.

"Yes, *Mademoiselle*, but?" de Grandin prompted.

She smiled, half bashfully, at him, and she was quite lovely when she smiled. It brightened the faintly sad expression of her mouth and raised her eyes, ever so little, at the corners. "It can't have been so long since you were young, Doctor," she returned. "What did you do on moonlight summer nights when you were alone with someone you loved terribly?"

"*Morbleu*," the little Frenchman chuckled, "the same as you, *petite*, no more, I think, and certainly no less!"

She smiled again, a trifle sadly, this time. "That's just the trouble," she lamented. "I couldn't."

"*Hein*, how is it you say, *Mademoiselle*?"

"I wanted to, Lord knows my lips were hungry and my arms were aching for him, but something seemed to come between us. It was as if I'd had a dish of food before me and hadn't eaten for a long, long time, then, just before I tasted it, a whisper came, 'It's poisoned!'

"Karl was hurt and puzzled, naturally, and I tried my best to overcome my feeling of aversion, but for a moment when his lips were pressed to mine I had a positive sensation of revulsion. I felt I couldn't bear his touch, his kisses seemed to stifle me; if he hadn't let me go I think that I'd have fainted.

"I ran right in the house when we got home, just flinging a good-night to Karl across my shoulder, and rushed up to my room. 'Perhaps a shower will pull me out of it,' I thought, and so I started to disrobe, when—" Once more she paused, and now there was no doubt of it: the girl was terrified.

"Yes, *Mademoiselle*, and then?" the Frenchman prompted softly.

"I'd slipped my jumper and culottes off, and let down my hair, preparatory to knotting it up to fit inside my shower cap, when I chanced to look into the mirror. I hadn't turned the light on, but the moonlight slanted through the window and struck right on the glass; so I could see myself as a sort of silhouette, only"—again she paused, and her narrow nostrils dilated—"only it wasn't I!"

"*Sacré nom d'un fromage vert*, what is it that you tell us, *Mademoiselle?*" asked Jules de Grandin.

"It wasn't I reflected in that mirror. As I looked, the moonlight seemed to break and separate into a million little points of light, so that it was more like a mist powdered with diamond dust than a solid shaft of light; it seemed to be at once opaque yet startlingly translucent, with a sheen like that of flowing water, yet absorbing all reflections. Then suddenly, where I should have seen myself reflected in the mirror, I saw another form take shape, half veiled in the sparkling mist that seemed to fill the room, yet startlingly distinct. It was a woman, a girl, perhaps, a little older than I, but not much. She was tall and exquisitely slender, with full-blown, high-set breasts and skin as pale as ivory. Her hair was black and silken-fine and rippled down across her shoulders till it almost reached her knees, and her deep-blue eyes and lovely features held a look of such intense distress that I thought involuntarily of those horribly realistic mediæval pictures of the Crucifixion. Her shoulders were braced back, for she held her hands behind her as though they had been tied, and on her breast and throat and sides were numerous little wounds as though she had been stabbed repeatedly with something sharp and slender, and from every wound the fresh blood welled and trickled out upon the pale, smooth skin."

"She was—" began de Grandin, but the girl anticipated him.

"Yes," she told him, "she was nude. Nothing clothed her but her glorious hair and the bright blood streaming from her wounds.

"For a minute, maybe for an hour, we looked into each other's eyes, this lovely, naked girl and I, and it seemed to me that she tried desperately to tell me something, but though I saw the veins and muscles stand out on her throat with the effort that she made, no sound came from her tortured lips. Somehow, as we stood there, I felt a queer, uncanny feeling creeping over me. I seemed in some way to be identified with this other girl, and with that feeling of a loss of personality, a bitter, blinding rage seemed surging up in me. Gradually, it seemed to take some sort of form, to bend itself against a certain object, and with a start I realized that I was consumed with hatred; dreadful, crushing, killing hatred toward someone named Karl Pettersen. Not my Karl, especially, but toward everybody in the world who chanced to bear that name. It was a sort of all-inclusive hatred, something like the hatred of the Germans which your generation had in the World War. 'I can't—I won't hate Karl!' I heard myself exclaiming, and turned to face the other girl. But she was not there.

"There I stood alone in the darkened, empty room with nothing but the moonlight—ordinary moonlight, now-slanting down across the floor.

"I turned the lights on right away and took a dose of aromatic spirits of ammonia, for my nerves were pretty badly shot. Finally I got calmed down and went into the bathroom for my shower.

"I was just about to step into the spray, when I heard a little plaintive *mew* outside the window. When I crossed the room, there was the sweetest little fluffy white kitten perched on the sill outside the screen, its green eyes blinking in the light which streamed down from the ceiling-lamp and the tip of its pink tongue sticking out like the little end of thin-sliced ham you sometimes see peeping from behind the rolls in railway station sandwiches. I unhooked the screen and let the little creature in, and it snuggled up against my breast and puffed and blinked its knowing eyes at me, and then put up a tiny, pink-toed paw and began to wash its face.

"'Would you like to take a shower with me, pussy?' I asked it, and it stopped its washing and looked up at me as if to ask, 'What did you say?' then stuck its little nose against my side and began to lick me. You can't imagine how its little rough tongue tickled."

"And then, *Mademoiselle?*" de Grandin asked as Greta broke off smilingly and lay back on her pillows.

"Then? Oh, there wasn't any then, sir. Next thing I knew I was in bed, with you and Doctor Trowbridge bending over me and looking as solemn and learned as a pair of owls. But the funny part of it all was that I wasn't ill at all; just too tired to answer when you spoke to me."

"And what became of this small kitten, *Mademoiselle?*" de Grandin asked.

"Mother didn't see it. I'm afraid the little thing was frightened when I fell, and jumped out of the bathroom window."

"U'm?" Jules de Grandin teased the needle-points of his mustache between a thoughtful thumb and forefinger; then: "And this so mysterious lady without clothing whom you saw reflected in your mirror, *Mademoiselle?* Could you, by any chance, identify her?"

"Of course," responded Greta, matter-of-factly as though he'd asked her if she had studied algebra at school, "she was the girl whose portrait's in the living-room downstairs, Kristina Friebergh."

"WILL YOU LEAVE ME in the village?" asked de Grandin as we left the Friebergh house. "I would supplement the so strange story which we heard last night by searching through the records at the church and court-house, too."

Dinner was long overdue when he returned that evening, and, intent upon his dressing, he waved my questioning aside while he shaved and took a hasty shower. Finally, when he had done justice to the salad and meringue glacé, he leant his elbows on the table, lit a cigarette and faced me with a level, serious glance.

"I have found out many things today, my friend," he told me solemnly. "Some supplement the story which Monsieur Friebergh related; some cast new light upon it; others are, I fear, disquieting.

"By example: There is a story of the little kitten of which Monsieur Friebergh told us, the kitten which refused to grow into a cat. When poor Madame Kristina was first haled before the magistrates for trial, a most careful search was made for it, but nowhere could the searchers find it; yet during the *al fresco* trial several persons saw it now here, now there, keeping just outside the range of stone-throw, but at all times present. Further, when the ban of witchcraft had apparently been lifted by Madame Kristina's inability to float and her burial within the churchyard close had been permitted, this so little kitten was seen nightly at her grave, curled up like a patch of snow against the greenery of the growing grass. Small boys shied stones at it, and more than once the village men went to the graveyard and took shots at it, but stone and bullet both were ineffective; the small animal would raise its head and look at those who sought to harm it with a sadly thoughtful glance, then go back to its napping on the grave. Only when approached too closely would it rouse itself, and when the hunter had almost succeeded in tiptoeing close enough to strike it with a club or sword it would completely vanish, only to reappear upon the grave when, tired out with waiting, its assailant had withdrawn to a safe distance.

"Eventually the townsfolk became used to it, but no horse would pass the cemetery while it lay upon its mistress' grave without shying violently, and the most courageous of the village dogs shunned the graveyard as a place accursed. Once, indeed, a citizen took out a pair of savage mastiffs, determined to exterminate the little haunting beast, but the giant dogs, which would attack a maddened bull without a moment's hesitation, quailed and cowered from the tiny bit of fluffy fur, nor could their master's kicks and blows and insults force them past the graveyard gateway."

"Well, what's disquieting in that?" I asked. "It seems to me that if there were any sort of supernatural intervention in the case, it was more divine than diabolical. Apparently the townsfolk tried to persecute the little harmless cat to death exactly as they had its mistress. The poor thing died eventually, I suppose?"

"One wonders," he returned as he pursed his lips and blew a geometrically perfect smoke-ring.

"Wonders what?"

"Many things, *parbleu*. Especially concerning its death and its harmlessness. Attend me, if you please: For several years the small cat persisted in its nightly vigils at the grave. Then it disappeared, and people thought no more about it. One evening Sarah Spotswood, a young farmer's daughter, was passing by the graveyard, when she was accosted by a small white cat. The little creature came out in the road near where it winds within a stone's-throw of the grave of Kristina Friebergh. It was most friendly, and when she stooped to fondle it, it leaped into her arms."

He paused and blew another smoke-ring.

"Yes?" I prompted as he watched the cloudy circle sail a lazy course across the table-candles.

"Quite yes," he answered imperturbably. "Sarah Spotswood went insane within a fortnight. She died without regaining reason. Generally she was a harmless, docile imbecile, but occasionally she broke out raving in delirium. At such times she would shriek and writhe as though in torment, and bleeding wounds appeared upon her sides and breast and throat. The madhouse-keepers thought she had inflicted injury upon herself, and placed her in a straitjacket when they saw the signs of the seizure coming on. It made no difference: the wounds accompanied each spell of madness, as though they were stigmata. Also, I think it worth while mentioning, a small white kitten, unknown to anybody in the madhouse, was always observed somewhere about the place when Sarah's periods of mania came.

"Her end came tragically, too. She escaped surveillance on a summer afternoon, fled to a little near-by stream and cast herself into it. Though the water was a scant six inches deep, she lay upon her face until she died by drowning.

"Two other similar cases are recorded. Since Sarah Spotswood died in 1750 there have been three young women similarly seized, the history of each case revealing that the maniac had taken a stray white kitten for pet shortly before the onset of incurable madness, and that in every instance the re-appearance of this kitten, or an animal just like it, had coincided with return of manic seizures. Like their predecessor, each of these unfortunate young women succeeded in drowning herself. In view of these things would you call this kitten either dead or harmless?"

"You have a theory?" I countered.

"Yes—and no," he answered enigmatically. "From such information as we have I am inclined to think the verdict rendered in Madame Kristina's witch trial was a false one. While not an ill-intentioned one—unknowingly, indeed, perhaps—I think the lady was what we might call a witch; one who had power, whether she chose to exercise it or not, of working good or bad to fellow humans by means of supernatural agencies. It seems this little kitten which never grew to cathood, which lay in mourning on her grave and which afflicted four unfortunate young women with insanity, was her familiar—a beast-formed demon through whose aid she might accomplish magic."

"But that's too utterly absurd!" I scoffed. "Kristina Friebergh died three centuries ago, while this kitten—"

"Did not necessarily die with her," he interjected. "Indeed, my friend, there are many instances in witch-lore where the familiar has outlived its witch."

"But why should it seek out other girls—"

"*Précisément*," he answered soberly. "That, I damn think, is most significant. Witches' imps, though they may be ambassadors from hell, are clothed in pseudo-natural bodies. Thus they have need of sustenance. This the witch supplies with her blood. It is at the insensitive spot known as the witch-mark or witch's teat that the familiar is suckled. When Monsieur Friebergh told us of Madame Kristina's trial, you will recall that he described the spot in which she felt no pain as an area roughly square in shape marked off by four small scars which looked like needle-wounds set about three-quarters of an inch apart? Consider, my friend—think carefully—where have you seen a cicatrix like that within the last few days?" His eyes, round and unwinking as those of a thoughtfully inclined tom-cat, never left mine as he asked the question.

"Why"—I temporized—"oh, it's too absurd, de Grandin!"

"You do not answer, but I see you recognize the similarity," he returned. "Those little 'needle-wounds,' *mon vieux*, were made by little kitten-teeth which pierced the white and tender skin of Mademoiselle Greta just before she swooned. She exhibited the signs of hemorrhage, that you will agree; yet we found no blood. *Pourquoi?* Because the little fluffy kitten which she took into her arms, the little beast which licked her with its tongue a moment before she lost consciousness, *sucked it from her body.* This cat-thing seems immortal, but it is not truly so. Once in so many years it must have sustenance, the only kind of sustenance which will enable it to mock at time, the blood of a young woman. Sarah Spotswood gave it nourishment, and lost her reason in the process, becoming, apparently, identified with the unfortunate Madame Kristina, even to showing the stigmata of the needle-wounds which that poor creature suffered at her trial. The manner of her death—by drowning—paralleled Kristina's, also, as did those of the other three who followed her in madness—*after having been accosted by a small white kitten.*"

"Then what d'ye suggest?" I asked him somewhat irritably, but the cachinnation of the telephone cut in upon the question.

"Good Lord!" I told him as I hung up the receiver. "Now it's young Karl Pettersen! His mother 'phoned to tell me he's been hurt, and—"

"Right away, at once; immediately," he broke in. "Let us hasten to him with all speed. Unless I make a sad mistake, his is no ordinary hurt, but one which casts a challenge in our faces. Yes, assuredly!"

I DO NOT THINK I ever saw a man more utterly unstrung than young Karl Pettersen. His injury was trivial, amounting to scarcely more than a briar-scratch across his throat, but the agony of grief and horror showing in his face was truly pitiful, and when we asked him how the accident occurred his only answer was a wild-eyed stare and a sob-torn sentence he reiterated endlessly: "Greta, oh, Greta, how could you?"

"I think that there is something devilish here, Friend Trowbridge," whispered Jules de Grandin.

"So do I," I answered grimly. "From that wound I'd say the little fool has tried to kill himself after a puppy-lovers' quarrel. See how the cut starts underneath the condyle of the jaw, and tapers off and loses depth as it nears the median line? I've seen such cuts a hundred times, and—"

"But no," he interrupted sharply. "Unless the young *Monsieur* is left-handed he would have made the cut across the left side of his throat; this wound describes a slant across the right side. It was made by someone else—someone seated on his right, as, by example, in a motorcar.

"*Monsieur!*" he seized the boy by both his shoulders and shook him roughly. "Stop this childish weeping. Your wound is but a skin-scratch. It will heal almost with one night's sleep, but its cause is of importance. How did you get it, if you please?"

"Oh, Greta—" Karl began again, but the smacking impact of de Grandin's hand against his cheek cut short his wail.

"*Nom d'un coq*, you make me to lose patience with you!" cried the Frenchman. "Here, take a dose of this!" From his jacket pocket he produced a flask of cognac, poured a liberal portion out into a cup and thrust it into Karl's unsteady hand. "Ah, so; that is better," he pronounced as the lad gulped down the liquor. "Now, take more, *mon vieux*; we need the truth, and quickly, and never have I seen a better application of the proverb that in alcohol dwells truth."

Within five minutes he had forced the better portion of a pint of brandy down the young man's throat, and as the potent draft began to work, his incoherent babbling gave way to a melancholy but considered gravity which in other circumstances would have appeared comic.

"Now, man to man, *compagnon de débauche*, inform us what took place," the Frenchman ordered solemnly.

"Greta and I were out driving after dinner," answered Karl. "We've been nuts about each other ever since we met, and today I asked her if she'd marry me. She'd been actin' sort o' queer and distant lately, so I thought that maybe she'd been fallin' for another bird, and I'd better hurry up and get my brand on her. Catch on?"

De Grandin nodded somewhat doubtfully. "I think I apprehend your meaning," he replied, "though the language which you use is slightly strange to me. And when you had completed your proposal—"

"She didn't say a word, but just pointed to the sky, as though she'd seen some object up there that astonished her."

"Quite so. One understands; and then?"

"Naturally, I looked up, and before I realized what was happening she slashed a penknife across my throat and jumped out of the car screaming with laughter. I wasn't very badly hurt, but—" He paused, and we could fairly see his alcoholic aplomb melt and a look of infantile distress spread on his features. "O-o-o!" he wailed disconsolately. "Greta, my dear, why did you—"

"The needle, if you please, Friend Trowbridge," Jules de Grandin whispered. "There is nothing further to be learned, and the opiate will give him merciful oblivion. Half a grain of morphine should be more than ample."

"T HIS IS POSITIVELY THE craziest piece of business I ever heard of!" I exclaimed as we left the house. "Only the other night she told us that she loved the lad so much that her heart ached with it; this afternoon she interrupts his declaration by slashing at his throat. I never heard of anything so utterly fantastic—"

"Except, perhaps, the case of Sarah Spotswood and the other three unfortunates who followed her to madness and the grave?" he interrupted in a level voice. "I grant the little *demoiselle* has acted in a most demented manner. *Ha*, but is she crazier than—"

"Oh, for the love of mercy, stop it!" I commanded querulously. "Those cases were most likely mere coincidences. There's not a grain of proof—"

"If a thing exists we must believe it, whether it is susceptible of proof or not," he told me seriously. "As for coincidence—had only one girl graduated into death from madness after encountering a kitten such as that which figures in each of these occurrences, we might apply the term; but when three young women are so similarly stricken, *parbleu*, to fall back on coincidence is but to shut your eyes against the facts, *mon vieux*. One case, yes; two cases, perhaps; three cases—*non*, it is to pull the long arm of coincidence completely out of joint, by blue!"

"Oh, well," I answered wearily, "if you—good Lord!"

Driven at road-burning speed a small, light car with no lamps burning came careening crazily around the elbow of the highway, missed our left fender by a hair and whizzed past us like a bullet from a rifle.

"Is it any wonder our insurance rates are high with idiots like that out upon the public roads?" I stuttered, inarticulate with fury, but the whining signal of a motorcycle's siren cut my protest short as a state policeman catapulted around the bend in hot pursuit of the wild driver.

"D'ye see 'um?" he inquired as he stopped beside us with a scream of brakes. "Which way did 'e go?"

"Took the turn to the right," I answered. "Running like a streak with no lights going, and—"

"My friend mistakes," de Grandin interrupted as he smiled at the policeman; "the wild one turned abruptly to the left, and should be nearly to the village by this time."

"Why, I'm positive he took the right-hand turn—" I began, when a vicious kick upon my shin served notice that de Grandin wished deliberately to send the trooper on a wild-goose chase. Accordingly: "Perhaps I was mistaken," I amended lamely; then, as the officer set out:

"What was your idea in that?" I asked.

"The speeder whom the gendarme followed was Mademoiselle Greta," he replied. "I recognized her in our headlights' flash as she went by, and I suggest we follow her."

"Perhaps we'd better," I conceded; "driving as she was, she's likely to end up in a ditch before she reaches home."

"WHY, GREFA'S NOT BEEN out to-night," said Mrs. Friebergh when we reached the house. "She went out walking in the afternoon and came home shortly after dinner and went directly to her room. I'm sure she's sleeping."

"But may we see her anyway, *Madame?*" de Grandin asked. "If she sleeps we shall not waken her."

"Of course," the mother answered as she led the way upstairs.

It was dark and quiet as a tomb in Greta's bedroom, and when we switched on the night-light we saw her sleeping peacefully, her head turned from us, the bedclothes drawn up close about her chin.

"You see, the poor, dear child's exhausted," Mrs. Friebergh said as she paused upon the threshold.

De Grandin nodded acquiescence as he tiptoed to the bed and bent an ear above the sleeping girl. For a moment he leant forward; then, "I regret that we should so intrude, *Madame,*" he apologized, "but in cases such as this—" An eloquently non-committal shrug completed the unfinished sentence.

Outside, he ordered in a sharp-edged whisper: "This way, my friend, here, beneath this arbor!" In the vine-draped pergola which spanned the driveway running past the house, he pointed to a little single-seated roadster. "You recognize him?" he demanded.

"Well, it *looks* like the car that passed us on the road—"

"Feel him!" he commanded, taking my hand in his and pressing it against the radiator top.

I drew away with a suppressed ejaculation. The metal was hot as a teakettle full of boiling water.

"Not only that, *mon vieux*," he added as we turned away; "when I pretended to be counting Mademoiselle Greta's respiration I took occasion to turn back the covers of her bed. She was asleep, but most curiously, she was also fully dressed, even to her shoes. Her window was wide open, and a far less active one than she could climb from it to earth and back again."

"Then you think—"

"*Non, non*, I do not think; I wish I did; I merely speculate, my friend. Her mother told us that she went out walking in the afternoon. That is what she thought. Plainly, that is what she was meant to think. Mademoiselle Greta walked out, met the young Monsieur Pettersen and drove with him, cut him with her ninety-six times cursed knife, then leaped from his car and walked back home. Anon, when all the house was quiet, she clambered from her window, drove away upon some secret errand, then returned in haste, re-entered her room as she had left it, and"—he pursed his lips and raised his shoulders in a shrug—"there we are, my friend, but just where is it that we are, I ask to know."

"On our way to home and bed," I answered with a laugh. "After all this mystery and nonsense, I'm about ready for a drink and several hours' sleep."

"An excellent idea," he nodded, "but I should like to stop a moment at the cemetery, if you will be so kind. I desire to see if what I damn suspect is true."

Fifteen minutes' drive sufficed to bring us to the lich-gate of the ancient burying-ground where generations of the county's founders slept. Unerringly he led the way between the sentinel tombstones till, a little distance from the ivy-mantled wall which bordered on the highway, he pointed to a moss-grown marker.

"There is Madame Kristina's tomb," he told me in a whisper. "It was there— by blue! Behold, my friend!"

Following his indicating finger's line I saw a little spot of white against the mossy grass about the tombstone's base, and even as I looked, the little patch of lightness moved, took shape, and showed itself a small, white, fluffy kitten. The tiny animal uncoiled itself, raised to a sitting posture, and regarded us with round and shining eyes.

"Why, the poor little thing!" I began, advancing toward it with extended hand. "It's lost, de Grandin—"

"*Pardieu*, I think that it is quite at home," he interrupted as he stooped and snatched a piece of gravel from the grave beneath his feet. "*Regardez, s'il vous plait!*"

In all the years I'd known him I had never seen him do an unkind thing to woman, child or animal; so it was with something like a gasp of consternation that I saw him hurl the stone straight at the little, inoffensive kitten. But great as my surprise had been at his unwonted cruelty, it was swallowed up in sheer astonishment as I saw the stone strike through the little body, drive against the granite tombstone at its back, then bounce against the grave-turf with a muffled thud. And all the while the little cat regarded him with a fixed and slightly amused stare, making no movement to evade his missile, showing not the slightest fear at his approach.

"You see?" he asked me simply.

"I—I thought—I could have sworn—" I stammered, and the laugh with which he greeted my discomfiture was far from mirthful.

"You saw, my friend, nor is there any reason for you to forswear the testimony of your sight," he assured me. "A hundred others have done just as I did. If all the missiles which have been directed at that small white cat-thing were gathered in a pile, I think that they would reach a tall man's height; yet never one of them has caused it to forsake its vigil on this grave. It has visited this spot at will for the past two hundred years and more, and always it has meant disaster to some girl in the vicinity. Come, let us leave it to its brooding; we have plans to make and things to do. Of course."

"GRAND DIEU DES CHATS, c'est l'explication terrible!" de Grandin's exclamation called me from perusal of the morning's mail as we completed breakfast the next day.

"What is it?" I demanded.

"Parbleu, what is it not?" he answered as he passed a folded copy of the Journal to me, indicating the brief item with a well-groomed forefinger.

TREASURE HUNTERS VIOLATE THE DEAD

the headline read, followed by the short account:

Shortly after eleven o'clock last night vandals entered the home of the late Timothy McCaffrey, Argyle Road near Scandia, and stole two of the candles which were burning by his casket while he lay awaiting burial. The body was reposing in the front room of the house, and several members of the family were in the room adjoining.

Miss Monica McCaffrey, 17, daughter of the deceased, was sitting near the doorway leading to the front room where the body lay, and heard somebody softly opening the front door of the house. Thinking it was a neighbor come to pay respects to the dead, she did not rise immediately, not wishing to disturb the visitor at his devotions, but when she noticed an abrupt diminution of the light in the room in which her father's body lay, as though several of the candles had been extinguished, she rose to investigate.

As she stepped through the communicating doorway she saw what she took to be a young man in a light tan sports coat running out the front door of the house. She followed the intruder to the porch and was in time to see him jump into a small sports roadster standing by the front gate with its engine running, and drive away at breakneck speed.

Later, questioned by state troopers, she was undetermined whether the trespasser was a man or woman, as the overcoat worn by the intruder reached from neck to knees, and she could not definitely say whether the figure wore a skirt or knickerbockers underneath the coat.

When Miss McCaffrey returned to the house she found that all the vigil lights standing by the coffin had been extinguished and two of the candles had been taken.

Police believe the act of wanton vandalism was committed by some member of the fashionable summer colony at Scandia who were engaged in a "treasure hunt," since nothing but two candles had been taken by the intruder.

"For goodness' sake!" I looked at de Grandin in blank amazement.

His eyes, wide, round and challenging, were fixed on mine unwinkingly. "*Non*," he answered shortly, "not for goodness' sake, my friend; far from it, I assure you. The thief who stole these candles from the dead passed us on her homeward way last night."

"Her homeward way? You mean—"

"But certainly. Mademoiselle Greta wore such a coat as that *le journal* mentions. Indubitably it was she returning from her gruesome foray."

"But what could she be wanting corpse-lights for?"

"Those candles had been exorcised and blessed, my friend; they were, as one might say, spiritually antiseptic, and it was a law of the old witch covens that things stolen from the church be used to celebrate their unclean rites. All evidence points to a single horrid issue, and tonight we put it to the test."

"Tonight?"

"*Précisément*. This is the twenty-third of June, Midsummer's Eve. Tonight in half the world the bonfires spring in sudden flame on mountain and in valley, by rushing river and by quiet lake. In France and Norway, Hungary and Spain, Rumania and Sweden, you could see the flares stand out against the blackness of the night while people dance about them and chant charms against the powers of Evil. On Midsummer's Eve the witches and the wizards wake to power;

tonight, if ever, that which menaces our little friend will manifest itself. Let us be on hand to thwart it—if we can."

"GRETA'S DANCING AT THE Country Club," said Mrs. Friebergh when we called to see our patient late that evening. "I didn't want her to go, she's seemed so feverish and nervous all day long, but she insisted she was well enough, so—"

"Precisely, *Madame*," Jules de Grandin nodded. "It is entirely probable that she will feel no ill effects, but for precaution's sake we will look in at the dance and see how she sustains the strain of exercise."

"But I thought you said that we were going to the club," I remonstrated as he touched my arm to signal a left turn. "But we are headed toward the cemetery—"

"But naturally, my friend; there is the grave of Madame Kristina; there the small white cat-thing keeps its watch; there we must go to see the final act played to its final curtain."

He shifted the small bundle on his knees and began unfastening the knots which bound it.

"What's that?" I asked.

For answer he tore off the paper and displayed a twelve-gage shotgun, its double barrels sawed off short against the wood.

"Good Lord!" I murmured; "whatever have you brought that for?"

He smiled a trifle grimly as he answered, "To test the soundness of the advice which I bestowed upon myself this morning."

"Advice you gave yourself—good heavens, man, you're raving!"

"Perhapsly so," he grinned. "There are those who would assure you that de Grandin's cleverness is really madness, while others will maintain his madness is but cleverness disguised. We shall know more before we grow much older, I damn think."

THE AIR SEEMED THICK and heavy with a brooding menace as we made our way across the mounded graves. Silence, choking as the dust of ages in a mummy-tomb, seemed to bear down on us, and the chirping of a cricket in the grass seemed as loud and sharp as the scraping of metal against metal as we picked our path between the tombstones. The stars, caught in a web of over-hanging cloud, were paling in the luminance which spread from the late-rising moon, and despite myself I felt the ripple of a chill run up my back and neck. The dead had lain here quietly two hundred years and more, they were harmless, powerless, but—reason plays no part when instinct holds the reins, and my heart beat faster and my breathing quickened as we halted by the tombstone which marked Kristina Friebergh's grave.

I cannot compute the time we waited. Perhaps it was an hour, perhaps several, but I felt as though we had crouched centuries among the moon-stained shrubbery and the halftones of the purple shadows when de Grandin's fingers on my elbow brought me from my semi-dream to a sort of terrified alertness. Down by the ancient lich-gate through which ten generations of the village dead had come to their last resting-place, a shadow moved among the shadows. Now it lost itself a moment; now it stood in silhouette against the shifting highlights on the corpse-road where the laurel bushes swayed in the light breeze. Terror touched me like a blast of icy wind. I was like a little, frightened boy who finds himself deserted in the darkness.

Now a tiny spot of lightness showed against the blackened background of the night; a second spot of orange light shone out, and I descried the form of Greta Friebergh coming slowly toward us. She was dressed in red, a bright-red evening dress of pleated net with surplice sleeves and fluted hem, fitted tightly, at the waistline, molding her slender, shapely hips, swirling about her toeless silver sandals. In each hand she bore a candle which licked hungrily against the shadows with its little, flickering tongue of orange flame. Just before her, at the outer fringe of candlelight, walked a little chalk-white kitten, stepping soundlessly on dainty paws, leading her unhurriedly toward the grave where Kristina Friebergh lay as a blind man's poodle might escort its master.

I would have spoken, but de Grandin's warning pressure on my arm prevented utterance as he pointed silently across the graveyard to the entrance through which Greta had just come.

Following cautiously, dodging back of tombstones, taking cover behind bushes, but keeping at an even distance from the slowly pacing girl, was another figure. At a second glance I recognized him. It was young Karl Pettersen.

Straight across the churchyard Greta marched behind her strange conductor, halted by the tombstone at the head of Kristina's grave, and set her feebly flaring candles in the earth as though upon an altar.

For a moment she stood statue-still, profiled against the moon, and I saw her fingers interlace and writhe together as if she prayed for mercy from inexorable fate; then she raised her hands, undid snap-fasteners beneath her arms and shook her body with a sort of lazy undulation, like a figure in a slowed-down motion picture, freeing herself from the scarlet evening gown and letting it fall from her.

Straight, white and slim she posed her ivory nakedness in silhouette against the moon, so still that she seemed the image of a woman rather than a thing of flesh and blood, and we saw her clasp her hands behind her, straining wrists and elbows pressed together as though they had been bound with knotted thongs, and on her features came a look of such excruciating pain that I was forcibly reminded of the pictures of the martyrs which the mediæval artists painted with such dreadful realism.

She turned and writhed as though in deadly torment, her head swayed toward one shoulder, then the other; her eyes were staring, almost starting from their sockets; her lips showed ruddy froth where she gnashed them with her teeth; and on her sides and slim, white flanks, upon her satin-gleaming shoulders, her torture-corded neck and sweetly rounded breasts, there flowered sudden spots of red, cruel, blood-marked wounds which spouted little streams of ruby fluid as though a merciless, sharp skewer probed and stabbed and pierced the tender, wincing flesh.

A wave of movement at the grave's foot drew our glance away from the tormented girl. Karl Pettersen stood there at the outer zone of candlelight, his face agleam with perspiration, eyes bright and dilated as though they had been filled with belladonna. His mouth began to twist convulsively and his hands shook in a nervous frenzy.

"Look—look," he slobbered thickly, "she's turning to the witch! She's not my Greta, but the wicked witch they killed so long ago. They're testing her to find the witch-mark; soon they'll drown her in the bay—I know the story; every fifty years the witch-cat claims another victim to go through the needle-torture, then—"

"You have right, *mon vieux*, but I damn think it has found its last one," interrupted Jules de Grandin as he rested his shotgun in the crook of his left elbow and pulled both triggers with a jerk of his right hand.

Through a smoky pompon flashed twin flares of flame, and the shotgun's bellow was drowned out by a strangling scream of agony. Yet it was not so much a cry of pain as of wild anger, maniacal, frenzied with thwarted rage. It spouted up, a marrow-freezing geyser of terrifying sound, and the kitten which had crouched at Greta's feet seemed literally to fly to pieces. Though the double charge of shotgun slugs had hit it squarely, it did not seem to me that it was ripped to shreds, but rather as though its tiny body had been filled with some form of high explosive, or a gas held at tremendous pressure, and that the penetrating slugs had liberated this and caused a detonation which annihilated every vestige of the small, white, furry form.

As the kitten vanished, Greta dropped down to the ground unconscious, and, astoundingly, as though they had been wiped away by magic, every sign of pulsing, bleeding wounds was gone, leaving her pale skin unscarred and without blemish in the faintly gleaming candlelight.

"And now, *Monsieur, s'il vous plait!*" With an agile leap de Grandin crossed the grave, drew back his sawed-off shotgun and brought its butt-plate down upon Karl's head.

"Good heavens, man, have you gone crazy?" I demanded as the youngster slumped down like a pole-axed ox.

"Not at all, by no means; otherwise, entirely, I assure you," he answered as he gazed down at his victim speculatively. "Look to *Mademoiselle*, if you will be so kind; then help me carry this one to the motorcar."

Clumsily, I drew the scarlet ballgown over Greta's shoulders, then grasped her underneath the arms, stood her on unconscious feet a moment and let the garment fall about her. She was scarcely heavier than a child, and I bore her to the car with little effort, then returned to help de Grandin with Karl Pettersen.

"What ever made you do it?" I demanded as we set out for my office.

Pleased immensely with himself, he hummed a snatch of tune before he answered: "It was expedient that he should be unconscious at this time, my friend. Undoubtlessly he followed Mademoiselle Greta from the dance, saw her light the candles and disrobe herself, then show the bleeding stigma of the witch. You heard what he cried out?"

"Yes."

"*Très bon.* They love each other, these two, but the memory of the things which he has seen tonight would come between them and their happiness like a loathsome specter. We must eliminate every vestige of that memory, and of the wound she dealt him, too. But certainly. When they recover consciousness I shall be ready for them. I shall wipe their memories clean of those unpleasant things. Assuredly; of course."

"How can you do that?"

"By hypnotism. You know I am an adept at it, and these two, exhausted, all weakened with the slowly leaving burden of unconsciousness, will offer little opposition to my will. To implant suggestions which shall ripen and bear fruit within their minds will be but child's play for me."

We drove along in silence a few minutes; then, chuckling, he announced: "*Tiens*, she is the lucky girl that Jules de Grandin is so clever. Those other ones were not so fortunate. There was no Jules de Grandin to rescue Sarah Spotswood from her fate, nor the others, either. No. The same process was beginning in this case. First came a feeling of aversion for her lover, a reluctance to embrace him. That was the will of wickedness displacing her volition. Then, all unconsciously, she struck him with a knife, but the subjugation of her will was not complete. The will of evilness forced her hand to strike the blow, but her love for him withheld it, so that he suffered but a little so small scratch."

"Do you mean to tell me Kristina Friebergh was responsible for all these goings-on?" I asked.

"No-o, I would not say it," he responded thoughtfully. "I think she was a most unfortunate young woman, more sinned against than sinning. That *sacré petit chat*—that wicked little cat-thing—was her evil genius, and that of Sarah Spotswood and the other girls, as well as Mademoiselle Greta. You remember Monsieur Friebergh's story, how his several times great-uncle found the little Kristina trying to force her way into the flames which burnt her parents, with a little kitten clutched tight in her arms? That is the explanation. Her parents were undoubtlessly convicted justly for the crime of witchcraft, and the little cat-thing was the imp by which they worked their evil spells. When they were burnt, the cat-familiar lingered on and attached itself to their poor daughter. It had no evil work to do, for there is no record that Kristina indulged in witchery. But it was a devil's imp, instinct with wickedness, and her very piety and goodness angered it; accordingly it brought her to a tragic death. Then it must find fresh source of nourishment, since witches' imps, like vampires, perpetuate themselves by sucking human blood. Accordingly it seized on Sarah Spotswood as a victim, and took her blood and sanity, finally her life. For half a century it lived on the vitality it took from that unfortunate young woman, then—*pouf!*—another victim suffers, goes insane and dies. Each fifty years the process is repeated till at last it comes to Mademoiselle Greta—and to me. Now all is finished."

"But I saw you toss a stone at it last night without effect," I argued, "yet tonight—"

"*Précisément.* That gave me to think. 'It can make a joke of ordinary missiles,' I inform me when I saw it let the stone I threw pass through its body. 'This being so, what are we to do with it, Jules de Grandin?'

"'Phantoms and werewolves which are proof against the ordinary bullet can be killed by shots of silver,' I reply.

"'Very well, then, Jules de Grandin,' I say to me; 'let us use a silver bullet.'

"'*Ha,* but this small cat-thing are an artful dodger, you might miss it,' I remind me; so I make sure there shall be no missing. From the silversmith I get some silver filings, and with these I stuff some shotgun shells. 'Now, *Monsieur le Chat,*' I say, 'if you succeed in dodging these, you will astonish me.'

"*Eh bien,* it was not I who was astonished, I damn think."

W E TOOK THE CHILDREN to my surgery, and while I went to seek some wine and biscuit at de Grandin's urgent request, he placed them side by side upon the couch and took his stance before them.

When I tiptoed back some fifteen minutes later, Greta lay sleeping peacefully upon the sofa, while Karl was gazing fascinated into Jules de Grandin's eyes.

". . . and you will remember nothing but that you love her and she loves you, *Monsieur,*" I heard de Grandin say, and heard the boy sigh sleepily in acquiescence.

"Why, we're in Doctor Trowbridge's surgery!" exclaimed Greta as she opened her eyes.

"But yes, of course," de Grandin answered. "You and Monsieur Karl had a little, trifling accident upon the road, and we brought you here."

"Karl dear"—for the first time she seemed to notice the scratch upon his neck—"you've been hurt!"

"*Ah bah,* it is of no importance, *Mademoiselle,*" de Grandin told her with a laugh. "Those injuries are of the past, and tonight the past is dead. See, we are ready to convey you home, but first"—he filled the glasses with champagne and handed them each one—"first we shall drink to your happiness and forgetfulness of all the things which happened in the bad old days."

Children of the Bat

J ULES DE GRANDIN BEAT his hands together softly in perfunctory applause as the slim young bubble-dancer, birth-nude save for a liberal application of pearl powder, poised on slender, painted toes an instant with the shimmering thirty-inch rubber balloon forming a pellucid barrier between her nakedness and the audience, then ran lightly as a wind-blown thistle-fluff from the semi-lighted dance quadrangle framed by the rows of tables.

"*Parbleu*," he murmured with a grin, "facilities for studying anatomy have been enlarged since you and I were at *l'école de médecine, n'est-ce-pas*, my friend?"

With the deftness of much practise he maneuvered the cherry at the bottom of his old-fashioned cocktail onto the flange of his muddler and raised it to his lips as a Chinaman might raise rice upon his chopsticks. He ruminated on the candied fruit a moment, washed it down with the cocktail's final draft and turned his eyes again toward the dancing-floor, where an amber spotlight's shaft stabbed through the violet darkness as the orchestra began to play a waltz tune softly.

Memories of moonlit straw-rides, of college proms and midwinter cotillions came to me as I recognized the gliding melody of *Sobre las Olas*, but no partners at a college hop or ballroom German of my dancing-days ever matched the couple who flowed out upon the floor. The man was tall and slim, virtually hipless in his molded evening clothes, with a tiny wisp of black mustache and gleaming hair pomaded and stretched back so tightly from his brow that it almost seemed to make his eyeballs pop. The girl was gold and cinnabar and ivory. Her hair, cut in a rippling shoulder-bob, was a mixture of pale gold and red, and the spotlight which played on her made it glimmer like a cataract of coruscating molten metal. Her gown of uncut velvet was brilliant yellow-red, throat-high in front, backless to the waist behind, and slit to the knee at either side to show the gleam of slender, sleekly depilated legs. Mandarin rouge was on her cheeks and lips, the filbert-shaped nails of her hands and feet were lacquered bright vermilion, her spool-heeled sandals were of gilded leather. The oval face, long-lashed blue eyes and provocative red mouth were perfect, yet her vibrant youthfulness was overlaid with a veneer of hardness. The girl had lived and looked at life, not always in its most alluring aspects.

Their dance was neatly executed but purely routine. Turn followed pirouette and lift succeeded turn in an acrobatic version of the waltz, and applause was merely courteous in volume when the couple paused at length and made their salutations to the audience.

The music muted to a slow, soft, sobbing undertone, and a purl of babbling conversation had began to buzz as the dancers turned to leave the floor. I looked about the darkened cabaret, searching for our waiter. A final drink of Dubonnet, the check, then home seemed the best immediate program, for I had an appendectomy at seven the next morning. The servitor had lost himself among the tables, according to the habit of his kind, and I half rose from my chair to get a better vision, when my glance strayed upward to the entrance stairway. Framed against the silken hangings of vermilion, multi-folded by reflections of opposing gilt-framed mirrors, stood a woman.

So startling was the silhouette she made that she seemed to be a figure out of allegory, Perhaps Lachesis grown weary of her task of measuring the thread of human destiny. Tall she was, and slender, an aureole of old-world glamor hovering round her; black hair shining smoothly back from a forehead of magnolia-white, wide-set black eyes beneath black-penciled brows, lips full and red and richly curved, a little mocking, more than a little scornful. Her gown was midnight velvet, its somberness lightened only by a diamond buckle at her belt, and, molding shapely hips, fell swirling down about the brocade sandals on her long and narrow feet. As she threw her velvet evening wrap back from her shoulders it seemed to spread and billow between her outstretched arms, and I had the momentarily unpleasant impression that her graceful shoulders were adorned with sable bat-wings.

"Mon Dieu!" de Grandin's exclamation called my wandering attention to the dance floor; "she is distrait, she is unwell, she swoons, my friend!"

The little danseuse's glance had caught the woman at the stairhead as she rose from her deep curtsy, and the set, professional smile faded from her features as though wiped away. A sudden deathly pallor spread across her face, making the vermilion rouge stand out in shocking contrast, like an undertaker's pigments on the features of a corpse. She paused abruptly, seemed to shiver as though chilled, then sank down to the floor, not in a toppling faint, but with a kind of slow deliberation which reminded me of the collapse of something formed of wax when heat is applied to it. Yet it was not an ordinary fainting fit which bore her down; rather, it seemed to me, she groveled on the polished floor in utter self-abasement, like a dog which, caught in fault, pleads with its master to withhold the whip.

As her dancing-partner raised her in his arms and bore her to the dressing-rooms the orchestra burst out into a fox trot, trumpets and saxophones bellowing the melody, piano, bass viol and drums beating the rhythm, and in a moment the sharp whisper of the dancers' sliding feet mingled with the jungloid music and the cachinnation of high, half-drunken laughter to drown out the memory of the girl's indisposition.

"Doctor," Mike Caldes, proprietor of *La Pantoufle Dorée*, tiptoed to our table, "will you step back to th' dressin'-rooms? Rita's pretty sick an' we'd like to keep th' customers from knowin' it, so—"

"Of course, immediately; at once," de Grandin whispered. "We observed her difficulty, my friend, and were about to offer our assistance when you came."

THE DANCER RITA LAY upon the couch in her narrow, cell-like dressing-room, and one look at her convinced us that she suffered from a case of paralyzing shock. Her face was absolutely colorless, her skin was utterly devoid of warmth, and tiny nodules of horripilation showed upon her forearms. When she sought to speak, an ululating groan was all that issued from between her writhing lips, for the muscles of her throat were contracted nearly to the choking-point by the *globus hystericus*; in a moment she was trembling in a spasm of uncontrollable successive shudders, while her eyeballs rolled back underneath the lids till the pupils disappeared, leaving but a line of oyster-white framed by her lashes.

"Has she got an epileptic fit, Doc?" Caldes asked. "Th' dirty little double-crosser told me she was strong an' healthy; now she goes an'—"

"Be silent," ordered Jules de Grandin, "it is not epilepsy, but hysteria. She has been badly frightened, this one. Hasten, if you please, *Monsieur*, and bring us brandy and a pan of boiling water and some towels. Be quick; we wait on you, but not with patience."

Quickly he wrung the steaming towels out, enveloped them in dry cloths and placed them on the trembling girl's neck, wrists and feet. This done, he wrapped her in a blanket and proceeded to administer the brandy by the spoonful till the tremors passed and her eyelids slowly lowered.

A little moan escaped her as her tautened nerves relaxed and the anesthesia of sleep came on. "What is it, *Mademoiselle?*" he asked, bending till his ear lay nearly level with her lips.

"*La—La Murciélaga*," she responded sleepily. "*La—Mur—*" her whisper trailed to silence and her bosom fluttered with a tired sigh as she sank into unconsciousness.

"What did she say?" I asked.

"I don't know," he responded with a shrug. "Perhaps a line of chorus from some song. They say absurd things at such times, my friend.

"She should be recovered in an hour, at most," he told Caldes as he rose and slipped his dinner jacket on. "Let someone sit with her until she has regained her strength; then see that she goes home. She must not dance again tonight."

"O.K., Doc; much obliged," responded Caldes. "I'll see she's taken care of." But the greedy gleam between his heavy lids served notice that the girl would carry out her schedule on the dance floor if her partner had to bear her in his arms.

I MIGHT HAVE BEEN ASLEEP an hour when the fretful rattle of the bedside telephone awakened me. "Hullo, Doctor Trowbridge, sor," a richly brogued Hibernian voice announced, "this is Detective Sergeant Costello. Will ye an' Doctor de Grandin be afther comin' to th' Pantuflay Dory on th' run, sor? I'll take it kindly if ye will."

"Come where?" I answered sleepily.

"Th' Pantuflay Dory, sor. Mike Caldes' joint. There's all hell to pay here an' no pitch hot."

"What's happened?"

"'Tis a pore young gur-rl's been murthered, sor; kilt dead entirely by a gang o' sacrilegious haythens, an'—can ye come at onct, sor? Ye'll be interested; leastwise, Doctor de Grandin will."

De Grandin joined me as I drove the car from the garage. He had not waited to don shirt and collar, but had wound a mauve silk scarf around his neck and tied it ascot fashion, then slipped his jacket over his pajamas. As he climbed into the motor he was busy teasing needle-points upon the tips of his small blond mustache.

"Who is it who is done to death?" he asked. "In what manner was the killing done?"

"You know as much as I," I answered as we slid into the street, and, headlights blazing, rushed across town to the *Pantoufle Dorée*.

COSTELLO HAD NOT MADE an overstatement when he told me that the murder was the work of "sacrilegious haythens."

The door communicating from the outer lobby to the club's wide entrance stairs was built of heavy mortised timbers—a relic of the Prohibition days when ax-armed raiders might swoop down upon the place unheralded—and these were overlaid with a smooth coat of bright vermilion lacquer on which were painted golden dragons in the Chinese manner. Bone-white against this brilliant background, crucified with railway spikes, hung the naked body of a girl. From nail-pierced hands and feet small rivulets of bright-red blood writhed down like ruby-colored worms. In haste, perhaps, the slayers had neglected to strip off both her sandals, so that one foot showed gilt cross-straps on each side of the cruel spike which held it to the painted door, while the other was unclothed except for the stigmata of bright blood which ran down from the pierced instep.

In the orange glow of a great Chinese lantern she hung against the red and golden panels in a hush of horror; yet she made a picture of appealing, tragic beauty. Her long, slim limbs, the slender waist, the hips which swelled in gracious curves, were beautiful as anything shaped by a master sculptor. Her breasts, drawn upward by the outstretched arms, were lovely as twin hemispheres of alabaster jeweled with coral. Her head had fallen forward in the utter flaccidity of death, and the fine, bright hair cascaded downward from her brow, veiling the horror of half-closed, glazing eyes and limp lips fallen open.

Upon the Peking-blue of the rich Chinese rug spread on the floor before her the sandal she had lost gleamed emptily upon its side, its buckle broken, its golden heel and instep straps ripped almost clear away from the gilt sole. Somehow, death seemed incongruous here. In this resort of opulent magnificence, this temple dedicated to enjoyment of the vanities of life, death was as out of place as a murder scene injected in a Johann Strauss operetta. An odd place, surely, for a woman to be crucified!

De Grandin stood before the lovely, piteous crucifix, arms akimbo, blond mustache a-twitch. "When did you find her?" he demanded of Costello.

"We didn't, sor," the Irishman replied. "Th' watchman o' th' place ran onto 'er whilst he wuz makin' his rounds a little afther three o'clock. He came a-runnin' like the divil's self wuz afther him, an' bawled his sthory to the desk sergeant down at Number Three; so they sends a harness bull around here to invistigate, an' rings th' homicide squad at headquarters. Gilligan an' I gits detailed to th' job, an' th' first thing I does when I sees how things is, is to ring fer you an' Doctor Trowbridge, sor."

"One comprehends. And where is this *gardien de nuit*—this how do you call him?—watchman?—if you please?"

"Come here, youse!" Costello bawled, and at the hail a heavy-set, bow-legged man of thirty-five or -six came from the checkroom where evidently he had been in durance. Despite the neat gray uniform he wore, the man reminded me of something simian. His shoulders were enormous, his chest so much developed that it seemed to dwarf his abdomen; his legs were strong and heavy, but bowed almost to the point of deformity; his arms hung down quite to his knees, and his forehead was so low it made his hairline seem to rest upon his brows. As he turned his head to keep his gaze averted from the pale corpse on the door, I saw the telltale cauliflower ear which proclaimed his past experience in the prize ring.

"I wuz goin' on me rounds, y'understan'," he said, "just after three o'clock this mornin'—th' three-ten box is by th' checkroom door—an' I had to come through there." He jerked a thumb across his shoulder toward the panels where the dead girl hung, but kept his eyes averted. "Th' door's always kind o' hard to open, y'understan,' but tonight seems like it wuz stuck, or sumpin, an' I has to lean me shoulder to it. Th' office is out here, an' th' first thing that I thinks about is that some yegg is monkeyin' wid th' safe an' one o' his pals is holdin' th' door on me; so I pulls out me rod an' jams me shoulder agin th' door wid all me might an' busts in here. But if they's anybody here, they're awful quiet, thinks I; so I flashes me light aroun,' an' then I sees her hangin' there—" He paused in his recital and a tremor shook his heavy frame.

"*Précisément*, you saw her; and then?" de Grandin prompted.

"Then I goes all haywire, I gits so deadly sick I busts out to th' street an' pukes; then I beats it for th' station house. Th' coppers brung me back, but I don't know nothin' about it. Honest to Gawd, I don't!"

"Did you hear no sounds before you found the body?"

"No, sir. I don't come on till two o'clock when th' kitchen gang signs off, an' dis wuz me first trip roun' tonight. I starts off down by th' kitchen an' storerooms, an' these doors is pretty thick, an' wid th' hangin's an' rugs an' things they has here, you wouldn't be apt to hear nothin' much goin' on in one end o' th' place when you wuz at th' other."

"*Très bien*," de Grandin answered. "You may wait outside, my friend." To Costello:

"Have you called the others?"

"Yis, sor. There's a squad car wid Mike Caldes on its way here, now."

The Frenchman nodded toward the pendent body on the door. "How long has she been dead, Friend Trowbridge?"

"H'm, not very long," I returned. "There's no sign of *rigor mortis*, and scarcely any perceptible clotting of blood around the wounds. No hypostasis apparent. My guess is that she could not have been dead much more than half an hour when the watchman found her."

He studied the pale body thoughtfully. "Does it not seem to you that there should be more hemorrhage?" he demanded. "Those spikes are blunt and more than half an inch in thickness, and the tissues round the wounds are badly torn; yet I doubt that she has bled as much as fifteen cubic centimeters."

"Why—er—" I temporized, but he was paying no attention.

Like a tom-cat pouncing on a mouse, he dropped upon his knees and snatched at something lying at the margin of the rug, half hidden by the shadow of the dead girl's feet. "*Tiens*, what have we here?" he asked, holding his find up to the light.

"A bat's wing," I replied as I looked at it, "but what in heaven's name could it be doing here?"

"God and the devil know, not I," he answered with a shrug as he wrapped the leathery pinion in a sheet of notepaper and stowed it in an inner pocket of his jacket.

Stepping softly, almost reverently, he crossed the room and surveyed the body pendent on the door through half-closed eyes, then mounting a chair brushed back the rippling wave of bright, fair hair and put a hand beneath her chin.

"*Que diable?*" he exclaimed as the back-brushed tresses unveiled the pale, dead face. "What do you make of this, *mon vieux?*" With a well-groomed forefinger he pointed to the tip of her tongue, which, prolapsed in death, lay across her teeth and hung a quarter-inch or so beyond her lower lip. Against the pale pink of the membrane showed a ruby globule, a little gout of blood.

"Probably the poor child gnashed her tongue in torment when they nailed her to the door," I hazarded, but:

"No, I do not think so," he denied. "See, here is the trail of blood"—he pointed to a narrow track of red which marked the center of the tongue—"and besides, her lips have not been injured. She would have bitten them to ribbons in her agony if—*ah?* Observe him, if you please!"

Lowering the girl's head he bent it downward on her chest and brushed the hair up from her neck. About three inches from the skull-base showed a tiny cross-shaped wound, its arms a scant half-inch in length. Apparently it had been made by some sharp, square instrument, and from the faintly bluish cast about the edges of the puncture I reasoned that the weapon had been forced deep into the tissues.

"Ritual, *pardieu!*" he murmured. "It is obvious. Of course, but—"

"What's obvious?"

"That they hanged her on the door as part of some vile ceremony. She was dead before they touched a hammer to a spike. That drop of blood upon her tongue explains the manner of her death. They drove the lethal instrument clear through her spine, so deeply that it penetrated to her throat. She died instantly and silently; probably painlessly, as well. That accounts for the watchman's having heard no outcry, and also for the small amount of blood she shed when they pierced her hands and feet with nails."

"But why?" I asked. "If they'd already killed her, why should they hang her body up like this?"

"That is a question we must answer, but I fear we shall not answer it tonight," he replied as he stepped down from the chair. "Now, if—"

A blustering bellow drowned his observation as Mike Caldes, flanked by two policemen, bustled through the vestibule.

"What's this?—what's all this?" he shouted. "Someone's broken in my place? Where's that dam' lazy watchman? I'll fire 'um! Sleepin' on th' job an' lettin'—" Striding forward wrathfully and glowering about him, he was almost face to face with the girl's body before he saw it.

The change that swept across his fat and swarthy countenance would have been comic if it had not been so terrible. Perspiration spouted on his forehead, trickling down until it formed in little pools above his bushy brows. His jowls hung heavily, like the dewlaps of a hound, and his black eyes widened suddenly and shone with an unnatural brightness, as though they were reacting to a drug. His lips began to twist convulsively and his hands twitched in a perfect paroxysm of abysmal terror. For half a minute he stared mutely at the body; then a dreadful, choking cry, retched from him.

"*Santissima Maria!*" he sobbed, bending an arm across his eyes to shut the vision out. "Not that—not here—they can't do this in my place! No—no—*no!*"

De Grandin bent a fixed, unwinking stare on him. "Be good enough to tell us more, *Monsieur*," he ordered. "Who is it that did this thing which could not be accomplished in your place? You were forewarned of this?"

"No!" Caldes gasped. "Not me! I didn't know—I didn't think—"

The Frenchman nodded to Costello. "Take him to the office, *sergent*," he commanded. "We can talk with more convenience there."

Turning to an officer he bade: "Have them take her down with gentleness, my friend. Do not let them tear her hands and feet unnecessarily when they withdraw the nails.

"A ND NOW, *MONSIEUR*, WE shall be grateful for such information as you have," he said to Caldes as we joined Costello in the office. "You may speak with freedom, but you must be truthful, too, for we are most unpleasant fellows to attempt the monkey business with."

Caldes' hands shook so that he had to make a number of attempts before he managed to set fire to his cigar. Finally, when he had drawn a deep whiff of pungent smoke into his lungs: "Read this," he ordered, drawing a sheet of paper from his pocket and thrusting it into de Grandin's hand.

"*Hace abierto la ventana de su oficina mañana por la noche*—leave your office window open tomorrow night," the missive ordered. It was without signature, but the silhouette of a flying bat was appended to the legend.

"*Ha!*" exclaimed de Grandin. "*La Murciélaga*—the she-bat! It was that the poor one babbled in her delirium of fear. What does the message mean?"

Caldes squirmed uncomfortably, looked about the room as though he sought an inspiration from the frankly displayed charms of the photographed young women hanging on the walls, finally:

"I was born in Tupulo," he answered, and we noticed that his usual boastful manner had departed. "They have societies down there, something like th' Black Hand they used to have in Italy, only worse. When they say to do a thing you do it, no matter what it is. Down in Yucatan th' orders of these people always have th' picture of a bat—a female bat, *la Murciélaga*—on them. Everyone, from th' *alcalde* down, knows what happens when you get a note with th' picture of a bat signed to it. I've been up here twenty years, but when I got that letter yesterday I didn't ask no questions—I left th' window open like they said. That's why I scrammed home early tonight an' had th' watchman come on duty late. They didn't ask for money, or tell me to stay an' meet 'em, so—"

"An' I don't suppose ye had th' faintest idea what they wuz up to, eh?" Costello interrupted cynically.

"*Dios mio, no!*" exclaimed the Mexican. "How should I know they wuz goin' to murder someone, least of all Rita, who's an American gal, an' never did a thing to cross 'em, far's I know?"

"A woman came into the club just as Mademoiselle Rita was finishing her dance; it was then that she was taken ill," mused Jules de Grandin. "Did you recognize her?"

"Who, me? No, sir. I wuz in th' bar when Rita pulled her faintin'-fit. I didn't know about it till they'd took her to her dressin'-room."

"And did you later recognize anyone whom you knew to be connected with these people of the bat?"

A grimace which might have been intended for a smile, but which bore small family resemblance to it, swept over Caldes' face, making the knife-scar on his cheek do a macabre dance. "Outsiders don't know th' members of th' bat society," he responded. "You don't live long if you ever find out who's a member, either. But—say, was this dame you're speakin' of a tall, dark woman—looked like a princess, or sumpin? If she wuz, I know her—she just blew into town, an' lives at—"

"*Jesusito!*" the shrill scream broke his words as he leapt from his chair, his face a writhen mask of pain and fright. Frantically he clawed at his throat, as if he slapped at some stinging insect which had lighted there. But it was no insect which he held between his fingers as he waved a trembling hand at us. It was a bit of brownish wood, no longer and no thicker than a match-stick, pointed at the tip and slightly rounded at the base.

I looked at it in mute inquiry, but de Grandin seemed to recognize it, for with a bound he dashed around the desk and seized the stricken man by the shoulders, easing him to the floor. With his thumb and forefinger he seized a fold of the smooth-shaven skin encasing Caldes' neck and, pinching the tiny wound up, put his lips to it.

"Look out for 'em, Clancy!" Costello roared, dashing to the open window of the office and leaning out to bawl his order down the alley. "Oh, ye would, would ye?"

Snatching the revolver from his shoulder holster he leant across the window-sill and fired two shots in quick succession, and the detonation of his weapon was repeated by a third shot from the alley-mouth. Nimble as a cat despite his bulk, he clambered through the window and went racing down the brick-paved passage.

"Send someone for potassium permanganate," de Grandin ordered as he raised his head from Caldes' wounded throat and expelled a mouthful of blood. "Quickly, if you please; we must make haste!"

I hurried to the lobby and dispatched an officer post-haste for the permanganate, then rejoined him in the office.

Caldes lay upon the floor, lips quivering, emitting little whimpering noises. Even as I joined de Grandin he drew his legs up with a sharp, convulsive jerk, then straightened them with a sharp kick, and his heels began to beat the floor with a constantly increasing rhythm. He drew his arms across his breast, clenching his fists together, then threw them out to right and left, bowling de Grandin over and upsetting a bronze smoking-stand which stood beside the desk.

"Ar-wa-ar-war-war!" thickly the choked syllables came from his throat as he fought for breath. The man was dying of asphyxia before our eyes.

We turned him on his face and begin administering artificial respiration, but before we had more than started the man gasped once or twice, shook with a hideous spasm, then went limp beneath our hands.

"Good heavens, what was it?" I asked as de Grandin rose and began matter-of-factly to brush the dust from his knees.

"Kurare poisoning. It was a dart from a soplete, or blow-gun, which struck him in the throat. The thing was poisoned with a strychnos extract which acts like cobra venom, causing death within an hour by paralysis of the respiratory muscles. Had it struck him on a limb we could have used a tourniquet to stop the flow of poison to the blood stream. But no! The dart struck into his external jugular, and the venom spread like wildfire through his system. I think that fright increased its action, too, for he had doubtless seen men die in such a way before, and gave himself no hope when he discovered he was wounded. Usually the poison does not act so quickly—"

"I got 'im, sor," announced Costello jubilantly from the doorway. "Bad cess to 'im, he tried to shoot me wid his bean-blower, so I give 'im a dose o' lead poisonin' an' Clancy let 'im have another pill jist for—howly Mither, what's this?"

"This, my friend, is murder," answered Jules de Grandin evenly. "It seems he spoke more truly than he realized when he said that those who recognized the members of this gang are seldom troubled by infirmities of age. Come, let us see the other."

Costello's victim was an undersized dark man, thin to emaciation, swarthy-skinned, smooth-shaven save for a small black mustache, and dressed impeccably in dinner clothes. A quick search failed to show a single clue to his identity. Nothing but a pack of Violetta cigarettes, ten dollars in bills and change and a book of paper matches occupied his pockets. The maker's labels had been taken from his clothes, his linen had apparently been worn that evening for the first time; there were no laundry marks upon it. Ten feet or so from where the man had fallen we found a tube of smoothly polished hollow reed some eighteen inches long, and beside it, like a clip of cartridges, a folded sheet of cardboard through which were thrust three four-inch splints of wood like that with which the night-club owner had been wounded. Near the window where it had fallen harmlessly to the pavement lay the dart he had blown at Costello.

"Be careful how you handle them," de Grandin warned as Officer Clancy picked up the paper clip of darts; "a scratch from them is death!"

"Humph," Costello murmured as he viewed the body of the murderer, "they wuzn't takin' any chances, wuz they, Doctor de Grandin, sor? This felly's as bare o' clues as Billy-be-damned. Th' woman Mike wuz tellin' us about is our best bet. A dame as sthrikin' as ye tell me this one wuz ought not to be so hard to locate. If she just blew into town, like Caldes said, an' if she's been around enough for him to notice her, she's likely livin' at some swank hotel. We'll put th' dragnet out for her immejiately, an' when we find her I'm afther thinkin' she'll have some mighty fancy answerin' to do."

W E WERE ENJOYING COFFEE and Chartreuse in the study after dinner the next evening when Nora McGinnis announced: "Sergeant Costello an' a lady's here to see yez, sors. Shall I have 'em wait?"

"Not at all; by no means; show them in," de Grandin bade, and, as the burly Irishman loomed in the doorway, "Welcome, *mon sergent*; is it news of the strange woman that you bring?"

'Well, sor, yis an' no, as th' felly sez," Costello answered with a rather sheepish grin as he beckoned to someone behind him. "This here young lady's got a sthory which may shed some light on last night's monkey-business."

The girl who entered at his gesture seemed absurdly small and fragile in comparison to his great bulk, though in fact she was something over middle height. It was not until she took a seat upon the sofa at de Grandin's invitation that I recognized her as the bubble-dancer at the Caldes cabaret. How a young female who dances naked dresses when she is not working at her trade had never been a subject of my thought, but certainly I was not prepared for any costume such as that our visitor wore. She was almost nun-like in her sheer black dinner dress of marquisette trimmed with tiny ruffles of white organdy, her corsage of gardenias, her small black hat, and her white-kid gloves. She might have been a clergyman's daughter, or a member of the Junior League, judging from appearances.

"I'm Nancy Meigs," she told us as she folded white-gloved hands demurely in her lap and looked at us with wide, grave, troubled eyes. "Rita Smith, the girl they killed last night, and I were pals."

"Smith! *Mon Dieu*, her name was Smith, and she so beautiful!" de Grandin murmured sadly. "This English, what a language!"

"It was *Los Niños de la Murciélaga*—the 'Children of the Bat'—who killed her," Nancy added. "I was sure—"

"Perfectly, *Mademoiselle*, and so are we," de Grandin interrupted, "but who are these sixty-times-accursèd ones, where may they be found, and why, especially, should they kill and crucify a young girl in New Jersey?"

Her gray eyes were clear and soft and steady as they looked at him, but they were frightened, too. "Was—did you find a bat wing by her body?" she responded.

"By blue, I did!" he answered. "Wait, I have it in my room."

He hurried out, returning in a moment with the sheet of paper wrapped around the wing he had retrieved the night before.

She took the folded wing between her thumbs and forefingers, extending it against the light cast by the study lamp. "Can you read it?" she demanded, moving the membranes across the field of light.

Scratched upon the leathery skin was a five-word legend:

Así SIEMPRE Á LOS TRAIDORES.

"Howly St. Patrick!" swore Costello.

"*Précisément*," de Grandin nodded.

"What's it mean?" I asked.

"'Thus always to traitors,' sor," Costello answered. "I picked up enough o' th' lingo whilst I wuz servin' in th' Fillypines to read that much."

De Grandin poured two glasses of Chartreuse and handed them to our visitors; then, as he refilled his own:

"Just what connection did this poor young woman have with these so naughty murderers, *Mademoiselle*?"

"Rita and I were members of the order—once," replied the girl. "It was back in '29, just before the bottom fell out of the show business; we were touring South America with a troupe of entertainers. Fan and bubble dancing hadn't been invented then, but we did a rumba routine that was popular, and went over almost as big as the performing seals. We'd gotten up the coast as far as Tupulo when the crash came. Tupulo's an oil town, you know, and all orders from the wells had been canceled; so the place was like a western mining-camp when the ore ran out. We didn't draw a corporal's guard at shows, and then one night our manager, Samuelson, got into a fight in a gambling-hall and they put him in jail and seized the animals and properties of the show. Rita and I were stranded with only about ten *pesos* between us. That didn't last us long and presently they threatened to jail us, too, for non-payment of rent. We were desperate."

"One understands," de Grandin nodded. "And then?"

"We got an engagement dancing in one of the saloons. It was pretty dreadful, for the patrons of the place were the off-scum of the oil fields, and we had to do the *danza de las dos tetas*—dancing in unbuttoned blouses and shaking our shoulders till our breasts protruded through the opening, you know—but stranded actresses can't very well afford to quarrel with their bread and butter.

"One night it was especially terrible. The drunken loafers in the place called insults at us and even pelted us with bits of bread and vegetables as we danced; we were both about to collapse when the evening's work was done. Rita cried all the way to our lodgings. 'I can't stand this another night,' she wept. 'I'd sooner go lose myself in the jungle and die than do another shimmy in that dreadful place!'

"'One may go into the jungle, yet not die, *Señorita*,' someone told us from the darkness, and a man stepped out from the shadow of a building, raising his sombrero.

"We thought at first it was one of the barroom loafers who'd followed us, and I drew my hands back to write the Ten Commandments on his cheeks with my nails, but the street lamp showed us he was a stranger and a *caballero*.

"'I have watched you for some time,' he told us. 'You were made for better things than twinkling your little, perfect feet before such swine as those you entertain. If you will let me, I can help you.'

"We sized him up. He was little, very neat and extremely ugly, but he didn't look particularly dangerous. 'All right,' said Rita, 'what's your proposition?'

"'One I serve has need of women with discretion—and beauty,' he answered. 'She can offer you a life of luxury, everything which you deserve—fine clothes, fine food, luxurious surroundings. But it will not be a life of ease or safety. There will be much work and more danger. Also, no one in this service ever makes a second mistake. However'—he shrugged his shoulders as only a Mexican can— 'it will be better than the life you're leading now.'

"Our contract was concluded then and there. We didn't even go back to our lodgings to collect and pack what clothes we had.

"He had a motor waiting at the outskirts of the town, and in this we rode till daylight, stopping at a little *hacienda* at the jungle edge to sleep all day. When darkness came he wakened us, and we rode on mule-back through the bush till it was nearly dawn again.

"Our destination was an old abandoned Mayan temple, one of those ruins that dot the jungle all through Yucatan, and it seemed deserted as a graveyard when we rode up to it, but we found the jungle had been cleared away and the debris of fallen stones removed till the place was made quite habitable.

"We rested all next day and were wakened in the evening by the sound of tom-toms. An Indian woman came and led us to a stone tank like a swimming pool, and when we finished bathing we found she'd taken our soiled clothes and left us gowns of beautifully woven cotton and *huaraches*, or native sandals. When we'd dressed in these she took us to another room, where she gave us stewed meat and beans and cool, tart wine, after which she signaled us to follow her.

"We walked out to the square before the pyramid, which was all ablaze with lighted torches, and I nearly fainted at the sight that met our eyes. All around the square was a solid rank of men and women, all in native costume—a simple, straight gown like a nightdress for the women, a shirt and pair of cotton trousers for the men—and all masked by having huge artificial bats' heads drawn over their faces like hoods. Everywhere we looked they were, as much alike as grains of rice from the same bag, all with their eyes flashing in the torchlight at us through the peep-holes in their masks.

"Four of the bat-men took our arms and turned us toward the steps of the great pyramid. Then we saw *La Murciélaga!*"

"*La Murciélaga?*" echoed Jules de Grandin. "Was it then a bat that these strange people worshipped?"

"No, sir. It was a woman. She was tall and slender and beautifully made, as we could see at a glance; for every inch of her was encased in a skin-tight suit of sheer black webbing, like the finest of silk stockings, and her face was hidden by a bat-mask like the rest, only hers seemed made of shimmering black feathers while theirs were made of coarse black fur. Joining her arms to her body were folds of sheer black silk so that when she raised her hands it spread and stretched like a bat spreading its wings to fly.

"Some kind of trial seemed to be in progress, for two bat-men held another one between them, and the woman in the bat costume seemed questioning the prisoner, though we couldn't hear what she said or he replied from where we stood.

"After a little while she seemed to have arrived at a decision, for she raised her hands, spreading out her bat-wings, and curved her fingers at him as though she were about to claw his face. The poor thing dropped upon his knees and held his hands extended, asking mercy, but *La Murciélaga* never changed her pose, just stood there with her claws stretched out and her eyes gleaming horribly through her mask.

"Before we realized what was happening some men had brought a blood-stained wooden cross and laid it down upon the pavement. Then they stripped the prisoner's clothing off and nailed him to the cross while the tom-toms beat so loudly that we could not hear his shrieks, and all the masked bat-people screamed, '*Así siempre á los traidores!*' over and over again.

"'That's what comes to those who disobey or fail *La Murciélaga!*' someone whispered in my ear, and I recognized the voice of the man who had brought us out from Tupulo.

"'But we don't want to join any such terrible society as this!' I cried. 'We won't—'

"'There are other crosses waiting,' he warned me. 'Will you hang beside that traitor or will you take the oath of fealty to the Bat Mother and become her true and faithful servants?'

"The poor wretch on the cross kept shrieking, and though we couldn't hear him for the tom-toms' noise, we could see his mouth gape open and the blood run down his chin where he gnashed his lips and tongue. He beat his head against the cross and arched his body forward till the spikes tore greater wounds in his pierced hands and feet, and all the time *La Murciélaga* stood there statue-still with her bat-wings spread out and her fingers curved like talons.

"Finally, when the crucified man's screams had muted to a low, exhausted moan, they led us up to the 'Bat Mother,' and there in the shadow cast by the cross with its writhing, groaning burden, we knelt down on the stones and swore to do whatever we were bidden, promising to give ourselves up for crucifixion if we ever disobeyed an order or attempted to leave the bat society or divulge its secrets. They made us put our hands out straight before us on the ground, and *La Murciélaga* came and stood on them while we kissed her feet and vowed we were her slaves for ever. Then we were given bat-masks and told to take our places in the ranks which stood about the square before the pyramid."

"And how did you escape that place of torment, *Mademoiselle?*"

"We didn't have to, sir. In the morning we were wakened and taken to the coast, where they put us on a boat and sent us up to Vera Cruz.

"May I have a cigarette?" she asked; and, as de Grandin passed the box to her, then held his lighter while she set it glowing, "Do you remember how the Spanish freighter *Gato* apparently sailed off the earth?"

De Grandin and Costello nodded.

"We did that, Rita and I. They told us to make love to the master and chief engineer, and with the memory of that horrid scene out in the jungle to spur us on, we did just as they told us. We teased the engineer to let us go and see his engines, and Rita took a little box they'd given her aboard, and hid it in the bunkers. What was in it we don't know, but when they threw the coal where it had rested in the furnace the whole side of the ship was ripped away, and everyone on board was lost."

"But this is purest idiocy, *Mademoiselle!*" protested Jules de Grandin. "Why should anyone in wanton cruelty desire to destroy a ship?"

"The *Gato* carried half a million dollars' worth of jewels," the girl replied. "She sank in less than fifteen fathoms, and the hole blown in her side made it easy for the divers to go in and loot her strongroom."

She took a final long draw at her cigarette, then crushed its fire out in the ash-tray. "You remember when MacPherson Briarly, the insurance magnate's son, was held for ransom in Chihuahua?" she asked. "Rita was the lure—posed as an American girl stranded in El Centro and traded on his chivalry. He went out riding with her one afternoon and—it cost his father fifty thousand dollars to get him back alive."

"But why didn't you attempt escape?" I asked. "Surely, if you went as far north as Chihuahua you were out of reach of the jungle headquarters in Yucatan?"

A queer look passed across her face, wiping away her youth and leaving her features old and utterly exhausted-looking. "You don't escape *Los Niños de la Murciélaga*, sir," she answered simply. "They are everywhere. The loafer in the doorway, the policeman in the street, the conductor of the tram-car or the train, is as likely as not a member of the band, and if he fails to prevent your breaking your oath of obedience—there's a cross waiting for him in the jungle. You may be dining in a fashionable hotel, sitting in a box at the opera in Mexico City or walking in the plaza when someone—a beggar, a stylish woman or an elegantly dressed man—will open his hand and display a bat wing. That is the signal, the summons not to be ignored on pain of crucifixion."

"But you finally escaped," I insisted somewhat fatuously.

Again that queer, senescent-seeming look spread on her face. "We ran away," she corrected. "They sent us up to Tia Juana and when we found ourselves so near the American border we decided to make a dash for it. We were well supplied with funds—we always were—so we had no trouble getting up to San Diego, but we knew we'd not be safe in California, or anywhere within a thousand miles of Mexico, for that matter, so we hurried back East.

"The movies had killed vaudeville, and no new musical shows were outfitting that season, but we managed to get jobs in burlesque. Finally I heard about an opening at Mike Caldes' place and sold him the idea of letting me go on as a bubble-dancer. I hadn't been there long when the girl who did the waltz routine left the show to marry, and I got Rita her place. We thought we'd be safe out here in New Jersey," she finished bitterly.

"And this so unpleasant female, this *Murciélaga*, you can tell us what she looks like?" asked de Grandin.

"*You're* asking *me?*" she answered. "You saw her when she came into the club before they took revenge on Rita."

"That lovely woman?" I exclaimed incredulously.

"That lovely woman," she repeated in a flat and toneless voice. "Did you see the way she held her cloak before she took it off? That's her sign. The others carry bat wings for identification. Only *La Murciélaga* is allowed to wear them."

"Well, I'll be damned," declared Costello.

"Assuredly, unless you mend your ways," agreed de Grandin with a grin. Then, sobering abruptly:

"Tell me, *ma petite*," he asked, "have you any idea the unfortunate Mike Caldes knew of your connection with these people of the bat?"

"No, sir," she answered positively. "Mike had never been a member of the order, but he'd lived in Tupulo and knew its power. He'd no more have dared shelter us if he'd suspected we were wanted by *La Murciélaga* than he'd have given us jobs if he'd thought we had the smallpox. As far as any Mexican from Yucatan is concerned, any fugitive from the vengeance of the Bat is hotter than counterfeit money or stolen Government bonds."

"And what of you, my friend?" de Grandin asked Costello. "Have you been able to locate this strange woman whose advent heralded these murders?"

"No, sor, we haven't," answered the detective. "We spread th' dragnet for 'er, like I told ye at th' joint last night, but we can't find hide nor hair o' her. P'raps she's stayin' in New York—there's lots o' furriners—axin' yer pardon, sor—always hangin' out there, an' we've asked th' police to be on th' lookout fer her, but you know how it is. Pretty much like lookin' fer a needle in a haystack, as th' felly says. So when Nancy—beg pardon, I mane Miss Meigs—come an' told me she might be able for to shed some light on all this monkey-business, I thought I'd better bring her over."

"Precisely," nodded Jules de Grandin. "And in the meantime, while we seek the so elusive Lady of the Bat, how shall we make things safe for Mademoiselle Nancy?"

"H'm, I might lock 'er up as a material witness," Costello offered with a grin, "but—"

"Oh, would you—*please?*" broke in the girl. "I never wanted to be anywhere in all my life as much as I want to be behind jail bars right now!"

"Sold," Costello agreed. "We'll go over to your place an' get your clothes; then you can trot along to jail wid me."

"One moment, *Mademoiselle*, before you go to the *bastille*," de Grandin interrupted. "It is entirely unlikely that the search for this Bat Woman will produce results. They are clever, these ones. I do not doubt that they have covered up their trail so well that long before the gendarmes realize the search is useless she will have fled the country. Tell me, would you know your way—could you retrace your steps to that so odious temple where the Children of the Bat have made their lair?"

A little frown of concentration wrinkled her smooth forehead. "I think I could," she answered finally.

"And will you lead us there? Remember, it is in the cause of justice, to avenge the ruthless murder of your friend and to save *le bon Dieu* knows how many others from a similar fate."

She looked at him with widened eyes, eyes in which the pupils seemed to swell and spread till they almost hid the irises. Her eyes were blank, but not expressionless. Rather, they seemed to me like openings to hell, as though they mirrored all the nightmares she had seen within their depths.

"I suppose I might as well," she answered with a little shudder. "If I go there they will nail me to a cross. If I stay here they'll do it sooner or later, anyway."

She was like a lovely, lifeless robot as she rose to go with Costello. The certain knowledge of foreshadowed death, cold and ominous as some great snake, had seized her in its paralyzing grip.

CAPTAIN HILARIO CÉSAR RAMIREZ de Quesada y Revilla, Commandant of Tupulo, courteously replenished our glasses from the straw-sheathed flask of *habañero*, then poured himself a drink out of all proportion to his own diminutive stature. "*Señores, Señorita*," he bowed to us and Nancy Meigs in turn, "your visit is more welcome than I can express. *Valgame Dios!* For a year I have stormed and sweated here in impotence; now you come with explanations and in offer of assistance. Crime is rampant in this neighborhood, and the police are powerless. A man is murdered, a business house is robbed at night, no one knows who did it; there are no clues, there are no complainants. The very persons who are injured place their fingers on their lips and shrug their shoulders. '*La Murciélaga*,' they say, as though they said it was inexorable fate. They tell us nothing; we are helpless. Nor is that all. People, women as well as men, disappear; they vanish as though swallowed by an earthquake. 'Where is so and so?' we ask, and 'S-s-sh—*La Murciélaga!*' is the only answer. I came here with a full company a year ago. Today I have but two platoons; the others are all dead, deserted or vanished—*La Murciélaga!*

"*Por Dios*, until you came here with this explanation I had thought she was a legend, like Tezcatlipoca or the Thunder-Bird!"

"Then we may count upon your help, *Monsieur le Capitaine?*" de Grandin asked.

"With all my heart. *Carajo*, I would give this head of mine to lay my eyes upon *La Murciélaga*—"

An orderly tapped at the door, and he looked up with a frown. "*Que cosa?*" he demanded.

"A young *caballero* waits to see the captain," the man explained apologetically. "His *hacienda* was burglarized last night. Much livestock was driven off; the family plate was stolen. He is sure it was *La Murciélaga*, and has come to make complaint."

"*Un milagro*—a miracle!" the Commandant cried exultantly. "Two in one day, *amigos*. First come you with information of this cursed bat society, then comes a man with courage to denounce them for their thievery.

"Bring him in, *muy pronto!*" he commanded.

The man the orderly showed in was scarcely more than a lad, dark, slender, almost womanish in build, his sole claim to masculinity seeming to be based upon a tiny black mustache and a little tuft of beard immediately below his mouth, so small and black that it reminded me of a beetle perched between his chin and lip. He wore the old-time Mexican costume, short jacket and loose-bottomed trousers of black velveteen, a scarlet cummerbund about his waist, exceedingly high-heeled boots, a bright silk handkerchief about his head. In one hand he bore a felt *sombrero*, the brim of which seemed only the necessary groundwork to support row on row of glittering silver braid.

At sight of us he paused abashed, but when the Commandant presented us, his teeth shone in a glittering smile. "We are well met, *Señores y Señorita*," he declared; "you are come to seek these Children of the Bat, I am come to ask the *commandante*'s aid. Last night they picked my house as clean as ever vultures plucked a carcass, and my craven peons refused to lift a hand to stop them. They said that it was death to offer opposition to *La Murciélaga*, but me, I am brave. I will not be intimidated. No, I have come to the police for aid."

"What makes you think it was *La Murciélaga*, sir?" the Commandant inquired. "These people of the bat are criminals, yes; but there are other robbers, too. Might not it be that—"

"*Señor Commandante*," broke in the other in a low, half-frightened voice, "would other robbers dare to leave *this* at my house?" Opening his small gloved hand he dropped a folded bat-wing on the desk.

"Bring a file of soldiers quickly," he besought. "We can reach my house by sundown, and begin pursuit tomorrow morning. Señorita Meigs can lead us to the secret stronghold in the jungle, and we can take them by surprise."

PREPARATIONS WERE COMPLETED QUICKLY. Two squads of cavalry with two machine-guns were quickly mustered at the barracks, and with young Señor Epilar to guide us, we set out for the scene of *La Murciélaga's* latest depredation. The sun dropped down behind the jungle wall as we arrived at the old *hacienda*.

The soldiers were bivouacked in the *patio*, and escorted by our host, we made our way to a wide, long drawing-room lighted by wax candles in tall wrought-iron standards and sparsely furnished with chairs and tables of massive oak.

"I bid you welcome to my humble home, my friends," said Señor Epilar with charming Spanish courtesy. "If you will indulge me a few moments I will have refreshment—"

"What's that?" the Commandant broke in as a sharp, shrill cry, followed by the detonation of a carbine shot, came from the *patio*.

"Perhaps one of my people plucked up courage to fire at a coyote," answered Epilar. "They showed little enough desire to shoot last night—"

"No, that was an army rifle," the Commandant insisted. "If you will excuse me—"

"And if I do not choose to do so?" calmly asked our host.

"*Très mil diablos*—if you do not choose—"

"*Precisamente, Señor Commandante*," answered Epilar. "I should like to claim my forfeit."

De Grandin's small blue eyes were sparkling in the candlelight. "*Dieu de Dieu de Dieu de Dieu!*" he murmured. "I was certain; I was sure; I could not be mistaken!"

The Commandant regarded Señor Epilar in round-eyed wonder. "Your forfeit?" he demanded. "In the devil's name——"

"Not quite the devil, though something like it," cut in Epilar with a soft laugh. "*La Murciélaga, Commandante mio.* As I came into your office you declared that you would give your head if you could but lay your eyes upon the Bat-Woman. Look, my friend, your wish is granted."

With one hand he tore off the tiny black mustache and goatee which adorned his face; with the other he unwound the gaudy handkerchief which bound his head, and a wealth of raven hair came tumbling down about his face and rippled round his shoulders. Stripped of its masculine adornments I recognized that lovely, cold, impassive face as belonging to the woman who had stood upon the stairs the night that Caldes and the dancer met their deaths.

"*Dios!*" the Commandant exclaimed, reaching for the pistol at his belt; but: "I would not try to do it," warned the woman. "Look about you."

At every window of the room masked men were stationed, each with a deadly blow-gun poised and ready at his lips.

"Your soldiers are far happier, I know," the woman announced softly. "All of them, I'm sure, had been to mass this morning. Now they are conversing with the holy saints. "As for you"—she threw us the dry flick of a Mona Lisa smile—"if you will be kind enough to come, I shall take pleasure in entertaining you at my jungle headquarters." For a moment her sardonic gaze fixed on Nancy Meigs; then: "Your fair companion will be glad to furnish some amusement, I am sure," she added softly.

W E RODE ALL NIGHT. Strapped tightly to the saddles of our mules, hands bound behind us and with *tapojos*, or mule-blinds, drawn across our faces, we plodded through the jungle, claws of acacia and mesquite slapping and scratching against us, the chafing of our rawhide bonds becoming more intolerable each mile.

It was full daylight when they took our hoodwinks off. We had reached an open space several hundred feet in breadth, tiled with squared stones and facing on the ruins of a topless Mayan pyramid which towered ninety or a hundred feet against the thick-set wall of jungle. On each side of us ranked a file of bat-masked men, each with a blow-gun in his hand. Of *La Murciélaga* we could see nothing.

"*Holá, mes enfants,* we have come through nobly thus far, *n'est-ce-pas?*" de Grandin called as he twisted in his saddle to throw a cheerful grin in our direction. "If—*par Dieu et le Diable!*" he broke off as his small blue eyes went wide with horror and commiseration. Turning, I followed the direction of his glance and felt a sickening sensation at my stomach.

Behind us, bound upon a mule, sat Nancy Meigs. They had stripped her shirt and bandeau off, leaving her stark naked to the belt, and obviously they had failed to tie a *tapojo* across her face, for from brow to waist she was a mass of crisscrossed slashes where the cruelly clawed thorn branches of the jungle had gashed and sheared her tender skin as she rode bound and helpless through the bush. Little streaks of blood-stain, some fresh, some dry and clotted, marked a pattern on her body and her khaki jodhpurs were bespattered with the dark discolorations. She slumped forward in her saddle, half unconscious, but sufficiently awake to feel the pain of her raw wounds, and we saw her bite her lips as she strove to keep from screaming with the torment which the buzzing jungle flies, her lacerations and the cruelly knotted rawhide bonds inflicted.

"Be all th' saints, 'tis meself as would like nothin' better than to git me hands on that she-devil!" swore Costello as he saw the claw-marks on the girl's white torso. "Bedad, I'd—

"*Andela*—forward!" came a sharp command beside us, and masked men seized the bridles of our mules and led them toward the pyramid.

Our prison was a large square room lighted by small slits pierced in the solid masonry and furnished with a wooden grating at its doorway. Here we stretched our limbs and strove to rub the circulation back into our hands and feet.

"*Soy un bobo*—what a fool I am!" the Commandant groaned as he rubbed his swollen wrists. "I should have known that no one in the neighborhood would have the courage to come to me with complaints against these Bat-Men. I should have taken warning—"

"Softly, *mon ami*," de Grandin comforted. "You acted in the only way you could. It was your duty to embrace the chance to wipe this gang of bandits out. Me, I should probably have done the same, if—"

A rattling at the wooden grating interrupted him. "*La Murciélaga* deigns to see you. Come!" a masked man told us.

For a moment I had hopes that we might overpower our guard, but the hope was short-lived; for a file of blowgun bearers waited in the corridor outside our cell, and with this watchful company we made our way along the passage till we came to a low doorway leading to a large apartment lighted by a score of silver lamps swinging from the painted ceiling.

The ancient walls were lined with frescoes, figures of strange dancing women posed in every posture of abandon, some wearing red, some clad in green, a few in somber black, but most entirely nude, flaunting their nakedness in a riot of contorted limbs and swaying bodies. There was a vigor to the art of the old Mayan painters who had limned these frescoes on the walls. Despite their crudity of execution there was an air of realness in the murals which made it seem that they might suddenly be waked to life and circle round the room in the frenzy of an orgiastic dance.

At the far end of the room a table of dark wood was laid with cotton napery and a wonderful old silver service which must at one time have graced the banquet hall of some old grandee in the days of Spanish dominance. Four chairs were drawn up to the board facing the end where a couch of carven wood heaped high with silken cushions stood beneath the fitful luminance cast by a hanging silver lamp.

"This must have been the priestess' hall," the Commandant informed us in a whisper. "This temple is supposed to have contained a college of priests and priestesses, something like a convent and monastery."

"*Parbleu*, if that is so, I think those old ones did not mortify the flesh to any great extent," the Frenchman answered with a grin. "But while we wait in this old mausoleum of the ancient ones, where is our charming hostess?"

As though his words had been a cue, a staff of bells chimed musically outside the door, and the guard of bat-men ranged about the walls sank to their knees.

The chime grew higher, shriller, sweeter, and a double file of women dressed in filmy cotton robes, each with a bat-mask on her face, came through the low-arched entrance, paused a moment, then, as though obeying an inaudible command, dropped prostrate to the floor, head to head, hand clasping hand, so that they made a living carpet on the pavement.

Framed in the arching entrance, *La Murciélaga* stood like some lovely life-sized portrait. A robe of finely woven cotton, dyed brilliant red with cochineal and almost sheer as veiling, flowed from a jeweled belt clasped below her bosoms to the insteps of her narrow, high-arched feet. On throat and arms, on her thumbs and little-fingers, flashed great emeralds, any one of which was worth a princely ransom. Long golden pendants throbbing with the flash of blood-bright rubies reached from the tiny lobes of little ears almost to naked, cream-white shoulders. Each move she made was musical, for bands of pure gold were clasped in tiers about her wrists and on her slender ankles, and clashed tunefully together with each step she took. Upon the great and little-toe of each slim foot there gleamed a giant emerald so that as her feet advanced beneath the swirling hem of her red robe it seemed that green-eyed serpents darted forth their heads.

"*Madre de Dios!*" I heard the Commandant exclaim, and his voice seemed choked with sobs. "*Que hermosa*—how beautiful!"

"So is the tiger or the cobra," murmured Jules de Grandin as *La Murciélaga* trod upon the prostrate women as unconcernedly as though they had been figures woven in a carpet.

She greeted us with a bright smile. "Good morning, gentlemen. I hope you did not suffer too much inconvenience from your ride last night?"

None of us made reply, but she seemed in nowise fazed. "Breakfast is prepared," she announced, sinking down upon the heaped-up cushions of the couch and motioning us to the chairs which stood about the table. "I regret I cannot offer you such food as you are used to, but I do my poor best."

Oranges and cherimoya, grapes, sweet limes, guavas and plates of flat, crisp native bread composed the meal, with coffee, chocolate and lemonade for beverages. Finally came long, thick cigars of rich lowland-grown tobacco and a sweet, strong wine which tasted like angelica.

THE WOMAN LEANT BACK on her cushioned divan and regarded us through half-closed eyes as she let a little streamlet of gray smoke flow from her lips. "The question, gentlemen, is, 'What are we to do with you?'" she stated in a voice which held that throaty, velvety quality of the southern races. "I cannot very well afford to let you go; I have no wish to keep you here against your will. Would you care to join our ranks? I can find work for you."

"And if we should refuse, *Madame?*" de Grandin asked.

Her shrug lifted the creamy shoulders till they touched the jeweled earpendants and set their gems to flashing in the lamplight. "There is always *el crucifijo,*" she replied, turning black-fringed, curious eyes upon him. "It would be interesting to see four bodies hanging up at once. You, my friend, would doubtless scream in charming tenor, *el Commandante* would shriek baritone, I think, while I do not doubt that the old bearded one and the big Irishman would be the bassos of the concert. It should make an interesting quartet. I have more than half a mind to hear it."

A frigid grimace, the mere parody of a smile, congealed upon the Commandant's pale lips. "You make a gruesome jest, *Señora,*" he asserted feebly.

"*Cabrón!*" she shot the deadly insult at him as a snake might spew its poison. "*La Murciélaga* never jests!" Her face had gone skull-white, with narrowed, venomous eyes, the chin and mouth thrust forward and the lips pressed taut against the teeth.

"Down," she ordered, "down on your faces, all of you! Lick my feet like the dogs you are, and pray for mercy! Down, I say, for as surely as I reign supreme here I'll crucify the one who hesitates!"

De Grandin looked at Costello, and his Gallic blue eyes met prompt answer in the black-fringed eyes of Irish blue of the detective. With one accord they turned to me, and instinctively I nodded.

The little Frenchman rose, heels clicked together, and faced the termagant she-fiend with a glance as cold and polished as a leveled bayonet. "*Madame,*" he announced in a metallic voice, "we are men, we four. To men there are things worse than death."

"*Bueno,* my little one," she answered; "then I shall hear your quartet after all. I had hoped that you would choose to play the hero." Turning to her guards she ordered sharply: "Take them away."

"No, no; not me, *Señora!*" the Commandant implored, falling on his knees before her. "Do not crucify me, I beseech you!"

Across his shoulder he cried frenziedly: "Save yourselves, *amigos.* Beg mercy. What good is honor to a corpse? I saw a man whom they had crucified—they flung his body in the city square at night. It was terrible. His wounds gaped horribly and the middle fingers had been torn away where his hands had ripped loose from the spikes!"

"You would have mercy, little puppy?" asked the woman softly, regarding him with a slow, mocking smile.

"Yes, yes, *Señora!* Of your pity spare me—"

"Then, since you are a cringing dog, deport yourself becomingly." With the condescension of a queen who graciously extends her hand for salutation, she stretched out a slim, ring-jeweled foot.

It was shocking to behold him stultify his manhood. "*Misericordia muy Señora graciosa*—have mercy, gracious lady!" he whimpered, and I turned away my head with a shudder of repulsion as he put his hand beneath her instep, raised the gemmed foot to his mouth, and, thrusting forth his tongue, began to lick it as a famished dog might lap at food.

"*Cordieu,*" de Grandin murmured as the guards closed round us and began to crowd us from the room, "she may murder us to death, but I damn think she can do no worse to us than she has done to him!"

"Thrue fer ye, Doctor de Grandin, sor," Costello rumbled. "You an' me wuz soldiers an' Doctor Trowbridge is a gintleman. Thank God we ain't more scared o' dyin' than o' dishonorin' ourselves!"

THE SQUARE BEFORE THE pyramid blazed bright with torchlight. On three sides, ranked elbow to elbow, stood the "Children of the Bat" looking through the peep-holes of their masks with frenzied, hot-eyed gloating. Before the temple steps there crouched a line of drummers who beat out a steady, mind-destroying rhythm. We stood, legs hobbled, between our guards, looking toward the temple stairs, and I noticed with a shudder that at intervals of some eight feet four paving-blocks had been removed, and beside each gaping opening was a little pile of earth. The crosspits had been dug.

"Courage, *mes enfants,*" de Grandin whispered. "If all goes well—"

Costello's lips were moving almost soundlessly. His eyes were fixed in fascinated awe upon the cross-holes in the pavement; the expression on his face showed more of wonder than of fear. "To hang upon a cross," I heard him whisper, "I am not worthy, Lord!"

"*Morbleu,* she comes, my friends!" the little Frenchman warned.

Tiny tom-toms, scarcely larger than a tea-cup, beat out a low, continuous roar beneath the thumbs and knuckles of the double line of bat-masked women filing from a doorway in the temple. Behind them came an awe-inspiring figure. Skin-tight, a sheath of finely woven jet-black silk, sheer and gleaming as the finest stocking, cased her supple form from throat to ankles, its close-looped meshes serving rather to accentuate than hide the gracious curves of her long, slim limbs. Moccasins of cloth of gold were on her feet, her head was covered with a hood which bore the pointed snout and tufted ears of a great vampire bat. In the eyeholes we could see the red reflection of the torchlight. Joined to her body from arm-pits to hips were folds of black-silk tissue, and these, in turn, were fastened to her tightly fitting sleeves, so that when she spread her arms it seemed that great black wings stretched from her. Her hands were bare, and we could see the blood-red lacquer gleaming on her nails as she curved her fingers forward like predatory talons.

"*La Murciélaga! La Murciélaga!*" rose a mighty shout of homage from the crowd of bat-masked men and women. It was not so much a cry of greeting as of stark insanity—of strange disease and maniacal excitement. It spouted up, cleaving the heavy, torchlit air like a terrible geyser of sound.

The drums redoubled their wild rataplan, and the shouting grew more frenzied as *La Murciélaga* mounted a low block of stone and stood outlined in torchlight, great sable wings a-flutter, as though she were in very truth the dread Death Angel come to grace the sacrifice of poor lives with her presence.

"Look, sors, for th' love o' hivin!" bade Costello.

Across the torchlit square there walked, or rather danced, a man. In his hand he held a tether, and I felt a wave of sick revulsion as I recognized the thing he led. It was the Commandant of Tupulo. He was chained and muzzled like a dog, and he went upon all fours, like a brute beast. As his keeper led him to the altar-stone on which the Bat-Woman was poised, he sank back on his heels, threw back his head and held his hands, drooped at the wrists, before him in simulation of a begging dog. At a kick from his keeper he sank down at the altar's base, drew up his knees and folded arms around them. His depth of degradation reached, he crouched in canine imitation at his mistress' feet.

"*Corbleu*, I think that we three chose the better part, *n'est-ce-pas*, my friends?" de Grandin asked.

The hot breath rising in my throat choked off my answer. Four men were staggering from the shadows with a cross, a monstrous thing of mortised timbers, and despite myself I felt my knees grow weak as I saw the red stains which disfigured it. "Mine will be there soon," a voice seemed dinning in my ears. "They'll stretch my limbs and drive the great spikes through my hands and feet; they'll hang me there—"

"*La Traidora—la Traidora*—the Traitress!" came a great shout from the crowd, as three masked women struggled forward with a fourth. All were garbed identically, but we knew before they stripped her mask and gown and sandals off that the captive was poor Nancy Meigs.

There was no pretense of a trial. "Á la muerte—á la muerte!" screamed the congregation, and the executioners leapt forward to their task.

Birth-nude, they stretched her on the blood-stained cross and I saw a hulking ruffian poise a great nail over her left palm while in his free hand he drew back a heavy hammer.

Costello started it. Hands joined, he dropped upon his knees and in a firm, strong voice began:

"Hail, Mary, full of grace, blessèd art Thou among women . . ."

De Grandin and I followed suit, and in chorus we repeated that petition of the motherless to Heaven's Queen. ". . . Mary, Mother of God, pray for us sinners now and in the hour of death."

"Amen," concluded Jules de Grandin. And, in the next breath: "Sang de Dieu, my friends, they come! Observe them!"

Their motor roars drowned by the screaming of the crowd, three planes zoomed down above the square, and a sudden squall of bullets spewed its deadly rain upon the close-packed ranks which lined the quadrangle.

I saw the executioner fall forward on his victim's body, a spate of life-blood gushing from his mouth; saw the Commandant leap up, then clutch his breast and topple drunkenly against the altar-stone; saw La Murciélaga's outspread wings in tatters as the steel-sheathed slugs ripped through them and cut a bloody kerf across her bosom; then de Grandin and Costello pulled me down, and we lay upon the stones while gusts of bullets spattered round us or ricocheted with high, thin, irritable whines.

The carnage was complete. Close-packed, illuminated by their own torch flares, and taken wholly by surprise, the bat-men fell before the planes' machine-gun fire like grain before the reaper.

That the three of us escaped annihilation was at least a minor miracle, but when the squadron leader gave the signal for the fire to cease, and, sub-machine guns held alertly, the aviators clambered from their planes, we rose unharmed, though far from steady on our feet.

"Muchas gracias, Señor Capitán," de Grandin greeted as he halted fifteen paces from the flight commander and executed a meticulous salute. "I assure you that you did not come one little minute in advance of urgent need.

"Come, let us see to Mademoiselle Nancy," he urged Costello and me. "Perchance she still survives."

She did. Shielded by the bodies of her executioners and the upright of the cross beside which she had rolled when the gunfire struck the bat-man down, she lay unconscious in a welter of warm blood, and it was not till we had sponged her off that we found her only hurts were those inflicted by the jungle vines the night before.

Carefully they placed the Commandant's shot-riddled body in a plane for transportation back to Tupulo, and a military funeral.

"He died a hero's death, *no?*" the flight commander asked.

"Was he not an officer and gentleman?" de Grandin answered disingenuously.

"B UT NO, MY FRIENDS," he told us as we lay sprawled out in deck chairs on the steamship *Golondrina* as she plowed her way toward New York "it was no magic, I assure you. That commandant at Tupulo, I mistrusted his good sense. There was a weakness in his face, and lack of judgment, too. 'This one loves himself too much, he is a strutting jackdaw, he has what Friend Costello would call the silly pan,' I say to me while we were talking with him. Besides—

"We knew the countryside was terrified of *La Murciélaga*; the bare mention of her name drove men indoors and women into swoons. That anyone would have the courage to complain of her—to come to the police and ask that they send out an expeditionary force—*pardieu*, it had the smell of fish upon it!

"Furthermore, I am no fool. Not at all, by no means, and it is seldom that I do forget a face. When I saw this Señor Epilar, there was a reminiscence in his features. He reminded me too much of one whom I had seen the night poor Mademoiselle Rita met her tragic death. Also, there was a savage gleam within his eye when it rested on our Nancy—the sort of gleam a cat may show when he finds that he has run the little helpless mouse to earth.

"'Jules de Grandin, my friend, are you going into the jungle with this so idiotic Commandant and this young man who looks uncomfortably like the Lady of the Bat?' I ask me.

"'Jules de Grandin, my esteemed self, I am going,' I reply to me, 'but I shall take precautions, too!'

"Accordingly, while *Monsieur le Capitaine* was fitting out his force and you were packing for the trip, I hied me to a telephone and put a call through to the military airport at Merida. '*Monsieur le Commandant*,' I tell the officer in charge, 'we are going in the jungle. We go to seek that almost legendary lady, *La Murciélaga*. I fear it is a foolish thing we do, for it is more than possible that we shall be ambushed. Therefore I would that you make use of us for bait. Have flyers fly above the jungle, and if we do not return by tomorrow noon, have them investigate anything suspicious which they may see. And, *Monsieur le Commandant*,' I tell him in conclusion, 'it might be well to order them to make investigation with machine-gun fire.'

"*Eh bien*, I think they carried out their orders very well, those ones."

Nancy laid slim fingers on his arm. "We owe our lives to you—all of us—you little darling!" Impulsively, she leant forward and kissed him on the mouth.

Tiny wrinkles crinkled round de Grandin's eyes and in their blue depths flashed an impish gleam.

"Behold, *ma chère*," he told her solemnly, "I save our lives again.

"*Mozo*," he hailed a passing deck steward, "bring us four gin slings, *muy pronto!*"

Satan's Palimpsest

IT WAS A MERRY though oddly assorted party Philip Classon entertained at Saint's Rest, his big house beside the Shrewsbury: a motion-picture star, a playwright quietly and industriously drinking himself to death, one or two bankers, a lawyer, several unattached ladies living comfortably on their dower or their alimony, Jules de Grandin and me. Dinner had been perfect, with turtle soup, filet of lemon sole in sauce bercy, Canada grouse and an assortment of wines which caused my little friend's blue eyes to sparkle with appreciation. Now, as he sat with Karen Kirsten on the big divan before the roaring fire of apple logs and sipped his Jérôme Napoléon from a lotus-bud shaped brandy snifter, he was obviously at peace with all the world.

"*Mais certainement, ma belle*," I heard him tell the actress in an interval between the efforts of the duet at the piano to retail the nostalgic longings of the old cowhand from the Rio Grande, "it is indubitably a fact. Thoughts are things. We may not see or handle them, nor can we weigh them in a balance, but they have a certain substance of their own. They can penetrate, they can permeate the hardest matter, and like the rose-scent in Monsieur Moore's poem, they will cling to it when it is all but worn away by time or smashed by violence."

"Sure of that, are you, de Grandin?" our host asked quizzically as he leant across the sofa back and rested one hand on the little Frenchman's black-clad shoulder, the other on the actress' gleaming arm.

"As sure as one can be of anything—only fools are positive," de Grandin answered with a smile.

"You're certain?"

"Positive, *parbleu!*"

As the laughter died away Classon nodded toward the curtained doorway. "We've a chance to test Doctor de Grandin's theory," he announced. "There's something in the gunroom I'd like to show you and see what effect it has."

Amid murmurs of mystified conjecture he led the way across the wide hall lit by a pair of swinging boat-shaped lamps which gave that odd, pale light that comes only from burning olive oil, swept aside the heavy Turkish hangings at the door and motioned us to enter.

The "gunroom" was a relic of the days when New Jersey had no need of conservation laws for game, and the fowling-piece and rifle were as much a source of daily meat as were the meadow, the pig-sty and the poultry yard. An ancestor of Classon's who built ships when Yankee mariners dropped anchor in every port from Bombay to Southampton had built Saint's Rest as sturdily as he built his craft, and though slaves' quarters and summer kitchens had long been turned to modern usages, like the gunrooms they still retained their ancient designations.

It was a lovely place. There was a walnut table of Italian make surely not a year younger than the Fifteenth Century, French rosewood chairs upholstered in brocade which must have been worth its measurement in gold, a lacquered Chinese cabinet dating from the days when the Son of Heaven bore the surname Han; across one wall was hung a lovely verdure tapestry from Sixteenth Century Flanders depicting decidedly naughty *al fresco* goings-on with the same lack of restraint as that displayed by that amazing little manikin in Brussels which every year decants champagne with utter unconventionality.

With a taper Classon lit two oil-dish lamps—the house was wired for electricity, but I'd seen nothing thus far but the light of lamps and candles—and directed our attention to a white-wood table like an altar which stood just within their zone of radiance. "This is it," he told us, and it seemed to me there was a sharp intake of breath, almost like a sigh of pain, as he made the brusk announcement.

Something like the tabernacle of a Catholic altar showed aureately in the lamplight. Two feet in height by eighteen inches wide, pointed like a Gothic arch, plain and unadorned with ornament as a siege gun's shell, its dull mat gold shone dimly in the mounting luminance cast by the gently swaying lamps.

"What is it? Is it a—" the querying babble started, but Classon raised his hand.

"This is just the frame," he answered. "Look."

He pressed a hidden spring and twin doors sprang apart, revealing three pictures integrated into one, all worked in deft mosaic. On the inside of the left-hand door there ranged a group of dancing youths and maidens clad in the chiton of the classic Greeks as modified for use in Constantine's Byzantium. The other panel bore a group of creeping children, nude and chubby with the chubbiness so dearly loved by early artists, while in the center, deep-set between the back-flung doors, there stood a slender, pale ascetic figure with a clout of camel's hair about his loins, rough sandals on his feet and a cross-topped staff in his right hand. The ancient artist had worked cunningly, so cunningly that the tiny lines between the variegated-colored marble were finer than the minute crevices in Chinese crackle-wear, and no detail of the groups or portrait had been lost. The saint's blue eyes, wide, deep and extraordinarily sad, seemed to look into our own with a searching, deep intensity, as though to chide us for the worldliness that lay within our hearts and say: "Behold these dancing youths, these creeping, puling babes; the babes grow into youth and maidenhood and have their hour of silly pleasure, then comes old age and death and dissolution. Vanity, vanity; all is vanity!"

"Well?" Classon asked when we had gazed upon the ikon for a long moment in silence. "What d'ye see?"

"A sacred picture."—"Beautiful!"—"Exquisite!"—"Sweet!"—"Divine!"—"Superb!"—"Swell!"

The fatuous comments fluttered thick as snowflakes, phrased according to the speaker's wealth or paucity of diction.

"Yes, of course, but what d'ye *see*? What's the picture of?"

"A saint?" I hazarded when no one else seemed willing to express conjecture.

"That's what you all see?" asked Classon, and it seemed to me there was an eagerness about his question and an air of quick relief entirely unwarranted by the triviality of the entire business.

I was turning to examine the Chinese cabinet when de Grandin's hand upon my elbow brought me round.

"Observe her, if you will, Friend Trowbridge," he commanded, motioning toward Karen Kirsten with his eyes.

She had not replied to Classon's questions nor expressed opinion of the ikon's artistry, I realized, but I was unprepared for what I saw. She was standing looking at the triple picture, head thrown back, hands hanging limply open at her sides. The lamplight played across her, accentuating her unusual beauty in a way no cameraman had ever managed. Tall she was, almost six feet, and every line of her was long, but definitely feminine. Her hair, like silver-silken filaments, was smoothed and plaited in long braids about her head; her dazzling fairness was set off by a slim gown of apple-green baghera draped in Grecian fashion; there were bracelets of carved gold upon her arms and a strand of pearls about her throat, and I caught my breath in sudden wonder, for lustrous pearls and lucent skin almost exactly matched each other. Her ice-blue Nordic eyes habitually held the commanding look which is the heritage of Northern races, but now there was another, different look in them. The pupils seemed to spread until they stained the blue irises black; I could see fear stealing into them, stark, abysmal fear which radiated from a sickened heart and was mirrored in her eyes.

"All right, folks," Classon's brusk announcement broke the spell; "that's all there is. Let's go back and have another drink."

"But why did you insist we tell you what we saw, Phil?" asked Mrs. Durstin as we reassembled in the drawing-room. "It's just an ordinary lovely piece of mosaic, isn't it?"

Classon laughed shamefacedly. "Just a gag, Clara," he assured her. "Didn't you ever notice how the average person can be bullied out of sticking to the evidence of his own senses? Why, I've had people here who declared they saw all sorts of things—even swore they saw the figures move—when I kept asking 'em what they saw in those pictures. Seems as if this is a pretty level-headed crowd, though; I didn't have a bit of luck with you."

The evening passed with a surprising variety of liquid refreshment, some passable singing, much ultra-modernistic dancing and a number of stories, some of which were funny and risqué, some merely ribald. By midnight I had managed to convince myself that the vision of Miss Kirsten's terror in the gunroom had been due to some illness which had stricken her—any doctor knows what changes indigestion-pangs can work in patients' faces—and dismissed the recollection from my mind.

But as we paused to say good-night beside the stairs, Miss Kirsten laid her hand upon my arm.

"You and Doctor de Grandin drove down from Harrisonville, didn't you, Doctor Trowbridge?" she asked, and again I saw that flicker of stark terror in her eyes.

"Yes," I answered.

"How long are you staying?"

"Only to breakfast, unfortunately. I should have liked the opportunity of talking more with you, but—"

"Won't you take me with you, please?" she broke in on my clumsy gallantry. "There isn't any train till noon tomorrow, and I've been going utterly mad in this house all day. I must get away as quickly as I can. I must—I *must!*"

"Why, certainly," I soothed. "Doctor de Grandin and I shall be pleased to have you with us on the homeward drive."

"Oh"—her long, slim, delicately articulated fingers closed upon my arm with a grip of surprising strength—"thank you, Doctor!"

She made me the offer of a grateful, half-frightened smile, lit her candle from the lamp of hammered bronze which burned upon the table by the newel post, and turned to mount the stairs.

ARRAYED IN VIOLET-SILK PAJAMAS and mauve dressing-gown, de Grandin stood before the window of our bedroom, looking out upon the snow-flecked darkness of the winter night as if he sought to light it with something burning in his mind.

"What's the matter, old fellow?" I asked, smothering a yawn as I made for the bathroom, tooth-brush in hand.

"I wonder," he returned without taking his meditative gaze from the black square of the window, "I ponder, I cogitate; there is a black dog running through my brain."

"Eh?" I shot back. "A black—"

"*Précisément.* An exceedingly troublesome and active small black poodle, my friend. Why?"

"I don't think that I follow—"

"*Ah bah,* you are literal as a platter of boiled codfish! When I ask why, I mean why. Why, by example, does our friend Classon want to have the testimony of his guests that that ikon in his gunroom is but the pretty picture of some danc-ing children and some creeping babes who act as foils for an ascetic saint? Why is he relieved when they tell him what they see. Why—"

"Didn't you hear what he told Mrs. Durstin?" I broke in. "It's some silly sort of game he played; he wanted to see if he could bully us into thinking that we saw—"

"What he has seen, maybe?"

"What *he* saw? Why, what could he see that we couldn't?"

"That which Mademoiselle Kirsten saw, perhaps."

"See here," I dropped into the armchair by the fire and felt for my cigar-case, "all this mystery has me slowly going crazy. Classon didn't seem in any jocose mood when he asked us what we saw while looking at that picture. Indeed, it seemed to me that he was definitely frightened, and when we told him that we saw the picture of a saint he seemed relieved, yet a little disappointed, too."

"Then take Karen Kirsten. I can't understand her. She's more like Brunhilde than Griselda; I'd say she never was afraid of anything. Twelve hundred years ago women like her swung double-bladed axes and tugged twenty-foot oars beside their men, and spat back curses and defiance in the face of god and devil; yet if that woman wasn't absolutely mad with horror of some sort—if she isn't hag-rid-den and almost wild to leave this house this very minute—I never saw terror in a human face. Have you any idea what it's all about?"

He turned from the window and tore the blue wrapping from a packet of "Marylands," selected one of the evil-smelling things with infinite care and set it alight. "Not an idea, my friend, merely a thought; one of those vague, elusive thoughts that fade like dewdrops in the sun when you seek to put them into words. But—" He shook his head impatiently, as though to clear his brain, then recommenced:

"You saw the composition of those pictures, how they are constructed of cleverly matched bits of colored stone. Very good. Between the little colored fragments are tiny, so small lines, *n'est-ce-pas?*"

"Of course, it's a mosaic—"

"*Bien.* It was only for a moment, for the fraction of the twinkling of an eye, but as I looked upon those pictures I thought the colored marbles ran together, separated, turned about one another like the bright glass of a kaleidoscope and formed a different pattern. It was over quickly, *parbleu,* so quickly that it could hardly have been said to have occurred, but—" He paused and puffed reflectively at his cigarette, letting twin rivulets of smoke trickle slowly from his nostrils.

"What was it that you saw?"

"*Mordieu*, that is what taunts me. I cannot say. So quickly it came, so fast it disappeared that I had not time to realize it. But I am certain that it was an evil, an obscene and wicked thing I saw, like a monkey dancing on a consecrated altar."

"But that's absurd."

"The line of demarcation that divides absurdity from horror is often very finely drawn, my friend." For a moment he stared straight before him, and his little round blue eyes seemed misted, as though, still open, they shut out vision while he racked his inner consciousness for an answer to the riddle. Abruptly: "Come, let us go and look at it," he bade. "It may be in the quiet of the empty room we shall be able to congeal and hold that fleeting metamorphosis which mocked me when we stood there with the others."

We tiptoed toward the stairs, but hardly had we gone ten feet when his hand upon my arm brought me to a halt. In the dim light cast by a single swinging oil lamp someone was coming from the floor below, someone who walked in silence and whose presence we should not have realized had it not been for the shadow cast across the stairhead.

"Back into this doorway if you please, my friend," de Grandin whispered, and as we shrank into the recess of the deepset door Karen Kirsten glided up the stairs, paused a moment with one hand upon the baluster and threw back her head with up-turned eyes as though imploring mercy from kind Providence. She was tense as a drawn harp-string, and her face was set in lines of suffering, but the faint light seeping up the stair-well from behind her rippled through her golden hair and cast shadows on her brows which seemed to deepen the cerulean of her eyes. In her sleeveless, neckless nightrobe of white crepe, with a slender hand laid humbly on her heaving bosom, it seemed to me she bore a likeness to the pictures of Saint Barbara.

"Ah, God!" she breathed in a high, quivering sigh. "God have pity!"

Filled with compassion I took a half-step toward her, but the sudden pressure of de Grandin's small hand on my elbow halted me.

"Observe," he breathed—"*le sang!*"

I felt a retching wave of sickness as he spoke. Across the bodice of her night-dress where her slender hand had rested, was a dark, rubescent stain.

For an endless moment we three, watched and watchers, stood in statue-like stillness; then with another sobbing sigh the woman turned and glided down the hall, her white, bare feet as soundless as a zephyr on the polished boards.

"Wh—what can have happened?" I faltered, but his only answer was to urge me toward the stairs.

The pale glow of a single lamp burning like a vigil light above the altar-table where the ikon stood shone through the gunroom as we entered. At a glance I saw the little doors were open and the triple picture on display, but before de Grandin's quickly indrawn breath had sounded I had also seen the thing that lay before the table on the floor.

It was—it had been—Wyndham Farraday, the dissolute young playwright, and a single glance assured us he was dead. His head lay back, and in the staring, sunken eyes, pinched nose, drooping jaw and idiotically half-protruding tongue we read the signs that to the practised eye are unmistakable. He lay upon his back with arms thrown out to right and left as though he had been crucified upon the hardwood floor, and from the left breast of his pajama jacket thrust the gilded cross-shaped handle of a slender dagger, a mediæval misericord, thin as a darning-needle, pointed as a bee-sting, designed to slip between the links of fine chain-mail and deal the death blow where a larger weapon would have failed. A little sluggish stream of blood had stained his jacket round the knife-wound. He was not handsome or majestic as he lay there with the chill of *rigor mortis* even then beginning to congeal his loose-hung lower jaw. Poets and romantic writers to the contrary, there is little dignity or beauty in raw death, as every soldier, doctor and embalmer knows. The majesty of death is largely artificial.

"Do you think she—" I began, but de Grandin's sudden exclamation broke my words.

"*L'idole*—the picture, my friend—observe her, if you please!" he breathed.

I looked, then blinked my eyes in wondering disbelief. The little bits of colored marble which composed the triple picture seemed sliding past, around and *through* one another with a bewildering kaleidoscopic motion, losing their old pattern, making vague, unformed designs upon their golden background, then rearranging themselves in new and terrifying groupings. It was hard—impossible—to say what scenes they formed, but I felt a wave of nausea sweeping over me, a physical sickness such as that I felt when as a young interne I had been assigned to duty at the city morgue and for the first time smelled the fulsome odor of decaying human flesh.

Then sanity returned. The lamp! It was swaying pendulum-like above the ikon. That was it; the changing light and shadow as the light swung back and forth had caused an optical illusion. I took the boat-shaped bowl of burnished copper in my hands and steadied it. When I looked again the pictures had resumed their lovely wont. The youths and maidens once again danced joyously upon the tender, blue-green grass against a background of fresh-budding willows; the chubby cooing infants rolled and sported on a flowering sward; the pale, ascetic saint looked out with admonition and reproach upon a world which wooed the pomps and pleasures of the carnal life.

"Oh, thou empty-headed zany, thou species of an elephant, thou—oh, *le bon Dieu* give me patience with this witless one!" de Grandin fairly chattered, his round blue eyes ablaze with indignation, his small hands twitching to close round my throat.

"Why, what's the matter now?" I asked. "That swaying lamp obscured our vision; we'll need a steady light to see—"

"If kindly Providence will defend me from my well-intentioned friends, I think that I can guard against my enemies!" he broke in sharply, looking at me with a heaven-grant-me-fortitude expression. "In your attempt at helpfulness you have blocked the path of justice, human and divine. That swinging lamp was not set in motion by itself, *par consequent* it must have started swaying by some outside force. I would make bold to venture that some human hand had touched it in the recent past, for it was still in motion when we came here. Accordingly, there were unquestionably finger-prints upon it. Whose? *Hélas*, that we shall never know. You must needs stop the light from swinging because it made you see things which were not there to see—and left your great and ugly paw-prints on it in the process. Twenty expert tracers cannot now find the prints which were left there by the person who had touched that lamp a little while before. And that person, I damn think, was none other than the murderer of this poor one.

"Also, the distortion of this picture, as you call it, which you have attributed to the swaying of that lamp, may be the very crux of all this cursèd mystery. Why was Monsieur Classon anxious to have the testimony of his guests that this pretty picture was nothing but a pretty picture? Because, I think, he had seen it show another scene, *pardieu!* Why did *la Kirsten* show such signs of fear when she looked upon this seventy-times-damned ikon? Because she saw a something which was not good to see while the others saw but pretty figures! Why did Jules de Grandin have impressions of some sacrilegious scene when first he looked upon this piece of what seems innocent mosaic? Because I am attuned to superphysical appearances; I see deeper into such things than the ordinary man. Finally, why did you look sick, as if your dinner had most vilely disagreed with you, when you looked at this cursèd picture but a moment since? Because you, too, saw something dreadful taking shape. A moment more and we had captured it—but you must be helpful and dispel the atmosphere of evil which was gathering thick as fog.

"And now you ask me what's the matter! You should abase yourself. You should repent in sackcloth; you should walk barefoot through the snow; you should abstain from liquor for a week, *parbleu!*

"No matter," he put aside annoyance with true French practicality and turned toward the door. "This is now a matter for police investigation. Let us telephone the state constabulary."

"THIS IS POSITIVELY THE most uncanny business I've ever seen," Captain Chenevert of the State Police informed us.

De Grandin eyed him saturninely. "You are informing me, *mon capitaine?*"

"I certainly am. Look here: We've checked and double-checked that room for finger-prints, and what do we find? Nothing. Not a thing!"

"Nothing?"

"Well, practically. Or, rather, something worse. There are plain and unmistakable prints on the dagger handle, but they're Wyndham Farraday's. Now, that just doesn't make sense. Farraday might have stabbed himself through the heart, though this job's so neatly done it almost seems as if a surgeon did it; but if he did it himself one of two things would have followed the infliction of the wound. Either he'd have staggered forward and fallen in a heap, probably on his side, or he'd have collapsed at once; in which case he would either have fallen face-forward or dropped upon his back with his legs partly doubled under him. Possibly—though this usually happens in cases of shooting through the brain—he'd have been seized with a cadaveric spasm, all his muscles would have tightened into knots, and his fingers would have closed round the dagger-hilt in an almost unbreakable grip."

He paused and looked at Jules de Grandin questioningly. "Do you agree?"

"Perfectly, *mon capitaine*; you have exhausted the possibilities of the situation from a scientific standpoint."

"Then why in blazing hell was he lying so neatly spread out on the floor with his heels together like a soldier at attention and his arms flung out at right angles to his body?"

"Mightn't someone wearing gloves have stabbed him after he'd had the dagger in his hand?" I hazarded; but:

"Not a chance!" Chenevert smiled bleakly. "We've considered that, but if it had been done that way Farraday's finger-prints would have been practically obliterated, or at least smudged to some extent. They're not; they're clean and clear as any I've ever seen. This thing's got me going nutty. The finger-prints say 'suicide' with a capital S; all collateral evidence points to murder. If such a thing weren't palpably absurd here, I'd say it looked like *hari-kari*—ritual suicide with the assistance of a second party, you know. I saw a case of it in Kobe some years ago. A man had disemboweled himself in the approved Japanese manner, but the friend who acted as his second had waited to compose his limbs so that he lay as peacefully as Wyndham Farraday, though he must have threshed around terribly during the death agony."

Suddenly I saw it all. Karen Kirsten's frenzy to get away, her terror when she entered the gunroom last night, the blood on her nightgown when we saw her in the upper hall! It had been a suicide pact, and the woman lost her courage at the last. "By, George," I exclaimed, "Miss—"

The kick de Grandin gave me underneath the table nearly broke my tibia, but it had the desired effect. "Mistakes like that are easy to make in such cases," I ended lamely as Chenevert cast a questioning look at me.

"Friend Trowbridge has the right of it," de Grandin nodded. "There are many angles to this case, my captain; the trail is long and winding, and involved. Perhaps it would be well to lay the household under interdict."

"Eh? Inter—"

"Perfectly. Until the guilty party is arrested or the case marked permanently unsolved, every person in the building is suspect. People have a way of disappearing, my captain, once they leave the jurisdiction. While all of us are here you can put the finger on us at convenience. Once we are scattered—"

"I gotcha," Chenevert laughed. "You bet I'll put the clamp on, Doctor. Can't hold 'em here indefinitely, but I'll post a couple of the boys here with orders not to let anybody leave for thirty-six hours. We should know where we stand by that time. Meantime," he wound his muffler round his neck and buttoned up his short coat, "there's the body to dispose of and reports to be prepared. Call me at the barracks if anything comes up. I'll be over again sometime this afternoon."

"OH, THIS IS TERRIBLE!" Karen Kirsten wailed when we told her the police had forbidden us to leave. "I have shopping to do in New York, and my lawyers to consult about a new contract. I have to take a plane for the Coast immediately!" Her blue eyes blazed and her long hands folded and unfolded as she strode across the floor with her characteristic long-limbed, effortless walk. "I can't—I won't be cooped up in this dreadful place another minute, I tell you!"

True to the traditions of her trade, she was working herself into a temperamental tantrum, but beneath de Grandin's level stare she calmed amazingly.

"It would be better if we told ourselves the truth without reservation of any sort, Mademoiselle," he spoke in a level, almost toneless voice. "We are your friends; moreover, our experience has taught us to give credence to many things which the ordinary man would brush aside as nonsense. Nevertheless, we cannot help you if you are not frank."

"Why shouldn't I be frank?" she blazed. "I've nothing to hide. I know nothing of this dreadful business."

"You did not know that Monsieur Farraday was dead until they told you?"

"Of course not!"

"Not even when you left your room at dead of night and crept mouse-quiet to the gunroom where he lay like one crucified before that so queer ikon?"

"What do you mean? I never left my room last night—"

"Mademoiselle," he interrupted harshly, "you are lying. It was Doctor Trowbridge and I who notified the police of Monsieur Farraday's death when we stumbled on his body in the gunroom. As we were about to leave our room we saw you coming up the stairs, we saw the agitation under which you labored, we saw the blood upon your *robe de nuit*. We have not spoken of this, *Mademoiselle*, for there are some things best left unsaid, for the present, at any rate; but if you persist in this pretense of ignorance—if you will not help us to help you"—he spread his hands and raised his shoulders, brows and elbows in a shrug—"*eh bien*, it is a crime to withhold information from the officers, *Mademoiselle*. You would not have us become criminals, surely?"

She went absolutely rigid. There had never been much natural color in her cheeks; now they were positively corpse-gray. And her eyes were terrible in their fixed stare.

"You mean you saw me come upstairs last night?" she whispered. Her words were so low that we could scarcely hear them, her voice flat, expressionless, almost mechanical.

"Perfectly, *Mademoiselle*." The ghost of a hard smile curved the lips beneath the trimly waxed wheat-blond mustache.

Surrender showed in the sudden drooping of her shoulders, in the lines of weariness that suddenly etched themselves in her carefully tended face.

"Very well," she answered in a voice dull with fatigue, "I was there; I saw him—found him huddled up before the altar where that dreadful picture stands. He seemed so young, so helpless, lying there like that. I composed his limbs"— her blue eyes filled with tears and her firm chin quivered with unbidden sobs—"I stretched his arms out, too. It was a dreadful thing he'd done; it's terrible to kill yourself, and I thought that if I stretched his arms out like a cross it might help him plead for pardon—"

"That was the *only* reason you arranged him so, *Mademoiselle?*" Again the flicker of a disbelieving smile showed upon his mobile lips.

"Oh"—the woman turned on him, her eyes gone flat with fright—"you're dreadful, uncanny, devilish! No, if you must have the truth! I stretched his arms out like a cross because I was afraid. There's an old belief in Sweden that the dead ride hard, that suicides are lonely on their way through hell, and come back to the world to look for company; but if you lay a cross across their path, their way back to this world is barred. They can't come at you, then. We forget these things in practical America, but Death's not practical; it's as old and terrible as Odin's raven or the Storm Sisters; it brings back thoughts of olden days, so—"

"Precisely, *Mademoiselle*, one understands. Now tell us, if you please, what made you seek the gunroom in the first place?"

"Give me a cigarette," she begged, and he held his open case before her, then held his lighter forward. As she touched her cigarette tip to the fire she looked at him across the tiny flame that gleamed its echo fascinatingly in her brilliant eyes.

"I've had devils ever since I came here," she told us. Her voice was slurred and languorous, almost somnolent, yet strangely mechanical, as though an unseen hand played a gramophone on which her words had been recorded. "I don't know what it was; ordinarily I'm not subject to nerves, even when I'm tired, but something in the very atmosphere of this house seemed to frighten me. Perhaps it was the eery half-light the place has even in the day, maybe the lamplight, so different from the bright glow of electricity to which I'm used. At any rate, I had the creeps from the moment I crossed the threshold; everywhere I went I seemed to feel eyes, dozens of pairs of eyes—evil, wicked, calculating eyes—boring right into my brain from behind. I'd turn around a dozen times in the process of crossing the room to see if someone really were staring at me, but it was no use, the eyes were quicker. No matter how fast I'd turn they'd get around behind me, and keep staring—*leering*—at me from the back."

She ground the fire of her cigarette out against the bottom of an ashtray. "Last year I visited a psycho-analyst in Hollywood, and he hypnotized me. I can remember how I fought against it just as I was going off to sleep. I kept shrieking to myself inside my brain: 'No, no; I won't give up my consciousness; I won't let this man inside my secret soul!' but by that time it had gone too far, and I fell asleep despite myself. That's how it was here. Someone—some *thing*—seemed trying to creep inside my brain; to steal my mind—no, not quite that, rather, to crowd it out. I could feel the force of impact of an alien presence trying steadily to get inside me, and just as I fought against the hypnotist, so I fought against this threat here at Saint's Rest. Only this time I was prepared; I was warned against the attack in time; I felt the subtle influence that probed and clawed and dug at my integrity. And I fought it—God, how I fought it!

"It was through Wyndham Farraday that I met Mr. Classon. I'd known Wyndham out on the Coast when he was doing some writing for Cosmic Films, and looked him up when I came East. He told me of a friend of his who had this wonderful old house filled with the most astonishing old relics, and said the pride of the collection was a reliquary brought from Constantinople when the Crusaders under Baldwin sacked it in 1204.

"I love old things. I've spent a fortune on them for my house in Beverly, and the thought of something like this fascinated me. Wyndham wanted Mr. Classon to take me to the gunroom right away, but he put us off with first one excuse and then another. We didn't go in till he took the others to see it after dinner last night, and by that time I was almost frantic. I felt that if only I could get away from this awful place I'd have nothing more to ask.

"The moment Mr. Classon took us in to see the ikon I *knew*. There, I realized, was the spider that sat in the center of the dreadful web which was entangling me. A spider—ugh! Spiders suck their victims' blood, I'm told, and just so this—this *thing*—had been sucking at my soul and sanity. I looked at the horrible, lovely thing with the same feeling of repulsion I'd have felt while looking at some beautiful venomous reptile in its cage. Only this thing wasn't caged. It was loose, and nothing stood between it and me. Then, as I looked, the colored stones in the mosaics all seemed to melt and run together, and form a sort of toneless gray. It seemed as though there were dull, lead-colored mirrors in the golden frames, and as I looked in them other pictures seemed to form. The dancing youths and maidens seemed to age before my eyes till they were dreadful dotards and hags, the little babies seemed to swell and puff to monstrous parodies of human children. The saint—" her voice trailed off and her eyes became lack-luster, dead as painted eyes in a wooden statue's painted face.

"Yes, *Mademoiselle?*" de Grandin prompted softly.

"I—don't—remember," she said softly. "It was something terrible, some dreadful transformation that shook me like a chill, but I can't describe it."

"One appreciates your difficulty," the little Frenchman murmured. "And then?"

"Like a voice in a dream I heard Mr. Classon telling us to go back to the drawing-room, and it seemed to awaken me from a sort of trance I'd fallen into. I drank more than I should last night, but if I could get drunk, I thought, I might be able to escape the memory of those frightful figures in the pictures. Finally, when we said good-night, I asked Doctor Trowbridge if I might ride up with you this morning.

"I couldn't sleep. The recollection of the things I'd seen—all the more terrifying because I couldn't recall them clearly—kept torturing me, and I made up my mind to go down to the gunroom and have another look at the reliquary."

A faint smile raised the drooping comers of her mouth, and she looked at us diffidently, as though she begged for understanding.

"When I was a little girl we had a picture-book that scared me dreadfully. It was the story of Strongheart and the Dragon, and I'd feel my breath all hot and sulfurous in my throat when I looked at some of the illustrations. But I kept going back to it. I'd creep into the library, take it down from its shelf and, beginning at the first page, slowly turn the pages back, leaf by leaf, till I came at last to the picture showing Strongheart grappling with the Monster. 'It won't frighten you so much this time, you're getting used to it,' I'd tell myself as I came nearer and nearer to the terrifying picture. But it always did. When at last I'd turned the final leaf and saw the awful, scaly thing with protruding, fiery eyes and forked red tongue and clutching claws staring at me, I'd seem to suffocate again, and run shrieking from the library to hide my face in Mother's apron.

"It was like that last night. I knew I'd be frightened almost past endurance if I looked at the ikon again, but I couldn't resist the morbid urge to go downstairs. Finally I gave up the struggle and crept down, fighting with myself at every step, and losing the contest at each stride. I was fairly running when I reached the lower hall.

"A light was burning in the gunroom, and it must have been set going recently, for the lamp was still swaying like a pendulum when I entered. I started for the picture, but before I reached it my foot struck something, and when I looked down there was poor Wyndham lying dead before me. I tried to scream, but the breath seemed to stick in my throat. I just stood there trembling, and in my brain a thought kept pounding: 'The picture made him do it—the picture made him do it!'"

"You say you knew he did it. One does not doubt your intuition, but how were you certain it was suicide, *Mademoiselle?*"

"Because there was a smear of blood on the heel of his hand, as if it had spurted out when he drove the dagger through his heart. If someone else had stabbed him he'd have thrown his hand up to his heart or tried to pluck the dagger out; the blood would have been on his palm or on his fingers."

"*Bravo*, an excellent deduction. And then—"

"I wiped the blood off his poor hand and wiped my own hands on my nightdress, then composed his limbs and laid him like a cross to bar his wandering spirit if it came back seeking company. Then I crept back upstairs without stopping even to extinguish the lamp."

An agony of entreaty was in her face, and she clasped her hands imploringly, not theatrically, but instinctively, as she begged: "Please, please believe me. I've told you nothing but the truth. You don't think that I murdered Wyndham, do you?"

"We believe you utterly, *Mademoiselle*," de Grandin answered. "But what the police would think is something else again. It would be better if we kept our counsel, we three, and said nothing till we have had time to think."

"**N**OW WHAT?" I ASKED as we closed our interview with Karen Kirsten.

"I think that I should like a word or several with Monsieur Classon," he replied. "His anxiety to test his guests' reactions to that *sacré* picture was founded on no idle whim, my friend; there is something much decidedly more than meets the naked eye in all this business of the monkey, or I am vastly more mistaken than I think. Yes, of course."

But Philip Classon was nowhere to be found. We sought him in the drawing-room, the library, the little combination office and retreat which he had made above the ancient carriage house. Finally, all other places failing, we ventured to the gunroom. The night before we had observed that only a heavy Turkish tapestry closed off the gunroom from the wide central hall. Now, as we put the drapery back, we found our passage barred by a heavy sliding door which had been drawn and locked.

"*Sang du diable!*" de Grandin muttered when neither repeated knockings nor calls could elicit a response; "this is more than merely strange! He cannot have gone out, the police will not permit that any leave the premises without a pass from Captain Chenevert; he is not in any of the other rooms; *alors*, he is in there. But who would go into that devil-haunted place, and why does he persist in keeping silent? *Parbleu*, but I should like to tweak him by the nose."

"Perhaps he doesn't want to be disturbed," I ventured. "Events of the last twelve hours have been enough to make him worry. If—"

"If he does not answer our next summons I shall force the door," the little Frenchman interrupted. "I do not trust that gunroom, me. No, it is an evil place, the very temple of the evil genius which has haunted Mademoiselle Kirsten since she came here. *Holà*, Monsieur Classon, are you within? We have important matters to discuss!"

Utter silence answered him and with a sigh of vexation he went to seek the trooper who stood guard at the front door.

The young state constable was diffident. His orders were to watch the house and see that no one left. Regulations forbade the injury of private property unless a crime had been committed.

"*Morbleu*, a crime will be committed, that of assault and battery, if you refuse us aid," the little Frenchman blazed. "Am I not in charge here in Captain Chenevert's absence? But certainly. Are not *Monsieur le Capitaine* and I close friends, boon companions? Indubitably. Have we not been drunk together? It is entirely so. Break in the door, *mon vieux*; I will shoulder full responsibility."

Whoever built that door had understood his business, for it was not until de Grandin had added his weight to the stalwart young trooper's that the lock gave way and the heavy oaken panels slid aside.

"Good heavens!" I exclaimed as the gunroom stood revealed.

"Well, I'll be damned!" the trooper swore.

"*Dieu de Dieu de Dieu de Dieu!*" said Jules de Grandin.

No lamp was burning in the room, and the heavy, rep-bound curtains had been drawn across the windows to shut out the howling storm, but enough light filtered through to make large objects visible. Almost in the selfsame spot where Wyndham Farraday had stretched out cruciform in death something half leant, half knelt in the gloom, its outlines proclaiming it a man, but its attitude terrifyingly inhuman.

It was—or rather had been—Philip Classon, and he leant obliquely forward with half-bent knees and dangling hands that almost touched the floor, and head bent oddly sidewise, mouth partly opened to permit a quarter-inch of livid, blood-empurpled tongue to find escape between the teeth displayed by curled-back upper lip and limply hanging, flaccid lower jaw. A strand of knotted rope was round his neck, its upper end made fast to the bronze ringbolt which secured the hanging lamp. The rope had been too long and Classon too tall to permit conventional suicide. It had been necessary for him to lean, almost kneel, in order to secure sufficient downward drag to strangle himself. Any time within the first few seconds after dropping forward he could have saved himself by merely standing upright, but unconsciousness follows swiftly on compression of the great blood-vessels of the neck. . . . He was grotesque but placid. There had been no death agony.

D E GRANDIN AND I were regaling ourselves with black coffee liberally flavored with araq when Captain Chenevert stormed in after battling fifteen miles of snow-blocked roads.

"Another one?" he shouted angrily. "In the same room—within twelve hours? God A'mighty, this things gettin' to be a habit!"

Functionaries filled the house with utter chaos the remainder of the day. Photographers and finger-print experts from the police barracks; a sheriff's deputy, not quite clear as to either functions, rights or duties, but officiously anxious to impress us and the cynically polite state troopers with his own importance; the coroner, who being also the neighborhood mortician was wrung between the necessity of appearing appropriately grave and the difficultly suppressed delight at acquiring two cases from the same house in a single day. Finally the coroner's physician, a superannuated quack whose knowledge of postmortem phenomena of suicide was plainly inferior to the state policemen's expert training. But at last the grisly business finished, and Classon left his house feet-first upon a stretcher, his mortality concealed but not disguised beneath a not-too-fresh white sheet.

Dinner was a dismal rite, its only spot of color Karen Kirsten's golden hair and vivid, scarlet lips. No one strove for conversation, no one had much appetite for food, but when we went into the drawing-room for coffee and liqueurs the appetite for alcohol was something more than obvious. By nine o'clock the women were thick-tongued and maudlin, the men sunk in the utter taciturnity of saturnine intoxication.

Karen Kirsten left us early, pleading headache, and de Grandin and I followed her as quickly as we could. There was too much of the solemnity and none of the jollity of a wake about that dim-lit drawing-room.

"Y OU'VE SOME THEORY," I accused as we shut our bedroom door against the dismal crowd downstairs, "What is it?"

"This afternoon I have been reading in the library of our late host," de Grandin answered as he fit a cigarette, "and what I read may throw some light upon these self-destructions. Mademoiselle Kirsten furnished us the clue when she told us that accursèd picture came from Constantinople. You are familiar with the culture of Byzantium?"

"Only vaguely."

"One assumed as much. Very well: The Greeks of that old city were an evil lot. For the most part they conformed to Christianity only outwardly, and conformity with them was largely but an overlaying of the ancient cults with a thin veneer of outward faith. At heart they never lost their paganism, and paganism, my friend, is far from being the sweet, pretty thing our pastoral poets would depict it.

"Diana of the Ephesians, the All Mother, sometimes known as *Magna Mater*, was no prototype of the Blessèd Virgin; quite otherwise, I do assure you. There were dark mysteries in the groves of Aricia beside the lake men called the Mirror of Diana. Dionysos, who has been so celebrated by our neopagan poets that we commonly regard him as a hearty boon companion, was far from being so. True, he was the god of women, wine and song, but his women were harlots, his wine was drunkenness, his songs the ditties of the brothel. At his midnight festivals men and women cast their garments off and ran with staring eyes and unbound hair between the swaying trees, frenzied with the worship of their god, and his worship was unbridled lust. Little children were caught up by grown men and women, oftentimes their own parents, and forcibly initiated in the rites of drunkenness and carnal love. Aphrodite's priestesses were mere strumpets, working openly in competition with the common women of the town. Adonis, that pale lovely boy so famed in poetry and picture, was worshiped with the sacrifice of boars. *Ha*, but there were places where his female votaries, anxious to assimilate their god through the intervention of his sacred animals, assumed the name and rôle of sows!

"Such were the deities of paganism. They were not gods, but devils. Yet for hundreds of years they had been worshipped with revolting ceremonies. Would people long accustomed to a religion of drunkenness and lechery willingly forgo it for the gentle, simple rites of Christianity? Not willingly, but Constantine the Great gave them their choice of Cross or sword, and they chose the Cross. Yet ever the old and wicked faith persisted, always there were found some worshippers of the old ones in the secret places.

"*Bien*. It was not safe to flaunt their heathen practises. The lictors of the Emperor were ever on the watch for those who frequented suspicious gatherings; so, like the gambling-houses in your puritanical communities where gaming is prohibited, they must perforce resort to subterfuge. They had chapels to all outward seeming dedicated to the holy saints, and in those chapels they had furniture which seemed devoted to the Christian worship. But as the witty Monsieur Gilbert says in his opera *Pinafore*, 'Things are seldom what they seem.' A quick change here, the drawing of a curtain or pressing of a hidden spring there, and the sacred Christian ikons become horrid instruments of evil, base scenes which pander to the passions like those which graced the obscene sanctuary of the goddess Aphrodite.

"But in some instances these Christians-who-were-no-Christians did not depend on anything so crude as mere mechanical appliances. They had skilled workmen make the holy images, sacred pictures, sacerdotal vessels which by means of cunning spells and conjurations were endowed with power to change their aspect of their own accord when the concentrated thought of evil persons focused on them. Happily, we do not know just what these wicked old ones' magic was; we do know that it comprehended human sacrifice and defilement of the sacred things of Christianity. We know also that periodically it was necessary that a victim be immolated, else the evil power of these Jekyll-Hyde things made of gold and stone and silver would be lost.

"Now, Friend Trowbridge, thoughts are things. Who is it that is not unpleasantly impressed when standing in a dungeon of the bad old Middle Ages? Who can look upon the blade of that blood-thirsty guillotine with which so many brave and lovely necks were severed while the Terror raged in *la belle France* and forbear to shiver? Who can hold a hangman's rope within his hands and not have feelings of a vague uneasiness? No one but the veriest clod, *pardieu!* For why? Because, I tell you, thoughts are things. The evil passions, the emotions of hatred, anger or despair which flowed so freely round these solid objects soaked into them as water penetrates a porous stone. And ever and anon those very thoughts are loosed—exhaled, if you prefer the term—upon the world again.

"*Bien. Très bien. Tout va bien.* In Monsieur Classon's books I read something of the history of this so hateful picture which he showed us. The Crusaders under Baldwin stole it from a place they thought to be a Christian chapel when they sacked Constantinople. *Ha,* but the one who brought it back to Venice soon discovered his mistake! He set it up upon the altar of a church, and straightway evil things began to happen. Good women praying at that altar turned to strumpets; mild, godly men were roused to deeds of lust and violence. At last the good priests exorcised the lovely, evil thing; then to make assurance doubly sure, got rid of it.

"But Italians were Italians then as now. Instead of throwing it away, destroying it, they sold it to a Frenchman!

"Piously, my guileless countryman took the vile thing home with him and made an offering of it to a house of Benedictines. *Nom d'un rat,* within a month all hell had broken loose in that community! The monks forgot their vows, and I regret to state the nuns did likewise. They mortified the flesh with mutton pie on Fridays, they drank sweet wines and sang some tunes which had a most unchurchly air, and other things they did which more befitted soldiers and women of the camp than sober-lifed conventuals. It was a gay and naughty time they had until the bishop heard of it.

"Came the Revolution. Tired of being trodden underfoot the people rose, and like a rabid, sightless beast struck right and left in frenzy, cutting down the just and unjust in their anger. The convents and religious houses were suppressed and sacred vessels melted down and turned to money to assist the Government in waging war against the foreign despots who would seat a king again upon the throne of France and place the tyrant's heel once more upon the people's neck. But not this one, *hélas!*

"An English milord bought it and took it to his *triste* and foggy little island. *Eh bien*, he was quite a fellow, that one! The things he did were shocking, even to a generation which was noted for its tolerance. If he coveted a neighbor's wife that neighbor would have been advised to say his paternosters, for our gallant lord was skilled in sword-play and could crack a wine-glass stem at twenty paces with his pistol bullet. Also it appeared that Satan was a loving guardian of his own; for when the injured gentleman sent friends to wait on the seducer of his wife or fiancée or daughter, he might have saved his heirs much trouble if he had sent messengers to interview the clerk, the parson and the sexton, for he soon had need of all their offices.

"*Tiens*, the devil is a mocker, always. After many years of startlingly success-ful sin our noble lord was caught red-handed as a card cheat. His fortune had been wasted by extravagance, the Jews of Lombard Street refused to lend him further money on his lands, he became a bankrupt and perished miserably in debtor's prison.

"Among the items seized by creditors was this same accursèd picture. For years it gathered dust in storage, then was put on sale at auction. Monsieur Clas-son's uncle purchased it, but luckily for him he kept it in a safe deposit box, and not until a year ago was it brought out and placed among the treasures of the gunroom. Again his luck held good, for he was much away from home, and though there were some stories of some naughty intrigues in the servants' quar-ters, who knows if these were influenced by the presence of the picture in this house or simply the result of poor, weak human nature?

"At any rate *Monsieur* the Senior Classon died and his nephew took posses-sion of this house and all things in it. When did he first perceive this picture of the saint was not as other pictures? One wonders. Surely, he must have noticed it, for it had him greatly worried. A Frenchman, an Italian, an Irishman or High-land Scot, even a Spaniard, perhaps, would at once have recognized that there was something *outré*, other-worldly, in the way that picture seemed to change its scenes and in the feeling of repulsion yet attraction it engendered in him. But certainly. These people have imagination. But Americans and Englishmen? *Non!* 'This thing is not in keeping with the general rule of things,' they would tell themselves. 'Me, I have seen things, things which most certainly are not there to be seen. Therefore it is my eyes which are at fault. I shall consult an oculist. I have felt things I never felt before; I have felt the power of utter, con-centrated wickedness. I am not like that, me. No, I go to church five Sundays in the year, and pay my taxes and obey such laws as it is convenient to obey. I am a thoroughly good citizen, an Anglo-Saxon; I do not believe in fairies, Santa Claus or witchcraft, even if I do put credence in the literature that stock-promoters send me. This feeling of malaise I have whenever I am near that picture is due to indigestion. *Voilà*, I shall buy some pills next time I pass a pharmacy.' Yes, my, friend, that is the way of it.

"But Monsieur Classon was not easy in his mind. He had seen things, he had felt things that neither spectacles nor patent medicines could cure. And so instead of seeking someone competent to give advice, he tried experiments upon his friends, asked them to the gunroom, bade them look upon this old Greek ikon and tell him what it was they saw. If they saw nothing strange he took their testimony as evidence that his feelings of discomfort and his visions of unpleasant things had come from his disordered faculties, not from some outside source. *Tiens*, that way madness lay."

"But granting all you say, and it seems incredible, what induced Farraday to stab himself?" I asked.

He teased the needle-points of his mustache between a thoughtful thumb and forefinger. At length:

"Ecstasy is hard to reason with," he answered slowly. "We see it manifest itself in various phases. The nun who kneels in breathless adoration at the altar feels no discomfort though the cold stones bite her knees till the flesh is almost separated from the bone. The Indian fakir and the Moslem dervish inflict unutterable tortures on themselves, yet feel no pain. Devotees of olden gods, Aphrodite, Moloch, Dionysos, Adonis, cut and hacked and cruelly mutilated their bodies while ecstatic fervor gripped them. Monsieur Farraday was a highly nervous, highly imaginative, highly organized man. Influences which would not affect the average person took tremendous hold on him. He had lived not long, but much. It is probable there was no sensation which he had not tasted sometime. The lure to self-destruction grows more potent as we deplete the possibility of fresh experience. That the evil influence of this picture swayed him we can hardly doubt. He had hidden it, but he induced Mademoiselle Kirsten to come and see it. Why? Merely because it was an ancient thing of lovely workmanship? I cannot think so. Deliberately, having felt the lure and terror and excitement which inevitably followed a period of gazing at that evil picture, he desired to initiate her into them. It was like the drug addict who seeks to corrupt others to his evil practises. Yes, that is so."

"And Classon?"

"We cannot surely know. He has sealed his lips; but I think if he could talk he would tell a tale of slowly mounting terror, yet a fascination which would not let him leave off looking at the dreadful scenes he saw when the picture changed its aspect. Like Mademoiselle Kirsten and the book which terrified her so, he must needs go back and back to look and look again upon that which no human eye should see. It was like a siren-song luring him to sure destruction. When his friend Farraday had broken with the strain and sacrificed himself a votive offering to sin, the strain on Monsieur Classon was past beating. Perhaps his reason snapped, perhaps he felt an impulse to emulate his friend—any police officer knows that suicidal impulses are contagious. *En tout cas*, there it is. Farraday is dead, self-murdered, Classon is dead by his own hand—"

"And Miss Kirsten?" I broke in.

"*Précisément*, Mademoiselle Kirsten. I think we shall do well to watch that lovely one, both for her sake and ours."

"Ours?"

"Perfectly. If we keep close watch on her we shall prevent her emulation of those other poor ones; also we may find that she will guide us to an explanation of this Christian-heathen ikon."

"But good heavens, man! We've been chatting here for hours; she may have gone and—"

"No fear," he interrupted with a smile. "Me, I took the care. The gunroom door I nailed tight shut, for I was certain if she meant to harm herself it would be on the same spot where the others offered up their lives, and—*mordieu—nom de nom de nom de nom!* Why had I not thought of it before?"

"What in the world—"

"*S-s-sh*, my friend, keep still; be silent as the *chauve-souris* when she goes flitter-flitting in the twilight. Me, I have the inspiration, the idea, the—what you call him?—hunch. Yes."

He tiptoed down the corridor till he stood outside Miss Kirsten's door, then, almost in a shout, announced, "Yes, my friend, it is amazing. I cannot think how I forgot it. The gunroom door is nailed tight shut, but the windows are unfastened. I must have them nailed the first thing in the morning."

Making more noise than the occasion seemed to warrant, he tramped back to our door and slammed it, shoved me unceremoniously aside and seized his woolen muffler from the dresser.

"Come," he commanded as he wound the reefer round his neck, "I do not think we shall have long to wait."

"What the dickens are you up to?" I demanded as he led me down the stairs, taking care to step on the innermost edges of the treads so that no telltale squeak should give warning of our descent.

"Cannot you see? I have given her the hint, shown her how the way is open. If she feels the mastering-urge to seek the gunroom, perhaps intent on suicide, she will surely do it now, and through the open window. We must be there first."

I T WAS COLD AND quiet as a mausoleum in the empty gunroom as we clambered through the window. In accordance with custom a fire had been laid on the andirons, but no logs had burned there since the night before, and the eery chill which permeates all empty places filled the darkened chamber to its farthest corner. Stabbing through the darkness with his flashlight, de Grandin finally decided on the space behind a yellow-taffeta upholstered sofa as the spot to lay our ambush and we sank down to begin our vigil.

I had no way of telling time, for de Grandin had insisted that we leave our watches off lest their ticking warn our quarry of our presence. My feet grew cold, then stiff, then "full of pins and needles" as I crouched behind the couch. We dared not talk, we hardly dared to change position lest the creaking of a board betray us. At last, when I was willing to affirm on oath our vigil had endured a month, I felt the pressure of de Grandin's fingers on my elbow. Slowly, sound-lessly, but steadily, the window opposite to where we crouched was being raised. In the half-light shining from the snow outside we descried a figure almost shapeless in the gloom, but plainly feminine.

The rasping of a match, the little flare of orange flame against Egyptian darkness, the pale, clear glow of burning olive oil as the hanging lamps were lighted, showed us Karen Kirsten.

She had thrust her bare feet into fur-lined carriage boots, and with one hand she held her coat of priceless sable tight across her breast. Her eyes shone phosphorescent in the lamplight's glow, like the eyes of an animal. Her lips' moist crimson and the pearl-hard sheen of little teeth between them fascinated me. Unbidden came the thought of Clarimonde, of Margarita Hauffe and her victims.

She faced the ikon and we saw her bosom heave beneath its sheath of gleaming fur. Her breath came rasping, grindingly, almost like the labored breathing of a patient *in extremis* with nephritis. A little skirl of laughter stung her scarlet mouth, not loud, but terribly intense. I thought that never had I heard a cry more blasphemous than that light cachinnation.

Her eyes were straining toward the ikon which she had thrown open so its triple picture caught the full force of the ever-shifting beams which slanted downward from the swinging lamps. They were fixed, intense, half closed, as though the violence of her gaze was too annihilating to be loosed direct; it seemed as though the very substance of her soul and body would pour out of those set, staring eyes.

"Master," came her thin-edged whisper, mordant as a storm-blast in December, "lord, possessor, ever-living conqueror of flesh and soul and spirit—I am here!"

She kicked the fur-topped boots from off her feet and put her hands up to the collar of her coat, throwing back the garment and permitting it to fall in coruscating brown-black coils upon the floor behind her. Then with a wrench she tore her marigold-hued negligée from throat to hem.

Whiter than a figure carved from Parian marble, whiter than an image fresh-cut from new ivory she stood before the altar-table with its golden-gleaming ikon in her pallid slenderness.

It was no wonder that two hundred million movie-fans were mad about her, for she was beautiful almost past describing. Her graciously turned arms, her slender, gently swelling hips, her tapering legs, her full, high, pointed breasts were utterly breath-taking in their loveliness. The Greeks had a word for her, *chryselephantinos*—formed of gold and ivory!

Strangely mystic she stood there; more mysterious, the odd thought came to me, in the starkness of her nudity, than when hidden in the swathe of clinging garments.

Statue-still she stood, only her left hand moving a little as it fluttered upward toward her breast, then forward, like a tower toppling when its cornerstone is wrenched away, like a silver-birch tree crashing when the axman's final stroke cuts through its roots, she fell face-downward on the floor and lay there motion-less.

The lamplight glimmered on the whiteness of her body and the bright gold of her hair, flecking, flowing shadows interchanging quickly with bright spots of light as she clasped her hands behind her neck and beat her forehead softly on the floor before the ikon.

"The pictures—*mort d'un rat!*—see the pictures, good Friend Trowbridge; do you see them now?" de Grandin whispered in my ear.

I saw, and a wave of retching nausea swept across me as I looked.

How it happened I know not, but the little bits of colored stone which formed the pictures in the ikon had rearranged themselves, leaving the compositions of the scenes unchanged, but the subject matter utterly transformed. Where the group of laughing youths and maidens had been dancing there was now a ring of naked, scrawny parodies of men and women holding hands and dancing back to back in the dreadful rigadoon which marked the witches' sabbat. Where the pretty babes had crept in infantile delight was now a crowd of edematous, hid-eously bloated monsters, obscenely tumefied, their faces formless as the features of a creature molded out of dough, yet with enough resemblance to the human countenance to show the nightmare grins which stretched their livid mouths and creased their puffy cheeks. They crept and crawled and sprawled upon each other like sightless slugs which come to light when rotting logs are lifted, nor could I say if they were filled with loathing or obscene affection for each other as they intermingled all but formless bodies in a sort of fictive struggle.

But the center panel showed the greatest metamorphosis of all. The saint had shed his penitential garment of rough camel's hair and in its place his loins were girded with a leopardskin. The cross-topped staff was now a spear with gleaming lance-head; rawhide clogs had turned to golden buskins laced up the leg with straps of scarlet leather; a wreath of wild wood-roses bound his hair. It was a figure of sheer beauty, slender, straight, white-limbed and white-bodied as a girl, with a face too delicate to be a man's, not soft enough to be a woman's. The stern, forbidding glance had vanished, yet the eyes had lost no whit of their compulsion. They seemed to catch and hold all other eyes, they burned and smoldered with an intolerable sadness, yet their brightness was so great that it was fairly dazzling.

"*Mon Dieu*, it is the Lord of Evil!" Jules de Grandin whispered. "Satanas, Lucifer, Adonis!"

A chill we had not felt before came through the room. It was not the hard bitterness of the storm wind thrusting through the partly opened window, nor the close, still cold of a place long empty and unheated; there was an otherworldliness to it, the utter gelidness of the freezing eternities of interstellar space, a cold which seemed to paralyze the soul and spirit even as it numbed the body. Perhaps it was a trick of shifting lights caused by the swaying of the swinging lamps, but I could swear that on the wall behind the altar where the ikon stood there formed a patch of gloom, a shadow-shape which etched a figure in dull silhouette. And it was a figure of fear. Bat-winged it was, and horribly malformed, with slanting brow, protruding chin and great tusks jutting upward toward a nose which had the outline of a predatory vulture-beak. Great claw-armed hands attached to scaly arms seemed reaching outward through the semi-dark to fasten on the woman prostrate on the floor.

"*Attendez-moi*, my friend," de Grandin whispered; "do exactly as I say, or we shall lose our lives, perhaps our souls as well. When I step forward, do you take up anything that comes to hand and with it strike that cursèd ikon from its place. When you have struck, strike on, and keep on striking till you have demolished it completely. Oh, do not stop to bandy silly questions, friend; three lives depend upon your doing as I say, believe it!"

Mystified, but willing to obey his orders, I nodded mute assent, and reached up for a double-bladed Tartar ax which hung clamped to the wall above us.

"*Monsieur*"—de Grandin stepped from his concealment and bent his body stiffly from the hips as though addressing someone formally—"*Monsieur le Démon*, we will fight you for her. We are but mortal men, but by the faith we hold and by the strength that faith imparts, we fling our gage into your face, and offer you wager of battle for this woman's soul and body. More, if that is not enough, we will pledge our own, as well!"

It was not quite a laugh that answered him, indeed, it was not any sound which human ears can record; rather, it was as if a feeling, a subjective impression, of boundless and colossal scorn swept through the room, and like a dried leaf borne before the wind the little Frenchman was hurled back against the wall with an impact so terrific that I heard his bones crack as he struck the plaster-covered brick.

"Remember my instructions, good Friend Trowbridge—strike!" he gasped while he strove to wrench himself from the position into which he had been forced by that unseen malevolence.

He was suffering, I could see. The force with which he struck the wall had knocked the breath out of him, and something which I could not see was pressing on his throat, his diaphragm, his limbs, and held him with his arms outstretched and head thrown back as though he had been crucified. He gasped and fought for breath, but the struggle was uneven. In a moment he would fall unconscious from asphyxia, for no air could reach his lungs, and his lips were even then beginning to show blue while his eyeballs started from their sockets.

Across the room I leapt, swinging my double-bladed ax: about my head and bringing it down with all my might upon the golden ikon on the altar.

It seemed for an instant that I had cut into an electric cable, for a shock of numbing pain ran up my forearms, and I all but dropped my weapon as I staggered back.

"*Bravo, bravissimo*, my friend; that was nobly done!" De Grandin's voice was stronger, now; he had managed to inhale a breath of air, but even as he cheered me came a rattling in his throat. He was being throttled by his unseen adversary.

I struck again, and this time swept the ikon to the floor. It fell face-downward, its pictures hidden from my sight.

A surge of sudden wild, insensate anger swept through me. How or why I did not know, but this picture somehow was responsible for Jules de Grandin's plight. When I assaulted it he gained a temporary respite, in the momentary pause between my blows he suffered strangulation. I went stark, raving mad. For a wild, exhilarated moment I knew the fury and the joy our Saxon forebears felt when they went berserker and, armor cast aside, leapt bare-breasted into battle.

I felt my ax-blade cleave the ikon's golden plates, wrenched it free and struck again; chopping, hewing, battering. The heavy golden plates were bent and broken, now, and little bits of colored stone were strewn about the floor where my furious assault had smashed the priceless mosaics. I drove my axhead through the center panel, cleft the figure of the beautiful young man in twain, cut the dancing horrors into bits, smashed the crawling infantile monstrosities to utter formlessness; finally, insane with murderous rage, drove the battered golden casque into the fireplace as a hockey-player might shoot the puck into the goalnet, then reached up frenziedly, dragged down a hanging lamp and dashed it on the logs which lay in order ready for the match.

The dry wood kindled like a torch, and as the leaping ocherous flame licked hungrily at the shapeless mass which had a moment earlier been a priceless relic of the tessellater's art, de Grandin staggered forward, gasping thirstily for air like a diver coming to the surface after long immersion.

"Oh, excellent Friend Trowbridge, *brave camarade; camarade brave comme l'epée qu'il porte, parbleu,* but I do love you!" he exclaimed, and before I could defend myself had flung his arms around me, drawn me to him and planted a resounding kiss upon each cheek.

"I'm sorry that I lost my head and wrecked that lovely thing," I muttered, gazing ruefully at the melting gold and flame-discolored fragments of bright marble in the fireplace.

"Sorry? *Mort de ma vie,* it is your sober reason that speaks now—and when has truth been found in staid sobriety? Your instinct was truer when it urged that you consign this loathsome thing to cleansing fire. *Tiens,* had someone had the wit to do it seven hundred years ago, how much misery would have been averted! *Pah*"—he seized the poker and probed viciously at the remnants of the reliquary—"burn, curse you! Your makers and your votaries have stewed and fried in hell for centuries; go thou to join them, naughty thing!" Abruptly:

"Come, we have work to do, Friend Trowbridge; let us be about it."

We draped the sable coat round Karen Kirsten, drew the fur-trimmed boots upon her feet, bundled up her tattered negligée, then, quietly as a pair of burglars, took her through the window, through the service-pantry door, and upstairs to her bedroom.

"It is well *Monsieur le Capitaine* had but two men set to watch the house," de Grandin chuckled as we got the girl's pajamas on and drew the bedclothes over her. "The young man who snores so watchfully before the kitchen door would be surprised if he could know with what impunity his charges come and go at will, I think."

"I SUPPOSE YOU'RE GOING TO tell me thoughts are things, and that explains the goings-on we've witnessed?" I accused as we got into bed.

"By damn, I am," he answered with a sleepy laugh. "If it were not so I should have had a merry chase to find a reason for these evil doings. Attend me, if you please: That ikon might be called a devil's palimpsest. First the olden, wicked tessellaters contrived the scenes we saw tonight, the wicked worshipers of evil gods who danced together back to back, as in the days when dancing widdershins paid honor to the pig-faced Moloch, the terrible, amorphous things which typified primeval wickedness, finally the Lord Adonis. Then by a trick of cunning workmanship they overlaid their true design with those sweet, innocuous scenes of innocence, and in the center set the picture of a saint. 'Beauty is in the beholder's eye,' the ancient proverb says. It might have added that wickedness and goodness are to a great extent the same. Only when summoned by deliberate thought of evil did the underlying pictures dedicated to the unclean worship of the evil old ones come to light; at other times the ikon showed an air of innocence. *Ha,* but that was in the very long ago, my friend. Like a jar of porous earthenware filled constantly with aromatic liquids, this ikon was the center of a very evil worship, the receptacle of concentrated thoughts of wickedness and hate. Thoughts are things; they filled the very substance of the ikon as the aromatic liquors will in time so permeate the fiber of the earthen jug that it will always afterward give off their scent. Yes, certainly.

"In time the evil principle became so strongly concentrated in this ikon that it changed unbidden from its good to wicked aspect, and this was so especially when the person who beheld it harbored secret thoughts of sin. More, it added to, it strengthened these desires for evil. Did the person in its presence have suppressed longings to forsake the ways of soberness and take to drink? His resolution to remain a sober citizen was straightway weakened to the breaking-point, his thirst for drink increased tenfold. And so right through the Decalogue. Whatever secret evil one had struggled with and conquered became so magnified when he came in this ikon's presence that be was unable to resist the sinful urge. He was vanquished, beaten, routed, lost in sin.

"And as person after person yielded to its wicked influence this devil's tool waxed ever greater in its strength. Eventually it was not necessary for the one corrupted to have harbored evil thought; he need only be impressionable, psychic, to behold the changing of the pictures and, unless he had unusual strength of character, to succumb to their foul lure. Karen Kirsten realized this when first she stepped into the gunroom; Wyndham Farraday had suffered from the same experience; often Philippe Classon must have seen those pictures change; it was that which preyed upon his mind and made him seek to lull his fears by having others look at them and hear the testimony which they gave. You see? It is quite simple, Yes. Thoughts most assuredly are things."

"But why should they select Adonis as typifying Evil?" I demanded. "As I recall it, he was a shy young man whom Venus wooed—"

"In Monsieur Shakespeare's poems, yes," he interrupted, "but not in the belief of those who worshiped Evil for its evil self. No, not at all; by no means.

"When those wicked ones were gathered to make mock of holy things and bend the knee to sinfulness, they invoked some god or goddess of the ancient days, or, in later times, the devil. At gatherings of devil-worshipers it was not always as a hairy man or goat that the devil was adored. He had other aspects, too. Sometimes he came as a most beautiful young man, Lucifer the Lightbearer; as Baron Satanas, cold, haughty, proud, but most distinguished in appearance; sometimes as Adonis, the young man beautiful and cold as ice, impervious alike to little children's lisping pleas or woman's charming beauty—it was not bashfulness, but utter, cold indifference that made Adonis proof against the blandishments of the Queen of Love and Beauty. He it was— still is, *parbleu!*—who gave nothing in return for worship but lies and bitter disappointments.

"Besides, the men who made those pictures and the worshippers who bent the knee before it were Greeks; degenerate Greeks, of course, but still inheritors of the culture that was Athens. A Greek could not do homage to a god, even to a god of evil, who was anything but beautiful."

"That dreadful shadow that we saw, the shadow that seemed to detach itself from the wall and reach toward Karen Kirsten just before you challenged it?" I asked. "That was—"

"Thought made manifest, my friend. The evil thought which for generation upon generation had been poured upon that cursèd ikon, that devil's palimpsest. It was the same thought that induced rebellion in the heavens against the power of good, the thought which prompted Cain to slay his brother, which brought the sacrificial babes to Moloch; *parbleu*, it was everything that is detestable and vile concresced into that little reservoir which was that never-to-be-sufficiently-anathematized palimpsest of Satan!"

"It's positively the damnedest thing I ever saw, swore Captain Chenevert next day. "Two killings in that room with no more clues to 'em than if they'd been in China. Then someone sneaks in there last night and smashes up a piece of *bric-à-brac* so valuable that no one can appraise it. Hanged if it doesn't almost seem as if the place were haunted!"

"I damn think you have right, *Monsieur le Capitaine*," de Grandin answered, his face expressionless as a death mask.

He reached out for the bell-pull: "Will you have Scots or Irish with your soda water, gentlemen?"

Pledged to the Dead

T HE AUTUMN DUSK HAD stained the sky with shadows and orange oblongs traced the windows in my neighbors' homes as Jules de Grandin and I sat sipping *kaiserschmarrn* and coffee in the study after dinner. "*Mon Dieu*," the little Frenchman sighed, "I have the *mal du pays*, my friend. The little children run and play along the roadways at Saint Cloud, and on the Île de France the pastry cooks set up their booths. *Corbleu*, it takes the strength of character not to stop and buy those cakes of so much taste and fancy! The Napoléons, they are crisp and fragile as a coquette's promise, the éclairs filled with cool, sweet cream, the cream-puffs all aglow with cherries. Just to see them is to love life better. They—"

The shrilling of the door-bell startled me. The pressure on the button must have been that of one who leant against it. "Doctor Trowbridge; I must see him right away!" a woman's voice demanded as Nora McGinnis, my household facto-tum, grudgingly responded to the hail.

"Th' docthor's offiss hours is over, ma'am," Nora answered frigidly. "Ha'f past nine ter eleven in th' marnin', an' two ter four in th' afthernoon is when he sees his patients. If it's an urgent case ye have there's lots o' good young docthors in th' neighborhood, but Docthor Trowbridge—"

"Is he here?" the visitor demanded sharply.

"He is, an' he's afther digestin' his dinner—an' an illigant dinner it wuz, though I do say so as shouldn't—an' he can't be disturbed—"

"He'll see me, all right. Tell him it's Nella Bentley, and I've *got* to talk to him!"

De Grandin raised an eyebrow eloquently. "The fish at the aquarium have greater privacy than we, my friend," he murmured, but broke off as the visitor came clacking down the hall on high French heels and rushed into the study half a dozen paces in advance of my thoroughly disapproving and more than semi-scandalized Nora.

"Doctor Trowbridge, won't you help me?" cried the girl as she fairly leaped across the study and flung her arms about my shoulders. "I can't tell Dad or Mother, they wouldn't understand; so you're the only one—oh, excuse me, I thought you were alone!" Her face went crimson as she saw de Grandin standing by the fire.

"It's quite all right, my dear," I soothed, freeing myself from her almost hysterical clutch. "This is Doctor de Grandin, with whom I've been associated many times; I'd be glad to have the benefit of his advice, if you don't mind."

She gave him her hand and a wan smile as I performed the introduction, but her eyes warmed quickly as he raised her fingers to his lips with a soft "*Enchanté, Mademoiselle.*" Women, animals and children took instinctively to Jules de Grandin.

Nella dropped her coat of silky shaven lamb and sank down on the study couch, her slim young figure molded in her knitted dress of coral rayon as revealingly as though she had been cased in plastic cellulose. She has long, violet eyes and a long mouth; smooth, dark hair parted in the middle; a small straight nose, and a small pointed chin. Every line of her is long, but definitely feminine; breasts and hips and throat and legs all delicately curved, without a hint of angularity.

"I've come to see you about Ned," she volunteered as de Grandin lit her cigarette and she sent a nervous smoke stream gushing from between red, trembling lips. "He—he's trying to run out on me!"

"You mean Ned Minton?" I asked, wondering what a middle-aged physician could prescribe for wandering Romeos.

"I certainly do mean Ned Minton," she replied, "and I mean business, too. The darn, romantic fool!"

De Grandin's slender brows arched upward till they nearly met the beige-blond hair that slanted sleekly backward from his forehead. "*Pardonnez-moi,*" he murmured. "Did I understand correctly, *Mademoiselle?* Your *amoureux*—how do you say him?—sweetheart?—has shown a disposition toward unfaithfulness, yet you accuse him of romanticism?"

"He's not unfaithful, that's the worst of it. He's faithful as Tristan and the chevalier Bayard lumped together, *sans peur et sans reproche*, you know. Says we can't get married, 'cause—"

"Just a moment, dear," I interrupted as I felt my indignation mounting. "D'ye mean the miserable young puppy cheated, and now wants to welch—"

Her blue eyes widened, then the little laughter-wrinkles formed around them. "You dear old mid-Victorian!" she broke in. "No, he ain't done wrong by our Nell, and I'm not asking you to take your shotgun down and force him to make me an honest woman. Suppose we start at the beginning: then we'll get things straight.

"You assisted at both our débuts, I've been told; you've known Ned and me since we were a second old apiece, haven't you?"

I nodded.

"Know we've always been crazy about each other, too; in grammar school, high school and college, don't you?"

"Yes," I agreed.

"All right. We've been engaged ever since our freshman year at Beaver. Ned just had his frat pin long enough to pin it on my shoulder-strap at the first fresh-man dance. Everything was set for us to stand up in the chancel and say 'I do' this June; then Ned's company sent him to New Orleans last December." She paused, drew deeply at her cigarette, crushed its fire out in an ash-tray, and set a fresh one glowing.

"That started it. While he was down there it seemed that he got playful. Mixed up with some glamorous Creole gal." Once more she lapsed into silence and I could see the heartbreak showing through the armor of her flippant manner.

"You mean he fell in love—"

"I certainly do *not!* If he had, I'd have handed back his ring and said 'Bless you, me children', even if I had to bite my heart in two to do it; but this is no case of a new love crowding out the old. Ned still loves me; never stopped lov-ing me. That's what makes it all seem crazy as a hashish-eater's dream. He was on the loose in New Orleans, doing the town with a crowd of local boys, and prob'bly had too many Ramos fizzes. Then he barged into this Creole dame's place, and—" she broke off with a gallant effort at a smile. "I guess young fel-lows aren't so different nowadays than they were when you were growing up, sir. Only today we don't believe in sprinkling perfume in the family cesspool. Ned cheated, that's the bald truth of it; he didn't stop loving me, and he hasn't stopped now, but I wasn't there and that other girl was, and there were no con-ventions to be recognized. Now he's fairly melting with remorse, says he's not worthy of me—wants to break off our engagement, while he spends a lifetime doing penance for a moment's folly."

"But good heavens," I expostulated, "if you're willing to forgive—"

"You're telling me!" she answered bitterly. "We've been over it a hundred times. This isn't 1892; even nice girls know the facts of life today, and while I'm no more anxious than the next one to put through a deal in shopworn goods, I still love Ned, and I don't intend to let a single indiscretion rob us of our happiness. I—" the hard exterior veneer of modernism melted from her like an autumn ice-glaze melting in the warm October sun, and the tears coursed down her cheeks, cutting little valleys in her carefully applied make-up. "He's my man, Doctor," she sobbed bitterly. "I've loved him since we made mud-pies together; I'm hungry, thirsty for him. He's everything to me, and if he follows out this fool renunciation he seems set on, it'll kill me!"

De Grandin tweaked a waxed mustache-end thoughtfully. "You exemplify the practicality of woman, *Mademoiselle*; I applaud your sound, hard common sense," he told her. "Bring this silly young romantic foolish one to me. I will tell him—"

"But he won't come," I interrupted. "I know these hard-minded young asses. When a lad is set on being stubborn—"

"Will you go to work on him if I can get him here?" interjected Nella.

"Of a certitude, *Mademoiselle*."

"You won't think me forward or unmaidenly?"

"This is a medical consultation, *Mademoiselle*."

"All right; be in the office this time tomorrow night. I'll have my wandering boy friend here if I have to bring him in an ambulance."

H ER PERFORMANCE MATCHED HER promise almost too closely for our comfort. We had just finished dinner next night when the frenzied shriek of tortured brakes, followed by a crash and the tinkling spatter of smashed glass, sounded in the street before the house, and in a moment feet dragged heavily across the porch. We were at the door before the bell could buzz, and in the disk of brightness sent down by the porch light saw Nella bent half double, stumbling forward with a man's arm draped across her shoulders. His feet scuffed blindly on the boards, as though they had forgot the trick of walking, or as if all strength had left his knees. His head hung forward, lolling drunkenly; a spate of blood ran down his face and smeared his collar.

"Good Lord!" I gasped. "What—"

"Get him in the surgery—quick!" the girl commanded in a whisper. "I'm afraid I rather overdid it."

Examination showed the cut across Ned's forehead was more bloody than extensive, while the scalp-wound which plowed backward from his hairline needed but a few quick stitches.

Nella whispered to us as we worked. "I got him to go riding with me in my runabout. Just as we got here I let out a scream and swung the wheel hard over to the right. I was braced for it, but Ned was unprepared, and went right through the windshield when I ran the car into the curb. Lord, I thought I'd killed him when I saw the blood—you do think he'll come through all right, don't you, Doctor?"

"No thanks to you if he does, you little ninny!" I retorted angrily. "You might have cut his jugular with your confounded foolishness. If—"

"S-s-sh, he's coming out of it!" she warned. "Start talking to him like a Dutch uncle; I'll be waiting in the study if you want me," and with a tattoo of high heels she left us with our patient.

"Nella! Is she all right?" Ned cried as he half roused from the surgery table. "We had an accident—"

"But certainly, *Monsieur*," de Grandin soothed. "You were driving past our house when a child ran out before your car and *Mademoiselle* was forced to swerve aside to keep from hitting it. You were cut about the face, but she escaped all injury. Here"—he raised a glass of brandy to the patient's lips—"drink this. Ah, so. That is better, *n'est-ce-pas?*"

For a moment he regarded Ned in silence, then, abruptly: "You are distrait, *Monsieur*. When we brought you in we were forced to give you a small whiff of ether while we patched your cuts, and in your delirium you said—"

The color which had come into Ned's cheeks as the fiery cognac warmed his veins drained out again, leaving him as ghastly as a corpse. "Did Nella hear me?" he asked hoarsely. "Did I blab—"

"Compose yourself, *Monsieur*," de Grandin bade. "She heard nothing, but it would be well if we heard more. I think I understand your difficulty. I am a physician and a Frenchman and no prude. This renunciation which you make is but the noble gesture. You have been unfortunate, and now you fear. Have courage; no infection is so bad there is no remedy—"

Ned's laugh was hard and brittle as the tinkle of a breaking glass. "I only wish it were the thing you think," he interrupted. "I'd have you give me salvarsan and see what happened; but there isn't any treatment I can take for this. I'm not delirious, and I'm not crazy, gentlemen; I know just what I'm saying. Insane as it may sound, I'm pledged to the dead, and there isn't any way to bail me out."

"*Eh*, what is it you say?" de Grandin's small blue eyes were gleaming with the light of battle as he caught the occult implication in Ned's declaration. "Pledged to the dead? *Comment cela?*"

Ned raised himself unsteadily and balanced on the table edge.

"It happened in New Orleans last winter," he answered. "I'd finished up my business and was on the loose, and thought I'd walk alone through the *Vieux Carré*—the old French Quarter. I'd had dinner at Antoine's and stopped around at the Old Absinthe House for a few drinks, then strolled down to the French Market for a cup of chicory coffee and some doughnuts. Finally I walked down Royal Street to look at Madame Lalaurie's old mansion; that's the famous haunted house, you know. I wanted to see if I could find a ghost. Good Lord, I *wanted* to!

"The moon was full that night, but the house was still as old Saint Denis Cemetery, so after Peering through the iron grilles that shut the courtyard from the street for half an hour or so, I started back toward Canal Street.

"I'd almost reached Bienville Street when just as I passed one of those funny two-storied iron-grilled balconies so many of the old houses have I heard something drop on the sidewalk at my feet. It was a japonica, one of those rose-like flowers they grow in the courtyard gardens down there. When I looked up, a girl was laughing at me from the second story of the balcony. '*Mon fleuron, monsieur, s'il vous plaît*,' she called, stretching down a white arm for the bloom.

"The moonlight hung about her like a veil of silver tissue, and I could see her plainly as though it had been noon. Most New Orleans girls are dark. She was fair, her hair was very fine and silky and about the color of a frosted chestnut-burr. She wore it in a long bob with curls around her face and neck, and I knew without being told that those ringlets weren't put in with a hot iron. Her face was pale, colorless and fine-textured as a magnolia petal, but her lips were brilliant crimson. There was something reminiscent of those ladies you see pictured in Directoire prints about her; small, regular features, straight, white, high-waisted gown tied with a wide girdle underneath her bosom, low, round-cut neck and tiny, ball-puff sleeves that left her lovely arms uncovered to the shoulder. She was like Rose Beauharnais or Madame de Fontenay, except for her fair hair, and her eyes. Her eyes were like an Eastern slave's, languishing and passionate, even when she laughed. And she was laughing then, with a throaty, almost caressing laugh as I tossed the flower up to her and she leant across the iron railing, snatching at it futilely as it fell just short of reach.

"'C'est sans profit,' she laughed at last. 'Your skill is too small or my arm too short, m'sieur. Bring it up to me.'

"'You mean for me to come up there?' I asked.

"'But certainly. I have teeth, but will not bite you—maybe.'

"The street door to the house was open; I pushed it back, groped my way along a narrow hall and climbed a flight of winding stairs. She was waiting for me on the balcony, lovelier, close up, if that were possible, than when I'd seen her from the sidewalk. Her gown was China silk, so sheer and clinging that the shadow of her charming figure showed against its rippling folds like a lovely silhouette; the sash which bound it was a six-foot length of rainbow ribbon tied coquettishly beneath her shoulders and trailing in fringed ends almost to her dress-hem at the back; her feet were stockingless and shod with sandals fastened with cross-straps of purple grosgrain laced about the ankles. Save for the small gold rings that scintillated in her ears, she wore no ornaments of any kind.

"'Mon fleur, m'sieur,' she ordered haughtily, stretching out her hand; then her eyes lighted with sudden laughter and she turned her back to me, bending her head forward. 'But no, it fell into your hands; it is that you must put it in its place again,' she ordered, pointing to a curl where she wished the flower set. 'Come, m'sieur, I wait upon you.'

"On the settee by the wall a guitar lay. She picked it up and ran her slim, pale fingers twice across the strings, sounding a soft, melancholy chord. When she began to sing, her words were slurred and languorous, and I had trouble understanding them; for the song was ancient when Bienville turned the first spadeful of earth that marked the ramparts of New Orleans:

O knights of gay Toulouse
And sweet Beaucaire,
Greet me my own true love
And speak him fair . . .

"Her voice had the throaty, velvety quality one hears in people of the Southern countries, and the words of the song seemed fairly to yearn with the sadness and passionate longing of the love-bereft. But she smiled as she put by her instrument, a curious smile, which heightened the mystery of her face, and her wide eyes seemed suddenly half questing, half drowsy, as she asked, 'Would you ride off upon your grim, pale horse and leave poor little Julie d'Ayen famishing for love, m'sieur?'

"'Ride off from you?' I answered gallantly. 'How can you ask?' A verse from Burns came to me:

Then fare thee well, my bonny lass,
And fare thee well awhile,
And I will come to thee again
An it were ten thousand mile.

"There was something avid in the look she gave me. Something more than mere gratified vanity shone in her eyes as she turned her face up to me in the moonlight. 'You mean it?' she demanded in a quivering, breathless voice.

"'Of course,' I bantered. 'How could you doubt it?'

"'Then swear it—seal the oath with blood!'

"Her eyes were almost closed, and her lips were lightly parted as she leant toward me. I could see the thin, white line of tiny, gleaming teeth behind the lush red of her lips; the tip of a pink tongue swept across her mouth, leaving it warmer, moister, redder than before; in her throat a small pulse throbbed palpitatingly. Her lips were smooth and soft as the flower-petals in her hair, but as they crushed on mine they seemed to creep about them as though endowed with a volition of their own. I could feel them gliding almost stealthily, searching greedily, it seemed, until they covered my entire mouth. Then came a sudden searing burn of pain which passed as quickly as it flashed across my lips, and she seemed inhaling deeply, desperately, as though to pump the last faint gasp of breath up from my lungs. A humming sounded in my ears; everything went dark around me as if I had been plunged in some abysmal flood; a spell of dreamy lassitude was stealing over me when she pushed me from her so abruptly that I staggered back against the iron railing of the gallery.

"I gasped and fought for breath like a winded swimmer coming from the water, but the half-recaptured breath seemed suddenly to catch itself unbidden in my throat, and a tingling chill went rippling up my spine. The girl had dropped down to her knees, staring at the door which let into the house, and as I looked I saw a shadow writhe across the little pool of moonlight which lay upon the sill. Three feet or so in length it was, thick through as a man's wrist, the faint light shining dully on its scaly armor and disclosing the forked lightning of its darting tongue. It was a cotton-mouth—a water moccasin—deadly as a rattlesnake, but more dangerous, for it sounds no warning before striking, and can strike when only half coiled. How it came there on the second-story gallery of a house so far from any swampland I had no means of knowing, but there it lay, bent in the design of a double S its wedge-shaped head swaying on upreared neck a scant six inches from the girl's soft bosom, its forked tongue darting deathly menace. Half paralyzed with fear and loathing, I stood there in a perfect ecstasy of horror, not daring to move hand or foot lest I aggravate the reptile into striking. But my terror changed to stark amazement as my senses slowly registered the scene. The girl was talking to the snake and—it listened as a person might have done!

"'*Non, non, grand'tante; halte là!*' she whispered. '*Cela est à moi—il est dévoué!*'

"The serpent seemed to pause uncertainly, grudgingly, as though but half convinced, then shook its head from side to side, much as an aged person might when only half persuaded by a youngster's argument. Finally, silently as a shadow, it slithered back again into the darkness of the house.

"Julie bounded to her feet and put her hands upon my shoulders.

"'You mus' go, my friend,' she whispered fiercely. 'Quickly, ere she comes again. It was not easy to convince her; she is old and very doubting. O, I am afraid—afraid!'

"She hid her face against my arm, and I could feel the throbbing of her heart against me. Her hands stole upward to my cheeks and pressed them between palms as cold as graveyard clay as she whispered, 'Look at me, *mon beau*.' Her eyes were closed, her lips were slightly parted, and beneath the arc of her long lashes I could see the glimmer of fast-forming tears. '*Embrasse moi*,' she commanded in a trembling breath. 'Kiss me and go quickly, but O *mon chèr*, do not forget poor little foolish Julie d'Ayen who has put her trust in you. Come to me again tomorrow night!'

"I was reeling as from vertigo as I walked back to the Greenwald, and the bartender looked at me suspiciously when I ordered a sazarac. They've a strict rule against serving drunken men at that hotel. The liquor stung my lips like liquid flame, and I put the cocktail down half finished. When I set the fan to going and switched the light on in my room I looked into the mirror and saw two little beads of fresh, bright blood upon my lips. 'Good Lord!' I murmured stupidly as I brushed the blood away; 'she bit me!'

"It all seemed so incredible that if I had not seen the blood upon my mouth I'd have thought I suffered from some lunatic hallucination, or one too many frappés at the Absinthe House. Julie was as quaint and out of time as a Directoire print, even in a city where time stands still as it does in old New Orleans. Her costume, her half-shy boldness, her—this was simply madness, nothing less!—her conversation with that snake!

"What was it she had said? My French was none too good, and in the circumstances it was hardly possible to pay attention to her words, but if I'd understood her, she'd declared, 'He's mine; he has dedicated himself to me!' And she'd addressed that crawling horror as '*grand'tante*—great-aunt!'

"'Feller, you're as crazy as a cockroach!' I admonished my reflection in the mirror. 'But I know what'll cure you. You're taking the first train north tomorrow morning, and if I ever catch you in the *Vieux Carré* again, I'll—'

"A sibilating hiss, no louder than the noise made by steam escaping from a kettle-spout, sounded close beside my foot. There on the rug, coiled in readiness to strike, was a three-foot cottonmouth, head swaying viciously from side to side, wicked eyes shining in the bright light from the chandelier. I saw the muscles in the creatures fore-part swell, and in a sort of horror-trance I watched its head dart forward, but, miraculously, it stopped its stroke half-way, and drew its head back, turning to glance menacingly at me first from one eye, then the other. Somehow, it seemed to me, the thing was playing with me as a cat might play a mouse, threatening, intimidating, letting me know it was master of the situation and could kill me any time it wished, but deliberately refraining from the death-stroke.

"With one leap I was in the middle of my bed, and when a squad of bellboys came running in response to the frantic call for help I telephoned, they found me crouched against the headboard, almost wild with fear.

"They turned the room completely inside out, rolling back the rugs, probing into chairs and sofa, emptying the bureau drawers, even taking down the towels from the bathroom rack, but nowhere was there any sign of the water moccasin that had terrified me. At the end of fifteen minutes' search they accepted half a dollar each and went grinning from the room. I knew it would be useless to appeal for help again, for I heard one whisper to another as they paused outside my door: 'It ain't right to let them Yankees loose in N'Orleans; they don't know how to hold their licker.'

"I didn't take a train next morning. Somehow, I'd an idea—crazy as it seemed—that my promise to myself and the sudden, inexplicable appearance of the snake beside my foot were related in some way. Just after luncheon I thought I'd put the theory to a test.

"'Well,' I said aloud, 'I guess I might as well start packing. Don't want to let the sun go down and find me here—'

"My theory was right. I hadn't finished speaking when I heard the warning hiss, and there, poised ready for the stroke, the snake was coiled before the door.

And it was no phantom, either, no figment of an overwrought imagination. It lay upon a rug the hotel management had placed before the door to take the wear of constant passage from the carpet, and I could see the high pile of the rug crushed down beneath its weight. It was flesh and scales—and fangs!—and it coiled and threatened me in my twelfth-floor room in the bright sunlight of the afternoon.

"Little chills of terror chased each other up my back, and I could feel the short hairs on my neck grow stiff and scratch against my collar, but I kept myself in hand. Pretending to ignore the loathsome thing, I flung myself upon the bed.

"'Oh, well,' I said aloud, 'there really isn't any need of hurrying. I promised Julie that I'd come to her tonight, and I mustn't disappoint her.' Half a minute later I roused myself upon my elbow and glanced toward the door. The snake was gone.

"'Here's a letter for you, Mr. Minton,' said the desk clerk as I paused to leave my key. The note was on gray paper edged with silver-gilt, and very highly scented. The penmanship was tiny, stilted and ill-formed, as though the author were unused to writing, but I could make it out:

Adoré
Meet me in St. Denis Cemetery at sunset
À vous de cœur pour l'éternité
Julie

"I stuffed the note back in my pocket. The more I thought about the whole affair the less I liked it. The flirtation had begun harmlessly enough, and Julie was as lovely and appealing as a figure in a fairy-tale, but there are unpleasant aspects to most fairy-tales, and this was no exception. That scene last night when she had seemed to argue with a full-grown cottonmouth, and the mysterious appearance of the snake whenever I spoke of breaking my promise to go back to her—there was something too much like black magic in it. Now she addressed me as her adored and signed herself for eternity; finally named a graveyard as our rendezvous. Things had become a little bit too thick.

"I was standing at the corner of Canal and Batonne Streets, and crowds of office workers and late shoppers elbowed past me. 'I'll be damned if I'll meet her in a cemetery, or anywhere else,' I muttered. 'I've had enough of all this nonsense—'

"A woman's shrill scream, echoed by a man's hoarse shout of terror, interrupted me. On the marble pavement of Canal Street, with half a thousand people bustling by, lay coiled a three-foot water moccasin. Here was proof. I'd seen it twice in my room at the hotel, but I'd been alone each time. Some form of weird hypnosis might have made me think I saw it, but the screaming woman and the shouting man, these panic-stricken people in Canal Street, couldn't all be victims of a spell which had been cast on me. 'All right, I'll go,' I almost shouted, and instantly, as though it had been but a puff of smoke, the snake was gone, the half-fainting woman and a crowd of curious bystanders asking what was wrong left to prove I had not been the victim of some strange delusion.

"Old Saint Denis Cemetery lay drowsing in the blue, faint twilight. It has no graves as we know them, for when the city was laid out it was below sea-level and bodies were stored away in crypts set row on row like lines of pigeonholes in walls as thick as those of mediæval castles. Grass-grown aisles run between the rows of vaults, and the effect is a true city of the dead with narrow streets shut in by close-set houses. The rattle of a trolley car in Rampart Street came to me faintly as I walked between the rows of tombs; from the river came the mellow-throated bellow of a steamer's whistle, but both sounds were muted as though heard from a great distance. The tomb-lined bastions of Saint Denis hold the present out as firmly as they hold the memories of the past within.

"Down one aisle and up another I walked, the close-clipped turf deadening my footfalls so I might have been a ghost come back to haunt the ancient burial ground, but nowhere was there sign or trace of Julie. I made the circuit of the labyrinth and finally paused before one of the more pretentious tombs.

"'Looks as if she'd stood me up,' murmured. 'If she has, I have a good excuse to—'

"'But non, mon coeur, I have not disappointed you!' a soft voice whispered in my ear. 'See, I am here.'

"I think I must have jumped at sound of her greeting, for she clapped her hands delightedly before she put them on my shoulders and turned her face up for a kiss. 'Silly one,' she chided, 'did you think your Julie was unfaithful?'

"I put her hands away as gently as I could, for her utter self-surrender was embarrassing. 'Where were you?' I asked, striving to make neutral conversation. 'I've been prowling round this graveyard for the last half-hour, and came through this aisle not a minute ago, but I didn't see you—'

"'Ah, but I saw you, chéri; I have watched you as you made your solemn rounds like a watchman of the night. Ohé, but it was hard to wait until the sun went down to greet you, mon petit!'

"She laughed again, and her mirth was mellowly musical as the gurgle of cool water poured from a silver vase.

"'How could you have seen me?' I demanded. 'Where were you all this time?'

"'But here, of course,' she answered naïvely, resting one hand against the graystone slab that scaled the tomb.

"I shook my head bewilderedly. The tomb, like all the others in the deeply recessed wall, was of rough cement encrusted with small seashells, and its sides were straight and blank without a spear of ivy clinging to them. A sparrow could not have found cover there, yet . . .

"Julie raised herself on tiptoe and stretched her arms out right and left while she looked at me through half-closed, smiling eyes. '*Je suis engourdie*—I am stiff with sleep,' she told me, stifling a yawn. 'But now that you are come, *mon cher*, I am wakeful as the pussy-cat that rouses at the scampering of the mouse. Come, let us walk in this garden of mine.' She linked her arm through mine and started down the grassy, grave-lined path.

"Tiny shivers—not of cold—were flickering through my cheeks and down my neck beneath my ears. I *had* to have an explanation . . . the snake, her declaration that she watched me as I searched the cemetery—and from a tomb where a beetle could not have found a hiding-place—her announcement she was still stiff from sleeping, now her reference to a half-forgotten graveyard as her garden.

"'See here, I want to know—' I started, but she laid her hand across my lips.

"'Do not ask to know too soon, *mon coeur*,' she bade. 'Look at me, am I not veritably *élégante?*' She stood back a step, gathered up her skirts and swept me a deep curtsy.

"There was no denying she was beautiful. Her tightly curling hair had been combed high and tied back with a fillet of bright violet tissue which bound her brows like a diadem and at the front of which an aigret plume was set. In her ears were hung two beautifully matched cameos, outlined in gold and seed-pearls, and almost large as silver dollars; a necklace of antique dull-gold hung round her throat, and its pendant was a duplicate of her ear-cameos, while a bracelet of matte-gold set with a fourth matched anaglyph was clasped about her left arm just above the elbow. Her gown was sheer white muslin, low cut at front and back, with little puff-sleeves at the shoulders, fitted tightly at the bodice and flaring sharply from a high-set waist. Over it she wore a narrow scarf of violet silk, hung behind her neck and dropping down on either side in front like a clergyman's stole. Her sandals were gilt leather, heel-less as a ballet dancer's shoes and laced with violet ribbons. Her lovely, pearl-white hands were bare of rings, but on the second toe of her right foot there showed a little cameo which matched the others which she wore.

"I could feel my heart begin to pound and my breath come quicker as I looked at her, but:

"'You look as if you're going to a masquerade,' I said.

"A look of hurt surprise showed in her eyes. 'A masquerade?' she echoed. 'But no, it is my best, my very finest, that I wear for you tonight, *mon adoré*. Do not you like it; do you not love me, Édouard?'

"'No,' I answered shortly, 'I do not. We might as well understand each other Julie. I'm not in love with you and never was. It's been a pretty flirtation nothing more. I'm going home tomorrow, and—'

"'But you will come again? Surely you will come again?' she pleaded. 'You can not mean it when you say you do not love me, Édouard. Tell me that you spoke so but to tease me—'

"A warning hiss sounded in the grass beside my foot, but I was too angry to be frightened. 'Go ahead, set your devilish snake on me,' I taunted. 'Let it bite me. I'd as soon be dead as—'

"The snake was quick, but Julie quicker. In the split-second required for the thing to drive at me she leaped across the grass-grown aisle and pushed me back. So violent was the shove she gave me that I fell against the tomb, struck my head against a small projecting stone and stumbled to my knees. As I fought for footing on the slippery grass I saw the deadly, wedge-shaped head strike full against the girl's bare ankle and heard her gasp with pain. The snake recoiled and swung its head toward me, but Julie dropped down to her knees and spread her arms protectingly about me.

"'Non, non, grand'tante!' she screamed; 'not this one! Let me—' Her voice broke on a little gasp and with a retching hiccup she sank limply to the grass.

"I tried to rise, but my foot slipped on the grass and I fell back heavily against the tomb, crashing my brow against its shell-set cement wall. I saw Julie lying in a little huddled heap of white against the blackness of the sward, and, shadowy but clearly visible, an aged, wrinkled Negress with turbaned head and cambric apron bending over her, nursing her head against her bosom and rocking back and forth grotesquely while she crooned a wordless threnody. Where had she come from? I wondered idly. Where had the snake gone? Why did the moonlight seem to fade and flicker like a dying lamp? Once more I tried to rise, but slipped back to the grass before the tomb as everything went black before me.

"The lavender light of early morning was streaming over the tomb-walls of the cemetery when I waked. I lay quiet for a little while, wondering sleepily how I came there. Then, just as the first rays of the sun shot through the thinning shadows, I remembered. Julie! The snake had bitten her when she flung herself before me. She was gone; the old Negress—where had *she* come from?—was gone, too, and I was utterly alone in the old graveyard.

"Stiff from lying on the ground, I got myself up awkwardly, grasping at the flower-shelf projecting from the tomb. As my eyes came level with the slab that scaled the crypt I felt the breath catch in my throat. The crypt, like all its fellows, looked for all the world like an old oven let into a brick wall overlaid with peeling plaster. The sealing-stone was probably once white, but years had stained it to a dirty gray, and time had all but rubbed its legend out. Still, I could see the faint inscription carved in quaint, old-fashioned letters, and disbelief gave way to incredulity, which was replaced by panic terror as I read:

Ici repose malheureusement
Julie Amélie Marie d'Ayen
Nationale de Paris France
Née le 29 Aout 1788
Décédée a la N O le 2 Juillet 1807

"Julie! Little Julie whom I'd held in my arms, whose mouth had lain on mine in eager kisses, was a corpse! Dead and in her grave more than a century!"

The silence lengthened. Ned stared miserably before him, his outward eyes unseeing, but his mind's eye turned upon that scene in old Saint Denis Cemetery. De Grandin tugged and tugged again at the ends of his mustache till I thought he'd drag the hairs out by the roots. I could think of nothing which might ease the tension till:

"Of course, the name cut on the tombstone was a piece of pure coincidence," I hazarded. "Most likely the young woman deliberately assumed it to mislead you—"

"And the snake which threatened our young friend, he was an assumption, also, one infers?" de Grandin interrupted.

"N-o, but it could have been a trick. Ned saw an aged Negress in the cemetery, and those old Southern darkies have strange powers—"

"I damn think that you hit the thumb upon the nail that time, my friend," the little Frenchman nodded, "though you do not realize how accurate your diagnosis is." To Ned:

"Have you seen this snake again since coming North?"

"Yes," Ned replied. "I have. I was too stunned to speak when I read the epitaph, and I wandered back to the hotel in a sort of daze and packed my bags in silence. Possibly that's why there was no further visitation there. I don't know. I do know nothing further happened, though, and when several months had passed with nothing but my memories to remind me of the incident, I began to think I'd suffered from some sort of walking nightmare. Nella and I went ahead with preparations for our wedding, but three weeks ago the postman brought me this—"

He reached into an inner pocket and drew out an envelope. It was of soft gray paper, edged with silver-gilt, and the address was in tiny, almost unreadable script:

M. Édouard Minton,
30 Rue Carteret 30,
Harrisonville, N.J.

"U'm?" de Grandin commented as he inspected it. "It is addressed à la française. And the letter, may one read it?"

"Of course," Ned answered. "I'd like you to."

Across de Grandin's shoulder I made out the hastily scrawled missive:

Adoré
Remember your promise and the kiss of blood that sealed it. Soon I shall call and you must come.

Pour le temps et pour l'éternité.
Julie.

"You recognize the writing?" de Grandin asked. "It is—"

"Oh, yes," Ned answered bitterly. "I recognize it; it's the same the other note was written in."

"And then?"

The boy smiled bleakly. "I crushed the thing into a ball and threw it on the floor and stamped on it. Swore I'd die before I'd keep another rendezvous with her, and—" He broke off, and put trembling hands up to his face.

"The so mysterious serpent came again, one may assume?" de Grandin prompted.

"But it's only a phantom snake," I interjected. "At worst it's nothing more than a terrifying vision—"

"Think so?" Ned broke in. "D'ye remember Rowdy, my Airedale terrier?"

I nodded.

"He was in the room when I opened this letter, and when the cottonmouth appeared beside me on the floor he made a dash for it. Whether it would have struck me I don't know, but it struck at him as he leaped and caught him squarely in the throat, He thrashed and fought and the thing held on with locked jaw till I grabbed a fire-shovel and made for it; then, before I could strike, it vanished.

"But its venom didn't. Poor old Rowdy was dead before I could get him out of the house, but I took his corpse to Doctor Kirchoff, the veterinary, and told him Rowdy died suddenly and I wanted him to make an autopsy. He went back to his operating-room and stayed there half an hour. When he came back to the office he was wiping his glasses and wore the most astonished look I've ever seen on a human face. 'You say your dog died suddenly—in the house?' he asked.

"'Yes,' I told him; 'just rolled over and died.'

"'Well, bless my soul, that's the most amazing thing I ever heard!' he answered. 'I can't account for it. That dog died from snake-bite; copperhead, I'd say, and the marks of the fangs show plainly on his throat.'"

"But I thought you said it was a water moccasin," I objected. Now Doctor Kirchoff says it was a copperhead—"

"*Ah bah!*" de Grandin laughed a thought unpleasantly. "Did no one ever tell you that the copperhead and moccasin are of close kind, my friend? Have not you heard some ophiologists maintain the moccasin is but a dark variety of copperhead?" He did not pause for my reply, but turned again to Ned:

"One understands your chivalry, *Monsieur.* For yourself you have no fear, since after all at times life can be bought too dearly, but the death of your small dog has put a different aspect on the matter. If this never-to-be-sufficiently-anathematized serpent which comes and goes like the *boîte à surprise* the how do you call him? Jack from the box?—is enough a ghost thing to appear at any time and place it wills, but sufficiently physical to exude venom which will kill a strong and healthy terrier, you have the fear for Mademoiselle Nella, *n'est-ce-pas?*"

"Precisely, you—"

"And you are well advised to have the caution, my young friend. We face a serious condition."

"What do you advise?"

The Frenchman teased his needlepoint mustache-tip with a thoughtful thumb and forefinger. "For the present, nothing," he replied at length. "Let me look this situation over; let me view it from all angles. Whatever I might tell you now would probably be wrong. Suppose we meet again one week from now. By that time I should have my data well in hand."

"And in the meantime—"

"Continue to be coy with Mademoiselle Nella. Perhaps it would be well if you recalled important business which requires that you leave town till you hear from me again. There is no need to put her life in peril at this time."

"IF IT WEREN'T FOR Kirchoff's testimony I'd say Ned Minton had gone raving crazy," I declared as the door closed on our visitors. "The whole thing's wilder than an opium smoker's dream—that meeting with the girl in New Orleans, the snake that comes and disappears, the assignation in the cemetery—it's all too preposterous. But I know Kirchoff. He's as unimaginative as a side of sole-leather, and as efficient as he is unimaginative. If he says Minton's dog died of snake-bite that's what it died of, but the whole affair's so utterly fantastic—"

"Agreed," de Grandin nodded; "but what is fantasy but the appearance of mental images as such, severed from ordinary relations? The 'ordinary relations' of images are those to which we are accustomed, which conform to our experience. The wider that experience, the more ordinary will we find extraordinary relations. By example, take yourself: You sit in a dark auditorium and see a railway train come rushing at you. Now, it is not at all in ordinary experience for a locomotive to come dashing in a theater filled with people, it is quite otherwise; but you keep your seat, you do not flinch, you are not frightened. It is nothing but a motion picture, which you understand. But if you were a savage from New Guinea you would rise and fly in panic from this steaming, shrieking iron monster which bears down on you. *Tiens*, it is a matter of experience, you see. To you it is an everyday event, to the savage it would be a new and terrifying thing.

"Or, perhaps, you are at the hospital. You place a patient between you and the Crookes' tube of an X-ray, you turn on the current, you observe him through the fluoroscope and *pouf!* his flesh all melts away and his bones spring out in sharp relief. Three hundred years ago you would have howled like a stoned dog at the sight, and prayed to be delivered from the witchcraft which produced it. Today you curse and swear like twenty drunken pirates if the Roentgenologist is but thirty seconds late in setting up the apparatus. These things are 'scientific,' you understand their underlying formulae, therefore they seem natural. But mention what you please to call the occult, and you scoff, and that is but admitting that you are opposed to something which you do not understand. The credible and believable is that to which we are accustomed, the fantastic and incredible is what we cannot explain in terms of previous experience. *Voilà, c'est, très simple, n'est-ce-pas?*"

"You mean to say you understand all this?"

"Not at all by any means; I am clever, me, but not that clever. No, my friend, I am as much in the dark as you, only I do not refuse to credit what our young friend tells us. I believe the things he has related happened, exactly as he has recounted them. I do not understand, but I believe. Accordingly, I must probe, I must sift, I must examine this matter. We see it now as a group of unrelated and irrelevant occurrences, but somewhere lies the key which will enable us to make harmony from this discord, to gather these stray, tangled threads into an ordered pattern. I go to seek that key."

"Where?"

"To New Orleans, of course. Tonight I pack my portmanteaux, tomorrow I entrain. Just now"—he smothered a tremendous yawn—"now I do what every wise man does as often as he can. I take a drink."

SEVEN EVENINGS LATER WE gathered in my study, de Grandin, Ned and I, and from the little Frenchman's shining eyes I knew his quest had been productive of results.

"My friends," he told us solemnly, "I am a clever person, and a lucky one, as well. The morning after my arrival at New Orleans I enjoyed three Ramos fizzes, then went to sit in City Park by the old Dueling-Oak and wished with all my heart that I had taken four. And while I sat in self-reproachful thought, sorrowing for the drink that I had missed, behold, one passed by whom I recognized. He was my old schoolfellow, Paul Dubois, now a priest in holy orders and attached to the Cathedral of Saint Louis.

"He took me to his quarters, that good, pious man, and gave me luncheon. It was Friday and a fast day, so we fasted. *Mon Dieu*, but we did fast! On créole gumbo and oysters à la Rockefeller, and baked pompano and little shrimp fried crisp in olive oil and chicory salad and seven different kinds of cheese and wine. When we were so filled with fasting that we could not eat another morsel my old friend took me to another priest, a native of New Orleans whose stock of local lore was second only to his marvelous capacity for fine champagne. *Morbleu*, how I admire that one! And now, attend me very carefully, my friends. What he disclosed to me makes many hidden mysteries all clear:

"In New Orleans there lived a wealthy family named d'Ayen. They possessed much gold and land, a thousand slaves or more, and one fair daughter by the name of Julie. When this country bought the Louisiana Territory from Napoléon and your army came to occupy the forts, this young girl fell in love with a young officer, a Lieutenant Philip Merriwell. *Tenez*, army love in those times was no different than it is today, it seems. This gay young lieutenant, he came, he wooed, he won, he rode away, and little Julie wept and sighed and finally died of heartbreak. In her lovesick illness she had for constant company a slave, an old mulatress known to most as Maman Dragonne, but to Julie simply as *grand'tante*, great-aunt. She had nursed our little Julie at the breast, and all her life she fostered and attended her. To her little white *'mamselle'* she was all gentleness and kindness, but to others she was fierce and frightful, for she was a 'conjon woman,' adept at obeah, the black magic of the Congo, and among the blacks she ruled as queen by force of fear, while the whites were wont to treat her with respect and, it was more than merely whispered, retain her services upon occasion. She could sell protection to the duelist, and he who bore her charm would surely conquer on the field of honor; she brewed love-drafts which turned the hearts and heads of the most capricious coquettes or the most constant wives, as occasion warranted; by merely staring fixedly at someone she could cause him to take sick and die, and-here we commence to tread upon our own terrain—she was said to have the power of changing to a snake at will.

"Very good. You follow? When poor young Julie died of heartbreak it was old Maman Dragonne—the little white one's *grand'tante*—who watched beside her bed. It is said she stood beside her mistress' coffin and called a curse upon the fickle lover; swore he would come back and die beside the body of the sweetheart he deserted. She also made a prophecy. Julie should have many loves, but her body should not know corruption nor her spirit rest until she could find one to keep his promise and return to her with words of love upon his lips. Those who failed her should die horribly, but he who kept his pledge would bring her rest and peace. This augury she made while she stood beside her mistress' coffin just before they sealed it in the tomb in old Saint Denis Cemetery. Then she disappeared."

"You mean she ran away?" I asked.

"I mean she disappeared, vanished, evanesced, evaporated. She was never seen again, not even by the people who stood next to her when she pronounced her prophecy."

"But—"

"No buts, my friend, if you will be so kind. Years later, when the British stormed New Orleans, Lieutenant Merriwell was there with General Andrew

Jackson. He survived the battle like a man whose life is charmed, though all around him comrades fell and three horses were shot under him. Then, when the strife was done, he went to the grand banquet tendered to the victors. While gayety was at its height he abruptly left the table. Next morning he was found upon the grass before the tomb of Julie d'Ayen. He was dead. He died from snake-bite.

"The years marched on and stories spread about the town, stories of a strange and lovely *belle dame sans merci*, a modern Circe who lured young gallants to their doom. Time and again some gay young blade of New Orleans would boast a conquest. Passing late at night through Royal Street, he would have a flower dropped to him as he walked underneath a balcony. He would meet a lovely girl dressed in the early Empire style, and be surprised at the ease with which he pushed his suit; then—upon the trees in Chartres Street appeared his funeral notices. He was dead, invariably he was dead of snake-bite. *Parbleu*, it got to be a saying that he who died mysteriously must have met the Lady of the Moonlight as he walked through Royal Street!"

He paused and poured a thimbleful of brandy in his coffee. "You see?" he asked.

"No, I'm shot if I do!" I answered. "I can't see the connection between—"

"Night and breaking dawn, perhaps?" he asked sarcastically. "If two and two make four, my friend, and even you will not deny they do, then these things I have told you give an explanation of our young friend's trouble. This girl he met was most indubitably Julie, poor little Julie d'Ayen on whose tombstone it is carved: '*Ici repose malheureusement*—here lies unhappily.' The so mysterious snake which menaces young Monsieur Minton is none other than the aged Maman Dragonne—*grand'tante*, as Julie called her."

"But Ned's already failed to keep his tryst," I objected. "Why didn't this snake-woman sting him in the hotel, or—"

"Do you recall what Julie said when first the snake appeared?" he interrupted. 'Not this one, *grand'tante*.' And again, in the old cemetery when the serpent actually struck at him, she threw herself before him and received the blow. It could not permanently injure her; to earthly injuries the dead are proof, but the shock of it caused her to swoon, it seems. *Monsieur*," he bowed to Ned, "you are more fortunate than any of those others. Several times you have been close to death, but each time you escaped. You have been given chance and chance again to keep your pledged word to the dead, a thing no other faithless lover of the little Julie ever had. It seems, *monsieur*, this dead girl truly loves you."

"How horrible!" I muttered.

"You said it, Doctor Trowbridge!" Ned seconded. "It looks as if I'm in a spot, all right."

"*Mais non*," de Grandin contradicted. "Escape is obvious, my friend."

"How, in heaven's name?"

"Keep your promised word; go back to her."

"Good Lord, I can't do that! Go back to a corpse, take her in my arms—kiss her?"

"*Certainement*, why not?"

"Why—why, she's *dead!*"

"Is she not beautiful?"

"She's lovely. and alluring as a siren's song. I think she's the most exquisite thing I've ever seen, but—" he rose and walked unsteadily across the room. If it weren't for Nella," he said slowly, "I might not find it hard to follow your advice. Julie's sweet and beautiful, and artless and affectionate as a child; kind, too, the way she stood between me and that awful snake-thing, but—oh, it's out of the question!"

"Then we must expand the question to accommodate it, my friend. For the safety of the living—for Mademoiselle Nella's sake—and for the repose of the dead, you must keep the oath you swore to little Julie d'Ayen. You must go back to New Orleans and keep your rendezvous."

THE DEAD OF OLD Saint Denis lay in dreamless sleep beneath the palely argent rays of the fast-waxing moon. The oven-like tombs were gay with hardly wilted flowers; for two days before was All Saints' Day, and no grave in all New Orleans is so lowly, no dead so long interred, that pious hands do not bear blossoms of remembrance to them on that feast of memories.

De Grandin had been busily engaged all afternoon, making mysterious trips to the old Negro quarter in company with a patriarchal scion of Indian and Negro ancestry who professed ability to guide him to the city's foremost practitioner of voodoo; returning to the hotel only to dash out again to consult his friend at the Cathedral; coming back to stare with thoughtful eyes upon the changing panorama of Canal Street while Ned, nervous as a race-horse at the barrier, tramped up and down the room lighting cigarette from cigarette and drinking absinthe frappé alternating with sharp, bitter sazarac cocktails till I wondered that he did not fall in utter alcoholic collapse. By evening I had that eery feeling that the sane experience when alone with mad folk. I was ready to shriek at any unexpected noise or turn and run at sight of a strange shadow.

"My friend," de Grandin ordered as we reached the grass-paved corridor of tombs where Ned had told us the d'Ayen vaults were, "I suggest that you drink this." From an inner pocket he drew out a tiny flask of ruby glass and snapped its stopper loose. A strong and slightly acrid scent came to me, sweet and spicy, faintly reminiscent of the odor of the aromatic herbs one smells about a mummy's wrappings.

"Thanks, I've had enough to drink already," Ned said shortly.

"You are informing me, *mon vieux?*" the little Frenchman answered with a smile. "It is for that I brought this draft along. It will help you draw yourself together. You have need of all your faculties this time, believe me."

Ned put the bottle to his lips, drained its contents, hiccuped lightly, then braced his shoulders. "That *is* a pick-up," he complimented. "Too bad you didn't let me have it sooner, sir. I think I can go through the ordeal now."

"One is sure you can," the Frenchman answered confidently. "Walk slowly toward the spot where you last saw Julie, if you please. We shall await you here, in easy call if we are needed."

The aisle of tombs was empty as Ned left us. The turf had been fresh-mown for the day of visitation and was as smooth and short as a lawn tennis court. A field-mouse could not have run across the pathway without our seeing it. This much I noticed idly as Ned trudged away from us, walking more like a man on his way to the gallows than one who went to keep a lovers' rendezvous . . . and suddenly he was not alone. There was another with him, a girl dressed in a clinging robe of sheer white muslin cut in the charming fashion of the First Empire, girdled high beneath the bosom with a sash of light-blue ribbon. A wreath of pale gardenias lay upon her bright, fair hair; her slender arms were pearl-white in the moonlight. As she stepped toward Ned I thought involuntarily of a line from Sir John Suckling:

Her feet . . . like little mice stole in and out.

"*Édouard, chêri! O, coeur de mon coeur, c'est véritablement toi?* Thou hast come willingly, unasked, *petit amant?*"

"I'm here," Ned answered steadily, "but only—" He paused and drew a sudden gasping breath, as though a hand had been laid on his throat.

"*Chèri,*" the girl asked in a trembling voice, "you are cold to me; do not you love me, then—you are not here because your heart heard my heart calling? O heart of my heart's heart, if you but knew how I have longed and waited! It has been *triste, mon Édouard,* lying in my narrow bed alone while winter rains and summer suns beat down, listening for your footfall. I could have gone out at my pleasure whenever moonlight made the nights all bright with silver; I could have sought for other lovers, but I would not. You held release for me within your hands, and if I might not have it from you I would forfeit it for ever. Do not you bring release for me, my Édouard? Say that it is so!"

An odd look came into the boy's face. He might have seen her for the first time, and been dazzled by her beauty and the winsome sweetness of her voice.

"Julie!" he whispered softly. "Poor, patient, faithful little Julie!"

In a single stride he crossed the intervening turf and was on his knees before her, kissing her hands, the hem of her gown, her sandaled feet, and babbling half-coherent, broken words of love.

She put her hands upon his head as if in benediction, then turned them, holding them palm-forward to his lips, finally crooked her fingers underneath his chin and raised his face. "Nay, love, Sweet love, art thou a worshipper and I a saint that thou should kneel to me?" she asked him tenderly. "See, my lips are famishing for thine, and wilt thou waste thy kisses on my hands and feet and garment? Make haste, my heart, we have but little time, and I would know the kisses of redemption ere—"

They clung together in the moonlight, her white-robed, lissome form and his somberly clad body seemed to melt and merge in one while her hands reached up to clasp his cheeks and draw his face down to her yearning, scarlet mouth.

De Grandin was reciting something in a mumbling monotone; his words were scarcely audible, but I caught a phrase occasionally: ". . . rest eternal grant to her, O Lord . . . let light eternal shine upon her . . . from the gates of hell her soul deliver . . . *Kyrie eleison*. . ."

"Julie!" we heard Ned's despairing cry, and:

"*Ha*, it comes, it has begun; it finishes!" de Grandin whispered gratingly.

The girl had sunk down to the grass as though she swooned; one arm had fallen limply from Ned's shoulder, but the other still was clasped about his neck as we raced toward them. "*Adieu, mon amoureux; adieu pour ce monde, adieu pour l'autre; adieu pour l'éternité!*" we heard her sob. When we reached him, Ned knelt empty-armed before the tomb. Of Julie there was neither sign nor trace.

"So, assist him, if you will, my friend," de Grandin bade, motioning me to take Ned's elbow. "Help him to the gate. I follow quickly, but first I have a task to do."

As I led Ned, staggering like a drunken man, toward the cemetery exit, I heard the clang of metal striking metal at the tomb behind us.

"WHAT DID YOU STOP behind to do?" I asked as we prepared for bed at the hotel.

He flashed his quick, infectious smile at me, and tweaked his mustache ends for all the world like a self-satisfied tom cat furbishing his whiskers after finishing a bowl of cream. "There was an alteration to that epitaph I had to make you recall it read, '*Ici repose malheureusement*—here lies unhappily Julie d'Ayen'? That is no longer true. I chiseled off the *malheureusement*. Thanks to Monsieur Édouard's courage and my cleverness the old one's prophecy was fulfilled tonight; and poor, small Julie has found rest at last. Tomorrow morning they celebrate the first of a series of masses I have arranged for her at the Cathedral."

"What was that drink you gave Ned just before he left us?" I asked curiously. "It smelled like—"

"*Le bon Dieu* and the devil know—not I," he answered with a grin. "It was a voodoo love-potion. I found the realization that she had been dead a century and more so greatly troubled our young friend that he swore he could not be affectionate to our poor Julie; so I went down to the Negro quarter in the afternoon and arranged to have a philtre brewed. *Eh bien*, that aged black one who concocted it assured me that she could inspire love for the image of a crocodile in the heart of anyone who looked upon it after taking but a drop of her decoction, and she charged me twenty dollars for it. But I think I had my money's worth. Did it not work marvelously?"

"Then Julie's really gone? Ned's coming back released her from the spell—"

"Not wholly gone," he corrected. "Her little body now is but a small handful of dust, her spirit is no longer earthbound, and the familiar demon who in life was old Maman Dragonne has left the earth with her, as well. No longer will she metamorphosize into a snake and kill the faithless ones who kiss her little mistress and then forswear their troth, but—*non*, my friend, Julie is not gone entirely, I think. In the years to come when Ned and Nella have long been joined in wedded bliss, there will be minutes when Julie's face and Julie's voice and the touch of Julie's little hands will haunt his memory. There will always be one little corner of his heart which never will belong to Madame Nella Minton, for it will be for ever Julie's. Yes, I think that it is so."

Slowly, deliberately, almost ritualistically, he poured a glass of wine and raised it. "To you, my little poor one," he said softly as he looked across the sleeping city toward old Saint Denis Cemetery. "You quit earth with a kiss upon your lips; may you sleep serene in Paradise until another kiss shall waken you."

Living Buddhess

T HE HOT, EROTIC RHYTHM of the rumba beat upon our ears with the repercussive vibrance of a voodoo drum. White dinner coated men guided partners clad in sheerest of sheer crêpes or air-light muslin in the mazes of the Negroid dance across the umber tiles which floored the Graystone Towers Roof. Waiters hastened silent-footed with their trays of tall, iced drinks. The purple, star-gemmed sky seemed near enough to touch.

"Tired, old chap?" I asked de Grandin as he patted back a yawn and gazed disconsolately at his glass of Dubonnet. "Shall we be going?"

"*Tiens*, we might as well," he answered with a slightly weary smile; "there is small pleasure in watching others—*grand cochon vert*, and what is that?"

"What's what?" I asked, noting with surprise how his air of boredom dropped away and little wrinkles of intensive thought etched suddenly about the corners of his eyes.

"The illumination yonder," he nodded toward the bunting-wrapped stanchions on the parapet between which swung the gently swaying festoons of electric lights, "surely that is not provided by the management. It looks like *feu Saint-Elme*."

Following his glance I noticed that a globe of luminosity flickered from the tallest of the light-poles, wavering to and fro like a yellow candle-flame blown by the wind; but there was no wind; the night was absolutely stirless.

"H'm, it does look like St. Elmo's fire, at that," I acquiesced, "but how—"

"*Ps-s-s-t!*" he shut me off. "Observe him, if you please!"

Bobbing aimlessly, like a wasp that bounces on the ceiling of the room to which it has made inadvertent entrance, the pear-shaped globe of luminance had detached itself from the gilt ball at the top of the light standard, and was weaving an erratic pattern back and forth above the dancers. Almost at the center of the floor it paused uncertainly, as if it had been a balloon caught between two rival drafts, then suddenly dropped down, landing on the high-coiled copper-colored hair of a young woman.

It fluttered weavingly above the clustered curls of her coiffure a moment like a Pentecostal flame, then with a sudden dip descended on the cupric hair, spread about it like a halo for an instant, and vanished; not like a bursting bubble, but slowly, like a ponderable substance being sucked in, as milk in a tall goblet vanishes when imbibed through a straw.

I do not think that anybody else observed the strange occurrence, for the dancers were too hypnotized by sensuous motion and the moaning rhythm of the music, while the diners were preoccupied with food; but the scream the girl emitted as the flickering flame sank through her high-dressed hair brought everyone up standing. It was, I thought, not so much a cry of pain as of insanity, of strange disease and maniacal excitement. It frothed and spouted from her tortured mouth like a geyser of unutterable anguish.

"*Mordieu*, see to her, my friend, she swoons!" de Grandin cried as we dashed across the dance floor where the girl lay in a heap, like a lovely tailor's dummy overturned and broken.

With the assistance of two waiters, chaperoned by an assistant manager in near-hysterics, we took her to the ladies' rest room and laid her on a couch. She was breathing stertorously, her hands were clenched, and as I reached to feel her pulse I noticed that her skin was cold and clammy as a frog's, and little hummocks of horripilation showed upon her forearms. "Every symptom of lightning-stroke," I murmured as I felt her feeble, fluttering pulse and turned her lids back to find pupils so dilated that they all but hid her irides; "is there any sign of burns?"

"One moment, we will see," de Grandin answered, stripping off her flaring-skirted frock of white organza and the clinging slip of primavera printed satin as one might turn a glove. We had no difficulty in examination, for except for a lace bandeau bound about her bosom and a pair of absolutely minimal gilt-leather sandals she was, as Jules de Grandin might have said, "as naked as his hand." Her skin was white and fine and smooth, with that appearance of translucence seen so often in red-headed people, and nowhere did it show a trace of burn or blemish. But even as we finished our inspection a choking, rasping wheeze came in her throat, and her stiffened body fell back lax and flaccid.

"Quickly," cried de Grandin as he turned her on her face, knelt above her and began administering artificial respiration; "have warm blankets and some brandy brought, my friend. I will keep her heart and lungs in action till the stimulants arrive."

ALMOST AN HOUR HAD elapsed when the girl's lids finally fluttered up, disclosing sea-green eyes that held a dreamy, slightly melancholy look. "Where am—I?" she asked feebly, voicing the almost universal question of the fainting. "Why—you're *men*, aren't you?"

"We are so taken and considered, *Mademoiselle*," de Grandin answered with a smile. "You had expected otherwise?"

"I—don't—know," she answered listlessly; then, as she saw her badly frightened escort at the door: "Oh, George, I think I must have died for a few moments!"

De Grandin motioned the young man to a chair beside the couch, tucked a blanket-end more snugly round the girl's slim shoulders, and bent a smile of almost fatherly affection on the lovers. "*Corbleu, Mademoiselle*, we—Doctor Trowbridge and I—feared you were going to die permanently," he assured her. "You were a very ill young woman."

"But what was it?" asked the young man. "One moment Sylvia and I were dancing peacefully, the next she screamed and fainted, and—"

"*Précisément, Monsieur*, one is permitted to indulge in speculation as to what it was," de Grandin nodded. "One wonders greatly. To all appearances *le feu Saint Elme*—the how do you call him? Saint Elmo's light?—took form upon a flagstaff by the dancing-roof, but that should happen only during periods of storm when the air is charged with electricity. No matter, it appeared to form and dance about the pole-tops like a naughty little child who torments a wandering blind man, then *pouf!* the globe of fire, he did detach himself and fall like twenty thousand bricks on *Mademoiselle*. This should not be. Saint Elmo's light is usually harmless as the gleaming of the firefly in the dark. Like good old wine, it is beautiful but mild. Yet there it is; it struck your lady's head and struck her all unconscious at the selfsame time.

"What was your sensation, *Mademoiselle*?" he added, turning from the young man to the girl.

"I hardly know," she answered in a voice so weak it seemed to be an echo. "I had no warning. I was dancing with George and thinking how nice it would be when the rumba finished and we could go back and get a drink, when suddenly something seemed to fall on me—no, that's not quite right, I didn't feel as if a falling object struck me, but rather as if I had received a heavy, stunning blow from a club or some such weapon, and as though every hair in my head was being pulled out by the roots at the same time. Then something seemed to spread and grow inside my head, pushing out against my skull and flesh and skin until the pain became so great I couldn't stand it. Then my whole head seemed to burst apart, like an exploding bomb, and—"

"And there you were," the young man interrupted with a nervous laugh.

She gave him a long, troubled look from heavily fringed eyes. "There I was," she assented. "But where?"

"Why, knocked all in a heap, my dear. We thought you were a goner. You would have been, too, if these two gentlemen hadn't happened to be doctors, and dining at the table next to us."

"That isn't what I mean," she answered with a little, puzzled frown. "I was—I *went* somewhere while I was unconscious, dear. I—I half believe I died and had a glimpse of Paradise—only it wasn't at all as I'd imagined it."

"Oh, nonsense, Syl," her sweetheart chided. "Maybe you imagined you saw something while you were out cold, but—"

"Tell us what it was you saw, *Mademoiselle*," de Grandin interrupted in a soothing voice. "How did your vision differ from your preconceived idea of Paradise?"

She lay in quiet thought a moment, her green eyes wide and dreamy, almost wistful. Finally: "I seemed to be in a great Oriental city. The buildings were of stone and towered like the Empire State and Chrysler buildings. Their tops were overlaid with gold leaf or sheet copper that shone so brilliantly that it fairly burned my eyes as the fierce sun beat down from a cloudless sky. I was on a portico or terrace of some sort, looking down a wide street reaching to a thick, high-gated wall, and through this gate came a procession. Hundreds of men on horseback carried lances from which silk flags fluttered, and after them came musicians with drums and flutes and tambourines and cymbals, and the music that they made was lovely. Then there were marching women, walking with a kind of dancing step and singing as they came. There were jewels and flowers in their straight, black hair, jewels in their ears and noses, necklaces of beaten gold and pearls and rubies and carved coral around their throats, and jeweled bands of gold around their arms and wrists. Bright gems flashed in the chain-gold belts that clasped their waists; around their ankles they had wire circlets hung with bells that chimed like laughter as they walked. They wore skirts of bright vermilion tied with girdles of blue silk, and their hands and toes and lips and nipples were all dyed brilliant red. Next came a great array of soldiers bearing shields and lances, then more musicians, and finally a herd of elephants which, like the women, wore belled bands of gold around their ankles. But while the women's bells were sweet and clear and high, the gongs upon the elephants were deep and soft and mellow, like the deep notes of marimbas, and the bass and treble bell-notes blended in a harmony that set the pulses going like the beat of syncopated music."

"*Eh bien, Mademoiselle*, this Paradise you saw was colorful, however much it may have lacked in orthodoxy," de Grandin smiled. But there was no answering gleam of humor in the girl's green eyes as she looked at him almost beseechingly.

"It thrilled me and elated me," she said. "I seemed to understand it all, and to know that this procession was for me, and me alone; but it frightened me, as well."

"You were afraid? But why?"

"Because, although I knew what it was all about, I didn't."

De Grandin cast a look of humorous entreaty at the young man seated by the couch. "Will you translate for me, *Monsieur*? Me, I have resided in your so splendid country but a scant twelve years, and I fear I do not understand the English fluently. I thought I heard her say she understood, yet failed to understand. But no, it cannot be. My ears or wits play the *mauvaise farce* with me."

"I don't quite know how to express it," the girl responded. "I seemed to be two people, myself and another. It was that other one who understood the pageant and who gloried in it, and that's what frightened me, for that other one who knew that the procession was to honor him was a man, while I was still a woman, and—" She paused, and tears formed in her eyes, but whether she were weeping for lost womanhood or from vexation at her inability to find the words to frame her explanation I could not decide.

"Come, come, young lady; that's enough," I ordered in my sternest bedside manner. "You've suffered from a heavy shock, and people in such cases often have queer visions. There's nothing medically curious in your having seen this circus parade while you were unconscious, and that feeling of dual personality is quite in keeping, too. If you feel strong enough, I suggest you get your clothes on and let us take you home."

"QUEER WHAT ABERRATIONS PEOPLE have following electric shock," I mused as we paused in the pantry for a final good-night drink. "I remember when I was an interne at City Hospital I had an ambulance case where a woman had been struck by a live wire fallen from a trolley pole. All the way back to the hospital she insisted that she was a cow, and lowed continuously. Now, take this Dearborn girl—"

"Precisely, take her, if you please," de Grandin nodded, his mouth half full of cheese and biscuit, a foaming mug of beer raised half-way to his lips. "Is hers not a case to marvel at? She is struck down all but dead by a ball of harmless *feu Saint-Elme*, and while unconscious sees the vision of a thing entirely outside her experience or background. She could not have dreamed it, for we dream only that of which we know at least a little, yet—" He drained his mug of beer, dusted off his fingers and raised his shoulders in a shrug. "*Tenez,*" he yawned, "let the devil worry with it. Me, I have the craving for ten hours' sleep."

IT WAS SHORTLY AFTER dinner the next evening that my office telephone began a clangor which refused to be denied. When, worn down at last by the persistence of the caller, I barked a curt "Hullo?" into the instrument, a woman's voice came tremblingly. "Doctor Trowbridge, this is Mrs. Henry Dearborn of 1216 Passaic Boulevard. You and Doctor de Grandin attended my daughter Sylvia when she fainted at Graystone Towers last night?"

"Yes," I admitted.

"May I ask you to come over? Doctor Rusholt, our family physician, is out of town, and since you're already familiar with Sylvia's case—"

"What seems to be the trouble?" I cut in. "Any evidence of burning? Sometimes that develops later in such cases, and—"

"No, thank heaven, physically she seems all right, but a little while ago she complained of feeling nervous, and declared she couldn't be comfortable in any position. She took some aromatic spirits of ammonia and lay down, thinking it would pass away, but found herself too much wrought up to rest. Then she started walking up and down, and suddenly she began muttering to herself, clasping and unclasping her hands and twitching her face like a person with Saint Vitus' dance. A few minutes ago she fainted, and seems to be in some sort of delirium, for she's still muttering and twitching her hands and feet—"

"All right," I cut the flow of symptoms short; "we'll be right over.

"Looks as if the Dearborn girl's developing chorea following her shock last night," I told de Grandin as we headed for the patient's house. "Poor child, I'm afraid she's in for a bad time."

"Agreed," he nodded solemnly. "I fear that he has managed to break in—"

"Whatever are you maundering about?—at your confounded ghost-hunting again?" I interrupted testily.

"Not at all, by no means; quite the contrary," he assured me. "This time, my friend, I damn think that the ghost has hunted us. He has, to use your quaint American expression, absconded with our garments while we bathed."

Sylvia Dearborn lay upon the high-dressed bed, her burnished-copper hair and milky skin a charming contrast to her apple-green percale pajamas. She was not conscious, but certainly she was not sleeping, for at times her eyes would open violently, as though they had been actuated by an unoiled mechanism, and her arms and legs would twitch with sharp, erratic gestures. Sometimes she moaned as though in frightful torment; again her lips would writhe and twist as though they had volition of their own, and once or twice she seemed about to speak, but only senseless jabber issued from her drooling mouth.

De Grandin leant across the bed, listening intently to the gibberish she babbled, finally straightened with a shrug and turned to me. "*La morphine?*" he suggested.

"I should think so," I replied, preparing a half-grain injection. "We must control these spasms or she'll wear herself out."

Deftly he swabbed her arm with alcohol, took a fold of skin between his thumb and forefinger and held it ready for the needle. I shot the mercy-bearing liquid home, and stood to wait results. Gradually her grotesque movements quieted, her moans became more feeble, and in a little while she slept.

"Give her this three times a day, and see that she remains in bed," I ordered, writing a prescription for Fowler's solution. "I don't think you'll need us, but if any change occurs please don't hesitate to call."

M RS. DEARBORN TOOK ME at my word. The blue, fading twilight of early dawn limned the windows of my chamber when the bedside telephone began its heartless, sleep-destroying stutter, and I groaned with something close akin to anguish as I reached for it.

"Oh, Doctor Trowbridge, won't you come at once?" the mother's frightened voice implored. "Sylvia's had another seizure, worse—much worse—this time. She's talking almost constantly, but it seems she's speaking in a foreign language, and somehow she seems changed!"

Years of practise had made me adept at quick dressing, but de Grandin bettered my best efforts. He was waiting for me in the hall, debonair and well-groomed with his usual spruce immaculateness, and had even found time to select a flower for his buttonhole from the *epergne* in the dining-room.

A single glance sufficed to tell us that our patient suffered something more than simple chorea. The pseudo-purposive gesticulations were no longer evident; indeed, she seemed as rigid as she had been the night before when we treated her for lightning-shock, and her skin was corpse-cold to the touch. But her lips were working constantly, and a steady flow of words ran from them. At first I thought it only senseless gabble, but a moment's listening told me that the sounds were words, though of what language I could not determine. They were sing-songed, now high, now low, with irregularly stressed accents, and, somehow, reminded me of the jargon Chinese laundrymen are wont to use when talking to each other. Queerly, too, at times her voice assumed a different timbre, almost high falsetto, but definitely masculine. Constantly recurring through her mumbled gabble was the phrase: "*Oom mani padme—oom mani padme! Hong!*"

"Do something for her, Doctor! Oh, for the love of heaven, help her!" Mrs. Dearborn begged as she ushered us into her daughter's bedroom; then, as I laid my kit upon a chair: "Look—look at her face!"

Whatever changes may be present in his patients'—or his patients' relatives'—appearance, a doctor has to keep a poker face, but retaining even outward semblance of unruffled nerves was hard as I looked in Sylvia Dearborn's countenance. A weird, uncanny metamorphosis seemed taking place. As though her features had been formed of plastic substance, and that substance was being worked by the unseen hands of some invisible modeler, her very cast of countenance was in process of transshaping. Somehow, the lips seemed thickened, bulbous, and drooped at the comers like those of one whose facial muscles had been weakened by prolonged indulgence in the practise of all seven deadly sins, and as the mouth sagged, so the outer comers of the eyes appeared to lift, the cast of features was definitely Mongol; the slant-eyed, thick-lipped face of a Mongolian idiot was replacing Sylvia Dearborn's cameo-clear countenance.

"*Oom mani padme—oom mani padme!*" moaned the girl upon the bed, and at each repetition her voice rose till the chant became a wail and the wail became a scream; dry-throated, rasping, horrible in its intensity: *"Oom mani padme—oom mani padme! Hong!"*

"Whatever—" I began, but de Grandin leaped across the room, staring as in fascination at the sick girl's changing features, then turned to me with a low command:

"Morphine; much more morphine, good Friend Trowbridge, if you please! Make the dose so strong that one more millionth of a grain would cause her death; but give it quickly. We must throw her speaking-apparatus out of gear, make it utterly impossible for her to go through the mechanics of repeating that vile invocation!"

I hastened to comply, and as Sylvia sink into inertia from the drug:

"Come, my friend, come away," he bade. "We must go at once and get advice from one who knows whereof he speaks. She will be all right for a short time; the drug will not wear off for several hours."

"Where the dickens are we going?" I demanded as he urged me to make haste.

"To New York, my friend, to that potpourri of intermixed humanity that they call Chinatown. Oh, make speed, my friend! We must hasten, we must rush; we must travel with the speed of light if we would be in time, believe me!"

WHERE DOYERS STREET MAKES a snake-back turn on its way toward the Bowery stood the taciturn-faced red-brick house, flanked on one side by a curio-dealer's ménage whose windows showed a bewildering miscellany of Chinese curiosa designed for sale at swollen prices to the tourist trade and on the other by a dingy eating-house grandiloquently mislabeled The Palace of Seven Thousand Gustatory Felicities. Shuttered windows like sleeping eyes faced toward the narrow, winding street; the door was flush with the front wall and seemed at first glance to be rather inexpertly grained wood. A second look showed it was painted metal, and from the sharp, unvibrant sound the knocker gave as de Grandin jerked it up and down, I knew the metal was as thick and solid as the steel wall of a safe.

Three times the little Frenchman plied the knocker, beating a sharp, broken rhythm, and as he let the ring fall with a final thump there came an almost soundless *click* and a hidden panel in the door slipped back, disclosing a small peep-hole. Behind the spy-hole was an eye, small, sharp and piercing as a bird's, curious as a monkey's, which inspected us from head to foot. Then came a guttural *"Kungskee-kungskee,"* and the metal door swung open to admit us to a hall where a lantern of pierced brass cast a subdued orange glow on apricot-hung walls, floors strewn with thick-piled Chinese rugs, carved black-wood chairs and tables, last of all a crystal image of the Buddha enthroned upon a pedestal of onyx.

Our usher was a small man dressed in the black-silk jacket and loose trousers once common to Celestials everywhere, but now as out of date with them as Gladstone collars and bell-shaped beaver hats are in New York. Tucking hands demurely in his jacket sleeves, he made three quick bows to de Grandin, murmuring the courteous "*Kungskee-kungskee*" at each bow. The little Frenchman responded in the same way, and, the ceremony finished, asked slowly, "Your honorable master, is he to be seen? We have traveled far and fast, and seek his counsel in a pressing matter."

The Oriental bowed again and motioned toward a chair. "Deign to take honorable seating—while this inconsequential person sees if the Most Worshipful may be approached," he answered in a flat and level voice. There was hardly any trace of accent in his words, but somehow I knew that he first formulated his reply in Chinese, then laboriously translated each syllable into English before uttering it.

"Who is it we have come to see?" I asked as the servant vanished silently, his footfalls noiseless on the deep-piled rugs as if he walked on sand.

"Doctor Wong Kim Tien, greatest living authority on Mongolian lore and Oriental magic in the world," de Grandin answered soberly. "If he cannot help us—"

"Good Lord, you mean you've dragged me from the bedside of a desperately sick girl to consult a mumbo-jumbo occultist—and a Chinaman in the bargain?" I blazed.

"Not a Chinaman, a Mongol and a Manchu," he corrected.

"Well, what the devil is the difference—"

"The difference between the rabbit and the stoat, *parbleu!* Do you not know history, my friend? Have you not read how this people conquered all the country from Tibet to the Caspian and from the Dnieper to the China Sea—how they laid the castles of the terrible Assassins in heaps of smoking ruins—"

"Who cares what they did before Columbus crossed the ocean? The fact remains we've left a critically ill patient to go gallivanting over the country to consult this faker, and—"

"I would not use such words if I were you, my friend," he warned. "A Manchu's honor is a precious thing and his vanity is very brittle. If you were overheard—"

The messenger's return cut short our budding quarrel. "The Master bids you come," he told us as if he were about to usher us into the presence of some potentate.

We climbed flight after flight of winding stairs, and as we went I was impressed with the fact that the place seemed more a fortress than an ordinary house. Steel doors were everywhere, shutting off the corridors, closing stairheads, making it impossible for anything less potent than a battery of field guns to force a passage from one floor to another, or even from the front to the rear of the building. Thick bars were at each window, and in the ceilings I caught glimpses of ammonia atomizers such as those they have in prisons to subdue unruly convicts. But if the place was strong, it was also lovely. Porcelains, silks, carved jades, choice pieces of the goldsmith's art, were everywhere. Walls were hung with draperies which even I could recognize as priceless, and the rugs we trod must have been well worth their area in treasury notes. Finally, when it seemed to me we had ascended more steps than those leading to the Woolworth Building's tower, our guide came to a halt, held aside a brocade curtain and motioned us to pass through the steel door which had been opened for our coming. De Grandin led the way and we stepped into the study of Doctor Wong Kim Tien.

I HAD NO PRECONCEIVED IMPRESSION of the man we were to meet, save that he would probably look like any Chinaman, butter-colored, broad-faced, button-nosed, probably immensely fat, and certainly a full head shorter than the average Caucasian.

The man who crossed the room to greet de Grandin was the opposite of my mind's picture. He was exceptionally tall, six feet three, at least, and lean and hard-conditioned as an athlete. Straight, black hair slanted sleekly upward from a high and rather narrow forehead, his nose was large and aquiline, his smooth-shaved lips were thin and firm, his high cheek-bones cased in skin of ruddy bronze, like that of a Sioux Indian. But most of all it was his eyes that fascinated me. Only slightly slanting, they were hooded by low-drooping lids, and were an indeterminate color, slate-gray, perhaps, possibly agate; certainly not black. They were meaningful eyes, knowing, weary, slightly bitter—as if they had seen from their first opening that the world was a tiresome place and that its ever-changing foibles were as meaningless as ripples on a shallow brooklet's surface.

The room in which we stood was as unusual in appearance as its owner. It was thirty feet in length, at least, and occupied the full width of the house. Casement windows, glazed with richly painted glass, looked out upon the roof-tops of the buildings opposite and the festooned backyard clotheslines of the tenements that clustered to the north. Chinese rugs woven when the Son of Heaven bore the surname Ming strewed the polished floors, and the place was warmly lighted by two monster lamps with pierced brass shades. The furniture was oddly mixed, lacquered Chinese pieces mingling with Turkish ottomans like overgrown boudoir pillows, and here and there a bit of Indian cane-ware. Book-shelves ran along one wall, bound volumes in every language of the Occident and Orient sharing space with scrolls of silk wound on ivory rods. Other shelves were filled with vases, small and large, with rounding surfaces of cream-colored crackle, or blood-red glaze or green or blue-and-white that threw back iridescent lights like reflections from a softly changing kaleidoscope. Upon a high stand was an aquarium in which swam several goldfish of the most gorgeous coloring I had ever seen, while near the northern windows was a refectory table of old oak littered with chemical apparatus. Glass-sided cases held a startling miscellany—mummified heads and hands and feet, old weapons, ancient tablets marked with cuneiform inscriptions. An articulated skeleton swung from a metal stand and leered at us sardonically.

"*Kungskee-kungskee*, little brother," our host greeted, clasping his hands before his blue-and-yellow robe and bowing to de Grandin, then advancing to shake hands in Western fashion. "What fair wind has brought you here?"

"*Tiens*, I hardly know myself," the little Frenchman answered as he performed the rites of introduction and the Manchu almost crushed my knuckles in a vise-like grip. "It is about a woman that we come, an American young woman who suffered from a seeming lightning-stroke two nights ago and now lies babbling in her bed. "

The Manchu doctor smiled at him ironically. "This one is honored that the learned, skillful Jules de Grandin, graduate of the Sorbonne and once professor at the *École Médical de Paris* should seek his humble aid," he murmured. "Have you perhaps administered the usual remedies, given her hypnotics to control her nervousness—"

"*Grand Dieu des artichauts!*" the Frenchman interrupted; "this is no time to jest, my old one. I said a *seeming* lightning-stroke, if you will recall, and if you will attend me carefully I shall show you why it is I seek your so distinguished help."

Quickly he rehearsed the incidents of Sylvia's mishap, recalled the floating ball of fire which struck her down, told of her vision of the Orient city; finally, dramatically: "Now she lies and murmurs, '*Oom mani padme—oom mani padme!*'" he concluded. "Am I, or am I not, entitled to your counsel?"

"My little one, you are!" the other answered. "Wait while I change my clothes and I will go at once to see this girl who chants the Buddhist litany in her delirium, yet has never been outside this country."

Arrayed in tweeds and Panama the Oriental savant joined us in a little while and we set out for Sylvia Dearborn's.

"What is that chant she keeps repeating?" I asked as we left the tunnel and started on the road across the meadows.

"'*Oom mani padme*' is literally 'Hail the Jewel of the Lotus,'" Doctor Wong replied, "but actually it has far more significance than its bare translation into English would suggest. Gautama Siddhartha, or Buddha, as you know him, generally shown as seated in a giant lotus blossom, you know, and for that reason is poetically referred to as the Jewel of the Lotus. But this phrase of worship has acquired a special significance through countless repetitions. It is the constant prayer of the devout Buddhist, it is inscribed on his sacred banners and on his prayer wheels, and one 'acquires merit'—something like obtaining an indulgence in the Roman Catholic faith—by constantly repeating it. To the followers of Buddha it is like the *Allah Akbar* to the Mohammedan or the *Gloria Patri* to the Christian. It is at once praise and prayer in all Buddhistic ceremonies, and with it they are all begun and ended. For a Buddhist to say it is as natural as to draw his breath, but for an American young lady, especially of such narrow background as your patient's, to begin intoning it is more than merely strange; it is incredible, perhaps indicative of something very dreadful."

THE MORPHINE TORPOR WAS relinquishing its hold on Sylvia when we readied her. From time to time she rolled her head upon the pillow, moaning like a person who dreams dreadful dreams. Once or twice she seemed about to speak, but only thick-tongued sounds proceeded from her mouth. De Grandin tiptoed to the window and raised the blind to bring the patient's face in clearer definition and as the lances of bright sunlight slanted sharply down upon the bed the girl rose to a sitting posture, flung out her arms as though to ward off an assailant and cried out in a voice honed sharp with fear, "No, no, I tell you; I won't let you! You can't have me! I won't—" As suddenly as it had commenced, her outburst ceased, and she fell back on the pillows, breathing with the heavy, gasping respiration of one totally exhausted.

De Grandin bent and rearranged the bed-clothes. "You see?" he asked the Manchu. "She suffers from the fixed idea that someone or some thing seeks to enter in her—*grand Dieu*, it comes again, *l'extase perverse!* Behold her, how she metamorphosizes!"

A subtle change had come into the young girl's face. The corners of her eyes went up, her mouth drooped at the corners, and her firmly molded lips appeared to swell and thicken. A sly, triumphant smile spread across her altered countenance, and she roused again, glancing sidewise at us with a cunning leer.

"*Empad inam moo!*" she exclaimed suddenly, for all the world like a naughty child who giggles a forbidden phrase. "*Empad inam moo!*" But the voice that spoke the singsong words was never hers. It was a high, cracked tone, like the utterance of an adolescent whose voice has not quite finished changing, or the treble of a senile graybeard, but it was definitely masculine.

"*Dor-je-tshe-ring!*" Doctor Wong exclaimed, and:

"*Kilao yeh hsieh ti to lo!*" that alien voice replied ironically, speaking through the girl's fast-thickening lips as a ventriloquist might make his words appear to issue from his dummy's painted mouth.

Doctor Wong addressed a very diatribe of hissing gutturals at the girl, and she answered with a flow of singsong syllables, shaking her head, grinning at him with a sly malevolence. They seemed to be in deadly argument, Wong urging something with great earnestness, Sylvia replying with cool irony, as though she were defying him.

At last the Manchu turned away. "Renew the opiate, my friend," he ordered wearily. "It will not last as long this time, but while she is unconscious she will rest. Afterward"—he smiled a hard-lipped smile—"we shall see what can be done."

"You have a plan of treatment?" I inquired.

"I have," he answered earnestly, "and unless it is successful it would be much better that you made this dose of morphine fatal."

The girl fought like a tigress when we tried to give her the narcotic. Scratching, biting, screaming imprecations in that strange heathen tongue, she beat us off repeatedly with the frenzied strength of madness, and it was not until they fairly hurled themselves upon her and held her fast that I was able to administer the morphine. This time the drug worked slowly, and almost an hour had elapsed before we saw her eyelids droop and she sank into a troubled sleep.

"I think it would be well if we secured two nurses used to handling the insane," advised de Grandin as we quit our bedside vigil. "It would be nothing less than murder to administer another dose of morphine after this; yet she must be protected from herself and we cannot remain here. We have important duties to perform elsewhere."

I telephoned the agency and in less than half an hour two stout females who looked as if they might be champion wrestlers in their leisure time reported at the Dearborn home. "*Pipe d'un chameau!*" de Grandin chuckled as he viewed our new recruits; "I damn think Mademoiselle Sylvia will have more trouble with those ones than she had with Doctor Wong and me, should she take a notion to go walking in our absence!"

Instructions given to the nurses, we set out once more for New York, Wong and de Grandin talking earnestly in whispers, I with a feeling I had blundered inadvertently into a fairy-tale, or come upon a modern version of the Mad Hatter's tea party.

L UNCHEON WAITED AT THE house in Chinatown and was served by Doctor Wong's diminutive factotum, who had changed his black-silk uniform for a short jacket of bright red worn above a skirt of blue, both embroidered in large circles of lotus flowers around centers of conventional good-fortune designs. The meal consisted of a clear soup in which boiled chestnuts and dice of apple floated, followed by stewed shellfish and mushrooms, steamed shark fin served with ham and crabmeat, roast duck stuffed with young pine needles, preserved pomegranates and plums, finally small cups of rice wine. Throughout the courses our cups of steaming, fragrant jasmine tea were never allowed to be more than half empty.

"A question, *mon ami*," de Grandin asked as he raised his thrice-replenished cup of rice wine; "what was it Mademoiselle Dearborn said when first the change came on her? It sounded like—"

"It was the anagram of '*Oom mani padme—empad inam moo.*'" Doctor Wong's words were crisp and brittle, without a trace of accent. "To say it in a Buddhist's presence is gratuitous sacrilege, much like repeating a Christian prayer back-ward, as the witches of the Middle Ages were supposed to do when meeting for their sabbats. It is the *bong* or sign manual of certain heretical Buddhist sects, notably those who have blended the *Bon-Pal,* or ancient devil-worship of Tibet, with Buddhist teachings."

"And what was it you said to her?" I asked.

Doctor Wong broke the porcelain stopper from a teapot-shaped container of *n'gapi* and decanted a double-thimbleful of the potent, amber-colored liquid into his cup before he answered. "Buddhism, Doctor Trowbridge, is like every other old religion. It far outdates Christianity, you know, and for that reason has had just that many more centuries in which to acquire incrustations of heresy. Like Christianity and Mohammedanism, it has been preached around the world, and its convents number millions. But the old gods die hard. Indeed, I think it might be said they never truly die; they merely change their names. Exactly as one may see survivals of the deities of ancient Rome none too thickly veiled in the pantheon of Christian saints, or discern strong vestiges of Gallic Druidism in the pow-wows and Hex practises of the Pennsylvania yokels, so the informed observer has no difficulty in seeing the ill-favored visages of the savage elder gods peering through the fabric of many heretical Buddhist sects. Some of these are harmless, as the Maryology of certain sects of Christians is. Some are extremely mischievous, as was the grafting of demonolatry on mediæval Christianity, with witchcraft persecutions, heresy huntings and other bloody consequences."

He lit an amber-scented cigarette, almost as long and thick as a cigar, and blew a cloud of fragrant smoke toward the red-and-gold ceiling, looking quizzi-cally at me through the drifting wreaths. "You know the Khmers?"

"Never heard of them," I confessed.

His thin lips drew back in a smile, and little wrinkles formed against the ruddy-yellow skin stretched tight across his temples, but his heavy-hooded eyes retained their look of brooding speculation. "I should have strongly doubted your veracity if you had answered otherwise," he told me frankly.

"Long ago, so long that archaeologists have refused to place the time, there boiled up out of India one of those strange migrations which have marked Asia since the first tick on the clock of time. It was a people on the march; across the lowlands, up the foothills, over the dragon-toothed mountains they came, kings with their elephants, priests in their golden carts, warriors a-horseback, the com-mon people trudging arm to arm with their goods and chattels and their house-hold gods in bundles on their backs. They swarmed across broad rivers, splashed neck-deep through marshes, crashed through the darkness of the matted jungle land. And finally they came to rest in that part of lower Asia which we call

Cambodia today. There they built a mighty nation. They raised great cities in the jungle waste—not only Angkor Thom, their capital, which had a population of a million and a half—but other towns of brick, and stone, stretching clear across the Cambodian peninsula. Brahmanism was their state religion, and the temples which they built to Siva the Destroyer are the puzzle and despair of modem archaeologists. Later—sometime in the Fifth Century as the West reckons time—missionaries came preaching the religion of the Lord Gautama, and Buddhism became the chief faith in the land. But the old gods die hard, Doctor Trowbridge. While images of Buddha replaced the Siva idols in the temples the philosophy of Buddha did not replace Brahmanism in the people's hearts, and the old religion mingled with and fouled the new system. In their sculpture they show the Lord Gautama seated side by side with the seven-headed cobra; some of their ornamental friezes show whole rows of Buddhas carrying a giant serpent. It was a degenerate and schismatic sect that flourished in the jungle."

He paused and helped himself daintily to another stoup of rice wine. Then:

"Two hundred years after Indian missionaries had preached the doctrines of the Buddha to the Khmers, other zealous *bonzes* penetrated far Tibet. The new faith took quick root, but it was like the seed that fell on stony ground in your Gospel parable. Pure Buddhism could not flourish into blossom in those devil-haunted uplands of the Himalayas. The thing which finally grew was a superstitious system which resembled Indian and Chinese Buddhism about as closely as the hierarchy of the Abyssinian Orthodox Church did the Twelve Apostles who followed your great teacher. With its crude admixture of the *Bon-Pal* of ancient Tibet and degenerate Buddhism, it is almost pure demonolatry, and the outgrowth of it is that queer system known as Lamaism. Sacrilegiously—when everything is taken into account—the leading lamas please to call themselves Buddhas, and centuries ago the doctrine that the Buddha never dies, but is reincarnated in his priests and lamas from one generation to another, was announced.

"There is more than one 'Living Buddha.' Besides the Dalai Lama of Tibet there are several 'living gods' in outer Mongolia, all lineal descendants of the Lord Gautama through infant-reincarnation."

"Infant-reincarnation?" I echoed, mystified.

"Exactly. As each successive Living Buddha falls into his final illness, subordinate lamas seek a fitting substitute in some infant born at the time the Living Buddha breathes his last, and into the body of the new-born child the soul of Buddha passes. So, according to tradition, it has been passed and repassed for countless generations.

"But there was among the ancient lamas a man who did not wish to have his soul incorporated in the new flesh of a whimpering infant; who did not want to start life with no recollection of his former incarnation, and this man, named

'The Thunderbolt'—*Dor-je-tshe-ring* in the Tibetan—decided to develop magic powers whereby he could pass consciously into the body of a living adult person, crowd out the other's soul—or consciousness or personality, whichever term you choose—and continue living with the full retention of his faculties and in the vigor of young manhood. It came about as close to immortality as any earthly thing could, you see."

"I should say so, if it could be worked."

"It could, and has. There is ample testimony in the ancient records that he did it not once but many times. Nor was it merely poetry that named him Thunderbolt. When he was about to expire from one body, the records tell us, his soul was seen to issue from his lips in the form of a small ball of fire, and pass from his old body to the new one. The body of the person struck by this fiery ball at once collapsed, with every evidence of being struck by lightning. Sometimes it would struggle, as if it had been seized with nervous spasms, but eventually these fits of resistance passed, and when they did, the stricken body spoke with Dor-je-tshe-ring's voice, acted as he had in his former fleshy habitation and, to a great degree, assumed his facial aspects.

"Tibet is superstition-ridden and the sorcerers and lamas can do things there no other country would permit, but it appears the Thunderbolt became unbearable even there; so with a thousand vengeful hillmen in pursuit, he fled down to the lowlands of Cambodia where, sometime in the period corresponding to the Western calendar's Eighth Century, he appeared in all his glory, having assumed the body of the reigning Buddhist dignitary as his own. Dor-je-tshe-ring was probably the foremost heretic of his day. He was among the earliest, if not the very first, to institute recital of *Oom mani padme* in reverse—offering conscious and intended insult to the Buddha by chanting *Empad inam moo* at Buddhist ceremonies.

"He ruled high-handedly in Angkor Thom for many years, and—this is believed by many historians—it was he who led them to oblivion. However that may be, the fact remains that the disappearance of the Khmers is one of the great mysteries of all time. There they were, a mighty nation with a high degree of culture, owners of proud cities, populous and powerful. Then one day, as abruptly and mysteriously as they came, they vanished. Their crowded cities were left empty as a tomb despoiled by grave-robbers, their market-places were deserted, their sanctuaries had no priests to serve them. Overnight, apparently, the Khmer Empire, the Khmer culture, the entire Khmer nation, disappeared. They did not die. Explorers have found no skeletal remains to evidence a plague or widespread massacre in their great, empty cities. They simply vanished, and the tiger and the lizard occupied their courts, the jungle flowed back to their streets and squares and palaces and temples."

"Quite so, but what's all this to do with Sylvia Dearborn?" I asked.

"Everything, by blue!" de Grandin answered quickly. "Tell him, *mon vieux*—tell him what you told me of the Khmer capital!"

Doctor Wong inclined his head. "Doctor de Grandin is correct," he nodded. "I think there is a strong connection. You recall Miss Dearborn's telling you about her vision of an ancient Oriental city? Her description closely parallels that of a countryman of mine, Tcheou-Ta-Quan, who was ambassador to Angkor Thom in the early Thirteenth Century."

Going to a lacquered bookcase he took down a slim volume bound in vellum, thumbed through its crackling parchment pages, and began to read:

When the king of Angkor leaves his palace be moves with a troop of horsemen at the head of his column. After the guard of cavalry are standard-bearers with fluttering flags, and behind them march the music-makers. Next in the procession are hundreds of concubines and girls of the palace . . . after them are other women of the palace carrying objects of gold and silver. Following them are the men-at-arms, the soldiers of the palace guard. In their wake come chariots and royal carriages all of gold and drawn by bulls. Behind these are the elephants in which ride nobles and ministers of the government. Each rides beneath a red umbrella.

In carriages or golden chairs or thrones borne on the backs of elephants are the wives and favorite concubines of the king, and their parasols are golden.

The king himself comes last, standing on an elephant and holding in his hand the sacred sword, while soldiers riding elephants or horses crowd closely by his side as he proceeds through the city.

The similarity between Miss Dearborn's vision and Tcheou-Ta-Quan's description of a state procession in the Khmer capital is very close, and when it is remembered that the Living Buddha of Angkor occupied an ecclesiastical position analogous to that of the Archbishop of Canterbury, if not quite as exalted as that of mediæval Popes, the meaning of her vision is quite plain. In my mind there is no doubt that *through the eyes of Dor-je-tshe-ring* she watched a ceremonial procession in which the king and his retinue marched through Angkor Thom to do their Living Buddha honor. That accounts for her saying 'one part of me seemed to understand it, while the other didn't', and also for her feeling of a dual personality, as if she were man and woman in one body.

"You see?" de Grandin asked.

"I don't think—"

"Then in heaven's name, do not boast of it, my friend. Cannot you understand? How else could this American young lady, this girl who never in her life had been to Europe, much less to lower Asia, behold that ceremonial march of ghosts from a long-forgotten past? This never-sufficiently-to-be-deprecated old one has struck down Mademoiselle Dearborn with his 'thunderbolt' and has entered into her. He is forcing forth her mind, he is making her assume the features of his so vile monkey-face; he is leaving her a living body while he kills her soul!"

"But how could he come over here, and why should he assume a woman's body? I thought the Living Buddha always is a man—"

Doctor Wong smiled frostily. "'The best-laid schemes of mice and men gang aft a-gley,'" he quoted. "According to the ancient chronicles his soul in fire-ball form passed seven times about the earth with the speed of sound before it struck the body of his victim. We do not know where Dor-je-tshe-ring's former body was when physical death took place, but we may allow for some deviation in his calculations. Instead of returning to China, or Manchukuo, or perhaps Korea or Siam, where his expiring body lay, his malignant spirit came to rest on that hotel rooftop in New Jersey. He may have been disconcerted by this happening, or, more probably, he intended to strike down the nearest masculine body to his place of rest, but through another error in his calculations, he struck Miss Dearborn's body instead. There seems to be a definite limit to his power. Once before he made an error; that time he entered the body of a cripple, and as he could not leave his earthly tenement till natural death ensued, he led the poor, unfortunate bit of deformed flesh to a miserable dance until he literally wore it out. Then he was able to transfer his headquarters to a home more suited to his wishes."

"But certainly," de Grandin seconded. "Our learned friend knew all these things, and being a mathematician as well as a philosopher, he found that two and two made four when added. Accordingly he damn suspected that the finger of this execrable Dor-je-tshe-ring was in the pie up to the elbow, and when he heard the poor young woman reciting Buddhist invocations in reverse, he taxed the villain with his act of trespass, calling him by name. And what was it he said? '*Ki lao yeh hsieh ti to lo*,—the honorable gentleman has my thanks,' by dammit. The sixty-times-accursed scoundrel not only admitted his so vile identity, he thanked our friend for recognizing him!"

My senses whirled from their wild talk no less than from the unfamiliar rice wine. "If what you say is true," I asked, "how are we to call back Sylvia's wandering spirit and expel this other from her?"

"That is for Doctor Wong to say," de Grandin answered.

"That is for me to *try*," the Oriental amended. "I will do the best I can. Whether I succeed or fail is for whatever gods may be to say. If you have completed luncheon, we can begin to make our preparations, gentlemen."

Wong's apparatus was assembled quickly. At his sharply spoken order the servant brought a slab of lucent, polished jade from one of the tall lacquered cabinets and laid it on the long refectory table. It must have been of priceless value, for it was at least a foot in length by a full eight inches wide, and certainly not less than one inch thick. Going to a locked steel chest Wong took a tiny phial of bright ruby glass, spilled a single drop of amber fluid from it on the slab of jade and began to polish it with a wad of gleaming yellow silk. As he rubbed the oil across the jade slab's gleaming face there crept through the room a perfume of an almost nameless sweetness, so rich and heady that my senses fairly reeled with it. For perhaps five minutes he worked silently, then, apparently satisfied, laid his silken buffer by and wrapped the jade block in a bolt of violet tissue.

In a tall, glass-fronted case stood a row of ancient bottles, fragile objects of exquisite delicacy, flat-bodied, small-mouthed, each with a tiny spoon attached to its stopper. One of shadowed malachite, one of glowing amber, one of richly gleaming coral he lifted from their shelves, and from each he scooped a minute portion of fine powder, stirred them carefully with a thin amber rod, then dusted them into a phial of gray agate and closed the bottle-neck with a rock crystal plug.

Finally, while the servant brought a Buddhist prayer wheel with disk of polished silver and uprights of age-black poplar wood, he took two tall, thick candles of blue wax set in crystal standards, wrapped them in a length of silken tissue, drew a censer of antique red gold from its case of cinnabar and ivory, and nodded to us.

"If you are quite ready, let us go," he suggested courteously.

"Has she rested quietly, *Mademoiselle?*" de Grandin asked the more feminine-looking of the Amazonian nurses when we arrived at Sylvia's room.

"Yes, sir, mostly. Once or twice she's been delirious, muttering and groaning, but she really hasn't given us much trouble."

"Thank you," he responded with a bow. "Now if you and your companion will await us in the hall, we shall begin our treatment. Come quickly if we call, but on no account come in the room or permit anyone else to enter till we give the word."

They made their preparations quickly. Sylvia's bed was moved until her head lay to the west and her feet east, that she might receive the natural magnetic currents of the earth. They stripped her green pajamas off, anointed her forehead, breasts, hands and feet with some pungently sweet-smelling oil, then crossed her hands upon her bosom, the right one uppermost, and bound her wrists together with a length of purple silk, that she might not change her posture. Her slender ankles were then crossed as they had crossed her wrists, and bound firmly with a red-silk sash. Beneath her head they put a pillow of bright-yellow silk embroidered with a swastika design in black. At one side of the bed they set the jade slab upright, and across from it they stood the dark-blue candles with the silver prayer wheel behind them. Doctor Wong filled the golden censer from the agate bottle, snapped a very modern cigarette-lighter into flame, lit the candles and set the incense glowing.

The scented smoke filled the room as wine may fill a bottle, penetrating every cranny, every crevice, every nook, sinking deep into the rugs and draperies, billowing and rolling back from walls and ceiling. It was curiously and pungently sweet, yet lacked the heavy, cloying fragrance of the usual incense.

They had drawn the blinds and pulled the curtains to, and the only light within the chamber came from the two tall candles which burned straight-flamed in the unwavering air, sending their yellow rays to beat upon the mirror-lustered surface of the slab of jade.

De Grandin put his hand upon the prayer wheel and at a word from Wong began to spin its disk. Astonishingly, the polished silver of the whirling disk caught up the candle rays, focused them as a lens will focus sunlight, and shot them back in a single sword-straight ray against the slab of glowing jade. Queerly, too, although he did not move the wheel's base, the beam of light moved up and down and crosswise on the jade mirror; then, as though it were a liquid stream, it seemed to ebb and flow as moonlight spreads on gently running water.

Doctor Wong was chanting in a low, monotonous voice, long, singsong words which rose and fell and seemed to slip and glide into one another until his canticle was more like a continuous flow of sound than words and sentences and phrases.

The nude girl on the bed stirred restlessly. She sought to take her hands down from her bosom, to uncross her feet, but the bandages prevented, and she lapsed back in what seemed a quiet sleep.

The long-drawn, uninflected chant proceeded, and the incense thickened in the room until I felt that I was being smothered. Where the prayer wheel whirled there came a low, monotonous humming, something like the droning hum made by an electric fan, but more penetrating, more insistent. It seemed to come from earth and air and sky, from the walls themselves, and to fill the atmosphere to overflowing with a spate of quivering sound that tore the nerves to tatters, shattering all inhibitions and dredging up dark memories and hates from the murk of the subconscious mind. I felt that I was going mad, that in another instant I should scream and tear my garments, or fall driveling and mouthing to the floor, when the sudden change in Sylvia's face caught and centered my attention.

Something alien had flowed into her features. Atop the perfect, cream-white body lying bound upon the bed was another face, an old face, a wicked face, a face with Mongoloid features steeped and sodden in foul malice.

A whining child-moan trickled from the thickening lips; then with a scream of fear surcharged with hatred she sat up struggling on the bed, tearing at the bonds that held her wrists, fighting like a thing possessed against the bandages that held her long, slim feet crossed on each other. But the silken fetters held—they had been tied with seven knots and sealed with red wax stamped with the ideograph of Lord Gautama!

And the low, monotonous chant went on, the incense foamed and frothed and billowed through the room, the gleaming candlelight pulsed throbbingly against the jade reflector, the silver wheel whirled on, giving off its nerve-destroying murmur.

"*Grand Dieu!*" I heard de Grandin's whisper rasping through the whirring of the wheel. "Observe her—look, Friend Trowbridge, he comes; he is emerging!"

Wearied by her futile struggles, Sylvia had fallen back upon the bed, and as her head sank flaccidly upon the black-embroidered yellow pillow, from her mouth, squared in a scream, there came a flow of luminance. Yet it was not merely light, it was a shining thing of ponderable substance, swelling as it reached the air till it hung above her face like a pear-shaped phosphorescent bubble joined to her by a single gossamer thread of fiery brilliance.

Idiotically—like a nervous woman tittering at a funeral—I giggled. More than anything else the dreadful tableau reminded me of a conjurer disgorging the collapsible property egg he has pretended to swallow.

The beam reflected from the swiftly whirling prayer wheel's silver disk cut athwart her face and, as if it had been a sharpened sword, clipped the ligature of luminance tethering the pyriform excrescence to her lips.

The brightly glowing globe seemed to shrink in upon itself, to acquire added weight and solidarity, yet oddly to become more buoyant. For an instant it hovered in midair above her face, as though undecided which way it should float; then, suddenly, like an iron-filing drawn to a strong magnet, it dropped upon the light-beam slanting from the prayer wheel to the plinth of jade and slid along the lucent track like a brakeless motor car gone headlong down a hill.

The impact was terrific. The jade rang like a smitten gong, a dreadful clang of sound, a shrill, high, wailing note as though it—or the ball of luminosity—had cried out in mortal anguish, a note of tortured outcry that thinned and lengthened to a sickening scream of torment. It hung and quivered in the incense-saturated air for what seemed an eternity, until I could not say if I still heard it or if tortured ear-drums held it in remembrance, and would go on remembering it till madness wiped the recollection out.

The jade was shattered in a thousand slivered fragments and the light-globe was dissolved in vapor thin as cirrous clouds that race before the rushing storm-wind, and blended with the hovering brume of incense. But a foul odor, rank and sickening as the fetor from decaying flesh, spread through the room, blotting out the perfume of the incense, bringing tears to our eyes and retchings to our stomachs.

"*Barbe bleu*, he had the fragrance of the rotten fish, that one!" exclaimed de Grandin as he raced across the room to fling the windows open and began to fan the air with a bath towel.

I looked at Sylvia. The invading presence had withdrawn and her lovely features were composed and calm. She lay there flaccidly, only the light flutter of her bosom telling us she was alive. I took her wrist between my thumb and forefinger. Her pulse was striking eighty clear-cut beats a minute. Normal. She was well.

They cut the silken bandages from wrists and ankles, drew her green pajamas on and tucked her in beneath the bed-clothes. Then, while I went to order broth and brandy ready for her waking, Wong and de Grandin packed their apparatus in its soft silk swaddling clothes, swept up the bits of shattered jade and drew their chairs up to the bedside.

We sat beside her till the dawnlight blushed across the eastern sky and day, advancing, trod upon the heels of night.

With the coming of the day she wakened. She lay against the heaped-up pillows, warm, relaxed and faintly smiling. One arm was underneath her head and the attitude showed her lines of gracious femininity; charming, tenderly and softly curved. Against the whiteness of the pillows and the counterpane her copper hair and fresh-blown cheeks glowed like an apricot that ripens in the sun.

But when she sat up with a sudden start her lovely color drained away and violet semicircles showed beneath her eyes. The glint of waking laughter that had kindled in her face was stilled and we could see fear flooding in her glance as blood wells through a sodden bandage. She licked dry lips with a tongue that had gone stiff, and her hands fluttered to her mouth in the immemorial, unconscious gesture of a woman sick with mortal terror. "Oh"—she began, and we heard the hot breath press against her words, as if her laboring heart were forcing it against them—"I thought—"

"Do not attempt to do so, *Mademoiselle*," de Grandin told her with firm gentleness. "You have been severely ill; this is no time for thought, unless you wish to think of getting well all soon, and of the one who comes tonight—*eh bien*, my little pigeon, have I not seen it in his eyes? But certainly! Drink this, if you please; then compose yourself to think of Monsieur Georges and the pretty compliments that he will whisper when he sees you lying here so beautiful—and filled to overflowing with returning strength. But certainly; yes, of course!"

WE PAUSED UPON THE Dearborn porch, weary with our vigil, but happy with the happiness of men who see their plans succeed. "How did you do it—" I began, but de Grandin cut my question off half uttered.

"Those things of Doctor Wong's were ancient things—and good things," he explained. "For more generations than the three of us have hairs upon our heads they have served the good of mankind—the sacred incense from the very tree beneath which Buddha sat in contemplation, the oil with which the Emperors of China were anointed, the clear, pellucid jade that casts back only good reflections, the candles made from wax of bees that drew their nectar in the very fields in which Gautama walked and preached, and last of all the prayer wheel that has recorded countless holy men's devout petitions to the Lord of Good—call Him what you will, He is the same in every heart filled with the love of man, whatever name He bears.

"Against these things, and against the ancient formulæ our friend Wong chanted, the evil one was powerless. *Parbleu*, they drew him forth from her as one withdraws the fish of April from the brooklet with a hook!"

"But," I ventured doubtfully, "is there a chance he may come back to plague—"

"I hardly think so," Doctor Wong replied. "He smashed the sacred mirror of *pi yü*—jade, that is—but in breaking it he also broke himself. You smelled the stench? That was his evil spirit vanishing. For almost countless generations he had occupied the flesh, first in one body then another. Dissolution—putrefaction—was long in overtaking him, but at last it sought him out. No, Doctor Trowbridge, I think the world has seen the last of Dor-je-tshe-ring, 'The Thunderbolt.' He has struck down his last victim, he has sucked in his last—"

"*Morbleu*, I am reminded by your reference to the sucking in!" de Grandin interrupted as he glanced at the small watch strapped on his wrist.

We looked at him in wonder. "Of what are you reminded, little brother?" asked Doctor Wong.

"In fifteen little minutes they will open. If we hurry, we can be among the first!"

"The first? What is it that you want?"

"Three, four, perhaps half a dozen of those magnificent old-fashioned cocktails; those with the so lovely whisky in them. Come, let us hasten!"

Flames of Vengeance

WITH INTENTLY NARROWED EYES, lips pursed in concentration, Jules de Grandin stood enveloped in a gayly flowered apron while he measured out the olive oil as an apothecary might decant a precious drug. In the casserole before him lay the lobster meat, the shredded bass, the oysters, the crab-meat and the eel. Across the stove from him Nora McGinnis, my household factotum and the finest cook in northern Jersey, gazed at him like a nun breathless with adoration.

"*Mon Dieu*," he whispered reverently, "one little drop too much and he is ruined, a single drop too few and he is simply spoiled! Observe me, *ma petite*, see how I drop *l'essence de l'olive*—"

The door-bell's clangor broke the silence like a raucous laugh occurring at a funeral service. Nora jumped a full six inches, the olive oil ran trickling from the cruet, splashing on the prepared sea-food in the sauce-pan. Small Frenchman and big Irishwoman exchanged a look of consternation, a look such as the Lord Chancellor might give the Lord Chief Justice if at the moment of anointment the Archbishop were to pour the ampulla's entire contents on the unsuspecting head of Britain's new-crowned king. The bouillabaisse was ruined!

"Bring him here!" bade Jules de Grandin in a choking voice. "Bring the vile miscreant here, and I shall cut his black heart out; I shall pull his so vile nose! I shall—"

"Indade an' ye'll not," protested Nora. "'Tis meself as'll take me hand off'n th' side of 'is face—"

"I'd better leave you with your sorrow," I broke in as I tiptoed toward the door. "It's probably a patient, and I can't afford to have you commit mayhem on my customers."

"Doctor de Grandin?" asked the young man at the door. "I've a letter to you from—"

"Come into the study," I invited. "Doctor de Grandin's occupied right now, but he'll see you in a minute."

The visitor was tall and lean, not thin, but trained down to bone and muscle, and his face possessed that brownish tinge which tells of residence in the tropics. His big nose, high cheekbones and sandy hair, together with his smartly clipped mustache, would have labeled him a Briton, even had he lacked the careless nonchalance of dress and Oxford accent which completed his ensemble.

"Jolly good of Sergeant Costello to give me a chit to you," he told de Grandin as the little Frenchman came into the study and eyed him with cold hatred. "I'm sure I don't know where I could have looked for help if he'd not thought of you."

De Grandin's frigid manner showed no sign of thawing. "What can I do for you, *Monsieur le Capitaine*—or is it *lieutenant?*" he asked.

The caller gave a start. "You know me?" he demanded.

"I have never had the pleasure of beholding you before," the Frenchman answered. His tone implied he was not anxious to prolong the scrutiny.

"But you knew I was in the service?"

"Naturally. You are obviously English and a gentleman. You were at least eighteen in 1914. That assures one you were in the war. Your complexion shows you have resided in the tropics, which might mean either India or Africa, but you called the sergeant's note a chit, which means you've spent some time in India. Now, if you will kindly state your business—" he paused with raised eyebrows.

"It's a funny, mixed-up sort o' thing," the other answered. "You're right in saying that I've been in India; I was out there almost twenty years. Chucked it up and went to farmin'; then a cousin died here in the province of New Jersey, leavin' me a mass o' rock and rubble and about two hundred thousand pounds, to boot."

The look of long-enduring patience deepened on de Grandin's features. "And what is one to do?" he rejoined wearily. "Help you find a buyer for the land? You will be going back to England with the cash, of course."

The caller's tanned complexion deepened with a flush, but he ignored the studied insult of the question. "No such luck. I'd not be takin' up your time if things were simple as that. What I need is someone to help me duck the family curse until I can comply with the will's terms. He was a queer blighter, this American cousin of mine. His great-grandfather came out to the provinces— the States, I should say—without so much as a pot to drink his beer from or a window he could toss it out of; cadet of the family, and all that, you know. He must have prospered, though, for when he burned to death he left half the bally county to his heirs at law, and provided in his will that whoever took the estate must live at least twelve months in the old mansion house. Sort o' period of probation, you see. No member of the family can get a penny of the cash till he's finished out his year of residence. I fancy the old duffer got the wind up at the last and was bound he'd show the heathens that their blighted curse was all a lot of silly rot."

De Grandin's air of cold hostility had been moderating steadily. As the caller finished speaking he leant forward with a smile. "You have spoken of a family curse, *Monsieur*; just what is it, if you please?"

An embarrassed look came in the other's face. "Don't think that I'm an utter ass," he begged. "I know it sounds a bit thick when you put it into words, but— well, the thing *has* seemed to work, and I'd rather not take chances. All right for me, of course; but there's Avis and the little chap to think of.

"Old Albert Pemberton, my great-grandfather's brother and the founder of the family in America, left two sons, John and Albert, junior. They were willing enough to pass their year of residence, but neither of 'em finished it. John left two sons, and they died trying to live out the year at Foxcroft. So did their two sisters, and their husbands. The chap I take it from was the younger daughter's son, and not born on the property. There's never been a birth in the old manor house, though there have been twelve sudden deaths there; for every legatee attempting to observe the dictates of old Albert's will has died. Yet each generation has passed the estate down with the same proviso for a year's residence as condition precedent to inheritance. Seems as if they're all determined to defy the curse—"

"*Mille tourments*, this everlasting curse; what is this seven times accursèd curse of which you speak so glibly and tell us absolutely nothing?"

For answer Pemberton reached in his jacket and produced a locket. It was made of gold, slightly larger than an old-time watch, and set with rows of seed-pearls round the edge. Snapping it open, he disclosed two portraits painted with minute detail on ivory plaques. One was of a young man in a tightly buttoned jacket of white cloth, high-collared, gilt-braided, with insignia of some military rank upon the shoulders. Upon his head he wore a military cap shaped something like the képi which the French wore in Algeria about the middle of the Nineteenth Century, hooded in a linen sheath which terminated in a neck-cloth trailing down between his shoulders. Despite the mustache and long sideburns the face was youthful; the man could not have been much more than three and twenty.

"That's Albert Pemberton," our visitor announced. "And that's his wife Maria, or, as she was originally known, Sarastai."

"*Parbleu!*"

"Quite so. Lovely, wasn't she?"

She was, indeed. Her hair, so black it seemed to have the blue lights of a cockerel's ruff within its depths, was smoothly parted in the middle and brought down each side her face across the small and low-set ears, framing an oleander-white forehead. Her wide-spaced, large, dark eyes and her full-lipped mouth were exquisite.

Her nose was small and straight, with fine-cut nostrils; her chin, inclined to point-edness, was cleft across the middle by a dimple. Brows of almost startling black curved in circumflexes over her fine eyes in the "flying gull" formation so much prized by beauty connoisseurs of the early eighteen hundreds. Pearl-set pendants dangled from her ear-lobes nearly to the creamy shoulders which her low-necked gown exposed. One hand was laid upon her bosom, and the fingers were so fine and tapering that they seemed almost transparent, and were tipped by narrow, pointed nails almost as red as strawberries. She was younger than her husband by some three or four years, and her youthful look was heightened by the half-afraid, half-pleading glance that lay in her dark eyes.

"*Que c'est belle; que c'est jeune!*" de Grandin breathed. "And it was through her—"

Our caller started forward in his chair. "Yes! How'd you guess it?"

I looked at them in wonder. That they understood each other perfectly was obvious, but what it was they were agreed on I could not imagine.

De Grandin chuckled as he noticed my bewilderment. "Tell him, *mon ami*," he bade the Englishman. "He cannot understand how one so lovely—*morbleu*, my friend," he turned to me, "I bet myself five francs you do not more than half suspect the lady's nationality!"

"Of course I do," I answered shortly. "She's English. Anyone can see that much. She was Mrs. Pemberton, and—"

"*Non, non,*" he answered with a laugh, "that is the beauty of the tropics which we see upon her face. She was—correct me if I err, *Monsieur*"—he bowed to Pemberton—"she was an Indian lady, and, unless I miss my guess, a high-caste Hindoo, one of those in whom the blood of Alexander's conquering Greeks ran almost undefiled. *Nest-ce-pas?*"

"Correct!" our visitor agreed. "My great-great-uncle met her just before the Mutiny, in 1856. It was through her that he came here, and through her that the curse began, according to the family legend."

Lights were playing in de Grandin's eyes, little flashes like heat-lightning flickering in a summer sky, as he bent and tapped our caller on the knee with an imperative forefinger. "At the beginning, if you please, *Monsieur*," he bade. "Start at the beginning and relate the tale. It may help to guide us when we come to formulate our strategy. This Monsieur Albert Pemberton met his lady while he served with the East India Company in the days before the Sepoy Mutiny. How was it that he met her, and where did it occur?"

Pemberton smiled quizzically as he lighted the cigar the Frenchman proffered. "I have it from his journal," he replied. "They were great diarists, those old boys, and my uncle rated a double first when it came to setting down the happenings of the day with photographic detail. In the fall of '56 he was scouting up Bithoor way with a detail of North Country *sowars*—mounted troops, you know—henna-bearded, swaggering followers of the Prophet who would cheerfully have slit every Hindoo throat between the Himalayas and the Bay of Bengal. They made temporary camp for tiffin in a patch of wooded land, and the fires had just been lighted underneath the troopers' cook-pots when there came a sort of ominous murmur from the roadway which wound past the woodland toward the river and the burning-ghats beyond. Little flickers of the flame that was about to burst into a holocaust next year were already beginning to show, and my uncle thought it best to take no chances; so he sent a file of troopers with a *subadar* to see what it was all about. In ten or fifteen minutes they came back, swearing such oaths as only Afghan Mussulmans can use when speaking of despised Hindoos.

"'*Wah*, it is a burning, Captain *Sahib*,' the *subadar* reported. 'The Infidels— may Allah make their faces black!—drag forth a widow to be burnt upon her husband's funeral pyre.'

"Now the British Raj forbade suttee in 1829, and made those taking any part in it accessories to murder. Technically, therefore, my uncle's duty was to stop the show, but he had but twenty *sowars* in his detail, and the Hindoos probably would number hundreds. He was, as you Americans say, in a decided spot. If he interfered with the religious rite, even though the law forbade it, he'd have a first-class riot on his hands, and probably lose half of his command, if the whole detail weren't massacred. Besides, his orders were to scout and bring reports in to the Residency, and he'd not be able to perform his mission if he lost too many men, or was killed in putting down a riot. On the other hand, here was a crime in process of commission under his immediate observation, and his duty was to stop it, so—"

"*Morbleu*, one understands!" de Grandin chuckled. "He was, as one might say, between the devil and the ocean. What did he do, this amiable ancestor of yours, *Monsieur*? One moment, if you please—" he raised his hand to shut off Pemberton's reply. "I make the wager with myself. I bet me twenty francs I know the answer to his conduct ere you tell it. *Bon*, the wager is recorded. Now, if you please, proceed."

A boyish grin was on the Briton's face as he replied: "It was a tight fix to be in, but I think the old boy used his head, at that. First of all, he bundled his dispatches in a packet and told a *sowar* off to take them to the Residency. It was no child's-play to select a messenger, for every man in his command itched to sink a saber-blade in Hindoo flesh; so finally they compromised by drawing lots. They're a bunch of fatalistic johnnies, those Mohammedans, and the chap who drew the short straw said it was the will of Allah that he be denied the pleasure of engaging in the shindy, and rode away without another murmur. Then my uncle told the men to stand to arms while he left them with the *subadar* and took two others to go scouting with him.

"At the forest edge they saw the Hindoos coming; and it must have been a sight, according to his diary. They were raising merry hell with drums and cymbals and tom-toms, singing and wailing and shrieking as if their luncheon disagreed with them. In the van came Brahmin priests, all decked out in robes of state and marching like a squad of sergeants major on parade. Then came a crowd of *gurus*—they're holy men, you know, and my uncle knew at once that these were specially holy; for whereas the average fakir shows enough bare hide to let you guess at his complexion, these fellows were so smeared with filth and ashes that you couldn't tell if they were black or white, and you could smell 'em half a mile away if you happened to get down-wind of 'em. They were jumpin' and contortin' round a four-wheeled cart to which a span of bullocks had been harnessed, and in which stood a ten-foot image of the goddess Kali, who's supposed to manifest the principles of love and death. If you've ever seen those idols you know what this one looked like—black as sin and smeared with goat's blood, four arms branchin' from its shoulders, tongue hangin' out and all awash with betel-juice and henna. There's a collar o' skulls strung round its neck and a belt of human hands tied round its waist. Not an appetizin' sight at any time, when it's plastered thick with half-dried blood and rancid butter it's enough to make a feller gag.

"Followin' the Kali-cart was another crowd o' Brahmins, all dressed up for a party, and in their midst they dragged—for she could scarcely walk—a girl as white as you or I."

"A white woman, you say?" I interrupted.

"You ought to know, you've just looked at her picture," answered Pemberton, raising the locket from his knee and holding out the sweet, pale face for my inspection. "That was my Aunt Maria—or Sarastai, as she was then.

"I suppose she must have looked a little different in her native dress, but I'll wager she was no less beautiful. My uncle's diary records that she was fairly loaded down with jewels. Everywhere a gem could find a resting-place had been devoted to her decoration. There was a diadem of pearls and rubies on her head; a 'golden flower,' or fan-like ornament of filigree in which small emeralds and seed-pearls were set, had been hung in her nose, and dropped so low across her lips that he could hardly see her mouth. Her ears and neck and shoulders and arms and wrists and ankles and every toe and finger bore some sort of jewel, and her gold-embroidered sari was sewn about the border with more gems, and even her white-muslin veil was edged with seed-pearls.

"Two Brahmins held her elbows, half leading and half dragging her along, and her head swayed drunkenly, now forward on her breast, now falling to one shoulder or the other as she lurched and staggered on the road.

"Last of all there marched a company of men with scimitars and pistols and a few long-barreled muskets. In their midst they bore a bier on which a corpse lay in full-dress regalia, pearl-embroidered turban, robe of woven silk and gold, waist-shawl set with diamonds. From the richness of the widow's jewels and the magnificent accouterments the corpse displayed, as well as by the size of the escort, my uncle knew the dead man was of great importance in the neighborhood; certainly a wealthy landlord, probably an influential nobleman or even petty prince."

"Poor child!" I murmured. "No wonder she was frightened to the point of fainting. To be burned alive—"

"It wasn't terror, sir," said Pemberton. "You see, to be *sati*, that is, to offer oneself as a voluntary sacrifice upon the funeral pyre, was considered not only the most pious act a widow could perform, it enhanced her husband's standing in the future world. Indian women of that day—and even nowadays—had that drilled into them from infancy, but sometimes the flesh is weaker than the spirit. In Sarastai's case her husband was an old man, so old that she had never been his wife in anything but name, and when he died she flinched at the decree that she must burn herself upon his funeral pyre. To have a widow backslide, especially the widow of such an influential man as he had been, would have cast dishonor on the family and brought undying scandal to the neighborhood; so they filled her up with opium and *gunjah*, put her best clothes on her and marched her to the burning-ghat half conscious and all but paralyzed with drugs—"

"Ah, yes, one comprehends completely," broke in Jules de Grandin. "But your uncle, what of him? What did he then do?"

"You can't use cavalry in wooded terrain, and the forest came down thick each side the road. Besides, my uncle had but two men with him, and to attempt a sortie would have meant sure death. Accordingly he waited till the procession filed past, then hurried back to his command and led them toward the burning-ghat. This lay in a depression by the river bank, so that the partly burned corpses could be conveniently thrown into the stream when cremation rites were finished. The Hindoos had a quarter-hour start, but that was just as well, as they took more time than that to make their preparations. The funeral pyre had been erected, and over it they poured a quantity of sandal-oil and melted butter. Paraffin was not so common in the Orient those days.

"When all had been prepared they took the dead man's costly garments off and stripped the widow of her jewels and gorgeous sari, wrapping each of them in plain white cotton cloth like winding-sheets and pouring rancid butter over them. They laid the corpse upon the pyre and marched the widow seven times around it with a lighted torch held in her hand. Then they lifted her up to the pyre, for the poor kid still was only semi-conscious, made her squat cross-legged, and laid the dead man's head upon her knees. A Brahmin gave the signal and the dead man's eldest son ran forward with a torch to set the oil-soaked wood afire, when my uncle rode out from the woods and ordered them to halt. He spoke Hindustani fluently, and there was no mistaking what he said when he told them that the Raj had banned suttee and commanded them to take the widow down.

"The thing the blighters didn't know was that nineteen Afghan cavalrymen were waiting in the underbrush; praying as hard as pious men could pray that the Hindoos would refuse to heed my uncle's orders.

"Allah heard their prayers, for the only answer that the Brahmins gave was a chorus of shrill curses and a barrage of stones and cow-dung. The dead man's son ran forward to complete the rite, but before he could apply the torch my uncle drew his pistol and shot him very neatly through the head.

"Then all hell broke loose. The guard of honor brought their muskets into play and fired a volley, wounding several of the crowd and cutting branches from the trees behind my uncle. But when they drew their swords and rushed at him it was no laughing-matter, for there must have been two hundred of them, and those fellows are mean hands with the bare steel.

"'Troop advance! Draw sabers! Trot, gallop, charge!' When the natives heard my uncle's order they halted momentarily, and it would have been a lot more healthy if they'd turned and run, for before they could say 'knife' the Afghans were among 'em, and the fat was in the fire.

"'*Yah Allah, Allah—Allah!*' cried the *subadar*, and his men gave tongue to the pack-cry that men of the North Country have used when hunting lowland Hindoos since the days when Moslem missionaries first converted Afghanistan.

"There were only nineteen of them, and my uncle, while the Hindoos must have totaled half a thousand, but"—the pride an honest man takes in his trade shone in his eyes as Pemberton grinned at us—"you don't need more than twenty professional soldiers to scatter a mob of scum like that any more than you need even numbers when you set the beagles on a flock of rabbits!"

"À *merveille!*" de Grandin cried. "I knew that I should win my bet. Before you told us of your uncle's actions you recall I made a wager with myself? *Bien.* I bet me that he would not let that lot of monkey-faces commit murder. *Très bon.* Jules de Grandin, pay me what you owe!" Solemnly he extracted a dollar from his trouser pocket, passed it from his right hand to his left, and stowed it in his waistcoat. "And now—the curse?" he prompted.

"Quite so, the curse. They took Sarastai from the funeral pyre and carried her to safety at the station, but before they went a *guru* put a curse on all of them. None should die in bed, he swore. Moreover, none of them should ever take inheritance of land or goods till kinsman had shed kinsman's blood upon the land to be inherited.

"And the maledictions seemed to work," he ended gloomily.—My Uncle Albert married Sarastai shortly after he had rescued her, and though she was as beautiful as any English girl, he found that he was ostracized, and had to give up his commission. English folk were no more cordial when he brought his 'tarbrush' bride back home to Surrey. So he emigrated to the States, fought the full four years of your great Civil War, and founded what has since become one of the largest fortunes in New Jersey. Still, see the toll the thing has taken. Not one of Albert Pemberton's descendants has long enjoyed the estate which he built, and death by fire has come to all his heirs. Looks as if I'm next in line."

De Grandin looked at him with narrowed eyes. "Death by fire, *Monsieur?*"

"Quite. Foxcroft's been burned down eight times, and every time it burned one or more of Albert Pemberton's descendants died. The first fire killed old Albert and his wife; the second took his eldest son, and—"

"One would think rebuilding with materials impervious to fire would have occurred to them—"

"Ha!" Our visitor's short laugh was far from mirthful. "It did, sir. In 1900 Robert Pemberton rebuilt Foxcroft of stone, with cement walls and floors. He was sitting in his libr'y alone at night when the curse took him. No fire was burning on the hearth, for it was early summer, but somehow the hearthrug got afire and the flames spread to the armchair where he dozed. They found him, burned almost to a crisp, next morning. Cyril Pemberton, from whom I take the estate, died in his motorcar three months ago. The thing caught fire just as he drove in the garage, and he fried like an eel before he could so much as turn the handle of the door.

"See here, Doctor de Grandin, you've just got to help me. When little Jim was born I resigned from the army so I could be with Avis and the kid. I bought a little farm in Hampshire and had settled down to be a country gentleman of sorts when Cyril died and news of this inheritance came. I sold the farm off at a loss to raise funds to come here. If I fail to meet the will's provisions and complete the twelve months' residence I'm ruined, utterly. You see the fix I'm in?"

"Completely," Jules de Grandin nodded. "Is there any other of your family who could claim this estate?"

"H'm. Yes, there is. I've a distant cousin named John Ritter who might be next in line. We were at Harrow together. Jolly rotten chap he was, too. Sent down from Oxford when they caught him cheatin' in a game o' cards, fired out o' the Indian Civil Administration for a lack of recognition of *meum et tuum* where other fellows' wives were concerned. Now, if Avis and I don't make good and live in this old rookery for a full twelve months, we forfeit our succession and the whole estate goes to this bounder. Not that he could make much use of it, but—"

"How so? Is he uninterested in money?"

"Oh, he's interested enough, but he's in jail."

"*Hein?* In durance?"

"Quite. In a Bombay jail, doin' a life stretch for killin' an outraged husband in a brawl. Jolly lucky he was that the jury didn't bring him in guilty of willful murder, too."

"One sees. And how long have you resided at Foxcroft?"

"Just six weeks, sir, and some dam queer things have taken place already."

"By example—"

"Our first night there the bedroom furniture caught fire. My wife and I were sound asleep, dog-tired from gettin' things in shape, and neither of us would have smelled the smoke until it was too late, but Laird, my Scottish terrier, was sleepin' by the bed, and he raised such a row he woke us up. Queer thing about it, too. There was no fire laid in the room, and neither Avis nor I'd been smokin', but the bedclothes caught fire, just the same, and we didn't have a second's spare time standin' clear. Two days later Laird died. Some stinkin' blighter poisoned him.

"The second week I was ridin' out from the village with some supplies when something whizzed past my head, almost cuttin' the tip o' my nose off. When I dismounted for a look around I found a knife-blade almost buried in a tree beside the road.

"We'd stocked the place with poultry, so that we could have fresh eggs, and every bloomin' chicken died. We can't keep a fowl in the hen-house overnight.

"Not only that; we've heard the damn'dest noises round the house—things crashing through the underbrush, bangings at the doors and windows, and the most infernal laughter from the woods at dead of night. It's got us nervy as a lot o' cats, sir.

"My wife and I both want to stick it, as much from principle as for the money, but Annie, Avis' old nurse, not to mention Appleby, my batman, are all for chuckin' the whole business. They're sure the curse is workin'."

De Grandin eyed him thoughtfully. "Your case has interest, Monsieur Pemberton," he said at last. "If it is convenient, Doctor Trowbridge and I will come to Foxcroft tomorrow afternoon."

We shook hands at the front door. "See you tomorrow afternoon," I promised as our caller turned away, "if anything—"

Whir-r-r-rr! Something flashing silver-gray beneath the street lamp's light came hurtling past my head, and a dull thud sounded as the missile struck the panel of the door.

"Ha, scélérat, coquin, assassin!" cried de Grandin, rushing out into the darkened street. "I have you!"

But he was mistaken. The sound of flying footsteps pounding down the street and vanishing around the corner was the sole clue to the mystery.

Breathing hard with rage as much as from exertion, he returned and wrenched the missile from my scarred front door. It was the blade of a cheap iron knife, such as may be bought at any ten-cent store, its point and edges ground to razor sharpness, its wooden helve removed and the blade-heel weighted with ten ounces of crude lead, roughly welded on.

"*Ah-ha!*" the little Frenchman murmured as he balanced the crude weapon in his palm. "*Ah-ha-ha!* One begins to understand. Tell me, *Monsieur*, was the other knife thrown at you like this one?"

"Yes, sir, just exactly!" gasped the Englishman.

"One sees, one comprehends; one understands. You may be out of India, my friend, but you are not away from it."

"What d'ye mean?"

"Me, I have seen the knife-blade weighted in this manner for assassination, but only in one place."

"Where?" asked Pemberton and I in chorus.

"In the interior of Burma. This weapon is as much like those used by *dakaits* of Upper Burma as one pea is like another in the pod. Tell me, *Monsieur le Capitaine*, did you ever come to grips with them in India?"

"No, sir," Pemberton replied. "All my service was in the South. I never got over into Burma."

"And you never had a quarrel with Indian priests or fakirs?"

"Positive. Fact is, I always rather liked the beggars and got on with 'em first rate."

"This adds the *moutarde piquante* to our dish. The coincidence of strange deaths you relate might be the workings of a fakir's curse; this knife is wholly physical, and very deadly. It would seem we are attacked on two sides, by super-physical assailants operating through the thought-waves of that old one's maledictions, and by some others who have reasons of their own for wishing you to be the center of attraction at a funeral. Good-night again, *Monsieur*, and a healthy journey home."

Foxcroft lay among the mountains almost at the Pennsylvania border, and after consulting road maps we voted to go there by train. It was necessary to change cars at a small way station, and when the local finally came we found ourselves unable to get seats together. Fortunately for me there was a vacant place beside a window, and after stowing my duffle in the rack I settled down to read an interesting but not too plausible article on the use of tetraiodophenolphthalein in the diagnosis of diseases of the gall bladder.

Glancing up from my magazine once or twice while the baggage car was being filled, I noticed several young yokels white and black, lounging on the station platform, and wondered idly why two young Negroes failed to join the laughing group. Instead, they seemed intent or something down the track, finally rose from the luggage truck on which they lounged and walked slowly toward the train. Beneath the window where I sat they paused a moment, and I noticed they were thin almost to emaciation, with skins of muddy brown rather than the chocolate of the Negro full-blood. Their hair, too, was straight as wire, and their eyes slate-gray rather than the usual brown of Africans.

"Odd-looking chaps," I mused as I resumed my reading.

Like most trains used in strictly local service, ours was composed of the railway's almost cast-off stock. Doors would not stay shut, windows would not open. Before we'd gone two miles the air within our coach was almost fetid. I rose and staggered up the swaying aisle to get a drink of water, only to find the tank was empty. After several unsuccessful efforts I succeeded in forcing back the door to the next coach and was inserting a cent in the cup-vending machine when a furious hissing forward told me someone had yanked the emergency cord. The train came to a bumping stop within its length, and I stumbled back to our coach to find de Grandin, a trainman and several passengers gathered in a knot about the seat I had just vacated.

"This is *hideux*, my friend!" the little Frenchman whispered. "Observe him, if you please."

I looked, and turned sick at the sight. The big countryman who had shared the seat with me was slumped down on the green-plush covered bench, his throat so deeply gashed the head sagged horribly upon one shoulder. A spate of blood from a severed jugular smeared clothing, seat and floor. The window beside which I'd sat was smashed to slivers, and bits of broken glass lay all around.

"How—what—" I stammered, and for answer Jules de Grandin pointed to the floor. Midway in the aisle lay something that gleamed dully, the counterpart of the lead-weighted blade which had been thrown at Pemberton as he left my house the night before.

"Good heavens!" I exclaimed; "if I hadn't gone for water—"

"*Mais oui*," de Grandin interrupted. "For the first time in a long and useful life I find that I can say a word for water as a beverage. Undoubtlessly that knife was meant for you, my friend."

"But why?"

"Are you not a friend of Monsieur Pemberton's?"

"Of course, but—"

"No buts, Friend Trowbridge. Consider. There were two of those assassins at your house last night; at least I judge so from the noise they made in flight. You stood directly in the light from the hall lamp when we bid our guest goodnight; they must have made a note of your appearance. Apparently we have been under surveillance since then, and it is highly probable they heard us say that we would visit him today. *Voilà.*"

We descended from the car and walked along the track. "*Regardez-vous!*" he ordered as we reached the window where I had been seated.

Upon the car-side was the crude outline of a grinning skull drawn in white crayon.

"Good Lord—those brown men at the station!" I jerked out. "They must have drawn this—it seemed to me they were not Negroes—"

"But no. But yes!" he nodded in agreement. "Indubitably they were not Africans, but Burmans. And very bad ones, too. This skull is the official signet of the goddess Kali, patron deity of *thags*, and the cult of *thaggee* makes its headquarters in Burma. It is useless to attempt to apprehend the thrower of the knife. By now he has had time to run half-way to Burma. But it behooves us to he careful how we step. We know not where to look for it, or when the blow will fall, but deadly peril walks with us from this time on. I do not think this task which we have undertaken is a very healthy one, my friend."

D RESSED IN SHABBY OXFORD bags and a khaki shooting-coat, Pemberton was waiting for us at the little railway station.

"Cheerio!" he greeted as we joined him. "All quiet on the jolly old Potomac, what?"

"Decidedly," de Grandin answered, then told him of the tragedy.

"By Jove!" our host exclaimed; "I'm shot if I don't feel like cutting the whole rotten business. Taking chances is all right for me, just part of the game, but to lug my wife into this hornets' nest—" he cranked the antiquated flivver standing by the platform, and we drove in moody silence through the groves of black-boughed, whispering pines that edged the roadway.

British genius for getting order out of chaos was evident as we arrived at Foxcroft. The straggling lawn was neatly trimmed, the raffish privet hedge was clipped, on the small grass plot were several wicker chairs with brightly colored sailcloth cushions. A line of lush green weeping willows formed a background for the weather-mellowed, ivy-covered house with its many gables, mullioned windows and projecting bays. As we chugged and wheezed between the tall posts of the gateless entranceway a young woman quit a gayly colored canvas hammock and walked toward us, waving cheerful greeting.

"Don't say anything about what happened on the train, please," begged Pemberton as he brought the coughing motor to a halt.

Though definitely brunette, Avis Pemberton was just as definitely British. She had wide-spaced, slightly slanting hazel eyes, straight, dark hair smoothly parted in the middle and drawn low across her ears, a broad, white forehead, a small straight nose set above a full-lipped rather wide and humorous mouth, and a small and pointed chin marked with the faint suspicion of a cleft. When she smiled, two dimples showed low in her cheeks, making a merrily incongruous combination with her exotic eyes. She was dressed in a twin sweater combination, a kilted skirt of Harris tweed, Shetland socks and a pair of Scotch grain brogues which, clumsy as they were, could not disguise the slimness of her feet. Every line of her was long, fine cut, and British as a breath of lavender.

"Hullo-hullo, old thing," her husband greeted. "Anything untoward occur while the good old bread-winner was off?"

"Nothing, Lord and Master," she answered smilingly as she acknowledged his quick introductions, but her hazel eyes were wide and thoughtful as the little Frenchman raised her fingers to his lips at presentation, and I thought I saw her cast a frightened glance across her shoulder as her husband turned to help us drag our duffle from the car.

Dinner was a rite at Foxcroft, as dinner always is with Britons. A flat bouquet of roses graced the table, four tall candles flickered in tall silver standards; the soup was cool and under-seasoned, the joint of mutton tough and underdone, the burgundy a little sour, the apple tart a sadly soggy thing which might have made a billy-goat have nightmares. But Pemberton looked spick and span in dinner clothes and his wife was a misty vision in rose lace. Appleby, the "bat man" who served Pemberton as servant through three army terms and quit the service to accompany him in civil life, served the meal with faultless technique and brought us something he called coffee when the meal was over and we congregated on the lawn beneath a spreading poplar tree. De Grandin's air of gloom grew deeper by the minute. When the servant tendered him a Sèvres cup filled with the off-brown, faintly steaming mixture, I thought he would assault him. Instead, he managed something like a smile as he turned to our hostess.

"I have heard Monsieur Pemberton speak of your son, *Madame*; is he with you in America?" he asked.

"Oh, dear, no; he's with my father at Lerwick-on-Tyne. You see, we didn't know just what conditions here might be, and thought that he'd be safer at the vicarage."

"Your father is a churchman, then?"

"Very much so. It was not till after we had Little Jim that he managed to forgive me; even now I'm not quite sure that he regards me as a proper person to have custody of a small boy."

"*Madame*, I am confused. How is it you say—"

The girl laughed merrily. "Father's terribly low church and mid-Victorian. He classes foreigners and Anglo-Catholics, heathens, actors and Theosophists together. When I joined a troupe of unit dancers at the Palace he said public prayers for me; when I went out to the colonies to dance he disowned me as a vagabond. I met Big Jim while dancing in Bombay, and when I wrote I'd married him the only answer Father sent was a note congratulating me on having found an officer and gentleman to make an honest woman of me. I almost died when Little Jim was born, and the doctors said I could not stand the Indian climate, so Big Jim gave up his commission and we all went back to England. Father wouldn't see us for almost a year, but when we finally took our baby to him for baptism he capitulated utterly. He's really an old dear, when you penetrate his shell, but if he ever saw me do an Indian dance—"

"You'd have to start from scratch again, old thing," her husband chuckled as he lit his pipe.

"She used to sneak off every chance she got and take instructions from the native dancers. Got so perfect in the technique that if she'd been a little darker-skinned she could have passed in any temple as a *deva-dasi*—by Jove, I say!" He looked at her as though he saw her for the first time.

"What is it, Jim?"

"I say, you know, I never noticed it before, but there's a look about you like Sarastai. Fine and beautiful, and all that sort of—"

"Oh, Jim darling, stop it! Anyone would think—what's that?"

"'elp, 'elp, somebody—'elp!" the shriek came from the house behind us, each quavering syllable raw-edged with terror.

We rushed around the angle of the building, through the neatly planted kitchen garden and up the three low steps that reached the kitchen door.

"What is it—who is here?" cried de Grandin as we paused upon the big room's threshold.

In the corner farthest from the door crouched an aged woman, or perhaps I should have said a creature with a woman's body, but a face like nothing human. Seasoned and lined with countless wrinkles, yellowed teeth bared in a senseless grin, she squatted by an open casement, elbows stiffly bent, hands hanging loosely, as a begging terrier might hold its paws, and mouthed and gibbered at us as we stared.

"Good God!" our host ejaculated. "Annie—"

"Annie! Oh, my poor dear Annie!" cried our hostess as she rushed across the lamp-lit kitchen and threw her arms around the human caricature crouching in the angle of the wall. "What's wrong with her?" she called across her shoulder as she hugged the mouthing crone against her bosom. "What's—O God, she's mad!"

The woman cringed away from the encircling arms. "You won't 'urt ole Annie, will 'ee?" she whimpered. "You won't let the black man get 'er? See"—she bared a skinny forearm—"'e 'urt me! 'e 'urt me with a shiny thing!"

De Grandin drew his breath in sharply as he examined the tiny wound which showed against the woman's wrinkled skin. "Up to the elbow, *mes amis*," he told us solemnly. "We have stepped in it up to the elbow. Me, I know this mark. But yes, I have seen him before. The devotees of Kali sometimes shoot a serum in a victim's arm with such results. I know not what this serum is—and probably no white man does—but the Indian police know it. 'Whom the gods destroy they first make mad' is no idle proverb with the *thags* of Burma. *Non*. There is no antidote for it. This poor one will be gone by morning. Meantime"—he put his hands beneath the woman's arms and raised her—"she might as well die in bed in Christian fashion. Will you lead us to her room, Friend Pemberton?"

De Grandin on one side, I on the other, we half led, half carried the chuckling, weeping crone along the passageway. A gust of wind swung the long casement open and I crossed to close it. From the night outside where thickly growing rhododendron shut the moonlight out there came a laugh like that the fiends of hell might give at the arrival of a new consignment of lost souls. "Ha-ha!—ha-ha-ha!—ha-ha!"

"Sacré nom, I'll make you laugh upon the other side of your misshapen face!" de Grandin cried, dropping the old woman's arm and rushing to the window where he leant across the sill and poured the contents of his automatic pistol at the shadows whence the ghostly laughter came.

A crash of twigs and the flapping-back of displaced branches answered, and from the further distance came an echo of the wild, malignant cachinnation: "Ha-ha!—ha-ha-ha!—ha-ha!"

"AND NOW, MY FRIENDS, it is for us to formulate our strategy," de Grandin told us as we finished breakfast. "From the things which we have seen and heard I'd say we are beset by human and subhuman agencies; possibly working independently, more probably in concert. First of all I must go to the village to make some purchases and notify the coroner of your late lamented servant's death. I shall return, but"—he cast the phantom of a wink at me—"not for luncheon."

He was back a little after noon with a large, impressive bundle which clanked mysteriously each time he shifted it. When the papers were removed he showed a set of heavy padlocks, each complete with hasp and staple. Together we went round the big house, fixing locks at doors and windows, testing fastenings repeatedly; finally, when our task was done, repairing to the lawn where Appleby awaited us with a teacart-load of toasted muffins, strawberry preserve and steaming oolong.

"What was in that old beer bottle that you stood beside the bed?" I asked. "It looked like ordinary water."

"Water, yes," he answered with a grin, "but not ordinary, I assure you. I have the—what you call him?—hunch?—my friend. Tonight, perhaps tomorrow, we shall have use for what I brought out from the village."

"But what—"

"Hullo, there, ready for a spot of tea?" called Pemberton. "I'm famished, and the little woman's just about to haul her colors down."

"You are distrait, Madame?" de Grandin asked, dropping into a willow chair and casting a suspicious glance upon the tray of muffins Appleby extended.

"Indeed, I am. I've been feeling devils all day long." She smiled at him a little wearily above her teacup rim. "Something's seemed to boil up in me—it's the queerest thing, but I've had an urge to dance, an almost irresistible impulse to put an Indian costume on and do the *Bramara*—the Bee-dance. I know it's dreadful to feel so, with poor old Annie's body lying by the wall and this menace hanging over us, but something seems to urge me almost past resistance to put my costume on and dance—"

"*Tiens, Madame*, one comprehends," he smiled agreement. "I, too, have felt these so queer urges. *Regardez, s'il vous plaît*: We are beset by mental stress, we look about us for escape and there seems none; then suddenly from some-where comes an urge unbidden. Perhaps it is to take a drink of tea; maybe we feel impelled to walk out in the rain; quite possibly the urge comes to sit down and strum at the piano, or, as in your case, to dance. Reason is a makeshift thing, at best. We have used it but a scant half-million years; our instincts reach back to the days when we crawled in primeval ooze. Trust instinct, *Madame*. Something boils within you, you declare? *Très bien*. It is your ego seeking liberation. Permit the boiling to continue; then, when the effete mat-ter rises to the top, we skim him off"—with his hand he made a gesture as of scooping something up—"and throw him out. *Voilà*. We have got rid of that which worries us!"

"You think I should give way to it?"

"But certainly, of course; why not? This evening after dinner, if you still have the urge to dance, we shall delight to watch you and applaud your art."

TEA FINISHED, APPLEBY, DE Grandin and I set out on a reconnaissance. We walked across the grass plot to the copse of evergreens from which the weird laughter came the night before and searched the ground on hands and knees. Our search was fruitless, for pine needles lay so thick upon the ground that noth-ing like a footprint could be found.

Behind the house stood barn and hen-coops, the latter empty, Pemberton's archaic flivver and two saddle-horses tenanting the former. "It's queer the place should he so much run down, considering the family's wealth," I murmured as we neared the stable.

"The former howner was a most hexcentric man, sir," Appleby supplied. "'e never seemed to care about the plyce, and didn't live 'ere hany more than necess'ry. Hi've 'eard 'e honly used hit as a sort o'—my Gawd, wot's that?" He pointed to a little mound of earth beside the barn foundation.

De Grandin took a step or two in the direction of the little hillock, then paused, his small nose wrinkled in disgust. "It has the perfume of corruption," he remarked.

"W'y, hit's pore hold Laird, the master's dawg, sir," Appleby returned excit-edly. "Who's done this thing to 'im? Hi dug 'is gryve meself, sir, w'en we found 'im dead, hand Hi took partic'lar pynes to myke hit deep hand strong. 'eaped a thumpin' boulder hon 'im, sir, Hi did, but now—"

"One sees, and smells," de Grandin interrupted. "He has been resurrected, but not restored to life."

The cockney leant above the violated grave to push the earth back in. "Picked clean 'e is, sir," he reported. "'e couldn't be no cleaner hif a stinkin' buzzard 'ad been hat 'im."

The little Frenchman tweaked the needle-points of his wheat-blond mustache between a thoughtful thumb and forefinger. "It is possible—quite probable," he murmured. "They have imported every other sort of devilment; why not this one?"

"What?" I demanded. "Who's imported what—"

"Zut! We have work to do, my friend. Do you begin here at this spot and walk in ever-widening circles. Eventually, unless I miss my guess, you will come upon the tracks of a large dog. When you have found them, call me, if you please."

I followed his instructions while he and Appleby walked toward the house.

In fifteen or twenty minutes I reached a patch of soft earth where pine needles did not lie too thick to cover tracks, and there, plain as the cannibals' mark on the sands of Crusoe's island, showed the paw-print of a giant dog.

"Hullo, de Grandin!" I began. "I've found—"

A crashing in the undergrowth near by cut short my hail, and I drew the pistol which de Grandin had insisted that I carry as the thing or person neared me.

The rhododendron branches parted as a pair of groping hands thrust forth, and Appleby came staggering out. "Th' black 'un, sir," he gasped in a hoarse voice. "Hi passed 'im 'fore I knew it, sir, then seen 'is turban shinin' hin th' leaves. I myde to shoot 'im, but 'e stuck me with a forked stick. Hi'm a-dyin', sir, a-dy—"

He dropped upon the grass, the fatal word half uttered, made one or two convulsive efforts to regain his feet, then slumped down on his face.

"De Grandin!" I called frenziedly. "I say, de Grandin—"

He was beside me almost as I finished calling, and together we cut the poor chap's trouser leg away, disclosing two small parallel pin-pricks in the calf of his left leg. A little spot of ecchymosis, like the bruise left by a blow, was round the wounds, and beyond it showed an area of swelled and reddened skin, almost like a scald. When de Grandin made a small incision with his knife in the bruised flesh, then pressed each side the wounds, the blood oozed thickly, almost like a semi-hardened gelatin.

"C'est fini," he pronounced as he rose and brushed his knees. "He did not have a chance, that poor one. This settles it."

"What settles what?"

"This, parbleu! If we needed further proof that we are menaced by a band of desperate *dakaits* we have it now. It is the mark and sign-manual of the criminal tribes of Burma. The man is dead of cobra venom—but these wounds were not made by a snake's fangs."

"But good heavens, man, if this keeps up there won't be one of us to tell the tale!" cried Pemberton as we completed ministering to Appleby's remains. "Twice they almost got me with their knives; they almost murdered Doctor Trowbridge; they've done for Annie and poor Appleby—"

"*Exactement*," de Grandin nodded. "But this will not keep up. Tonight, this very evening, we shall call their promontory—*non*, I mean their bluff. The coincidences of your kinsmen's deaths by fire, those might have been attributed to Hindoo curses; myself, I think they are; but these deliberate murders and attempts at murder are purely human doings. Your cousin, Monsieur Ritter—"

"Not an earthly!" Pemberton smiled grimly. "Did you ever see a British Indian jail? Not quite as easy to walk out of 'em as it is from an American prison—"

"Notwithstanding which, *Monsieur*"—the little Frenchman smiled sarcastically—"this Monsieur Ritter is at large, and probably within a gun-shot of us now. When I was in the village this forenoon I cabled the police at Bombay. The answer came within three hours:

John Ritter, serving a life term, escaped four months ago. His whereabouts unknown.

"You see? His jail-break almost coincided with the passing of your kinsman in America. He knew about the family curse, undoubtlessly, and determined to make profit by it. But he was practical, that one. *Mais oui*. He did not intend to wait the working of a curse which might be real or only fanciful. Not he, by blue! He bought the service of a crew of Burman cutthroats, and they came with all their bag of villain's tricks—their knives, their subtle poisons, even a hyena! That it was your servants and not you who met their deaths is not attributable to any kindness on his part, but merely to good fortune. Your turns will come, unless—"

"Unless we hook it while we have the chance!"

"Unless you do exactly as I say," de Grandin finished without notice of the interruption. "In five minutes it will be ten o'clock. I suggest we seek our rooms, but not to sleep. You, *Monsieur*, and you, *Madame*, will see that both your doors and windows are securely fastened. Meantime, Doctor Trowbridge and I will repair to our chamber and—*eh bien*, I think we shall see things!"

DESPITE DE GRANDIN'S ADMONITION, I fell fast asleep. How long I'd slept I do not know, nor do I recall what wakened me. There was no perceptible sound, but suddenly I was sitting bolt-upright, staring fascinated at our window's shadowed oblong. "Lucky thing we put those locks on," I reassured myself; "almost anything might—"

The words died on my tongue, and a prickling sensation traced my spine. What it was I did not know, but every sense seemed warning me of dreadful danger.

"De Grandin!" I whispered hoarsely. "De Grandin—"

I reached across the bed to waken him. My hand encountered nothing but the blanket. I was in that tomb-black room with nothing but my fears for company.

Slowly, scarcely faster than the hand that marks the minutes on the clock, the window-sash swung back. The heavy lock we'd stapled on was gone or broken. I heard the creak of rusty hinges, caught the faint rasp of a bar against the outer sill, and my breath went hot and sulfurous in my throat as a shadow scarcely darker than the outside night obscured the casement.

It was like some giant dog—a mastiff or great Dane—but taller, heavier, with a mane of unkempt hair about its neck. Pointed ears cocked forward, great eyes gleaming palely phosphorescent, it pressed against the slowly yielding window-frame. And now I caught the silhouette of its hog-snouted head against the window, saw its parted, sneering lips, smelled the retching stench that emanated from it, and went sick with horror. The thing was a hyena, a grave-robber, offal-eater, most loathsome of all animals.

Slowly, inch by cautious inch, it crept into the room, fangs bared in a snarl that held the horrible suggestion of a sneer. "Help, de Grandin—help!" I shrieked, leaping from the bed and dragging tangled blankets with me as a shield.

The hyena sprang. With a cry that was half growl, half obscene parody of a human chuckle, it launched itself through the intervening gloom, and next instant I was smothered underneath its weight as it worried savagely at the protecting blanket.

"Sa-ha, Monsieur l'Hyène, you seek a meal? Take this!" Close above me Jules de Grandin swung a heavy kukri knife as though it were a headsman's ax, striking through the wiry mane, driving deep into the brute's thick neck, almost decapitating it.

"Get up, my friend; arise," he ordered as he hauled me from beneath the bedclothes, already soaking with the foul beast's blood. "Me, I have squatted none too patiently behind the bed, waiting for the advent of that one. *Morbleu*, I thought that he would never come!"

"How'd you know about it—" I began, but he cut me short with a soft chuckle.

"The laughter in the bush that night, the small dog's ravished grave, finally the tracks you found today. They made the case complete. I made elaborate show of opening our window, and they must have found the others fastened; so they determined to send their pet before them to prepare the way. He was savage, that one, but so am I, by blue! Come, let us tell our host and hostess of our visitor."

T HE NEXT DAY WAS a busy one. Sheriff's deputies and coroner's assistants came in almost ceaseless streams, questioning endlessly, making notes of everything, surveying the thicket where Appleby was killed and the kitchen where old Annie met her fate. At last the dreary routine ended, the mortician took away the bodies, and the Pembertons faced us solemn-eyed across the dinner table.

"I'm for chucking the whole rotten business," our host declared. "They've got two of us—"

"And we have one of them," supplied de Grandin. "Anon we shall have—"

"We're cutting out of here tomorrow," broke in Pemberton. "I'll go to selling cotton in the city, managing estates or clerking in a shop before I'll subject Avis to this peril one more day."

"*C'est l'enfantillage!*" declared de Grandin. "When success is almost in your hand you would retreat? *Fi donc, Monsieur!*"

"*Fi donc* or otherwise, we're going in the morning," Pemberton replied determinedly.

"Very well, let it be as you desire. Meantime, have you still the urge to dance, *Madame?*"

Avis Pemberton glanced up from her teacup with something like a guilty look. "More than ever," she returned so low that we could scarcely catch her words.

"*Très bien.* Since this will be our last night in the house, permit that we enjoy your artistry."

Her preparations were made quickly. We cleared a space in the big drawing-room, rolling back the rugs to bare the polished umber tiles of which the floor was made. Upon a chair she set a small hand-gramophone, needle ready poised, then hurried to her room to don her costume.

"*Écoutez, s'il vous plaît,*" de Grandin begged, tiptoeing from the drawing-room, returning in a moment with the water-filled beer bottle which he had brought from the village, the kukri knife with which he killed the hyena, and a pair of automatic pistols. One of these he pressed on me, the other on our host. "Have watchfulness, my friends," he bade in a low whisper. "When the music for the dance commences it is likely to attract an uninvited audience. Should anyone appear at either window, I beg you to shoot first and make inquiries afterward."

"Hadn't we better close the blinds?" I asked. "Because if we're likely to be watched—"

"*Mais non,*" he negatived. "See, there is no light here save that the central lamp casts down, and that will shine directly on *Madame.* We shall be in shadow, but anyone who seeks to peer in through the window will be visible against the moonlight. You comprehend?"

"I'd like to have a final go at 'em," our host replied. "Even if I got only one, it'd help to even things for Appleby and Annie."

"I quite agree," de Grandin nodded. "Now—s-s-sh; silence. *Madame* comes!"

The chiming clink of ankle bells announced her advent, and as she crossed the threshold with a slow, sensuous walk, hips rolling, feet flat to floor, one set directly before the other, I leant forward in amazement. Never had I thought that change of costume could so change a personality. Yet there it was. In tweeds and Shetlands Avis Pemberton was British as a sunrise over Surrey, or a Christmas pageant Columbine; this sleekly black-haired figure rippling past us with the grace of softly flowing water was a daughter of the gods, a temple *deva-dasi*, the mystery and allure and unfathomable riddle of the East incarnate. Her bodice was of saffron silk, sheer as net. Cut with short shoulder-sleeves and rounded neck it terminated just below her small, firm breasts and was edged with imitation emeralds and small opals which kindled into witch-fires in the lamplight's glow. From breast to waist her slim, firm form was bare, slender as an adolescent boy's, yet full enough to keep her ribs from showing in white lines against the creamy skin. A smalt-blue cincture had been tightly bound about her slender waist, emphasizing gently swelling hips and supporting a full, many-pleated skirt of cinnabar-red silken gauze. Across her smoothly parted blue-black hair was thrown a sari of deep blue with silver edging, falling down across one shoulder and caught coquettishly within the curve of a bent elbow. Silver bracelets hung with little hawk-bells bound her wrists; heavy bands of hammered silver with a fringe of silver tassels that flowed rippling to the floor and almost hid her feet were ringed about each ankle. Between her startlingly black brows there burned the bright vermilion of a caste mark.

Pemberton pressed the lever of the gramophone and a flood of liquid music flowed into the room. Deep, plaintive chords came from the guitar, the viols wept and crooned by turns, and the drums beat out an amatory rhythm. She paused a moment in the swing-lamp's golden disk of light, feet close together, knees straight, arms raised above her head, wrists interlaced, the right hand facing left, the left turned to the right, and each pressed to the other, palm to palm and finger against finger. The music quickened and she moved her feet in a swift, shuffling step, setting ankle bells a-chime, swaying like a palm tree in the rising breeze. She took the folds of her full skirt between joined thumbs and forefingers, daintily, as one might take a pinch of snuff, spread the gleaming, many-pleated tissue out fanwise, and advanced with a slow, gliding step. Her head bent sidewise, now toward this sleek shoulder, now toward that; then slowly it sank back, her long eyes almost closed, like those of one who falls into a swoon of unsupportable delight; her red lips parted, fell apart as though they had gone flaccid with satiety after ecstasy. Then she dropped forward in a deep salaam, head bent submissively, both hands upraised with thumbs and forefingers together.

I was about to beat my hands together in applause when de Grandin's grip upon my elbow halted me. "*Les flammes, mon ami, regardez-vous—les flammes!*" he whispered.

Across the vitric umber tiles that made the floor, a line of flame was rising, flickering and dancing, wavering, flaunting, advancing steadily, and I could smell the spicy-sweet aroma of burnt sandalwood. "It is the flame from that old, cheated funeral pyre," he breathed. "The vengeance-flame that burned the old one to a crisp while he lay in a fireproof room; the flame that set this house afire eight times; the flame of evil genius that pursues this family. See how easily I conquer it!"

With an agile leap he crossed the room, raised the bottle he had brought and spilled a splash of water on the crackling, leaping fire-tongues. It was as if a picture drawn in chalks were wiped away, or an image on a motion picture screen obliterated as the light behind the film dies; for everywhere the drops of water fell, the flames died into blackness with a sullen, scolding hiss. Back and forth across the line of fire he hurried, throwing water on the fluttering, dazzling flares till all were dead and cold.

"The window, *mes amis*, look to the window! Shoot if you see faces!" he ordered as he fought the dying fire.

Both Pemberton and I looked up as he called out, and I felt a sudden tightening in my throat as my eyes came level with the window. Framed in the panes were three faces, two malignant, brown and scowling, one a sun-burned white, but no less savage. The dark men I remembered instantly. It was they who stood beside the train the day the knife was thrown to kill the man who shared the seat with me. But the frowning, cursing white man was a stranger.

Even as I looked I saw one of the brown men draw his hand back and caught the glimmer of a poised knife blade. I raised my pistol and squeezed hard upon the trigger, but the mechanism jammed, and I realized the knifeman had me at his mercy.

But Pemberton's small weapon answered to his pressure, and the stream of bullets crashed against the glass, sent it shattering in fragments, and bored straight through the scowling countenances, making little sharp-edged pits in them like those a stream of sprinkled water makes when turned upon damp clay, except that where these little pockmarks showed there spread a smear of crimson.

There was something almost comic in the look of pained surprise the faces showed as the storm of bullets swept across them. Almost, it seemed to me, they voiced a protest at an unexpected trick; as though they'd come to witness an amusing spectacle, only to discover that the joke was turned on them, and they had no relish for the rôle of victim.

"Yes, it's Ritter, all right," Pemberton pronounced as we turned the bodies over in the light of an electric torch. "Of course, he was a filthy rotter and all that, but—hang it all, it's tough to know you have a kinsman's blood upon your hands, even if—"

"*Parbleu; tu parles, mon ami!*—you've said it!" cried de Grandin in delight. "The ancient curse has been fulfilled, the wicked one's condition met. A kinsman has shed kinsman's blood upon the property inherited!"

"Why—"

"'Why' be doubled-damned stewed in Satan's sauce-pan; I tell you it is so!" He swung his arm in an all-comprehensive gesture. "We have at once disposed of everything, my friend. The human villains who would murder you and Madame Pemberton, the working of the ancient curse pronounced so many years ago—all are eliminated!"

He leant above the body of a prostrate Indian, searching through his jacket with careful fingers. "Ah-ha, behold him!" he commanded. "Here is the thing that killed your so unfortunate retainer." He held a length of bamboo stick fitted at the end with something like a tuning-fork to which a rubber bulb was fixed. "Careful!" he warned as I reached out to touch it. "The merest prick of those sharp points is certain death."

Pressing the queer instrument against the wall, he pointed to twin spots of viscid, yellow liquid sticking to the stones. "Cobric acid—concentrated essence of the cobra's venom," he explained. "One drives these points into his victim's body—the sharp steel penetrates through clothing where a snake's fangs might not pierce—and *pouf!* enough snake-poison goes into the poor one's veins to cause death in three minutes. *Tiens*, it is a clever little piece of devilment *n'est-ce-pas*."

"D'ye think we got em all?" asked Pemberton.

"Indubitably. Had there been more, they would have been here. Consider: First they set their foul beast on us, believing he will kill some one of us, at least. He does not return, and they are puzzled. Could it be that we disposed of him? They do not know, but they are worried. Anon they hear the strains of Indian music in the house. This are not the way things had been planned by them. There should be no celebration here. They wonder more, and come to see what happens. They observe *Madame* concluding her so lovely dance; they also see us all unharmed, and are about to use their knives when you forestall them with your pistol."

"But there were two Burmese at the railway station the other day, yet someone threw the knife intended to kill Doctor Trowbridge," objected Pemberton. "That would indicate a third one in reserve—"

De Grandin touched the white man's sprawling body with the tip of his small shoe. "There was, my friend, and this is he," he answered shortly. "Your charming cousin, Monsieur Ritter. It was he who hid beside the tracks and hurled the knife when he beheld the mark of Kali. The Burmans knew friend Trowbridge; had it been one of them who lay in ambush he would not have wasted knife or energy in killing the wrong man, but Ritter had no other guide than the skull chalked on the car. *Tenez*, he threw the knife that killed the poor young man to death."

"How do you account for the fire that broke out just as Mrs. Pemberton had finished dancing?" I asked.

"There is no scientific explanation for it, at least no explanation known to modern chemistry or physics. We must seek deeper—farther—for its reason. Those Hindoo *gurus*, they know things. They can cast a rope into the air and make it stand so rigidly that one may climb it. They take a little, tiny seed and place it in the earth, and there, before your doubting eyes, it grows and puts forth leaves and flowers. Me, I have seen them take a piece of ordinary wood—my walking-stick, *parbleu!*—make passes over it, and make it burst in flames. Now, if their ordinary showmen can do things like that, how much more able are their true adepts to bring forth fire at will, or on the happening of specific things? The rescue of the Hindoo girl Sarastai left the funeral pyre without a victim, and so the old priests placed a curse on her and hers, decreeing fire should take its toll of all her husband's family till kinsman had shed kinsman's blood. That was the fire that followed every generation of the Pembertons. This fire burned this house again, and yet again, burned one when he lay in safety in a fireproof room—even set a motorcar afire to kill the late proprietor of the estate.

"Tonight conditions were ideal. The sacred music of the temple sounded from the gramophone, Madame Avis danced in Hindoo costume; danced an old, old dance, perhaps the very dance Sarastai used to dance. Our thoughts were tuned to India—indeed, there is no doubt the urge which prompted Madame Pemberton to dance a Hindoo dance in Hindoo costume came directly from the thought-waves set in motion by those old priests in the days of long ago. The very stones of this old house are saturated in malignant thought-waves—thoughts of vengeance—and Madame Avis was caught up in them and forced along the pathway toward destruction. All was prepared, conditions were ideal, the victims waited ready for the flames. Only one thing that old priest forgot to foresee.

"Jolly interestin'," murmured Pemberton. "What was it he forgot?"

"That you would ask advice of Jules de Grandin!" my little friend grinned shamelessly. "There it was he missed his trick. I am very clever. I looked the situation over and saw we were confronted by both physical and ghostly menaces. For the men we have the sword, the pistol and the fist. For the ghostly enemy we need a subtler weapon.

"Accordingly, when I go to the village to obtain the locks for doors and windows, I also stop to visit with the *curé* of the little church. Fortunately, he is Irish, and I do not have to waste a day convincing him. 'Mon père,' I say, 'we are confronted with the devil of a situation. A crew of monkey-faces who give worship to the wicked ones of India are menacing a Christian family. They will undoubtlessly attempt to burn them up with fire—not ordinary fire, but fire they make by wicked, sinful, heathen incantations. Now, for ordinary fire we use the ordinary water; what should we use to put out fire that comes from hell, or hell's assistants?'

"That old priest smiles at me. He is no fool. 'My son,' he say, 'long, long ago the fathers of the Church discovered that it is hot work to fight the devil with fire. Therefore they invent holy water. How much of it will you be needing for your work?'

"He was a good and hospitable man, that priest. He had no whisky in the house, but he had beer. So we made a lunch of beer and cheese and biscuit, and when we finish, we clean a bottle out and fill him to the neck with *eau bénite*.

"'Bonjour, mon fils,' the old priest say, 'and when you win your fight with Satan's henchmen, remember that our church could use a new baptismal font.' You will remember that, I trust, *Monsieur*, when you get your inheritance?"

"By George, I'll build a new church for him, if he wants it!" promised Pemberton.

THE LOCOMOTIVE GAVE A long-drawn, mournful wail as the train drew near the station and the smiling porter hurried through the car collecting luggage. "Well, we're home again," I remarked as the train slid to a stop.

"Yes, *grâce à Dieu*, we have escaped," de Grandin answered piously.

"It did look pretty bad at times," I nodded. "Especially when that fellow at the window poised his knife, and those devilish flames began to flicker—"

"Ah bah," he interrupted scornfully. "Those things? *Pouf*, they were not to be considered! I speak of something far more hideous we have escaped. That dreadful English cooking, that cuisine of the savage. That roast of mutton, that hell-brew they call coffee, that abominable apple tart!

"Come, let us take the fastest cab and hasten home. There a decent drink awaits us, and tonight in hell's despite I shall complete construction of the perfect bouillabaisse!"

Frozen Beauty

T HE HEAT HAD BEEN intolerable all day, but now a rain was falling, a soft and cooling summer rain that spread a gleaming black veneer across the highway pavement and marked the traffic lamps with cross-shaped fuzzy glows of green and ruby. Falling on our faces as we drove home from the club with the roadster's canvas cover folded back it was cool and gracious, delicate and calm upon our brows as the light touch of a skillful nurse's fingers on a fever-patient's forehead, soothing nerves stretched taut by eighteen holes of golf played in a blistering sun.

My friend Jules de Grandin's satisfaction with himself was most annoying. He had ceased playing at the second hole, found a wicker rocker on the clubhouse porch and devoted the entire afternoon to devastation of gin swizzles.

"*Tiens*," he chuckled, "you are droll, my friend, you English and Americans. You work like Turks and Tartars at your professional vocations, then rest by doing manual labor in the sun. Not I, by blue; I have the self-respect!"

He leant back on the cushions, turning up his forehead to the cooling rain and hummed a snatch of tune:

La vie est vaine,
Un peu d'amour—

With a strident screech of brakes I brought the roadster to a stop in time to keep from running down the man who stood before us in the headlights' glare, arm raised imperatively. "Good heavens, man," I rasped, "d'ye want to be run over? You almost—"

"You're a doctor?" he demanded in a sharp, thin voice, pointing to the Medical Society's green cross and gold caduceus on my radiator.

"Yes, but—"

"Please come at once, sir. It's the master, Doctor Pavlovitch. I—I think he's very ill, sir."

The ethics of the medical profession take no account of work-worn nerves, and with a sigh I headed toward the tall gate in the roadside hedge the fellow pointed out. "What seems to be the matter with the doctor?" I inquired as our guide hopped nimbly on the running-board after swinging back the driveway gate.

"I—I don't know, sir," he replied. "Some kind o' stroke, I think. Th' telephone went out of order just at dinner-time—lightning musta hit th' line when th' storm was blowin' up—an' I took th' station wagon to th' village for some things th' grocer hadn't sent. When I got back everythink was dark an' couldn't seem to make th' lights work, but they flashed on all sudden-like, an there was Doctor Pavlovitch a-layin' in th' middle o' th' floor, with everythink all messed up in th' study, an' I couldn' seem to rouse him; so I tried to get th' village on th' phone, but it still won't work, and when I tried to start th' station wagon up I found that somethink had gone wrong with it; so I starts to walk down to th' village, an' just then you come down th' road, an' I seen th' little green cross on your car, so—"

"I'll have that darn thing taken off tomorrow," I assured myself; then, aloud, to stop the servant's endless chatter: "All right, we'll do everything we can, but we haven't any medicines or instruments; so maybe we shall have to send you for supplies."

"Yes, sir," he replied respectfully, and to my relief lapsed into momentary silence.

THE BIG HOUSE DOCTOR Michail Pavlovitch had purchased two years previously and in which he lived in churlish solitude, attended only by his English houseman, sat back on a deep lawn thick-set with huge old trees, fenced against the highway by an eight-foot privet hedge and surrounded on the three remaining sides by tall brick walls topped with broken bottles set in mortar. As we circled up the driveway I could feel the eery atmosphere that hovered round the place. It was, I think, the lights which struck me queerly, or, to be more accurate, the absence of familiar lights in a place we knew to be inhabited. Blinds were drawn down tightly, with forbidding secrecy, at every window; yet between their bottoms and the sills were little lines of luminance which showed against the darkness like a line of gray-white eyeball glimpsed between the lowered eyelids of a corpse.

We hurried down the wide hall to a big room at the rear and paused upon the threshold as the glare of half a dozen strong, unshaded lamps stabbed at our eyes. Everything about the place was topsy-turvy. Drawers had been jerked from desks and literally turned out upon the floor, their contents scattered in fantastic heaps as though they had been stirred with a gigantic spoon. The davenport was pulled apart, its mattress tipped insanely sidewise; pillows were ripped open and gaped like dying things, their gasping mouths disgorging down and kapok. The whole room might have been a movie set at the conclusion of a slapstick farce, except for that which occupied the center of the floor.

In the midst of the fantastic jumble lay a man in dinner clothes, save for the jacket which, sleeves turned half out and linings slit to tatters, was crumpled on a chair. He lay upon his back, his partly opened eyes fixed on the ceiling where a cluster of electric bulbs blazed white and hard as limelight. He was a big man with a big mustache curled in the fashion of the pre-war days, and what hair he had was touched with gray.

"Gawd, sir, he ain't moved since I left 'im!" the houseman whispered. "Is 'e paralyzed, d'ye think?"

"Completely," nodded Jules de Grandin. "He is very dead, my friend."

"Dead?"

"Like a herring, and unless I miss my guess, he died of murder."

"But there's no blood, no sign of any wound," I interrupted. "I don't believe there was a struggle, even. The place has been ransacked, but-"

"No wound, you say, *mon vieux?*" he broke in as he knelt beside the dead man's head. "*Regardez, s'il vous plaît.*" He raised the massive, almost hairless head, and pointed with a well-groomed finger to a gleaming silver stud protruding from the flesh. Plunged in the rather beefy neck a tiny silver-headed bodkin showed. Less than half an inch of haft protruded, for the little awl was driven deep into that fatal spot, the medulla oblongata, with deadly accuracy. Death had been instantaneous and bloodless.

"How—" I began, but he shut me off with an unpleasant laugh as he rose and brushed his knees.

"*Cherchez la femme,*" he murmured. "This is undoubtlessly a woman's work, and the work of one who knew him quite well. All the evidence suggests it. A little, tiny bodkin driven into the brain; a woman's weapon. Probably she did it with her arms about his neck; a woman's finesse, that. Who she was and why she did it, and what she and her confederates looked for when they made a bears' den of this place is for the police to determine."

Turning to the servant he demanded: "This Doctor Pavlovitch, did he have callers in the afternoon?"

"No, sir, not as I knows of. He was a queer 'un, sir, though he was a proper gentleman. Never had no callers I remember, never used th' telephone while I was here. If anybody ever come to see 'im they done it while I was away."

"One sees. Did he ever mention fearing anyone, or suspecting that he might be robbed?"

"Him? Lor, sir, no! Six foot three in 'is stockin's, 'e was, an' could bend iron bars in 'is bare hands. I seen 'im do it more'n once. Had a regular harsenal o' guns an' things, too, 'e did, an' kept th' house locked like a jail. Didn't take no chances on a robbery, sir, but I wouldn't say he was afraid. He'd 'a been a nasty customer in a row; if anyone 'ad broken in he'd 'a give 'em what-for good an' proper, sir."

"U'm?" Going to the telephone the little Frenchman raised the instrument from its forked cradle and held it to his ear. "*Parbleu!*" he pressed the contact bar down with a triple rattle, then dropped the speaking-tube back in its rack. "Remain here, if you please," he bade the servant as he motioned me to follow. Outside, he whispered: "There is no dial tone discernible. The line is cut."

W E CIRCLED ROUND THE house seeking the connection, and beside a chimney found the inlet. The wires had been neatly clipped, and the fresh-cut copper showed as bright against the severed insulation as a wound against dark flesh.

"What d'ye make of it?" I asked as he knelt on the wet grass and searched the ground for traces of the wire-cutters. "Think that chap inside knows more than he pretends?"

"Less, if possible," he said shortly. "Such stupidity as his could not be simulated. Besides, I know his type. Had he been implicated in a murder or a robbery he would have set as great a distance between him and the crime-scene as he could." With a shrug of resignation he straightened to his feet and brushed the leaf-mold from his trousers. "No tracks of any sort," he murmured. "The grass grows close against the house, and the rain has washed away what little tale the miscreants' footprints might have told. Let us go back. We must inform the police and the coroner."

"Want me to take the car and notify 'em?" I asked as we turned the corner of the house. "It's hardly safe to trust the servant out of sight before the officers have had a chance to question him, and you don't drive, so—"

The pressure of his fingers on my elbow silenced me, and we drew back in the shelter of the ivy-hung wall as the crunch of wheels came to us from the lower driveway.

"What the deuce?" I wondered as I glimpsed the vehicle between the rain-drenched trees. "What's an express van doing here this time o' night?"

"Let us make ourselves as inconspicuous as possible," he cautioned in a whisper. "It may be that they plan a ruse for entering the house, and—"

"But good heavens, man, they've already gone through it like termites through a log," I interjected.

"*Ah bah*, you overlook the patent possibilities, my friend. What do we really know? Only that Doctor Pavlovitch was murdered and his study ransacked. But why do people search a place? To find something they want, *n'est-ce-pas?* That much is obvious. Still, we do not know they found the thing they sought, or, if they found it, we cannot say that others do not also seek it. It must have been a thing of value to have caused them to do murder."

"You mean there may be two gangs hunting something Pavlovitch had hidden in his house?"

"It is quite possible. He was a Russian, and Russia is synonymous with mystery today. The old *noblesse* have smuggled fortunes from the country, or have plans for getting out the treasures they could not take with them in flights; plots and counterplots, intrigue, plans for assassination or revenge are natural to a Russian as fleas are to a dog. I think it wholly possible that more than one conspiracy to deprive the amiable Pavlovitch of life and fortune has been in progress, and he would not have been a good insurance risk even if the ones who murdered him tonight had done their work less thoroughly."

The big green truck had drawn up at the steps and a man in express uniform hopped out. "Doctor Pavlovitch?" he asked when the houseman answered to his thunderous banging at the knocker.

"No-o, sir," gulped the servant, "the doctor isn't home just now—"

"Okay, pal. Will you sign for this consignment and give us a lift with it? It's marked urgent."

With grunts and exclamations of exertion, plus a liberal allowance of the sort of language prized by soldiers, stevedores and sailors, the great packing-case was finally wrestled up the steps and dropped unceremoniously in the hall. The express van turned down the drive, and we slipped from our concealment to find Pavlovitch's houseman gazing at the giant parcel ruefully.

"What'll I do with it now, sir?" he asked de Grandin. "I know th' doctor was expectin' somethink of th' sort, for he told me so hisself this mornin'; but 'e didn't tell me what it was, an' I don't know whether I should open it or leave it for th' officers."

De Grandin tweaked an end of waxed mustache between his thumb and forefinger as he regarded the great crate. It was more than six feet long, something more than three feet wide, and better than a yard in height.

"*Eh bien*," he answered, "I think the citizens of Troy were faced with the same problem. They forbore to open that which came to them, with most deplorable results. Let us not be guilty of the same mistake. Have you a crowbar handy?"

WHOEVER PUT THAT CASE together had intended it to stand rough usage, for the two-inch planks that formed it were secured with mortises and water-swollen dowels, so though the three of us attacked it furiously it was upward of an hour ere we forced the first board loose; and that proved only the beginning, for so strongly were the shooks attached to one another that our task was more like breaking through a solid log than ripping a joined box apart. Finally the last plank of the lid came off and revealed a packing of thick felt.

"*Que diable?*" snapped de Grandin as he struck his crowbar on the heavy wadding. "What is this?"

"What did you expect?" I queried as I mopped a handkerchief across my face.

"A man, perhaps a pair of them, by blue!" he answered. "It would have made an ideal hiding-place. Equipped with inside fasteners, it could have been thrown open in the night, permitting those who occupied it to come forth and search the place at leisure."

"Humph, there's certainly room for a man or two in there," I nodded, prodding tentatively at the black felt wadding with my finger, "but how would he get air—I say!"

"What is it?" he demanded. "You have discovered something—"

"Feel this," I interrupted, "it seems to me it's—"

"*Parbleu*, but you have right!" he exclaimed as he laid his hand against the felt. "It is cool, at least ten degrees cooler than the atmosphere. Let us hasten to unearth the secret of this *sacré* chest, my friends, but let us also work with caution. It may contain a charge of liquid air."

"Liquid air?" I echoed as with the heavy shears the servant brought he started cutting at the layers of laminated felt.

"*Certainement*. Liquid air, my friend. Brought in sudden contact with warm atmosphere it would vaporize so quickly that the force of its expansion would be equal to a dynamite explosion. I have seen it—"

"But that's fantastic," I objected. "Who would choose such an elaborate—"

"Who would choose a woman's bodkin to dispatch the learned Doctor Pavlovitch?" he countered. "it would have been much simpler to have shot him; yet—*morbleu*, what have we here?"

The final layer of felt had been laid back, and before us gleamed a chest of polished dark red wood, oblong in shape, with slightly rounded top with chamfered edges and a group of Chinese ideographs incised upon it. I had seen a case like that but once before, but I recognized it instantly. A friend of mine had died while traveling in Mongolia, and when they shipped his body home . . . "Why, it's a Chinese coffin!" I exclaimed.

"*Précisément, un cercueil de bois chinois*, but what in Satan's name does it do here? And behold, observe, my friend; it, too, is cold."

He was correct. The polished puncheon of Mongolian cedar was so cold that I could hardly bear to rest my hand upon it.

"I wonder what those characters stand for?" I mused. "If we could read them they might give some clue—"

"I do not think so," he replied. "I can make them out; they are the customary *hong* for Chinese coffins, and mean *cheung sang*—long life."

"'Long life!'—on a coffin lid?"

"But yes. *C'est drôle ça*," he agreed. "It seems the heathen in his blindness has hopes of immortality, and does not decorate his tombs with skulls and crossbones, or with pious, gloomy verses in the Christian manner. However"—he raised his narrow shoulders in a shrug—"we have still the puzzle of this so cold coffin to be solved. Let us be about it, but with caution."

With more care than the average dentist shows when he explores a tooth, he bored a small hole in the cedar with an auger, pausing every now and then to test the temperature of the small bit against his hand. Some thirty seconds later he leaped back. "I have struck nothingness; the bit is through—stand clear!" he cautioned, and a gentle hissing followed like an echo of his warning as a plume-like jet of feathery remex geysered upward from the coffin lid.

"Carbon dioxide snow!" we chorused, and:

"*Tiens*, it seems we shall not listen to the angels' songs immediately," added Jules de Grandin with a laugh.

The casket followed usual Chinese patterns. Made from a single hollowed log with top and bottom joined by dowels, it was covered with successive coats of lacquer which made it seem an undivided whole, and it was not till we searched some time that we were able to discern the line between the lid and body. A series of small auger-holes was driven in the wood, and with these for starting points we had begun the arduous task of prizing off the heavy lid when the sudden screech of brakes before the house gave warning of a new arrival.

"Take cover!" bade de Grandin, dropping down behind the massive coffin as he drew his pistol. "If they think to carry us by storm we shall be ready for—"

"Michail—Michailovitch, has it come? Proudhon and Matrona are here; we must make haste! Where are you, man?" Rattling at the knob, kicking on the panels, someone clamored at the front door furiously, then, as we gave no sign, burst out in a torrent of entreaty phrased in words that seemed entirely consonants.

De Grandin left his ambush, tiptoed down the hall and shot the bolt back from the door, leaping quickly to one side and poising with bent knees, his pistol held in readiness. The heavy door swung inward with a bang and a young man almost fell across the sill.

"Michail," he called hysterically, "they're here; I saw them on the road today. Has it come, Michail—oh, my God!—as he saw the coffin stripped of its enclosures standing in the glaring light from the hall chandelier—"too late; too late!" He stumbled blindly a few steps, slumped down to his knees, then crept across the polished floor, dropping head and hands upon the coffin lid and sobbing broken-heartedly. "Nikakova, *radost moya!*" he entreated. "Oh, too late; too late!"

"*Tenez, Monsieur*, you seem in trouble," de Grandin moved from his concealment and advanced a step, pistol lowered but eyes wary.

"Proudhon!" the stranger half rose from his knees and a look of utter loathing swept his face. "You—" His furious expression faded and gave way to one of wonder. "You're not—who are you?" he stammered.

"*Eh bien*, my friend, I think that we might say the same to you," de Grandin answered. "It might be well if you explained yourself without delay. A murder has been done here and we seek the perpetrators—"

"A murder? Who—"

"Doctor Pavlovitch was murdered something like an hour ago; we are expecting the police—"

"Pavlovitch killed? It must be Proudhon was here, then," the young man breathed. "Was this coffin like this when you found it?"

"It was not. It came after Doctor Pavlovitch was murdered. We suspected it might be connected with the crime and were about to force it when you came howling at the door—"

"Quick, then! We must take it off before—"

"One moment, if you please, Monsieur. A murder has been done and everyone about the place is suspect till he clears himself. This so mysterious parcel came while we were seeking clues, and neither it not any other thing may be removed until the police—"

"We can't wait for the police! They wouldn't understand; they'd not believe; they'd wait until it is too late—oh, Monsieur, I don't know who you are, but I beg that you will help me. I must remove this coffin right away; get it to a safe place and have medical assistance, or—"

"I am Doctor Jules de Grandin and this is Doctor Samuel Trowbridge, both at your service if you can convince us that you have no criminal intent," the little Frenchman said. "Why must you rush away this casket which was brought here but a little while ago, and why should you desire to keep its presence hidden from the officers?"

A look of desperation crossed the other's face. He laid his forehead on the chilly coffin top again and burst into a fit of weeping. Finally: "You are educated men, physicians, and may understand," he murmured between sobs. "You must believe me when I tell you that unless we take this coffin out at once a terrible calamity will follow!"

De Grandin eyed him speculatively. "I will take the chance that what you say is true, Monsieur," he answered. "You have a motorcar outside? Good. Doctor Trowbridge will accompany you and guide you to our house. I shall stay and wait until the police have been notified and aid them with such information as I have. Then I shall rejoin you."

Turning to the servant he commanded: "Help us place this box upon the motor, if you please; then hasten to the nearest neighbor's and telephone the officers. I await you here."

WITH THE LONG BOX hidden in the tonneau of his touring-car the young man hugged my rear fender all the way to town, and was at my side and ready to assist in packing the unwieldy case into the house almost before I shut my motor off. Once in the surgery, he crept furtively from one window to another, drawing down the blinds and listening intently, as though he were in mortal fear of spies.

"Well, now, young fellow," I began as he completed his mysterious precautions, "what's all this about? Let me warn you, if you've got a body hidden in that casket it's likely to go hard with you. I'm armed, and if you make a false move—" Reaching in my jacket pocket I snapped my glasses-case to simulate—I hoped!—the clicking of a pistol being cocked, and frowned at him severely.

The smile of child-like confidence he gave me was completely reassuring. "I've no wish to run away, sir," he assured me. "If it hadn't been for you they might have—Jesu-Mary, what is that?" He thrust himself before the red wood coffin as though to shield it with his body as a rattle sounded at the office door.

"Salut, mes amis!" de Grandin greeted as he strode into the surgery. "I am fortunate. The gendarmes kept me but a little while, and I rode back to town with the mortician who brought in the doctor's body. You have not opened it? Très bon. I shall be delighted to assist you."

"Yes, let us hurry, please," our visitor begged. "It has been so long—" a sob choked in his throat, and he put his hand across his eyes.

The wood was heavy but not hard, and our tools cut through it easily. In fifteen minutes we had forced a lengthwise girdle round the box, and bent to lift the lid.

"Nikakova!" breathed the young man as a worshipper might speak the name of some saint he adored.

"Sacré nom d'un fromage vert!" de Grandin swore.

"Good heavens!" I ejaculated.

A coat of hoarfrost fell away in flakes, and beneath it showed a glassy dome with little traceries of rime upon it. Between the lace-like meshes of the gelid veil we glimpsed a woman lying quiet as in sleep. There was a sort of wavering radiance about her not entirely attributable to the icy envelope enclosing her. Rather, it seemed to me, she matched the brilliant beams of the electric light with some luminescence of her own. Nude she was as any Aphrodite sculptured by the master-craftsmen of the Isle of Melos; a cloven tide of pale-gold hair fell down each side her face and rippled over ivory shoulders, veiling the pink nipples of the full-blown, low-set bosoms and coursing down the beautifully shaped thighs until it reached the knees. The slender, shapely feet were crossed like those on mediaeval tombs whose tenants have in life made pilgrimage to Rome or Palestine; her elbows were bent sharply so her hands were joined together palm to palm between her breasts with fingertips against her chin. I could make out gold-flecked lashes lying in smooth arcs against her pallid checks, the faint shadows round her eyes, the wistful, half-pathetic droop of her small mouth. Oddly, I was conscious that this pallid, lovely figure typified in combination the austerity of sculptured saint, lush, provocative young womanhood and the innocent appeal of childhood budding into adolescence. Somehow, it seemed to me, she had lain down to die with a trustful resignation like that of Juliet when she drained the draft that sent her living to her family's mausoleum.

"Nikakova!" whispered our companion in a sort of breathless ecstasy, gazing at the quiet figure with a look of rapture.

"*Hein?*" de Grandin shook himself as though to free his senses from the meshes of a dream. "What is this, *Monsieur?* A woman tombed in ice, a beautiful, dead woman—"

"She is not dead," the other interrupted. "She sleeps."

"*Tiens,*" a look of pity glimmered in the little Frenchman's small blue eyes, "I fear it is the sleep that knows no waking, *mon ami.*"

"No, no, I tell you," almost screamed the young man, "she's not dead! Pavlovitch assured me she could be revived. We were to begin work tonight, but they found him first, and—"

"*Halte la!*" de Grandin bade. "This is the conversation of the madhouse, as meaningless as babies' babble. Who was this Doctor Pavlovitch, and who was this young woman? Who, by blue, are you, *Monsieur?*"

The young man paid no heed, but hastened around the coffin, feeling with familiar fingers for a series of small buttons which he pressed in quick succession. As the final little knob was pressed we heard a slowly rising, prolonged hiss, and half a dozen feathery jets of snowflakes seemed to issue from the icy dome above the body. The room grew cold and colder. In a moment we could see the vapor of our breaths before our mouths and noses, and I felt a chill run through me as an almost overwhelming urge to sneeze began to manifest itself.

"*Corbleu,*" de Grandin's teeth were chattering with the sudden chill, "I shall take pneumonia; I shall contract coryza; I shall perish miserably if this continues!" He crossed the room and threw a window open, then leant across the sill, fairly soaking in the moist, warm summer air.

"Quick, shut the lights off!" cried our visitor. "They must not see us!" He snapped the switch with frenzied fingers, then leaned against the door-jamb breathing heavily, like one who has escaped some deadly peril by the narrowest of margins.

As the outside air swept through the room and neutralized the chill, de Grandin turned again to the young man. "*Monsieur,*" he warned, "my nose is short, but my patience is still shorter. I have had enough—too much, *parbleu!* Will you explain this business of the monkey now, or do I call the officers and tell them that you carry round the body of a woman, one whom you doubtless foully murdered, and—"

"No, no, not that!" the visitor besought. "Please don't betray me. Listen, please; try to realize what I say is true."

"My friend, you cannot put too great a strain on my credulity," de Grandin answered. "Me, I have traveled much, seen much, know much. The thing which I know to be true would make a less experienced man believe himself the victim of hallucinations. Say on, *mon vieux*; I listen."

With steamer rugs draped around our shoulders we faced each other in the light of a small, shaded lamp. Our breath fanned out in vapory cumuli each time we spoke; before us gleamed the crystal-hooded coffin, like a great *memento mori* fashioned out of polar ice, and as it radiated ever-growing cold I caught myself involuntarily recalling a couplet from Bartholomew Dowling:

And thus does the warmth of feeling
Turn chill in the coldness of death . . .

Till then the rush of action had prevented any inventory of our visitor. Now as I studied him I found it difficult to fit him into any category furnished by a lifetime's medical experience. He was young, though not as young as he appeared, for pale-blond coloring and slenderness lent him a specious air of youth which was denied by drooping shoulders, trouble-lines about his mouth and deep-set, melancholy eyes. His chin was small and gentle, not actually receding, but soft and almost feminine in outline. The mouth, beneath a scarcely visible ash-blond mustache, suggested extreme sensitiveness, and he held his lips compressed against each other as though the trait of self-suppression had become habitual. His brow was wider and more high than common, his blue eyes almost childishly ingenuous. When he spoke, it was with hesitancy and with a painfully correct pronunciation which betrayed as plainly as an accent that his English came from study rather than inheritance and use.

"I am Serge Aksakoff," he told us in his flat, accentless voice. "I met Nikakova Gapon when I was a student at the University of Petrograd and she a pupil at the Imperial Ballet Academy. Russia in 1916 was honeycombed with secret liberal societies, all loyal to the Little Father, but all intent on securing something of democracy for a land which had lain prostrate underneath the iron heel of autocrats for twenty generations. Perhaps it was the thrill of danger which we shared; perhaps it was a stronger thing; at any rate we felt a mutual attraction at first meeting, and before the summer ended I was desperately in love with her and she returned my passion.

"Our society numbered folk of every social stratum, workmen, artisans, artists and professional people, but mostly we were students ranging anywhere from twenty to sixteen years old. Two of our foremost members were Boris Proudhon and Matrona Rimsky. He was a tailor, she the mistress of Professor Michail Pavlovitch of the University of Petrograd, who as a physicist was equal to Soloviev in learning and surpassed him in his daring of experiment. Proudhon was always loudest in debate, always most insistent on aggressive action. If one of us prepared a plan for introducing social legislation in the Duma he scoffed at the idea and insisted on a show of force, often on assassination of officials whose duties were to carry out unpopular ukases. Matrona always seconded his violent proposals and insisted that we take direct and violent action. Finally, at their suggestion, we signed our names beneath theirs to a declaration of intention in which we stated that if peaceful measures failed we favored violence to gain our ends.

"That night the officers of the Okhrana roused me from my bed and dragged me to the fortress of St. Peter and St. Paul. They locked me in a stinking, vermin-swarming cell and left me there three weeks. Then they led me out and told me that because I was but seventeen they had decided to extend me clemency, so instead of being hanged or sent to the Siberian mines with most of my companions I was merely to be exiled to Ekaterinburg for a term of sixty months. During that time I was to be subjected to continuous surveillance, to hold no communication with my family or friends in Russia, and not engage in any occupation without express permission."

"But you'd done nothing!" I protested. "The paper that you signed declared specifically that you favored peaceful measures; you merely said that if these measures failed—"

Aksakoff smiled sadly. "You didn't have to be a criminal to be exiled," he explained. "'Political unreliability' was sufficient cause, and the officers of the political police were sole judges of the case. You see, administrative exile, as they called it, was technically not a punishment."

"Oh, that's different," I replied. "If you were merely forced to live away from home—"

"And to make a journey longer than from New York to Los Angeles dressed in prison clothes and handcuffed to a condemned felon, shuffling in irons so heavy that it was impossible to lift your feet, to be fed infrequently, and then on offal that nothing but a half-starved dog—or man—would touch," he interrupted bitterly. "My only consolation was that Nikakova had been also granted 'clemency' and accompanied me in exile.

"The officer commanding our escort came from a family some of whom had also suffered exile, and this made him pity us. He allowed us to converse an hour a day, although this was prohibited, and several times he gave us food and tea from his own rations. It was from him we learned that Proudhon and Matrona were *agents provocateurs* of the political police, paid spies whose duty was not only to worm their way into the confidence of unsuspecting children such as we, but to incite us to unlawful acts so we might be arrested and deported.

"Since I had no money and the Government did not care to fee me, I was graciously permitted to take service with a cobbler at Ekaterinburg, and Nikakova was allowed to do work for a seamstress. Presently I found a little cottage and she came to live with me."

"It must have been some consolation to be married to the girl you loved, even in such terrible conditions—" I began, but the cynicism of the look he gave me stopped my well-meant comment.

"I said she came to live with me," he repeated. "'Politicos' were not permitted marriage without special dispensation from the police, and this we could not get. We had no money to pay bribes. But whatever church and state might say, we were as truly man and wife as if we'd stood before the altar of St. Isaac's and been married by the Patriarch. We pledged our love for time and all eternity kneeling on the floor of our mean cabin with a blessèd ikon for our witness, and because we had no rings to give each other I took two nails and beat them into circlets. Look—"

He thrust his hand out, displaying a thin band of flattened wire on the second shaft of the third finger.

"She had one, too," he added, beckoning us to look upon the body in the frost-domed coffin. Through the envelope of shrouding ice we saw the dull gleam of the narrow iron ring upon one of the shapely folded hands.

"In that northern latitude the twilight lasts till after ten o'clock, and my labors with the cobbler started with the sunrise and did not end till dark," Aksakoff continued as he resumed his seat and lit the cigarette de Grandin proffered. "There is an English saying that shoemakers' children go unshod. It was almost literally true in my case, for the tiny wage I earned made it utterly impossible for me to purchase leather shoes, and so I wound rags round my feet and ankles. Nikakova had a pair of shoes, but wore them only out of doors. As for stockings, we hadn't owned a pair between us since the first month of our exile.

"One evening as I shuffled home in my rag boots I heard a groan come from the shadows, and when I went to look I found an old man fallen by the way. He was pitifully thin and ragged, and his matted, unkempt beard was almost stiff with filth and slime. We who lived in utter poverty could recognize starvation when we saw it, and it needed but a single glance to see the man was famishing. He was taller by a head than I, but I had no trouble lifting him, for he weighed scarcely ninety pounds, and when I put my arm round him to steady him it was as if I held a rag-clothed skeleton.

"Nikakova helped me get his ragged clothing off and wash away the clotted filth and vermin; then we laid him on a pile of straw, for we had no bedsteads, and fed him milk and brandy with a spoon. At first we thought him too far gone for rescue, but after we had worked with him an hour or so his eyes came open and he murmured, 'Thank you, *Gaspadin Aksakoff.*'

"'*Gaspadin!*' It was the first time I had heard that title of respect since the night the police dragged me from my bed almost a year before, and I burst out crying when the old man mumbled it. Then we fell to wondering. Who was this old rack of bones, clothed in stinking rags, filthy as a *mujik* and verminous as a mangy dog, who knew my name and addressed me with a courteous title? Exiles learn to suspect every change of light and shadow, and Nikakova and I spent a night of terror, starting at each footstep in the alley, almost fainting every time a creak came at our lockless door for fear it might be officers of the *gendarmerie* come to take us for affording shelter to a fugitive.

"The starving stranger rallied in the night and by morning had sufficient strength to tell us he was Doctor Pavlovitch, seized by the Okhrana as a politically dangerous person and exiled for five years to Ekaterinburg. Less fortunate than we, he had been unable to obtain employment even as a manual laborer when the Government, preoccupied with war and threat of revolution, had turned him out to live or starve as fate decreed. For months he'd wandered through the streets like a stray animal, begging *kopeks* here and there, fighting ownerless dogs and cats for salvage from swill-barrels; finally he dropped exhausted in his tracks within a hundred yards of our poor cabin.

"We had hardly food enough for two, and often less than the equivalent of a dime a week in cash, but somehow we contrived to keep our guest alive through the next winter, and when spring came he found work upon a farm.

"The forces of revolt had passed to stronger hands than ours, and while we starved at Ekaterinburg Tsar Nicholas came there as an exile, too. But though the *Bolsheviki* ruled instead of Nicholas it only meant a change of masters for the three of us. Petrograd and all of Russia was in the hands of revolutionists so busy with their massacres and vengeances that they had no time or inclination to release us from our exile, and even if we had been freed we had no place to go. With the coming of the second revolution everything was communized; the Red Guards took whatever they desired with no thought of payment; tradesmen closed their shops and peasants planted just enough to keep themselves. We had been poor before; now we were destitute. Sometimes we had but one crust of black bread to share among us, often not even that. For a week we lived on Nikakova's shoes, cutting them in little strips and boiling them for hours to make broth.

"The Bolsheviks shot Nicholas and his family on July 17, and eight days later Kolchak and the Czechs moved into Ekaterinburg. Pavlovitch was recognized and retained to assist in the investigation of the murder of the royal family, and we acted as his secretaries. When the White Guards moved back toward Mongolia we went with them. Pavlovitch set up a laboratory and hospital at Tisingol, and Nikakova and I acted as assistants. We were very happy there."

"One rejoices in your happiness, *Monsieur*," de Grandin murmured when the young man's silence lengthened, "but how was it that Madame Aksakoff was frozen in this never quite sufficiently to be reprobated coffin?"

Our visitor started from his revery. "There was fighting everywhere," he answered. "Town after town changed hands as Red and White Guards moved like chessmen on the Mongol plains, but we seemed safe enough at Tisingol till Nikakova fell a victim to taiga fever. She hovered between life and death for weeks, and was still too weak to walk, or even stand, when word came that the Red horde was advancing and destroying everything before it. If we stayed our dooms were sealed; to attempt to move her meant sure death for Nikakova.

"I told you Pavlovitch was one of Russia's foremost scientists. In his work at Tisingol he had forestalled discoveries made at great universities of the outside world. The Leningrad physicians' formula for keeping blood ionized and fluid, that it might be in readiness for instant use when transfusions were required, was an everyday occurrence at the Tisingol infirmary, and Carrell's experiment of keeping life in chicken hearts after they were taken from the fowls had been surpassed by him. His greatest scientific feat, however, was to take a small warm-blooded animal—a little cat or dog—drug it with an opiate, then freeze it solid with carbonic oxide snow, keep it in refrigeration for a month or two, then, after gently thawing it, release it, apparently no worse for its experience.

"'There is hope for Nikakova,' he told me when the news came that the Bolsheviks were but two days away. 'If you will let me treat her as I do my pets, she can be moved ten thousand miles in safety, and revived at any time we wish.'

"I would not consent, but Nikakova did. 'If Doctor Pavlovitch succeeds we shall be together once again,' she told me, 'but if we stay here we must surely die. If I do not live through the ordeal—*nichevo*, I am so near death already that the step is but a little one, and thou shalt live, my Serge. Let us try this one chance of escape.'

"Pavlovitch secured a great Mongolian coffin and we set about our work. Nikakova was too weak to take me in her arms, but we kissed each other on the mouth before she drank ten drops of laudanum which sent her into a deep sleep within half an hour. The freezing process had to be immediate, so that animation would come to a halt at once; otherwise her little strength would be depleted by contending with the chill and she would really die, and not just halt her vital processes. We stripped her bedrobe off and set her hands in prayer and crossed her feet as though she came back from a pious pilgrimage, then sealed her lips with flexible collodion and stopped her nasal orifices; then, before she had a chance to suffocate, we laid her on a sheet stretched on carbonic oxide snow, spread another sheet above her and covered her with a sheet-copper dome into which we forced compressed carbonic oxide. The temperature inside her prison was so low her body stiffened with a spasm, every drop of blood and moisture in her system almost instantly congealing. Then we laid her in a shallow bath of distilled water which we froze as hard as steel with dry ice, and left her there while we prepared the coffin which was to be her home until we reached a place of safety.

"Pavlovitch had made the coffin ready, putting tanks of liquefied carbonic oxide underneath the space reserved for the ice plinth and arranging vents so that the gas escaping from the liquid's slow evaporation might circulate continuously about the icy tomb in which my darling lay. Around the ice block we set a hollow form of ice to catch and hold escaping gases, then wrapped the whole in layer on layer of *yurta*, or tent-felt, and put it in the coffin, which we sealed with several coats of Chinese lacquer. Thus my loved one lay as still as any sculptured saint, sealed in a tomb of ice as cold as those *zaberegas*, or ice mountains, that form along the banks of rivers in Siberia when the mercury goes down to eighty marks below the zero line.

"We trekked across the Shamo desert till we came to Dolo Nor, then started down the Huang Ho, but just north of Chiangchun a band of Chahar bandits raided us. Me they carried off to hold for ransom, and it was three days before I made them understand I was a penniless White Russian for whom no one cared a *kopek*. They would have killed me out of hand had not an English prisoner offered them five pounds in ransom for me. Six months later I arrived at Shanghai with nothing but the rags I stood in.

"White Russians have no status in the East, but this was helpful to me, for jobs no other foreigner would touch were offered me. I was in turn a ricksha boy, a German secret agent, a runner for a gambling-house, an opium smuggler and gun runner. At every turn my fortunes mounted. In ten years I was rich, the owner of concessions in Kalgan, Tientsin and Peiping, not much respected, but much catered to. *Maskee*"—he raised his shoulders in a shrug—"I'd have traded everything I owned for that red coffin that had vanished when the Chahars captured me.

"Then at last I heard of Pavlovitch. He had been made the surgeon of the bandit party which co-operated with the one that captured me, and when they were incorporated in the Chinese army had become a colonel. When he saved a war lord's life by transfusion of canned blood they presented him with half a City's loot. Shortly afterward he emigrated to America. The coffin? When the Chahars first saw it they assumed that it was filled with treasure and were about to smash it open, but its unnatural coldness frightened them, and they buried it beneath the ice near Bouir Nor and scuttled off pell-mell in mortal fear of the ten thousand devils which Pavlovitch assured them were confined in it.

"It cost me two years and a fortune to locate Nikakova's burial-place, but finally we found it, and so deeply had they buried her beneath the *zaberega's* never-melting ice that we had to blast to get my darling out. We wrapped the coffin in ten folds of tent-felt wet with ice-and-salt solution, and took it overland to Tientsin, where I put it in a ship's refrigeration chamber and brought it to America. Yesterday I reached this city with it, having brought it here in a refrigeration car, and all arrangements had been made for Pavlovitch to revive

Nikakova when—this afternoon I saw Proudhon and the Rimsky woman driving down the road toward Pavlovitch's house and knew that we must hasten."

"*Pardonnez-moi, Monsieur*, but why should seeing your confrères of Russian days impress you with this need for desperate haste?" de Grandin asked.

Aksakoff smiled bleakly. "Do you remember what befell the people who investigated the assassination of the Tsar?" he answered. "The assassins covered up their bloody work completely, so they thought; burned the bodies in a bonfire and threw the ashes down the shaft of an abandoned mine, but patient research under Sokoloff made all precautions useless. It was Pavlovitch whose work unearthed the evidence of crime. From the ashes in the old Isetsky mine he sifted little bits of evidence, the Emperor's Maltese cross, six sets of steels from women's corsets, a mixed assortment of charred buttons, buckles, parts of slippers, hooks and eyes, and a number of small dirty pebbles which, when cleaned and treated chemically, turned out to be pure diamonds. It was this evidence which proved the *Bolsheviki's* guilt—after they bare-facedly denied all implication in the regicide, and all who helped to prove their guilt were marked for 'execution'—even those who occupied the posts of clerks have been run down and murdered by their secret agents. There is no doubt Proudhon and the woman who was Pavlovitch's mistress—and whose betrayal caused his exile in the Tsarist days—were sent here to assassinate him. It was unquestionably that female Judas who killed Pavlovitch, and after he was dead she and Proudhon rummaged through his papers. Their task is not only to stop oral testimony of their Government's guilt, but to destroy incriminating documents, as well."

"One sees. And it is highly probable they found messages from you to him, advising him of your arrival. *Tiens*, I think that you were well advised to take this coffin from the house of death without delay."

"But in killing Pavlovitch they killed my darling, too!" sobbed Aksakoff. "The technique of his work was secret. No one else can bring belovèd Nikakova from her trance—"

"I would not say as much," denied the little Frenchman. "I am Jules de Grandin, and a devilish clever fellow. Let us see what we shall see, my friend."

"IT'S THE MOST FANTASTIC thing I ever heard!" I told him as we went to bed. "There's no doubt the freezing process has preserved her wonderfully, but to hope to bring her back to life—that's utterly absurd. When a person dies, he's dead, and I'd stake my reputation that's nothing but a lovely corpse in there," I nodded toward the bathroom where the plinth of ice stood in the tub and Aksakoff stretched on a pallet by the bolted door, a pistol ready in his hand.

De Grandin pursed his lips, then turned an impish grin on me. "You have logic and the background of experience to support your claims," he nodded, "but as Monsieur Shakespeare says, heaven and earth contain things our philosophy has not yet dreamed of. As for logic, *eh bien*, what is it? A reasoning from collated data, from known facts, *n'est-ce-pas?* But certainly. Logically, therefore, wireless telegraphy was scientifically impossible before Marconi. Radio communication was logically an absurd dream till invention of the vacuum tube made former scientific logic asinine. Yet the principles that underlay these things were known to physicists for years; they simply had not been assembled in their proper order. Let us view this case:

"Take, by example, hibernating animals, the tortoise of our northern climates, the frog, the snake; every autumn they put by their animation as a housewife folds up summer clothes for winter storage. They appear to die, yet in the spring they sally forth as active as they were before. One not versed in natural lore might come upon them in their state of hibernation and say as you just said, 'This is a corpse.' His experience would tell him so, yet he would be in error. Or take the fish who freezes in the ice. When spring dissolves his icy prison he swims off in search of food as hungrily as if he had not paused a moment in his quest. The toad encrusted in a block of slate, such as we see unearthed in coal mines now and then, may have been 'dead' *le bon Dieu* only knows how many centuries; yet once release him from encasement and he hops away in search of bugs to fill his little belly. Again—"

"But these are all cold-blooded creatures," I protested. "Mammals can't suspend the vital process—"

"Not even bears?" he interrupted with mock-mildness. "Or those Indians who when hypnotized fall into such deep trances that accredited physicians do not hesitate to call them dead, and are thereafter buried for so long a time that crops of grain are sown and harvested above them, then, disinterred, are reawakened at the hypnotist's command?"

"Humph," I answered, nettled. "I've never seen such things."

"*Précisément.* I have. I do not know how they can be. I only know they are. When things exist we know that they are so, whether logic favors them or not."

"Then you think that this preposterous tale is true; that we can thaw this woman out and awaken her, after she's lain dead and tombed in ice for almost twenty years?"

"I did not say so—"

"Why, you did, too!"

"It was you, not I, who called her dead. Somatically she may be dead—clinically dead, in that her heart and lungs and brain have ceased to function, but that is not true death. You yourself have seen such cases revived, even when somatic death has lasted an appreciable time. She was not diseased when animation was suspended, and her body has been insulated from deteriorative changes. I think it possible the vital spark still slumbers dormant and can be revived to flame if we have care—and luck."

T HE BATHROOM VIGIL LASTED five full days and nights. There seemed a steel-like quality to the icy catafalque that defied summer heat and gently dripping water from the shower alike, as if the ice had stored up extra chill in the long years it lay locked in the frost-bound earth of Outer Mongolia, and several times I saw it freeze the water they dropped on it instead of yielding to the liquid's higher temperature. At last the casing melted off and they laid the stiff, marmoreal body in the tub, then ran a stream of water from the faucet. For ten hours this was cool, and the gelid body showed no signs of yielding to it. Time after time we felt the stone-hard arms and hands, the legs and feet that seemed for ever locked in algid *rigor mortis*, the little flower-like breasts that showed no promise of waking from their frigid unresponsiveness. Indeed, far from responding to the water's thermal action, the frozen body seemed to chill its bath, and we noticed little thread-like lines of ice take form upon the skin, standing stiffly out like oversized mold-spores and overlaying the white form with a coat of jewel-bright, quill-like pelage.

"*Excellent, parfait, splendide; magnifique!*" de Grandin nodded in delight as the ice-fur coat took form. "The chill is coming forth; we are progressing splendidly."

When the tiny icicles cleared away, they raised the water's temperature a little, gradually blending it from tepid to blood-warm, and fifteen hours of immersion in the warmer bath brought noticeable results. The skin became resilient to the touch, the flesh was firm but flexible, the folded hands relaxed and slipped down to the sides, slim ankles loosed their interlocking grip and the feet lay side by side.

"Behold them, if you please, my friend," de Grandin whispered tensely. "Her feet, see how they hold themselves!"

"Well?" I responded, "What—"

"*Ah bah*, has it been so long then since your student days that you do not remember the flaccidity of death? Think of the cadavers which you worked upon—were their feet like those ones yonder? By blue, they were not! They were prolapsed, they hung down on the ankles like extensions of the leg, for their flexor muscles had gone soft and inelastic. These feet stand out at obtuse angles to the legs."

"Well—"

"*Précisément; tu parles, mon ami.* It is very well, I think. It may not be a sign of life, but certainly it negatives the flaccidity of death."

Periodically they pressed the thorax and abdomen, feeling for the hardness of deep-seated frozen organs. At length, "I think we can proceed, my friends," de Grandin told us, and we lifted the limp body from the bath and dried it hurriedly with warm, soft towels. De Grandin drew the plugs of cotton from the nostrils and wiped the lips with ether to dissolve the seal of flexible collodion, and this done he and Aksakoff began to rub the skin with heated olive oil, kneading with firm gentleness, massaging downward toward the hands and feet, bending arms and legs, wrists, neck and ankles. Somehow, the process repulsed me. I had seen a similar technique used by embalmers when they broke up *rigor mortis*, and the certitude of death seemed emphasized by everything they did.

"Now, *Dei gratia*, we shall succeed!" the Frenchman whispered as he turned the body on its face and knelt over it, applying his hands to the costal margins, bearing down with all his might. There was a gentle, sighing sound, as of breath slowly exhaled, and Aksakoff went pale as death.

"She lives!" he whispered. "O Nikakova, *lubimuimi moï, radost moya—*"

I felt a sob of sympathy rise in my throat. Too often I had heard that vital simulation when air was forced between a corpse's lips by sudden pressure. No physician of experience, no morgue attendant, no embalmer can be fooled by that. . . .

"*Mordieu*, I think . . . I think—" de Grandin's soft, excited whisper sounded from the bed. He had leant back, releasing pressure on the corpse, and as he did so I was startled to observe a swelling of the lower thorax. Of course it could be nothing but mechanical reaction, the natural tendency of air to rush into an emptied space, I told myself, but . . .

He bent forward swiftly, pushing down upon the body with both hands, retained the pressure for a moment, then swung back again. Forward—back; forward—back, twenty times a minute by the swiftly clicking second hand of his wrist watch he went through the movements of the Schaefer method of forced respiration, patiently, methodically, almost mechanically.

I shook my head despairingly. This hopeless labor, this unfounded optimism . . .

"Quick, quick, my friend, the supradrenalin!" he gasped. "Put fifteen minims in the syringe, and hurry, if you please. I can feel a little, so small stirring here, but we must perform a cardiocentesis!"

I hastened to the surgery to prepare the suprarenal extract, hopeless as I knew the task to be. No miracle of medicine could revive a woman dead and buried almost twenty years. I had not spent a lifetime as a doctor to no purpose; death was death, and this was death if I had ever seen it.

De Grandin poised the trocar's point against the pallid flesh beneath the swell of the left breast, and I saw the pale skin dimple, as though it winced instinctively. He thrust with swift, relentless pressure, and I marveled at the skill which guided pointed, hollow needle straight into the heart, yet missed the tangled maze of vein and artery.

Aksakoff was on his knees, hands clasped, eyes closed, prayers in strangled Russian gushing from his livid lips. De Grandin pressed the plunger home, shooting the astringent mixture deep into a heart which had not felt warm blood in half a generation.

A quick, spasmodic shudder shook the pallid body and I could have sworn I saw the lowered eyelids flutter.

The Frenchman gazed intently in the calm, immobile face a moment; then: "*Non?*" he whispered tensely. "*Pardieu*, I say you shall! I will it!"

Snatching up a length of sterile gauze he folded it across her lightly parted lips, drew a deep breath and laid his mouth to hers. I saw his temple-veins stand out as he drained his lungs of air, raised his head to gasp more breath, then bent and breathed again straight in the corpse's mouth. Tears stood in his eyes, his cheeks seemed losing every trace of color, he was becoming cyanotic. "Stop it, de Grandin!" I exclaimed. "It's no use, man, you're simply—"

"*Triomphe, victoire; succès!*" he gasped exultantly. "She breathes, she lives, my friends; we have vanquished twenty years of death. *Embrasse-moi!*" Before I realized what he was about he had thrown both arms around me and planted a resounding kiss on both cheeks, then served the Russian in like manner.

"Nikakova—Nikakova, *radost moya*—joy of life!" sobbed Aksakoff. The almost-golden lashes fluttered for an instant; then a pair of gray-green eyes looked vaguely toward the sobbing man, unfocussed, unperceiving, like the eyes of new-born infants struggling with the mystery of light.

It was impossible, absurd and utterly preposterous. Such a thing could not have happened, but . . . there it was. In the upper chamber of my house I had seen a woman called back from the grave. Sealed in a tomb of ice for almost twenty years, this woman lived and breathed and looked at me!

P HYSICALLY SHE MENDED RAPIDLY. We increased her diet of albumins, milk and brandy to light broth and well-cooked porridges in two days. She was able to take solid food within a week; but for all this she was but an infant magnified in size. Her eyes were utterly unfocussed, she seemed unable to do more than tell the difference of light and shade, when we spoke to her she gave no answer; the only sounds she made were little whimpering noises, not cries of pain or fear, but merely the mechanical responses of vocal cords reacting to the breath. Two nurses were installed and de Grandin scarcely left her side, but as the time drew out and it became increasingly apparent that the patient whom he nursed was nothing but a living organism without volition or intelligence, the lines about his eyes appeared more deeply etched each day.

A month went by without improvement; then one day he came fairly bouncing in to the study. "Trowbridge, *mon vieux*, come and see, but step softly, I implore you!" he commanded, clutching at my elbow and dragging me upstairs. At the bedroom door he paused and nodded, smiling broadly, like a showman who invites attention to a spectacle. Aksakoff knelt by the bed, and from the piled-up pillows Nikakova looked at him, but there was nothing infantile about her gaze.

"Nikakova, *radost moya*—joy of life!" he whispered, and:

"Serge, my love, my soul, my life!" came her murmured answer. Her pale hands lay like small white flowers in his clasp, and when he leant to her, her kisses flecked his cheeks, his brow, his eyelids like lightly fluttering butterflies.

"*Tiens*," de Grandin murmured, "our Snow Queen has awakened, it seems; the frosts of burial have melted, and—come away, my friend; this is not for us to see!"

He tweaked my sleeve to urge me down the hall. The lovers' mouths were joined in a fierce, passionate embrace, and the little Frenchman turned away his eyes as though to look on them were profanation.

NIKAKOVA SEEMED INTENT ON catching up the thread of interrupted life, and she and Serge with de Grandin spent long hours shopping, going to the theatre, visiting museums and art galleries or merely taking in the myriad scenes of city life. The semi-nudity of modern styles at first appalled her, but she soon revised her pre-war viewpoint and took to the unstockinged, corsetless existence of the day as if she had been born when Verdun and the Argonne were but memories, instead of in the reign of Nicholas the Last. When she finally had her flowing pale-gold hair cut short and permanently waved in little tight-laid poodle curls she might have passed as twin to any of a million of the current crop of high school seniors. She had an oddly incomplete mode of expression, almost devoid of pronouns and thickly strewn with participles, a shy but briar-sharp sense of humor, and an almost infinite capacity for sweets.

"No, recalling nothing," she assured us when we questioned her about her long interment. "Drinking laudanum and saying good-bye to my Serge. Then sleep. Awaking finds Serge beside me. Nothing more—a sleep, a waking. Wondering could death—true death—be that way? To fall asleep and wake in heaven?"

As soon as Nikakova's strength returned they were to go to China where Serge's business needed personal direction, for now he had recovered his belovèd the matter of accumulating wealth had reassumed importance in his eyes. "We suffered poverty together; now we shall share the joy of riches, *radost moya*," he declared.

DE GRANDIN HAD GONE to the county medical society, where his fund of technical experience and his Rabelaisian wit made him an always welcome guest. Nikakova, Aksakoff and I were in the drawing-room, the curtains drawn against the howling storm outside, a light fire crackling on the hearth. She had been singing for us, sad, nostalgic songs of her orphaned homeland; now she sat at the piano, ivory hands flitting fitfully across the ivory keys as she improvised, pausing every now and then to nibble at a peppermint, then, with the spicy morsel still upon her tongue, to take a sip of coffee. I watched her musingly. Serge looked his adoration. She bore little semblance to the pale corpse in its icebound coffin, this gloriously happy girl who sat swaying to the rhythm of her music in the glow of the piano lamp. She wore a gown of striped silk that flashed from green to orange and from gold to crimson as she moved. It was negligible as to bodice, but very full and long of skirt. Brilliants glittered on her cross-strapped sandals, long pendants of white jade swayed from her ears.

In the trees outside, the wind rose to a wail, and a flock of gulls which flew storm-driven from the bay skirked like lost souls as they wheeled over-head. A mile away a Lackawanna locomotive hooted long and mournfully as it approached a crossing. Nikakova whirled up from her seat on the piano bench and crossed the room with the quick, feline stride of the trained dancer, her full skirt swirling round her feet, the firelight gleaming on her jewel-set sandals and on brightly lacquered toenails.

"Feeling devils," she announced as she dropped upon the hearth rug and crouched before the fire, chin resting in her palms, her fingers pressed against her temples. "Seeming to hear *zagovór*—'ow you call heem?—weetches' spell-charm? On nights like this the weetches and the wairwolves riding—dead men coming up from graves; ghosts from dead past flocking back—"

She straightened to her knees and took a match-box from the tabouret, bent a match stave till it formed an *L* turned upside down and drove the end of the long arm into the box top. Breaking off another stave to make it match the first in height, she stood it with its head against that of the upturned *L*, then pressed her cigarette against the touching sulfurous heads.

"Now watching!" she commanded. A sudden flare of flame ensued, and as the fire ran down the staves the upright match curled upward and seemed to dangle from the crossbar of the L. "What is?" she asked us almost gleefully.

"The man on the flying trapeze?" I ventured, but she shook her head until her ear-drops scintillated in the firelight.

"But no, great stupid one!" she chided. "Is execution—hanging. See, this one"—she pointed to the fire-curled match—"is criminal hanged on gibbet. Perhaps he was—"

"A Menshevik who suffered justly for his crimes against the People's Revolution?" Softly pronounced, the interruption came in slurring, almost hissing accents from the doorway, and we turned with one accord to see a man and woman standing on the threshold.

He was a lean, compactly put together man of something more than medium height, exceedingly ugly, with thin black eyebrows and yellowish-tinted skin. His head was absolutely hairless, yet his scalp had not that quality of glossiness we ordinarily associate with baldness. Rather, it seemed to have a suède-like dullness which threw no answering gleam back from the hall lamp under which he stood. His small, side-slanting eyes were black as obsidian and his pointed chin thrust out. His companion wore a blue raincoat, tight-buttoned to the throat, and above its collar showed her face, dead-white beneath short, jet-black hair brushed flat against her head. Her brows were straight and narrow, the eyes below them black as prunes; her lips were a thin, scarlet line. She looked hard and muscular, not masculine, but sexless as a hatchet.

I saw terror like cold flame wither my companions' faces as they looked up at the trespassers. Although they said no word I knew the chill and ominous foreknowledge of sure death was on them.

"See here," I snapped as I rose from my chair, "what d'ye mean by coming in this way—"

"Sit down, old man," the woman interrupted in a low, cold voice. "Keep still and we'll not hurt you—"

"'Old man?' I choked. To have my house invaded in this way was injury, to be called an old man—that was added insult. "Get out!" I ordered sharply. "Get out of here, or—" The gleam of light upon the visitors' pistol barrels robbed my protest of authority.

"We have come to execute these traitors to the People's Cause," the man announced. "You have doubtless heard of us from them. I am Boris Proudhon, commissar of People's Justice. This is Matrona Rimsky—"

"And you will both oblige me greatly if you elevate your hands!" Standing framed in the front door, Jules de Grandin swung his automatic pistol in a threatening arc before him. He was smiling, but not pleasantly, and from the flush upon his ordinarily pale cheeks I knew he must have hurried through the rain.

There was corrosive, vitriolic hatred in the woman's voice as she wheeled toward him. "Bourgeois swine; capitalistic dog!" she spat, her pistol raised.

There was no flicker in de Grandin's smile as he shot her neatly through the forehead, nor did he change expression as he told the man, "It is a pity she should go to hell alone, *Monsieur*. You had better keep her company." His pistol snapped a second spiteful, whip-like crack, and Boris Proudhon stumbled forward on the body of his companion spy and fellow murderer.

"*Tiens*, I've followed them for hours," the Frenchman said as he came into the drawing-room, stepping daintily around the huddled bodies. "I saw them lurking in the shadows when I left the house, and knew they had no good intentions. Accordingly I circled back when I had reached the corner, and lay in wait to watch them. When they moved, so did I. When they so skillfully undid the front door lock all silently, I was at their elbows. When they announced intention to commit another murder—*eh bien*, it is not healthy to do things like that when Jules de Grandin is about."

"But it was scarcely eight o'clock when you went out; it's past eleven now.

Surely you could have summoned the police," I protested. 'Was it necessary that you shoot—"

"Not necessary, but desirable," he interrupted. "I know what's in your thought, Friend Trowbridge. Me, I can fairly see that Anglo-Saxon mind of yours at work. 'He shot a woman!' you accuse, and are most greatly shocked. *Pourquoi?* I have also shot the female of the leopard and the tiger when occasion called for it. I have set my heel upon the heads of female snakes. Had it been a rabid bitch I shot in time to save two lives you would have thought I did a noble service. Why, then, do you shudder with smug horror when I eliminate a blood-mad female woman? These two sent countless innocents to Siberia and death when they worked for the Tsarist government. As agents of the Soviets they fed their blood-lust by a hundred heartless killings. They murdered the great savant Pavlovitch in cold blood, they would have done the same for Nikakova and Serge had I not stopped them. *Tenez*, it was no vengeance that I did; it was an execution."

Aksakoff and Nikakova crossed the room and knelt before him, and in solemn turn took his right hand and raised it to their brows and lips. To me it seemed absurd, degrading, even, but they were Russians, and the things they did were ingrained as their thoughts. Also—I realized it with a start of something like surprise—Jules de Grandin was a Frenchman, emotional, mercurial, lovable and loving, but—a Frenchman. Therefore, he was logical as Fate, He lived by sentiment, but of sentimentality he had not a trace.

It was this realization which enabled me to stifle my instinctive feeling of repugnance as he calmly called police headquarters and informed them that the murderers of Doctor Pavlovitch were waiting at my house—"for the wagon of the morgue."

Incense of Abomination

"... incense is an abomination unto me."

—*Isaiah* 1: 13

DETECTIVE SERGEANT COSTELLO LOOKED fixedly at the quarter-inch of ash on his cigar, as though he sought solution of his problem in its fire-cored grayness. "'Tis th' damndest mixed-up mess I've iver happened up against," he told us solemnly. "Here's this Eldridge felly, young an' rich an' idle, wid niver a care ter 'is name, savin' maybe, how he'd spend th' next month's income, then zowie! he ups an' hangs hisself. We finds him swingin' from th' doorpost of his bedroom wid his bathrobe girdle knotted around 'is neck an' about a mile o' tongue sthickin' out. Suicide? Sure, an' what else could it be wid a felly found sthrung up in a tight-locked flat like that?

"Then, widin a week there comes a call fer us to take it on th' lam up to th' house where Stanley Trivers lived. There he is, a-layin' on his bathroom floor wid a cut across 'is throat that ye could put yer foot into, a'most. In his pajammies he is, an' th' blood's run down an' spoilt 'em good an' proper. Suicide again? Well, maybe so an' maybe no, fer in all me time I've niver seen a suicidal cut across a felly's throat that was as deep where it wound up as where it stharted. They mostly gits remorse afore th' cut is ended, as ye know, an' th' pressure on th' knife gits less an' less; so th' cut's a whole lot shallower at th' end than 'twas at th' beginnin'. However, th' coroner says it's suicide, so suicide it is, as far as we're concerned. Anyhow, gintlemen, in both these cases th' dead men wuz locked in their houses, from th' inside, as wus plain by th' keys still bein' in th' locks.

"Now comes th' third one. 'Tis this Donald Atkins felly, over to th' Kensington Apartments. Sthretched on th' floor he is, wid a hole bored in 'is forehead an' th' blood a-runnin' over everything. He's on 'is back wid a pearl-stocked pistol in 'is hand. Suicide again, says Schultz, me partner, an' I'm not th' one ter say as how it ain't, all signs pointin' as they do, still—" He paused and puffed at his cigar till its gray tip glowed with sullen rose.

Jules de Grandin tweaked a needle-sharp mustache tip. "Tell me, my sergeant," he commanded, "what is it you have withheld? Somewhere in the history of these cases is a factor you have not revealed, some denominator common to them all which makes your police instinct doubt your senses' evidence—"

"How'd ye guess it, sor?" the big Irishman looked at him admiringly. "Ye've put yer finger right upon it, but—" He stifled an embarrassed cough, then, turning slightly red: "'Tis th' perfume, sor, as makes me wonder."

"Perfume?" the little Frenchman echoed. "What in Satan's foul name—"

"Well, sor, I ain't one o' them as sees a woman's skirts a-hidin' back of ivery crime, though you an' I both knows there's mighty few crimes committed that ain't concerned wid cash or women, savin' when they're done fer both. But these here cases have me worried. None o' these men wuz married, an', so far as I've found out, none o' them wuz kapin' steady company, yet—git this, sor; 'tis small, but maybe it's important—there wuz a smell o' perfume hangin' round each one of 'em, an' 'twas th' same in ivery case. No sooner had I got a look at this pore Eldridge felly hangin' like a joint o' beef from his own doorpost than me nose begins a-twitchin'. 'Wuz he a pansy, maybe?' I wonders when I smelt it first, for 'twas no shavin' lotion or toilet water, but a woman's heavy scent, strong an' swate an'—what's it that th' ads all say?—distinctive. Yis, sor, that's th' word fer it, distinctive. Not like anything I've smelt before, but kind o' like a mixin' up o' this here ether that they use ter put a man ter slape before they takes 'is leg off, an' kind o' like th' incense they use in church, an' maybe there wuz sumpin mixed wid it that wasn't perfume afther all, sumpin that smelt rank an' sickly-like, th' kind o' smell ye smell when they takes a floater from th' bay, sor.

"Well, I looks around ter see where it's a-comin' from, an' it's strongest in th' bedroom; but divil a sign o' any woman bein' there I find, 'ceptin' fer th' smell o' perfume.

"So when we runs in on th' Trivers suicide, an' I smells th' same perfume again, I say that this is sumpin more than mere coincidence, but th' same thing happens there. Th' smell is strongest in th' bedroom, but there ain't any sign that he'd had company th' night before; so just ter make sure I takes th' casin's off th' pillows an' has th' boys at th' crime lab'ratory look at 'em. Divil a trace o' rouge or powder do they find.

"Both these other fellies kilt theirselves at night or early in th' mornin', so, o' course, their beds wuz all unmade, but when we hustle over ter th' Kensington Apartments ter see about this Misther Atkins, 'tis just past three o'clock. Th' doctor says that he's been dead a hour or more; yet when I goes into his bedroom th' covers is pushed down, like he's been slapin' there an' got up in a hurry, an' th' perfume's strong enough ter knock ye down, a'most. Th' boys at th' crime lab say there's not a trace o' powder on th' linen, an' by th' time I gits th' pillows to 'em th' perfume's faded out."

He looked at us with vaguely troubled eyes and ran his hand across his mouth. "'Tis meself that's goin' nuts about these suicides a-comin' one on top th' other, an' this perfume bobbin' up in every case!" he finished.

De Grandin pursed his lips. "You would know this so strange scent if you encountered it again?"

"Faith, sor, I'd know it in me slape!"

"And you have never met with it before?"

"Indade an' I had not, nayther before nor since, savin' in th' imayjate pris-ence o' them three dead corpses."

"One regrets it is so evanescent. Perhaps if I could smell it I might be able to identify it. I recall when I was serving with *le sûreté* we came upon a band of scoundrels making use of a strange Indian drug called by the Hindoos *chhota maut*, or little death. It was a subtle powder which made those inhaling it go mad, or fall into a coma simulating death if they inspired enough. Those naughty fellows mixed the drug with incense which they caused to be burned in their vic-tims' rooms. Some went mad and some appeared to die. One of those who went insane committed suicide—"

"Howly Mither, an' ye think we may be up against a gang like that, sor?"

"One cannot say, *mon vieux*. Had I the chance to sniff this scent, perhaps I could have told you. Its odor is not one that was soon forgotten. As it is"—he raised his shoulders in a shrug—"what can one do?"

"Will ye be afther holdin' yerself in readiness ter come a-runnin' if they's another o' these suicides, sor?" the big detective asked as he rose to say good-night. "I'd take it kindly if ye would."

"You may count on me, my friend. À *bientôt*," the little Frenchman answered with a smile.

THE STORM HAD BLOWN itself out early in the evening, but the streets were still bright with the filmy remnant of the sleety rain and the moon was awash in a breaking surf of wind-clouds. It was longer by the north road, but with the pavements slick as burnished glass I preferred to take no chances and had throttled down my engine almost to a walking pace as we climbed the gradient leading to North Bridge. De Grandin sank his chin into the fur of his upturned coat collar and nodded sleepily. The party at the Merrivales had been not at all amusing, and we were due at City Hospital at seven in the morning. "Ah, *bah*," he murmured drowsily, "we were a pair of fools, my friend; we forgot a thing of great importance when we left the house tonight."

"U'm?" I grunted. "What?"

"To stay there," he returned. "Had we but the sense *le bon Dieu* gives an unfledged gosling, we should have—*sapristi!* Stop him, he is intent on self-destruction!"

At his shouted warning I looked toward the footwalk and descried a figure in a heavy ulster climbing up the guard rail. Shooting on my power, I jerked the car ahead, then cut the clutch and jammed the brakes down hard, swinging us against the curb abreast of the intending suicide. I kicked the door aside and raced around the engine-hood, but de Grandin disdained such delays and vaulted overside, half leaping, half sliding on the slippery pavement and cannoning full-tilt against the man who sought to climb the breast-high railing. "*Parbleu*, you shall not!" he exclaimed as he grasped the other's legs with outflung arms. "It is wet down there, *Monsieur*, and most abominably cold. Wait for summer if you care to practise diving!"

The man kicked viciously, but the little Frenchman hung on doggedly, and as the other loosed his hold upon the rail they both came crashing to the pavement where they rolled and thrashed like fighting dogs.

I hovered near the mêlée, intent on giving such assistance as I could, but my help was not required; for as I reached to snatch the stranger's collar, de Grandin gave a quick twist, arched his body upon neck and heels and with a blow as rapid as a striking snake's chopped his adversary on the Adam's apple with his stiffened hand. The result was instantaneous. The larger man collapsed as if he had been shot, and my little friend slipped out from underneath him, teeth flashing in an impish grin, small blue eyes agleam. "A knowledge of jiu-jitsu comes in handy now and then," he panted as he rearranged his clothing. "For a moment I had fears that he would take me with him to a watery bed."

"Well, what shall we do with him?" I asked. "He's out completely, and we can't afford to leave him here. He'll surely try to kill himself again if—"

"*Parbleu! Attendez, s'il vous plaît!*" he interrupted. "*Le parfum*—do you smell him?" He paused with back-thrown head, narrow nostrils quivering as he sniffed the moist, cold air.

There was no doubt of it. Faint and growing quickly fainter, but plainly noticeable, the aura of a scent hung in the atmosphere. It was an odd aroma, not wholly pleasant, yet distinctly fascinating, seeming to combine the heavy sweetness of patchouli with the bitterness of frankincense and the penetrating qualities of musk and civet; yet underlying it there was a faint and slightly sickening odor of corruption.

"Why, I never smelled—" I began, but de Grandin waved aside my observation.

"Nor I," he nodded shortly, "but unless I am at fault this is the perfume which the good Costello told us of. Cannot you see, my friend? We have here our laboratory specimen, an uncompleted suicide with the redolence of this mysterious scent upon it. Help me lift him in the car, *mon vieux*, we have things to say to this one. We shall ask him, by example, why it was—"

"Suppose that he won't talk?" I broke in.

"*Ha*, you suppose that! If your supposition proves correct and he is of the obstinacy, you shall see a beautiful example of the third degree. You shall see me turn him inside out as if he were a lady's glove. I shall creep into his mind, me. I shall—*mordieu*, before the night is done I damn think I shall have at least a partial answer to the good Costello's puzzle! Come, let us be of haste; *en avant!*"

DESPITE HIS HEIGHT THE salvaged man did not weigh much, and we had no trouble getting him inside the car. In fifteen minutes we were home, just as our rescued human flotsam showed signs of returning consciousness.

"Be careful," warned de Grandin as he helped the passenger alight. "If you behave we shall treat you with the kindness, but if you try the monkey's tricks I have in readiness a second portion of the dish I served you on the *Pont du Nord*.

"Here," he added as we led our captive to the study, "this is the medicine for those who feel at odds with life." He poured a gill of Scots into a tumbler and poised the siphon over it. "Will you have soda with your whisky," he inquired, "or do you like it unpolluted?"

"Soda, please," the other answered sulkily, drained his glass in two huge gulps and held it out again.

"*Eh bien*," the Frenchman chuckled, "your troubles have not dulled your appetite, it seems. Drink, my friend, drink all you wish, for the evening is still young and we have many things to talk of, thou and I."

The visitor eyed him sullenly as he took a sip from his fresh glass. "I suppose you think you've done your Boy Scout's good deed for today?" he muttered.

"*Mais oui, mais certainement*," the Frenchman nodded vigorously. "We have saved you from irreparable wrong, my friend. *Le bon Dieu* did not put us here to—"

"That's comic!" the other burst out with a cackling laugh. "'*Le bon Dieu*'— much use *He* has for me!"

De Grandin lowered his arching brows a little; the effect was a deceptively mild, thoughtful frown. "So-o," he murmured, "that is the way of it? You feel that you have been cast off, that—"

"Why not? Didn't we—I—cast Him out? Didn't I deny Him, take service with His enemies, mock at Him—"

"Be not deceived, my friend"—the double lines between the Frenchman's narrow brows was etched a little deeper as he answered in an even voice—"God is not mocked. It is easier to spit against the hurricane than jeer at Him. Besides, He is most merciful, He is compassionate, and His patience transcends understanding. Wicked we may be, but if we offer true repentance—"

"Even if you've committed the unpardonable sin?"

"*Tiens*, this *péché irrémissible* of which the theologians prate so learnedly, yet which none of them defines? You had a mother, one assumes; you may have sinned against her grievously, disappointed her high hopes in you, shown ingratitude as black as Satan's shadow, abused her trust or even done her bodily hurt. Yet if you went to her sincerely penitent and told her you were sorry, that you truly loved her and would sin no more, *parbleu*, she would forgive, you know it! Will the Heavenly Father be less merciful than earthly parents? Very well, then. Who can say that he has sinned past reconciliation?"

"I can; I did—we all did! We cast God out and embraced Satan—" Something that was lurking horror seemed to take form in his eyes, giving them a stony, glazed appearance. It was as if a filmy curtain were drawn down across them, hiding everything within, mirroring only a swift-mounting terror.

"Ah?" de Grandin murmured thoughtfully. "Now we begin to make the progress." Abruptly he demanded:

"You knew Messieurs Eldridge, Trivers and Atkins?" He flung the words more like a challenging accusation than a query.

"Yes!"

"And they, too, thought they had sinned past redemption; they saw in suicide the last hope of escape; they were concerned with you in this iniquity?"

"They were, but no interfering busybody stopped them. Let me out of here, I'm going to—"

"*Monsieur*," de Grandin did not raise his voice, but the look he bent upon the other was as hard and merciless as though it were a leveled bayonet, "you are going to remain right here and tell us how it came about. You will tell of this transgression which has caused three deaths already and almost caused a fourth. Do not fear to speak, my friend. We are physicians, and your confidence will be respected. On the other hand, if you persist in silence we shall surely place you in restraint. You would like to be lodged in a madhouse, have your every action watched, be strapped in a straitjacket if you attempted self-destruction, *hein?*" Slowly spoken, his words had the impact of a bodily assault, and the other reeled as from a beating.

"Not that!" he gasped. "O God, anything but that! I'll tell you everything if you will promise—"

"You have our word, *Monsieur*; say on."

The visitor drew his chair up closer to the fire, as if a sudden cold had chilled his marrow. He was some forty years of age, slim and quite attractive, immaculately dressed, well groomed. His eyes were brown, deep-set and drawn, as if unutterably weary, with little pouches under them. His shoulders sagged as if the weight they bore was too much for them. His hair was almost wholly gray. "Beaten" was the only adjective to modify him.

"I think perhaps you knew my parents, Doctor Trowbridge," he began. "My father was James Balderson."

I nodded. Jim Balderson had been a senior when I entered college, and his escapades were bywords on the campus. Nothing but the tolerance which stamps a rich youth's viciousness as merely indication of high spirits had kept him from dismissal since his freshman year, and faculty and townsfolk sighed with relief when he took his sheepskin and departed simultaneously. The Balderson and Aldridge fortunes were combined when he married Bronson Aldridge's sole heir and daughter, and though he settled down in the walnut-paneled office of the Farmers Loan & Trust Company, his sons had carried on his youthful zest for getting into trouble. Drunken driving, divorce cases, scandals which involved both criminal and civil courts, were their daily fare. Two of them had died by violence, one in a motor smash-up, one when an outraged husband showed better marksmanship than self-restraint. One had died of poison liquor in the Prohibition era. We had just saved the sole survivor from attempted suicide. "Yes, I knew your father," I responded.

"Do you remember Horton Hall?" he asked.

I bent my brows a moment. "Wasn't that the school down by the Shrewsbury where they had a scandal?—something about the headmaster committing suicide, or—"

"You're right. That's it. I was in the last class there. So were Eldridge, Trivers and Atkins.

"I was finishing my junior year when the war broke out in 'seventeen. Dad got bulletproof commissions for the older boys, but wouldn't hear of my enlisting in the Navy. 'You've a job to do right there at Horton,' he told me. 'Get your certificate; then we'll see about your joining up.' So back I went to finish out my senior year. Dad didn't know what he was doing to me. Things might have turned out differently if I'd gone in the service.

"Everyone who could was getting in the Army or the Navy. We'd lost most of our faculty when I went back in '18, and they'd put a new headmaster in, a Doctor Herbules. Fellows were leaving right and left, enlisting from the campus or being called by draft boards, and I was pretty miserable. One day as I was walking back from science lab, I ran full-tilt into old Herbules.

"'What's the matter, Balderson?' he asked. 'You look as if you'd lost your last friend.'

"'Well, I have, almost,' I answered. 'With so many fellows off at training-camp, having all kinds of excitement—'

"'You want excitement, eh?' he interrupted. 'I can give it to you; such excitement as you've never dreamed of. I can make you—' He stopped abruptly, and it seemed to me he looked ashamed of something, but he'd got my curiosity roused.

"'You're on, sir,' I told him. 'What is it, a prize-fight?'

"Herbules was queer. Everybody said so. He couldn't have been much past thirty; yet his hair was almost snowwhite and there was a funny sort o' peaceful expression on his smooth face that reminded me of something that I couldn't quite identify. He had the schoolmaster's trick of speaking with a sort of pedantic precision, and he never raised his voice; yet when he spoke in chapel we could understand him perfectly, no matter how far from the platform we were sitting. I'd never seen him show signs of excitement before, but now he was breathing hard and was in such deadly earnest that his lips were fairly trembling. 'What do you most want from life?' he asked me in a whisper.

"'Why, I don't know, just now I'd like best of all to get into the Army; I'd like to go to France and bat around with the *mademoiselles*, and get drunk any time I wanted—'

"'You'd like that sort of thing?' he laughed. 'I can give it to you, and more; more than you ever imagined. Wine and song and gayety and women—beautiful lovely, cultured women, not the street-trulls that you'd meet in France—you can have all this and more, if you want to, Balderson.'

"'Lead me to it,' I replied. 'When do we start?'

"'Ah, my boy, nothing's given for nothing. There are some things you'll have to do, some promises to make, something to be paid—"

"'All right; how much?' I asked. Dad was liberal with me. I had a hundred dollars every month for spending money, and I could always get as much again from Mother if I worked it right.

"'No, no; not money,' he almost laughed in my face. 'The price of all this can't be paid in money. All we ask is that you give the Master something which I greatly doubt you realize you have, my boy.'

"It sounded pretty cock-eyed to me, but if the old boy really had something up his sleeve I wanted to know about it. 'Count me in,' I told him. 'What do I do next?"

"There was no one within fifty yards of us, but he bent until his lips were almost in my ear before be whispered: 'Next Wednesday at midnight, come to my house.'

"'Private party, or could I bring a friend or two?'

"His features seemed to freeze. 'Who is the friend?' he asked.

"'Well, I'd like to bring Eldridge and Trivers, and maybe Atkins, too. They're all pretty good eggs, and I know they crave excitement—'

"'Oh, by all means, yes. Be sure to bring them. It's agreed, then? Next Wednesday night at twelve, at my house.'

"Herbules was waiting for us in a perfect fever of excitement when we tiptoed up his front-porch steps on Wednesday night. He had a domino and mask for each of us. The dominoes were fiery red, with hoods that pulled up like monks' cowls; the masks were black, and hideous. They represented long, thin faces with out-jutting chins; the lips were purple and set in horrid grins; the eyebrows were bright scarlet wool and at the top there was another patch of bright red worsted curled and cut to simulate a fringe of hair. 'Good Lord,' said Atkins as he tried his on, 'I look just like the Devil!'

"I thought that Herbules would have a stroke when he heard Atkins speak. 'You'll use that name with more respect after tonight, my boy,' he said.

"After that we all got in his car and drove down toward Red Bank.

"We stopped about a mile outside of town and parked the car in a small patch of woods, walked some distance down the road, climbed a fence and cut across a field till we reached an old deserted house. I'd seen the place as I drove past, and had often wondered why it was unoccupied, for it stood up on a hill surrounded by tall trees and would have made an ideal summer home, but I'd been told its well was dry, and as there was no other source of water, nobody wanted it.

"We didn't go to the front door, but tiptoed round the back, where Herbules struck three quick raps, waited for a moment, then knocked four more.

"We'd all put on our robes and masks while he was knocking, and when the door was opened on a crack we saw the porter was robed and masked as we were. Nobody said a word, and we walked through a basement entrance, down a long and narrow hall, and turned a corner where we met another door. Here Herbules went through the same procedure, and the door swung back to let us in.

"We were in a big room, twenty by forty feet, I guess, and we knew it was a cellar by the smell—stiflingly close, but clammy as a tomb at once. Rows of folding chairs like those used at bridge games—or funerals—were arranged in double rows with a passage like an aisle between, and at the farther end of the big room we saw an altar.

"In all my life I don't believe I'd been to church ten times, but we were nominally Protestants, so what I saw had less effect on me than if I'd been a Catholic or Episcopalian; but I knew at once the altar wasn't regulation. Oh, it was sufficiently impressive, but it had a sort of comic—no, not comic, grotesque, rather—note about it. A reredos of black cloth was hung against the wall, and before it stood a heavy table more than eight feet long and at least six wide, covered by a black cloth edged with white. It reminded me of something, though I couldn't quite identify it for a moment; then I knew. I'd seen a Jewish funeral once, and this cloth was like the black-serge pall they used to hide the plain pine coffin! At each end of the altar stood a seven-branched candelabrum made of brass, each with a set of tall black candles in it. These were burning and gave off a pale blue glow. They seemed to be perfumed, too, and the odor which they burned with was pleasant—at first. Then, as I sniffed a second time it seemed to me there was a faint suspicion of a stench about it, something like the fetor that you smell if you're driving down the road and pass a dog or cat that's been run over and has lain a while out in the sun—just a momentary whiff, but nauseating, just the same. Between the candelabra, right exactly in the center of the altar, but back against the wall, was a yard-high crucifix of some black wood with an ivory figure on it, upside down. Before the cross there was a silver wine goblet and a box of gilt inlay about the size and shape of a lady's powder-puff box.

"I heard Atkins catch his breath and give a sort of groan. He'd been brought up an Episcopalian and knew about such things. He turned half round to leave, but I caught him by the sleeve.

"'Come on, you fool, don't be a sissy!' I admonished, and next moment we were all so interested that he had no thought of leaving.

"There was a sort of congregation in the chapel; every seat was occupied by someone masked and robed just as we were, save three vacant places by the altar steps. These, we knew, were kept for us, but when we looked about for Herbules he was nowhere to be seen; so we went forward to our seats alone. We could hear a hum of whispering as we walked up the aisle, and we knew some of the voices were from women; but who was man and who was woman was impossible to tell, for each one looked just like his neighbor in his shrouding robe.

"The whispering suddenly became intense, like the susurrus of a hive of swarming bees. Every neck seemed suddenly to crane, every eye to look in one direction, and as we turned our glances toward the right side of the cellar we saw a woman entering through a curtained doorway. She wore a long, loose scarlet cape which she held together with one hand, her hair was very black, her eyes were large and luminously dark, seeming to have a glance of overbearing sensuousness and sweet humility at once. Her white, set face was an imponderable mask; her full red lips were fixed in an uneven, bitter line. Beneath the hem of her red cloak we saw the small feet in the golden, high-heeled slippers were unstockinged. As she neared the altar she sank low in genuflection, then wheeled about and faced us. For a moment she stood there, svelte, graceful, mysteriously beautiful with that thin white face and scarlet lips so like a mask; then with a sudden kicking motion she unshod her feet, opened wide her cloak and let it fall in scarlet billows on the dull-black carpet of the altar steps.

"She was so beautiful it almost hurt the eyes to look at her as she stood there in white silhouette against the ebon background of the black-draped altar, with her narrow, boy-like hips, slim thighs and full, high, pointed breasts. She was a thing of snow and fire, her body palely cool and virginal, her lips like flame, her eyes like embers blazing when a sudden wind stirs them to brightness.

"The modern strip-tease routine was unthought of in those days, and though I was sophisticated far beyond my eighteen years I had never seen a woman in the nude before. The flame of her raced in my blood and crashed against my brain with almost numbing impact. I felt myself go faint and sick with sudden weakness and desire.

"A long-drawn sign came from the audience; then the tableau was abruptly broken as the girl turned from us, mounted nimbly to the black-draped altar and stretched herself full length upon it, crossed her ankles and thrust her arms out right and left, so that her body made a white cross on the sable altar-cloth. Her eyes were closed as though in peaceful sleep, but her bosoms rose and fell with her tumultuous breathing. She had become the altar!

"Silence fell upon the congregation like a shadow, and next instant Herbules came in. He wore a priest's vestments, a long red cassock, over it the alb and stole, and in his hand he bore a small red book. Behind him came his acolyte, but it was not an altar-boy. It was a girl, slender, copper-haired, *petite*. She wore a short surcoat of scarlet, cut low around the shoulders, sleeveless, reaching just below the hips, like the tabards worn by mediæval heralds. Over it she wore a lace-edged cotta. Otherwise she was unclothed. We could hear the softly slapping patter of her small bare feet upon the altar-sill as she changed her place from side to side, genuflecting as she passed the reversed crucifix. She swung a brazen censer to and fro before her and the gray smoke curled in spurting puffs from it, filling the entire place with a perfume like that generated by the candles, but stronger, more intense, intoxicating.

"Herbules began the service with a muttered Latin prayer, and though he seemed to follow a set ritual even I could see it was not that prescribed by any church, for when he knelt he did so with his back turned toward the altar; when he crossed himself he did it with the thumb of his left hand, and made the sign beginning at the bottom, rather than the top. But even in this mummers' parody the service was majestic. I could feel its power and compulsion as it swept on toward its climax. Herbules took up the silver chalice and held it high above his head, then rested it upon the living altar, placing it between her breasts, and we could see the flesh around her nails grow white as she grasped the black-palled altar table with her fingers. Her body, shining palely on the coffin-pall under the flickering candles' light, was arched up like a tauted bow, she shook as if a sudden chill had seized her, and from her tight-drawn, scarlet lips there issued little whimpering sounds, not cries nor yet quite groans, but something which partook of both, and at the same time made me think of the soft, whining sounds a newborn puppy makes.

"The kneeling acolyte chimed a sacring-bell and the congregation bent and swayed like a wheat-field swept across by sudden wind.

"When all was finished we were bidden to come forward and kneel before the altar steps. Herbules came down and stood above us, and each of us was made to kiss the red book which he held and take a fearful oath, swearing that he would abstain from good and embrace evil, serve Satan faithfully and well, and do his best to bring fresh converts to the worship of the Devil. Should we in any manner break our oath, we all agreed that Satan might at once foreclose upon his mortgage on our souls, and bear us still alive to hell, and the sign that we were come for was to be the odor of the perfume which the candles and the censer gave that night.

"When this ritual was finished we were bidden name our dearest wish, and told it would be granted. I could hear the others mumble something, but could not understand their words. I don't know what possessed me when it came my turn to ask a boon of Satan—possibly he put the thought into my mind, maybe it was my longing to get out of school and go to France before the war was ended. At any rate, when Herbules bent over me I muttered, 'I wish the pater would bump off.'

"He leaned toward me with a smile and whispered, 'You begin your postulancy well, my son,' then held his hand out to me, signifying that I should return his clasp with both of mine. As I put out my hands to take his I saw by my wristwatch that it was exactly half-past twelve.

"What followed was the wildest party I had ever seen or dreamt of. The farmhouse windows had been boarded up and curtained, and inside the rooms were literally ablaze with light. Men and women, some draped in their red dominoes, some in evening dress, some naked as the moment that they first drew breath, mingled in a perfect saturnalia of unrestrained salacity. On tables stood ice-buckets with champagne, and beside them tall decanters of cut glass filled with port and sherry, tokay, madeira, muscatel and malaga. Also there was bottled brandy, vodka and whisky, trays of cigarettes, boxes of cigars, sandwiches, cake and sweetmeats. It was like the carnival at New Orleans, only ten times gayer, madder, more abandoned. I was grasped by naked men and women, whirled furiously around in a wild dance, then let go only to be seized by some new partner and spun around until I almost fell from dizziness. Between times I drank, mixing wine and spirits without thought, stuffed sandwiches and cake and candy in my mouth, then drank fresh drafts of chilled champagne or sharptoned brandy.

"Staggering drunkenly about the table I was reaching for another glass when I felt a hand upon my shoulder. Turning, I beheld a pair of flashing eyes laughing at me through the peep-holes of a mask. 'Come with me, my neophyte,' the masked girl whispered; 'there is still a chalice you have left untasted.'

"She pulled me through the crowd, led me up the stairs and thrust a door ajar. The little room we entered was entirely oriental. A Persian lamp hung like a blazing ruby from the ceiling, on the floor were thick, soft rugs and piles of down-filled pillows. There was no other furniture.

"With a laugh she turned her back to me, motioning me to slip the knot which held the girdle of her domino; then she bent her head while I withdrew the pins that held her hair. It rippled in a cascade to her waist—below, nearly to her knees—black and glossy as the plumage of a grackle's throat, and as it cataracted down she swung around, shrugging her shoulders quickly, and let the scarlet domino fall from her. An upswing of her hand displaced the black-faced, purple, grinning mask, and I looked directly in the face of the pale girl who half an hour earlier had lain upon the altar of the Devil. 'Kiss me!' she commanded. 'Kiss me!' Her arms were tight about my neck, pulling my lips to hers, drawing her slender, unclothed body tight against me. Her lips clung to my mouth as though they were a pair of scarlet leeches; through her half-closed lids I saw the glimmer of her bright black eyes, burning like twin points of quenchless fire. . . .

"It was daylight when we reached the dorm next day, and all of us reported sick at chapel. Sometime about eleven, as I rose to get a drink of water, a knock came at my door. It was a telegram that stated:

Father dropped dead in his study at twelve forty-five. Come.   MOTHER.

"I hurried back to school as soon as possible. My father's death had startled—frightened—me, but I put it down to coincidence, He'd been suffering from Bright's disease for several years, and probably his number'd just turned up, I told myself. Besides, the longing for the celebration of the sacrilegious Mass with its sensual stimulation, followed by the orgiastic parties, had me in a grip as strong as that which opium exerts upon its addicts.

"Twice a week, each Wednesday and Friday, my three friends and I attended the salacious services held in the old farmhouse cellar, followed by the revels in the upper rooms, and bit by bit we learned about our fellow cultists. Herbules, the head and center of the cult, was a priest stripped of his orders. Pastor of a parish in the suburbs of Vienna, he had dabbled in the Black Art, seduced a number of his congregation from their faith, finally celebrated the Black Mass. The ecclesiastical authorities unfrocked him, the civil government jailed him on a morals charge, but disgrace could not impair his splendid education or his brilliant mind, and as soon as his imprisonment was over he emigrated to America and at once secured a post as teacher. Though his talents were unquestionable, his morals were not, and scandal followed every post he held. He was at the end of his string when he managed to worm his way into the Horton trustees' confidence and secured the post left vacant by the former headmaster's entrance in the Army.

"Our companion Devil-worshippers were mostly college and preparatory students looking for a thrill, now tangled in the net of fascination that the cult spun round its devotees, but a few of them were simply vicious, while others turned to demonolatry because they had lost faith in God.

"One of these was Marescha Nurmi, the girl who acted as the living altar. She was my constant partner at the orgies, and bit by bit I learned her history. Only nineteen, she was the victim of a heart affliction and the doctors gave her but a year to live. When they pronounced sentence she was almost prostrated; then in desperation she turned to religion, going every day to church and spending hours on her knees in private prayer. But medical examination showed her illness was progressing, and when she chanced to hear of Herbules' devil-cult she came to it. 'I'm too young, too beautiful to die!' she told me as we lay locked in each others' arms one night. 'Why should God take my life? I never injured Him. All right, if He won't have me, Satan will. He'll give me life and happiness and power, let me live for years and years; keep me young and beautiful when all these sniveling Christian girls are old and faded. What do I care if I go to Hell to pay for it? I'll take my heaven here on earth, and when the bill's presented I won't welch!'

"There's an old saying that each time God makes a beautiful woman the Devil opens a new page in his ledger. He must have had to put in a whole set of books when Marescha was converted to our cult. She was attractive as a witch, had no more conscience than a snake, and positively burned with ardor to do evil. Night after night she brought new converts to the cult, sometimes young men, sometimes girls. 'Come on, you little fool,' I heard her urge a girl who shrank from the wild orgy following initiation. 'Take off your robe; that's what we're here for. This is our religion, the oldest in the world; it's revolt against the goody-goodies, revolt against the narrowness of God; we live for pleasure and unbridled passion instead of abnegation and renunciation—life and love and pleasure in a world of vivid scarlet, instead of fear and dreariness in a world all cold and gray. That's our creed and faith. We're set apart, we're marked for pleasure, we worshippers of Satan.'"

"*Tiens*, the lady was a competent saleswoman," de Grandin murmured. "Did she realize her dreams?"

The laugh that prefaced Balderson's reply was like the echo of a chuckle in a vaulted tomb. "I don't know if she got her money's worth, but certainly she paid," he answered. "It was nearing graduation time, and the celebrations were about to stop until the fall, for it would be impossible to keep the farmhouse windows shuttered so they'd show no gleam of light, especially with so many people on the roads in summer. Herbules had just completed invocation, raised the chalice overhead and set it on Marescha's breast when we saw her twitch convulsively. The little whimpering animal-cries she always made when the climax of the obscene parody was reached gave way to a choked gasping, and we saw the hand that clutched the altar-table suddenly relax. She raised her head and stared around the chapel with a look that sent the chill of horror rippling through me, then cried out in a strangled voice: 'O Lord, be pitiful!' Then she fell back on the coffin-pall that draped the altar and her fingers dangled loosely on its edge, her feet uncrossed and lay beside each other.

"Herbules was going on as if nothing had happened, but the woman who sat next to me let out a sudden wail. 'Look at her,' she screamed. 'Look at her face!'

"Marescha's head had turned a little to one side, and we saw her features in the altar-candles' light. Her dark hair had come unbound and fell about her face as though it sought to hide it. Her eyes were not quite closed, nor fully open, for a thread of gray eyeball was visible between the long black lashes. Her mouth was partly open, not as though she breathed through it, but lax, slack, as though she were exhausted. Where a line of white defined the lower teeth we saw her tongue had fallen forward, lying level with the full, red lip.

"Somewhere in the rear of the chapel another woman's voice, shrilly pitched, but controlled, cried out: 'She's dead!'

"There was a wave of movement in the worshippers. Chairs were overturned, gowns rustled, whispered questions buzzed like angry bees. Then the woman sitting next me screamed again: 'This is no natural death, no illness killed her; she's been stricken dead for sacrilege, she's sacrificed for our sins—fly, fly before the wrath of God blasts all of us!'

"Herbules stood at the altar facing us. A mask as of some inner feeling, of strange, forbidden passions, of things that raced on scurrying feet within his brain, seemed to drop across his features. His face seemed old and ancient, yet at the same time ageless; his eyes took on a glaze like polished agate. He raised both hands above his head, the fingers flexed like talons, and laughed as if at some dark jest known only to himself. 'Whoso leaves the temple of his Lord without partaking of this most unholy sacrament, the same will Satan cast aside, defenseless from the vengeance of an outraged God!' he cried.

"Then I knew. Karl Erik Herbules, renegade Christian priest, brilliant scholar, poisoner of souls and votary of Satan, was mad as any Tom o' Bedlam!

"He stood there by the Devil's altar hurling curses at us, threatening us with Heaven's vengeance, casting an anathema upon us with such vile insults and filthy language as a fishwife would not dare to use.

"But panic had the congregation by the throat. They pushed and fought and scratched and bit like frenzied cats, clawing and slashing at one another till they gained the exit, then rushing pell-mell down the hill to their parked cars with out a backward look, leaving Herbules alone beside the altar he had raised to Satan, with the dead girl stretched upon it.

"There was no chance that Herbules would help. He kept reciting passages from the Black Mass, genuflecting to the altar, filling and refilling the wine-cup and stuffing his mouth with the wafers meant to parody the Host. So Trivers, Eldridge, Atkins and I took Marescha's body to the river, weighted it with window-irons and dropped it in the water. But the knots we tied must have been loose, or else the weights were insufficient, for as we turned to leave, her body floated almost to the surface and one white arm raised above the river's glassy face, as though to wave a mute farewell. It must have been a trick the current played as the tide bore her away, but to us it seemed that her dead hand pointed to us each in turn; certainly there was no doubt it bobbed four times above the river's surface before the swirling waters sucked it out of sight.

"You've probably heard garbled rumors of what happened afterward. The farmhouse burned that night, and because there was no water to be had, there was no salvage. Still, a few things were not utterly destroyed, and people in the neighborhood still wonder how those Persian lamps and brazen candlesticks came to be in that deserted house.

"Herbules committed suicide that night, and when the auditors went over his accounts they found he'd practically wrecked Horton. There was hardly a cent left, for he'd financed his whole grisly farce of Devil worship with the money he embezzled. The trustees made the losses good and gave up in disgust. Ours was the last class graduated.

"They found Marescha's body floating in the Shrewsbury two days later, and at first the coroner was sure she'd been the victim of a murder; for while the window-weights had fallen off, the cords that tied them were still knotted round her ankles. When the autopsy disclosed she'd not been drowned, but had been put into the river after death from heart disease, the mystery was deepened, but until tonight only four people knew its answer. Now there are only three."

"Three, Monsieur?" de Grandin asked.

"That's right. Trivers, Atkins and Eldridge are dead. I'm still here, and you and Doctor Trowbridge—"

"Your figures are at fault, my friend. You forget we are physicians, and your narrative was given us in confidence."

"But see here," I asked as the silence lengthened, "what is there about all this to make you want to kill yourself? If you'd been grown men when you joined these Devil-worshippers it would have been more serious, but college boys are always in some sort of mischief, and this all happened twenty years ago. You say you are sincerely sorry for it, and after all, the leaders in the movement died, so—"

Balderson broke through my moralizing with a short, hard laugh. "Men die more easily than memories, Doctor. Besides—"

"Yes, *Monsieur*, besides?" de Grandin prompted as our guest stared silently into the study fire.

"Do you believe the spirits of the dead—the dead who are in Hell, or at least cut off from Heaven—can come back to plague the living?" he demanded.

De Grandin brushed the ends of his small waxed mustache with that gesture which always reminded me of a tomcat combing his whiskers. "You have experienced such a visitation?"

"I have. So did the others."

"*Mordieu!* How was it?"

"You may remember reading that Ted Eldridge hanged himself? Three days before it happened, he met me on the street, and I could see that he was almost frantic. 'I saw Marescha last night!' he told me in a frightened whisper.

"'Marescha? You must be off your rocker, man! We put her in the Shrewsbury—'

"'And she's come back again. Remember the perfume of the candles and the incense Herbules used in celebrating the Black Mass? I'd come home from New York last night, and was getting ready for a drink before I went to bed, when I began to smell it. At first I thought it was some fool trick that my senses played on me, but the scent kept getting stronger. It seemed as if I were back in that dreadful chapel with the tall black candles burning and the hellish incense smoldering, Herbules in his red vestments and Marescha lying naked on the altar—I could almost hear the chanting of inverted prayers and the little whimpering noises that she made. I gulped my drink down in two swallows and turned round. She was standing there, with water on her face and streaming from her hair, and her hands held out to me—'

"'You're crazy as a goat!' I told him. 'Come have a drink.'

"He looked at me a moment, then turned away, walking quickly down the street and muttering to himself.

"'I'd not have thought so much about it if I hadn't read about his suicide next day, and if Stanley Trivers hadn't called me on the telephone. 'Hear about Ted Eldridge?' he asked the moment I had said hello. When I told him I'd just read about it he demanded: 'Did you see him—recently?'

"'Yes, ran into him in Broad Street yesterday,' I answered.

"'Seemed worried, didn't he? Did he tell you anything about Marescha?'

"'Say, what is this?' I asked. 'Did he say anything to you—'

"'Yes, he did, and I thought he had a belfry full o' bats.'

"'There's not much doubt the poor old lad was cuckoo—'

"'That's where you're mistaken, Balderson. According to the paper he'd been dead for something like four hours when they found him. That would have made it something like four o'clock when he died.'

"'So what?'

"'So this: I waked up at four o'clock this morning and the room was positively stifling with the odor of the incense they used in the Black Chapel—'

"'Yeah? I suppose you saw Marescha, too?'

"'I did! She was standing by my bed, with water streaming from her face and body, and tears were in her eyes.'

"I tried to talk him out of it, tell him that it was a trick of his imagination stimulated by Ted Eldridge's wild talk, but he insisted that he'd really seen her. Two days later he committed suicide.

"Don Atkins followed. I didn't talk with him before he shot himself, but I'll wager that he saw her, too, and smelled that Devil's incense."

De Grandin looked at me with upraised brows, then shook his head to caution silence ere he turned to face our guest. "And you, *Monsieur?*" he asked.

"Yes, I too. Don killed himself sometime in early afternoon, and I was home that day. I'd say that it was shortly after two, for I'd lunched at the City Club and come home to pack a bag and take a trip to Nantakee. I had the highboy open and was taking out some shirts when I began to notice a strange odor in the air. But it wasn't strange for long; as it grew stronger I recognized it as the scent of Herbules' incense. It grew so strong that it was almost overpowering. I stood there by the chest of drawers, smelling the increasing scent, and determined that I'd not turn round. You know how Coleridge puts it:

Like one, that on a lonesome road
Doth walk in fear and dread,
And having once turned round, walks on,
And turns no more his head;
Because he knows a frightful fiend
Doth close behind him tread . . .

"The odor of the incense grew until I could have sworn somebody swung a censer right behind me. Then, suddenly, I heard the sound of falling water. '*Drip—drip—drip!*' it fell upon the floor, drop by deliberate drop. The suspense was more than I could bear, and I wheeled about.

"Marescha stood behind me, almost close enough to touch. Water trickled from the hair that hung in gleaming strands across her breast and shoulders, it hung in little gleaming globules on her pale, smooth skin, ran in little rivulets across her forehead, down her beautifully shaped legs, made tiny puddles on the polished floor beside each slim bare foot. I went almost sick with horror as I saw the knotted cords we'd used to tie the window-weights on her still bound about her ankles, water oozing from their coils. She did not seem dead. Her lovely slender body seemed as vital as when I had held it in my arms, her full and mobile lips were red with rouge, her eyes were neither set and staring nor expressionless. But they were sad, immeasurably sad. They seemed to probe into my spirit's very depths, asking, beseeching, entreating. And to make their plea more eloquent, she slowly raised her lovely hands and held them out to me, palms upward, fingers slightly curled, as though she besought alms.

"There was a faint resemblance to her bitter, crooked smile upon her lips, but it was so sad, so hopelessly entreating, that it almost made me weep to see it.

"'Mar—' I began, but the name stuck in my throat. This couldn't be the body that I'd held against my heart, those lips were not the lips I'd kissed a thousand times; this was no girl of flesh and blood. Marescha, lay deep in a grave in Shadow Lawns Cemetery; had lain there almost twenty years. Dust had filled those sad, entreating eyes long before the college freshmen of this year were born. The worms . . .

"Somewhere I had heard that if you called upon the Trinity a ghost would vanish. 'In the name of the Father—' I began, but it seemed as if a clap of thunder sounded in my ears.

"'What right have you to call upon the Triune God?' a mighty voice seemed to be asking. 'You who have mocked at Heaven, taken every sacred name in vain, made a jest of every holy thing—how dare you invoke Deity? Your sacrilegious lips cannot pronounce the sacred name!'

"And it was true. I tried again, but the words clogged in my throat; I tried to force them out, but only strangling inarticulacies sounded.

"Marescha's smile was almost pityingly tender, but still she stood there pleading, entreating, begging me, though what it was she wanted I could not divine. I threw my arm across my eyes to shut the vision out, but when I took it down she was still there, and still the water dripped from her entreating hands, ran in little courses from her dankly hanging hair, fell drop by drop from the sopping cords that ringed her ankles.

"I stumbled blindly from the house and walked the streets for hours. Presently I bought a paper, and the headlines told me Donald Atkins had been found, a suicide, in his apartment.

"When I reached my house again the incense still hung in the air, but the vision of Marescha was not there. I drank almost a pint of brandy, neat, and fell across my bed. When I recovered from my alcoholic stupor Marescha stood beside me, her great eyes luminous with tears, her hands outstretched in mute entreaty.

"She's been with me almost every waking instant since that night. I drank myself into oblivion, but every time I sobered she was standing by me. I'd walk the streets for hours, but every time I halted she would be there, always silent, always with her hands held out, always with that look of supplication in her tear-filled eyes. I'd rush at her and try to drive her off with blows and kicks. She seemed to float away, staying just outside my reach, however savagely I ran at her, and though I cursed her, using every foul word I knew, she never changed expression, never showed resentment; just stood and looked at me with sad, imploring eyes, always seeming to be begging me for something.

"I can't endure it any longer, gentlemen. Tonight she stood beside me when I halted on North Bridge, and I'd have been at peace by now if you'd not come along—"

"*Non*, there you are mistaken, *mon ami*," de Grandin contradicted. "Had you carried your intention out and leaped into the river you would have sealed your doom irrevocably. Instead of leaving her you would have joined her for eternity."

"All right," Balderson asked raspingly, "I suppose you have a better plan?"

"I think I have," the little Frenchman answered. "First, I would suggest you let us give you sedatives. You will not be troubled while you sleep, and while you rest we shall be active."

"SHAKESPEARE WAS RIGHT," I said as we left our patient sleeping from a dose of chloral hydrate. "Conscience does make cowards of us all. The memory of that early indiscretion has haunted that quartet of worthless youngsters twenty years. No wonder they kept seeing that poor girl after they'd thrown her so callously into the Shrewsbury. Of all the heartless, despicable things—"

He emerged from a brown study long enough to interrupt: "And is your conscience clean, my friend?"

"What has my conscience to do with it? I didn't throw a dead girl in the river; I didn't—"

"*Précisément*, neither did the good Costello, yet both of you described the odor of that Devil's incense: Costello when he went to view the bodies of the suicides, you when we halted Monsieur Balderson's attempt at self-destruction. Were you also haunted by that scent, or were you not?"

"I smelled it," I responded frigidly, "but I wasn't haunted by it. Just what is it you're driving at?"

"That the odor of that incense, or even the perception of the dead Marescha's *revenant*, is no optical illusion caused by guilty conscience. It is my firm conviction that the apparition which appeared to these unfortunate young men was the earthbound spirit of a girl who begged a boon from them."

"Then you don't think that she haunted them because they'd thrown her body in the river?"

"Entirely no. I think she came to ask their help, and in their fear and horror at beholding her they could not understand her plea. First one and then another, lashed with the scorpion-whip of an accusing conscience, destroyed himself because he dared not look into her pleading eyes, thinking they accused him of mistreating her poor body, when all the *pauvre belle créature* asked was that they help her to secure release from her earthbound condition."

"Why should she have appealed to them?"

"In all that congregation of benighted worshippers of evil, she knew them best. They saw her die, they gave her body sepulture; one of them, at least, had been her lover, and was, presumably, bound to her by ties of mutual passion. She was most strongly in their minds and memories. It was but natural that she should appeal to them for succor. Did not you notice one outstanding fact in all the testimony—the poor Marescha appeared to them in turn, looking not reproachfully, but pleadingly? Her lips were held, she might not put her plea in words. She could but come to them as they had last beheld her, entreat them by dumb show, and hope that they would understand. One by one they failed her; one by one they failed to understand—"

"Well, is there anything that we can do about it?"

"I think there is. Come, let us be upon our way."

"Where the deuce—"

"To the rectory of St. Chrysostom. I would interview the Reverend Doctor Bentley."

"At this time of night?"

"*Mais certainement*, clergymen and doctors, they have no privacy, my friend. Surely, you need not be told that."

THE FRESHLY LIGHTED FIRE burned brightly in the Reverend Peter Bentley's study, the blue smoke spiraled upward from the tips of our cigars, the gray steam curled in fragrant clouds from the glasses of hot Scots which stood upon the coffee-table. Looking anything but clerical in red-flannel bathrobe, black pajamas and red Turkish slippers, Doctor Bentley listened with surprising tolerance to de Grandin's argument.

"But it seems the poor girl died in mortal sin," he murmured, obviously more in sorrow than in righteous indignation. "According to your statement, her last frantic words called on the Devil to fulfill his bargain: 'O Lord, be pitiful—'"

"*Précisément, mon père*, but who can say her prayer was made to Satan? True, those so bewildered, misled followers of evil were wont to call the Devil Lord and Master, but is it not entirely possible that she repented and addressed her dying prayer to the real Lord of the heaven and earth? Somewhere an English poet says of the last-minute prayer of a not-wholly-righteous fox-hunter who was unhorsed and broke his sinful neck:

Betwixt the stirrup and the ground
I mercy asked; mercy I found.

"Me, I believe in all sincerity that her repentance was as true as that the thief upon the cross expressed; that in the last dread moment she perceived the grievous error of her ways and made at once confession of sin and prayer for pity with her dying breath.

"But she had bent the knee at Satan's shrine. With her fair body—that body which was given her to wear as if it were a garment to the greater glory of the Lord—she parodied the sacred faircloth of the altar. By such things she had cut herself adrift, she had put herself beyond communion with the righteous which is the blessèd company of all the faithful. There was no priest to shrive her sin-encumbered soul, no one to read words of forgiveness and redemption above her lifeless clay. Until some one of her companions in iniquity will perform the service of contrition for her, until the office for the burial of Christian dead is read above her grave, she lies excommunicate and earthbound. She cannot even expiate her faults in Purgatory till forgiveness of sins has been formally pronounced. Sincerely repentant, Hell is not for her; unshrived, and with no formal statement of conditional forgiveness, she cannot quit the earth, but must wander here among the scenes of her brief and sadly misspent life. Do we dare withhold our hands to save her from a fate like that?"

Doctor Bentley sipped thoughtfully at his hot Scots. "There may be something in your theory," he admitted. "I'm not especially strong on doctrine, but I can't believe the fathers of the early church were the crude nincompoops some of our modern theologians call them. They preached posthumous absolution, and there are instances recorded where excommunicated persons who had hovered round the scenes they'd known in life were given rest and peace when absolution was pronounced above their graves. Tell me, is this Balderson sincerely sorry for his misdeeds?"

"I could swear it, *mon père*."

"Then bring him to the chapel in the morning. If he will make confession and declare sincere repentance, then submit himself to holy baptism, I'll do what you request. It's rather mediæval, but—I'd hate to think that I'm so modern that I would not take a chance to save two souls."

THE PENITENTIAL SERVICE IN the Chapel of the Intercession was a brief but most impressive one. Only Balderson, I and de Grandin occupied the pews, with Doctor Bentley in his stole and cassock, but without his surplice, at the little altar:

". . . we have followed too much the devices and desires of our own hearts, we have offended against Thy holy laws . . . remember not, Lord, our offenses nor the offenses of our forefathers, neither take Thou vengeance of our sins . . . we acknowledge and bewail our manifold sins and wickednesses; the memory of them is grievous unto us, the burden of them is intolerable . . ."

After absolution followed the short service ordered for the baptism of adults; then we set out for Shadow Lawns.

Now Doctor Bentley wore his full canonicals, and his surplice glinted almost whiter than the snow that wrapped the mounded graves as he paused beside an unmarked hillock in the Nurmi family plot.

Slowly he began in that low, full voice with which he fills a great church to its farthest corner; "I am the resurrection and the life, saith the Lord; he that believeth in me, though he were dead, yet shall he live. . . ."

It was one of those still winter days, quieter than an afternoon in August, for no chirp of bird or whir of insect sounded no breath of breeze disturbed the evergreens; yet as he read the opening sentence of the office for the burial of the dead a low wail sounded in the copse of yew and hemlock on the hill, as though a sudden wind moaned in the branches, and I stiffened as a scent was borne across the snow-capped grave mounds. Incense! Yet not exactly incense, either.

There was an undertone of fetor in it, a faint, distinctly charnel smell. Balderson was trembling, and despite myself I flinched, but Doctor Bentley and de Grandin gave no sign of recognition.

"Thou knowest, Lord, the secrets of our hearts, shut not Thy merciful ears to our prayer, but spare us, Lord most holy. . ." intoned the clergyman, and,

"Amen," said Jules de Grandin firmly as the prayer concluded.

The Æolian wailing in the evergreens died to a sobbing, low clamation as Doctor Bentley traced in sand a cross upon the snow-capped grave, declaring: "Unto Almighty God we commend the soul of our departed sister, and we commit her body to the ground: earth to earth, ashes to ashes, dust to dust, in the *sure and certain hope of the Resurrection into eternal life. . . .*"

And now there was no odor of corruption in the ghostly perfume, but the clean, inspiring scent of frankincense, redolent of worship at a thousand consecrated altars.

As the last amen was said and Doctor Bentley turned away I could have sworn I heard a gentle slapping sound and saw the blond hairs of de Grandin's small mustache bend inward, as though a pair of lips invisible to me had kissed him on the mouth.

DOCTOR BENTLEY DINED WITH us that night, and over coffee and liqueurs we discussed the case.

"It was a fine thing you did," the cleric told de Grandin. "Six men in seven would have sent him packing and bid him work out his salvation—or damnation—for himself. There's an essential nastiness in Devil-worship which is revolting to the average man, not to mention its abysmal wickedness—"

"*Tiens*, who of us can judge another's wickedness?" the little Frenchman answered. "The young man was repentant, and repentance is the purchase price of heavenly forgiveness. Besides"—a look of strain, like a nostalgic longing, came into his eyes—"before the altar of a convent in *la belle France* kneels one whom I have loved as I can never love another in this life. Ceaselessly, except the little time she sleeps, she makes prayer and intercession for a sinful world. Could I hold fast the memory of our love if I refused to match in works the prayer she makes in faith? *Eh bien, mon père*, my inclination was to give him a smart kick in the posterior; to bid him go and sin no more, but sinfully or otherwise, to go. *Ha*, but I am strong, me. I overcame that inclination."

The earnestness of his expression faded and an impish grin replaced it as he poured a liberal potion of Napoléon 1811 in his brandy-snifter. "Jules de Grandin," he apostrophized himself, "you have acted like a true man. You have overcome your natural desires; you have kept the faith.

"Jules de Grandin, my good and much admired self—be pleased to take a drink!"

The Complete Tales of Jules de Grandin by Seabury Quinn
is collected by Night Shade Books in the following volumes:

The Horror on the Links
The Devil's Rosary
The Dark Angel
A Rival from the Grave
Black Moon